LORD OF CHAOS

Rob Sanders

LORD OF CHAOS

Rob Sanders

BLACK LIBRARY

A BLACK LIBRARY PUBLICATION

Archaon: Everchosen first published in 2014.
Archaon: Lord of Chaos first published in 2015.
Archaon: The Fall and the Rise first published in 2014.
This edition published in Great Britain in 2016 by
Black Library,
Games Workshop Ltd.,
Willow Road,
Nottingham,
NG7 2WS, UK.

10 9 8 7 6 5 4 3 2 1

Produced by Games Workshop in Nottingham.

Lord of Chaos © Copyright Games Workshop Limited 2016. Warhammer, the Warhammer logo, GW, Games Workshop, The Game of Fantasy Battles, the twin-tailed comet logo, and all associated logos, illustrations, images, names, creatures, races, vehicles, locations, weapons, characters, and the distinctive likeness thereof, are either ® or TM, and/or © Games Workshop Limited, variably registered around the world, and used under licence. Creative Assembly, the Creative Assembly logo, Total War and the Total War logo are either registered trade marks or trade marks of The Creative Assembly Limited. SEGA and the SEGA logo are either registered trade marks or trade marks of SEGA Holdings Co., Ltd. or its affiliates.
All rights reserved.

A CIP record for this book is available from the British Library.

UK ISBN 13: 978 1 78496 404 7
US ISBN 13: 978 1 78496 405 4

No part of this publication may be reproduced, stored in a retrieval system, or transmitted in any form or by any means, electronic, mechanical, photocopying, recording or otherwise, without the prior permission of the publishers.

This is a work of fiction. All the characters and events portrayed in this book are fictional, and any resemblance to real people or incidents is purely coincidental.

See Black Library on the internet at
blacklibrary.com

Find out more about Games Workshop
and the world of Warhammer 40,000 at
games-workshop.com

Printed and bound by CPI Group (UK) Ltd, Croydon, CR0 4YY

This is a dark age, a bloody age, an age of daemons and of sorcery. It is an age of battle and death, and of the world's ending. Amidst all of the fire, flame and fury it is a time, too, of mighty heroes, of bold deeds and great courage.

At the heart of the Old World sprawls the Empire, the largest and most powerful of the human realms. Known for its engineers, sorcerers, traders and soldiers, it is a land of great mountains, mighty rivers, dark forests and vast cities. And from his throne in Altdorf reigns the Emperor Karl Franz, sacred descendant of the founder of these lands, Sigmar, and wielder of his magical warhammer.

But these are far from civilised times. Across the length and breadth of the Old World, from the knightly palaces of Bretonnia to ice-bound Kislev in the far north, come rumblings of war. In the towering Worlds Edge Mountains, the orc tribes are gathering for another assault. Bandits and renegades harry the wild southern lands of the Border Princes. There are rumours of rat-things, the skaven, emerging from the sewers and swamps across the land. And from the northern wildernesses there is the ever-present threat of Chaos, of daemons and beastmen corrupted by the foul powers of the Dark Gods.
As the time of battle draws ever near, the Empire needs heroes like never before.

TOTAL WAR WARHAMMER

The Old World echoes to the clamour of ceaseless battle. The only constant is WAR!

A fantasy strategy game of legendary proportions, Total War: WARHAMMER combines an addictive turn-based campaign of epic empire-building with explosive, colossal, real-time battles, set in the brooding and bloody world of Warhammer Fantasy Battles.

Command one of four wholly different Races: The Empire of Men, the stoic Dwarfs, the bloodthirsty Greenskin hordes and the dark and elegant lords of the undead, the Vampire Counts. In Total War: WARHAMMER, it is up to you to consolidate and expand your territory, marshalling powerful armies and using them to carve a path of conquest across the Old World, shaping it to your liking as you go.

Train mighty wizards and shamans to heal the wounded, raise the dead or consume your enemies in maelstroms of magic. Take to the skies for the first time in a Total War game as you field a host of flying creatures and monsters, from majestic griffons to mighty dragons. Lead you forces into battle with Legendary Lords from the Warhammer Fantasy Battles world, arming them with epic weapons, armour and deadly battle-magic. Unlock narrative quest-chains for your Legendary Lords and engage in hand-crafted spectacular quest-battles.

As you spread your influence throughout the Old World, you'll form strong alliances and bitter rivalries, tallied in blood and gold. Will you become a magnanimous and diplomatic leader, protected by treaties and agreements between friends? Or will you make a name for yourself as a ruthless warlord, mercilessly slaughtering any and all who stand in your way as you sculpt a sanguine path to total domination.

Whether you lead by sword or silver, the enemies you make on the campaign map, the mighty foes that render your troops asunder and plague your general's nightmares will in time be overshadowed by a far more terrible threat.

Those sensitive to the changing Winds of Magic spread hushed rumours of fluctuations; dread vibrations in these energies stemming from their ethereal source. The fabric of reality itself begins to buckle and bend, threatening to come undone altogether. The Realm of Chaos swells.

Unspeakable things gather in the northernmost parts of the Old World. Here, the physical world and the realm of Chaos overlap, and the nefarious energies from beyond ebb and flow. The Ruinous Powers that have, for time immemorial, presided over this seething place of unnatural darkness grow restless. Talons, claws, tentacles, shapes without form, name or number itch for new territories to torment and new flesh to tear.

The true power of Chaos comes from an immaterial reality, parallel to the mortal realm of the Old World. Here, the formless flux has coagulated to form many abominations, four of which have grown to be creatures of unimaginable power, the Four Chaos Gods. Nurgle is the god of decay, despair and disease. Slaanesh represents decadence, excess, pleasure and self-indulgence. Tzeentch is the god of change and magic. Khorne is associated with hatred, rage, bloodshed and war. Chaos is a seductive force. Those who embrace it and devote themselves to the Ruinous Powers become increasingly corrupted by its influence. Some develop physical mutations to better serve their dark lords' nefarious purposes whilst some are affected in more subtle ways.

To these Dark Gods, the squabbles of the mortal realms are as two rats fighting over scraps. Whatever differences they possess are meaningless. All are mere vermin to be exterminated. As ill winds howl southwards, they set in motion the wheels of a prophecy conceived to eclipse all light and plunge the Old World into the pitch darkness of pure Chaos.

Chaos energy is the source of all magic in the world. It first entered the Old World long ago. This event, known as the Coming of Chaos, engulfed the polar areas of the world in dark energy, creating uncontrollable gateways from which the forces of Chaos spill forth.

As these energies interact with those of the physical world, they are transmuted into the Winds of Magic. Sorcerers and shamans are able to harness and refine this energy in its various forms to serve their own purposes. The risks of commanding such powers should not be underestimated however, and the arrogance and lust for power of mortal spellcasters has often seen them consumed entirely, their souls cast for eternity to the unending torments of the Chaos dimension.

Just south of the hellish Chaos Wastes, lie many a desolate, vast and inhospitable land: The Norsca Peninsula to name but one. These places and the wild folks that populate them have long acted as a buffer, stemming the flow of Chaos from reaching the mortal realms.

Though they are raised in devout worship of the Chaos Gods, their constant squabbling and infighting keeps them occupied and save for occasional bands of marauders they rarely venture southwards. To these people, the bleak Wastes to the north are a venerated and sacred place, worthy of pilgrimage. They are the true embodiment of Warriors of Chaos.

It is the dream of many of the tribespeople to journey to this ruined place and offer themselves fully to the Ruinous Powers as tools of their malevolent will. Those that survive the journey and ensuing ordeals are anointed, and return altered.

Clad in dark armour, bearing dread marks of ruinous favour and possessing skill and strength far beyond mortal means these Chaos Champions are able to take their place as exalted rulers of the bickering tribespeople below. The most revered of these may even become Daemon Princes. So it has been for countless generations.

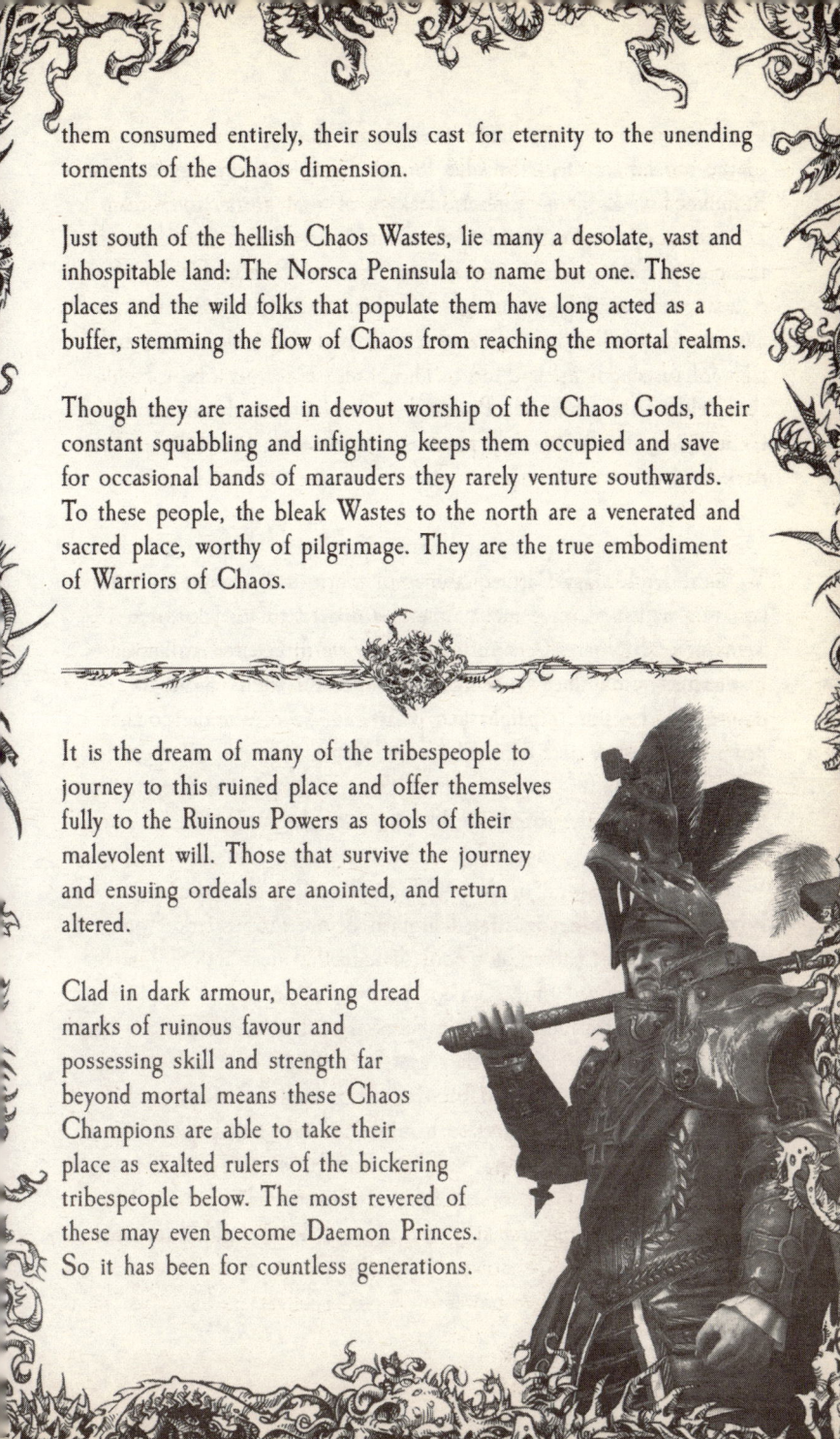

In recent times however, the clamour of infighting that has kept Chaos-worshipping tribes divided for millennia has begun to fade. Rumours have begun to spread, speaking of a far greater force than any Chaos Champion bringing these unruly lands to heel and uniting them under the banner of the one true favoured Son of Chaos. A being of pure malevolence and sheer will, this figure represents the culmination of the Ruinous Powers' machinations. A warlord to end all wars, he stands at the head of an unbreakable army whose ranks swell with horrors beyond count. He is the supreme champion of the Dark Gods, the Everchosen, and the Three-Eyed King. His name is Archaon.

One of the most infamous and iconic characters in the world of Warhammer Fantasy Battles, Archaon's story is one written in blood coursing with loss, rage and hatred. Rumoured to be a former Templar of Sigmar, Archaon is said to have discovered an ancient manuscript. Contained within this were certain truths about the nature of Chaos. His perceptions shattered, he cursed the gods he had lived to serve and then took great lengths to sever all mortal tethers before setting out on a path towards his inevitable destiny: to become the Everchosen, the harbinger of the End Times.

When he finally stood in that perilous place that the Ruinous Powers call home he prostrated himself before those Dark Gods, offering himself to them as a tool of unilateral destruction. His life unnaturally extended by his Chaos patrons, his next task would be to gather the Artefacts of Chaos necessary for his coronation.

With this done, his quest to become the Everchosen would be completed, but his true mission would only have just begun. It is at his behest that the followers of Chaos will bend the knee. It is under his banner that the Warriors of Chaos will unite. The world shall quake at his footsteps and at his command, it will fall to darkness.

In Total War: WARHAMMER, the threat of the expanding Chaos realm may not seem too pressing at the outset of your campaign. As your dominion grows and you conquer new lands and foes however, it will develop into a palpable danger that will require all your wisdom and guile to deal with effectively. The armies of Chaos are gathering, with Archaon the Everchosen leading the march.

Whether you build your empire on diplomacy or subjugation, the alliances and conflicts of the Old World will be but shadows in the light of what is to come. Nations, borders, races. All are meaningless to the encroaching forces of Ruin. As leader, will you remain distracted with the enemies that plague your borders and ignore the encroaching northern hordes until it's too late? Or, will you rally your populace, call in all favours and galvanise your forces, riding to meet the Chaos onslaught with sword in hand?

Chaos is an insidious force indeed, one that poses just as much of a threat from within as it does from without. Even with the strongest fortifications to defend from the northerly Chaos hordes, if you neglect your own lands you may find that the seeds of Chaos begin to sprout within your own walls.

Desperate people will often look to dark places for salvation, and if you cannot keep yours happy, you may find them abandoning their native faith to devote themselves to the Ruinous Powers. Should this occur, you may find pockets of dissent blooming into fully-fledged religious uprisings. Deal with these cultists quickly or else watch helplessly as your hard-won provinces fall to the Dark Gods' will.

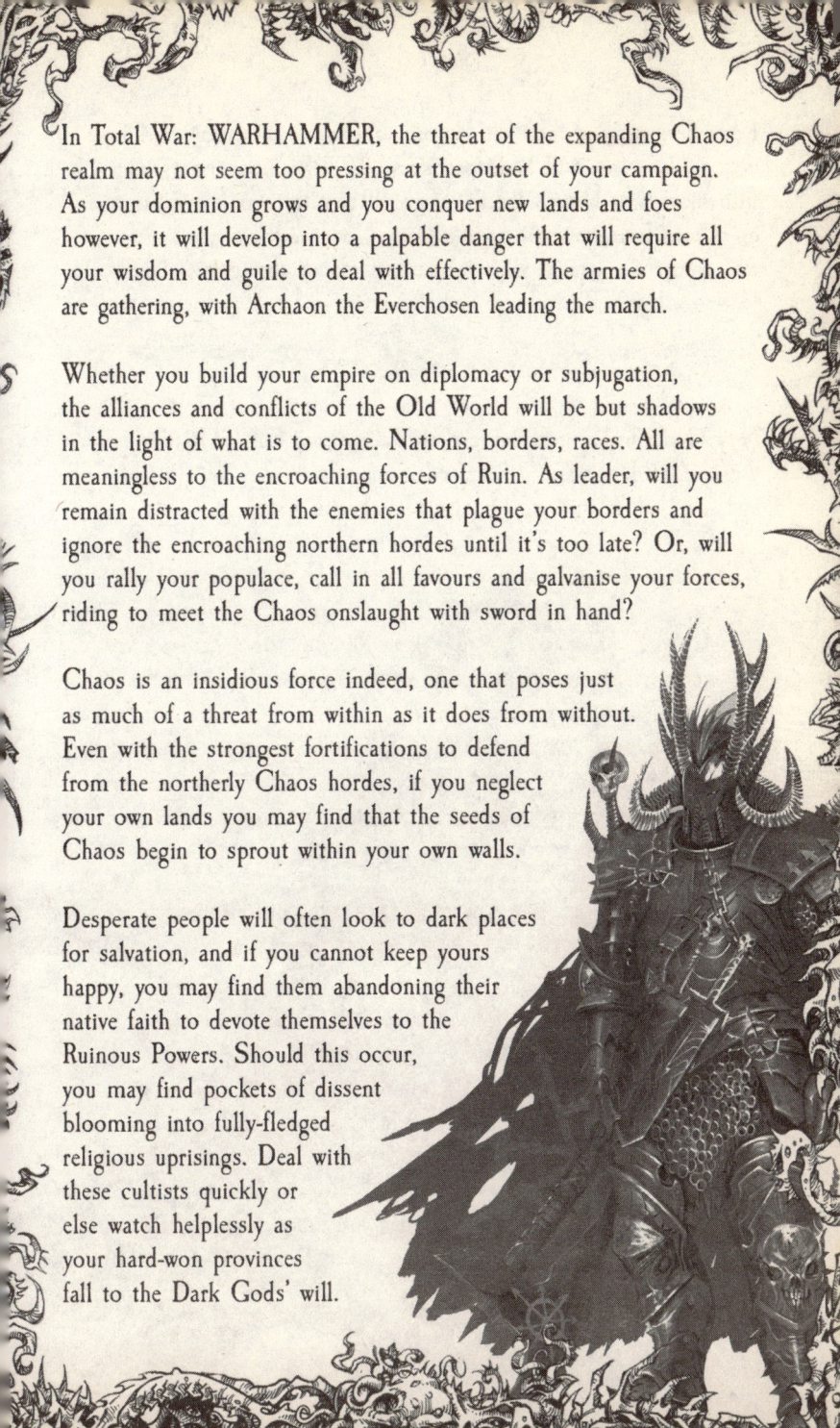

Regardless of what race you choose to play as, the threat of Chaos is something you will have to address. Whether you occupy yourself with matters at home, dissolving conflicts within your own borders, or ride to face the wrath of the Dark Gods head on, your actions will dictate the fate of your people and indeed the entire Old World.

Now, delve further into the lore of Warhammer Fantasy Battles with these selected stories which helped inspire Total War: WARHAMMER and may help inspire you on your campaigns within it...

CONTENTS

Archaon: Everchosen   17

Archaon: Lord of Chaos   495

Archaon: The Fall and the Rise   919

ARCHAON: EVERCHOSEN

'Mortals are free to do as they will. The gods give them no choice.'

– *Imperial proverb*

VOLUME ONE
BORN ✷F BLOOD

*'Smothered in the midnight
Draped in woe, sits dread itself,
Meditating misfortunes unknown.'*
– Anspracher, *The Threads of Fate*

PROLOGUE

*'O'er those unborn, whose ruin the light
will grieve
wing'd harbingers sit to receive
and set such servants the world to cleave.'*
— Fliessbach, *Tales Untold*

*The Republic of Remas – Tilea
The Lands of the South
The Year of Light and Law (IC 1586)*

'You shall know me by my works,' the prognosticator howled.

They knew him by his pain. The agonies erupting from his ruined face. The gasps of relief and hope – both sweet and dangerous – that escaped his broken body inbetween tortures. They called it the Cracker. An ugly name for an ugly contraption. With the victim's head braced between the unforgiving metal of a chin bar and a closing crown-cap, the two were drawn together by the slow turn of a handle screw. It had earned such a name for its effectiveness in producing confessions.

'Battista Gaspar Necrodomo,' a priestly witch hunter read from a blood-spattered scroll, 'his holy vengefulness, Solkan – God of Light and Law – has judged you witchfilth and false prophet, denying the poor and ignorant of this republic the comforts of his guidance.'

'You will know me by my works,' Necrodomo spat. His words escaped the clenched mantrap of his own jaw in a hissing rasp. Bloody lip-spittle sprayed the interrogator sitting opposite. One of the priests milling in the dungeon-darkness beyond tore a strip from his ragged grey robes.

'Grand inquisitori,' he mumbled, kissing the rag and handing it to his spiritual superior. The interrogator dabbed his speckled cheeks and the whiteness of his beard.

'Again,' the grand inquisitori said.

'No,' Necrodomo groaned, his pleadings pathetic and palsied. A priestly servant of Solkan turned the screw and fresh agonies filled the dungeon chamber. Necrodomo's screams were muffled shrieks of gargling desperation. As the turns of the screw abated, the freshly blinded seer sobbed and moaned.

'You are a charlatan,' the grand inquisitori said slowly, his voice threaded with the certainty of his age and station. He was the Avenger's high hand in these low dealings of the world. 'You are the herald of lies. You are an artist of nothings. You read the eye, the lip, the face and write false prophecy on the stars. You tell gullible widows what they want to hear, no? A sayer of soothings. Saw you this coming, prognosticator?'

'No...' Necrodomo managed through his shattered jaw.

'If you had stuck to prattlemongering,' the venerable inquisitori told him, 'you just might have escaped the attentions of the brotherhood. Though Avenger knows, your professed haruspexery would have been known to him – he who sees all and judges all. Your time would have come, Necrodomo. Necrodomo the foreteller. Necrodomo the skygazer. Necrodomo the reader of futures dark. Now to be known – if known at all – as Necrodomo the Insane. By my order.'

'No…' Necrodomo whimpered. 'Know…'

'This, however,' the grand inquisitori continued, picking up a bony fistful of pamphlets that littered the table, 'this goes beyond the pilfering of credulous coin. *The Celestine Prophecies. Signs and Wonders. Transcendentia. The Days of Doom to Come. The End Times.* This is heresy in our midst. This is demagoguery, spreading fear through the people. It is a challenge to the Republic. It is a corruption advertised and an invitation of vengeance. It is what brought us to you, Necrodomo. It is what brought you to this.'

The grand inquisitori gestured at the quill and pots of ink on the table and the thick, unmarked tome that sat before the groaning Necrodomo, its pages clean and waiting for his confession. 'Help me by helping yourself, Necrodomo. Confess your crimes to the brotherhood. Allow Solkan into your heart and I promise a death swift and clean enough to take you to his judgement. Why dally here in the meaningless filth of lies and conspiracy? Why suffer here as well as before the Lord of Light and Law? Commit your contrition to these pages and let me grant you the relief of death.'

'Forgive…' Necrodomo begged through shattered teeth.

'It is not for me to do so. Only the Avenger can grant you that. All I can grant you is an unburdened conscience and free passage. Your crimes are grievous. These bold pronouncements of coming apocalypse, printed and passed between the people. We are the light in the ignorance you sought to spread with your writings of the trembling world and the End Times you profess are to come. The world already trembles, Necrodomo. It trembles with the vengeance of Solkan the Mighty. It trembles with his judgement on the unnatural and the wicked. This is the greatest of your sins, false prophet. Fear is not your weapon to wield. It is ours. Armageddon is not yours to portend. The world is the Avenger's to destroy at a time of his choosing. If his servants fail, if the land can bear no more evil and the filth of corruption floods the–'

The oratory was shattered by a single clap. Followed by another. And another. Like the grand inquisitori, the witch hunters and priestly torturers of the chamber turned to the entrance. Stepping down from the rusted ladder that led from the trapdoor in the dungeon's ceiling, a lone priest in the hooded, ragged robes of the Avenger stood in slow applause. Sallow clouds of brimstone drifted down from the chamber above and descended about the interloper.

'How dare you interrupt the holy work of–' a priest began.

'Enough,' the interloper said, the word drenched in the sickly, mellifluous urgency of an infernal order. The final clap was louder and more insistent than the caustic applause that had preceded it. With the sound echoing about the dungeon like a thunderclap, the priests and servants of Solkan proceeded to untie the ropes about their waists and disrobe.

'What do you think you are doing?' the grand inquisitori barked at them. As he stared about in righteous incredulity, the witch hunters and interrogators crafted swift nooses from their belts. The grand inquisitori was out of his seat, his beard shaking and his eyes screwed up with rage. 'Stop this madness at once. The Avenger compels you.' He turned back to the priest standing at the ladder. Within the darkness of the interloper's hood, the inquisitori could make out the pin-prick glow of eyes ancient and burning like the embers of eternity. The inquisitori hadn't realised that he had soiled himself. A pool of urine was gathering on the filthy dungeon floor about him. 'Guards! Guards!' he roared. Above he could hear the clink of the plate, helms and halberds of the Reman Republican Guard.

The interloper looked up through the open trapdoor entrance. Something like a momentary storm passed through the chamber above, the influence of the sudden tempest felt on Necrodomo's apocalyptic pamphlets, which were blown from the table. The screams were brief. With the interloper still staring through the dungeon opening, it began to rain blood. The Republican Guard gaolers were now nothing but a cruel drizzle drifting, dripping and dribbling from the trapdoor entrance. The interloper allowed the downpour to blotch his robes to a gory crimson. As his ghastly gaze returned to the grand inquisitori, the trapdoor slammed shut and thundered with heavy chains securing the dungeon entrance.

The robed thing moved across the chamber with the dread purpose of something unreal. As it passed them the servants of Solkan dropped from stools and improvised furniture to dance a spasmodic jig from their belt-nooses and the rings set in the dungeon ceiling. The interloper drifted through the forest of hanging priests.

'Sit,' it commanded.

The grand inquisitori wailed as his knees gave way, causing him to fall back into his interrogator's throne.

The interloper moved towards the throne like an ancient evil. It pulled back its hood, revealing the full, unspeakable horror of its daemonic visage to the chamber. The robes fell like a fearful whisper from its barbed unflesh. It grew with each flagstone-pulverising step of its taloned feet, twisted bones blooming with muscle that ruptured into existence about them, lending the beast a glorious brawn and sinew. It dragged a serpentine tail, shot through with spikes, behind its infernal form, while both the daemon-crown of horns warping their way out of its head and the thumb-claws erupting from the dreadful magnificence of its wings scraped the dungeon ceiling.

Like a nightmare, it lowered its blood-curdling skull and moved up behind the interrogator's throne. Necrodomo, still clamped between the bar and crown-cap of the torture device, had no eyes with which to behold the beast. The grand inquisitori found, with his heart in the grasp of terror, cold, dark and despair that he could not move. As the daemon brought its unseen face forward, both the venerable priest and the prognosticator found their cheeks bathed in the radiance of infernal royalty. A princely power of hellish birthright; a creature of unimaginable darkness; horror incarnate.

The grand inquisitori felt the thing touch him. At once all that had remained pure and noble in the man shrivelled within his soul. Darkness blossomed within the priest. Every ill-deed committed in the service of selfish weakness and temptation grew through his being like a rampant cancer. His eyes turned to inky twilight as his face became a cadaverous mask of ghoulish anticipation. The daemon clasped the grand inquisitori's head in its claws.

'You search for darkness in wretched madmen,' the daemon prince whispered to the venerable priest – every word falling on the inquisitori with the force of a furnace, 'when you should have been searching for it within your own ranks. No matter… You are mine now and have no need for this vessel of flesh. Before I take your soul, there is something you should know, priest. A gift for the journey *you* are about to take.' The daemon leant in closer. 'Your. God. Is. A. Lie.' With that, the daemon prince crushed the grand inquisitori's skull between its claws with effortless ease.

Slashing both the headless body and the back of the throne from the seat with a swoosh of its serpent tail, the daemon prince took a seat before Necrodomo. Necrodomo the foreteller. Necrodomo the reader of futures dark. Necrodomo the Insane. The thing drummed its talons across the desk, prompting the torturous contraption known as the Cracker to rust to disintegration about the blind prisoner's head. Necrodomo pulled away immediately. The prognosticator was out of his mind with pain, but something spiritual and instinctive told him that he was in the presence of a dangerous evil. He felt fear without sight. Dread without sanity. Being contorted within the vice for so long, Necrodomo found that his legs no longer supported him. Crashing to the filthy floor he scrabbled away from the daemon prince like an animal until he felt his back against the cold stone of the dungeon wall.

'Do not fear me,' the beast told him. 'I am your saviour – as you are mine. My name, for all it matters to you, madman, is Be'lakor.' The monster allowed the 'r' of its name to hang like a forlorn echo. 'I am known by many titles: the Harbinger, the Herald and the Bearer. To the northmen, I am the Shadowlord. In the Empire and the *civilised* lands of the south, I am the Dark Master. To you, mortal, I am simply Master.'

Necrodomo curled up in agony. He was rocking, shaking and whimpering.

'You are Necrodomo. Though your heretic name shall be whispered in the shadows, your work shall echo through eternity.'

Be'lakor looked down on the pamphlets decorating the desk. 'I am an appreciator of your work – charlatan or not. Now I wish to become facilitator. Your masterpiece is yet to be written.'

The beast laid its claw on the empty tome intended for the prognosticator's confession. Under the touch of its talons, the leather of the cover moaned and warped to a gruesome ghastliness. Its spine became as barbed bone and the bronze lock-clasps holding its pages closed melted into sets of jaws that snapped open. The cover smoked as hellfire scorched fresh lettering into the leather. As the tome writhed to stillness and Be'lakor removed his talon, the words *LIBER CAELESTIOR* afflicted the cover in the dark tongue of his Ruinous masters, accompanied by the name BATTISTA GASPAR NECRODOMO.

'We shall wield your prophecies like a weapon,' the Dark Master told him. 'We shall make history together, you and I. We shall unite the gods and harness war, famine and plague in honour of a champion of ultimate darkness. We shall craft through destiny a warrior worthy of the challenges to come. Worthy to bear the blessing of each of my Ruinous masters in equal measure and be called Everchosen of Chaos. He will be the key, as I am the keeper of the coming apocalypse. Between us, we shall herald the coming of the End Times – the doom you spoke of, my friend. Rejoice, soothsayer. They are coming. When we do… when I have no more need of your words or his deeds, I shall assume the Everchosen's flesh in true coronation – the flesh your prophecies shall exalt to the status of legend – and I shall take my rightful place as

Lord of the End Times. Once more the world will be mine to plunge into darkness and ruin.'

Necrodomo groaned and shrieked. If the pain of torture hadn't driven him into the embrace of insanity, then the daemon prince's words had. He was gone – a willing host to oblivion that, like a leech, sapped him of the last of his mental strength. The prognosticator moaned insensibilities. He laughed at his agonies and shrieked at nothing. Necrodomo let go and Be'lakor let him.

'No matter,' the daemon prince said to the madman. He opened the tome to its first blank page and selecting a quill, dipped it into the ink on the table. 'I will assist you. I will transcribe. I have a name already. The name I shall bequeath my champion. The name I shall eventually take, with the body of the Everchosen I shall possess and assume. A name of your southern tongue, prognosticator, honouring both the ancient I have been and the eternity I have yet to become. We shall be known as… Archaon.'

*'There comes to the Emperor's shores
one night, driven before a storm,
a gift in the guise of a child
unknowing, unknown and unsought.*

*'From womb to sea he is returned,
a victim of the churning surf –
to be saved by a fisherman
who sees the gift and not the curse.*

*'The error of the innocent –
a commoner baseborn and bred,
will never cost the land so dear
or put its people to the test.*

*'If murder comes more easily –
or rude compassion shows its heel,
then worlds old and new will be saved
from the coming catastrophe.*

*'For despite early clemency,
and the God-King's watchful gaze
The child finds its path to darkness
and returns not man but plague.'*

– Necrodomo the Insane,
The Liber Caelestior
(The Celestine Book of Divination)

CHAPTER I

'–Art thou some darknid thing?
Wielding accident and advantage from the
shadows?
Some spirit, some fiend, some godless fury
from afar, that stays the dice and winds
the thread of life about its claws,
that turns blood to ice and shivers the
spine,
With dark providence and blessed
tragedies?
Tell me devil, what thou art.'

– Geisenberg, *Destinations*

The village of Hargendorf
Nordland Coast – The Empire
Dunkelstag, IC 2390

The north. The north. Always the north. Out of the north they came, riding the storm. The rough wool cloth of their sails knew it. The rotting timbers of their clinkered hulls knew it. The marauders knew it in their hot bones and salt-stained flesh. This was no natural tempest. A wretched squall that had slammed the northmen from their bloody course and swept them south before gales serrated like their weapons, and rain fell like pellets of frosted iron. A blessing from the north. From the Wastes. From the Powers allowed to be.

Vargs, far from home. Like fire on the water, they lived for the basest expression of their miserable existence. War – wherever it could be found, women and the favours that could be ripped from them, and the cruel laughter that could be drawn from mens' bellies in the face of calamities wrought. When not engaged in such mordant pursuits, the northmen might have remembered to eat or sleep or attend to their weapons, their vessels or the monstrous darkness to which they had pledged their lives. Their names were made up of consonants that cut the mouth and their hearts were hollow and black. Some bore the ghastly afflictions of their calling but most were ugly enough before – being grizzled of limb, scarred of flesh and ragged of beard. They cursed the elements and spat in the face of Manann, god of the seas for his free passage. They honoured their patron Powers with action. They honoured them with the wolfish howls they roared at the tumultuous skies, as their boats cut through the range of mountainous waves before them and revealed the glint of torches and lanterns. The coast of some victim nation. The darkened shore.

As the storm smashed them on, lightning seethed through the sky. The world was fit to break. The furious flashes revealed a shale beach. On the shore sat a collection of beached fishing boats, rocking in the storm. Beyond lay a fishing village. Innocent. Provocative. Vulnerable. The barbarians stood in their dripping furs and spiked armour. They could already feel the spray of hot blood across their faces. The screams and the begging that aroused them so, soothing the mind and ear. The ache of omnipotence flooded their being. Hands stain-speckled with death reached for the tools of their trade – wicked blades, slender axes and spear shafts of saturated gore. They were the storm. The sudden and sickening eruption of forces unknown upon the helpless and afeared. The stinking and smoking ruin that their progress left in its path – the northmen's advertisement to the world. They were there. They robbed. They ravaged. They murdered. And they lived.

The hovel's roof flashed white in the storm. Rain lashed the windows clean and the shrieking north wind battered the door with the insistence that it be admitted. As the oldest homestead in Hargendorf and one of the closest to the beach, the hovel bore the full fury of the coming storm. Within, a fish broth bubbled above the fire, both being attended by Viktoria Rothschild. It was cold for the time of year but storms didn't bother Viktoria. She was a fisherman's daughter and a fisherman's wife. The north winds warranted nothing more than a shawl. She had nets to mend and three young boys to tend to.

Otto pretended to be asleep in his bunk. He had never liked the Nordland storms and his father feared for the kind of fisherman he would make. His brother Dietfried, on the other hand, pushed his face to the window, feeling the drum of droplets through the glass and his nose. As thunder shook the hovel and lightning bleached the young boy's face, his mother called him away. Dietfried retreated. A little. Only Lutz seemed oblivious to the tempest, sitting with his mother by the fire. He had no intention of helping her. With a stomach like a grotto or sea cave, the boy merely waited for his broth and the salt bread that would go with it.

Viktoria sighed. Lutz's stomach was usually a good indicator of when her husband Roald was due to return. In weather like this she expected him even earlier but reasoned that the boats would need dragging further up the beach and securing in the storm. Between the claps of thunder she heard the sound of boots on shale. Roald was home. She handed bowls and wooden spoons to Lutz from the shelf.

'Set the table for your father,' Viktoria told the boy. 'Dietfried, help your brother.'

When Dietfried didn't reply, the fishwife turned on him with a face like the squall. 'Dietfried,' she carped, heading to unbar the door, her hands busy with salt bread. The boy was staring out of the window. He looked back at her, his face cast in shadows of concern by the flashing outside.

'Mother…' he began, turning back to the window.

There was shouting. Course and guttural. With bread in hand, Viktoria approached the window. Shadows passed before it in quick succession. The shadows of men in the village, but instead of nets and boat hooks and buckets, their hands glinted with the metal of blades, spear tips and axes.

Viktoria dropped the bread.

She grabbed Dietfried and went to pull him away from the window. The horror held them there, however. There was screaming now. Hedda Molinger was dead. Viktoria heard it. She had probably gone out to greet her husband, Edsel. The Rodeckers' dog was barking and then promptly stopped. Old Mother Irmgard was suddenly out in the street, the centre of a mob of kicking and stamping. Bertilda's boys Gelbert and Jorgan were straight out into the unfolding havoc but within moments were on their knees and pleading for their lives, but their entreaties went unheeded.

Viktoria couldn't quite catch her breath. She hauled Dietfried back and found both Lutz and Otto – awake and out of bed – clutching at her skirts. She looked about the hovel. They were fisherfolk and had little coin to spend on weapons like swords. She wouldn't know what to do with it even if she had one. The best they had was a wood axe but it was wedged in a log amongst the firewood piled outside the door.

She felt her heart hammer in her chest. As the shadows continued to flash by the window and she could hear the crunch of boots up the beach and into the village, she felt the hammering accelerate to a lightheaded flutter. She went to say something to her children but the words wouldn't come. A silhouette eclipsed the storm at the window. It was a man. Big in his furs and spiked armour. He wasn't running into the havoc unfolding in the centre of Hargendorf like the others. He had stayed to finish Old Mother Irmgard, while his barbarian battle-kin had surged on to pillage and slaughter children and womenfolk.

He stood still like a predator, the wind and rain whipping about him. The shape of a woman tore by, shrieking the name 'Brigette'. Through the glass, Viktoria saw it was Carla Vohssen. The marauder sprung like a trap, snatching the screaming woman by the hair and pulling her into the hovel wall. His shadow held hers there. She fought but the barbarian stood like a statue above her. Viktoria heard the slow sound of a blade escaping its scabbard. Carla Vohssen's voice was a strangled whisper. She alternated between begging and praying but the marauder silenced her with a single 'Sssshhhhhhh' from behind his helmet. As the tip of his broad blade dimpled her flesh, Viktoria heard Carla fall once again to screaming and struggling. Her elbow crashed through the hovel window, allowing the storm to scream inside. Viktoria clutched her children to her and retreated further into the hovel.

Viktoria felt her children cling to her. In the distance the shrine bells were ringing. The temple. It somehow calmed Viktoria. She knew she had to act. Pushing Dietfried, Otto and Lutz to the corner of the hovel, she lifted the mound of fishing nets waiting for her attention there. There was no time for words, even ones of maternal comfort. They were all too scared. The boys instinctively understood what their mother wanted and crawled beneath, Dietfried's hand lingering on Viktoria's as she positioned the netting over them. An impact on the hovel door sent the child's hand shooting back beneath the material. Viktoria stood bolt upright.

The shadow was missing from the window. The marauder's armoured boot slammed into the door but it was barred against the storm and held. Viktoria slipped the knife she had been using to gut the fish off the table. She backed towards the fire, the stinking blade behind her. She watched. She waited.

The third impact splintered the bar in two and the smashed door was battered aside, allowing the maelstrom in. Framed in the doorway, in the flaring storm, in her nightmares, was the marauder. Rain cascaded from his furs and the urchin-like outline of his armour. Where leather, mail and plate failed to contain the northman's brawn, his flesh was tattooed and scarred. Centred about his heart and crossing one great pectoral muscle, the warrior had a rough tattoo in the shape of an eight-pointed star. Viktoria felt both drawn to and despairing of the symbol but decided that it would be the best place to bury her knife when she had the chance. The warrior's helm was horned and covered his face. Light was admitted by a number of rough puncture holes in the faceplate that, for all Viktoria knew, afflicted the marauder's hidden face also. The tempest whipped Carla's lifeblood and gore from the huge blade of the sword in the marauder's mailed fist.

He entered. Slowly. Like his knife had the girl outside. His sea-drenched boots carried him calmly across the hovel. There was no frenzied attack. Nothing like the butchery behind him as marauders moved through the village like a pack of wolves, slashing, tearing and sharing. Viktoria picked up a plate and threw it, and another, but they bounced uselessly off the marauder's chest. He kept coming. Slow. Deliberate. His blade held in casual readiness. He reached out for her but she retreated, grabbing the pot of fish broth by one burning handle and flinging it awkwardly at the warrior. As the heavy pot clattered to the floor, the boiling broth steamed off the marauder's scalded flesh and armour. If he felt pain, the warrior didn't show it.

Viktoria backed away. She felt a sob erupt from her. Futility and frustration. She was about to die and she knew it. At the sound the boys beneath the fishing net stifled their own terror, as the marauder's helm drew around to the corner of the hovel. The action turned Viktoria's stomach to stone. She reached into the fire for a partially burning log. She would torch the northerner. His mailed fist snapped around her wrist like vice. She strained but the warrior held her there. She felt his balance change. The tip of his sword was up and resting on her stomach. He intended to skewer her like he had Carla.

And the marauder would have done, but Viktoria brought the knife from behind her back with her other hand and thrust the blade at the tattoo of the star across the monster's heart. The tip of the knife punctured the skin and slipped partly into the warrior's flesh. The marauder was no fish, however. Muscle, bone and whatever protection the unholy symbol offered barred the way to his heart. As Viktoria stood there, frozen with horror, an instant of dark connection was made between their two souls, their two bodies. Shocked and sickened, she released her grip on the weapon, and tried to pull away.

He looked down at the knife protruding from his flesh, then back at Viktoria. She thought she saw his eyes, the light of the fire penetrating the helmet and revealing the jaundiced, bloodshot peace of his gaze. He released her wrist but backhanded her away from the fire. The mailed palm took several of the fishwife's teeth and she hit the wall with an ugly, head-gashing crack. The children squealed from beneath the netting.

'Stay where you are,' Viktoria called to them. 'Mummy's all right.'

The knife clanged to the floor as the marauder swept his own weapon around, smashing the handle down and the blade tip from his flesh. He turned towards the mound of nets but Viktoria called, 'No'. She spat blood. She sobbed. 'Here. Here.'

She backed into the hovel's only other room. The bedroom. She was crying. The marauder stopped. He considered. Finally he slid his sword slowly back into its scabbard. The marauder advanced. Viktoria retreated. She cried out as the back of her legs hit the bed. She fell back into the blankets. The marauder entered. In his armour and helm he seemed to fill the tiny room. Thunder crashed. The wind moaned. The skies wept.

Viktoria lifted her back from the covers.

'No,' she wept.

The marauder brought his mail fist up to the helm and extended a finger. 'Sssshhhhhhh,' he told her.

Someone was behind him. The warrior went for his sword and turned. The boat hook smashed through the side of both his helm and skull. Roald Rothschild held him there for a moment, the fisherman's weapon keeping the marauder in place as he began to tremble and shake. Rothschild had no warrior skill. He had been fortunate in both his approach and the hook's destination. Fear had driven him on. A husband's wrath had carried him through doubt. The ungainly wickedness of his improvised weapon had done the rest. Lowering the warrior to his armoured knees, Roald shook the hook loose from the twisted metal of the helm and allowed his victim to fall. The marauder crashed onto the floor and fell into a brief fit, the insides of his head leaking out of the side of the helmet, before finally falling silent and still.

All Viktoria could see was her husband. His beard hid the grimness on his lips. Dietfried, Otto and Lutz were suddenly about his legs, crying. He put his finger to his lips and bid them be quiet before extending a hand to his wife. Viktoria took it and the family fled the hovel, heading into the storm – Roald's fishing boat waiting for them, a little way up the rain-lashed beach.

Legends are not made in this way…

The Dark Master will not be thwarted thus. What is a prophecy if not a truth promised to be? The skill is knowing where to exert force. It is true that with so many competing forces in the world, so many invested entities and powers, with so many destinies at odds, it is nigh but impossible to change the great happenings of the age – any age – directly. There is balance, except when there is not. With a lever long enough, however, I could balance it across the great mountains of the Worlds Edge and prise mighty Morrslieb from the night sky.

This world was once mine. A glorious ruin of ash and flame. It will be again. And so like the pages of a book, flicked back to read again that which was missed the first time, I bring forth my instrument of destruction. He, who is destined for Armageddon's crown. He, whose anointed flesh is destined to be my own. Archaon… will be.

Small changes can make a big difference – sometimes, all the difference.

Which is why this time the shrine bells of Hargendorf never rang.

CHAPTER I

*'Every new beginning comes from some
other beginning's end.'*
— Senectra the Younger, *Dialogues*

*The village of Hargendorf
Nordland Coast – The Empire
Mitterfruhl, IC 2391*

The water was cold, as was her purpose. Viktoria Rothschild stood in the shallows. She had been crouching there for some time and her legs were numb. The waters splashed up against her knees and swollen belly and on up along the shale beach. She looked out across the bay. Beyond extended the Sea of Claws and beyond that, only the gods knew what. The sea had been good to her family. To her father. To her father's father. To herself, Roald and the boys. It was a giver of life. Dietfried, Otto and Lutz had grown strong and healthy on whatever the sea had provided for them. Roald had his boat. She sold the fish he caught. The sea *had* been good to them.

Manann's realm could be fickle, however. As well as giver it was also the taker of life. Isolde Altoff's boy Hanke had drowned off Stukker Nook. Viktoria's cousin Gretel had been taken by a wyrm on the beaches of Lugren when Viktoria had been just a teenager. Three generations of the Lassowitz family had been lost in one night during a squall on the Hunderbank. The sea would take another that morning.

The slosh of the waves and the offshore breeze stole her grunts and exertions. She was a mother of three fine boys. She had done this before. About her the water was a murky crimson. She cried for the last few minutes. Above, dark clouds were gathering and the wind turned.

'Viktoria!'

It was Roald. He had been running up the beach calling her name. His boots took him into the shallows. 'Gods, woman, no,' he said, swirling about the bloody waters with his big hands. 'Viktoria, no.'

She turned to him and staggered. He caught her and held her for a moment. He looked out to sea while she peered back up the shale beach to the hovel. It was one of the last standing after the terrible night of slaughter nine months before. The hovel that had admitted the marauder and borne witness to the dark gift he had bestowed on Viktoria Rothschild. The gift of a child unwanted. Viktoria blinked the salt from her eyes. If only there had been a warning. If only the shrine bells had rung. If only Roald and the fishermen had returned earlier. But they hadn't and Viktoria had bought herself and her children time with her miseries.

'We shall be punished for this,' Roald told her. 'The gods will punish us.'

Viktoria held him a little longer.

'We've been punished enough,' Viktoria said bleakly, before wading out of the shallows and back up the shale. Otto and Lutz were playing outside, while Dietfried watched them from up the beach, from where he had been helping his father with the catch.

Roald Rothschild remained, the waves rising and falling

about him. He looked but saw nothing. The sea had taken the child. It was one with the depths. He cast his gaze up at the haemorrhaging sky. There would be another storm. It was the season. The fisherman's lips moved silently. Roald Rothschild prayed. He prayed to Manann. He prayed to Sigmar. He prayed to any and all that were listening. Little could he know that a force dark and powerful had indeed heard his fearful prayers.

You would consign fate, crafted in flesh and blood, to the depths? The gifts of Chaos are not to be refused. They are not demanded or earned, they are visited upon mortals at the pleasure of Dark Gods and the princes of ruin.

This story cannot be untold. The will of daemons cannot be undone. It is decided. Doom lives on. Damnation endures. From the darkness of the depths to the darkness of the womb, the gift shall be returned.

And so I petition the moons and turn back the tide. The black depths reject that which has been rejected. Once more the fruit is swollen with the seed of doom. This child shall live and in doing so bring about the death of all the world. Consider this already done. Done in the name of god-thwarted Be'lakor.

CHAPTER I

*Now it is the time of night,
when fears surmount their mighty sum,
and the grave gapes forth its welcome.*
— Nelkenthal, *The Raven's Call*

*The village of Hargendorf
Nordland
Nacht der Kranken, IC 2391*

Viktoria sent Dietfried for the midwife from Schlaghugel. Gunda Schnass had brought all three of her sons successfully into the world and Viktoria would have no one else for the fourth. Although a lapsed follower of Shallya, Gunda made her offerings to the God-King at Dempster's Rock. The temple was nearer and according to Dietfried – who she had also delivered – there was little time. Gunda didn't even know Viktoria was expecting. It seemed strange after the tragedy that had befallen Hargendorf. There was so much work to do in rebuilding and managing the catch alone that another child – so soon – struck Gunda as an extra burden. Asking for Sigmar's blessing on her work and strong sons for his Empire, the midwife made her way to Hargendorf with Dietfried Rothschild walking miserably behind. She tried to prise some conversation from the boy on their journey but he would not be drawn. He had turned into a serious child, hard of face and burdened by his thoughts. The midwife expected little else from the youngling: he had been taken by the heel and dipped in tragedy head first. He had seen things no one was meant to see.

Gunda had had no reason to visit the fishing village in the past few months. The marauder attack had been swift and brutal. Hovels and boats had been put to the flame while men, women and children had been put to the sword. Gunda waddled through the ash-drowned ruins, the slaughter and decimation evident everywhere: in the torched timbers, in the stains of old blood on the cobbles, in the absence of gossip and children's laughter on the air.

She found the Rothschilds' hovel at the edge of the shale where she had left it four years before, after bringing the angel-faced Otto into the world. It was easy to find. It was one of the only buildings left standing. The Rothschilds had been fortunate that terrible night. Roald had got Viktoria and the children out and to his boat, the family taking refuge in the storm-mauled bay while the village burned on the shore. Few others had been so fortunate. Others who had survived had left, leaving the atrocities at Hargendorf behind – though as a survivor of life's myriad misfortunes herself, Gunda knew that you could walk to the other side of the Empire and never quite escape the darkness of your past. It waited for you behind the closing of each eye, to be relived each night.

She didn't bother to knock. Viktoria's suffering could be heard up the empty street. The hovel was dark and muggy. Roald stood by the fire. He was impassive, like one of the wooden statues lining the temple at Dempster's Rock. He said nothing. A pot of water boiled over a spitting fire. The children were seated at the table, tearing material into the rags Gunda would need. There was no greeting from the younglings either. Dietfried joined them. Their eyes were directed through the bedroom door, on their mother and her pain. The last time they had heard their mother scream had been nine months before, on the night of the attack. The night the marauders arrived. The night the marauder crossed the doorstep and entered their lives.

'Well, let's get started then,' Gunda said, rolling up her sleeves. She thought she should say something. In reality, Viktoria was well on her way but it was proving to be a troublesome birth. The midwife washed her hands. She told Viktoria that everything would be all right. Roald and the children just stared, as though seeing something far off. Gunda wasn't happy. Viktoria's cries were unnaturally harsh for a mother already of three. The tide came in. The sun went down. The midwife pressed on with the difficult birth. Viktoria reached out for Roald but the fisherman stayed by the fire, sending the children across the room when Gunda needed something. Viktoria's suffering went on into the night. She became weaker and more frightened and Gunda felt the woman slipping from her grasp.

The baby was born to silence. It was a strong little thing, Gunda had to admit. A boy. Few children she had brought into the world had endured such a delivery. It had fought its way through the first trial of its life and emerged bloody, bonny and full of fight. Its screams seemed to produce a reaction in the family. The children too fell to sobbing but they were not tears of joy. No thanks were offered to the gods and so it fell to Gunda to mumble a prayer to Sigmar – as she had done in his temple some hours before – acknowledging that another son of the Empire had been born.

With the child wrapped in swaddling and placed on the bed, Gunda turned her attentions back to Viktoria. She told her how brave she had been. How well she had fought to see her son into the world. That she had attended few births so difficult. She lifted water to her lips from a ladle but

Viktoria would not take it. Her eyes fluttered and her head fell to one side.

'Don't do this, lassie,' Gunda said, but then the convulsions started. Viktoria was experiencing some kind of violent fit. Arms flew out and her legs kicked across the bed. 'The baby!' Gunda cried out. 'Get the baby.' Roald and the children just watched. Moving the child to the floor and away from the violence of his mother's passing, Gunda attempted to hold Viktoria down. Bracing a wound rag across her mouth like a bridle, the midwife tried to stop her biting down on her own tongue. 'Roald,' the midwife called. 'Get over here and help me.'

Putting one horrified foot in front of the other, Roald made it across the hovel and into the bedroom. The children, now descended into a sobbing mess, followed him. The four of them joined Gunda by the bed. Together they held their mother down. They felt the heat of her skin and the last of the fight within her, until finally she fell still. The children wept into the blankets. Roald bawled his grief at his wife's silence. The baby cried for attention it would not get. Gunda felt her own tears come. She backed away from the bed feeling like an intruder, knowing that the family needed this moment alone.

'I'm so sorry,' she murmured before making for the door. It seemed to take an eternity to reach it.

'Take it with you,' Roald managed, snatching a breath.

'Roald, no,' Gunda said.

'I beg you,' the fisherman cried, his sorrow cutting through him like a sword. His face was a contorted mask of unbearable woe.

'He's your son, man,' Gunda implored.

'He's not my son,' Roald barked, his anger driving his whimpers away. 'He's not my son.'

Gunda stared at them all. The inconsolable younglings. The fisherman, his shoulders broad and taut, as if under some fresh burden. Viktoria Rothschild, bloody and broken on the bed. She came to understand how tragedy might have intruded on the household that dreadful night nine months ago. How the Rothschilds might not have been as fortunate as gossip had supposed. 'Take it,' Roald hissed through his pain and gritted teeth. 'Or I will see to it that the tide will.'

The midwife nodded, picked up the child and held the swaddling to her chest. She opened the door. It was the dead of night. The sky was open and a chill breeze felt its way through the layers of her clothing.

'I'm truly sorry,' the midwife said, tears rolling down her rounded cheeks.

Gunda settled into her hood and, pulling the babe close to the warmth of her body, set off into the Nordland night.

CHAPTER II

*'Thus Gerreon's blade found its way to
Pendrag's heart and love,
and the winds took its wielder north to the
realm of bear and wolf,
Sigmar followed with a sword-brother's
rage – eager to avenge fair Pendrag's
blood,
He searched for dark Gereon through
mount and wood,
But vengeance turned to calling with
Sigmar crushing the Norsii beneath his
boot.'*

– Hollenstein, *Chronicles*

*The Schlaghugel Road
Nordland
Pendragstag, IC 2391*

The Schlaghugel Road was a ghoulish ribbon winding its way between the gurgling darkness that was the River Demst and the dread of Laurelorn Forest. *Road* was a charitable description for the channel-hugging pathway that couldn't decide whether it was wagon-hardened earth, moss-threaded gravel or the occasional lonely cobblestone. It was the small hours of the night and there were no merchant wagons travelling the road. Not a messenger. Not a mail coach. Not even a footpad or highwayman. Both Swift Nikolaus and 'Six-Fingered' Dirk were regular sights on the route. Killers both, Gunda Schnass would even have welcomed the company of such robbers on the Schlaghugel Road that night. The breeze hissed like a serpent through towering treetops, which drooped like closing jaws over the miserable path.

Gunda would never ordinarily have left a birth. Traditionally a midwife would remain until morning. Both mother and baby needed care, comfort and advice. The passage was safer during the day and with their wives resting, husbands were sometimes reticent about payment for the midwifery services rendered. The Rothschilds' tragedy did not allow for such luxury, however, and Gunda found herself out on the open road, late into the night with a mewling child drawing the attention of every wretched thing that haunted the edge of the forest. Gunda saw shapes moving through the brush and the glint of eyes in moonlight.

It was cold. The heavens were cloudless and the constellations hung above the forest like secret signs and indecipherable symbols. Gunda wasn't much of a reader as it was and her talents certainly didn't extend to interpreting the stars. The midwife peered up into the depths of the heavens with ignorance and suspicion. The sky didn't look good, whatever it said. It wasn't helped by the moons. Mannslieb's great disk was settled amongst the treetops, staining them a sickly yellow. Morrslieb was in the ascendant, rising high overhead, throwing its dread radiance down upon all that might walk, crawl or creep through the Laurelorn Forest.

Gunda hugged the child close to her. The boy was wet

and hungry. His bawling left the midwife in no doubt of his displeasure. Although she had taken the child at Roald's insistence, she had little idea what she was to do with him. She was too old to raise him herself. She was a midwife but her husband Ambros had long passed. Her daughter was a wet nurse in Beilen and there was an orphanage in distant Dieterschafen – but neither would take the boy if they knew the circumstances of his conception. The reavers and marauders of the north were known to be polluted from their compacts with dark forces and enjoyed visiting that pollution on others.

Gunda found herself singing a low tune. Something her father had taught her as a child – *The Knight's Dalliance* – about a knight's encounter one night with a beautiful elfin stranger on the empty roads of the Laurelorn Forest. It was a deceptively cheerful tune but did not end well. Despite the comfort it gave her, Gunda allowed the song to trail off on the breeze, lest it attract the attentions of some lonely member of the elder races, whose villages were rumoured to haunt the depths of the forest hereabouts.

She heard the growls first. Low, predacious rattles from the back of blood-slick throats. As she crunched her way along the Schlaghugel Road, Gunda couldn't help looking behind her – hoping for a farmer on a cart of hay or a fellow traveller on foot. Instead she discovered dark shapes that dribbled from the shadowy treeline, like an ink blot running on parchment. Ulric's children. Wolves drawn from the forest by Morrslieb's boldness. They snapped and snarled. They skulked up behind her in a loose pack, waspish in their wasted want. Their eyes glinted with craven hunger.

Even if the child's mewling hadn't drawn their ragged ears, the pack could probably smell the baby's unwashed body. Holding the babe to her bust, Gunda snatched a rock from the road and tossed it at the beasts. The crack of the stone off the road shot through the night. The wolves kept their distance, hugging her scent along the river. Their numbers grew and the midwife's heart sank with every step. The forest fiends would soon tire of their fearful game. Their number would overcome their feral caution with baying and the baring of teeth. They would attack. Before long all Gunda could think of was the sun rising over her bone-picked corpse. Darker thoughts still were prompted by the snapping of the emboldened monstrosities at her heels. She would not die for this child. This screeching orphan. This northman's mongrel.

Morrslieb, full and furious, leered over the treetops at her. With each of the midwife's prayer-mumbling steps, however, a silhouette rose from the canopy. Framed in the moon's lurid glare was Sigmar's glorious form. Cut out of the moon's surface like a shadow, the unmistakable outline of the Heldenhammer rose to greet her. It was the temple. It was Dempster's Rock. Sigmar's statue stood proud atop the tower-dome crowning the rugged brickwork of the temple. The pitch outline of the forest broke for the tree-sparse hillocks amongst which the temple nestled. Gunda Schnass had never been so pleased to see the God-King's bronze form. As her waddling step and the roll of her ample hips took her towards the tall temple doors she felt the wolf pack fall away. She could hear the hackle and snap of their frustration. The God-King was an imposing sight, even for the mindless, savage beasts of the world. The fearful power of Sigmar's image held sway even over them.

Under the temple's great archway, Gunda found the mighty doors closed and barred. Given the hour, this did not surprise the midwife. It was not unusual to find Father Dagobert late at study but it was the dead of night, when most god-fearing folk were wisely in their beds and not in need of a priest. Unlike Gunda. Unlike the child. Huddled beneath the protective stonework of the small temple, Gunda's tired, dread-addled mind came to a conclusion. She could not care for this child. She could not ask her daughter Ada or Mistress Buttenhauser in Dieterschafen to care for it either, not knowing where he came from. What if his father came for him one day? What if the child himself harboured an unknown darkness? He was safest there, Gunda realised, under Sigmar's unflinching gaze. The God-King would see the child right. Gunda – a humble midwife – had seen him safely to Sigmar's door. She had done her best. His fate was in the God-King's hands now.

Pulling the child away from the warmth of her breast and laying the swaddling package in the nook of the arch, Gunda laid a kiss on the boy's forehead with her cracked lips.

'Gods forgive me,' the midwife told him as the child's screams intensified. Gunda did not want to be seen and with heavy heart and tears on her wrinkled cheek, she hurried away – the shame of her steps carrying her off towards Schlaghugel and the hovel she called a home.

As night wore on and the child screamed, the fell radiance of the witchmoon probed the temple archway. The great disk of Morrslieb – like a great bauble in the sky – peered from behind the temple stonework and soothed the babe with its brilliance. The child stared up in infant wonder, its eyes wide and its cries stifled. Moonlight reached through the forest also, calling to its bestial acolytes. The ill-light of the moon eclipsed Sigmar's statue, shielding the coward-hearts of forest savages from the reproach of the God-King's gaze. The treeline bled its gathering darkness and soon the hillocks of Dempster's Rock were swarming with their vicious kind, baying to the moon and drooling their intention to tear and shred. What the sordid effulgence did for their night eyes the unchanged swaddling did for their empty bellies. The forest was saturated with the baby's smell. Its tender flesh called to them.

As the most brazen and ravenous of the wolves ventured before the great doors and into the arch, they snarled and snapped their claim, streams of slobber tossing this way and that as each advancing beast attempted to secure the prize for itself. They nipped experimentally at the swaddling, dragging the babe from the archway and down the steps. Again the child's screams shattered the night, as it became the object of a tug-of-war between two great black beasts.

The first barely managed a half-yelp before its skull was smashed into the ground. The second was allowed a fleeting moment of wide-eyed panic as it released the child. The spiked metal ball that had demolished its competitor came up on a chain. It accomplished a moon-scraping orbit before coming crashing down on the wolf with equal fervour. A second smash pulverised the beast and finished it.

'Get out of here!' the weapon's wielder roared. Father Hieronymous Dagobert's vestments hung down about his waist; the hairy belly that wobbled generously with every swing of the twin-entwined chains was pale in the moonlight. He had been woken by the cries of a baby before his temple's doors and had hurriedly donned his robes and his boots. The morning star clutched in his pudgy fists was in fact the temple censer, streaming incense from the heavy ball of its spiked thurible.

'Back, beast,' Dagobert compelled the pack savages, his boots kicking teeth from the jaws of skulking scavengers and breaking the backs of the fleeing creatures. 'Back, I say! In the name of Sigmar back, or you'll get a taste of the Herald.'

Dagobert swung the spiked ball about his great body on its twin chain, the gust-fed incense within glowing like a comet through the sky.

Within moments of the priest erupting from the doors of his temple, the ravenous pack recovered. Lurkers slinked in under the Herald's arc to snap at the child, who once again had become transfixed – this time by the streaming afterglow of the priest's Herald. Beasts left the ground and snapped for Dagobert's own ample flesh. He pounded them back with bloodied fists and tight swings of the chain. A rumble built within the priest's belly that became a growl of his own as he smashed the children of the night out of the air and into the ground. With his chest rising and falling, and the Herald burning bright at its chain-end, the pack broke off. Enough of the scavengers were dead to shake loose the moon-fuelled confederacy of their number.

'Back, you beasts,' Dagobert said finally, spitting his derision down on the mashed carcasses of wolves that had incurred the wrath of Sigmar's Herald. Beside him, the baby stared up in blood-speckled wonder.

'Now who are you,' the priest put to the child, 'abroad on such an evil night?' He looked about for any sign of who had left the infant before shrugging. 'You'd best come in with me then,' he said, the kindness of his words labouring against the catching of his breath.

With the babe in one hand, held against his rounded belly, and the Herald coiled in the other, Father Dagobert made his way back towards the temple. Beneath the bronze gaze of Sigmar he nodded silently, before stomping in under the archway and kicking the great temple doors closed behind him.

CHAPTER III

*'The corn is cut and the crops are reap'd.
Taal is praised and the gathering heap'd.
Thanks are given for the kindly skies,
And that fruit was not taken before it
was ripe.'*

– The Reaper's Danse (Anon)

*Dempster's Rock
Nordland
Vigil der Erntezeit, IC 2399*

Hieronymous Dagobert's footfalls were heavy on the scullery steps. The kitchen fire was roaring but there was nothing cooking on it. The priest was silent as he reached the basement flags.

'Father,' a voice came, just audible above the roar of the fire. It was tender with age. Young, fragile and broken. More of a devastated whisper than a voice. The word rattled off into a coughing fit, which prompted the priest to close his eyes. 'Hieronymous, is that you?'

Dagobert stood with his broad back to the child. His hand had formed a fist. He bit at his knuckle absently. His eyes were rheumy and his cheeks flushed but Lady Magdalena of the Salzenmund Hospice had assured him that it wasn't the pestilence and that he was merely overwrought in his tending to the child. She could not say the same of the boy, however. Worse, the priestess of Shallya told him that the disease was not known to her or her order and the best she could do was make him comfortable for the coming end.

'Father?'

'I'm here, my son,' Dagobert assured the young boy. He opened his misery-clutched eyes and walked to the scullery side where a pot of medicinal tea had been cooling. Ravenswort and ground Staffroot, Magdalena had told him. Something to help the suffering. If taken in quantity, something to help the sufferer slip away. 'You should take some more of your tea,' Dagobert called over the fire. 'As Lady Magdalena instructed.' He picked up the fire-burnished pot and poured the foul-smelling infusion into a wooden mug. He stopped. His hand was shaking. The misty liquid sloshed about the cup. Dagobert slammed it back down on the tabletop. 'No,' he said to himself. 'Sigmar forgive me. One more night.' Leaving the concoction, Dagobert crossed the scullery to where he had positioned the boy's bed before the fire.

'Oh, Little Diederick,' Dagobert said. The youngling looked terrible. A veritable corpse. He was shaking – his frame continually wracked by shivers that even the most furious fire failed to combat. Dagobert had called the boy Little Diederick, but for eight he had been quite tall and brawny. The pestilence, however, had wasted him to a husk. A field mouse could have lifted him from the bed. His young flesh was threaded through with a canker that opened up splits and welts that would not heal and in turn gave breed to a pox that had turned his skin to scab and scale. His fine, blond hair had fallen away and his sockets were bruised brown with corruption. The eyes within had clouded over and consigned the boy to darkness. Worst of all, a bloody and black treacle continually leaked from the corner of the youngling's mouth, proceeding from both his chest and his stomach, making it difficult for him to breathe and almost impossible for him to eat.

Despite the boy's myriad sufferings, the priest hardly ever heard him complain. He had a strength of body and mind that Dagobert both admired and dreaded. The more Little Diederick fought and the longer he endured the more he would suffer. Lady Magdalena told Dagobert that despite the boy's undeniable spirit, he was finished. Dagobert had wept before the priestess. He had raised Little Diederick at the temple. They had not been apart for eight years and Dagobert – who had no children of his own – discovered that the boy had brought meaning to his life he had not expected. The act of charity in saving him that fateful, moonlit night and taking him in had turned into an act of love. He was both a spiritual and substitute father to the child. He had named him, for Sigmar's sake. The truth was that the tears Dagobert shed were tinged with relief as well as sorrow. It was almost over for the poor boy. A day at most, the priestess had given him. Then she had given Dagobert the tea to ease both the boy's suffering and the way to Shallya's bosom.

'Father,' Little Diederick wheezed. 'Am I dying?'

'Yes, my boy,' Dagobert answered. The words came fast and easier than he expected. 'Not long... Not long. Your trials will soon be at an end and you will be free. Do you suffer, Diederick?' Dagobert asked.

'I don't feel much,' the boy said. Dagobert nodded. Lady Magdalena's concoction had been successful in cushioning her patient from the worst of his agonies. 'I'm frightened,' the boy admitted.

Dagobert took the small, silver hammer he wore about his fat neck in reverence to his God-King – the emblem of his holy office – and draped it about the child's neck. The boy didn't even feel it.

'Don't be,' Dagobert said. 'I'm here. I'll always be here – at your side.'

The boy was still shivering, despite the fire. Dagobert sidled around the bed and lay down behind Diederick. He put his arm about the child, trying to warm him further. The pair of them lay still awhile, staring into the raging kitchen fire. Minutes passed. The boy's breathing grew increasingly laboured. Dagobert held him through a savage coughing fit that shook the delicate child until he was almost insensible.

As he rescued his breath and returned to solemn silence, Dagobert spoke.

'Diederick?'

'Yes, father.'

'Do you think you might ever find it in yourself to forgive me?' the priest asked, his voice strained with emotion.

'For what?' Little Diederick hissed, his words reedy.

'This is my fault,' Dagobert admitted. 'I don't think you caught this pestilence in the forest or from the river. I don't think a visitor to the temple brought it to us. And neither does Lady Magdalena.'

'What's wrong with me?' the child asked with a chilling directness. Dagobert turned his eyes from the blinding flicker of the fire.

'I sent you for the books,' he told the boy. 'I was distracted. I left the vault door open. I never thought that…' The priest caught himself. 'These things are all my fault.'

'I don't understand,' Diederick said, moving his head, causing more black ooze to roll from the corner of his mouth.

'The vault is a special place,' Dagobert said. 'A secure place, where I am required to keep special things.'

'Special things?' Little Diederick asked.

'Tomes. Manuscripts. Works of great age.'

'Books?'

'Yes, but not the ones I sent you for. Those would never be found in such a place. The vault contains tomes of dangerous knowledge and ideas,' Dagobert said. 'Knowledge that can hurt people. Understanding for which the world will never be ready. Each temple has a vault of such heresies stored securely beneath the holy ground of its flagstones.'

'Why do you keep such things, father?' Diederick asked, devolving once more into a horrible coughing fit. Blood, fresh and raw from the lungs appeared on the boy's lips, prompting Dagobert to wipe it away with the tails of his priestly robe. Little Diederick appeared to be in greater discomfort. Every breath was an effort.

Dagobert thought on the question as the boy grew still once more.

'In order to better protect ourselves from the enemies of Sigmar,' the priest said, 'and the God-King has many. We must know what they know. We study and translate them to know how the servants and darkness might be stopped. Sigmar entrusts such a solemn and hazardous task to a chosen few.'

'Who?' Little Diederick rasped.

'His priests,' Dagobert said. 'His templar knights. You remember meeting Sieur Kastner, yes?'

'Yes...'

'He came searching for such a tome,' Dagobert told him. 'That was why the vault was open. You have to know, Diederick, it was a mistake. I would never have exposed you to such dangers intentionally.'

'I never found the books you asked for,' Diederick said.

'But you found others,' Dagobert pressed tautly.

'Yes...'

'Did you read them?'

'I knocked over a pile,' Diederick said, his face creasing with further pain and discomfort. 'One lay open. I leant in to look. It was covered in strange symbols. I did not understand.'

'Lady Magdalena and I found the toppled books in the vault,' Dagobert said.

'Does Lady Magdalena think I got this for reading one of the dangerous books?'

'No, my child.'

'Is Sigmar angry with me,' Diederick said, bloody tears welling in the mist of his eyes, 'for reading the book?'

'No, Little Diederick,' Dagobert told the boy, 'he is not. The God-King could not be prouder of your hard work in the temple and in your studies. Lady Magdalena thinks that you might have breathed something in: some ancient pestilence or contamination. Something left there a long time ago by one of Sigmar's enemies. The God-King is not angry with you. He is angry with me. I am the one to be punished.'

Diederick began to cough. This time it took several minutes to stop. Dagobert held him, lest the fragile boy shake himself to ruin. As they lay there, before the fury of the fire they both became still and silent.

'Father?' Diederick said, his voice but a strangled sigh.

'Yes, my dear child?' Dagobert dared to answer.

'I forgive you,' the boy mouthed.

The priest read the words on his dry, blackening lips. Tears rolled down the priest's fat cheeks. He laid the child on his back. It was time.

'The God-King waits for you,' Dagobert told him.

'There is something there,' Diederick hissed. 'In the darkness.'

'It is He,' Dagobert said. 'Don't be frightened. Go to him.'

The boy's face contorted with sudden horror and disgust. 'It's not the God-King…' Diederick said. The words were still on his lips as his last breath escaped him.

The Lord of All enjoys the songs, the chanting of children at play, holding hands and dancing around. They sing of flowers, of his plagues that sweep through the land and the ashes of bodies burned. They celebrate this life of death, for he is both the cause of their suffering and he who would save them from it. He defines the times with the pain and fear he brings into mortal lives. Though they would not know it, they sing and dance to the tune of the Great Pestilence's calling.

He takes so many souls in this way. Like the harvest, they are weighed and measured. They are his tithe. His reward for the architecture of agony that is his contribution to their mortal failing.

Like the scythe, the Lord of All does not choose between the one stalk and the other. With so many souls feeding his eternal appetite for affliction and end, he will not miss the one stalk. Does the mill miss the single grain? The bread bereft of flour that dusts the floor with its forgotten bounty? The mouth the crumb that falls from the lip?

He will not miss the one soul unpromised to him. The one soul destined for more than his plague or pestilence. For this one grain re-planted will yield a reaper's harvest. A celebration of death and suffering the like of which the world has never known. He will be a scourge, a disease all of his own. A plague from which the world will never recover. And so I release this soul from its suffering and send it back so that it might be a worm in the rotting carcass of the world. And not a carcass in itself.

CHAPTER III

*'The great and the good carry the same
flaws as you and I.
They are just buried deeper or concealed
with greater skill.
Accept this as truth. Though it is true also
that such revelations are a fall from which
we never truly recover.'*

– Eugen Kufka, *A History of the Empire v.XII*

*Holzbeck
Middenland
Jhardrung's Eve, IC 2404*

Oberon.

Diederick had always liked the horse's name. It rang of nobility. The kind of muscular majesty the monstrous, black stallion projected in its every step. Diederick would know. The page had one of the horse's goliath hooves between his thighs. He held it still, placing a new shoe on the foot. He was overdue a change. As page to Sieur Kastner's squire Nils, it had been Diederick's honour to attend the templar's horse.

Placing the shoe that Diederick had had specially made by Holzbeck's only farrier to accommodate the stallion's size, he positioned the first nail. The shoeing hammer made easy work of the hoof, sending the nail out of the hoof topside, where Diederick expertly bent and twisted it secure. As he went about his work, his hammer pendant swung like a pendulum from the chain about his neck. It had been given to him by Father Dagobert upon being appointed as Sieur Kastner's page, so that Sigmar would watch over him. Grabbing the hammer he held it to stillness. The coolness of the Middenland night crept into the blacksmith's stable. Diederick felt the chill through the wool of his hood and tabard. It was a patched cast-off that had formerly belonged to Nils. Diederick had inherited both the position and the ragged uniform. With both blacksmith and farrier enjoying the night's festivities at the Three Ways Inn across the road, Diederick and Nils were alone and without the blaze of the forge to warm them.

'Nils,' Diederick said. The squire ignored him. 'You cold, Nils?'

'I am,' Nils admitted, going to work with cloth and oil at the broad, heavy blade of Sieur Kastner's greatsword *Terminus*. It was a magnificent weapon. As tall as the squire cradling it. The weapon was ostentatious only in the shameless craft of its blade and the death-dealing certainty of its cleaving edge – although you wouldn't know it to watch Sieur Kastner hack at the unliving like a woodcutter or make a bludgeoned mess of forest-infesting goblinoids. The crusader blade had been in the Kastner family for generations – an heirloom passed from father to eldest son. The guard was inset with the bejewelled modesty of the Kastner family's wealth. The blade itself was inscribed with the weapon's honourable name – earned by Sieur Kastner's great-great grandfather a hundred years before at the side of Magnus the Pious. Along its holy length it bore the crafted design of the twin-tailed comet that heralded the Heldenhammer's coming. The pommel was a simple metal orb, into which the Imperial cross was crafted, honouring the Kastner family's service in the name of Sigmar. The weapon gleamed in the lantern-light of the stable. Nils was careful not to leave the greasy marks of his fingertips on the blade. He rubbed the metal with a cloth, holding it up to the light, his study of the weapon fastidious to the point of obsession. Such imprints would lead to corrosive blemishes, the like of which the squire had suffered for previously at his master's hand. 'Just busy yourself with your work,' Nils told the page. 'The burn of honest labours will warm you to your bed tonight.'

The young Diederick raised an eyebrow. It sounded like something Sieur Kastner would say in one of his more knightly moments but coming from Nils sounded like a hustle. Since there were three more shoes to be fitted and only the filthy straw of the stable waiting for him, Diederick found the invitation a hollow one. As the page finished the first shoe and allowed the steed's great hoof to fall, he walked up the beast's silky, black flank. He patted it softly, noticing the animal flinch a little as he reached the whipping scars on his hindquarters.

'Good Oberon,' Diederick said. 'That's it, boy – just three more to go.'

The night air did little to bother Oberon. He was a Sollander. A pureblood charger from the Upper Soll Valley – although Diederick suspected that in reality he had more than a little Bretonnian Draught in him. As a knight's destrier he was tall and strong. A wall of darkness and muscle standing next to the page.

The inn door opened and the gaiety of fiddle, raucous song and empty steins slammed on tables briefly intruded on the muddy road. It was Jhardrung's Eve, the turning of one year to another. The entirety of Holzbeck had crammed itself into the Three Ways – so called because the inn sat on a well-travelled junction between the City of the White Wolf, Grimminhagen and the Old Forest Road that took the unwary through the dark and dangerous Drakwald. Diederick found himself standing at the stable door as Nils went on with his oiling of the sword.

Without his plate and shield – also waiting for Nils's efforts with cloth and oil – Sieur Kastner cut an unimpressive figure. If it hadn't been for the worn finery of his garments or the dwindling weight of his purse, he could have been trader, cleric or blacksmith. The strength and skill of a warrior's body was long hidden beneath a small mountain of fat. Chicken scraps from an earlier feast clung to grease-spots on the silk of his tent-like smock, while beer-froth sat in his greasy beard like the webs of busy spiders.

The templar clutched his prize for the night to his massive frame. One of the innkeeper's buxom daughters. The innkeeper of the Three Ways wasn't about to argue with a Knight of the Twin-Tailed Orb and might even have hoped that issue from such a union might bright him connections to the Kastner family and their estates in the Gruber Marches. The girl had plenty of fight in her, however. She pushed. She slapped. She bit at the templar's fat, wandering fingers.

Too drunk to restrain her as intended and with festive indifference evident on his broad face, Kastner meandered through the filth and water pooling in the wheel-mulched road – the girl's wrist held in the grip of one meaty fist. She hauled at the man mountain and as he hauled back, drawing her to him, he let his pudgy palms travel across her. More slapping and scraping at the templar's face this time took him from a beer-fuelled daze to thunderous realisation. The palm of his hairy hand produced a stifled squeal from the girl and put her down in the quagmire. He blinked at her and a fat finger came up in warning but the innkeeper's daughter was already up. Filthy rainwater cascaded from her dress as she slipped and skidded away from him. Her face was fearful but her eyes full of defiance. Diederick found a squalid inspiration in the girl's determination. Pulling her drenched skirt-tails to her, she ran up the road, melting into the darkness. Kastner spat after the innkeeper's daughter, shouting something unintelligible after her. As he shrugged his disappointment and disgust away he stumbled to one side, slipping down into a wagon-cut crevasse in the road. He floundered back the other way, his boot losing purchase and putting the templar down on one knee. Furious, the knight rumbled half-heard threats to himself before slapping the pooling waters in frustration.

Diederick felt Nils standing behind him. Watching, like the page.

'Sieur Kastner is not what Sigmar intended,' Diederick said.

The squire didn't disagree, but as the beer-blind templar rose from the small lake in the road, mumbling to himself in a black mood, Nils returned to the greatsword *Terminus* and his work. Sieur Kastner listed back towards the Three Ways Inn before seeming to forget where he was going and settled on a course for the open stable door.

'Get back to work,' Nils instructed the page. Diederick nodded slowly and returned to Oberon's side.

Sieur Kastner stumbled into the stable. He tried to hold position for a moment as he glowered at Nils, furiously at work on the blade, and Diederick's back as the page selected a further shoe for the steed.

'What do you think you're looking at?' the knight slurred at them, despite the fact that no eyes had been raised in the templar's presence. Kastner fell to more grumbling, holding some kind of conversation with himself. Diederick could only make out intermittent words and phrases: 'cesspit', 'White Wolf', '...where a man of the God-King can be appreciated'.

He stomped through the straw to Oberon, who snorted his uncertainty. When the knight was in his cups, nothing was safe from his drunken wrath. The templar wasn't above whipping the horse for some perceived fault. Snatching for the spooked animal's noble head, it became apparent that Kastner intended on mounting the horse and riding north for Middenheim.

'My lord,' Nils braved finally, amongst the commotion. 'My

lord, what are you doing?' It was unwise to challenge the knight in such a state but if Kastner had ridden and fallen or if Oberon were lost, there would only be a greater price to pay the next morning. In his inebriated state, the squire could at least hope that the templar might tire easily or pass out.

'Are you telling me what to do?' Kastner growled, turning on Nils. Diederick watched the pair of them fall into a familiar routine. More slurred mumbling from the knight eventually formed the words, '…little dung-shoveller like you tell a templar of the Tail-Twinned Orb when he can ride and when he cannot…'

Nils didn't correct the knight but simply tried to convince him that the horse was without saddle, bridle and bereft of shoe.

'You want to do this?' Kastner asked with a fat snarl. His face moved between contortions of confusion and gall, falling away occasionally to the palsy of growing fatigue. Unconsciousness beckoned but the templar wouldn't let it take him. 'You want to do this, turd?'

'No, my lord,' Nils said, his voice rising with fear and his own face straining with the ordeal he knew was to come. 'Please, sir. I beg of you. My concern is but for the safety of your hallowed person. In Sigmar's name…'

Kastner's eyes closed for a moment and the fat nobleman drifted to the left. For a second it looked as if he might crash to the stable floor in a drunken malaise. His eyes shot back open suddenly at the mention of his God-King.

'You use his name to me?' the templar slurred. He advanced on the squire.

'F-f-forgive me, my lord,' Nils stammered, his eyes glassy and quivering. 'Diederick changed the shoes against my good counsel. It is he who is responsible for the unreadiness of your steed at this hour.'

Kastner turned his head towards Diederick, who stood trying to calm the snorting and disquieted Oberon. He stared at the page.

'You?' Sieur Kastner blurted.

Diederick stared back, his teenage face hard and unreadable. There was nothing of hurt and betrayal to be found there. Nils couldn't take another beating at the templar's hand. Diederick knew that. Kastner glared at him. He gave him the darkness of his eyes. As usual, the knight found it difficult to hold the boy's gaze. He always had – ever since he had reluctantly taken the young Diederick off Hieronymous Dagobert's hands. The drunken Kastner turned back to Nils.

'No, no, no,' the knight rumbled dangerously. 'The page is responsible to the squire, the squire to his lord. Punish him as you will. You are my servant. Your correction is my burden.'

With difficulty, Kastner unbuckled his belt and tossed the coils of heavy leather down on the ground before the squire. Stumbling at the stable wall, Kastner rummaged through the squire's saddlebags, hanging from a nearby stall.

'Please… sir,' Nils pleaded. The flush-faced knight found what he was looking for. He tossed a tied bundle of birching twigs and a length of knotted rope down with the thick belt. Nils almost seemed to crumble before them. Diederick watched in stony silence.

'Birch, braid or belt?' the templar put to the demolished Nils, spittle rolling down through his beard.

'No,' the squire moaned.

'What?' Kastner roared. 'I can't hear you. Birch, braid or belt. Choose your correction.' Nils just wheezed at his hulking master. 'Sigmar compels you, boy. Tell me now.'

The shoeing hammer flew across the stable, head over handle, before striking the templar in his mountainous backflesh. It thudded and fell. Kastner staggered forward, his face a mixture of pain and surprise, his brow like a growing storm. He turned slowly to look down at the hammer on the straw-strewn floor. The knight seemed to sober. He looked up at the page.

'I choose the hammer, you sack of wine,' Diederick told his master. The knight still couldn't believe what had just happened. He kicked the other implements of punishment at

Nils with his boot before leaning down to pick up the hammer. He must have been seeing several because it took him several attempts to acquire it.

'So be it, you little runt,' Kastner told him, advancing with the hammer. 'I knew you were more trouble than you were worth. Since your squire has clearly failed to beat such unruliness from you, it falls to me to take charge of your re-education. You want the hammer, boy, then you shall have it.'

Nils, bawling into the straw, went to crawl away.

'Don't you move,' Kastner seethed back at him. 'You're next.'

Diederick stepped fearlessly forward, drawing the templar's eyes back to his dark-eyed defiance. 'Tell me, boy,' Kastner said, lifting the tool in readiness to strike. 'Why the hammer?'

'Because Sigmar compels me,' Diederick told the templar. Kastner grunted his drunkard's derision and went to bring the hammer down on the boy.

Oberon snorted and whinnied. The stallion suddenly reared up on its hind legs, kicking out with its front hooves. Thinking that Kastner was coming for it, the horse had gone wild. Kastner stepped back from the flash of the hooves and the steam of the destrier's breath.

'Calm, Oberon, calm,' Diederick called, reaching out for the animal, but it bucked and turned, kicking out behind it and smashing the stall bar to splinters.

'Back you blasted thing,' Kastner raged, swinging the hammer before him. As Nils scrabbled away through the straw, Diederick snatched up the stallion's halter chains from the stable wall and moved in to calm the beast before it harmed itself. Oberon's flank came around suddenly, knocking the page to one side, before the frightened horse's back hooves kicked out, striking Diederick in the head.

The page's body was knocked from his feet, smashing into the opposite stall like a child's rag doll. Everything grew dark. Oberon's hooves thundered about him and the heat of the steed's snorts washed over his face. Then, within several hoof-falls it was gone, the horse having bolted from the stable.

The lantern-light was dim. Diederick's face felt wet. There was a dull ache where his head used to be. Something bad had happened, but the page's thoughts couldn't quite make their way to what. All he knew were the beams of the stable roof above him and the tools mounted there. Two heads moved slowly into view. Everything was blurred and the light was bleeding away, but Diederick could make out Nils and Sieur Kastner looking down at him – their faces wearing the same mask of dread stupefaction. The light withered and died. It was the last thing Diederick ever saw.

Accident. Chance. Providence. Doom. These are one and the same. How many heroes have been crafted of the misfortunes that befell them? But for the roll of a die, the flip of a coin or the turn of a card they would be happy nothings to the world. All gods – those of light and of darkness – operate in the enormity of these mere moments. They are in the quiver of the string that sends the arrow wide and the glance of the sword that fails to meet its mark.

I have saved my pawn, my small piece in a larger game, from a hundred such deaths. What is life but the journey of hapless mortals through the myriad dangers of their miserable existence? It is the tedious curse of princes such as I to watch the tangled deathtraps of entwined lives form knots before me. Sometimes I cut the skein free, damning all to whom it is attached. To mortals these are the battles, massacres and disasters of the world. The labyrinthine circumstances into which the doomed have been inescapably placed. Sometimes, however, I take the time to unravel the threads of existence and free the living of their present doom. This I do when I have investment in the game. This I do for my pawn. I set him free knowing that he will similarly set me free of fate – bonds no less intricate or inescapable. And so, my pawn, I release you from a death ordinary and unknown. You are meant for greater deeds.

CHAPTER III

*'But man's way
Lies through the twists and turns of forests
great and woodland dark,
Where savage and born of the earthen
spite before fancy's fearful eye,
the grotesques of the underwald come, as
they did before Sigmar.'*

– Stoltz and Kramer

*Near Suderberg
The Drakwald
Black Aubentag, IC 2406*

Nils called but the thick darkness of the forest gave them nothing. They were alone. They were wet. Deep in the Drakwald and getting deeper. Nils held out Sieur Kastner's dress sword before him. Kastner wore the short blade when not decked in his templar's plate and required at temple or before Graf Todbringer. Nils cared little for etiquette and court protocol now. He needed to put cold steel between himself and the dank darkness through which he was advancing. Diederick – having through hard work and study, also attained the rank of squire – followed with the reins of Oberon in hand. A lantern bobbed from a saddle-mounted staff, throwing a feeble circle of light about the three of them.

It had been raining and although it had long stopped, the heavens' issue had yet to work its way down through the Drakwald's twisted canopy. The darkness was a wall of sound. A cacophony of dripping. Droplets gathering, rolling and falling from leaf to branch to muddy pools and saturated undergrowth beneath. It made for a miserable passage.

Nils called out for the templar again. The action filled both squires with dread. 'What else can we do?' Nils had put to Diederick, but the boy didn't have an answer for him. In a place so thick with trees, tangle and shadow that they might walk straight past their master and not even know it, hollering his name through the night-drenched forest was all they could do. It didn't stop the fanciful imaginations of the pair conjuring images of beastmen, fang-faced lycanthropes and the wandering dead drawn down on them by their own foolish advertisements.

'Surely the barrow can't be that much further,' Diederick said. 'We've been walking for an age.'

Nils crunched on through the sodden undergrowth.

'Perhaps it just seems that way,' the squire mused.

Sieur Kastner's drunken boasts had once again drawn them into danger. Passing through the village of Suderberg, the knight had ventured into the Crooked Boar for a stein or four of spiced brew. When he hadn't emerged, the pair of squires assumed as usual that he had forgotten about them and had taken a room at the tavern. As the next morning spent in the stables rolled into the afternoon, the boys entered the tavern to enquire as to their master's whereabouts. They found that the templar had never made it to bed and had instead entertained them with a tale told by a grieving woodsman about his children, Franz and Frieda, who had disappeared about the Six Stones Barrow. Two trappers at the tavern told the squires that the old Teutogen burial ground was due west of the village and that was the direction the knight had set off in the previous night, after stein-clashing boasts in the tap room that he would find the children or destroy the evil that had.

The squires stopped in their soggy tracks. There were sounds from beyond. Wood cracking. Branches splintering. The agony of trees with their trunks rent apart by something monstrous and unseen moving through the wet forest. Nils crouched down in the brush. Diederick did likewise, holding Oberon's head down and praying to the God-King that the dense forest smothered their lantern-light. His other hand was preoccupied with holding the sacred hammer of Sigmar, the pendant that nestled coolly against his chest. The horse snuffled and blinked its alarm. The animal smelled something, for it too fell to stillness. Listening to the departing crash of the unseen thing through the crowded forest, Nils and Diederick exchanged glances of fearful relief.

'What if we don't find him?' Diederick said as they resumed their trek through the bleak wood.

'You mean Sieur Kastner?' Nils said.

'Yes.'

'We will.'

'What if we don't?' Diederick pressed. 'This is the Drakwald. Entire companies of troops have disappeared here without a trace.'

Nils nodded. Diederick wasn't exaggerating.

'Well you for one would return to your priest and temple on the Nordland coast,' Nils said with confidence, cutting through the knotted undergrowth with the edge of Sieur Kastner's short sword.

'Father Dagobert's moved,' Diederick said. 'I mean, he was moved. The Arch Lector said he was needed in Hochland. His way temple is near Esk, at the foot of the Middle Mountains.'

'Some bad country,' Nils said. 'So I've heard.'

'What about you?'

'You don't have to worry about me,' Nils assured the squire.

'Will you return to your parents?'

'I'm an orphan,' Nils told him. 'Like you.'

Diederick stopped for a moment, bringing Oberon and the lantern to a stop. He'd never known that about Nils. The squire found that he was hacking ahead of the grim halo of light that the lantern was casting in the tight confines of the ancient forest. 'Come on,' Nils scowled, prompting Diederick to follow.

Nils's blade cut through the darkness. 'Bring the lantern up,' he instructed. As Diederick brought it forward, the squires realised that they had hit a clearing. Where there had been trees there was now a dripping, thorny tangle. Leading with Oberon's mighty hooves, the horse trampled a way through for the boys. Through the squire-drowning foliage, they found that the lantern was not needed. Mannslieb was high in the sky – although Nils and Diederick wouldn't have known it under the thick forest canopy – and blessed the clearing with its ghoulish light. The clearing was roughly circular in shape, rising in the middle and dominated by stubby stones, standing upright out of the ground in a circle. Diederick counted them. The two squires looked at one another.

'The Six Stones Barrow,' Diederick said. The trappers had been right.

Climbing up the moon-glossed hummock, the pair moved through the stones.

Nils swore.

'What?' Diederick said.

'I've got bones over here,' the squire said. 'And here. They look human.'

'Probably an animal kill,' Diederick said, upon inspection. 'See the gnawing? Besides, they look old.'

'You don't know that,' Nils told him. 'This could be like Fassberg. Or last Geheimnisnacht.'

'Dark ceremonies? Human sacrifice? Look at the moss on the stones,' Diederick assured him. 'Teutogen all right. Nothing's happened here for a long time.'

'So where is he?' Nils put to the squire.

'Wish I knew.'

Nils kicked a rock at one of the standing stones. 'Let's go.'

'We should wait,' Diederick suggested.

'Are you out of your mind?'

'We've come all the way out here,' Diederick said. 'You want to just go back?'

'He's probably returned to the Crooked Boar and is snug in a bed with a farmer's wife as we speak.'

Diederick shook his head. 'Or passed out under a tree with an empty flask.'

Sieur Kastner kept several about his massive person, for when he was out of reach of an alehouse. 'We should wait. We'll probably hear him snore or fart or something.'

Diederick smiled his reassurance. Nils's anxious mask broke and the squire joined him in the joke.

'Just look for the trees shaking...'

'Or the ground...'

'Enough to wake the dead,' Nils's chuckle died in his throat as he looked down at the bones littering the barrow. Tying Oberon to one of the stubby stones, Diederick and Nils sat down on two of the others. The cascade of droplets from the surrounding forest fell to a puddle-plopping trill. Moonlight bathed the clearing. Nils looked about him.

'Seriously,' Diederick said, attempting to take the squire's mind from the ghastly moon, the dark suggestion of the treeline and the sepulchre beneath his boots. 'You have a plan?'

'What?'

'If we couldn't find him,' Diederick clarified, 'you said not to worry about you. Where would you go?'

Nils looked uncomfortable.

'I don't want to talk about it,' the squire said. Diederick nodded. Silence dominated the stone circle. It was eerie. Sounds reached out for them from the Drakwald beyond. Every scurry, every snapped twig and flutter through the foliage drew their eye-flitting gaze. 'All right,' Nils said suddenly.

'It's fine...'

'I've waited long enough,' Nils said. 'I'm going to Altdorf. To the cathedral. To the chapterhouse. I'm going to apply to be a knight. If the Knights of the Twin-Tailed Orb will have me. If Sigmar will have me.'

Diederick mulled over what the squire had said. 'I'm sure Sigmar will accept you into the ranks as he has accepted you into his heart. That's not the problem. Squire or not, only sons of noble birth can apply to the chapterhouse.'

'It's only a matter of time,' Nils said, his thoughts wandering. 'Even if we find him, sooner or later Kastner will end up with a sword in his gullet in one of his drunken duels or a pitchfork through his heart from some farmer, whose wife or daughter he wronged. That beastman in the Schadensumpf last month almost got the better of him. Or more likely, he will just fall to a tavern floor one night and not get back up.'

'All true,' Diederick admitted. 'But that doesn't help you.'

Nils leant in conspiratorially.

'For years, Sieur Kastner has been a menace to maidens all over the province. It was going on long before I joined him. It is said that his issue routinely arrive at his estates in the Gruber Marches – sent by their commoner mothers to find their father and seek their fortune.'

'I have heard such things,' Diederick agreed.

'Have you ever met Lady Kastner?' Nils asked.

'No.'

'Neither have I,' Nils said, 'which isn't surprising considering how often Kastner returns to his estates. She keeps a townhouse in the city also. It is well known that Lady Kastner is of good heart: a giver of alms to the poor, a good mistress of the Marches and – unlike her husband – a true Sigmarite.'

'Good to hear but so what?'

'What is less known,' Nils told him, 'is that partly out of good heart and partly out of resentment for her husband's disgraceful antics, Lady Kastner sponsors his baseborns' beginnings with wealth from the estate and allows them to carry his name.'

'You would present yourself as Sieur Kastner's issue?' Diederick asked.

Nils nodded slowly, looking down at his reflection in the short sword's oiled blade. There was a self-satisfied grin on his face. 'Would you tell her of his death?'

'I would take some small proof,' Nils said, thinking on it. 'Dead or alive, Lady Kastner is mistress of the Gruber Marches. Does she not deserve to re-marry? Does she not deserve some small happiness of her own?'

Diederick never got the opportunity to answer the squire's question. 'Did you hear that?' Nils said, getting to his feet. Diederick had and even if he hadn't, Oberon's ears had pricked up. Through the curtain of dripping and nocturnal movements the forest had to offer, it sounded like a distant and angry wail: some agonising roar of fear and frustration. The two boys looked at each other, their faces pale in the moonlight. Nils took several steps towards the sound with sword in hand. Snatching up the lantern and Oberon's reins, Diederick followed.

'Come on,' Nils said grimly, cutting his way back into the blackness of the tangled forest.

As they moved through the maze of midnight trunks and snarled foliage, they heard the dreadful call again. It was Sieur Kastner. They would know it anywhere. He sounded weak. Desperate. In pain. Nils went to call out to him but Diederick's hand grabbed his shoulder. The pair stopped. Oberon snorted its anxiety. There were whisperings about them. Voices harsh and hushed, hidden in the forest night. The boys stared about in neck-craning disconcertion. Sieur Kastner called out again. This time it was more of a miserable howl of agony. Much closer. Almost an echo.

Nils pushed on through the Drakwald but once again Diederick's hand shot out for his shoulder. Nils hacked through the rampant shrubbery of the ancient forest, his blade slicing its way back through to the moon's ailing glow. His boot found nothing before it and the squire slid down a collapsed bank of shredded roots and saturated earth. Diederick's hand slipped down his shoulder and arm, the two squires grabbing for one another as they ran out of limb. Snapping his hand closed about Nils's own, Diederick was almost pulled after the squire, as the pair of them hung off the edge of a forest sinkhole. With his other hand, Diederick held onto Oberon's reins, the weight of the horse the only thing preventing the pair from plunging into the gaping hollow.

The steed, also not wishing to fall, reared – which fortunately was what the squires needed it to do. With Nils back on solid ground and Diederick regaining the use of his arm, the pair clung to the trunks of rain-drenched trees and peered into the large sinkhole. It was lined with ancient trees and foliage fortunate enough not to have fallen in. Its walls were threaded with rotten roots and jagged with stones but everything was greasy with moss and mud, as rainwater from the surrounding woodland dribbled down into the depression. Diederick went to grab the staff-lantern but discovered that he didn't need it. Mannslieb gleamed down on the Drakwald, dusting the canopy with a sickly, silver light that penetrated and illuminated the sinkhole's depths. The hollow reached into the forest's black bowels. Its bottom was uneven. A landscape of root-strangled earth, mouldering logs and depressions, deep with collected rainwater. Then they saw him.

'Heldenhammer's sweet blood,' Nils said.

It was Sieur Kastner. He was lying broken and delirious at the bottom of the sinkhole, where he had fallen the night before. The sight of people peering into the hollow drew urgent groans from the knight, who was beyond words.

'We've got to get him out,' Diederick said. Nils said nothing. He just looked down on the fallen templar. 'We've got to get him out,' Diederick repeated.

'I'm thinking,' Nils said.

'I'll climb down,' Diederick suggested.

'And how are we supposed to get the sack of wine back up here?' the squire put to him.

'The man is suffering,' Diederick told Nils.

'Perhaps he deserves to,' Nils said, looking down on his master.

'He's a servant of Sigmar.'

'Have you ever known him serve anyone but himself and his appetites?' Nils put to the squire.

'One of us could go back to Suderberg for help,' Diederick suggested, looking back into the whisper-haunted darkness of the forest.

'Alone? Through the Drakwald? In the middle of the night?' Nils said. 'You think that a good idea? Look what happened to him.'

'Exactly,' Diederick pressed. 'Look what happened to him. You can't seriously be contemplating leaving him down there.'

'What can we do?'

'Like I said,' Diederick repeated, 'I'll climb down. You drop a rope to me. I'll tie it around him and we'll use Oberon to pull him out.'

Nils seemed to consider the plan.

'The rope is back at the stable,' he said dourly.

Diederick fixed the squire in a stony stare that gleamed in the moonlight.

'Nils,' he said, 'I know what you're thinking but we're not doing this. I'm going down into that hole. You are going to rig something up here with Oberon – take apart the harness – vines, roots, anything.' Diederick handed Nils the reins. 'Yes?'

'Yes,' the squire said finally.

With that, Diederick ventured into the sinkhole. Descent wasn't a problem. Climbing down the wall of the hollow, the squire found that the earth came away in his hand in squelchy sods but that the root systems of surrounding trees gave him all the handholds he could wish for. As he climbed down, he could hear the templar's ragged breathing and his agonised moans echo about the depths. Mannslieb looked down on them from above, like a great coin in the night sky, reflecting light from its blotched, silvery surface down into the sinkhole. Nearer the bottom of the hollow, where even the roots of the ancients above failed to reach, Diederick would be forced to drop the remainder of the distance. This would make climbing out all but impossible if Nils failed to rig something for their extraction.

'How's it coming?' Diederick called up. His voice assumed an empty desperation, as though the depth of the hollow sapped all of the strength and determination from his words. There was no reply from above but Diederick could see roots twitching at the hollow edge suggesting that the squire was hacking up material for an improvised rope of some kind. Clutching the hammer about his neck and offering a small prayer to his God-King, Diederick dropped.

It felt further than it looked. Something leapt in the pit of his stomach. His boots hit the sodden ground and he slipped, falling to one side into a sunken depression of collected rainwater. Pulling his face from the water, Diederick found the stinking pool to be choked with bones. Extricating his hand from a ribcage, while staring at a skull – jawless and cracked – Diederick found himself swarmed by a plague of frogs that had made their home in the dank underpool. The disturbed colony hopped about in filthy panic, croaking their disconcertion.

Scrabbling to his feet, Diederick made his way across the pit with difficulty. The bottom was a boot-clamping mire that threatened to drag the boy down further into its foetid depths. Clambering across a log that disintegrated in his hands, liberating infestations of lice and the segmented lengths of venomous centipedes, Diederick reached the templar. Sieur Kastner looked up at his squire with unseeing eyes. The knight was feverish and out of his mind with pain. His plate was bent and buckled, while beneath there were almost certainly bones broken. He clutched the length of the greatsword *Terminus* to him like a child he feared to let go of – a lethal, mud-splattered child, whose cleaving blade and inset jewellery glinted in Mannslieb's pallid blaze.

'We're going to get you out of here,' Diederick assured his master bleakly. 'Can you move?'

When the templar didn't reply, Diederick went to inspect his legs for injury. With heart-sinking realisation, Diederick saw that Sieur Kastner's legs were no longer there. The knight moaned miserably to himself. Diederick looked about the bottom of the pit. There were wretched holes – openings – in both sides of the hollow wall. The sinkhole had collapsed into a network of excavated misery running beneath the ancient forest. Something living both beneath the Drakwald and the ruined barrows of the Empire's long-dead tribes had been liberated. Diederick stared into the darkness of the nearest opening. He strained to see what was within and was greeted by the suggestion of beady, blood-hungry eyes staring back. Diederick stumbled back through a water-logged crater, only to turn and find the tunnel entrance behind him similarly haunted. Needle-toothed monstrosities were swarming the dribbling crawlspace of the passage, eager to catch a glimpse of their next meal.

'God's wounds,' Diederick cursed. He looked back down at Sieur Kastner. Whatever infested the tunnels seemed to fear the light. Where the knight's armoured body had fallen, in both presence of daylight filtering down through the Drakwald, and the fearful gleam of the moons during the horror of night, Sieur Kastner had remained untouched. Where his legs had lain in shadow, near the hollow's edge, things had ventured from the tight, muddy openings to feast on the knight's flesh. Opening his plate up, the monsters had begun to eat Sieur Kastner alive. Only the reach of *Terminus*, wildly swung, and the light of the sun and moons had kept the creatures at bay.

Diederick retched into the frog-writhing pool. Wiping his mouth, the squire suddenly felt something slither across his shoulder. Spinning around, the squire found a root-twined rope had fallen across him.

'Thank Sigmar,' Diederick murmured, grabbing at the improvised rope. The squire looked down at Sieur Kastner. There would be no saving him now. As his squire and a servant of the God-King, it was still Diederick's responsibility to see his master's body to a funeral pyre. He had to try. Father Dagobert would never have forgiven him otherwise.

Diederick pulled the length of entwined root. Something was wrong. Its length ran and it ran until finally the coils of its hasty construction fell down into the pit.

'Nils…' Diederick growled, his eyes drawn back up towards the forest above.

Something was happening. The squire could hear the sound of Oberon crashing about the trees. He listened to the fearful whinnying of the stallion and the thud of panicked hooves into the woodland earth.

'Nils!' Diederick called. There was something up there with them. The squire could make out the break of branch and the snapping of foliage as Oberon turned, bucked and kicked out at creatures of darkness emerging to claim him. Of Nils he heard nothing. No friendly face appeared at the sinkhole edge and no further root-twined rope dropped down to extricate him. All he could hear was the crunching of bones, the scissor-slice of needle teeth and the horrible passing of flesh down goblinoid gullets. Diederick felt a dank dread creep through him. Nils could not save him; Oberon would follow; the squire would be left in the pit with his dying master, to face a slow death by starvation or be flesh-stripped by swarms of subterranean fiends, the instant clouds covered the guardian moon.

The boy's lips tightened to a dogged snarl. He would not die here, in some arsehole of the Drakwald, as a full belly for an underclan of shadow-suckling goblinoids. This was not the death the God-King had planned for him.

Diederick turned back to Sieur Kastner. The knight still clung to *Terminus* with an almost religious fervour. Diederick looked about the grim pit for an exit. He made a decision. He needed that sword.

'My lord,' Diederick said, kneeling down in the mire beside the fallen templar. Kastner's eyes writhed about their sockets in delirium. 'Master, trust that I will see *Terminus* back to your family's lands.' The squire took hold of the great blade but Kastner would not let it go. 'Your great-grandfather, your grandfather and your father saw its honoured blade – a blade that shed blood at the side of Magnus the Pious – back to the Gruber Marches. There, Sigmar-willing, it will one day find service with one of your issue. A warrior, like yourself, pledged to the God-King's cause. Let me do this last service for you, master. Allow its example to live on. Let me see *Terminus* home.'

Diederick couldn't tell if the knight had heard him but the metal-cased digits of his gauntlets suddenly released the blade. Diederick nodded but the templar's eyes trembled shut. He fell to moaning away the last of his life – a life long with sin and regret. Despite the knight's failings, Diederick hoped he could find his way to peace.

Drawing the greatsword to him, Diederick gauged the weight. It was far too heavy for him to hurl from the pit like an anchor or grapnel. Above, a sliver of cloud was drifting before Mannslieb's full form. Diederick didn't have much time. Grabbing the rope Nils had thrown down to him, he climbed through the loop intended to haul Sieur Kastner back up the side of the hollow. The end Nils had failed to secure Diederick triple-knotted about the hilt and guard of the greatsword. Attached to *Terminus* by a line of entwined roots, Diederick held the heavy sword over his shoulder in the fashion of a pikeman or halberdier. Splashing through the bone-littered shallows, the squire launched the tip of the weapon at the sinkhole wall like a javelin. The broad blade passed into the damp earth, its weight and the keenness of its edge taking it with ease into the side of the pit.

Backing along the wall, with the horrid whispers of tunnel crawlers in his ears, Diederick prepared to save himself. He breathed in. He breathed out. With water erupting about his footfalls, the boy launched himself at the protruding hilt of the two-handed sword. Swinging about it like a tumbler or acrobat, the squire's legs came about and his boot tips reached the flat of the blade. Without waiting to lose his balance, Diederick bent his knees and pushed off from the embedded blade, leaping desperately for the wall-snaking roots of the trees. Like grapnels, his hands clawed through the strata of black soil, grasping for anything that might provide purchase. And there the squire hung, by the tips of the index and middle finger of his left hand, ensnared in a willowy root.

As the mire-smeared squire made his ascent through the under-tangle of the ancient forest, he could hear Oberon stamp and snort, whinny and haw. The steed was being attacked by the dark denizens of the below and beyond.

'I'm coming!' Diederick hollered up the sinkhole wall. He was terrified that the horse would bolt and abandon him. 'Nearly there, boy...' Diederick was exhausted, but managed to haul his mud-sleek form over the edge of the pit. There was no time to catch his breath. He could hear the steed stomping and skidding to a halt, hemmed in by the dense forest. The Drakwald darkness was sibilant with the hissing of shadow-hidden forms. Things that crawled from the earth to feast.

Diederick skidded about the edge of the pit, bathed in the silver safety of the dying moonlight. He slipped out of the roots looped about him like a harness. Upon reaching the far side of the hollow, he began to gather the rope in his arms. With the slack taken up, he hauled at the hairy roughness of the root line. His palms burned and his heels sank as he fought the sinkhole wall for possession of the embedded greatsword. Inch by inch it slipped out, until finally *Terminus* slurped free of its earthen prison, sending Diederick tumbling back into the blackness of the forest.

On his back, and with the weald about him alive with the sounds of famished evil, Diederick gathered the rope hand over hand like a sailor. Finally hauling the greatsword through the forest tangle and to him, the squire scrambled back to his feet. *Terminus* was far too heavy for the boy to wield. Grunting, Diederick laid its length across his shoulders. As he felt something come at him in the murk he used his body to lunge the blade tip at the threat, sometimes spinning on his heel to cut at his tormenters with the cleaving edge of the weapon.

The effort was back-breaking work, but through a snarl of exertion, Diederick found his way to a grim smile. He couldn't see them but he could feel the wariness of the goblinoids beyond. Even wielded in such a fashion, *Terminus* could take off a spindly limb or impale a wizened ribcage. Guided by the staff-lantern mounted on Oberon's saddle and the stallion's snorting alarm, Diederick found his way to the steed. The wildly swinging lantern had saved the animal's life under the sky-blanketing darkness of the forest canopy. Their fear no less for such artificial light than Mannslieb's gleam or the blinding fury of the sun, the night goblins had been wary of the beast. Instead of the shredded mound of horseflesh Oberon should have been, the steed had only suffered belly-bites and scratches along its muscular flanks. Allowing *Terminus* to tumble from his shoulders and stab upright in the forest soil, the mud-splattered squire held his arms up to calm the stallion.

'It's all right,' Diederick soothed. 'It's all right, boy.'

As the horse lowered its head and approached, it revealed the butchered body of Nils. The squire's ragged corpse was being dragged down a hole between the great roots of a twisted oak. The corpse twitched as the thing below attempted to wedge Nils through an opening too small to admit him.

'No!' Diederick yelled, skidding down beside the squire's corpse. As he grabbed for his body, something gave and Nils slipped suddenly below. Grabbing for his trailing hands, Diederick and the underdweller fought for the squire's body, until finally it was wrenched from the boy's grip. 'No!' Diederick roared down the hole, but something shot back out at him. A sneering mask of pallid underdweller gnarlflesh, stretched over a sordid skull and crowded with teeth like broken glass. Only its eyes sported any kind of colour – a murky crimson, like the blood its clan guzzled from the fresh corpses like piglets.

The night goblin dared not press its advantage further into the lanternlight and swiftly withdrew. Diederick kicked away from the hole and pulled *Terminus* from where it was speared in the ground. Slipping the muddy length of the templar sword down into the stallion's saddle-scabbard, the squire mounted his master's warsteed. Diederick could only imagine the hissing hordes of goblinoid hatred stalking him between the tree trunks, just out of sight. Holding the staff-lantern high, Diederick kept the monstrosities back as he guided Oberon to the sinkhole's edge.

Looking down into the hollow and with Mannslieb's waning light dying about them, Diederick found that Sieur Kastner, lying smashed and insensible on the pit bottom, was almost impossible to make out. He heard the crunching of small jaws through bone and gristle, and realised that in the twilight he was being watched. Scores of beady, red eyes peered up out of the pit at the squire. Drawn out by the dwindling glare of the moon, the night goblins had ventured out from their tunnels. They were swarming the snug shadow of the forest and were now creeping out into the open night and feasting on the Knight of the Twin-Tailed Orb. It was an ignoble end for a servant of Sigmar. Even Sieur Kastner. His body would never see the funeral pyre. His spirit would never rise to meet the God-King.

Diederick thought on the knight. His squireship was over. He thought on poor Nils and considered his daring plan. There, above the pit, Diederick came to a decision. He would not be returning to the temple. To Father Dagobert and his sermons. Diederick lifted the staff-lantern high before tossing it down into the sinkhole. The lantern smashed down on the pit bottom, splashing oil across the shallows. The flames raged, turning the pit into an inferno. Goblinoids screeched in blind agony, unable to find their way to mother-darkness. The underdwellers burned and the darkness of the surrounding forest was lit up by the blaze. The shadow creepers withdrew, spitting their simultaneous hunger and hatred of the pink flesh.

The squire felt the heat rise from the pit. With it, he hoped that Sieur Kastner's soul might reach for the skies – if only to atone to Sigmar himself for being such a despicable human being. Diederick turned the great Oberon about. He had never ridden the beast and the steed was huge. The squire gave the horse a little encouragement with his heels but Oberon didn't need it. The horse was happy to weave through the thick trunks and leave the goblin-haunted site of flame and slaughter.

Their path lay east. East of Suderberg. East of Middenland. East to the Gruber Marches – where, God-King willing – Diederick would return the sword *Terminus* to its ancestral home and lay false claim to a new one of his own.

CHAPTER IV

*''pon my soul, I could a mighty tale
unfold,
and upon the shoulders of our hero bestow
times of trial, transformation and woe.'*
– Kaufmann, *The Saga of Faramond* (Chorus)

*Flaschgang River Road
Hochland
Schlachtentide, IC 2420*

It was the first warm day of the Sommerzeit and Diederick Kastner felt the sun on the metal of his plate. He rolled in the saddle to the idle rhythm of Oberon's ambling gait. The Flaschgang buzzed with darting dragonflies and gurgled its meandering journey south, on its way to join the mighty Talabec.

'And the precepts that guide us?' Kastner put to his squire.

Emil Eckhardt rode beside his master, the young squire's horse in turn trailing a third pack animal. Over the beast of burden, hands and feet bound beneath the horse's belly, was a blanket-bundled corpse.

'To strengthen,' Emil said.

'And why?'

'The servants of Sigmar must be as strong–' Emil said.

'–in both mind and body,' Kastner added.

'...as the bonds that bind them, one Imperial to another.'

'Sigmar was unifier of the warring tribes that settled these ancient lands,' Kastner said. 'He gathered their strength so that they might face trials past, and those yet to come, as one. It is our sacred duty to maintain what he created. No one man can call himself an army, a nation, a people. It was Sigmar's wish that we be part of something greater than himself. He is both a generous and modest God-King. We love him for that. Go on.'

'To honour,' Emil told his master.

'How?'

'Leading by the Heldenhammer's example,' Emil said. 'By bringing his teachings to the people through action.'

'Sigmar was no teacher,' Kastner corrected, 'no mentor in a conventional sense. There are no writings of his to study. No body of works left to follow. His instruction lay in his deeds. His ways in his character. He trusts us to keep his spirit alive in our aspiration to his example. Brave in battle and loving of his land. And the third of the precepts that guide our order?'

'To protect.'

'Go on.'

'We are the blazing omen,' Emil said with confidence, 'throwing fear into those who would bring fear to the Empire. We are the griffon's talon, tearing the heart from the darkness within our own borders. We are the hammer in Sigmar's hands, to be swung through the ages at enemies out of his reach. The innocent are our charge, the weak our burden and those who would war in the God-King's name, we call brother. Does that satisfy you, master?'

'It will serve,' Kastner said, the merest curl of pride in his otherwise grim lips.

Content that he had pleased his lord, Emil fell to self-satisfied silence.

'Tell me, squire,' Kastner said. 'Why do we drag the maggot-ridden corpse of Yulian Spartak back to Flaschfurt?'

'To burn him, master.'

'But what does that serve?'

'We burn him before the people,' Emil said, 'so that they may always remember it. So they know him as but a man and not as some dark legend of their past.'

'You can't kill a legend,' Kastner said. 'Yulian Spartak needs to be dead in the hearts of the people. Only the certainty of his end should endure on tongues and be carried far on the wings of idle gossip. They must see the monster burn, for then they will not fear him. They will not fear what he has become. They will be better prepared to stand against such evil, should they encounter it again.'

'Does such an act not carry dangers, master?' Emil asked.

'Explain yourself.'

'Are we not simply exposing the innocent to a corruption that they would rather forget or have never seen at all?'

Kastner frowned.

'Do you not understand?' Kastner said, his voice grave.

'I have doubts…' the squire admitted.

'A spider crawls across your arm,' the templar hypothesised.

'Yes?'

'You brush it away,' Kastner continued. 'Moments later, you brush your arm off again – but there was no spider there.'

'Is that not a good thing?' Emil asked.

'It is your fear returned,' Kastner told him. 'A dread that now lives on inside you, giving function and form to your nightmares. It draws you to it and makes you part of that which you abhor. In your heart you would know that there was nothing to brush away, if the spider still sat crushed in your fist. We guard the borders of Sigmar's empire. We patrol the roads and forests of his ancient land. We cannot, however, stand sentinel over the souls of each and every one of his people. Actions will speak in our absence.'

'Yes, my lord,' Emil said obediently.

'How many womenfolk wake to infant screams of horrors relived? How many sons of Flaschfurt would have set off after Yurian Spartak and his Ruinous band? How many would have wanted to but for the chill of cowardice in their bones? Victimhood eats its way through the victim, leaving a darkness that the Ruinous Powers of this world can exploit. Sigmar did not give rise to a nation of victims. The people must be allowed their peace. There is a reason we burn and bury our dead. We must be able to move on in good conscience. To live our lives without wonder of what was and what might have been.'

'Yes, master.'

Kastner was not convinced that the squire truly understood. He pulled gently on the reins, prompting Oberon to fall back. He leant across Emil's trailing packhorse and, pulling at the rope that bound the body to it, Kastner liberated the blanket-bundle. The body fell to the road with a thud and a spray of rotten mulch and maggots. The filthy blanket fell open to reveal Yulian Spartak. Spartak of the Iron River. Spartak of Chernigov. Spartak of the Horde of Change. Spartak of the Flesh Capricious. The Kislevite had taken more names than forms, which would have made him difficult to track down were it not for the series of sorcery-slaughters committed by his warband in villages and homesteads along the Drakwasser. It had begun in Flaschfurt, however, and that was where Kastner was determined it would finally end. Emil stared at the hideous champion of Chaos before instinctively looking away.

'Look at it,' Kastner instructed harshly. Emil obeyed with disgust. 'Look at this evil. Not the manflesh it has riddled its way through, but the darkness still there in its Ruinous form. Even in death it wishes to take you from your thoughts – to a place of dread and doubt, where it reigns supreme. In death it does this as it did in its disgusting half-life, putting you from your shot.'

Emil looked down at the misshapen warrior. Its crossbow

bolt still sat in the hunch of one shoulder where a second horned head had grown, yearning to be flesh-separate from the first. Hideous arachnoid limbs of some fresh transformation hung uselessly from the bear furs of its armoured back, while the warrior's legs and feet were those of a terrible bird: scaly, taloned and powerful. Beyond that there was little to make out in the butchery and the rot. Kastner's sword *Terminus* had gouged, hewn and hacked pieces off the thing with cold efficiency. With its sickle-staff cleaved in two and the crowning emblem of its Ruinous patron smashed, the Knight of the Twin-Tailed Orb had spun around. His broad templar blade was like the cyclonic fleshstorm Yulion Spartak had cast through Flaschfurt, Garssen and Ahresdorf and had attempted to visit upon the Sigmarite templar. As *Terminus* had chopped through the armour and chitin of the damned warrior's back, severing the champion's spine and almost cutting the thing in half, Spartak of the Capricious Flesh had erupted in a vomit-inducing blossom of final transformations, until finally the changes slowed and grew still like solidifying wax about a candle.

'You can know your enemy,' Kastner said as the squire stared down at the ungodly corpse, 'without becoming him. That is the burden Sigmar left us to bear. It is a heavy one and it forces us to be strong for our own good. Do you understand?'

'I do,' Emil said, his eyes burning into the butchered corpse. He looked up at the knight and Kastner knew that he did.

'Shall we see this monster back to Flaschfurt?' Kastner asked.

'And watch him burn for his atrocities,' Emil said. The knight and the squire climbed down from their steeds and together bagged and replaced the miserable cadaver on the packhorse's back.

Kastner heard the scrape of sandals on the road. Meandering up the river road was Gorst. The flagellant seemed lost in his thoughts of impending doom and catastrophe to come. His head was hairless with obsession and worry – giving it the appearance of a skull – sitting inside the thick bars of an iron face-cage. His ragged robes hung off the sharp bones of his emaciated form. His lips mumbled a constant stream of madness – warnings and portents of little meaning or consequence. About his whippet-frame the flagellant had wrapped slender chains and the heavy locks that bound them to his purpose.

Kastner had found him sitting on the steps of Sigmar's mighty cathedral in Altdorf. Such doom-laden fanatics often gathered before the temple, watching for signs of some impending apocalypse or great war in the comings and goings of the God-King's priests and templars. When he left the cathedral two years before, Gorst had stood and started following the knight without explanation. The two men had never spoken of Gorst's reasons and, although seeming to understand what few instructions Kastner had given him over that time, he had never made any kind of sense in return. Kastner had come to think of the flagellant like a hound in this way. He was always following in his tracks, hanging his head for the favour of a word or scrap of food. Emil couldn't find it in his heart to take pity on the madman, taking him for at best a parasite or beggar and at worse a potential thief or slitter of throats. Kastner often joked that the squire would go before the flagellant – having given as reason the greater number of years of service.

'What was that?' Emil asked. There was a sound that if not carried on the wind, gurgled along on the lazy Flaschgang. It wasn't the rattle of Kastner's plate, nor the muffled jangle of Gorst's chains. 'Is that a child?'

Kastner bit at his bottom lip but held his tongue. Emil wandered from the packhorse to the river's edge. Kastner waited. The squire's call came. 'Master,' he said, 'it's an infant – a baby – on the water.'

Indeed, the sluggish channel carried a root-riddled sod of reeds and twigs downstream. In the nest lay a bundle of swaddling. From the swaddling came the cries of a newborn. 'My lord?'

'Go,' Kastner told him. 'If you think you need to.'

Emil trudged down the weed-strangled bank, his footfalls tearing through the foliage. Down in the water, where mud and silt attempted to claim his boots, the squire reached out for the sod and pulled it to him. The baby's cries subsided at the appearance of another face above it. With the swaddling clasped to him, Emil made the difficult ascent, careful that the infant did not fall or himself with it.

'Who could do such a thing?' Emil said as he approached his master with the rescued child. 'In Sigmar's name, have these people no shame, no decency?'

Kastner gave the squire the hardness of his eyes.

'Probably not,' he agreed. Waiting.

Emil pulled back the swaddling to inspect the child for injuries. He found none. He found something else entirely. The infant suddenly fell to the ground. The squire's arms were open. He had dropped the bundle of swaddling, the monstrous infant, the horror that the babe had been. His steps took him back towards the river. The baby screamed once more from the tall grass of the roadside. Emil looked up at Kastner and then back down at the uncovered altered form.

'You knew?'

'I suspected,' the templar said. 'It is not uncommon. The product of some deviant liaison. After carrying such a horror, a mother might not be able to bring herself to end her own issue. It is still her child, after all – despite bearing the hideous marks of dark favouring.' Emil said nothing. He just stared at the misshapen infant, screaming its misfortune to the sky. 'Perhaps she thinks her babe might find its way to someone with greater strength and stouter heart.'

Emil looked from the child to the crossbow hanging from his saddle.

'I couldn't,' the squire said.

'The servants of the Ruinous Powers will not always present themselves as Yulian Spartak, dripping with the blood of his innocent victims. You must end this thing of darkness,' the Sigmarite templar told his squire, 'as your calling dictates.'

'I can't,' Emil said miserably.

'Have you not read your Rendsberger? What would Von Bildhofen's *Daemonologie* say on the matter?'

Emil shook his head. The squire heard the sigh of *Terminus* clearing its saddle-scabbard. His head continued to shake.

'My lord, no.'

'You would defend such evil from Sigmar's steel?'

'Surely this child is not our enemy,' Emil said.

Holding the greatsword in two gauntlets, its heavy blade dangling above the screeching infant, Kastner prepared himself.

'We find our enemies on the dark path. Would you join them on it?'

'No, master.'

'Then you know what is necessary. What is needed. This thing presents with the blessings of the Ruinous Powers,' Kastner insisted grimly.

'Cannot the gods decide if it should live or die?'

'We are their instrument,' Kastner said, lifting the blade. 'It is decided.'

Emil looked away.

'I cannot watch,' the squire told him.

Kastner's gauntlets creaked about the sword's hilt. He paused.

'You have much to learn, squire,' the templar said finally, before removing his blade from above the infant's horrific form. 'Your education is my burden. I will not fail you as you fail yourself. Pick up the child.'

'My lord?' Emil said with a face contorted by mixed emotions: shame, concern and disgust. Kneeling, Emil wrapped the creature back up in its swaddling.

'Place it back on the water,' Kastner commanded. 'You will come to see the mistake in your mercy.'

Emil made his way down to the water and set the screaming child back on the sod of woven weeds before pushing it into the torpid current. By the time he returned, Kastner was in the saddle, his glare full of reproachful sadness.

Knowing that he had disappointed his master, the squire remained silent.

The knight prompted Oberon on with his heels, Emil and his packhorse trailing behind with the troubled Gorst mumbling incessantly to himself in their hoof steps. Kastner kept his distance from the shrieking child, the sod carried ahead of them on the sloshing waters, bouncing along the reed banks on the opposite side of the river. The templar and his squire had little to say to one another for the next hour. Emil knew better than to disturb Sieur Kastner in such a black mood.

The infant cried. The waters lapped at the muddy banks and the horses crunched through the grit of the road. Emil watched his master who in turn was looking downstream, watching the far bank. Kastner suddenly sat up in his saddle, craning his head for a better view. Drawing Oberon to a stop, the templar slid down from the steed and led the horse to the roadside. Emil followed suit and knelt down beside his crouching master. Kastner had but one word for his squire.

'Watch.'

Peering through the long grasses lining the river road, Emil saw that the sod of reeds had become tangled in a broken branch that lay off the bank. The infant screeched – its suffering rising with the heat of the dying day. Emil watched. He waited.

The squire's heart thudded in his chest as a figure darted from the tree line and down the riverbank. Its body was covered in piebald fur and its legs were long and cloven. Looking up and down the river, the beast – with a long face and stubby horns of a nanny goat – snatched the child from the reeds and clutched it to itself. Within moments, the creature had become one with the forest again.

'The gods decided,' Kastner said. 'Just not the ones you were counting on.' Emil felt the biting reproach of his master's words. 'Now the infant is our enemy.'

'My lord...'

'Now it suckles gall from a mother born of hate,' Kastner

continued, 'to take its place in a tribe of beastmen. To spread the canker of the Ruinous Powers through the ancient forests and hunt us through the darkness. To maim. To defile. To kill. To sire more of its monstrous kind for us to destroy.'

'I'm sorry, my master,' Emil told him, his eyes on the grit at his boots.

'Fortunately,' Kastner said, getting to his feet. 'Calamity is not without virtues of its own. There is a crossing not too far downstream. We shall pick up the trail at the riverbank and you will track the beast – as I have taught you – back to its foetid herd. There Sigmar's holy work will be done. Have no doubt. We shall end the beasts that walk like men, with all their foul get.'

'Yes, my lord,' Emil said. He was having difficulty finding his way to the same fervent enthusiasm for the fight ahead as his master. The feeling followed him across the Flaschgang and into the depths of the Drakwald. Light left them and the squire was forced to light a lantern. Reading tracks by lantern light was not ideal and several times the squire lost the trail, only to have the templar find a hoof print here or the broken pieces of a snapped twig there.

'Such foundlings,' Kastner told the squire, 'are considered by the beastmen to be gifts from their Dark Gods. Their ears are always open to the cries of the afflicted and abandoned.'

The tracks led the pair to the suggestion of a trail, a dark path winding its way through the broad trunks of the ancient forest. The haunting sound of creaking bark and hollowed bone-chimes hanging from the branches drifted on the dank air. Moss-ravaged stone markers started to signal the beginnings of a dark and shrouded route through the forest's ancient tangle. Once upon the winding trail, Kastner and Emil could hear the distant cries of the child. They were gaining on the beastwoman. Every step into the Drakwald depths took them into the creatures' accursed and ancient hunting grounds. Stinking water sat in leaf-choked puddles. Fungus ran rampant across dying trees while a miasma infected the very air they breathed. The stench of rot – of disease and of slow death – coated them with its rancid musk. Through it, bloated flies buzzed. Things that droned about them crawled across their skin and bit at their flesh.

At the glint of light through the blackness of the dense forest, Kastner told Emil to douse the lantern. Again the pair crouched to watch the beastwoman, foundling cradled in her filthy claws, approach some kind of concealed camp. The smothering forest broke ahead. Cankered leaves carpeted the floor – rustling with snakes, vermin and the large beetles they preyed upon – leaving the surrounding branches bare. Black birthing pools writhed with knots of foul worms. The fat trunks of dead trees seemed to thin, making way for a circle of rough menhirs and standing stones. At the centre raged a fire, threading the forest with a muggy smoke, and casting the beastwoman in silhouette.

There were others. Many others. Black outlines of muscle, hoof and horn. Some swigged blood and ale, while others roared a bestial laughter at one another. Several creatures butted thick skulls in drunken dispute as about them beasts were snarling, bleating and jostling each other in the shadows. Beyond the fire, Kastner could see a crude altar improvised atop a fallen stone, where some kind of bestial shaman was shaking a staff crowned with a star of bloodied antlers over a sacrificial offering. The creature was dressed in rags, its fur settled with moss and its flesh harvested by blooms of fungus. A single horn curled its way out of the creature's skull. Behind the monster, the herdstone it was honouring with innocent blood ached with unnatural energies.

'Sigmar has blessed us,' Kastner hissed. Emil couldn't find it in himself to agree. 'It's a warherd. Take courage, boy. You could not kill the child – the God-King has seen fit to pave the way to enemies you can. These beasts are the very children of Chaos. We shall take their hides in Sigmar's name and bring light once more to this benighted part of his Empire.'

Carefully and quietly, Kastner drew *Terminus* from his saddle-scabbard and climbed down from Oberon. Taking his crusader shield from its saddle-mounting on the steed's flank, Kastner slid his arm through the thick leather restraints. Even in the gloom, the Imperial cross was clear on the shield's battered surface – a symbol of unity across Sigmar's lands, with the God-King bringing tribes from the north, east and west of the Empire together with the under-dwelling dwarfs under one banner. Emil climbed down also, taking his crossbow and drawing the string back to its latch. Kastner shook his head. 'Must you? I don't mind you hunting our evening meal with that wretched thing but must it be used to slay the God-King's enemies?'

'Is this not a hunt of a kind, my lord?' Emil replied, placing a bolt in the groove. Kastner disapproved of the crossbow. It was not a knightly weapon. On the other hand, it would take little for it to slam a bolt straight through the thick plate of his armour. Or the thick hide of a beastman, for that matter. He looked back at the raucous celebration about the standing stones. The templar stared at the wizened shaman with suspicion as it conducted its primitive ritual above the butchery on the altar. Such primitives called on otherworldly powers against which a knight's armour offered as little protection as against a crossbow bolt.

'Then your first quarry can be that horned thing at the centre of the stones,' Kastner told the squire.

'You think it leads this herd?' Emil asked.

'Hopefully not for much longer,' Kastner said.

'I'll need to get closer.'

Kastner looked down at *Terminus*, the greatsword's blade shadowed by the darkness about it. 'You and me both.'

Emil thought on the deer and boar he hunted through the woods.

'Won't they smell us coming?'

Kastner nodded at the squire's packhorse. At the stinking corpse of Yurian Spartak draped over it.

'We are masked by the stench of corruption,' the templar said. He took his crusader's helm from the pommel-horn of Oberon's saddle. 'Fight well,' he said to Emil. 'Know that the

God-King is with us in this desperate place. That he fights at our side in the bloodshed to come. On my signal.'

Emil nodded.

'Good luck, my lord.'

'When your sword is guided by Sigmar, good fortune is not a factor,' Kastner said. 'Remember that.' Kastner's face disappeared behind his helm. Taking slow steps through the mud and mire, leading Oberon by the reins, Kastner advanced on the warherd. As he got nearer he could see that the gors' fighting, drinking and dancing was masking their approach. With Spartak's rotten stench hiding the sweet smell of their uncorrupted flesh from the host and their warhounds, the knight and his squire made it to the outlying circle of standing stones. Roughly carved runes and daemon-honouring symbols, splashed in old blood, covered the ancient obelisks. From the leafless branches of the canopy above swung gibbet cages of petrified wood. Each contained a miserable specimen. Prisoners – men, women and children – had been gathered by bestial hunting parties to provide fresh sacrifice for their unholy gods and flesh for their grumbling bellies. The warhounds that had hunted them had been chain-staked into the ground below the prisoners. They routinely leapt and snapped at the cages, snarls and feverish drool dribbling from their jaws.

The sound of an ugly death – wet and shrill – cut through the bombast of the bestial gathering. Risking a glance about the standing stone, Kastner saw the shaman, arms outstretched, holding his staff and a gore-oozing heart in his disgusting claws. He bleated something to the stars as a disturbed cloud of flies swarmed about his filthy robes. The shaman jabbed his staff at the cages, summoning another victim to his dark altar.

Moving his helm around, Kastner peered around the other side of his stone. A hulking beastman, a wall of muscle and wiry black hair emerged from behind the swollen trunk of a diseased oak. Upon its globed, shaggy shoulders sat a squat bovine skull. The mighty horns of a bull dominated the monstrous head, while its long face bore the curse of a thing sired by daemon on livestock. Steam smoked from its nostrils as it parted the braying and bestial merry-making. Several urn-swilling beastmen failed to move swiftly enough and produced from the monster's chest a rumble of thunder. A skull-crushing fist came down on the first goatly head, sending the beastman crashing into the mud. The second was grabbed by its furry shoulders and butted into savage unconsciousness by the oxen-headed beast. It too went down to the celebratory braying and bleating of the herd. The creatures parted for the beastman, leaving only the warhounds in its way. The bull broke one of the hunting dogs across its hoof with a furious kick. The carcass flew into the air before being torn back down to the ground on its staked chain. Within moments the gnashing mongrels were flat to the forest floor, whining their submission.

Kastner watched the bull take instruction badly from its bleating shaman. Barging through the gibbet cages and setting them to creak and swing, the monster's search produced sobs and doom-laden shrieks from the prisoners within. The people were broken. They had watched as their number had dwindled, one by one succumbing to the butchery on the altar and a bone-splintering feast for the hideous herd. Only one seemed to have any fight left in her. A mere girl by the look of her. Kastner watched as her legs flailed out at the monster from the gibbet cage. The girl gagged.

'Get away from me! You stink,' the girl called. The bull reached out for her but she pulled her legs within the cage. 'Are you deaf as well as lame of brain, you abomination? Go find a spit.'

Kastner was impressed with the girl's spirit – and she was a girl, seeming no older than Emil. She was dressed in rags that might once have been robes, made from material that might once have been white. The girl had the reckless abandon and wicked tongue of youth. Her eyes were dark and defiant while her hair was boyishly short and looked as if it had been scissored about a bowl. Kastner had seen such haircuts before – on the novice-sisters and vestals of religious orders. Standing in her gibbet, she clutched a package to her stomach: a pile of tomes, bound in a pile with twine. As the beastman grasped the wooden bars of the cage, the girl kicked at it with her sandals. 'Get off, you reeking freak.'

The girl certainly didn't sound like a sister. Ire dribbled from the bull's steaming snout. Its ears rang with the bleatings of its shaman and the girl's effrontery. With an effortless flex of its muscle-bound arms and shoulders, the monster tore the cage apart, causing the novice-sister to drop into the den of dogs below. A fang-faced hound brought up its head to snap at the girl. Swinging the books around on their length of twine, the girl smacked its snout aside. A great hoof came down beside her, crunching the dog into the ground for its impudence. The girl screamed as the bull snatched her up by the legs and dragged her through the mire towards the altar. Clawing at the muddy ground, the girl discovered that she had lost her pile of books. She reached out for the length of twine but the bull's monstrous stride swiftly took her out of reach. As the beastman stomped away, the warhounds rose from their subservience and closed about the package of tomes like the gates of a snarling enclosure.

Kastner moved back around the standing stone, *Terminus* seeming to burn in his grasp. The bull laid its colossal, blood-stained hands on the girl, producing another shriek of surprise, but the monster simply grabbed her like a sack of grain and slammed her down on the altar. Lying in the butchered remains of the previous sacrifice, the novice-sister thrashed out with her feet and small fists, knocking the heads of toadstools and settled fungus from the shaman's flesh. The bull glowered at the victim, its stench overpowering and its hot breath billowing about them. The goat-headed shaman seemed amused by the girl's resistance, its yellow teeth bared and its foetid form wracked by a sickly laughter.

'I hear your shepherd calling, whey-face,' the novice said, hitting out at the ancient. She was simple and coarse of tongue but her spirit was indomitable. The shaman reached out for her with mildewed hands. 'Don't you touch me,' she said, spitting at the beast. The girl tried to get up out of the gore but the shaman's staff suddenly came down across her throat. It both held her to the altar and restricted her breathing. She clawed at it but dark energies were flowing through the monster and it was as immovable as a tree. The goatly grin was gone from the ancient's furry lips. It moved in with a claw still wet with blood. The girl tried to cover herself as its hand explored her shredded robes, pulling from them a small silver hammer on a chain. It dawned on the shaman, as it had done on Kastner, that the girl was some kind of novice or the sister of a religious order. With the last of her breath and the staff across her throat, the girl hissed: 'My… God-King… will… smite… thee…'

The shaman erupted with bleating laughter. It was infectious. The creatures of the warherd joined the celebration in savage mirth. As the concubine of an enemy god, the girl's sacrifice would bring many blessings from their dark patrons. Selecting a flint knife from the altar, its razored blade stained red by the many lives it had taken, the shaman held it above the torso of the thrashing girl. The shaman's eyes closed and its lips fell to daemon-honouring bleats and incantations.

Kastner stood, the smooth metal of his plate gliding up the moss-threaded stone. The templar was tensed. His mind and body were ready for the slaughter to come. He had been watching and waiting. Enemies had been counted. Every brute silhouette had been allowed to reveal itself, the measure of its reach and its likely intention. The knight knew by horn and frame which beasts would fight and which would scatter. He knew which creatures were far from their brute weapons and which were out of their mind on ale. He knew the things that had to die first. The ones that would test him with their gifts and savagery. The gors. The bull. The wizened shaman. He looked to Emil. The squire's crossbow was already up, resting against an opposing stone.

'Now,' Kastner told him, his helm coming down and tapping against his breastplate.

The shaman's ragged ears pricked. His eyes opened and rotated in their sockets. Interlopers. Intruders on unholy ground. Fresh sacrifices for the herdstone. His thick tongue wrapped itself around curses and ancient bewitchments.

Emil's horse reared with sudden savagery. The squire instinctively moved, sending his bolt wide. The quarrel tugged at the shaman's rags and shattered off the herdstone behind. The squire's steed was not itself. The creature was glazed of eye and flashing out with its hooves. Emil ducked and backed from out of the cover of the obelisk as his horse's shoe sparked off the stone. The packhorse was similarly affected, hawing and bucking the corpse of Yurian Spartak from its back. This had nothing to do with the dead warrior of Chaos, Kastner decided. This was the shaman asserting its control over the wild natures of its beast-kin.

Kastner watched as Oberon's eyes glazed over like a northern lake. The stallion's lips curled back from the long pegs of its teeth. The knight had to act fast. Kastner ran at the steed, his mail and plated fist bringing his crusader shield up, smashing the horse's skull aside. The animal stumbled backwards, both the sense and spell's influence knocked from it. Legs faltered and the stallion crumbled and crashed to the ground unconscious. The Sigmarite templar's gauntlet creaked about the greatsword *Terminus*. He was less sentimental about his squire's steed and packhorse, which they had recently picked up in Bergsburg. The crusader blade went up between the savage hooves of the reared steed and into its chest. Pulling the broad blade from the punctured ruin of the horse's heart, Kastner spun around. *Terminus* passed through the packhorse's throat before Emil's steed hit the ground.

'Again,' the knight bawled through his helm at the squire who was reloading his crossbow.

The fire raged. The warherd remembered themselves. Ale-jars were flung into the standing stones of the circle. Muscle-bound silhouettes came at the templar. The longhorns first. Savages already tested in battle with greenskins and ratmen. Monsters who had killed enough and had lived long enough to enjoy the appreciations of their herd. They had never met a Knight of the Twin-Tailed Orb, however. They had never met Diederick Kastner. Their beastflesh was tough and wiry, shot through with sinew and strong bone. *Terminus* cleaved through it like clotted cream. Kastner became a silhouette amongst many – the fire framing both the clean, confident movements of his training and the invention he introduced inbetween.

The beastmen, in contrast, were bludgeoners, favouring scavenged axes and stone hammers. Their weapons were rude and rusted but the strength with which they swung them was hate-fuelled and barbaric. There was no organisation or consideration of tactics, only an animal cunning and a pecking order, with monsters of greater size and length of horn engaging first. It was easy for a warrior – even a templar knight moving within the exhausting constraints of metal plate – to lose himself in battle. To become such an animal.

The lost were in the thrall of the Blood God – their rage a mindless offering. Such men were no better than the beasts Kastner was taking apart with the disciplined strokes and thrusts of his templar blade. Kastner had reasoned that the best warriors thought their way through battle. They knew where their blade would be the moment before it landed. They knew where the service of their shield would be required before the fatal landing of the axe. A man that fought by instinct alone – like even the most capable savage – could not know such things. He could not predict the lethal preferences of his enemy and he could not learn from them mid-engagement. Battle was a serious game of strategy and skill, like those played with boards and fancy pieces. Able players could rely on rehearsed moves, while simultaneously exploiting the weaknesses of opponents as they were revealed before them.

Terminus hacked limbs from muscular torsos. Shoulder-cleaving swings took heads almost from shoulders. Streams of hot beast-blood sailed about the knight as the herd's best gors carpeted the ground within the circle.

Kastner's shield soaked up the frustration and desperation of axe-wielding monsters that roared at him as if it meant something. The onslaught continued as Kastner plunged his blade through the carcasses of their fellow savages. Inbetween such surgical thrusts, the templar found a moment to slam back at the creatures at his rear, smashing jaws from goat-skulls with the cross guard of his sword and kicking monstrosities back into the flames of the furious fire.

As the carnage unfolded and the warherd began to get over the drunken shock of the intrusion, the shaman slashed his flint knife through the air, motioning the hordes of lesser gors and brays on into the slaughter. As the herd's best butcherers were cleaved apart by the fearless knight, there were few beastmen that relished such a proposition. With the ale souring in their bellies and their spears and cudgels loose in their claws, they hesitated.

During a raid or the murderous slaughter of a village, the cogs of barbaric carnage were usually oiled by the blood spilled by beastlords and longhorns – the very creatures the plate-clad knight was hewing his way through. With lesser creatures and beastlings fleeing into the darkness of the forest, many of the herd's savages thought of doing the same. Several hoofsteps back, however, they were stopped in their tracks by the thunderous roar of the bull. The beast snatched a broad woodcutter's blade from a nearby creature and took its head clean off with a bellow-driven sweep. Both the sound and the violence drove the warherd on, like a storm at their backs, across the stone circle at the templar knight.

The shaman bleated its alarm at the bull, fearful of offending its gods and intent on completing the sacrifice. Spinning the axe in its colossal fist, the beast caught it and launched the weapon haft over blade at the tree supporting the gibbet cages of the prisoners. Embedding itself in the diseased trunk, the axe cut through the lines supporting them. The cages crashed to the ground amongst and on top of the herd's warhounds. Like the horses, the dogs had been driven to mindless savagery by the shaman's incantations.

The prisoners shrieked their terror as their cages shattered and the diseased maws of the dogs set upon them, tearing the flesh from their bones.

The last of the beastlords was a four-horned monstrosity that Kastner thought he had put down in the first few kills. The monstrous thing, driven on by some bestial refusal to die, swung a mace made up of the embedded fangs of some sabre-toothed conquest. Twice the weapon had punctured Kastner's shield and had even plunged through his plate pauldron and into his shoulder.

As Kastner cut pieces off the beastman with his greatsword and the creature mauled him in return with its thagomizer, Emil found it difficult to take the shot. He had held the crossbow to his eye for some time. Each time he prepared to take the shot, Kastner's armoured form or the flailing body of one of his brute victims moved before the target. As Emil had moved to get a better shot, beastmen had joined the fray – some bound for the squire and intercepted by Kastner.

The shaman, eyes closed and lips mouthing ritual incantations in some dark tongue, held his flint blade over the girl's chest. The novice's bosom rose and fell rapidly in alarm, the creature's staff holding her down on the altar. She pushed up against the staff but it would not move. The mumbling ended. The knife came up. Emil's target would not wait. The squire let the bolt fly. It whistled between Diederick Kastner and the four-horned beast he was exchanging blows with, but the pair barely noticed.

The shaman did notice. The quarrel – which had flown straight and true – had found its way between the creature's unsettling eyes. It stumbled against the mighty herdstone at its back as the flint knife clattered to the altar. The macabre staff followed. Sliding back down the herdstone, the shaman was dead by the time it reached the cankered earth. The novice-sister sat upright, clutching at her throat. She was coughing, cursing and trying to get her breath.

There was snarling. There was barking. And it was getting closer. Emil turned to see that the hulking bull had stomped through the flesh-stripped prisoners and released the warhounds. The beast towered over the chain-trailing creatures, snorting its hate at the squire before thundering its way back towards the Sigmarite knight and the horde of bestial kin it had unleashed at him. Emil hooked the stirrup over his boot and feverishly reloaded the crossbow.

'My lord,' he said, the words leaving his lips like a last regret. Bringing the crossbow up, he slammed the bolt into the lead creature, pinning it to the ground. He reloaded. The pack scrambled on.

Kastner looked to the squire and then back at the four-horned beast before him which refused to die. Behind the creature was a horde of bull-spooked beastmen, charging with spears and gnarled clubs. Another hound went down. 'Master,' Emil called, hammering a third mongrel into a tree trunk.

Kastner threw *Terminus* down at the ground, the blade quivering in the soft earth, and allowed the beastman's fanged mace to bury itself in his shield. Shrugging the weapon aside and with his gauntlets free, the knight seized the creature by the horns and butted it in the snout with his crusader helm. And again. And again. With the beastman's ruined face splattered across the helm, Kastner released it, allowing the creature to fall backwards.

'Present your blade,' Kastner roared across the stone circle, retrieving his own weapon.

The pack was almost upon the squire. Emil lined up his next shot but realised the futility of the action. Allowing the crossbow to drop, he tore his short blade from his scabbard, slashing the first of the hounds to one side. Another came at him and received the same treatment. Somehow, in the unfolding havoc, Emil found his way to his training. The disciplined cuts and slashes that Kastner had taught him. Moves that suited a short blade and an inexperienced swordsman. But there were too many. Too many sets of jaws. Too many blood-crazed hounds, savaging his legs, clamping onto his arms, leaping at the squire and dragging him down. Emil became a mound of emaciated bodies, whippet tails and diseased maws, tearing his body in different directions.

Kastner saw the occasional flash of the blade and the isolated yelps of animals unfortunate enough to find themselves skewered by it. The squire was down, however, and needed help. The templar took several determined steps towards the screaming squire, but the dogs were dragging his fang-slashed body into the trees. The templar's steps became an awkward run, exhaustion and the weight of his plate dragging him down. He felt the warherd slam into his shield like a team of charging stallions at the head of a runaway coach. Kastner fell to one side, almost tripping over his own armoured boots. He almost went over, which Kastner knew would have been the end of him. Down on the ground in full plate armour, he would have been an easy sitting target for crooked spears.

Self-reproach sizzled in his chest. He could not save the squire without saving himself. He was no use to the God-King dead. Kastner dug his boots into the sloppy earth. The horde pushed. With a roar the knight heaved back.

'Sigmar,' he hissed within his crusader helm. 'My god... my king...'

Kastner heaved. He heaved again. Blows began to rain down on his armour from the flanks. He gasped as a spear slipped inbetween his plates and cut, hot and wicked, into his side. Cutting through the shaft with *Terminus*, he pushed on into the centre of the mob. Every mongrel and half-breed wanted to own his death. The yellowness of their hearts was gone. Their bare chests beating with the confidence of their number, the success of their savage blows and the knight's impending death. Diederick Kastner had no intention of meeting such an expectation.

'Sigmar, grant me the strength to cleanse this land of your foes...' the knight snarled through his efforts. He heaved at the mob before him. His teeth gritted beneath his helmet and his boots stamped footholds in the ground. He hurled himself at the shield and the shield at the warherd. '...as the light cleanses the darkness.'

One final gargantuan push had driven the monstrosities before him into the embrace of their own fire. Kastner screwed his eyes shut against the brightness that flooded his helm. He felt heat pass rapidly through the metal of his plate. In driving the throng before him, the templar had half stepped into the fire himself. The silhouettes of his enemies, thrashing at the knight with their weapons moments before, were now thrashing at themselves, bleating and screeching, as the beastmen attempted to extinguish the flames licking their way through their shaggy fur.

Kastner turned, the heat scorching its way through his plate searing the skin. With part of the horde aflame and the rest unwilling to follow them, the knight found himself alone. The hammer of blows raining down on his buckled plate had ceased. Spears failed to lance his flesh. Muscular bodies no longer clashed with his own. The beastmen huddled together. They were a wall of spear-points and the crude presenting of weaponry. Kastner had reminded them why they should fear him.

The templar's steaming plate rattled as he shook himself back to composure. He stretched his tension-knotted neck from side to side. *Terminus* ached in his gauntlet and he clashed it three times against his mangled shield.

'Come on!' the knight roared at them. 'Come on! I have the God-King's absolution in my hand. Come and get it...'

One exhausted step followed another, taking the templar into the bestial ranks. A ram-headed beast came at him with a stone hammer. It died. An antlered monstrosity tried to impale him on a pitch-forked spear. It died. A stubby-horned fiend threw itself and its serrated hatchets at him. It died. Cut. Thrust. Shield-smash. Repeat. As his plate cooled, righteous hatred for the darkbreeds burned. He would kill them all. Holding back a pair of dead-eyed goat monsters, Kastner swung *Terminus* about him, severing head after bleating head. Pushing the beastmen back he pulled the shield aside and slammed the length of the greatsword blade through the pair of carcasses. He would kill them all. The stone circle stank of death like never before. Kastner found himself striding through mounds of corpses. The beastmen stumbled through their dead. *Terminus* sang through them, its blade an instrument upon which a ballad was played. A story of drama and death. Mostly death. Even as the herd thinned and the cowardly creatures went to flee, the knight cut them down, opening their shaggy beastflesh from their broad shoulders to their buttocks. He. Would. Kill. Them. All.

But he wouldn't. The bull – a ferocious tower of bovine fury – denied him. The colossus stomped forward, shaking its mighty horns and smashing remaining beastmen aside with its huge fists. As the broken bodies of its kindred hit trees and the standing stones of the circle, the bull grabbed the herd's final gor. The goat-faced wretch bleated in terror before the bull tore it in two. With gore and intestines dribbling through its huge fingers, the monster snorted pure hate at the knight standing before him.

'Come on,' Kastner said, beckoning it on with a gesture of his shield. 'In the God-King's name, let's finish it…'

The bull stormed at him, its hooves shaking the ground like thunder. Its head came down. Its horn-points came at the templar, dark with dried blood. Kastner assumed a fighting stance. He was ready to side-step the beast and use its own momentum to take it past him. There he would deliver a strike to fell the creature – or at least slow it down. The bull was fast for something so huge and at the last moment Kastner decided that he would not be able to evade the avalanche of muscle and rage coming at him. Bracing himself behind the shield for the impact, Kastner found himself driven backwards.

Corralled between the monster's two great horns, Kastner was slammed back into the rough stone of a primitive obelisk behind. The hulking beast grabbed the standing stone with its huge hands, and trapping Kastner between the unforgiving obelisk and its thick skull proceeded to pound the knight to oblivion. Kastner felt his shield buckle and his plate crumple about him. His head bounced back and forth within his helm as the bull smashed him into the standing stone.

The assault stopped and Kastner attempted to recover his breath. The beast's huge skull moved away, once again allowing the knight to see the light of the fire, the stone circle and the shadows that lay beyond. The only other living thing within the circle was the girl, who, benefitting from the bull's distraction, had picked her way back through what was left of the hound-mauled prisoners to find her precious pile of books.

Kastner pushed himself away from the obelisk, his plate having moulded itself to the stone's imperfections. Like a prize-fighter trapped in a corner by his opponent, Kastner was pushed back. His shield battered him into the rough stone, its metal surface pounded to uselessness by the beastman's colossal fists. Suddenly the shield was gone, torn away by the bull – the creature eager to pulverise the knight's armoured form and the soft flesh that lay within. A fist came at Kastner. He ducked. Barely in time. The woolly knuckles of the beast smashed stone from the monolith. Another fist almost took the knight's head off, settling instead for shattering away a section of the obelisk.

Kastner launched himself at the colossal creature's chest. It was like the side of a building, muscles bulging like bricks – it had its own brutal architecture. Kastner slammed it again with his battered pauldron – enough to make room for *Terminus*, and the chest-opening sweep of the blade that gashed the beast from navel to nipple. The monster bellowed its pain, smacking the broad blade from the knight's exhausted grip. As the sword clanged off the standing stone and onto the wet earth, the beast back-fisted Kastner across the circle.

For moments following, the knight had little idea where he was. The brightness of the fire eclipsed all else. Its crackle was a mind-aching torment. The ground seemed to move with a sickening motion. Suddenly Kastner was up. The bull was upon him once more. It lifted the armoured templar and flung him like a sack of grain back across the circle. He hit another of the standing stones. There was a sharp pain in the back of his skull. When he opened his eyes he found that his helm had gone. He was sitting at the base of an obelisk. All he could hear was the fury spilling out of the beastman. It charged.

Kastner toppled himself to one side, his plate rattling like a wagon on a rough road. He felt himself drifting in and out of consciousness. The brute's hoof smashed down into the base of the stone where the knight had been. Kastner crawled miserably away, plated arm over buckled arm. The creature raged above him like a storm. The knight dashed his face in the muddy pool he was crawling through, bringing him briefly back to clarity. The standing stone gave an excruciating moan as the bull tore at it, toppling it across the knight's scrabbling form. Trapping Kastner briefly, the irregularity of the obelisk and the marshiness of the ground beneath its fallen length allowed the knight to scrape his armoured legs free. Before Kastner knew it, the beast was bringing another stone down on him. The knight rolled to one side through the mud, the mire squelching in through the rents in his plate. The bull grasped a broken chunk of stone, bigger than the monster's own head, and held it above its horns. Mounting the fallen stones, the creature stood above the knight's prone form, snorting its clouded exertions into the night air. Its arms trembled. Kastner stopped crawling. He rolled back over to present himself to the bovine colossus... the squire's recovered crossbow in his muddy gauntlets. It was not a knightly weapon – but it would serve. Kastner fired.

The bolt stabbed up through the muscle of the bull's chest. The close range had buried the bolt right up to its feathered flight. The beastman snorted with sudden surprise. Its bludgeoning stone crashed to the ground, bouncing off the toppled obelisk from which it came. The bull staggered back across the slaughter of the circle. Gasping. Snorting. Moaning like a herd of frightened cattle.

Kastner pushed himself to his knees. His arms were shaking. His head felt light and the wound in his side burned with every excruciating movement. He got unsteadily to his feet, his plate rattling with exhaustion. Putting one foot in front of the other, the knight walked about the stone circle and recovered *Terminus* from where it lay, splattered with both mud and blood before the base of a rough obelisk. The sword felt heavy in his hands and the knight needed both to drag the blade across the stone circle. The bull had made it to the gore-dripping altar, bent over double, its great chest heaving with the difficulty of breathing.

With more effort than he could bear, Kastner heaved *Terminus* above his head, roaring his side-splitting agony. The greatsword crashed down on the altar surface, sending a crack through the ancient stone. The bull had pushed itself away through the slick blood on its surface and crashed down beside its shaman at the foot of the herdstone. It groaned, one hoofed slab of a leg shaking uncontrollably. It spread the fingers of one huge hand across its chest and around the bolt through its thunderous heart. Its other arm waved the Sigmarite knight away in silent pleading. With difficulty, Kastner moved around the broken altar and swayed above the bull in his own torment. The templar shook his head as clouds of the beastman's hot breath enveloped them both. The herdstone ached with the unnatural energies of its making and construction. Its wyrdstone gleamed like shadow, charged with the offering of so many souls slaughtered in the circle before it. The bull nestled its mighty horned skull against it, like an infant at its mother's bosom. Still it thought its Ruinous patrons would deliver it.

'No,' Kastner said, his lips bloodied and bruised. The beast closed eyes wet with fear and frustration. Its arm came down in monstrous acceptance. Kastner lifted *Terminus* once more and brought the blade down on the creature's thick skull with all the fury he could summon from his pain-wracked body. Blood sprayed the knight's ruined armour as he hacked down through horn and bone. The blade came down again and again, its cleaving movements becoming wilder and wilder. Although the fire in his arms succumbed to the effort, the fire in his heart did not. He. Would. Kill. Them. All.

The heavy blade went wide, missing the beastman's

demolished skull and clashing through the irregularity of the herdstone. The metal of the blade rang strangely against the material and Kastner felt a sudden agony burn through his mind like the tip of a fire-stoked poker. The hurt and surprise was such that the Knight of the Twin-Tailed Orb dropped *Terminus* in the gore of his ruined foe and stumbled at the altar, his gauntlet clasped across his right eye. A groan of delicate anguish escaped his lips. Blood, hot and thick, spilled through the metal digits and down his face. He tried to see but he could not. Blinking his left eye open through the blood and the pain he found that he could not do so with the right. His heart became a whisper. He roared his fears and fell to his armoured knees. All he could see with the right was the deep darkness of the world now gone. A throbbing woe. A feverish affliction. A white-hot absence. Doom in all its pure honesty.

Snatching his gauntlet from his hand he traced the tip of a finger through the bloody socket and across the ruined eye. He felt the prick of an object within and the simultaneous agony of a pain the like of he which he had never experienced. It was like a crash of lightning through the mind, throwing everything within into the dread, darkness and disorder that followed. Kastner tried to think. To focus his way through the constant torment. *Terminus* must have struck a flinty shard from the wyrdstone and sent it like an arrow head into his eye. Clutching his other hand, the knight smashed the metal fist into the herdstone in frustration and anger. He had been stupid. Rash. Irrational. And he had paid for it. He had lost something that he couldn't possibly get back. The realisation burned him.

The templar remained before the stone for a while, kneeling in the end of his enemies. The shame of tears rolled quietly down one blood-speckled cheek. Gore steamed from the ground. The fire began to die. The raw redness of the dawn reached through the open sky.

Kastner felt something nudge his arm. It was Oberon. The stallion pushed at him gently with its nose, as though unsure whether its master was dead or alive. The knight was so still. The steed was not the only one interested. Kastner looked up. The novice-sister was kneeling before him, her bound books in her lap, her lips parted as she stared at his eye. It was a botched mess. A spider-shaped puncture wound revealing the darkness within. Blood ran like tears from its ruination. The girl tore a strip of clean material from her chemise and proceeded to wrap it about Kastner's head, covering his blind eye. She had been talking but Kastner hadn't noticed.

'So you're a knight,' the girl said.

'What?'

'You're a knight?' she repeated. Her voice was annoyingly up-beat. Sing-song and provincial. She moved the pile of books closer, as though she were protecting them. Kastner grunted. From the sound of her voice, the templar found it difficult to believe that the girl had ever looked between the covers of one. 'I've never seen a knight close up. There were some that visited the Reverend Mother, you know, with important persons and such…'

'A knight is an important person,' Kastner said. He needed something to concentrate on other than the agony in his head. The girl didn't seem to have noticed that Kastner had spoken. She rambled on.

'The one I saw up closest, well he wore the same kind of armour as you. Different symbol, though. Some kind of animal, I think. One of the girls in the scullery said it was a griffon, whatever that is…'

'You're a sister?' Kastner put to her.

'Yes, well, no – I'm a novice,' the girl admitted. 'I work in the scullery…'

'I got that,' Kastner said. The blinding agony of his eye was making him short and sarcastic. 'A Sigmarite?'

'Why, yes, sieur,' the girl said. 'The Reverend Mother said that one day I'd make a very fine Sister of the Imperial Cross.' Kastner had heard of the order. Like his own knightly order, the Sisters of the Imperial Cross answered ultimately to the Grand Theogonist in Altdorf. The order maintained priories and convents of dutiful sisters throughout the Empire and took as their symbol the Imperial cross – the same cross that adorned the pommel of *Terminus*. North, south, east and west – the Sisters of the Imperial Cross honoured Sigmar as their patron and took as their solemn duty the spiritual unity of the God-King's Empire. 'She gave me this...' the girl told him. She pulled a silver hammer from her robes from where it was hanging on a chain.

'Where's your priory, girl?' Kastner demanded, pushing himself to his feet. He wobbled and the novice went to steady him.

'The Hammerfall,' the girl told him. 'In the Middle Mountains. Going on three years now.'

Kastner turned and put his head to Oberon's.

'Good boy,' the templar told him. Then to the novice, 'Girl, get my sword and my steed.'

'I have a name, you know,' the girl scowled.

Kastner nodded to himself. The girl really wasn't bright. She clearly knew no better than to answer back to a knight. If Kastner had truly been of noble birth he might have had her answer for it. It was the same pluck he had seen in the cage, before the bull. Three years at the Hammerfall and still a novice. Little wonder, given the mouth on her. Little wonder that she had found her services indispensable in the scullery, the knight reasoned. He turned.

'What's your name, girl?'

'Giselle,' she said.

Kastner nodded slowly.

'Girl,' he said, 'get my sword and steed.'

'Don't you have...?' Giselle began.

The knight turned his head, brought up his hand and slapped it down into his gauntlet.

'All right, all right,' the girl said, heaving *Terminus* out of the gore. 'I just thought you'd have a squire for this sort of thing.'

'I do,' Kastner said, finding his footing and striding for the woods. As he passed Emil's crossbow on the ground – the unknightly weapon that had saved the knight's life – he scooped it up.

With *Terminus's* bloody blade over one shoulder, Oberon's reins in the other hand and her pile of books under an arm, Giselle followed the templar out of the stone circle. Kastner stepped over the two warhounds Emil had shot. Even in the sliver of morning sun, the tracks were easy to follow. The pads of the savage dogs were everywhere. Emil's body had been dragged through the trees. There were scraps of clothing. Blood. Even a couple of the boy's fingers. There were also bodies. The bodies of emaciated hounds that the squire had managed to gut with his short sword or skinning knife. One by one the knight stepped over the carcasses of dead dogs. There were so many that it was hard to believe any of the herd's hunting pack had been left alive. They hadn't. Kastner found the last of the beasts, its tainted jaws still wrapped around Emil's neck.

Kastner trudged down into the bloody mire about the boy's body, pulling the warhound off him. A crossbow bolt, planted there by hand, was buried in the dog's stab-thrashed belly. Emil was a mess. Kastner felt cold emotion wash through his pain-wracked chest. Giselle came up behind with Oberon. She allowed the greatsword to fall and spear the ground and looked at the templar. The girl saw the grief – the responsibility – pass across Kastner's face.

'Is he alive?' she asked. Kastner didn't answer. 'Saw a man fed to the Graf's wolves once,' the girl said absently. 'He looked much like that.'

The boy's limbs were savaged, his ragged torso was a fang-punctured mess, his handsome features all but gone. Kastner brought his ear to the squire's mauled chest. He paused. He held his own breath. Then he heard it. Faint – but there. The beating of the boy's heart. He felt it. The slight rise and fall of his ribcage. Kastner closed his eye.

'Hang on, Emil,' the knight said.

Hauling the moaning Emil out of the puddle of his own blood, Kastner laid him across Oberon's saddle.

'Get up,' Kastner told the girl. She shook her head.

'I don't ride.'

'You do today,' Kastner said. 'Give me your foot.'

'I've never ridden a horse in my life, sir. My family couldn't even afford a broken mule…'

'Girl, I need you to do this,' Kastner said. '*He* needs you to do this. There is a small temple in the foothills of the Middle Mountains, near the village of Esk.'

'A temple to Sigmar?' the girl asked, suddenly interested.

'Yes, a way temple,' the templar replied.

'I need a temple,' she said and Kastner found the girl's delicate foot in his gauntlet. He pushed her up onto the mighty Oberon. There she uncertainly took the reins with Emil laid before her. She hugged her books to her.

'There you will find a priest named Dagobert. Tell him Sieur Kastner sent you. He will recognise my steed and my squire. This is Oberon.'

'This priest,' Giselle asked, 'he is a wise man?'

'Yes,' Kastner said. 'He will know what to do.'

'I mean,' Giselle said, 'is he a learned man? My Reverend Mother bade me promise, on the blood of the Founder, that I deliver these tomes to a learned man, a priest – a true servant of Sigmar.'

'Your books be damned, girl,' Kastner said, his agonies making him sharp and impatient. 'A man's life hangs in the balance.'

'My lady was very specific,' the girl said moodily. 'A learned man, she said. A true servant of Sigmar.'

'You'll find none truer,' Kastner said irritably. He pulled Oberon to a stop. He rubbed his blood-splattered forehead with his fingers. He needed the girl more than he cared to admit to her. His trials – his agonies – were making him discourteous. 'You were taken by the beasts of the forest on your way to deliver these tomes?'

'I was.'

'The Drakwald is not to be travelled lightly,' Kastner told her. 'Take my squire to Father Dagobert. He is a good man. A learned man. He will see to your tomes and answer any questions your Reverend Mother has. But please, take my man to him first.'

'My Lady seeks no answers from the books, sir,' Giselle said. 'She said take them. Take them far from the Hammerfall. To safety.'

Kastner frowned, but he did not have time for further questions. He handed her Emil's crossbow. 'If any bar your path, you tell them you are on the temple's business and put this in their face. They will think twice, I assure you.'

Giselle took the weapon.

'How might I find this temple?'

'Oberon knows the way,' Kastner told her.

'You would entrust this man's life to a horse?'

'No, I entrust him to you,' the templar told her. 'Gorst!' Kastner called to the forest. 'Gorst, get yourself out here, you mangy beggar.'

Giselle looked about. The fingertips of red morning radiance probed the dank forest. Then she saw him, emerging like a skittish animal from behind a tree. A wretched figure. A flagellant draped in chains, his head trapped within a small cage. Giselle's lip curled with obvious disgust. 'Girl, meet Gorst. Gorst, I want you to lead Oberon to Father Dagobert. You remember the temple at Esk?'

The flagellant nodded slowly. 'Gorst, the God-King asks this of you. Do you understand? You will not fail him. You will not fail me.' The flagellant nodded. Kastner slapped Oberon's hindquarters, prompting the stallion on. As the horse reached Gorst, the flagellant broke into a run, leading it into the forest at a trot. As Emil moaned at the movement and Giselle rolled in the saddle, the novice turned back to look at Kastner.

'What are you going to do?' the girl called over her shoulder.

'The God-King's work,' Kastner told her. 'There is stone to smash and bodies to burn. I shall ensure that this dark path leads nowhere. The Empire is no place for the children of Chaos. The next warherd to pass through here will know that.'

As the Knight of the Twin-Tailed Orb became lost to her in the halo of morning sun breaking through the trees, Giselle nodded and turned back to her path. She thought on the slaughter of the stone circle. 'I think they will,' she said to herself.

CHAPTER V

*'Why did chance its steps betray,
Far from friend and home –
On trails left by the hands of fate
Where only shadows roam.'*
– The Brothers Ziegler

*The Drakwald
Hochland
Sonstill, IC 2420*

Diederick Kastner was lost.

North had not taken him north. It had taken him to another place. Somewhere the sun rarely shone – and when it did, it bled across the sky like a wound, keeping impossible consort with the moons. Diederick wandered, his mindless steps and stumbles plunging him through forest he had never known. He dragged *Terminus* behind him in one trembling, white fist. The tip of the sword's broad blade left a furrow behind the templar, cutting through the tangle of the forest earth.

Kastner's battered armour felt like a fireplace, reflecting the feverish heat of his body inwards. Droplets fell from his brow and cheeks, pitter-patting against his breastplate. He moaned his exhaustion, madness dripping from his lips like Gorst or the madmen he'd seen in hospice cages. He tried to stem its flow but even the attempt to do so became a senseless rant.

Day and night danced about him, like lovers at a fête, swinging each other around, each revolution getting faster and faster. The sensation was sickening. The land moved beneath his feet and his stomach shifted, causing the knight to heave and vomit down the trunks of trees. He tumbled. He fell, his plate clattering like a tray of tankards to a tavern floor. His sweat dropped to the black forest earth. Buds on the trees erupted and buried the knight in blossom. Leaves glowed glorious green before bronzing, withering and raining down to the ground about him. Frost crept both through the naked woodland and the templar, harbinger of snowfall which dusted everything a dirty white. Within moments it was gone, leaving puddles in its wake that were guzzled by the thirsty earth and once again the twigs and branches of the canopy were dotted with shoots of green.

Kastner crawled. He pushed himself from tree to trunk. He stabbed the toe of his boots into the dirt for purchase, like the climber of a slope or mountain. Roots slithered about his footfalls while foliage seemed to reach out for him. Insects stung, bit and ate the templar alive. Birds and bats flew at him. Forest vermin raced before his unsteady feet. All were blurred and indistinct. Afterthoughts of their own noxious existence.

A snake shot out and snapped at his foot. Kastner blundered back into a tree, disturbing an owl which flapped its great wings at him. His next footfall wasn't there and neither was the one after that. The knight tumbled. He fell for what seemed like an eternity before hitting the ground. It was a steep slope, littered with logs and boulders pushing up out of the ground. Kastner hit one before bouncing and falling against another. Some were plate-scuffing glances while others knocked him briefly from what little sense he had left. Pieces of plate were torn from his suit and the sword *Terminus* was lost to him.

A short plummet later and the templar felt his body snap straight through the rotten branches of a dead pine. While his mind struggled with the impossibility of what he was experiencing, his body cleaved straight through dry wood. His armour crumpled as he slammed stomach first into a thicker, more resilient branchlet lower down the giant. Something like a rib broke inside the knight but before he could claw himself to safety, the weight of his plate dragged him down through the living boughs and branches. They beat him and smashed him to near unconsciousness before depositing the knight in a twisted pile at the foot of its trunk, his face in the dirt.

Kastner roared like a wild animal. Fire lanced through his left thigh, cutting through the malaise of other agonies squirming through him. Something had speared down through his leg, pinning him and his plate to the forest floor. Arching his back and tearing the wound in his side, Kastner saw that the sword *Terminus* had fallen after him, the broad blade stabbing down through the knight's plate, searing through his flesh and grazing the bone. The templar smacked his head into the ground and fisted the soil with his remaining gauntlet. Bellowing once more, Kastner reached back and took the blade in hand. Hauling it upwards, the metal made an excruciating sound against the plate through which it had punctured. The pain was unbearable, but Kastner found himself willing it on – the agony cauterising its way through his dismal torments. At last the blade came free and fell heavily to one side, sticky with the templar's blood.

Dragging the greatsword like a penitent burden and limping like an animal that had ripped itself from a trap, Kastner pushed miserably on through the changing forest. Hours passed. It could have been days or weeks, for all the knight knew. His body felt as if it were aflame. The fever brought the knight's heartbeat thundering to his ears. He was everywhere, yet felt nowhere. Each twist and turn about the trees was a dark discovery. Every decision, left or right, cost the knight a little shred of his soul, yet moment by moment he felt he was becoming something more.

He was shaking. The templar willed himself to stillness but felt even his resolution tremble. The hairs on his body stood up on end with the chill of fear and excitement. In the impossible forest about him, roots snaked through the earth beneath his feet as if bifurcating networks of midnight blue threaded his pallid flesh. Like a God-King distant and lost to him, the land was Kastner and Kastner was the land. A nation of competing afflictions. A living, breathing empire to master and control.

Thunder ripped the heavens apart above the dark canopy. A storm was descending – unseen and irresistible. What feeble light from the dying sun and shine-stealing moons found its way down to the clearing floor withered to twilight. The weald became an impenetrable labyrinth of gloom and dread. Kastner drew his miserable hobble to a stop, dragging his skewered leg in line with the other. All ways looked equally foreboding. Ahead was a fat log – a toppled trunk, bulbous with growths, nests and holes. Kastner could see the glint of eyes within. The bug-riddled timber was infested with vermin and the crawling, creeping, slithering things of the world. Beyond the woodland was a chorus of sickly creaking. From within the gaping darkness of the log, Kastner heard a dreadful, booming laughter. Its jovial invitation was infectious and ripe with a doom-laden mockery.

Turning from the log, which seemingly blocked the path ahead, the knight saw to his left a colossal oak – gnarled and broad. The kind of timber from which the great cannon-carrying vessels and siege machines of the Empire were crafted. Its branches were straight like a gallows. Its bark was rough and full of furious character, giving the knots and gnarled bumps the appearance of a rising column of leering skulls that barred his path, flashed white by the lightning that opened the sky up above them. As the thunder tore the very air apart around the knight, lightning struck the branches above. With an ear-splitting crack, the bolt split the great oak in two. Flame spread rapidly through its crooks and boughs, devouring the wood with hateful abandon. Kastner drank in the power of the scene. The spectacle of wanton destruction.

The templar hobbled back from the intense heat, turning his plated back to the furious inferno. Opposite, the pathway was no more certain. Trees seemed to meld one into another, as though they were one. The bark was uniformly scarred and stripped by the wicked claws of some animal, the rents dribbling sap down the wood. The more Kastner looked at the gliding curves, the rounded beauty, the arches, the twists and bends of the trunks and branches about one another, the more he was drawn to it. It reminded him not of inanimate trees but of people, men and women, embracing one another. In the opposing flames, Kastner found his face on every one of the male figures, while the girls were every woman he had ever yearned for.

'No...' he half-gasped, and forced his gaze from the perversity. To his right he found the log – which was impossible, since that was behind him. Except it wasn't. The flaming oak now occupied that space. Kastner stared about, searching for the way he had entered the clearing, but it wasn't there. The bodies. The flames. The laughter. The flames. The laughter. The bodies. The knight was lost in every way a man could be.

Kastner roared at the spuming heavens above. He had never seen such a storm. Rolling banks of clouds swallowing one another – spreading, surging and raging with lightning of pinks and blues. His chin fell and his gaze reached the clearing floor. He found tracks – the trench the greatsword had been carving behind him cross-crossed itself many times in a pattern of madness. Lines and circles. The black earth of the clearing was churned up in the impression of a star. An eight-pointed star.

Kastner reached for the name of his God-King but found that it wasn't there. The hallowed name that had sat on his lips for decades. His patron. His god and his king. The deity to whom the templar had pledged his life and service. His name... was gone. Kastner crumbled to his armoured knees.

'My lord,' he called up into the storm. 'Why have you forsaken me!'

'You are not forsaken...'

The voice was everywhere. It was the roar of the flame. The laughter in the darkness. The doom-laden rapture. The impossible storm. Kastner turned, dragging his injured leg after him. He spun around, the forest blurring to smeared darkness. Then he saw it. For an instant. In the clearing. Right next to him. Horror incarnate, leering at mortal insignificance. Stumbling to a stop, Kastner got the impression of some hideous thing of the beyond. Fiend. Gargoyle. Daemon. Black as night, with the horns and wings of infernal favour.

'Do not see meeeee...' the being said in a voice that seemed to burst the heart.

Pain. Incredible.

Kastner clutched his head and let slip a scream of honest agony. He covered his eye, but the searing torment proceeded in the socket of the one that was no longer there. He could see lightning inside his mind. Shards of colour that defied name or description. Ghostly impressions of a world beyond that of sense and sight. He could feel with his heart. Listen with his mind. He could taste a world ripe for destruction. It was too much. It was all too much. Make it stop.

CHAPTER VI

*'With a world of pleas to hark and heed,
Miracles begged and forgiveness received,
Recoveries to foster and babes to feed
How can fair Shallya offer aught but tears?'*
– Fliessbach, *The Daughter of Death*

Way Temple – the Sudenpass
Hochland
Niedrigstag, IC 2420

'Get him up, get him up.'

Being the hulking fellow that he was, Dagobert's attendant, Berndt, picked Kastner's body up from the hay cart, plate and all. 'Bring him inside,' the priest said, his voice like the gravel on the road running beside the way temple. He ran stubby fingers through his greyish hair. Berndt didn't reply. The attendant was a mute.

'Also had this,' the gruff farmer said, lifting with difficulty the deadweight of the gore-smeared *Terminus*. Dagobert ducked inside and snatched a pudgy fistful of coin from the donations box and put it in the hand of the bemused farmer who had found the Knight of the Twin-Tailed Orb unconscious on the side of the Sudenpass. He took the greatsword *Terminus*. 'Put him in the robing room,' Dagobert instructed, 'with his squire.'

As Berndt stomped through the temple with the knight in his arms, candles guttering as he went, the clatter of Kastner's ruined plate attracted the attention of the congregation. It was mostly travellers – skinners, pedlars, merchants and the like – taking the Sudenpass from Wolfenburg to Middenheim, with a few regulars from the goat farms up in the foothills. Disturbed from their devotions, the attendees' eyes were drawn from the God-King's sculpted form to the dreadful state of the templar.

'Apologies,' Dagobert said, waddling after Berndt and the templar. 'Pray return to your thoughts, brothers and sisters.'

Moving through the way temple, Berndt pushed through the curtains of the robing room. Emil was already there – like a preserved body in an ancient tomb, the hideousness of his injuries hidden in bandages and moist salves. A portly priestess of Shallya sat beside the squire in her white robes, giving motherly instruction to Giselle who was moving back and forth with fresh dressings.

'By the Dove,' the priestess said, 'what have we here now?'

'Another servant of Sigmar, Sister Arabella,' Dagobert said. 'Deserving, I fear, of your attentions.'

'Set him down on the other bunk,' the priestess directed. Berndt obeyed. 'I am going to need assistance with his armour.' Dagobert nodded, laying *Terminus* aside and moving across to help Berndt with the smashed plate.

'His wounds are grievous,' the priestess concluded as she unwound Giselle's handiwork about the templar's eye. 'An object. It still seems to be in there,' the priestess said. 'Hand me my satchel, child.' Giselle passed the priestess her bag of instruments and potions with no little petulance. 'It's going to have to come out. It'll get infected.'

'Whatever you think is best,' Dagobert said.

'Shallya knows,' the priestess said, 'this is dangerous. He could lose more than his sight – and he has lost that already. You'll take responsibility.'

'Aye,' Dagobert said slowly. 'Aye, I will at that.'

Selecting a pair of tongs that wouldn't have been out of place on a blacksmith's rack, the priestess dipped them into the ruin of the socket and tried to grasp the shard protruding from it. As the metal of the tong scraped the stone, Kastner's hand shot up, snatching the priestess's wrist and the tongs away from his eye.

'What are you doing?' the templar snarled, his other eye writhing about its socket, his gaze roaming the room like a frightened animal.

'Diederick,' Dagobert soothed. 'Diederick, it's me. You were brought to the temple.'

As the templar lifted his head and looked about him, he fixed Arabella and Giselle in a withering stare. He let go of Arabella's wrist.

'I don't know you.'

'This is Lady Arabella, new to Shallya's shelter from Hovelhof,' Dagobert said. 'And this is Giselle, from the Hammerfall. She brought Emil to us, thank the Founder. She said you sent her.'

Kastner burned into Giselle with his gaze, making the novice-sister bridle under the intensity of his attentions.

'Yes,' he said finally. 'You were there.'

'We've been expecting you,' Dagobert said. 'It's been a few days.'

Kastner laid back down, then turned his head towards the bandage-smothered Emil.

'Will he make it?'

'Lady Arabella doesn't like his chances, out here in the provinces,' Dagobert said.

'He needs the care of the hospice in Altdorf,' the priestess said. 'As might you.'

'I'm not going to Altdorf,' Kastner told her.

'The injury to your eye requires extraction of the offending object,' Arabella told him. 'I cannot lie to you. There will be pain.'

'I have known pain.'

'A great deal of pain,' the priestess said.

'Then leave it alone.'

'It will become infected and it will kill you. You will be slain from within, good templar. Would you have that? Taken in your bed during fever and delirium. Not the end a knight of Sigmar would pray for.'

'Do what you must,' Kastner said grimly.

'Before you were insensible,' Arabella told him. 'You must be rendered so again. Father Dagobert, please bring us a bottle of your strongest spirits.'

'Well, I...'

'Come, father. The God-King praises alcohol as a gift – if enjoyed in health, peace and moderation. This purpose is medicinal, after all.'

'Save it,' Kastner spat. He looked hard at the priestess. 'Just get it out. If it's going to be as painful as you say I'll be out soon enough.'

'As you wish, my son,' Arabella said to him. 'Hold him down.'

With Berndt's great form holding the knight's broken body down and Dagobert holding his skull against the bunk, Giselle hovered over them.

'What can I do?' the girl said.

'Take these,' Lady Arabella said, thrusting a handful of clean rags at her. 'There will be blood.'

Moving in once more with the tongs, Arabella felt the knight suddenly strain against them. His body spasmed and a grim moan erupted from his pursed lips. 'Hold him,' the priestess commanded. She took the tip of the shard – which still protruded a little way out from the ruined eye – and attempted to extract it. Moans became roars and roars shrieks as the priestess used all of her strength and skill to take the stone from his skull. Dagobert held Kastner down, his face a grave mask of care and determination. Blood streamed down the side of the templar's face, where Giselle tried her best to stem the flow. Soon the gathering were covered in the knight's blood, their hands slimy with his gore.

'Hold him,' Arabella carped, her frustration getting the best of her.

'I'm trying,' Dagobert shot back. 'He's so strong. Girl, help me here,' the priest of Sigmar said to Giselle. The bunk was already awash with blood.

'Why isn't he out?' Giselle asked, the templar's screams passing straight through her. 'My brother had my father pull a rusty nail from his foot once. The pain. He went out like a candle.'

'He has a strong will,' Arabella mumbled, no less rattled by the knight's grating agonies. 'I'll give him that.'

Even with both Dagobert and the novice-sister holding his head still, the priestess could not extract the shard's infectious presence. The stone seemed wedged in the bone of the socket, as well as lancing deep into the skull. Even her bodily attempts to twist the splinter of stone free – producing from Kastner the most dismal howls she had ever heard from a patient – failed to move it.

When the knight's screams finally subsided – to the relief of everyone – the priestess thought she might be able to exert more pressure but regardless of her efforts, the stone shard was there to stay. She finally sat back, letting the tension in her shoulders go. She seemed in shock.

'You're giving up?' Dagobert asked.

'The goddess forbids harm done in her name,' Arabella said, her face almost as white as her patient's.

'You said he would get an infection if it was left in,' Dagobert protested. 'You said he would die.'

Arabella looked from Dagobert, to Giselle to Berndt.

'He's already dead,' the priestess of Shallya said, withdrawing her hand from his chest. Dagobert moved around and put his ear to Kastner's heart. There was no life to be found there. 'I have offended my mistress,' Arabella said. 'I must make amends.' She got up from the bunk. 'I'm sorry, Hieronymous – I must leave you now.'

Dagobert lifted his ear from Kastner's blood-smeared chest.

'What of Emil?' the priest said miserably, his mind elsewhere.

'I will take my ponies back to Hovelhof,' she said, 'and leave you the hospice wagon. I can do no more for him. Take the boy to the Shallya temple in Altdorf. If he survives the journey, the high priestess will care for him there.'

As Arabella left them, Dagobert turned back to Kastner's lifeless form. He leant up and kissed the knight on the forehead. Even now, in the blood-battered corpse of the warrior before him, the priest could see the boy he had raised.

'Girl,' Dagobert said, getting to his feet.

'Yes, father,' Giselle said, the tautness of teenage ill-humour and irritability gone from her face.

'Strip and bathe the body for last rites,' the priest said with difficulty, as though he were forcing every word. Giselle nodded slowly. She drew Sigmar's hammer up out of her robes on its chain – the simple token of her simple faith – and kissed the silver of its form. 'I must send word to Grand Theogonist Lutzenschlager and Grand Master Schroeder of the Knights of the Twin-Tailed Orb,' Dagobert continued. 'Berndt, you will go ahead to the temple and the chapter house with my missives. They shall learn that one of their very best, a scholar and a warrior born – a true son of Sigmar – this day is lost to us.'

There are many who would mean you harm, shadow-of-mine. Many wretched gods and their misguided servants. The weakling God-King of the Empire. Ulric of Wolves and Winter. Even the merciful maiden Shallya, who would harm as much as she heals with her potions and instruments. They will cut you with their steel. They will burn you with their faith.

You are claimed, shadow-of-mine. You were begot of havoc. Orphaned in a world you will destroy. Baptised in the susceptibilities of your enemies. You have the attention of the Dark Gods. They look down on you as I do. With dread. With hope. With possibility. You cannot deny what you are. My gift to the world. Flesh, bone and the spirit that drives it on. A living doom.

In order to realise your terrible purpose, however, you must live, my creation. Live, shadow-of-mine. The Dark Gods know you now. Show them what you can do. Give them a glimpse of the calamity to come.

CHAPTER VI

*'Methinks the road to damnation cuts
unfairly through lands of fair intention.'*
   – Frederik III (ascribed – *the Great Crusade
against Araby*)

*The Drakwasser Road
Middenland
Klein Frederikstag, IC 2420*

Day and night. Day and night. Kastner's eyes were dry, for he could not close them. In the hours of day he endured the tedium of the world, viewed through the narrow opening between the curtains of the hospice wagon. At night he dreamt dark visions projected on the darkness beyond. He felt a living death. Every moment was so acutely experienced that it hurt to think and feel. He sensed his body healing. It was becoming stronger. More powerful. Assuming a formidability that even he, as a knight trained in the arts of death, had never enjoyed. He was becoming… something else. Something more. The flesh of his side and his leg itched as it knit itself back together. Breaks and fractures were now but dull aches and the dread fever a distant memory.

Only his eye still burned. The storm was still there, raging in the darkness of his mind. A constant torment, shredding at his nerves and his sanity. He could feel the shard of stone in his head. It was heavy and aching with wretched purpose. It was part of him now and wanted him to be part of it. The realisation of his desires and impulses might have distracted the templar from the ever-present agony that shot through his skull. A goal upon which to focus and channel the raw anguish that proceeded from the mind-splitting torture. Instead he was forced to simply lie and endure every single second of a torment without end. If a man knows his labours end as the sun goes down, then he can push on through to dusk. If a man knows his journey's destination, even though that destination might be far away, he can walk on – putting one boot ahead of the other, until finally he reaches journey's end. The agony ripping through one side of his face, his head, his mind, was a journey without destination and a day without end. At first Kastner didn't know if he could take it. Then he discovered that he didn't have a choice. He finally found that he could, but that it might have cost him his sanity.

He had awoken to horror. When he was but a small boy he would wake in the middle of the night. The temple dormitory was without windows and black with darkness. Down the corridor he could hear Dagobert snoring. It had been a reassuring noise to a boy all alone in the world. Some nights he would wake to silence, however. No sound. No light. Most dreadful of all was the feeling that there was something there in the darkness with him. Something stalking him. Watching him. He knew that to set eyes on it would be the end of him – but he had no choice because he could not move. The horror of vulnerability. It didn't matter how strong, how fast or lethal you were, if you couldn't move a muscle to defend yourself. Bumping about the cot in the back of the hospice wagon, that was what Kastner had woken to. Paralysis. Immobility. The insensitivity of the flesh.

He could not lift an arm, kick out with a leg, blink his eye or lick his lips. A fly crawling inbetween them could choke him. An insect could end him. It was the most dreadful feeling he had ever experienced. No bed wetting nightmare or courage-leeching doubt before combat could compare. He would rather feel the steel of his enemy skewer through him than live the soullessness of utter vulnerability. As he was wont to do – as it was the only thing to do – Kastner tried to reach out. He tried to sit up. He tried to move just one toe. But there was nothing. In his mind his body responded with force and enthusiasm for the task. He throbbed with possibility. The power of the things he wanted to do. The magnitude of coming accomplishment intoxicated him. His body was just waiting to catch up with such grand achievements. It was a useless study in flesh. A forgotten vessel housing a furious force. A living trap within which was buried a monster… a giant… a god.

Perhaps, when he had been able to walk, his every step had driven the shard of wyrdstone deeper into his brain. He could even have fallen and driven the sliver further into his skull. He thought on his surroundings. Perhaps some attempt to remove the object had done him more ill than good. Conversely, the thing might just have petrified its way into him and claimed him for its own. It didn't matter. What danger was he to the Empire, to others or himself lying in a cot like a cadaver? Whatever had happened, the shard had pierced into or pressed against something that had crippled him. His life as he knew it was over.

Kastner heard a moan. There was someone in the cot lining the other wall of the hospice wagon. The templar had never been able to turn his head to see who he shared the wagon with. He assumed it was Emil, his squire – although it didn't sound very much like him. Like Kastner, his injuries had warranted the long, uncomfortable journey to Altdorf, in search of healing hands at the Temple of Shallya. The boy groaned beneath his bandages and blankets – something between agony and ecstasy. Kastner hoped he was having a nice dream. The wretch would have little to look forward to upon waking.

The knight peered hard at the darkness between the doorway curtains. There used to be just darkness and light. The longer he stared at the only view he was allowed, the one constantly visited upon him, the more he came to appreciate the degrees of difference. With the rising of the sun, day was just the absence of darkness. With the setting of the sun, both the night and the knight were a canvas upon which darkness daubed its dread. Like a painter working colours on his palette, Kastner had observed darkness mixed in many shades – and found himself lost to them. They were to be his masterpiece. And he theirs.

For what seemed like forever, Kastner had watched their journey drop behind the wagon. That was how he knew for sure that they were heading for the Reikland. He had felt the winding path of the Sudenpass, the bump and crunch back up the Flaschgang Road and the rattle as they crossed the well-travelled crossways of the Old Forest. He had watched the trees change and even disappear for a spell as they trundled past the brigand-haunted Weiss Hills. Occasionally, he would spy one of the many individual homesteads and hamlets on the route. In some, peasants peered in with ghoulish curiosity. Not too close – in case the hospice wagon was carrying somebody infectious – but close enough to see the freakishness of the horrifically injured, the almost dead and the dying. Kastner watched the same disappointment cross their faces. He was the kind of freak they could not see. The kind of abomination that hid its true form and denied the morbidly inquisitive a sickening thrill.

It was with ghoulish curiosity, however, that Kastner found himself staring through the curtains as the wagon passed through the larger villages. He knew three through which they passed well: Bergendorf, Heedenhof and Gerzen-by-the-River. He knew the sounds of village life, the sing-song Hochlanden lilt and the bustle of passage on the crossroads – heavy goods moving north and south, regiments marching east-west along the Old Forest Road, both to and from Fort Schippel. The knight would not have recognised the villages through which the wagon had passed on its way south. The thoroughfares were dead but for the congress of ravens. Woodsmoke stung his nostrils and on his dry tongue he tasted the copper-tang of fresh death. He knew destruction without seeing it. Not the terror of beastmen or greenskins from the woods. Their needs were their own. Kastner sensed carnage absolute. A message in the massacre. Buildings had burned. The earth had drunk deep of innocent blood. Mutilated bodies were spread and hung as totems of annihilation. Advertisements to all who would now fear to tread where the archenemy had left its unholy works. Only the slaves to darkness worked in such ways. Ruinous doom from the north. The warriors of Chaos.

Night intruded on the hospice wagon. A kind of a moonless darkness reigned. He could hear the trees beyond, hissing in gentle movement, but he could not see them because the rear of the wagon was facing the other way. The Drakwasser sloshed and slurped not far in the distance. Kastner could hear its broadening banks and the unimpeded breeze coming off the lonely hills that the sunset positioned to the west. All of this and the smoothness of the wagon's passage through the well-worn ruts in the road told the templar that they were somewhere between Flaschfurt and Fort Denkh where the track broadened to allow camp to be made off the tree line. The knight's hearing – growing with his other senses – drew the world beyond to him. He could hear a fire, which the low-tinged blackness outside seemed to confirm. He could hear the sizzle of a spit, and the smell of scorched meat pulled at a powerful hunger in his belly like the strings of an instrument. He was ravenous as little had passed his lips in the preceding days but liquids – water and a little broth – for fear of choking. Horses loitered somewhere nearby. Kastner could hear the soft rumble of their hearts and the gush of hot blood through their veins. They snorted and kicked gently at the earth, their tails swishing about them in agitation. Something was bothering them.

It was probably Emil. The squire's withered moans had become more insistent. Despite being unconscious, the poor boy had become increasingly aware of his agonies and the little anyone could do to alleviate them. Kastner had seen the wreckage the pack of dogs had left behind. The wagon was thick with the squire's sickly stench, which with the constant groans and lack of conversation had made Emil a poor travelling companion. At least he could move – if the rippling covers, the periods of violent shuddering and the occasional thrash of a bandage-trailing limb were anything to go by. Kastner felt for the boy and felt responsibility for him. He might have felt more if it weren't for his own dismal prospects. The warherd and whatever Ruinous abominations to which they were making sacrifices had all but finished them both. Kastner was fairly certain that they were spending their last hours together in the back of the hospice wagon.

Sounds, both within and about the wagon fell away. The knight's concentration intensified. It hurt – as if his ears were bleeding – but the tiny details beyond became his. The nibbling of mice in the grass. Grubs boring through the wood of nearby trees. The imperceptible creak of stones expanding about the fire. Like the forest-shattering felling of a mighty larch or elm, Kastner could hear the turning of the pages of a book. The desiccated leather of the tome's covers soaked up the clamminess of the hands holding them. The pages, crisp with age and rough like southern parchments, rubbed against one another with an ancient sibilance. The knight could hear the ink, hundreds of years old, still drying in the dread formations of letters on the page.

There were voices. Mind-cleaving in the volume and clarity with which they came to Kastner. Gorst mumbled booming insanities some way off, enjoying the campfire from a distance. As his face-cage and chains rattled and the flagellations quietly bled and soaked into the filthy rags at his back, the fanatic spoke of one Kastner had thought lost to him. The man who became a king. The king who became a god. Sigmar… Kastner's mind burned to hear the Heldenhammer's name but it was an old pain – remembered and welcome.

'I don't understand any of this…'

'…any of this…'

'…any of this…'

New words intruded on the scene and echoed through the cavernous emptiness of Kastner's thoughts. A girl's voice: sing-song, coarse of cant, tender with teenage years. Unbroken. Unseasoned. Untouched. The grating insolence of youth to be tamed. The knight remembered. The prisoner. The novice-sister. Giselle, the Sister of the Imperial Cross. The girl from the Hammerfall. Kastner drank in the fear and uncertainty of her words.

'I'm not so sure anyone was ever meant to…'

Kastner detected a voice from his childhood. The warm rumble of Father Dagobert. He heard the gravelly rasp of the priest's chins and the weight he carried about his belly – in turn carrying the weight of his words with authority. Despite this, the knight sensed a sweet edge of doubt to the priest's declaration. It was like the stain of harvested fruit on a knife. It was meant to be an answer. A comfort – but it was anything but.

Kastner heard the priest select another tome from a stack warming near the fire. The creak of an opening spine. The whisper of pages. The priest was consulting. Comparing. Cross-referencing. The world died away. Only the conversation mattered. The frank exchange of hushed words across the crackle of the food and fire, heard by Kastner as though he were sitting there also.

'Well I don't,' the girl said honestly. 'All this brainworking – it's not for someone like me. I work in the scullery. I'm not even a sister.'

'Tell me again,' Dagobert said. 'It's important.'

'The Reverend Mother summoned us to the Repository,' Giselle said. 'Below even the undercloisters. Deep in the mountain. My mistress told us that it was where the most dangerous tomes, papers and artefacts collected by the Sisters of the Imperial Cross were stored. Things a novice was never meant to see, I can tell you that.'

'I know of it, child,' Dagobert informed her. 'Though I have never been honoured with an invitation.'

'Well I didn't know of it,' Giselle said. 'Sister Elissa told me she thought it was a myth. I was terrified.'

'As you should be, my child,' Dagobert said. 'For the Hammerfall's vault holds centuries of recovered deviancy, the life's work of madmen and knowledge of the damned once employed – or intended as such – against the God-King's subjects. Even the Arch Lectors require the Grand Theogonist's own permission to conduct their studies there, so secure a repository for darkness it is. Only Sigmar's own cathedral in Altdorf could boast better protection for such damned things than that mountain. Pray continue.'

'My mistress was acting oddly.'

'How so?'

'Out of sorts. Like she was afeared. I'd never seen her that way,' Giselle told him. 'There was this time, Sister Elissa and I–'

'Please, my child. To the bones of the matter.'

The girl paused. A demonstration of her childish hurt.

'The Reverend Mother's patience was thin and her instruction urgent,' Giselle said. 'That's all I meant to say. She set her sisters to work destroying the artefacts and burning the tomes of the Repository. Elissa, me and the other girls from the scullery, we were scared. It felt wrong, to destroy all that the sisterhood had worked hard to protect.'

'Then?'

'She had selected a number of items that she claimed were – well, as she put it, too dark, too rich in potential or too essential to the Empire's continued existence to be put to the hammer or flame. Grand boasts, from my Reverend Mother's lips, I can tell you.'

'This scared you even more, I suspect.'

'Yes, father,' Giselle acknowledged. 'It terrifies me to know that such dark treasures exist in the world.'

'They do,' the priest assured her. 'Such tomes – studied with care and precaution – are a great boon to our crusade against the Ruinous Powers. If they were to fall into the wrong hands, however, they could spell the end of the world. I exaggerate not, child. You carried such tomes to me from the indomitable Hammerfall.'

The pair were quiet for a moment.

'"Giselle Dantziger", my Reverend Mother said, "you came into the world a rude and inconstant thing, with a mouth more at home in the gutter than the cloister",' the novice told Dagobert. '"You may have lacked the study and serenity required to achieve the rank of sister so far but the one thing you do not lack is courage, girl."'

'You were not originally intended for the sisterhood?' Dagobert said. It was not really a question.

'I call the City of the White Wolf home, sir. My father thought some time at the isolated Hammerfall would tame my wilfulness and wild ways,' Giselle said.

'Not Ulric's own wolf priests?'

'The Al-Ulric and his holy men would not have me,' Giselle said. 'The God-King took me to him and for that I am thankful.'

'You have served him well, child.'

'She gave me the collection of tomes, grimoires and papers I presented to you,' Giselle continued, 'and sent me down the mountainside with orders to deliver them to a priest – a learned man – a true servant of Sigmar. She sent some of the other novice-sisters down the mountain in other directions. All ways were treacherous. I cannot tell you the number of times I nearly lost my life on those frozen heights.'

'She sent the novices? What of the older sisters?'

'The Reverend Mother said that since they were closer in age to meeting the God-King, they deserved to face him at the Hammerfall. I still don't understand what she meant. Myself. Amalie. Karletta. Marlene. Several more of the scullery girls. Each with a bundle of books or sack of artefacts. Karletta was but four and ten. I don't know how many of them made it off the Hammerfall alive. I heard screams across the valleys, but they could have been anyone's.'

'You were brave,' Dagobert commended. 'To climb down out of the Middle Mountains would have tested the most fearless of the God-King's subjects. Your Reverend Mother sent you south?'

'South-west, sir, yes. "Don't you stop girl", she said. "Not for man nor beast, until you pass your burden on to another." Well, I would'nt've – but for the beasts that walk like men. They didn't seem interested in the tomes in my care but it was good fortune that your man came by when he did.'

'Fortune of a sort,' Dagobert conceded darkly.

'You think it was the God-King's doing?'

'Perhaps,' Dagobert said. 'My child, the letter sent with the bundle of books. Did you not read it?'

'I did not, father,' Giselle said. 'I cannot. I cannot read.'

Dagobert gave a grave chuckle.

'I think it not amusing, sir. The Reverend Mother was teaching me, but I fought her in my studies.'

'I do not laugh at you child but with the world,' the priest assured her. 'The Reverend Mother sent you with some of the most dangerous texts I have had the dubious privilege to lay eyes upon. Your ignorance protected you, child, for if you had been tempted by even the titles of some of these tomes, it would have been your end.'

'My mistress sent a letter?'

'Between the books in the bundle, bearing the wax sigil of her order,' Dagobert said. 'You would like me to read it to you?'

'If you would, sir.'

'To whom this letter finds,' Dagobert read. 'I pray to the God-King that the works with which I have burdened this poor child find their way to a keeper of the faith – a true servant of the Heldenhammer. My name is Ottoline Hentshel, Reverend Mother of the Hammerfall Priory and proud

Sister of the Imperial Cross. It had been, with my sisterhood, the highest honour to stand sentry over such damned volumes as now find themselves in your possession. Two nights past, however, I was blessed with what I believe to be a vision of the God-King. He came to me. He told me that three days hence, the Hammerfall would receive a visitation from which it would not recover – from which my sisterhood would not recover. The Hammerfall, which has stood for centuries unmolested, atop the highest of peaks in the Middle Mountains, looking down on the God-King's Empire and watching over his people. If I hadn't heard it from the Heldenhammer's own lips, I would not have believed it. It has been my duty to destroy what I can of the dark hoard the Hammerfall has kept safe these generations past. There are some pieces, some texts and the dread knowledge they carry that even I am not permitted to erase from history. My sisters and I will greet our visitors in the way Sigmar intended before preparing to receive his own. Please welcome the child who carries these burdens with hospitality and care. She is a daughter of the Empire and emissary of the God-King's word. I beg you: see these dangerous works to safety, to the site of our patron's crowning – the Cathedral of Sigmar in Altdorf – where they may once more find sanctuary with the priests, scholars and holy knights of his church. The blessings of Sigmar upon you.'

Again, silence settled on the scene, with only the spitting of the fire filling the void.

'You think my mistress received the God-King?'

'I do not know,' Dagobert said. 'But the rider I stopped and had confidence with earlier today told me that Bergendorf, Gerzen and Heedenhof were not the only villages to suffer destruction. There is a storm sweeping through our lands, burning and butchering its way south with dread purpose. It has put others to the sword in our blessed ignorance. The township Esk – dear to my own heart – has similarly fallen to these fearless marauders. Perhaps Sigmar did warn your mistress. Warned her that a doom from the north was coming.

A warband or host intent on destruction. Men and monsters, who move through our lands unchecked, like vengeful ghosts, who slaughter with impunity in search of god knows what. Report is, my child, that the Hammerfall too smokes like the fiery anger of the mountain and that your sisters already sleep in Sigmar's delicate care. For all we know, you might be the last of your order…'

'This cannot be,' the girl sobbed.

'And yet it is,' Dagobert said. 'It is happening. Right now. Events move swiftly about us.'

'What do these marauders want?'

'No one can tell what truly drives such mockeries of men,' Dagobert said. 'The favour of some dark god? Immortality? Daemonhood?'

'But you think not?'

'This carnage is not the random path of some northern barbarian,' Dagobert said. 'The path has purpose. I believe that this host – whoever or whatever they might be – slaughtered the Sisters of the Imperial Cross at the Hammerfall in search of one of the godforsaken works you brought to me. I think that they followed it to Esk because the tomes were taken to the way temple nearby, and that they know it travels south on this road – accounting for the butchered villages and hamlets on our route.'

'Then they are already ahead of us,' Giselle said, her words rising with panic. 'How will we reach the city with these beasts between us and safety?'

'Calm yourself, girl,' Dagobert said. 'Don't forget that Sigmar watches over us.'

'Sigmar watches over us!'

'…or that I sent Berndt on ahead with my missives to the Grand Theogonist. There are soldiers stationed at Fort Denkh. We shall appeal to the company captain for sanctuary behind his walls. It is also where I requested Lord Lutzenschlager have a contingent of his finest knights meet us to escort us back to the Altdorf.'

'How do you know that he will answer such a call?' Giselle

put to the priest. 'Are you and the Grand Theogonist friends from temple?'

'Far from it, child,' Dagobert said coldly. 'But I included in my letter assertions that even the Grand Theogonist would dare not ignore.'

'Excuse me, sir. Assertions?'

Dagobert didn't answer at first, as though considering his words carefully.

'Some of the tomes you brought to me were undoubtedly dangerous and belonged in the secure vaults of the Hammerfall,' the priest said. 'But only one of the diabolic works could truly justify such a bold invasion of our lands. One worth risking so much for.'

'Which one?'

'This one, child. *The Celestine Book of Divination,*' the priest said. 'Or *The Liber Caelestior*. It was composed by a Tilean scryer or madman – depending upon whose version of history you trust – called Battista Gaspar Necrodomo. He used the stars, their relative positions and the patterns they cast across the night sky to make predictions about times that were to come to pass.'

'He knew of the future?'

'So say some,' Dagobert admitted. '*The Liber Caelestior*, however, is considered especially dangerous since it prophesises the coming of the End Times.'

'The End Times?'

'The days of doom, my child. The end of the world.'

'You have read of these End Times?' Giselle asked.

'*The Liber Caelestior* is on a list of prohibited texts that the Grand Theogonist forbids even his Sigmarite priests to read. The contents are considered too perilous to become common knowledge. As far as I know, the Grand Theogonist and his predecessors are the only ones to have read it in its entirety.'

'You *have* read this tome,' Giselle said. 'I can tell.'

Dagobert said nothing for a few moments. Then:

'Given the murderous circumstances surrounding the tome's acquisition,' Dagobert explained, 'and what presently is at stake, I thought it prudent to examine it for myself. The bundle you brought from the Hammerfall contained a primer – a text used to translate, at least in part, some of the other works. Our journey has afforded me time to translate the early sections.'

'And?'

'Though he seems to talk in dark riddles, some of what the madman says has already come to pass,' Dagobert admitted grimly.

'And what of the End Times?'

'The End Times are heralded by a coming of a warrior from the north, at the head of the greatest army in the history of man. He will be the Everchosen of the Ruinous Powers…'

'I don't know much,' Giselle said, 'but I know that does not sound good.'

'The Everchosen is a warlord bearing the favour of the Dark Gods and their blessings in equal measure. There have been few who have enjoyed such a title and unrivalled command of damnation's forces. Only a warrior worthy of the Powers' dread unity, through the completion of a series of unholy quests, can present himself to be crowned Everchosen of Chaos. Several such men have plagued the Empire and our God-King fought them even before that. As we have had our mighty champions like Magnus the Pious, so the Dark Gods have their own. To be Everchosen is to receive the gods' ultimate blessing: sole command of the legions of darkness and the honour of ushering in the End Times – the end of the world as we know it.'

'Then…' Giselle began. She seemed to be thinking. 'Who is this Lord of the End Times to be?'

'All I've learned so far is a single name,' Dagobert said. 'A name I have mercifully never heard before. The herald of the apocalypse is a man called Archaon. A southern name for a northern threat – with the Empire caught inbetween.'

'A name? Surely this Necrodomo must have said more of him than that?' Giselle argued, her tender years lending themselves to impatience. 'On account of these strange powers, and all.'

'He did,' Dagobert admitted, 'but the page bearing the burden of that secret had been torn from the tome. Perhaps someone, at some time, thought that such knowledge should be kept separate from the text. Or that it was better destroyed. Even Necrodomo himself could have removed the dangerous details of Archaon's identity upon truly considering the danger that they posed.'

'Do you think that the leader of the marauders is Archaon?' Giselle asked.

'Desiring confirmation and the secrets of his future?' the priest said. 'I think that such an idea is equally dreadful and possible, my child – and if true, makes getting this volume to Altdorf all the more necessary.'

'I can't believe this to be happening.'

'Do not fear, child,' Dagobert assured her, 'the Grand Theogonist will send his Templars for *The Liber Caelestior*, if not for us personally. Trust that they are on their way to us.'

'Did you hear that?'

Kastner's searing attentions were suddenly brought back to the hospice wagon. Beyond the incredible stench that now dominated the space, the knight could hear noises from the opposite bunk. Emil's moans had ceased. The knight could see the bottom of the squire's bunk. There were still movements beneath his bandages and blankets but they had assumed a horrid undulation, like a snake sloughing off its skin. The sounds from beneath were grisly. It was like the splinter of crackling on a roast pig and the collapse of liquefied flesh. Kastner wondered if Dagobert or the girl had checked the squire's dressings recently.

Then he heard it. Something new. In the tedium of wagon, new was usually good. The knight did not think this to be the case when he heard the slow, wet growl of what Kastner could only assume was some kind of dog. Outside, Kastner heard the horses bridle. The stink of predation was in the air.

The knight fought his body for control of his neck muscles. If he could just loll his head over to one side, he could see the thing with which he was trapped in the hospice wagon.

Pleading fed the knight's frustration which in turn stoked his anger – but it was no good. He could not even form a face of fury let alone act upon it. The cot opposite creaked as the thing that was no longer Emil shifted its weight.

'I'm sure I heard something,' Kastner thought he heard Giselle say.

'It's probably that malingering oaf, Gorst,' Dagobert said, putting the girl's fears to rest. 'Here. Eat something. You will need your strength.'

Inside his head, Kastner roared his defiance. He would not die a miserable, unknown death in the back of a wagon, slowly devoured by and horribly becoming one with some Chaotic spawn of corruption. Kastner willed his body to movement. He yearned for his arms to thrash out, or his legs to kick, his head to lift from the cot or his torso to buck. His mind burned with the effort but his body betrayed him. There was no life there. Not even a promising numbness. Just a terrifying absence.

The growling grew louder. A savage announcement of territorial assertion. Except the horror cared not for forest or hills. Its claim was the templar's own precious flesh. Although he could not see it, Kastner felt the wagon lean, ever so slightly, as Emil's unmade form pushed out from the blankets in its glistening stink and moved towards Kastner – led on by a new snout and a new sense of smell.

Kastner had started to entertain his blackest fears, when suddenly something wonderful happened. Kastner passed water. He hadn't realised it at first but the templar had been soaking the blankets and the cot – urine passing down through the boards of the hospice wagon. Kastner could hear the pitter-patter of his waters beneath the wagon. He heard Giselle grunt as she realised what had happened.

'I think our patients may need us,' the knight heard Dagobert say.

'I'll go,' Giselle said. 'There are fresh blankets in the driver seat.'

Kastner felt feeling return to the tip of his little finger and the knight waggled it for all he was worth. A celebration in miniature. This led to a twitch of the shoulder and the slight drift of his head to one side. There his sore eyes beheld the thing that was now Emil. Still a festering patchwork of mauled flesh, a hairless, eyeless dog snout had pushed free of the terrible changes that had overtaken the squire's wretched form. The grotesque head snarled at the templar as it sniffed his vulnerability. Lips curled back like an opening bud and the snaggle-toothed jaw – a twisted parody of the mongrels that had infected the boy with their corruption-frothing maws – yawned open with predacious intention.

A roar built within Kastner's chest, at first a miserable rasp, building to bombast and the raw announcement that the templar wanted to live. He reached out with soul-draining effort, bringing his hand up in defence. The fresh obedience of action to thought was sweet relief. It was instinct. The spawn moved in to consume the templar's flesh. Kastner's hand came up between them but suddenly stopped. For a heart-stricken moment, the knight thought his body had once again failed him. As he heard the jangle of chains through the cot side, Kastner came to realise that this was not paralysis. It was captivity. There were manacles about his wrists and thick chains between them. As the spawn moved in to feed on him, similar restraints thunked to the wagon floor, slipping from the squire's changing form.

As threaded slime dribbled from the spawn-jaws in expectation of its first meal, Kastner tore at the chains. Passed through the cot as they were, the restraints accomplished precisely what they were designed to do. Keep the templar in place.

'God's wounds,' Kastner heard Dagobert swear. He could see the priest through the curtain opening, where Giselle stood also, the girl struggling with what she was seeing. Kastner's mouth was moving but returning from insensibility, his throat couldn't manage anything as articulate as speech. The urgency of the bellow that escaped his lungs was enough to shake the priest from the spectacle.

'The crossbow,' Dagobert rumbled. 'The crossbow.'

The spawn's own hackle-roar erupted from the nest of teeth and tongues which had once been a head. Its transformations still underway beneath the blood-soaked mound of blankets, the abomination leant in for the kill.

Kastner punched for the wagon bonnet, dragging the length of chain between his manacles up against the cot rail. Once, twice, thrice. The rail gave and clattered free – just in time for the knight to land a punch on the dog-spawn's snout. He hit it again and again with his left fist, his right forced to follow, but the ravenous monstrosity would not surrender its first conquest. Within the spawn, bones snapped and flesh rearranged itself in its aching desire to feed and make Kastner part of its metamorphosis.

Allowing it an opening, Kastner felt his own lips retract with disgust. The blind snout slipped through the opportunity the templar had allowed it, bringing its stinking maw right up to his face. A growl like buried thunder issued from the beast's transformations. Kastner bellowed back at it, coiling the length of chain between his manacles about the spawn's alteration-slick neck. Kastner heaved the beast to him, holding its horrid, squirming flesh against his own, cutting across its throat with his restraints.

'Damnable contraption,' Dagobert said, having been handed the retrieved crossbow and a bolt from Giselle, but struggling to load the weapon.

Kastner heaved. His muscles enjoyed the ecstasy of movement. He willed the corrupted spawn dead and his body answered the call. His biceps bulged and the metal of the chain cut into the thing. The thrashings of primordial panic replaced the undulations of transformation on the opposite cot. The monstrous nest of butchery that was the creature's evolving form did not like what Kastner was doing to its mongrel head. It might have been some nightmare aberration of nature but it still needed to breathe.

The spawn bucked and flailed. A foul fluid bubbled, foamed and leaked from its hissing jaws. Kastner could feel it dying in his embrace. Somewhere, in the horror of it all, the templar's arms trembled to give his squire peace. With a final roar, Kastner strangled the loathsome aberration. A crunch and wet rattle left the grotesque's throat before the beast – moments before in the flesh-euphoria of new life – convulsed its way to a messy death.

Kastner heard the crossbow relieve itself of its bolt. With the priest awkwardly behind the weapon, the quarrel cleared the creature's horrific malformation and thudded into the wooden sideboards beside it.

Kastner released the spawn's blind, skinless muzzle and allowed the fang-heavy skull to hit the wagon floor. The sweet smell of corruption lingered. Giselle turned away, the food she had just eaten returning with a retch of disgust. Dagobert allowed the crossbow to dangle at his side, the priest's face hollow and sheepish. Kastner brought up his wrists, the manacles and chains rattling together. Finally, the word came. When it did, it was cold and imperious.

'Keys…'

CHAPTER VII

*'If history has taught us anything,
it's that one man fighting for his belief –
no matter how mistaken and misguided
his faith,
is measured to the worth of ten faithless
knights.'*

– Frederik III (ascribed – *the Great Crusade
against Araby*)

*Fort Denkh
Middenland
Nachfrederikstag IC 2420*

It was a dismal day and had started badly.

They had built a basic pyre and burned what remained of Emil Eckhardt on the mist-shrouded hills along the Drakwasser. Father Dagobert had deemed it the safest course of action, considering the extent of the boy's corruptions. The priest had reasoned that he must have been infected in some fashion from the bites he received from the beastmen's pack of hounds. He claimed that he had heard of herds hammering extra fangs into the jaws of their beasts, made from curse-carved bone and wyrdstone flints for just such a purpose.

Dagobert, Giselle and Kastner stood in attendance about the smoking pyre, with Gorst ghosting the impromptu funeral a little way off. The fire struggled to take in the early morning drizzle and Kastner brooded in his blood-stained arming doublet and leggings, with a blanket about his shoulders. Dagobert conducted the swift service, saying some nice things about the squire and his family. When asked if he had anything to add, Kastner said nothing, limping back to the camp and wagon.

The knight spent the morning and part of the dreary afternoon the same way, sitting morosely in the saddle, guiding Oberon ahead of the wagon on the Drakwasser Road. Dagobert had tried several times to engage the templar in conversation but Kastner had been deaf to the priest's entreaties.

Erupting like a pair of fat spear-points from the forest, the towers of Fort Denkh were a welcome sight. The sight of the towers drew a smile of relief from the priest, directed at Giselle sitting beside him on the wagon.

'I will ask to speak with the company captain,' Dagobert called to Kastner, but the templar rode on in silence. The priest's syllables grew sour and accusatory. 'You can be very surly sometimes.'

Kastner drew Oberon slowly to a stop. As the wagon caught up with him, the priest did the same. The templar gave him the grim gaze of his single eye, fresh bandages tied about his head, hiding the other. Giselle had offered him the dressings from the hospice wagon supplies but the knight had taken them from her in silence and changed the dressing himself. The material masked the darkness of the ruined socket and the dull glint of the protruding shard point. What it couldn't hide was the septic star of bruising that threaded outwards from the wound, reaching through the pale flesh surrounding the injury.

'You want to do this now?' Kastner said.

'You're right I do,' Dagobert said. 'We had no choice with the chains.'

'What does a paralysed patient need with chains?'

'Lady Arabella lent us the wagon,' the priest informed him, 'for your transportation and comfort. She indicated the restraints as a precaution. We knew little of the nature of Emil's injuries, or your own – and by Sigmar we were right to do so.'

'You served me up like some kind of sacrifice.'

'I can only say sorry so many times,' the priest said. 'I did what I thought was best. These are testing times, Diederick – but know that I am truly sorry my boy, for your suffering.'

'What know *you* of my suffering?' Kastner accused.

'I know the pain of change unsought,' Dagobert said. 'I had raised you like my own. I had hoped you might want to serve with me at the temple. You wished to travel with Sieur Kastner, however – I could see that. There was a deep yearning inside you to fight for the God-King with more than words – for men's souls, but not in their hearts, from before an altar. Sigmar had other plans for you and I accepted that. Loved and encouraged you. Arranged for your squireship. Your path from there you made yourself. Think not that it did not wound – it hurt me deeper than a sword can cut or a spear can pierce.'

The templar saw the priest's eyes glisten and allowed the harshness of his own features to soften. 'I cared for you then,' Dagobert said, 'as I care for you now. Which is why I want you to let me inspect your injuries.'

'They heal,' Kastner said.

'The priestess said they could become infected,' Dagobert said. 'Your fever, your malaise. They could all be part of–'

'I am returned to health,' Kastner said. 'With the sun, Sigmar gave me back my strength and my senses. I am his again as I am yours. My infirmity, Emil's fate – these are all tests to be endured as part of the God-King's work. It is dangerous but necessary. If I heard you right in the back of this wretched wagon, you carry burdens that deserve your attention far more, father.'

'You seem at the centre of those also,' Dagobert admitted. He nodded to Giselle beside him. 'If you hadn't delivered this child and the dark treasures she carried from the forest and its dangers – paying dearly for it yourself – then we would be living the doom of the Empire. Nay, the world, if that damned volume is to be believed.'

'Our concern with these dread, otherworldly matters will soon be at an end,' Kastner told him as the towers of Fort Denkh reached into the sky above them. 'Other servants of Sigmar will carry the weight of responsibility on their shoulders. Let ancient prophecies and Ruinous lunacy be Lutzenschlager's concern. Let the people be yours and the bold advance of this invading warband mine. We shall all be the God-King's hand in this, in our different ways, according to the gifts he has given us.'

'It fills me with joy to hear you speak in such ways,' Dagobert said with a bleak smile. 'I thought I had lost you, boy.'

When Kastner didn't reply, the priest looked to him and followed the templar's glare. It was directed up at the towers and the smoke trails that wound about their rounded elevations and stained the sky.

'Crossbow,' Kastner said. Dagobert nodded, his chins wobbling with the sudden effort of passing the reins to Giselle. Stuffing the bulk of *The Liber Caelestior* and its primer, wrapped in soft cloth, into his robes, Dagobert climbed into the back of the wagon.

'What is it?' Giselle asked, but neither of the men answered the girl.

Changing places with the novice, Dagobert returned with the loaded crossbow and Emil's quiver of bolts, standing about the driver seat like a coachman with a blunderbuss.

'This cannot be,' the priest said to himself. 'This cannot be.'

Giselle heard *Terminus* clear its saddle-scabbard. Kastner

held the sword upright, balancing the weight of the heavy blade. Without his plate, the templar wore only his doublet, leggings, boots and a blanket. He craned his head around and peered back at the sight of Gorst in his rags, chains and cage, tramping up the road some distance behind. The Knight of the Twin-Tailed Orb could see no one else on the road.

'Eyes open, girl,' Kastner said to Giselle at the wagon's reins, digging his heels into Oberon's side and prompting the horse ahead.

As Oberon and the hospice wagon rounded the corner approach and the fort crept out from behind the trees, the three of them saw bodies in the road. Some were merchants and farmers, cut down on the road with their packhorses and oxen where they had been waiting for admittance. The tall fort gates were open, however, with soldier sentries missing from the portly, conical-roofed half-towers of the gatehouse. Archers were also missing from the curtain wall of the fort. As they approached, Kastner cast a suspicious eye across the river but found only the fort's lonely reflection in the slow, glassy waters.

As Oberon's hooves and the wheels of the wagon hit the cobbles, the cacophony of their entrance bounced about the stone barbican and the courtyard beyond. It was eerily quiet. The buildings within the fort walls were black and burned out, trailing a breeze-blown smoke of cinders. The stables, outhouses and market exchange were gone and the gallows toppled. Only the stone of the petitioners' hall and barracks remained and the captain's quarters and company chapel still quietly smouldered. The dead carpeted the courtyard, their bodies lying broken and butchered across the blood-splattered cobbles or dumped in mounds that buzzed with feasting flies. Crowds of crows launched themselves from the slaughter at the visitors' approach, cawing about the courtyard before settling on the fort wall.

Kastner guided Oberon through the bodies, the steed's mighty hooves stepping through travellers and traders. The horse passed over the blue and white of Middenland soldiers.

State troops, garrison sentries, archers and halberdiers. All had been slaughtered where they stood. The bodies were not defiled or tainted with sorcery, and neither did they bear corruptions or display the hallmarks of butchery for butchery's sake. Despite the absence of these things, Kastner was confident that the massacre was the work of Chaotics or marauders. It wasn't something that betrayed itself to the eye or would bear explanation. The destruction had a taste to it. A murderous economy. The elegant butchery of an unsuspecting, unprepared and outclassed force, torn through by their martial superiors. Veteran dealers in death. It was a massacre – but a purposeful one, by warriors who enjoyed their work but to whom the swift and circumspect execution of their enemies was the only thing on their minds. Kastner had sensed the self-same purity of purpose as they had passed through Gerzen and Bergendorf.

'Take care, child,' Dagobert said to Giselle as the wagon bumped through the bodies, before calling across the carnage, 'Diederick?'

'It's them,' the templar confirmed. 'Expert bladework – one man, one mortal wound. No casualties. Some improvisation, with the fires. A distraction, maybe. Had to be something. The gates are open, bearing no damage of an assault. They were in without a fight.' Kastner moved Oberon around a toppled artillery piece. 'Cannon. Unfired.'

'What do we do? What do we do?' Dagobert said.

'We can't stay here,' Kastner said. 'That's for sure. You say that they're looking for that book. If they hit a provincial fort to find it, then your precious tome will only find security in the Altdorf, where the walls are thicker and their opponents more than just a borrowed weapon and a bright uniform.'

Kastner turned towards the far gate.

'Do you hear that?'

'Hear what?' Dagobert said. Giselle's confusion confirmed to the knight that he was the only one to hear the approach: the developing acuteness of his senses warning him of danger. Horses. Heavy, like his own. Plate and barding, rattling to the rhythm of a gallop. The deep breathing of both steed and rider. Eighteen. Kastner listened to the hoof falls. No. Twenty horses and riders. The knight turned to Dagobert and Giselle.

'Riders approaching,' Kastner said, turning his own steed. 'Conceal yourselves.'

Dagobert cursed, getting down from the wagon with difficulty carrying the crossbow. Giselle jumped down lightly behind him.

'Where?' the priest called, already flustered.

'Anywhere,' Kastner said, sidling Oberon up against the inside of the fort wall beside the southern gatehouse. The portcullis was open and it was through the entrance that the horses thundered in – like a battlefield charge. Kastner cast a glance across the courtyard and found that Dagobert and the girl had disappeared into the charred remains of a domed chapel.

Destriers flashed by the templar. White, wearing red barding. In the saddle, Kastner saw armoured figures in gleaming silver plate. The lead rider carried a standard advertising the host as Knights of the Fiery Heart. Templars out of Altdorf and personal guardians of the Grand Theogonist and the Cathedral of Sigmar. In their plated fists the knights carried the long hafts of silver warhammers. Their tabards bore the striking red of Imperial crosses, the arrow-points of each end terminating in the shape of a heart. The visor sights of their crowned crusader helms were cut to accommodate a similar pattern.

Despite being a vision to behold in their armour and on their magnificent steeds, the templars drew from Kastner the wrinkle of his lip. This was not a new feeling. Many of the Sigmarite Orders felt that both the Knights of the Fiery Heart and the Knights Griffon – responsible for safeguarding the God-King's temples in Altdorf and Nuln, capital city of the Empire – were glorious to behold. That they were expertly drilled and fearsome warriors. They also felt that they were far from the real work of the God-Emperor. Temples and personages needed protection but it was in the deep dark forests and provincial mountain ranges of the Empire that Sigmar's will was prosecuted – slaying greenskins, beastmen and the servants of the Dark Gods in His name. It was dirty, desperate work and the duty of orders like the Knights of the Twin-Tailed Orb, while the magnificent temples and cathedrals of the land, already situated in some of the most fortified areas of the Empire, were guarded by the Knights Griffon and the Knights of the Fiery Heart.

A preceptor riding behind the standard bearer raised the haft of his hammer, bringing the corpse-mulching entrance of the knights to a halt. As the horses slowed and stopped, the riders looked about the carnage – the smouldering of buildings and the sea of bodies. The preceptor raised his visor – a Reiklander, noble of face, black of hair and sporting the trimmed moustache and beard thought fashionable in the cities.

'Brotherhood!' the preceptor called crisply. 'Dismount.'

The templars stepped down from their steeds with hammers in hand. As Kastner motioned Oberon on in front of the open south gate, he heard Dagobert bawl from the ruined chapel.

'By Sigmar's blood, it's good to see you, sirs.'

As Dagobert and Giselle emerged – the priest resting the crossbow on a demolished wall – the preceptor ordered six of his knights forward. The templars were quite an intimidating sight, running forward in formation, glinting warhammers held in two gauntlets, their faces hidden in their crowned helms. As the Knights of the Fiery Heart surrounded them, Dagobert and Giselle slowed. Kastner felt his hand tighten about *Terminus*. Feeling the urgency of an explanation, Dagobert addressed the preceptor.

'My name is Hieronymous Dagobert of Nordland,' he said, his words fast and uncertain, 'priest of Sigmar's way temple on the Sudenpass near Esk.'

'You are the priest?' the preceptor asked.

'I am, good sir,' Dagobert replied, 'last time I checked. This is Giselle Dantziger, Sister of the Imperial Cross, late of the Hammerfall, in the Middle Mountains.' The priest looked to Giselle, not only to check that he had announced her name correctly but also to see the glow of pride on her face at hearing that she was now to be known as a Sister of the Imperial Cross. Dagobert didn't think that there would be anyone left alive at the Hammerfall to dispute the fact. Besides, the priest believed that the girl had earned it.

'Preceptor Riesenweiler of the Knights of the Fiery Heart,' the warrior told him. 'My orders come directly from the Grand Theogonist himself, Hedrich Lutzenschlager – though for the purposes of this conversation, sir, you may take them as coming from Sigmar himself.'

'Well, I don't know about tha–'

'You still have the tome?' Riesenweiler asked.

'I do, sir, by the God-King's good grace,' Dagobert said, uncomfortable being within a cordon of hammer-wielding knights. 'Though you can see from the massacre about us that you are not the only interested party.'

'I sincerely hope that you are not attempting to bargain with me you foolish old man,' Riesenweiler warned.

'No, sir,' Dagobert went on uncertainly, and with Giselle looking about them at the slowly closing templars.

'We have ridden far, at the Grand Theogonist's behest,' Riesenweiler continued. 'Be clear. Hedrich Lutzenschlager demands the whole truth of your heart, priest, and we nothing less.'

'I only meant to say that there has already been a great deal of blood spilt over these heretical works.'

'I swear, priest,' Riesenweiler spat with the impatience of nobility, 'that your man on the rack made more sense.'

'What?' Dagobert said. 'You mean Berndt? You racked him?'

'Speak up!' the knight bellowed imperiously.

'Why?'

'Because Hedrich Lutzenschlager demanded the whole truth of his heart.'

'But... he... he's a mute...'

'And yet on my master's rack, the words fell right out of him,' Riesenweiler said. 'One last time, priest. Or I shall have my man here open your skull with his hammer and search for the answers in there.'

Dagobert looked to a terrified Giselle – and then back to the preceptor with a face of stone.

'These poor fools died at the hand of marauders,' Dagobert said, nodding at the slaughter around them. 'Who, I suspect, would do as much as your master has empowered you to do – and more – to acquire the contents of the tome in our possession.'

'At last, we understand one another,' Riesenweiler said with a wolfish smile. 'The Grand Theogonist was also told that you had with you a pair of invalids. Men in need of Shallya's mercy.'

Dagobert's eyes narrowed.

'I should wonder that you did not send one of her priestesses to ease their suffering, sir,' Dagobert said, 'rather than a company of heavily armed knights. Men better equipped to inflict suffering than alleviate it.'

'I see you know us well, sir,' the preceptor said. 'Now, these men…'

'What does the Grand Theogonist want with them? Surely not to enquire as to their wellbeing?'

Riesenweiler nodded to one of the knights, who slammed the haft of his warhammer into Dagobert's ample gut, drawing a savage grunt from the priest and putting him down on his knees.

'Blackguards!' Giselle screeched at the knights.

'Do not make me ask again, you idiot provincials,' Riesenweiler said.

'The boy, Emil Eckhardt, passed,' Dagobert managed, attempting to get back his wind. 'Sieur Diederick Kastner–'

'–is right behind you.'

The courtyard echoed with the clatter of plate, as Preceptor Riesenweiler and his Knights of the Fiery Heart turned around in unison. There Kastner sat, blocking the south gate, on Oberon. He was armourless, bloodied, bandaged and holding the greatsword *Terminus* out before him. 'What would you have with him? And don't make *me* ask again, you bloody genteels.'

Something about Kastner amused the preceptor. Perhaps it was the knight's grim jest or his filthy attire, bereft of plate. It could simply have been the appalling odds. Nodding, Riesenweiler ordered his remaining templars to similarly surround Kastner and his steed. Oberon snorted and stamped as the Knights of the Fiery Heart formed a circle about him.

'Sieur Kastner – Diederick Kastner of the Gruber Marches,' Riesenweiler announced. 'By the order of the Hedrich Lutzenschlager – Grand Theogonist and Sigmar's Will in this world – you are charged with perfidy, wanton bloodshed, bringing terror to this land, the breach of your holy faith, consort with heretics and the worship of outlawed gods.

'Outrageous!' Dagobert said, getting to his feet, but the knight standing over him put him back down with another haft-slug to the gut.

'Your crimes have been weighed and measured,' Riesenweiler said, 'and your punishment devised. That punishment is death, sir. I have taken the liberty of informing your chapter master and claiming your ancestral lands.'

'Kind of you,' Kastner called, 'but you are mistaken, as the God-King is my witness.'

'And yet Sigmar stands as witness against you,' the preceptor replied, 'speaking through my master of your renouncement of his following and your service to the Ruinous Powers.'

'I don't suppose it matters that I have done none of those things.'

'You will,' Riesenweiler told him coldly. Kastner's lip curled into a snarl. It did not matter. This was no mistake. Some great betrayal had been fabricated and his life and work offered as a solution to some unknown problem. If the God-King had a failing, it was that he entrusted his Empire to sycophants and parasites that would pervert his cult for their own ends. Most who served in the ranks of his priesthood or martial orders knew this, believing that they might still do some small good in his name despite their suspicion that the leaders of his faith had lost their way. This was no mistake. The Grand Theogonist would not have sent twenty of his best templars out into the provinces with such specific accusations and orders as part of a misunderstanding. This was real and it was happening now. Kastner felt the careful life of advancement and devotion unravel about him. He had fooled himself into thinking that his next action would have great meaning and would change the direction of his life. The truth he admitted to himself was that his life had already turned a corner. There was nothing left to do but accept his fate.

'I will...'

'You will,' Riesenweiler repeated. Kastner lowered *Terminus* and pointed the tip of the broad blade at the Knight of the Fiery Heart.

'Wanton bloodshed I might grant you, preceptor,' Kastner growled.

'No,' Dagobert bawled from the ground. 'Diederick, don't. This is madness – the servants of Sigmar set against one another.'

'Diederick Kastner is no servant of Sigmar,' Riesenweiler seethed. 'Brotherhood! Do your duty.'

'No,' Dagobert roared. 'Desist in this insanity. We demand audience with the Grand Theogonist. We demand to hear this from him. We demand to hear his reasons.'

But the preceptor had done with the priest. He had heard the order from Lutzenschlager's own lips. 'The man Diederick Kastner must die...'

When Riesenweiler had proposed taking five knights, Lutzenschlager had said, 'Take twenty and see that it is done.' When Riesenweiler protested the number, the Grand Theogonist had told him, 'This man is cursed by the Dark Gods with a future of doom and damnation. A future that must be denied, for our sake as well as his own. Sigmar has granted us the opportunity to do that. He has entrusted me with this task and now I entrust you. Take twenty of your knights and end this enemy of the Empire. No life your holy weapons have taken has ever been more deserving.'

'Do your duty!' Riesenweiler commanded.

The knights moved in with their hammers, the dismal daylight reflecting off their immaculate plate. Kastner felt the pain in his eye intensify. The crackling torment felt its way through his mind like lightning searing between a thunderhead and the ground. With every snap of pain, the templar's face contorted. In the blinding after-agony of each mind-cleaving crack, he saw the bodies of brother templars cut down in the courtyard. The blood-splashed silver of their plate. Crowned helms, rolling about the cobbles with the decapitated heads of knights within. The blessed soldiers of Sigmar laid low.

'I will not be a slave to the perversity of these events any longer,' the templar told all. 'Servants of the Dark Gods or the servants of Sigmar – you all seem lost to me. I will not offer up my life in the name of such madness.'

'Diederick, no!'

But it was already done. The decision was made. With it came peace. With it came – for that moment at least – a mind free from soul-crippling pain. Oberon reared. Kastner lifted *Terminus* for a killing stroke. His first victim came in, his hammer swing drilled and predictable. Kastner would make him pay for the insult of such a routine manoeuvre. To think that Diederick Kastner could be felled by such lack of imagination. At least the forest creatures and the marauders of the north hit you with everything they had. All their skill, their passion, their blood-thirsty invention. Sigmar's knight would die for his presumption.

Suddenly there was movement.

It caught Kastner's attention, as it did his opponent – as it did his templar brothers. A nearby mound of bodies rose from the cobbles. Dead Middenlanders rained to the ground. Butchered torsos. Cleaved limbs. Spilled guts. Beneath were winged forms. Warriors in mail and plate of their own, the metal dark with age and stain. Their wings appeared to be extensions of their armour, infernal appendages of beetle-black. The warriors' helms were the colour of bronzed bone, almost seeming to be skull grown over the metal plate. They rose to their knees, their gauntlets empty, protecting themselves with the mound, shaking the blood and leakage from the surface of their wings.

'My god…' Preceptor Riesenweiler said, lifting his warhammer. He looked from Kastner to the eight marauder knights who had just revealed themselves. Oberon's hooves hit the ground once more. The templar's hammer hovered. Kastner held *Terminus* high above his head.

'The marauders!' Dagobert called out, retreating within the ruined chapel.

'Enemies of Sigmar in our midst,' Riesenweiler called to his knights. He jabbed an accusatory metal digit at Kastner. 'The forsaken reveals his dark servants. Destroy them!'

Knights of the Fiery Heart charged through the carpet of bodies at the Chaos warriors. The armoured figures walked calmly towards the templars, bringing the thumb-protrusions of their wings over their shoulders. Reaching up, the Chaos knights grabbed the protrusions with their gauntlets and withdrew from the hollow bone fingers between the wing membranes a pair of curved, bone swords. Like gnarled sabres of rachidian razors, the knights readied themselves for the charge.

It was just the kind of carnage Kastner had imagined in the courtyard. The marauder knights were cold and purposeful in their execution of their assault. While Riesenweiler's templars lifted and swung their warhammers with a confidence born of drill and prayer, the Chaos warriors were lopping, slashing and stabbing their way through their element – the blood and body parts of their victims. The Ruinous knights moved with the reactive fluidity not of one born to wear plate, like the highborn of the Empire, but of one who had become part of it. Drawing wings before them like shields, the warriors allowed silver hammers to bounce uselessly from the armoured membranes before erupting forth from behind them and scything down through gaps and between plates in the templars' silvered armour.

Kastner watched with simultaneous horror and exhilaration as the templars of Sigmar and the Ruinous knights fought for his soul. Oberon trotted about the bloodshed, with Kastner lifting *Terminus* to strike. Knights of the Fiery Heart, batted back by the wings of their silent foes, tripped through cadavers into the greatsword's reach. The rage in Kastner's belly caused *Terminus* to tremble in his grip, but he couldn't bring himself to strike Sigmar's servants down. As three silver knights smashed one of the damned warriors back through the carnage, its wings and bone blades turning the irresistible force of the warhammers aside, Kastner found himself above the knight.

Righteous fury washed through him like ice-water. The Ruinous warrior had to die. Every part of Kastner's being needed to end him. Almost every part. The wyrdstone within his skull grew warm. It was a strange sensation and the templar brought his hand up to the ruin of his punctured eye. The stone was hot to the touch. Every time Kastner brought his greatsword up, it pulsed a savage heat that he felt throughout his head. Kastner growled at himself in frustration. Within moments the Chaos warrior would turn or move out of reach. *Terminus* came up. Kastner's head came down with the searing thunder that peeled through his skull. Gritting his teeth through the agony, the templar unleashed the broad blade of his weapon. Hacking down between the warrior's wings, the sword cleaved through his neck and shoulder. Tearing *Terminus* skyward, Kastner brought the sword down through the flesh and armour fusion of the other shoulder.

Kastner didn't see the Chaos warrior crash to its armoured knees, its helm-heavy head lolling forward and falling from its gore-spuming torso. He was down on the cobbles, *Terminus* clattering to the ground beside him. Clutching his head with his hands, the templar looked up just in time to see a Knight of the Fiery Heart hammer aside the body of the winged warrior and bring his warhammer over his decorative helm. Kastner rolled across the blood-spattered courtyard, snatching for the hilt of his greatsword as he did. The warhammer came down, sparking off the cobbles. Kastner kicked back to his feet and put *Terminus* between him and the Sigmarite.

Two other knights, drawn down on the dismounted templar, charged from the right and for a moment it appeared as if Kastner would need to take the three of them. With the agony in his head subsiding, he brought his hand down and clutched his greatsword. The first of the charging knights suddenly went down, a Chaos warrior who had been matching him step for step, hacking his leg from his knee with the sweep of his heavy bone sabre. The second was knocked from his feet by a second warrior who slammed into the knight from the side. Tackling the Sigmarite to the ground in a pile of bodies, the Ruinous warrior encapsulated them both in its wings before rearing and stabbing one of its great sabres down through the knight's silver chest.

Kastner felt the God-King's wrath come down with the warhammer of the knight facing him. Holding the heavy blade of *Terminus* against the assault, the templar fought the desire to kill his opposite.

'I'm a Knight of the Twin-Tailed Orb,' Kastner roared at him. 'A templar of Sigmar. Like you.'

Kastner's protests didn't give the hammer-wielding knight a moment's pause. The weight of the weapon came down once, twice and a third time, each swing carrying more fervent force than the last.

'You are nothing like me,' the knight bellowed through his visor, his clipped and cultured voice that of a Reiklander. Kastner felt rage build within him. As the hammer's haft came down, the templar pushed it aside with his greatsword. Reaching for the knight's ornate helm with his other hand, Kastner flipped up the visor and found himself looking at a young nobleman. His couth features were screwed up with effort and righteous hatred for his enemy, the kind of righteous hatred that had once disfigured Kastner's face. Hooking his fingertips inside the crowned helm, Kastner pulled the knight violently to him. Bringing *Terminus* back with the other, he buried the cross-guard of the sword in the young knight's face. Allowing the dead Sigmarite to rattle to the courtyard cobbles, Kastner spat after him.

'You're right,' he said. 'We are nothing alike.'

He turned from the Knight of the Fiery Heart to the two marauder knights that had saved him. The templar expected vengeance. Instead he found cold acceptance. Kastner heard Riesenweiler direct his knights on with imperious disappointment, sending eager warriors his way. Kastner shook his head, raising *Terminus* before him.

'Fight me!' he bawled at the Chaos warriors. He ran at the first but it simply backed away, not even offering a bone sword or wing in defence. 'What's wrong with you? I'm your enemy.' Turning savagely at the second, Kastner brought his greatsword around with such frustration and force that it cut the Chaos knight's bone sword in two. As the marauder backed away, its skull-helm bowed in some kind of wretched deference to the templar, it reached for the gristle of a third protruding hilt and cleared a shorter bone blade from another winged finger-scabbard.

As Riesenweiler's company stormed at Kastner, the marauder knights stepped into their path, bone swords flashing in both hands – putting the holy Sigmarites from their prize. The templar felt his heart twist inside his chest. He had a cold loathing for everything in the courtyard but couldn't bring himself to butcher his damned saviours from behind with a sword in their backs. Looking about him, Kastner came to realise that the marauder knights had formed a skirmish line – a cordon of their own, facing outwards and keeping the devout Knights of the Fiery Heart from him. Sick to his soul, Kastner knew that without them he would have been bludgeoned mercilessly into the cobbles by the Grand Theogonist's armoured assassins. He knew that he wanted to live and had the marauders' intervention to thank for the possibility.

Looking beyond, Kastner saw Father Dagobert making an awkward run for the hospice wagon, his damned volume clutched to his chest. Giselle still sought the cover of the chapel ruins, while Riesenweiler put himself between the two of them. Clutching the haft of his hammer high in his hand, the preceptor rattled up behind the priest at a jog.

Grabbing Oberon's reins in his hand, Kastner mounted the horse and jabbed his heels into the animal's flanks. Urging the steed into a corpse-stomping gallop, Kastner rode for the preceptor. Pushing Dagobert against the wagon, Riesenweiler spun the priest around. *The Liber Caelestior* was buried in his chubby arms.

'Give it to me!' Riesenweiler shouted into the priest's face. As Dagobert struggled against the far stronger knight, Riesenweiler smashed the wood of the forward wagon bow to splinters with his hammer. He swung the weapon at Dagobert with murderous force. The second swing destroyed the wagon's handbrake, while the third put a hole through the sideboard. Between the weight of the weapon in one hand and the priest's struggles, the preceptor couldn't guarantee the hammer's destination. Riesenweiler roared. Dagobert roared back.

'Deviants all,' the Knight of the Fiery Heart accused the priest, the silver head of the hammer against his cheek, pinning him against the wagon. 'That tome belongs to my master now!'

With Kastner still riding through Riesenweiler's scattered company – evading the arcs of hammers and knocking the knights down with Oberon's flanks and turns – Giselle found herself grabbing at the back of the preceptor's plate.

'Leave him,' she called, but Riesenweiler shrugged her off and turned, grabbing the girl's short hair in his gauntlet. Hauling her into the wagon bed, the novice-sister hit the wood with a crack. Tearing her around, the knight found that it was the stock of the crossbow she had recovered from the derelict chapel that had made the noise rather than the girl's delicate bones. Holding it casually at her hip, Giselle pulled on the trigger. The weapon gave a buck and a sigh, sending the bolt the short distance into Riesenweiler's groin. The knight stumbled back, clutching at the mail skirt covering his lower abdomen. The chainmail had done nothing to halt the quarrel, which had slammed some depth into the preceptor's flesh.

Riesenweiler started to say something but he was distracted by the shaft of wood through his body and the blood splashing down the cuisse plates on his thighs. He went down with a cacophonous crash, looking between his gauntlet around the bolt at both Giselle and the priest.

'This is...' Riesenweiler began, 'this is not what Sigmar had planned for me.'

'Not for any of us,' Dagobert agreed, stepping forward. Black horseflesh suddenly flashed by, its passage rippling the priest's robes. Kastner rode Oberon straight through the Knight of the Fiery Heart, Riesenweiler ending up a trampled mess, some distance away – brained and broken beneath the stallion's colossal hooves.

As Kastner pulled the horse around, he discovered Father Dagobert and Giselle staring dumbfounded at him.

'Get in,' he shouted, bringing the pair back to their senses. Turning the greatsword about in his wrist, Kastner slapped the flat of the blade against Oberon's side, urging the horse on ahead of the wagon.

'On,' the priest yelled, sending ripples down the reins at the wagon horses. 'On, my beauties.'

Weaving Oberon through the silver knights, Kastner leant low and to one side, cutting down the desperate Sigmarites as he rode, creating a path for the wagon to bump across the courtyard bodies for the south gate. Turning aside warhammers and cleaving through the finest quality plate with well-aimed hacks and chops, Kastner discovered that the few knights who had made it back to their glorious white steeds had been set upon by the winged marauders.

Leaping the corpses of a Chaos warrior and the four knights whose lives it had cost to bring him down, Kastner and

Oberon thundered up to the gate. Reloading the crossbow, Giselle had little skill at range, but the threat of the weapon and the glancing whoosh of crossbow bolts off stone and cobble enabled Dagobert to whip the wagon horses through the stone gateway. Slashing the ropes of the barbican winch with *Terminus*, Kastner brought his head down low and nudged Oberon swiftly through the gate with the portcullis shuddering down behind him. Hammering his horse up the road away from the decimated Fort Denkh, Kastner could hear the slaughter of the leaderless knights by the warband of winged warriors – the same warband that was massacring its way south through the Empire. As he rode past the wagon, urging Dagobert to keep up the pace, the templar couldn't help feeling that he was trying to outrun both his past and his future in leaving the Sigmarites and marauder knights behind.

'Where are we going?' the priest shouted at the passing warrior.

Kastner considered. They needed a place to rest and collect themselves. Somewhere he could think and devise a more decisive course of action. He turned to look at the red-faced Dagobert and Giselle, who was still clutching Emil's crossbow. The templar made a decision.

'Home,' Kastner told him.

helped him with the bodies and was now sitting behind a finely trimmed hedge, unusually quiet. As the last few shovels of earth hit the mound, Kastner patted them down. On the simple marker he had painted the name 'Trudi'. He had never known the serving girl's family name.

A lantern approached from the manor house. It was Giselle, with a stein and a jug of milk. She hung the lantern off the handle of a pick buried in the ground. It rested with Kastner's hammer swinging from its chain – the silver hammer Father Dagobert had given him before the young Diederick had left to be a knight's page. The novice poured the milk in silence and handed it to the templar. Despite all they had been through, Kastner detected fear in a face unaccustomed to such an emotion.

'What is it, girl?' Kastner demanded.

'Father Dagobert said you should keep up your strength. You're still healing,' Giselle told him. Kastner drank deep. The milk was cool from the cellars. He thrust the stein forward for more. The sister obliged him. 'My cousin Johan once–'

'Tell Dagobert that I need him,' Kastner cut her off. 'Someone should say something for these people.'

'Then why don't you?' Dagobert's voice carried through the darkness. The priest walked up behind Giselle, the heretical tome both the Knights of the Fiery Heart and the winged marauders were searching for under one arm. 'You know the words.'

'They stick in the throat,' Kastner told him grimly.

'As a servant of Sigmar, you've presided over many funerals,' Dagobert said, walking into the lantern-light.

'I knew these people…'

'All the more reason you would want to honour them.'

'You think after today, it wise to lecture me on funeral etiquette?' Kastner said, his anger rising. 'Conduct the bloody lamentations – would you, please?'

'Humour me, Diederick,' Dagobert pressed. 'Help me with first rites.'

Kastner glared at the priest. His lips parted but nothing

proceeded from them. He tried again and again he failed. Kastner clenched his teeth and stabbed the shovel into the ground.

'You know the words won't come,' he said finally.

'And what of this,' Dagobert said, indicating the silver hammer he had given to the templar. The hammer he had worn around his own neck. He moved forward. Kastner flinched. Not afraid of Dagobert but himself. The priest took the lantern from the pick handle and held it up to the knight's chest. There, in the flesh, masquerading as a wound or injury, was a hammer-shaped mark. Like a burn, the silhouette was red, agitated and covered in scratches where it had irritated the templar's skin.

'You cannot speak His words, nor tolerate His sigil against your flesh,' Dagobert said.

Kastner looked down at the mark on his chest. His head rose slowly and thoughtfully. His pain and anger was spent. He felt tired. Looking up at the priest, he stared deep into Dagobert's eyes.

'What is happening to me?' Kastner asked, his voice barely a whisper on the night air.

'You are marked,' Giselle said. 'Any fool can see that. Marked by the Dark Gods…'

'Silence, woman,' Kastner snapped. 'Don't speak such things.'

'Someone must,' Dagobert said.

'Why didn't they kill us?' Giselle asked. 'In the fort, the marauders could have killed us with all those other people. Why didn't they? The Hammerfall. The villages. The fort – but not us. Are we marked with you?'

'I'm warning you…'

'They could have taken the book from our corpses,' Dagobert said, pulling the damned tome from beneath his arm.

'I don't know,' Kastner told them, his gaze on the ground.

'I think I do,' Dagobert said. 'In the manor house, in view of what has come to pass, I thought it worth the risk to consult this Ruinous volume further. While you were out digging graves for those whose blood is on your hands...' Kastner's head came up sharply, but the harsh words the templar had for Father Dagobert died on his lips. 'I have been using the primer to translate this wretched thing. It has answers for us, Diederick, but answers you are not going to want to hear.'

'But I think that we need to hear them,' Giselle said, her arms folded before her. She looked from Kastner to the priest.

'You accuse me of being marked by Ruinous Powers,' Kastner said, kicking at the earth, 'but it is the two of you with your noses in the pages of outlawed—'

'We seem to be at the heart of events of some significance. The marauders. The Knights of the Fiery Heart. The Grand Theogonist of the Empire. Sigmar himself, for all we know. I have been sitting for hours, trying to conceive of why Hedrich Lutzenschlager would have ordered his knights to destroy us. You know that I have few good words to say about that man. Court politics and cult conspiracy put a toad like Lutzenschlager on the Grand Theogonist's throne, not the God-King's will. Men who opposed him were banished to the way temples of the northern coast and the wilds of Hochland. He's deluded. He's devout. His soul is a bottomless well of ambition, tapped falsely in the name of the God-King. But a murderer of convenience?'

'He's a walking corpse,' Kastner hissed through his teeth. 'That's all we need to know.'

'You're going to march into one of the most fortified cities in the land?' Dagobert challenged. 'You are already a hunted man. You mean to execute the most well-protected man in the Empire – bar the Emperor himself – in his own cathedral? I wish you a miracle in such an endeavour, my son, because you are going to need one.'

'No,' Kastner said in words of flint, 'just a blade and powerful will.'

'And a heart full of vengeance?' Dagobert said. 'Would you not know what placed such fire there?'

Kastner's expression soured, 'Pray continue.'

Dagobert held the tome up before Giselle and the templar.

'Despite its macabre appearance,' he said, 'it seems free from any kind of physical corruption. Leather cover, iron clasps, ink and vellum. If evil resides in its pages, it hides itself well. The reason, it seems, for the tome's heretical status and inclusion in the vaults of the mighty Hammerfall, is the knowledge it has faithfully carried to us through the ages. It is called *The Liber Caelestior* or *The Celestine Book of Divination*. You have helped me catalogue such books brought to us at the temple, Diederick, false prophecies that preach the God-King's absence in the world, foretellings derived from celestial congress…'

'Nonsense,' Kastner said.

'Agreed,' Dagobert said, 'the ramblings of madmen, hardly worthy of notice, hardly worthy of cataloguing and securing. These writings are nearly a thousand years old and belong to a professed Tilean seer called Battista Gaspar Necrodomo. He was an astromancer who prophesied what he called the End Times – the end of the world, my friend.'

'Doesn't mean it's not–'

'The Reman priests and inquisitors of Law and Light didn't seem to think so,' Dagobert said, 'and neither did Sigmar's devout servants. When it found its way to the Empire, it was buried in the Hammerfall.'

'Even learned men can be wrong,' Kastner assured him.

'Necrodomo tells that the End Times will be heralded by the coming of a great warrior from the north, a man who would be favoured through his deeds by all of the Ruinous Powers in unison. A man who would be their chosen – their Everchosen, as the Tilean terms it.'

'And how might one man alone bring about the end of the world?' Kastner asked darkly.

'He wouldn't,' Dagobert replied. 'Warriors flock to stand beside great men for the promise of battle, glory and victory. Harnessing their strength, Necrodomo claims he would overcome the trials set for him by the Dark Gods and earn their sponsorship. With their armies – their unified power – his advance would be irresistible. He would destroy the

Empire – nay, the world. Without people to pray to them, gods like our own would be lost to history and the existence of man, with all other races, would be plunged into an eternal darkness.'

'Does this doom-monger have a name?'

'His name is Archaon.'

'Then perhaps this Archaon leads the marauders we saw yesterday,' Kastner said.

'Perhaps…'

'A dread tale indeed.'

'Not a tale, Diederick,' Dagobert said. 'Tales do not come true in the telling.' Kastner shook his head.

'It tells of truths?'

'That have already come to pass, my boy. How the tome itself came to be in our possession. The death and destruction in its wake. The doom to follow. Interpretations, true, as is the case with the translation of any ancient text. Even allowing for that, the predictions are uncanny.'

Kastner burned into Dagobert with his gaze.

'You think I am this Archaon?'

'From where I stand, it seems possible,' Dagobert said slowly.

Kastner roared, snatching up the shovel. Swinging it about him, he let the tool sail into the canopy of the surrounding trees.

'No!' Kastner bawled at the priest, as the shovel clanged its way through the branches and down into the earth below. He stabbed a finger at Dagobert. 'That cannot be so.'

'You are marked, good templar,' Giselle said.

'I should end you both for suggesting such a thing,' Kastner seethed. 'And burn that tome for the lies it tells.'

'Burning the book would not stop the prophecies coming to fruition,' Dagobert said. 'We would simply be blind to them.'

'How can you know?' Kastner said, his chest rising and falling, his face contorted and his eye filling. 'How can you know?'

'I don't,' Dagobert admitted, shamed by the pain of Kastner's reaction.

'What is your proof?'

'The north and the south meet in Archaon's blood.'

'What does that mean?' Kastner bawled.

'You were undoubtedly born here,' Dagobert said. 'You were brought to me a newborn. But look at your skin, your hair. You are a northerner from head to toe.'

'Proof of nothing…'

'Before serving the Ruinous Powers, Archaon found service in Sigmar's name.'

'So have many,' Kastner said. 'The Dark Gods delight in the corruption of virtue. Some of the God-King's boldest and best have fallen to that path.'

'Not many of his templars, I would hope, my son,' Dagobert said. 'Knights pledged in earnest to his cause. Men who were already chosen to stand as our protection against such darkness.'

'A templar?'

'The agreement of events and the people at the heart of them is compelling,' Dagobert said. 'The tome tells of this all, the unfolding tragedy of these times.'

'No,' Kastner spat. 'This is not true. You are wrong. You are deceived.'

'And sometimes we deceive ourselves,' Dagobert warned.

'I am a changed man,' Kastner admitted wretchedly. 'And events would seem to have conspired against me, certainly since this girl brought the calamitous thing into our lives. How can we know she is not a dark servant herself?'

Giselle took several steps back.

'You have already damned us all by your wretched company,' Giselle spat. 'I cannot return to the Hammerfall. This good father here will never see the inside of a temple as its priest. You wallow like a sow in its sorrow but cannot see the ruin you visit upon others.'

Giselle ran forward with her hand outstretched to slap him, but the templar's own came up, locking around her wrist.

He pushed her back with a snarl, causing the novice-sister to fall across Trudi's fresh grave.

Dagobert helped her up as Kastner glowered at them both.

'My child, even if Archaon stands before us,' the priest said to Giselle, 'as far as I can glean from the early sections of the volume, the Dark Gods complot against him. He is no more to blame than the animal in the hunter's trap. He did not choose but was chosen. It is the reason I stand with him – why we should stand with him – in hope that he might be extricated from the snare he finds himself in.'

'Is there no hope?' Kastner said, crumbling slowly to his knees.

'Always, my child.'

'Should I not just select a noose from the many that hang in these trees?'

'I doubt fate would allow such an ending,' Dagobert mused.

'What does that even mean?'

'I knew a young man once,' Dagobert said. 'A man the plague had left bereft of wife and child. He tried to follow them through the noose of a rope...' Dagobert seemed to stall, the story difficult to tell. Giselle and Kastner watched the priest struggle. 'The timbers of his cottage had been as rotten as his fortune, however, and they broke under the weight of the attempt.'

'What happened to him?' Giselle asked.

'He pledged the life that had been granted him, to helping others through their difficulties, rather than sinking into his own.'

The girl nodded, still not quite understanding, and attempted a weak smile.

'I never knew that,' Kastner said, still on his knees.

'Well here's something that you should know,' Dagobert said. 'There is a page missing from *The Liber Caelestior*. An important one. Torn straight from the tome itself. The page, it seemed, was going to reveal the identity of the warrior who was to become this Archaon. Without it, we cannot be certain of anything. We need that page.'

'Where is it?' Giselle asked.

'It must reside – for safety – with the only man with authority in the land to have your matriarch grant him access to the tome in the first place.'

'The Grand Theogonist?'

'Well that is it then,' Kastner said after a pause. 'Lutzenschlager sent the knights. The page has told him who he is looking for.'

'Even learned men can be wrong,' Dagobert said, attempting a smile of his own. 'Diederick, I can continue with my translations, but you will not know any kind of peace until you know for sure. We need that page. It's time to start praying for a miracle.'

Kastner looked down at the freshly turned grave earth. He didn't think he was capable of such prayers. Not to the God-King, at any rate. The devotions would close up his throat. He pushed himself to his feet, nodding slowly in agreement. He would know what business destiny had with him. Besides, there were marvels and miracles in the world for which the God-King was not responsible. Miracles that required neither prayer nor devotions.

Picking up his arming doublet from where it lay across a hedge, disturbing Gorst from his quiet mumblings, Kastner slipped into the blood-stained garment and made his way to the manor house. The new sensitivity of his hearing – one of many changes to the way the templar was beginning to experience his doomed world – picked up the sighs of relief that fell out of Dagobert and the girl. At what should have been well out of earshot, he heard them exchange words.

'The very Cathedral of Sigmar?' Giselle said.

'The lion's den, child.'

'Will he return?'

'No,' Dagobert said. 'I seriously doubt it.'

'Then why send your friend to his death?' Giselle asked.

'I sent him because he *is* my friend,' Dagobert said. 'I hope for his sake – and our own – that he does not return. That he finds peace in the God-King's holy temple. Knight of Sigmar or not, Diederick is polluted. Dread forces twist his soul in the same way they twisted the flesh of poor Emil Eckhardt.' Dagobert's manner became grim and brooding. 'If he does indeed return, with dark answers to dark questions... well then, we shall all be doomed.'

Kastner crossed the pitch-black lawn, heading for the untruth of his ancestral home. He nodded slowly to himself, his head burning with unanswerable questions. His past was a lie. He knew that. But would his future be similarly false?

'Kastner,' Giselle called.

Her voice echoed about the empty gardens of the manor house. It was morning and even the birds seemed to be paying their respects to the dead. The air smelt of freshly turned earth. 'Sieur Kastner!' Giselle hollered across the graves.

'He's not in the house?' Father Dagobert called back. He had just completed his lamentations for the dead. With the number of bodies buried, it had taken some time.

'No, father. Last I saw him,' Giselle said, 'he was looking over the suits in the hall.'

'Sieur Kastner's ancestral suits of armour,' Dagobert said. Giselle frowned as he approached her. 'The former Sieur Kastner,' the priest clarified. 'His great-great grandfather fought alongside Magnus the Pious, you know, during the Great War against Chaos.'

'Perhaps he just left for the city early this morning,' Giselle said.

'Without talking to me first – I wouldn't have thought so.'

'Perhaps he just wanted to be alone.'

'Understandable, I suppose,' Dagobert said. 'It's not every day you discover you might be the herald of the apocalypse.'

'He'll return when he's ready, yes?'

'Yes,' Dagobert considered. If the priest was right about *The Celestine Book of Divination*, then Kastner's whole life was in there. He was going to want to come back for it. Dagobert nodded, his chins wobbling. 'The tome, yes, indeed.

If we wish to know where he is, I should get back to my translations.'

'I'll make us some breakfast,' Giselle said.

'Yes, my child. You do that.'

As Giselle arrived at the well for fresh water, she discovered that the bucket had already been lowered. Heaving on the handle crank, she found that it wouldn't budge.

'The bucket is stuck,' Giselle called. While she tried her best to lever the handle round with her slight form, Dagobert walked back over to assist.

'It's probably the windlass,' the priest told her. As the pair of them heaved, the rope slowly wound its way around the spindle. 'What by gods?' Dagobert said. The weight on the rope was incredible.

'Perhaps it's caught or something.' As Giselle leant over to see the bucket rise from the darkness, leaving Dagobert on the crank, the rope almost ran. The commotion drew Gorst, who sniffed at the well like a curious hound.

'Get back on the handle, child, or all our efforts with be for naught,' the priest said, thick beads of sweat forming on his brow. 'It's caught on a root or something that's broken through the shaft wall. We're probably hauling up half a tree here.'

As the bucket rose above the stone rim of the well, Giselle and Father Dagobert could see that they were dragging no tree root. The bucket hung next to Diederick Kastner's body, the rope of which had been formed into a noose. The templar's face was a livid white – the black tracks of corruption clear to see, radiating through his flesh, away from his injured eye, like a star.

'Sigmar's blood…' Dagobert said. 'Sigmar's precious blood.'

'What does this mean?' Giselle said, her face still stricken with shock.

'It means I was wrong,' Dagobert said. 'It means that destiny cannot be compressed like a dead flower between the pages of a heavy tome. It lives. It is untamed and ever changing.' Giselle saw tears roll down the priest's rounded cheek.

It was a tear of grim happiness, rather than grief. 'It means,' Dagobert said finally, 'that fate is what you make of it.'

But fate is not what you make it, shadow-of-mine. Fate is as inescapable as I choose to make it. Your fate is tied to my own and I will not let us fail. You cannot give away what isn't yours. Your soul may flee this mortal vessel at my command. When I am ready to assume the Everchosen's anointed flesh. When I am once again ready to rule a world ripe for ruin. No coward's noose will deny me my eternity.

You think it took an indomitable will to deny me? To flee your mortality and consign your flesh to corruption? No, shadow-of-mine. It takes an indomitable will to bend, nay break, the very laws of existence. It takes an indomitable will to wrestle the reins of runaway fate and yoke destiny – that tramples even gods – like a beast of my burdens. It takes an indomitable will to send you back to redress your failures and begin again. To live in ignorance and do my daemon bidding. My indomitable will.

CHAPTER VIII

*'They called it the 'Miracle of Altdorf'.
For years the River Reik had served as
the city's latrine, with outpourings and
effusions dumped straight into broad
waters. It is from this time that Emperor
Siegfried declared the city "The Great
Reek" – the first recorded use of the
term – and transferred his court to Nuln.
Plagues of the Bloody Flux and Muddied
Waters decimated the population. It is
a little appreciated fact that the dwarf
engineers tasked with constructing the
Cathedral of Sigmar also established the
beginnings of the first brick sewer system
under the Domplatz District, on the river's
southern shore.*
*With the diffusion of waste spread along
the river's length, both the stench and the
plagues abated. The network and culverts*

> *would be greatly extended during the princedom of Wilhelm III. At the time, however, the sewer system was hailed the "Miracle of Altdorf" and the dwarf engineers responsible were given freedom of the city. Many decided to stay, establishing the city's first Dwarf Quarter.'*
>
> – Emmerich Siessl, *The Great Reek*

The Sewers
The City of Altdorf
Tag von den leered Thron, IC 2420

Kastner had stowed away on a riverboat called the *Mutter's Melken* at Ahlenhof. Narrow barges were a common sight on the mighty Talabec. The waters were slow but powerful there and heavily laden with the black earth of the mountains upriver. Still, the journey was swifter than that back upstream to Talabheim, where the use of horses and well-worn towpaths were required. From what Kastner could tell from the hold in which he was hiding and overheard conversations from above, the *Mutter's Melken* was transporting grain to Marienburg, with little intention of stopping off at Altdorf. The captain was capable and the small crew busy, making it easy for the templar to maintain his concealment amongst the cargo. It also gave him time to think. To feel. To decide.

Diederick Kastner would not be a puppet of fate. He would not be hunted for being what he was not. The champions of the Dark Gods were mistaken and the God-King's servants fools. This insanity would end. Diederick Kastner would end it.

For a large part of the journey downriver, Kastner dozed amongst the grain sacks. He had left the Kastner estates before daybreak, enjoying little in the way of sleep, and took back-forest trails through the Marches to Ahlenhof. He hadn't woken Giselle or Dagobert, leaving them to enjoy the lonely luxuries of the manor house, its many rooms and soft sheets.

He imagined that they would be relieved upon finding him gone. They were safer without him. Kastner was confident that the priest would know why he had left them and where he was going. On a table nearby, Kastner had seen *The Liber Caelestior* and the primer Dagobert was using to translate it. The knight had glowered at the pages with their meaningless words and symbols. The tome had been open at an early section, where, Kastner could see, a page had been torn out. He had studied the tattered edge of the vellum and the pattern of the tear, hoping to recognise it again. As he stood there, he fancied his life laid out in the macabre volume and imagined himself tearing all of the pages from its wicked spine and feeding them to the fire. His hand had hovered over the tome for a moment before he snatched his fist back.

Down in the Great Hall, Diederick had found Sieur Kastner's collection of suits. Armour belonging to the knight as a younger man. Plate worn by his father, his grandfather and his great-grandfathers. The noble family that Diederick Kastner had never had. With his own plate ruined and lost, the templar had selected a suit belonging to Sieur Kastner's great-great-grandfather. Sieur Adalbrecht Kastner – of the Gruberswald Kastners – who had fought in the Great War against Chaos beside Magnus the Pious. The irony was not lost on the knight. It wasn't an attractive suit, having suffered extensive repairs upon its return from service in Kislev. The work was of fine craftsmanship, however. It was a functional piece of mail and plate, lacking in the fashionable flourishes of the others, which were more demonstrations of status and calling. A boxy crusader helm with a protruding head-spike completed the armour, and Kastner had selected a single-handed battlehammer and round shield combination from a display in the hall that seemed to match the suit in style and brute function.

In the stables, Kastner had fed Oberon. Intending to stay off the roads and take the river downstream, the knight had decided to let Oberon sit the certain slaughter out. Patting the stallion, he had wandered to the gate where the saddle rested and unbelted the saddle-scabbard containing the greatsword *Terminus*. Belting the scabbard about his plate, Kastner settled the weapon across his back. *Terminus* had been earned at Magnus the Pious's side and complemented the style of the armour well. With that, Kastner had walked from the estates, morning breaking over the surrounding treetops.

Kastner smelled Altdorf before the calls on deck told him of the boat's approach. It was not called the Great Reek for nothing. Sieur Kastner had an untended townhouse in the Oberhausen District and Diederick had visited the capital on numerous occasions as part of his duties, the chapter house of his order and the Cathedral of Sigmar both residing in the Domplatz, south of the river. Altdorf was an abomination. A cancerous growth on the hide of the Empire. The city reached out with its slums into the Great Forest and the Reikwald, its boundary walls routinely extended and rebuilt about the more permanent developments. Towering above the surrounding tree tops, Altdorf had the power to steal the breath – which given the stench coming off the river and rising from the narrow streets, was a welcome consequence. Its ramshackle buildings appeared like children's toys, built precariously about and on top of one another. Towers trembled and steeples leaned about constructions of finer worksmanship – the palaces, colleges and temples – with the Cathedral of Sigmar shaming them all.

It was beautiful. The exquisite brickwork. The spired towers. The glorious windows of stained-glass and lead. The colossal temple-dome marking the spot where Sigmar was crowned the first Emperor. Visits to the cathedral – on cult business or private reflection at the side altars – were the only thing about the city that had brought Kastner any pleasure. The templar suspected that his present visit would be less enjoyable. His route to the cathedral would also be very different. No clatter of horseshoes on cobble. No citizens paying subdued respects to a Sigmarite Knight of the Twin-Tailed Orb.

Kastner felt the difference as the *Mutter's Melken* crossed the confluence of the Talabec and the River Reik. The narrowboat rocked as it hadn't done before on the journey, producing angry calls from the captain and liveliness from his small crew. He could hear the bustling business of the docks nearby, with boats offloaded or loaded with cargo bound for Marienburg and the considerably slower treks upriver to Talabheim and Nuln.

Kastner pushed the fore hatch open. The boatmen were all busy with negotiating the meeting of two rivers and the arches of a towering crossing. It was called the Three Tolls Bridge – or as Kastner knew it, the Ostlander Bridge. Dank weed hung from the underside of the arch like the hulls of galleons in drydock. Skeletal smugglers sat in gibbet cages that in turn were set into the stone of the bridge exterior, waiting for their deaths while riverside ravens circled. Along the shoreline Kastner saw a muddy embankment of collapsed stone blocks, where beggars had erected a small colony of tents and shanties. He watched. He waited.

'Oi, you!' one of the crew called. The templar had been spotted. 'Stowaway, captain.'

The captain came forward as the narrow boat cut through the current and angled itself for an approach to the bridge archway nearest the southern shore.

'Bring 'im 'ere,' the captain bawled above the heavy slop of the river against the flat-bottomed hull. 'Any man that travels on my boat has to pay for his passage. You gets to save your legs. What do I gets, ay?'

As several boatmen closed in on Kastner, the templar rose from a crouch and exited the fore hatch. As the boatmen saw he was clad in mail, plate and helmet, they slowed. They knew a warrior when they saw one.

'For my passage,' Kastner called at them, 'you get to keep your lives. It's a bargain, believe me.'

Kastner saw what he was looking for. He filled his lungs with as much air as his breastplate would allow, took several heavy steps to the side of the boat and dived into the murky waters.

'Well, would you look at that,' the captain said, as Kastner's fully armoured form disappeared below the stinking surface.

The weight of the plate took Kastner down. The pressure inside his lungs built. Water gushed in through his helmet, but Kastner's eyes were already closed. You couldn't see through the waters of either the Talabec or the Reik and certainly not where they met in confluence. Using his shield as a crude paddle, Kastner pushed himself through the weight of the water, all the while the bulk of his armour dragging him to a watery grave. Suddenly his boots hit stone, angular and slimy with algae and effluence. It wasn't the river bottom. The Reik was much deeper near the harbour dock. He had sunk to the collapsed blocks of the embankment. Pushing the weight of his plate forward and clawing at the architecture of the sunken collapse with the mail on his other hand, Kastner made for the shore.

The air in his lungs burned to be free. His underwater exertions had plunged him into dizziness and disorientation. He felt his way with more than his hands now. He was developing senses he had scarcely imagined a man could possess. Despite the fact that one eye was closed and the other gone, the templar felt that he could still see. Despite the darkness of his world and the cold, wet embrace of the river water smothering him, Kastner's goal drew him like a wolf to a bleating lamb. He could hear it. He could smell it. He could feel its resistance. He could taste its possibility. He could do all of these things and none of them. They were all part of the way he was changing. It repulsed and excited him. He felt the vulnerability of its power. The promise of doom. The objective in the blinding darkness. Or perhaps he was simply addled and drowning.

Kastner's helmet spike clanged against a stone block above his head. He had found it. The overhang he was looking for. With the spent air stabbing its way out of his chest and oblivion beckoning, the templar stomped on through the depths. Beneath the overhang in the ancient collapse, Kastner found a pocket of foetid air. As the helmet broke the surface, the templar hauled it off his head and breathed deep in the funk beyond. It was disgusting. He almost wretched but there was nothing in his stomach to bring up. All he knew was that he could breathe in the darkness.

He blinked river water and filth from his eye. Kastner stared into the darkness. He had rarely been in a place so absolutely bereft of light. The forest was never this lightless. Whether it was the glint of the stars or the pervasive gloom of the clouds, there was always something to see by. Impossibly, in the blackness of the embankment hollow – where light had not ventured for possibly centuries – Kastner found he could see. Not well. Perhaps only as well as the things that crept, crawled and slithered through the feculence about him, but he could see. He was not even sure that his remaining eye was responsible for the strange sensation. It was as if Kastner himself was giving off some kind of ghostly darkness, imperceptible to others, which cast everything about him in a contrasting and ominous light.

Kastner stared about him. Every crook and irregularity of the collapsed passage that the hollow fed into caught Kastner's darkness, throwing shadows of light beyond them. It was as if this sunless and forgotten place had been dusted with the feeblest shimmer. It was fainter than faint, but it was there.

Moving his armoured form up the incline of shattered stone and sludge, he came to the thick metal bars of a subterranean entrance. Kastner put his mailed fingers about the bars. Rust came away in his hands. It was in fact an exit. Kastner had been confident in the location of the passage even if the same confidence hadn't extended to reaching it. Few people knew of its existence, since few had ever taken an interest. As a templar of Sigmar, he knew of the Grand Theogonist's security arrangements and on occasion had been part of them – even though that wasn't the primary role of the Knights of the Twin-Tailed Orb. It was more likely that Kastner's love of the Cathedral of Sigmar as a squire and young templar had brought the existence of the passage to his attention. He adored the architecture of the temple and had familiarised himself with the history of its construction as well as its cult significance. The dwarf engineers responsible for the architectural wonder had built many functional features into the cathedral as well as flourishes of spiritual grandeur. Kastner knew of the secret staircases that wound through the colossal pillars of the Great Sanctuary. He knew of the ossuary below the catacombs that connected the Sun Chapel and the chapter house of the Knights of the Fiery Heart to the cathedral. He knew of the priest passage – a hidden subterranean route constructed by the engineers as a means of escape and for the evacuation of relics, should the cathedral ever be besieged. The priest passage, connecting the cathedral to the river and providing escape by means of the miracle of the city's first functional sewer system. The sewer system in which Kastner was standing.

Slipping his battlehammer from his belt, the templar smashed at the cage door set in the bars. There was a brief and blinding spray of sparks. Kastner hit it again. This time the door fell off its rust-eaten hinges in a shower of flakes. The passage beyond was round and buckled, as though weight from above had contorted its structure and foundations. Dwarf-crafted bricks sat uneasily against one another, some protruding, some angled awkwardly and others pulverised under the pressure. As Altdorf had grown in importance and Sigmar's ruling priesthood in their overconfidence, the priest passage had been largely forgotten. But Kastner hadn't forgotten it.

Kastner's armoured form sank down into the swamp that percolated the passage. The stench was horrendous. The collective feculence of the Domplatz District, gathering, stewing and creeping slowly downhill towards the river. Each step was a putrescent struggle. Each breath was a gag-stifling ordeal.

The waste soaked through his mail and smeared his plate. With his lip set in a permanent snarl of determination, Diederick Kastner pushed on through the endless length of the tunnel.

He encountered side-passages and turn-offs, ladders, hatches, and cage-ways but he would not be put from his purpose. Kastner thought of the sweet city air, high above, through the crumbling stone and the newer Imperial sewer networks, up through the gratings and hatch-covers. Rank in its own way but like a noblewoman's perfume compared to the muck he had been breathing down in the tunnel.

Besides, Kastner had a very good reason for taking the excruciating route that he had. If the Grand Theogonist had sent twenty of his finest templars out into the provinces to destroy the man Necrodomo's words had identified as Archaon, Herald of the End Times, then Kastner could expect heightened security about the city. Kastner tried to imagine the ordeal that would be waiting for him. Altdorf's mighty gates fortified with extra sentries and soldiers. The watch doubled. Reiklanders, armed with bills and shields, swarming the Templeplatz about the prince's palace, forming with engineers and their cannons a veritable gauntlet along the Templestrasse. Templars – perhaps even of Kastner's own order – Knights of the Fiery Heart and the temple's men-at-arms, all placed on high alert and ready to respond, should a threat manifest itself. Should a champion of Chaos called Archaon and his Ruinous allies make an attempt to push into the city. It made for a vision of hopeless futility. A vision that had driven the templar to find another way into the cathedral.

In the face of any such threat, it was unthinkable to all that the Grand Theogonist was in any actual danger. That the city walls could be breached by a single man and so small a force. That the Imperial Army would not be a match for any single threat. Those people could afford to be confident. None of those people had read *The Liber Caelestior*. None but the Grand Theogonist himself, and it was no doubt on Hedrich Lutzenschlager's unquestioned orders that the city be elevated to such a state of vigilance and security.

As his every doomed step took Kastner closer to the cathedral, the waste got deeper, the rats swimming through it bigger and the corpses more frequent. Every so often, something rotting in the sludge would groan and reach out for him, prompting Kastner to smash in its skull with a merciful swing of his hammer. Just as he allowed himself to believe that his trek through the city's bowels was almost over, the knight encountered an obstacle. A colossal stone ball, as tall, broad and round as the tunnel itself. Kastner leaned against the immovable object and tried to catch his breath but he couldn't take the foul air of the sewer down far enough to make a difference without retching. The thick river of excrement was being slowly fed by a side tunnel but the ball blocked Kastner's route to the cathedral. It was one of the technological wonders the dwarfs had built into the system. Such colossal balls were employed to prevent blockages. Rolling slowly and gently downhill, they pushed the swamp before them, out into the river at different times and intervals along the shoreline – before being winched back on hook-points inset in the ball's surface. This one had been jammed in the collapsing dimensions of the tunnel.

Kastner smashed at the ball with his hammer but time had not had the same effect on the ball as on the passage. It was a solid, if slime covered, ball of solid rock. The templar might as well have been pummelling a boulder on some mountainside. Resting the battlehammer by his side, the templar tried to clear his head of the rancid stench of the sewer. The side tunnel didn't take him to where he needed to go. Climbing out of the sewers in the middle of the Templestrasse was exactly the kind of suspicious activity that would bring a company of Altdorf's finest down on him. He stared about the rancid darkness. At the ball and the irregularity of the brickwork in the surrounding wall. Kastner grunted.

Moving around the side of the ball, he smashed at the wall where the ball had become wedged. The bricks – even dwarf-crafted bricks – came apart under the hammer's insistence with a great deal more forgiveness than the ball. It was hard work, but before long the knight had decimated the side of the tunnel about the huge ball. As the impacts echoed about him, up and down the passage, it dawned on Kastner that hammering might attract unwanted attention. Holding the hammer silent he listened through the blackness and fug. Even with the weapon doing its worst and shards of brick flying, the templar's keen senses had not abandoned him. Something had shuffled up through the sludge behind him. It was broken and awkward; it groaned at the thing it sensed in the darkness but could not see.

Kastner allowed the thing to bathe in his darkness. In the rich effluvium of the sewer, the templar couldn't smell it but suspected that the shambler was dead. From what he could make out, half the thing's head was missing. He began to wonder if this was one of the bodies he had already encountered in the sewer morass. It reached out for him. Batting the cadaver back against the tunnel wall, Kastner brought up his shield and sliced its rounded edge through the rotten meat of the corpse's neck. Shearing its head off against the brick, Kastner allowed the thing to die once and for all. The body dropped and sank below the effluence.

Reinvigorated by the kill, Kastner slid his own body around the slimy circumference of the ball. With his armour plates catching on the broken brick at his back, it was difficult to edge around the object. With a final push, Kastner tore through a section of wall. The muck that had collected beyond oozed forth, dribbling around the ball and almost swamping the knight. Once again, Kastner found himself up to his neck in the mire. The Reik had been a bath of rose petals compared to the faecal deluge beyond and the templar found it difficult to keep his footing below the surface. Every slip, slide and step was a gagging agony. There simply wasn't enough air left in the tunnel-space above the slurp and fester.

Then he felt it. Where his hand expected to find the rounded wall of the tunnel, he discovered a sludge-filled alcove. Wading into it, Kastner could make out the barest impression of rungs on a rusted ladder, which his mail digits confirmed moments later. Hauling himself from the suction of the muck, Kastner climbed the short distance to a metal hatch. Feeling about its edges, he found it to be unmistakably octagonal. It was the shape of the cathedral's Great Sanctuary and the shape of the dwarf-crafted bricks used to build it. Kastner rested his crusader helm against the hatch and risked a smile. Bringing up his shield and putting his shoulder against it, the templar smashed at the metal until the long-rusted bolt locks on the other side gave way and the hatch bucked. Hooking his fingertips about the hatch, he slid its weight to one side and climbed out of the sewer.

Effluence streamed from his armour, pooling about his boots. Within the plate his doublet and leggings were soaked through. Kastner could only imagine how he appeared – covered from helm to toe in the waste of ancients, freshly crawled from the sewer like a rat or roach. The priest passage was roughly hewn and led to a dead end, with only a crack of light giving the suggestion of a false door. After the darkness of the sewer, the sliver of golden light was almost blinding. Taking several heavy steps, Kastner smashed his boot down on stone, which promptly gave with a creak and toppled. Kastner blinked his way into the next chamber, his shield held up against the harshness of the light, but found only a single stubby candle, alight but almost spent.

As his boots crossed the uneven stone floor, the templar felt suddenly weaker, as though the raw determination that had got him through the sewers had abandoned him. He stumbled to one side, reaching out for a surface, and found a skull. A human skull, amongst many. Skulls set in stone. In fact, the chamber was filled with rough stone shelves stacked high with the browning bone of skull collections and presented skeletal remains. At intervals through the chamber, full skeletons were displayed in sarcophagi – some standing upright like the one Kastner had just smashed to the ground, others on horizontal slabs. Kastner felt dizzy. It was an effort even to walk. It was as though the very stone were sapping his strength.

The templar shook his head within his helm. He was in the ossuary – the charnel chambers below the catacombs – housing the remains of men and women who thousands of years before had pledged themselves to the cult of the God-King and the building of his holy Empire. Kastner bit at his lip. He was standing on holy ground. The stone beneath the soles of his boots – that had once filled him with such passion and devotion – now leeched his strength and plunged his heart into a deep well of dread.

He stumbled on through the ossuary, afflicted by the consecration of his surroundings. Rough steps took him up into the labyrinthine catacombs that riddled the foundations of the cathedral and the Templeplatz beyond. Here the subterranean tombs of distinguished priests, templars and even past Grand Theogonists were to be found. The catacombs marked the passing of more recent paragons and martyrs to the Sigmarite cause. Rather than be returned to a family estate to which he didn't belong, Kastner had hoped one day to earn his own place in the catacombs and be honoured as one of Sigmar's worthiest servants. Now he couldn't stand to be in the presence of such worthies. The templar slipped down to one knee at the foot of a flight of stone steps leading down into the catacombs.

The door creaked open and Kastner was forced to retreat noisily into the shadows. The door boomed shut and he heard the scuff of sandals on the steps. A priest was descending. Kastner felt his limbs tremble, as though he suffered a fever without the symptoms. Before, the Ruinous taint had fought the devotion in the templar's soul and the love, pure and true, that he held for his god and his calling. Something had prevailed, though for the life of him Kastner knew not what. Here in the catacombs, in the presence of a future not to be and surrounded on all sides by the holy ground of Sigmar's cathedral, the templar felt the corruption within him fight for its existence. Kastner clenched his mail fist. Shakes turned to quakes. Quakes to a cacophony of rattling plate.

'Is there someone there?' the priest asked with an imperious sneer. 'Present yourself. I don't have all day.'

Kastner heard the priest sniff the air. 'What is that god-awful smell? What is going on down here?' he demanded as he descended. Two steps from him, Kastner stepped out. Colour fell from the priest's harsh features. He had expected to find a novice or a sentry to be scolded, not a hammer-wielding warrior, dressed in faecal-splattered plate. Kastner fed off the fear in the priest's eyes. The shaking ceased. He brought up the hammer to strike the priest down. The hammer hovered above the terrified Sigmarite. But something in Kastner wouldn't let him do it. To murder an unarmed cleric, cowering on the cathedral steps. He turned away. 'It's you,' the priest said behind him. 'The extra men-at-arms – the templars. You're the one they're looking for.'

'And much more,' Kastner said, whipping around with his shield and dashing the priest into the stone wall of the stairwell. He bounced and fell back onto the stairs, tumbling head over shoulders down the harsh steps. Kastner looked down on his still form. He stared for what seemed like an eternity, his face a blank mask. There was blood. There was injury but the priest breathed still. 'Forgive me my sins, father,' Kastner said to the unconscious cleric, 'but I need to compound them. I'll be requiring your robes.'

CHAPTER IX

*'And Friar Helstrum told of Sigmar – a vision to behold.
Through the land his power, his virtues and memory extolled.
Sigmar knelt amongst the divines and before the Winter God.
A gold crown of immortality our Emperor did don.
Sigmar comes to us timely, almighty and reigning supreme –
This, the friar did attest, the God-King revealed in his sleep.'*

– Gottfried Hachenbacher, *the Ascended Sigmar*

*The Cathedral of Sigmar
The City of Altdorf
Tag von den leered Thron, IC 2420*

Kastner went down on his knees. This was a relief. He felt weak and unsteady. The knight certainly didn't want to attract any attention by falling over in his plate in the all but silent sanctuary. The floor hurt to walk upon. The stained-glass shards stung his eye. The very walls of the cathedral ached devotion. Somewhere deep inside the templar, the God-King's divinity was leeching his soul like a vampire.

His newly liberated robes barely fit about his armour but he wasn't the only visitor to the sanctuary bedecked as such. The colossal chamber – feeling ever more so below the vaulted dome above him – was playing host to a number of priests, Sigmarite sisters and templars of different orders – some also dressed in armour. Sigmar was a martial god. The wearing of armour in his place of worship did not offend him. It was a form of worship and respect. While wearing plate before the God-King was not considered disrespectful, disturbing another man's devotions was. This worked very much in Kastner's favour. Priests at prayer kept their distance from one another, spreading out about the chamber. Some favoured the side altars, others the spectacle of the magnificent stained-glass window. Some the colossus of Sigmar himself, wrought in gold and dominating the head of the chamber. Kastner suffered quietly before the mighty statue, the God-King looking down on him in silent, aureate reproach.

The priest's thick robes were doing their best to soak up the filth that covered his plate and leaked from his mail. He still reeked but there was little he could do about that and he hoped to pass for an afflicted begging Sigmar for relief. It seemed to be working. Many of those at prayer were too polite to comment on the smell or unwilling to engage such an unfortunate in conversation and simply moved away. Holding his crusader helm to his chest and pulling up his hood, the templar waited. Rather than blunder past sentries in an attempt to get in to cross to the heavily guarded Sun Chapel – the Grand Theogonist's private temple – Kastner had reckoned on waiting in the main sanctuary, confident that the Grand Theogonist would come to him.

Before Kastner was the Grand Theogonist's golden, octagonal throne – the throne from the comfort of which Hedrich Lutzenschlager would enjoy morning observances.

The templar rocked slightly on his armoured knees. It was just him and the God-King, in the holiest place in all the Empire.

'You have forsaken me,' Kastner hissed to himself, his dry lips pronouncing each word slowly within the confines of the hood. The templar looked up at the statue's proud features. The statue gleamed its goldenness and from the low angle, Sigmar looked like a haughty and disdainful god. 'I have lived a devout existence. Bettered myself with study, for your good grace. Trained to my limits and served you through the sword. I have honoured you. I have loved you. I have given you everything I have. Yet you have left me lost on a path to I know not where.'

The templar was bathed in shafts of coloured light from the stained-glass window and felt his harsh whispers rise on the heat of the morning sun.

'I am no longer an instrument of your design,' Kastner said. 'A yardstick to measure the purity of others, a weapon for you to wield in punishment and a shield to protect your Empire from foes near and far. I am changing. I am changed. I know it. Circumstance has turned me from my purpose, in service of others unknown. Like the warped arrow, I fly untrue, yet hit the mark. I will not be a nothing in your eyes. A dog to be put down in the street. I am not an error. An aberration. I am not history to be re-written. I am not a mistake to be corrected. Speak to me, my lord. My Emperor-of-all. My God-King. Show my heart the way. Lead me back to your light and love. I did all in service of you. Like the arrow shaft, I can be softened and straightened. Like the imperfect blade, I can be re-forged. I beg of you, my lord. Find use for me again.'

About Kastner, priests had started to gather for the morning observance. They stood in clusters, the daily business of cult politics dominating the conversation. The templar even heard several speak of the Grand Theogonist's mysterious orders and the extra security around the cathedral. Clusters became crowds as the numbers grew and the domed sanctuary filled with clerics standing before the colossal figure of their god. Still they gave the stinking templar a wide berth. Kastner rose to his feet. He felt sick to his stomach. His knees felt weak.

'Don't leave me,' Kastner pleaded with his lord, 'the plaything of fate. Show me a sign – in this place of all places. Anything, curse you.' But nothing came. Kastner's lifetime of devotion and service was rewarded with the kind of monumental silence only a towering statue could deliver. As the priestly gathering hushed and parted, Hedrich Lutzenschlager entered the Great Sanctuary. In robes of glorious white and golden thread, which trailed behind the Grand Theogonist for half the hall, the High Sigmarite made his way towards the throne. Lutzenschlager was known as an ardent but cold servant of the God-King. A puritanical and inflexible executor of his faith, his displeasure was easily earned. He wasn't a physically imposing man. He didn't need to be. The six Knights of the Fiery Heart escorting him in were imposing enough, in the gilding of their gold and silver plate, carrying the lengths of hammer-crowning pole-axes in their glorious gauntlets. Lutzenschlager's short steps took him with business-like speed through the masses. With him hurried a small group of attendants, bearing the Grand Theogonist's own ceremonial hammer, staff-sceptre and rolled readings. Lutzenschlager's head was shaved short, leaving a black shadow that almost gave the appearance of a skullcap, while his feathered brow framed hard eyes and a beaked nose.

As the Grand Theogonist made his long approach, Kastner glowered back up at the impassive mask of the golden god. Pulling back his hood, he slipped his crusader helm back over a snarl that threatened to split his face.

'You speak not,' Kastner mouthed within the darkness of his helmet, 'but I hear everything. Silence will be met with silence, God-King. Nothing so singularly personifies the prayer unanswered as a god powerless to save his people. So be it. You will watch your worshippers suffer and die – as I drag down your Empire into the embers of Armageddon. You will hear me then, God-King. You will hear me in the pleading prayers of your people, held under my blade. You will hear me in the ravenous fires that will eat all you have lived to build. You will hear me in the deafening silence of the End Times, where I will leave your petty Empire no world left to conquer. Though half blind, I see you for the fraud you have always been. The appealing ramblings of a mad friar. I renounce your false majesty – and will forge a path of my own making. I will champion my undoing and accept allegiance of those that already answer the hatred in my heart. I do this out of hatred for you, my lord. Out of hatred for all the fickle Powers of this world, who play at destiny with men's souls. With darkness lies a new beginning, as with me lies the end of man and all godkind.'

'Yessssss,' something dark and deep within him said. With the word, Kastner felt his heart suddenly thud within his chest. Like the unfastening of a lock, the heavy chains and shackles of his infirmity fell away. A dread potential had bloomed within the knight, at once allowing him to access all he once had been and the fearful doom he would one day become. Kastner savoured the troubled birth of darkness within his soul. The feeling was new. It was exciting. And yet it had always been there, its mouldering seed forever planted in his heart. He knew nothing of birth. It was lost to the darkness of ignorance. He had been begotten by darkness and to darkness he would return. Kastner allowed the cold rage to build within him, honing it like a blade on the eve of battle. It was time.

As Hedrich Lutzenschlager passed Kastner, he heard furious mutterings from within Kastner's helm. He turned to one of his escorting knights before ascending the steps leading to the statue of Sigmar, to take his place on the throne. The Knight of the Fiery Heart came to a stop beside Kastner and laid a gleaming gauntlet on his pauldron.

'Silence, brother,' the knight warned from within his own ornate helmet.

Kastner's mail fist came up behind his helmet and reached down the back of his hood. As the knight turned to retake his place in the Grand Theogonist's honour guard, *Terminus* cleared the scabbard at Kastner's back. The blade sang overhead, before Kastner brought its cleaving edge down through the knight's own armoured shoulder. With the force of the storm stirring within Kastner behind it, the greatsword cut through the ceremonial plate like ripe cheese. Blood fountained from the stump as the arm clattered to the ground, the knight falling swiftly after it. Like the sigh of a stirring volcano, shock passed through the congregation. But Kastner had barely begun.

While Reikland reinforcements milled on the Templeplatz and horses dragged cannons across the Three Tolls Bridge, a gauntlet of knights in full plate sat tall in saddles. Sentries and men-at-arms stood in double their number at the cathedral's archways and entrances. All waited without the great cathedral walls and doors for a threat that would never come.

Kastner had already announced his arrival within in blood. He called to his enemies with the death of their own. The world flooded him with its new sensations. He could hear the echo of confusion in Sigmarite hearts. He could taste the questions on their lips and drank in deep the fear filling their bellies. The rear three knights attempted the clatter of an urgent turn. Kastner wished them dead. And it was so.

The gold and silver of the knights' ceremonial plate did not look as impressive with Kastner's blade exploding from the chest plate or leaving the crimson of slashed throats cascading down its polished surface. There was running. And shouting. And screaming. The Great Sanctuary was emptying of Sigmar's false prophets. They shrieked with unmanly abandon, tearing at each other's vestments to get through the chamber doors and arches.

As his attendants fled with the only weapons the Grand Theogonist had – and called for the cathedral's men-at-arms – Hedrich Lutzenschlager fell back into his throne. He wore the shock of a man watching an accident unfold but feeling powerless to stop it. His face was a paralysed mask of horrified acceptance. Two Knights of the Fiery Heart crossed their pole-axes before the throne to prevent Kastner getting through, while the remaining warrior came for him with the kind of confidence and fervour Kastner himself had once reserved for the enemies of Sigmar. He swung the pole-axe with the full length of its haft, expertly guiding the weight of the hammer at its far end towards Kastner with irresistible force who brought up his shield and leaned into the impact. As it smashed into the shield surface, Kastner was sent skidding to the side. As tiles came up before the sliding side of his boot, Kastner threw himself straight back at the knight. Circling in a graceful arc, the pole-axe came at Kastner again – from the other side. Again the hammer fell like a thunderbolt at him and again he got his shield before it. Crunching up through the shattered tiles and sliding *Terminus* between his arm and the shield, Kastner slipped the toe of his boot beneath the haft of a pole-axe lying across the body of one of his victims. Scooping the weapon up with his foot, he caught it in his mail fist before launching it at the knight. The armoured warrior caught the haft-spike of the axehead in his chestplate, the point rupturing the knight's heart.

'Your god has abandoned you, sieurs,' Kastner told the two remaining honour guardsmen. 'As he has done me.'

The knights were not interested in exchanging conversation with heretics and as the first grabbed his master below the arm and man-handled him from the throne, the second came forward to keep Kastner occupied.

'One at a time,' Kastner questioned. 'Really?'

The Sigmarite held his pole-axe in two gauntlets, jabbing and thrusting at Kastner with well-practiced lunges. Kastner didn't even move to take *Terminus* from where the weapon was resting behind the handles of his shield. He watched the spear-point on the head of the weapon come for him and merely leaned back out of the weapon's path. To one side. Then the other. Having pushed the stunned Grand Theogonist in the direction of his escape, the second knight rattled up behind to aid his compatriot.

Kastner slapped the haft of the first knight's weapon aside with his shield before running straight at him. There was a clatter as the plate of the two knights clashed. Kastner had knocked the warrior back at the throne with his shield before turning to meet the oncoming head of the other knight's pole-axe. The Grand Theogonist, meanwhile, was backing rapidly towards the hordes of exiting priests, unable to take his eyes from the blood being spilled in Sigmar's Great Sanctuary.

Kastner allowed the head of the pole-axe to glance from the rounded surface of the shield, turning with the force of the weapon and moving out to one side. His hand slapped down at his side to remove the battlehammer from his belt. The Grand Theogonist had not heeded the calls and entreaties of his priests to follow them, but upon spying Kastner move in on him with the hammer, Lutzenschlager turned and ran. Three more steps took Kastner to the trailing tails of Lutzenschlager's extravagant robes. Stamping down on the material, Kastner stopped the Grand Theogonist in his tracks. As Lutzenschlager turned, gathering the robes in his hands to heave for his freedom, Kastner tossed his battlehammer with murderous force. Passing head over haft, the hammer struck Lutzenschlager in the chest, knocking him from his feet and turning him into a lifeless mound of robe and limbs.

The first mistake that Kastner's opponent made was turning his helm to check on his master. The second was turning back. Pulling *Terminus* from where it nestled behind his shield, Kastner cleaved through the knight's helmet. Dropping his pole-axe, the Knight of the Fiery Heart crashed onto his backside, struggling to push the rent visor up from his ruined face. Kastner could hear the footsteps of the knight behind him and didn't even turn to meet his attacker. The steps were not even, like those of a knight making a charge.

They sounded irregular, like the kind you might make to throw a ball or the weight of a pole-axe around on the length of its haft. Kastner waited. He allowed the knight to line up his target. Kastner took a step closer to the knight on the floor, fighting to pull the mess of his face from the mess of his helmet. Then Kastner suddenly lowered his head and swooped to one side. The crowning hammer of the pole-axe came straight down on the head of the sitting knight, smashing what was left of his skull to mulch. The knight couldn't believe what he had just done to his knightly comrade and his body remained frozen in stunned realisation. The Knight of the Fiery Heart had little time to contemplate the harrowing accident, as *Terminus* came down like the blade of an executioner's axe and took off his stricken head and helm.

Tearing the priest's robes from his muck-smeared plate, Kastner slipped his greatsword back in its scabbard on his back. Walking with a brisk clatter, he stood over the Grand Theogonist. Lutzenschlager – his former spiritual master. He picked up his battlehammer in one hand and the leg of the robed Grand Theogonist in the other. A novice priest stood apart from the fleeing crowd of Sigmarite priests. He looked at Kastner in stunned amazement, his eyes needlepoints of searing naivety and accusation.

'Come on,' another novice begged, pulling the boy but he resisted.

'That's it, boy,' Kastner mocked. 'Run along.'

He dragged Lutzenschlager back through the gore on the floor and towards his throne.

'For Sigmar's sake,' the novice priest's friend pleaded once more. 'Let's go. The Knights of the Fiery Heart will handle this.'

'They will try,' Kastner said to himself, as the novice was pulled away.

'Wherever you go,' the boy shouted, his voice tender with his years, 'wherever you run, wherever you hide, the God-King will find you.'

'He will not,' Kastner barked back, his words echoing about the Great Sanctuary. 'For I am already lost to him.'

'He will punish you,' the novice's voice faded as he was pulled back through the fearful confusion of priests exiting the chamber. 'For the desecration of his temple and the dark path your soul has taken.'

'A path my craven god put me on,' Kastner roared.

'You are deceived…'

'About a great many things,' Kastner said, turning and looking up at Sigmar's golden face. With the words dying on his lips, he set about tying the Grand Theogonist's wrists and ankles to arms and legs of his throne with belts from his ample robes.

Kastner sensed them coming. He heard the rhythmic clack of plate: Reiksguard, Sigmarite knights and templars summoned and running across the Templeplatz. The flutter of confusion and fear to be found in the chests of common soldiery – fighting men forming a perimeter with their halberds and spears. The patience of cannons, loaded, primed and dragged into position across the cobbles. There was shouting and the clearing of swords from scabbards as armoured figures strode into the cathedral and began issuing orders. As the last of the priests fled the Great Sanctuary, a river of plate cut through their numbers. Knights of the Fiery Heart, full of imperious dread to learn that their defences had been breached, accompanied by Sigmarite warriors of other orders, at liberty in the Domplatz to aid their knightly brothers and highlight further their failure. Knights Griffon. The Hammers. The Knights of Sigmar's Blood. Even a few of his own order: the Knights of the Twin-Tailed Orb. Grand Master Schroeder was present but at the head of the deluge of devout fury was Grand Master Boschkowitz of the Fiery Heart. Helmless, immaculate in silver and temple gold and with his huge warhammer already in his hands, Boschkowitz's great beard trembled with anger at the sight of the Grand Theogonist's honour guard cut down before Sigmar.

Using the head of his battlehammer, Kastner lifted Lutzenschlager's chin and held the unconscious Grand Theogonist's head against the back of the throne. The gesture slowed Boschkowitz and the advance of the knights.

'You'll be Diederick Kastner,' Boschkowitz bawled across the chamber, 'out of the Gruber Marches. Late of the shadow of the Middle Mountains. The deep shadow.'

Kastner said nothing to confirm or deny the Grand Master's accusation. He was not there to oblige Etzel Boschkowitz.

'If you take another step further,' Kastner assured the Grand Master, 'he dies.'

The serpentine certainty of Kastner's words halted the furious Boschkowitz, causing the knights to clash into one another. 'You storm the sanctuary – he dies. If you still grace my sight at the end of ten seconds – he dies.'

'You can't expect us to leave the Grand Theogonist,' Schroeder said, his eyes full of loathing for his own knight.

'One.'

'Would you?'

'Two... Three...'

'Out!' Grand Master Boschkowitz commanded.

'Four...'

'We can rush him,' Schroeder said.

'Out, I say,' Boschkowitz bawled, backing his knights out of the chamber and holding his warhammer out in front of the Master of the Twin-Tailed Orb. 'Care for the Grand Theogonist's person still falls to me and my knights. I have the Arch Lector's confidence and you will do as you're commanded.'

'Six... Seven...'

As the knights withdrew, Boschkowitz gestured to Kastner with his warhammer.

'I'll kill you, Kastner,' the Grand Master told him. 'In Sigmar's name, your life is mine.'

'Hedrich Lutzenschlager is Sigmar's representative in this world, Master Boschkowitz,' Kastner said. 'Concern yourself with his life, for it is only your cooperation and my forbearance that keeps him breathing. Now get out of my sight, blind pawn of a false god.'

Etzel Boschkowitz bit back a righteous retort and stepped back out of the Great Sanctuary, closing the archway doors with a boom. When Kastner turned his dark attentions back on Lutzenschlager, he found the Grand Theogonist's eyes open and staring at him up the haft of the battlehammer.

'What do you want?' Lutzenschlager said. His words spoke of cold indifference but the beads of sweat forming at his temples said otherwise. Kastner removed the hammer, allowing the Grand Theogonist to support his own head. He slipped his head out of his crusader helm and placed it on the floor before the throne. He looked down on the Grand Theogonist.

'What all men want,' Kastner told him. 'Answers.'

'The God-King has nothing for you,' Lutzenschlager said. 'You have spilt blood, the blood of his servants, in his great temple. Sigmar only has vengeance in his mighty heart for you.'

'I'm not asking Sigmar,' Kastner said. 'I'm asking you.'

'I have nothing for you either,' Lutzenschlager said, 'but the assurance that it does not matter whether I live or die and the promise that you will fail. Every true son of Sigmar will stand against you. You will be a thing hunted. Your life will not be worth living. End yourself, dark pilgrim, here in this place – before the god you once loved, and receive his forgiveness.'

'I'm not going to kill you, Lutzenschlager,' Kastner told him, the words of comfort cold on his lips like a nonchalant threat. 'You are weak. A weak man. A weak leader of the Sigmarite church. I like you just where you are. On the throne – divisive, inept, a slave to vanity. The God-King deserves you. As for killing myself, I already feel I've died a thousand times over. No more. No more. Death is easy. Death is quick. Only through the suffering and affliction that is a life long-lived can we expect to learn all of the answers to all of the questions that plague us. I'll start with yours.'

Kastner brought the battlehammer down hard on the arm of the throne. The domed roof of the Great Sanctuary rang with the shrieking anguish that ripped its way out of Hedrich Lutzenschlager.

'The heretic text I was escorting from the Hammerfall, back to the safety of these hallowed halls,' Kastner said, his patience wearing away with every moment. '*The Liber Caelestior*. It had a page missing. A page torn from the tome, bearing the identity of a man who would be end to the world. You have this page? From your visits to the Hammerfall.'

'You think… I would aid,' Lutzenschlager half-sobbed through his agony, '…a chosen of the Dark Powers?' An irrational guffaw burst forth from the man.

'I think you might save yourself further suffering,' Kastner said, 'knowing before your weakling god and in your coward's heart that you had no choice. Because you do not.'

'I will never…'

The battlehammer came down again. Hard. Blood sprayed Kastner's plate. The scream was longer this time. It tailed off into a livid moan that haunted the chamber with its miserable insistence before dying further to a dread whimper. Lutzenschlager began to fade.

'Wake up!' Kastner roared, slapping the Grand Theogonist about his pale and stricken face. 'The page…' Kastner said, kneeling slowly before the throne. Lutzenschlager looked at him through pain-clouded eyes. 'It contained details of this man – this chosen – this Archaon.'

When the Grand Theogonist didn't respond, Kastner raised the battlehammer again. 'Don't make me destroy what's left of you,' he told him. Kastner tapped the hammer against the gilding of the seat, making Lutzenschlager jump at each impact. The Grand Theogonist let out a wretched moan before nodding his pain and conflict-contorted face.

'Names?'

Lutzenschlager shook his head.

'Places?'

'No,' Lutzenschlager answered, miserably.

'A description,' Kastner demanded, pointing to his face. 'Some defining scar or mark of birth?'

'Sigmar forgive me,' the Grand Theogonist blubbered. 'No…'

'What then!' Kastner snapped. 'There have been others – knights, templars, good men of Sigmar who have fallen to the Ruinous Powers. How can you know that I am this Archaon? Without such details, how can you be so certain that you would have me, one of the most loyal and devoted of Sigmar's servants, hunted down by his brother templars and killed on sight?'

Kastner smashed the battlehammer back and forth between the sides of the throne, drawing wails of terror from the Grand Theogonist.

'Tell me! Tell me now – while some semblance of humanity yet remains within me.'

Lutzenschlager's strangled howls found their way to the words Kastner demanded but did not expect.

'He is the only one…'

'The only one?'

'The only one prophesised to come in search of his name,' Lutzenschlager wheezed.

Kastner dropped the battlehammer down before the throne and rose slowly to his feet. He turned away, his mind wrestling with what he had just heard. 'The page predicted its own accidental tearing from the tome.'

'What?' Kastner said, half listening, half thinking, half feeling. 'It what?'

'The page contained a prediction of its own removal,' Lutzenschlager said, his words punctuated by sobs of torment. 'Discovered only after its first translation. *The Liber Caelestior* told of the living end – a man called Archaon who would kill the world. He was a man both of the Empire and not of it. And yes, one of the Sigmar's most loyal and devoted servants. A knight of the God-King's realm.'

'You suspected I was this Archaon…'

'Your priest sent word that you were coming to the cathedral with *The Celestine Book of Divination*,' Lutzenschlager said, his voice struggling under the weight of the words. 'The tome, the attack on the Hammerfall and the villages on your route – the fact that you were, even Master Schroeder admits you were, one of the finest knights of his order.'

'But when I arrived, you knew.'

'Only Archaon himself is to come searching for confirmation of his true self – so the page claimed.'

Kastner stood in silence. He could hear the crowds outside on the Templeplatz. The orders being barked. The perimeter being established.

'Why not destroy both the page and the damned book?' Kastner asked. 'Why didn't you just wipe it from the face of the world?'

'You know better than anyone what we do,' Lutzenschlager croaked his suffering. 'Such texts have to be studied, despite their dangers. It was felt long ago, by one of my predecessors, that the knowledge in the tome itself could be used to combat the evil knowledge therein. That the best chance to destroy this harbinger of doom was to allow him to come. Grand Master Boschkowitz was uncomfortable with the risk and sent his men to intercept you – but I assume they failed, as they were destined to do.'

Kastner looked up at the golden face of Sigmar and then down at Lutzenschlager's demolished form, bound to the throne.

'And the Grand Master is unlikely to fail twice,' Kastner said, looking about the sanctuary. 'If you knew this was going to happen, what were your orders?'

'It doesn't matter.'

'It matters to me,' Kastner growled.

'Right at this moment,' the Grand Theogonist said, the ghost of a wicked smile crossing his pain-strained face, 'every fighting man in the city is being summoned to the Domplatz. Reinforcements have been called from Carroburg, Castle Reikguard and the surrounding weald. Any man of Sigmar has been promised eternity at the God-King's side for your death. On top of that, the palace great cannons and batteries have been turned on the cathedral. My orders are to level Sigmar's holy temple rather than allow one of his greatest foes to escape. I don't care if they have to fish both of our bodies out of the rubble. You will not leave this place.'

Kastner wandered about the chamber, his gaze drifting from the incense burners to the tapestries to the side altars to the Great Sanctuary doors. An army waited for him outside the cathedral. Sigmarites, drunk on their staunch devotions, baying for a heretic's blood. Would Kastner be cut down? Would he be burned on the Templeplatz for all to see or hung, drawn and quartered in the palace courtyard before the crowds? Would he be imprisoned, living out the last of his miserable days in some dank cell below a distant castle, buried in unbreakable chains with only daily tortures to look forward to? There was no end to the miseries the Empire could visit upon him. There was nothing left.

The priests and templar knights he had served now wanted him dead. The nobility, whose duchies, baronies and marches he had purged of evil, would come to regard *him* as evil, the very same. Worst of all, the people – who had enjoyed the protection of his knightly deeds – would forget the name Diederick Kastner and revel in his downfall. His execution would be a form of entertainment to the blood-thirsty crowds and his story would become a wretched ballad, the cautionary tale of a monster and virtue fallen from grace.

Kastner felt their future loathing and he hated them for it. He despised their double-dealing god and his Empire that sheltered them from the true darkness of the world. With the toe of his boot he pushed the stand of an incense burner forward, allowing the trailing material of a Sigmarite tapestry to dangle in the embers and catch light. The flame – simple flame – had Kastner entranced. The flame became a flicker and the flicker a dance. Soon fire was raging up the ancient cloth, devouring the material, the ink and the history it depicted in image and the language of the long dead Unberogens. Sigmar's comet-commemorating birth and his glorious deeds – the uniting of the tribes of men; his battle with Morkar, the first Everchosen of the Chaos gods; the Battle of Black Fire Pass and undeath from the south. Kastner watched the fires spread. Sigmar's trek towards the Worlds Edge with its dark peaks and crowning sunset finally fell to the flame. It was the last Diederick Kastner saw of the God-King. Sigmar was facing adventures new in unknown lands and had his back to the Empire he had built. His back turned to Kastner. Within moments, the scene was lost, raining to the floor as soot – for even the God-King couldn't outrun the ravenous fires of destruction, hungry for history and intent on turning all to ash and darkness.

As the fires crackled up the tapestries and scorched stone sanctuary walls, feasting on the beams and staining the great domed ceiling with soot, Kastner felt a rage build within him. The injustice of it turned his blood to ice. His heart froze and shattered within his chest. He had come so far on the God-King's path and yet had reached no destination. He had survived obscurity, sacrificed all in the God-King's devoted name, worked his whole life in study and training and taken the fight to Sigmar's enemies, defeating them with a scholar's mind and a warrior's nerve. All for naught.

His hard work, his accomplishments, his pain and his sacrifice had brought him to betrayal. Of Sigmar and his servants. The promise of Kastner's treachery, as written in the stars. The bottomless doom Archaon intended to fulfil. Archaon would avenge him. Archaon would bring the Empire, nay the world, to its knees and punish the gods that plagued it for their falsehood. The lesser races of the world – like maggots infesting the lands in their ignorance and indifference – would be alleviated of the burden of their meaningless lives. Their existence would find new expression in servitude or an end to all suffering in death. He would drown the sun and smash the moons. He would tear down the sky and turn the world inside out – a world of darkness and flame, worthy only of the blackest souls and the evil that they may commit upon one other. A doom perpetual. The End Times would be his for the earning.

Kastner turned towards the golden statue of his accursed god.

'This I pledge,' Kastner spat. 'I renounce your worship and the doubt ensconced in my heart. I curse you in word and deed, my craven-king. Your servants will be mine to slaughter. Your lands mine to burn. My body and soul I give to the darkness. This is my oath. Here – in this place – on the very spot where your Empire began, I pronounce myself as its living end...'

Kastner felt the warmth of Sigmar's hammer on its chain about his neck. A gift from Father Dagobert. The hammer began to melt, scarring the flesh beneath his plate and dribbling molten metal down his chest.

Taking several armoured steps towards the statue, Kastner tossed his battlehammer with all his terrible might. The hammer cut through the smoke gathering in the chamber, head over haft, until it smashed into Sigmar's aureate face. The soft gold of the sculpture crumpled about the heavy hammer-head, turning one half of the God-King's impassive face to unsightly ruin, leaving the haft of the weapon protruding from Sigmar's right eye.

'The Darkness is not without a sense of humour,' Kastner said, satisfied. 'Unlike you.'

Suddenly the flames about the chamber roared and jumped domeward, as though extra fuel had been poured upon them from above. Kastner drew *Terminus* from the scabbard at his back, at first suspecting that the forces outside had grown desperate enough to employ battle wizards from the colleges. Kastner felt a warmth pass through his body. The metal of his plate and the rings of his mail were growing hot to the touch. The knight felt his hair singe and his skin roast where it was in contact with the crusader armour. Before the Grand Theogonist's throne, Kastner watched his helm smoulder. Like his armour, its surface charred. Unlike Kastner, now pledged to the Ruinous Powers of the world and enjoying their protection, such instruments in service of darkness were scalded by their presence on the cathedral's holy ground. Kastner's helm and plate were scorched to a burnished black. Even the greatsword *Terminus* – which had done so much in Sigmar's service – suddenly erupted in strange flame, its blade a nexus of twisting and turning tongues, the colours of all damnation.

'This won't save your pig-priest,' Kastner said, marching up the steps towards Hedrich Lutzenschlager, still tied to his throne. Shouldering his shield on its straps, Kastner scooped up the hot metal of his helm and slammed it down on his head in defiance, the scorched smell stinging his nostrils. He lifted the burning *Terminus* above his head. The Grand Theogonist's eyes, weak and barely open suddenly came to fear-stung life. He tore at his bindings, his brave words to Kastner fleeing from his craven heart. 'You want to be a martyr, Lutzenschlager?' Kastner put to the Grand Theogonist. 'Let's go together – you to your doomed gods and me to mine...'

Thunder. Everywhere. An ear-splitting flash. A dazzling boom. The sanctuary dome rang like a bell. A great force passed furiously through the chamber. The smoke cleared. And Kastner with it.

Kastner was no longer on the steps. He was back on the sanctuary floor, bathed in grit and surrounded by chunks of crafted stone – some of which had struck his shielded shoulder and armoured body. This wasn't battle wizards or the wrath of a vengeful deity. This was *Big Bathilda*. The greatest of the palace great cannons, crafted at the Imperial Gunnery School in Nuln. It was famous more for the circumstances surrounding its crafting than the power of its broad barrel and gaping muzzle. It had been intended as a gift from the Emperor Dieter to his cousin Prince Wilhelm but had been insensitively named after the city prince's mother, Lady Bathilda. As a consequence, it had never been fired. Until now.

Kastner blinked brick-dust from his eye. It was everywhere. On the floor. In his helmet. Swirling about the chamber like a thick mist. Disorientated, and with *Big Bathilda*'s boom still between his ears, Kastner squinted about him. The blast – if not the cannonball – had blown him across the slippery stone floor of the chamber. He could make out the infernal blush of flames about him and the glow of daylight, presumably streaming in through a *Bathilda*-blasted hole in the cathedral wall. The glow flickered and it took Kastner a few moments to find his way back to his thoughts and the danger he was in. The flicker was the single-file entrance of knights and soldiers through the freshly created entrance.

Kastner slapped his gauntlet about the floor for his *Terminus*. Fortunately, the blade was still aflame with the purity of the place and Kastner found it just in time. Murky silhouettes closed in on him as he pushed himself to his feet. He could hear Lutzenschlager screeching for help and Kastner assumed that the Grand Theogonist was still bound to the throne where he had left him. He could also hear Grand Master Boschkowitz's Reikwald drawl through the dust, giving orders to his Knights of the Fiery Heart. There were shapes and shadows everywhere. The knights were cautious. In the chalky gloom, and in the heart of their sacred temple, they didn't want to injure or kill one of their own. Kastner didn't have to worry about that.

Rising into a swing, Kastner took down an armoured unfortunate with his blade. The warrior's death cry drew knights down on Kastner, as well as barking orders from Boschkowitz. *Terminus* clashed with a warhammer, lopping its ugly head from its haft before doing the same to its wielder. Another hammer glanced off Kastner's pauldron as he worked his way around. With knights coming down on him faster and in building numbers, he couldn't afford drawn-out textbook engagements. He didn't need to fight these men. There were no accolades to win for technique or tournamentship. The Dark Gods only demanded deaths: so that's what Kastner gave them.

He buried his blade through a breastplate. Withdrew it. Turned a broadsword aside, one hand on his hilt, while grabbing a hammer haft to stop it coming down on him. Kastner smashed Boschkowitz's man back with the cross-guard of *Terminus*, before dropping to his knees and sweeping the blade straight through the legs of the other knight. As he went down, Kastner saw that he was one of his own order. The warhammer was back. He turned it away with a swipe of his sword, allowing the swung weight of the weapon to take it off target. The silhouettes spliced. They doubled and took form. Soon there were knights all about him, all hungry for victory in the presence of their God-King. Kastner made them pay for their overconfidence. Regardless of the teeth-clenching effort behind their visors, the knights still fought in the way they had been trained. Their movements were restricted and measured for economy, trust being placed firmly in their plate's ability to resist the impact of enemy weapons. Kastner knew their manoeuvres. Their combinations of attack and defence. He was an expert in such pedestrian combat. He knew the weak spots of their plate, for so long he had been forced to guard them for his own survival.

With each death – with each limb-lopping, head-cleaving, heart-stabbing death – Kastner felt the favour of darkness flow through him. Plate clattered about him, forming a mound of metal bodies that Kastner ascended. The dust thinned. He could see the knights flooding into the chamber: the Reiksguard, the Knights of Sigmar's Blood, the Knights Griffon and the God-King's champions – the Knights of the Fiery Heart. Amongst their number were a selection from other orders, including Kastner's own, as well as temple men-at-arms and city state troops – though no common soldier would come between an honour-bound knight and his quarry. Like a sea of polished plate, catching the tinted sunlight of a stained-glass window, the knights were like waves crashing up against the shore of their demolished dead.

Like the captain of a ship reading the weather, Kastner guided the stroke of his sword through the parting plate and spuming surf of his enemies' end. The island of the fallen at the centre of the sanctuary became his to defend and step by step, death by death, he reclaimed lost territory from the silver seas. *Terminus* trailed unnatural flame like a banner, flapping from the blade. It cleaved lesser blades in half, struck the ponderous heads from warhammers and sliced shields in two. The broad blade clutched in his gauntlets was everywhere it needed to be. Turning aside the practiced clash of knightly sweeps and the thrusted points of halberds and tapering blades. Cleaving through helms. Smashing down through armoured torsos. Opening up silver bellies and trailing the guts that spilled from his brother templars.

An otherworldly exaltation had Kastner's heart in its grip. Something hidden in the shearing of armour, the crunch of bones and ugly parting of flesh was pleased. He could almost see its horrific form in the spectacular spraying of blood from lopped limbs and severed heads. He could smell its ambitions for him on the copper-tinged air. He could hear its encouragement ring in the ghastly peel of screams echoing about the helmets of his victims. He felt the presence of darkness in this death he dealt.

Like two farmer's sons fighting for the reins of a cart on its way to market, Kastner felt a fight within him for the murderous path and the plunge of the crusader blade. At moments, the vengeful thrust of the weapon's broad tip into a crunching helm or the unyielding, stone cold parry of a halberd blade that should have hewn him apart were his own. He was a knight. A templar. A battle-tempered warrior at the peak of his training and physical fitness. He still was, of a different following. At other moments, lives were taken before he had conceived of their ending. Feats of incredible strength or unknowable skill were performed by his hand. His body raged in fires of exhaustion and the weight of the greatsword was an agony in his arms but this didn't stop Kastner smashing knight after Sigmarite knight into the sanctuary floor, punching visors and jaws from his mailed fist and cutting clean through Gotz Schroeder – the Master of his own order – *Terminus* finding a path through every chink, hinge and weakness in the knight's finely crafted plate.

As the horror followed the blade everywhere it went and the torso and legs of Grand Master Schroeder fell to one side, Kastner suddenly realised that his eye was firmly shut. He was a raging bonfire, blinding in the darkness he threw across the stinging purity of the temple sanctuary. Blotted out by the brightness of the cathedral walls and the holy ground upon which they charged, the knights of Sigmar caught the full glare of Kastner's burgeoning malevolence and cast shadows of light – some blazing with the pious nobility of their hearts, some long and sallow with the doubt and dark secrets they hid deep within themselves. Kastner saw through their plate and the armour of their souls. He read them like heretical texts: their hopes, their needs, their flaws and their fears. He knew what they were going to do to him before they did and he killed them for it.

Kastner's darkness was only eclipsed by the deep inscrutability falling from the great, round stained-glass window in the cathedral wall. A great black sun, it looked down on him like a lens and Kastner felt the dread ancients of existence take turns to peer down on his miserable mortality in simultaneous celebration and judgement. As he hacked and skewered the God-King's warriors on *Terminus's* blazing length, Kastner both grew and withered under their infernal gaze. Stronger. Faster. More adamant and savage in mind and form. Hope shrivelled and crumbled within him like leaves during the Great Fall. His love of life, the architecture of his beliefs and the nobility of a man never to be, all turned to dust within him. It rained like loss through his soul, leaving a terrible emptiness for the darkness to fill. Perhaps it was this last moment of doubt – this scintilla of shattered honour – that allowed Etzel Boschkowitz through.

Kastner felt the Grand Master's warhammer smash into his back, pulverising his shield and the pauldron beneath it. Kastner was spun off balance by the weapon's brute force and was tossed off his mound of bodies and into a forest of halberd spikes and blades. Caught off-guard, the weapons clattered against his armour rather than through it, but as Kastner became swamped by knights eager for the kill, he rediscovered the hot sensation of steel passing through his plate and flesh. Pushing himself back and forth in the metallic throng, with knights finding it difficult to bring their weapons to bear on an enemy so close, Kastner gave back to his brothers. Messily grabbing knights from behind their helms, Kastner plunged the searing blade of *Terminus* blindly at guts, groins and thighs, feeling his enemies go down before him.

Suddenly the sound of clashing metal subsided and the knights pulled back. Kastner attempted a tight turn in his armour. It was difficult. *Terminus* was employed in swiping away the thrustings of spear-points and angled blades and he was off balance. He turned to see Boschkowitz before him, his beard shaking with righteous rage. He felt a mind-splitting smash as the Grand Master battered his helm aside with a swing of his hammer. The world suddenly spun. It felt as though the Grand Master had taken his head clean off. He hadn't. He had just sent Kastner tumbling back into the wall of knights and blades. Steel squealed once again through his armour. Pain lanced through his back and thigh.

Shaking sense back into his concussed skull, Kastner turned *Terminus* about and thrust the anguished blade straight into the knight behind. He pulled it out and forced it back into the armoured warrior unfortunate enough to take his place. Once again, the disorderly throng withdrew. Like Sigmar's fist, Boschkowitz's warhammer came down on Kastner. He went down on one knee to receive the God-King's blessing before bringing the flaming *Terminus* up, his gauntlet on both the hilt and blade like a staff to intercept the incredible force of the weapon. The warhammer's haft hit the blade, Kastner holding his sword above his head and keeping the weapon from smashing him into the flagstones of the sanctuary. A combination of the Grand Master's own strength and the cleaving edge of Kastner's crusader blade took the head of the hammer from it haft. Kastner stood to press his advantage but Boschkowitz kicked him straight in the breastplate, knocking him back into his knights.

'Hold him,' the Grand Master roared like a lion through his beard. 'Hold the Ruinous slave.'

A Knight Griffon took Kastner about the throat with his arm, while a gauntlet grabbed out for his plate, holding him fast. He felt his helmet crumple as Boschkowitz slammed into his helm with his great mail fists. One-two. One-two.

'Kill him!' Kastner heard the Grand Theogonist screech. 'Kill him now, Boschkowitz!'

Grand Master Boschkowitz held his mighty fists out to receive a pair of warhammers, tossed to him by Knights of the Fiery Heart on either side of the parting. He clenched his teeth and smashed the pair of hammers at each other, causing them to spark.

'Now you die,' Boschkowitz spat, bringing one of the warhammers up to strike Kastner's battered helm from his armoured shoulders. Kastner had no doubt that this time the Grand Master would send his head flying across the Great Sanctuary. Pulling on every ounce of strength he had left, Kastner dived. Lowering his head like a bull, he lurched forward, dragging the knights holding him from behind with him. As Grand Master Boschkowitz's warhammer pulverised its way through skull after knightly skull – several belonging to knights of his own order – the gauntlets released their grip on Kastner whosurged on, his battered helm lowered and its head-spike aimed at the exposed chest of the Grand Master. As his helm hammered into Boschkowitz's chestplate, the knight gave a grunt. The spike had slammed straight into his heart. Drawing on the strength of the God-King himself, still the knight fought on, holding Kastner to him and smashing down on his back with his other hammer.

Kastner pulled his head from his helm, leaving the head-spike buried in the Grand Master's chest, and stumbled into a fighting stance. Boschkowitz stared down at the spike and then back at Kastner, bringing both warhammers at him with as much force as the knight could muster. This time Kastner was ready for him, turning aside one warhammer, then the other, before sweeping *Terminus* back across the Grand Master's throat. All fell silent for a moment in the Great Sanctuary. Boschkowitz started to say something, but his final words were lost in the awful sound his neck made as his head lolled backwards to hang down between his shoulders. The chamber echoed with the clatter of his knees on the flagstones and the crash of his armoured body to the ground.

Silence reigned for a few moments more as the ring of the Grand Master's metal plate endured. It was broken by the imperious shrieks of Grand Theogonist Lutzenschlager as he was removed to safety from the chamber, throne and all.

'The cannon,' he called in a panic driven by the fact that only he of all Sigmar's servants in the sanctuary knew the extreme importance of Kastner's death. 'Fire the cannon. Destroy the interloper. Somebody end this now!'

As Lutzenschlager was removed through the brick-ragged hole in the cathedral wall, Kastner saw the monstrous muzzle of *Big Bathilda* wheeled awkwardly up to the opening. It didn't matter; the response from the knights was instantaneous. At the Grand Theogonist's order they fell on Kastner. *Terminus* smacked away the first hammers and halberds, but Kastner was soon clamped between the armoured bodies of knights. Some were driven by simple glory. Others by the grief of fallen brothers. Others still by the blessings of their God-King. Within seconds it became a plate-pulverising crush, with those most ardent in their attempts to end Kastner pushed against him by knights further away, eager to play their part in the downfall of a dangerous foe.

Kastner tore his body this way and that, attempting to create some room about him – at least enough to bring *Terminus* up from where it was trapped between the vice-like bodies of two Sigmarite knights. It was no use. There were too many knights, with a never-ending stream of armoured warriors filing into the Great Sanctuary from the blasted opening and the main doors. Beyond that, *Big Bathilda* was being loaded and primed. Kastner had no doubt that the Grand Theogonist would order the great cannon fired as soon as possible and wouldn't let a consideration like the lives of his knights get in the way of such a decision. Not to kill a man who would become the Everchosen of Chaos and the Lord of the End Times.

Kastner felt the axe blade of a halberd bite into him. The wicked point of a spear slid into his shoulder, cutting its hot way through meat and bone. Sword tips waggled their way between joints and split chainmail rings to knife at his flesh. These hot agonies and more, Kastner felt through his trapped form. He heaved. He pushed. He tried to extract the broad blade of *Terminus* where it sat extinguished between the backs of two equally immobile knights, but the greatsword would not budge. The tip of a crusader sword stabbed wildly at his face, opening up gashes across Kastner's forehead and cheek, but he couldn't even crane his neck out of the way. It suddenly became difficult to breathe as the spear-tip of a halberd that had been burrowing into his torso breached his plate and sank into his side.

Kastner reached up at the multi-coloured light coming in through the stained glass. His fingertips scraped at dust-defined beams. In his last moments, even a monster like Kastner could appreciate its beauty. He watched as he waited. Waited for the killing strike through the clash of bodies. Waited for the thunder of the great cannon turned on the mad throng of knights. Waited for a death well-earned.

It was raining. Inside the temple. Glass fell across the bloody scene, glinting as it caught sunlight that had blasted its way into the cathedral. The stained-glass window was no more. Dark shapes, like fallen angels, rocketed down towards the mob of Sigmarites. They landed in a circle about Kastner, crushing surrounding knights into the floor of the Great Sanctuary beneath their boots, producing fountains of gore that rained about them. The figures rose. Their dark armour was unmistakable. Their skull-helms of bronzed bone. Their armoured wings, now extended about them like the lengths of shields. They drew their bone swords from the finger-sheathes of the wings, one in each hand. The marauders. The Ruinous Warriors. The Swords of Chaos that Kastner had left behind at Fort Denkh to finish Riesenweiler's knights. It seemed that they had not left him.

The slaughter began almost immediately. The razored

rachidian edge of the warriors' bone swords cut a bloody swathe through the confusion of plate. They stabbed. They sliced. They cleaved. The air was thick with a bloody haze and the death that accompanied it. Like a closing star, the Swords of Chaos moved in on Kastner. The throng loosened in the knights' panicked attempt to turn their weapons outward to defend against the new threat. The winged marauders were like an elemental force. Overwhelming. Unstoppable.

As the bodies parted, Kastner fell to his knees. His armour was slick with gore and he was kneeling in a pool of blood – much of it his own. He swung *Terminus* wildly at passing knights, hamstringing several with the remaining strength he had left. Mostly he just drove knights into the armour-opening slashes of bone swords as the Chaos warriors closed in. They were suddenly about him. One winged marauder either side of Kastner. They were cold and deathly to the touch and promptly re-sheathed their weapons in their leathery wings. The other marauders had turned, forming a ring of bone swords about Kastner as the dark warriors supported him. Knights of the Fiery Heart stared in disbelief at the slaughter of fellow Sigmarites. Butchery in the temple of the God-King. There would be bellows of righteous revenge and a renewed call to charge the hated foe, but the knights were weary and their numbers decimated. Even knights and men-at-arms fresh to the death and destruction were given reason to pause.

The knights of Sigmar stared at their enemy, swaying in their armour and exhaustion. The winged marauders stared back before sheathing their bone swords, bending their knees and surging for the domed ceiling of the Great Sanctuary. Still clutching *Terminus* loosely in one hand, Kastner was held between two of them, who dragged him horribly up into the heavens. With powerful beats of their wings the warriors were soon high off the holy ground. There was a colossal crash. *Big Bathilda* had once again visited her fury on the scene of slaughter, the fat cannonball blasting through the bodies – both dead and dying – and out through the other wall. Knights still on their feet were knocked to the ground and slid through the gore of their brothers while a cloud of brick-dust erupted from the far wall, obscuring the horror below.

Kastner fell in and out of consciousness. The blood loss had made him faint. He felt pity for the birds and the bats. Flight was not a pleasant sensation.

He was high above the Cathedral of Sigmar. It was a sight not even the dwarf engineers had enjoyed during its construction. The wretched city of Altdorf fell away, its reek and rooftops melting into the tangled woodland of the Reikwald and the Great Forest. Roads cut sharply through the canopy while rivers snaked their lazy meandering way into the distance. His tense limbs slackened and his head slumped. As consciousness left him and obscurity crept in from the edges of his sight like the ash of a ravaged wasteland claiming everything he could see, Kastner saw his homeland and Sigmar's Empire darken.

It was a vision he promised himself he would realise… upon his doomed return.

VOLUME TWO
THE CHANGER OF WAYS

'Doom hath drowned more men than the sea.'

– Ignatz van Offen, *Offered Truths*

*'So the doom of man travelled north –
north through forests and shadows cold,
Through lands of iron, spice and ice –
through man-eating ogres and trolls.*

*'Bitter like winter's bite he was,
with the God-King's lands at his back.
His darkened heart beat to vengeance,
echoing with questions unasked.*

*'A new path lay before the knight,
a way of blood and butchery:
On which no sacred life was spared
and his dark patrons were appeased.*

*'Northern Wastes and warrior met,
where men's forlorn hopes go to die.
Accepting he was damned and lost,
to his gods he made sacrifice.*

*'Warrior of the Empire dead,
subject of the God-King deceived.
Great warlord of the Shadowlands,
of Ruinous treasures received.'*

– Necrodomo the Insane,
*The Liber Caelestior (The Celestine Book of
Divination)*

CHAPTER X

*'There are many ways north, for the path
is well-trodden,
There are none from the south, for the
route is forgotten.'*

– Ungol proverb

*The Worlds Edge Mountains
The Northlands
Poslekogot/Month of the After-Claw (Gospodarin Calendar)*

Hieronymous Dagobert had found the bloodied and broken knight in the stable, saddling Oberon. He looked like suffering itself. The priest had tensed as he discovered that they were not alone. The armoured marauders, the winged knights that had slaughtered the soldiers and templars at Fort Denkh, were leading some of Lady Kastner's finest horses from stalls deeper within. Dagobert looked to the templar, to the Ruinous knights and then back to his friend.

'So it has come to pass,' Dagobert said gravely.

The templar grunted. He sounded different, Dagobert decided.

'I'm in no mood for riddles, old man.'

It was still his voice, but there was something… more. Potent. Powerful. A slight echo, like that created when speaking in some great hall or chamber. A dark authority, even at a grunt or a whisper.

'You are Archaon.'

'I am… Archaon.'

'To be the Everchosen of the Dark Gods and Herald of the End Times.'

'In the flesh.'

The Chaos knights, deathly things with their dark armour, skull-helms and wings, led their steeds outside leaving the two men alone.

'Well, you will always be Diederick Kastner to me,' Dagobert said.

The knight tightened Oberon's harness and took *Terminus* from where it hung off the stalls on its cross-guard. The blade sizzled to afflicted flame at the templar's touch, a ghostly torment seething about the weapon's honourable history and service to the God-King. The knight slammed the greatsword down in the scabbard attached to Oberon's saddle.

'One of those names I stole,' the templar said. 'The other was given to me as an act of pitiable charity. You'll forgive me if I choose not to hear either of them ever again.'

'You expect me to call you… by that name?'

'It is the only one that is truly mine,' Archaon told him. 'Where's Gorst?'

'I think you frightened him off.'

'And the girl?'

'In the hall, with the crossbow,' Dagobert said.

'Whereas you opted for one of Sieur Kastner's duelling pistols from the mounting on the hall wall,' Archaon said. He could hear the weapon rattling in the priest's nervous grip. The warrior turned. 'Have you ever fired one of those things before?'

Dagobert shook his head and looked down. As he did he

felt the razor tip of a bone sword dimple his double-chin. One of the Chaos knights was beside him, arm and weapon outstretched.

'The weapon of a coward,' Archaon said, 'in the hands of a man who is anything but. Do not fear me, father.'

'Fear you?'

'I mean you no harm,' Archaon told him. 'You. Gorst. The girl. This horse. You're the only kindly souls I know in the entire world.'

'I don't fear you,' Dagobert said. 'I fear what you will become.'

'What I have already become,' Archaon said. 'Destiny has made its play. Fate has chosen a side. Now it's my turn. The gods of light and darkness have created this doom between them. Well, they will get more than they bargained for with my miserable soul. If I am to be end to all then all will end. Man and god will fear me for the annihilation I will bring. The rise and fall of the sun, the ever-lengthening horizon – wretched covenants with deathless damnation. Nothing will stop me. Do you hear?'

'I'm trying to save you, child,' Dagobert said desperately.

'And I you, father,' Archaon said. 'Lutzenschlager and his Sigmarites are out in force. They will scour their miserable Empire for me and any associated with me. They will capture you. They will torture you. They will kill you. I would save you from that. For the kindnesses you have done me, priest.'

'You would have me come with you?' Dagobert said incredulously. 'Betray my god? An entire lifetime's worth of prayer and devotion?'

'Your god is a liar,' Archaon hissed. 'A trader in souls who would betray those most in love with him. Those who, for him, have fought the hardest.'

'I cannot follow you into damnation.'

'Then come to save my soul, Dagobert,' Archaon said, lightening a little. 'I don't care for your reason. I care that you are by my side. With me or not, I would have the counsel of a man of the world – a wise man – in these tumultuous times.'

'So that we may all become the playthings of Dark Powers?'

'Dagobert,' Archaon said. 'We have a book of tomorrows and the means to translate and interpret its riddles. I mean not to be the pawn of the infernal powers any more than your pig of a God-King. Help me forge my own path – and save your life into the bargain.'

The tip of the bone sword tapped the priest on the chin. 'You'll have to excuse them,' Archaon said. 'They seem tediously intent on my continued existence.'

After a moment's reflection, the priest dropped the pistol to the stable floor with a thud. Archaon nodded. The tip of the bone sword drifted from the priest's chins.

'Just as well,' Archaon said. 'Wouldn't want you to hurt yourself. Balls, barrels, black powder. I don't trust them. The thing is just as likely to blow up in your hand as put its shot through me.'

But Dagobert couldn't find it in himself to derive any humour from the situation. He turned and the winged Chaos knight stood to one side. As he walked away, the lines of his face cutting deep with the gravest concern, Archaon stopped him at the stable door.

'Father.'

Dagobert looked down to one side at the straw on the floor in grim acknowledgement. 'Pack up the wagon with the tools and provisions for a considerable journey,' Archaon said. 'If you please. Have the girl and Gorst, if you can find him, assist you. Take anything from the manor house for your comfort. The rest will be put to the flame. Do you understand?'

Hieronymous Dagobert did understand. He understood that he was damning himself to Ruinous confederacy. He understood that he was doing it for the love he still bore both the man and the boy he had known.

'I understand,' the priest said, and left the stable.

And so Archaon went north. North through the dark woods of Hochland. Across the Middle Mountains, where the Hammerfall still smoked among the peaks, and through the wilds of Ostland and the Forest of Shadows. Riding at the head of the wagon, the white bonnet of which soon became a blood-splattered brown, Archaon watched the world of men unfold before him. His good eye took it all in. The life of the place was intoxicating. He had never really appreciated it before. The trees. The buzzing insects. The birds calling through the canopy. The people, everywhere, a plague on the land – living out their selfish existence in ignorance and obedience to lesser gods. Archaon had never appreciated the complex vitality of the world until he had wanted to destroy it. Though his ruined socket was covered by a leather eye-patch, the dark templar could still see. He saw ash. He saw smoke. He saw bodies burning beneath benighted skies. He saw the doom of the north clawing its way south and he the herald of its annihilation.

Behind him the wagon was flanked by four of his winged warriors on horseback. Archaon's Swords, as he came to call them, were five in number. There was little to tell the silent warriors apart and they were not much interested in conversation, so it was difficult for Archaon to set them apart in terms of character: they didn't seem to have any. Archaon let his imagination fill in the details, assuming that at some time, perhaps long before they were lost to Chaos, they had been men with hopes, dreams and fears, like everyone else. In the end, the dark templar simply took *Terminus* and cut numerals into the black of their pauldrons, naming the warrior who seemed to shadow him most closely 'Eins'. The other Swords became 'Zwei' and 'Drei' – who seemed to Archaon closer than the others, and Archaon fancied them brothers in a former existence. 'Vier' and 'Fünf' appeared to hold each other at a distance and the templar imagined that perhaps they harboured some secret dislike for one another, in the days before their dreadful damnation.

Archaon had two Swords travel on either side of the wagon at an ambling gait, while Eins drifted at the rear to ensure no one was following them. Gorst was always following them, but Archaon had informed the Swords that the flagellant wasn't a threat, and on occasion even had his uses.

Father Dagobert, sullen and silent since leaving the inferno of the Kastner estates, thought of the Swords as a prisoner escort. He couldn't so much as pass water in the trees without one of their number loitering nearby. There was little need for such precautions. He had decided to stay with Archaon and as the warrior had put it, attempt to 'save his soul'.

The girl Giselle had been another case entirely. The sister had no relationship with Archaon. She had not known him… before. She owed him her life, and that was about it. Being not especially bright, for Giselle the choice was simple. Travel with Archaon and Dagobert north into the terrifying unknown and damnation, or remain in the Empire. With the simple honesty of a girl innocent in the ways of the world, she had confessed to Dagobert that she intended to quietly leave the party and present herself to a temple or convent. It was not Archaon or his Swords that prevented the sister from leaving. Echoing Archaon's own words, Father Dagobert found himself warning her to stay. He told her that she would be turned over to the Grand Theogonist's men by any of Sigmar's servants. That she would be tortured for what she knew, imprisoned and executed as a heretic. He told her that he was protecting her – as Archaon had done Dagobert.

In reality, she became Dagobert's prisoner, the priest watching her as the Swords watched him. In truth, Dagobert saw his salvation in her. The girl was so stubborn and her simple faith so enduring that Dagobert found the fight in her something of an inspiration. In the insanity of such dark times, he found her to be a compass to guide him back to the light. He could trust in her unbreakable will. In order to save Archaon's soul, he needed to preserve his own: which meant he needed Sister Dantziger. This meant that on several occasions he was forced to betray her confidences. Sometimes the girl would just slip away. On other occasions, she simply ran for her life, appealing to those they encountered on the dismal roads of the Empire for assistance. Dagobert brought her back. Sometimes forcefully. When she slipped into the hamlet of Smallhof, begging the villagers to be hidden, the priest had been forced to tell Archaon, for their own safety, as well as the girl's. Archaon set his Swords on the hamlet, with instructions to find her. The search soon descended into a bloodbath, with Archaon and Dagobert looking on, as the Swords tore the village apart searching for the girl. They slaughtered all who would hide her, all who would inform on them and send word to the soldiers, templars and witch hunters on their tail. After Smallhof, Archaon had Father Dagobert chain one of the sister's wrists to the driver seat of the wagon. It was better than breaking her leg, which had been Archaon's other suggestion.

As time went on, the forests of the Empire gave way to the grim cold of Kislev. The sun was lower in the sickly sky, its light struggling to reach through the northern haze. The dreadful days and nightmares inbetween seemed to stretch into weeks uncounted and months that were marked by whether and how hard the snows came. The companies of soldiers and lone Sigmarite knights that had hunted them through the Imperial provinces were a mercifully rare experience in the lands of the Gospodar. Step by step, the warband's progress became less of an escape and more of a dark pilgrimage. They were no longer hunted, it seemed – bar the occasional and wretched attempt of lone witch hunters to bring them to Sigmar's justice. The dawn, feeble as it was, began to promise more to the warband than just an opportunity to put more distance between them and their persecutors.

The Kislevites themselves were as welcoming as their ice-threaded hovels. They were a backward and superstitious people, bleak and hard as iron. Unlike villagers in the Empire, they didn't run for their homes or send for their lord or baron at the sight of Archaon and his warband. They did nothing but work their farmsteads and watch with ghoulish, hollow expressions as another madman rode north to his destiny. Their only luxury seemed to be in the greasy extravagance of their facial hair and the impregnation of their womenfolk, who went about their backbreaking chores with swollen bellies and small armies of bedraggled urchins. Some said it was the cold that drove Kislevite men to their beds, since they were not known to be especially accomplished lovers. Some said that they spent much of their time this way with their wives out of necessity. It was part of their culture. To be ready – for the next incursion, the next invasion, the next war against Chaos. As Archaon rode along frost-shattered roads and through the smoky homesteads of the northern division he understood that the wastrels clinging to their mothers' dirty skirts were simply the hardened savages and horsemen he would have to fight on his way back through Kislev on his return to the Empire. The idea amused Archaon and on one occasion he even drank to Kislevite courage, toasting the northerners with their own potato swill, in an all but empty watering hole.

The crows gave way to vultures, the spice on the air to the cold, copper tang of old blood. The warband started to lose the little light they had across the Troll Country. There were no friendly faces to be found there. Even Ungol nomads and archers on horseback, despatched by the Tsarina to cull the beasts of the borderlands, were open in their hostility. On the frost-bitten plains and amongst the howling hills, Archaon encountered all manner of winter savagery. Prides of white sabretusks that slashed the wagon bonnet and leapt at Archaon in the saddle. Hordes of gnoblar cannibals, driven insensible with hunger and feasting on each other as well as themselves. Herds of northern rhinox and great mammoths, stampeding across the icy plain: hormone-fuelled and aggressive, charging anything in sight. Savage tribes of albino orcs, mounted on blind boars of war, observing the warband's passing from a distance. A pack of direwolves, struck down by some monstrous and unnatural mange, howling their torment through the blackened stakes of a dead forest. All manner of blood-crazed creatures, eking out an existence on the shadowy frontier of the Chaos realm. Monsters that would have long died out, were it not for the game trails leading north out of the Tsarina's lands, carrying lone maniacs and defectors. Men of death and destiny.

The savage lands tested Archaon and his Swords, more than their escape from the Empire or the harsh indifference of the Gospodars. Beyond the torchings of the God-King's way temples en route and the bloodshed necessary to secure passage, the warband had tasted little of the murder required to honour new and Dark Gods. Crossing the borderlands, Archaon had traded a magnificent bear skin for the life of the Ungol chieftain that wore it. With the cloak, Archaon received the blessing of the Ursun, father of the Bears and patron god of Kislev, from the nomad chief. It could have been custom, fearful courtesy or even an insult. Archaon didn't know. He did know that blessings from any power other than the dark, primordial entities he now served scorched his soul and within moments the Chaos warrior had reneged upon his deal and ended the chieftain as an offering to the Star of Universal Ruin. With the shaggy hide about his shoulders, keeping the worst of the chill from his bones, Archaon wiped the innocent blood of the Ungol from the searing blade of *Terminus* and bade his Swords slaughter the Ursun-worshipping nomads for the same purpose.

In the Troll Country the warband made scabbards of the low beasts – things of horn and fang, some that walked on four legs and some that walked on two. Though the monstrosities had all the advantage of number and brute nature, they had only been lightly bathed in the darkness of the north. Though hard won, the warband's victories were ones of survival against packs and predators, and as such, were squalid offerings to the dread pantheon. Oddly for a place with such a name, the warband never encountered such a thing as a troll.

All through their journey, with the ancient forests of the Empire behind them and the cruel Kislevite winter a recent memory, Dagobert continued his translations. Having the miserable Giselle take the wagon's reins and with the wind and the beast-things howling through the tears in the bonnet, Dagobert tried to unlock the secrets of their destination and destiny. Like everything *The Liber Caelestior* had delivered, all but the most significant of details were vague and open to interpretation. Deliberately so, the priest thought. Necrodomo the Insane had a dark gift, but he was no less a charlatan than other prophets of his ilk. Sometimes, Necrodomo hedged his bets. For such a prognosticator the unfolding moments in an hour, a day, a year or a lifetime were like drops of water in a river, flowing by. Sometimes the waters were crystal clear. At other times, the waters were white with the violent churning of their passage or murky with the silty burden of past meanderings.

Archaon would routinely interrogate the priest as to the tome and its secrets. Whereas before, Dagobert's interest ran to Archaon's salvation and opportunities the volume might provide. Now, reading Necrodomo's revelations had become a duty. As the warband's steeds climbed and the wagon struggled through the heavy snow of Black Blood Pass, Dagobert read of the northmen's ambush. The avalanche of ice and rock that tumbled down before the warband, blocking its path and the riders that rode up behind them. The greasy marauders of Edric Ulfensbane seated on their shaggy mounts, cutting silhouettes of horn, fur and axe into the blinding glare of the Worlds Edge Mountains. The northman was known as Red Edric in the Jottenheim and it was said that he and his Norscans charged a heavy toll for those travelling the pass. One traveller – one life. The horsemeat of accompanying steeds was considered an added bonus for a job well done, and Red Edric's men had grown fat on a diet of horsemeat and death.

Archaon and his Swords were outnumbered four to one by the marauders, but it made little difference. Ulfensbane's murderers were no match for the dark templar and his knights of Chaos. Archaon decorated the snow with their lopped limbs and livid gushings. With their winter steeds slain and axe-brothers butchered, the last of the northmen abandoned their leader to the Chaos warriors, choosing to leap from the crag upon which Archaon had cornered them. Taking their chances with gravity, rather than the certainty of a horrible and immediate death at Archaon's hand, the northmen might have made the terrible drop if the snows below had been deep enough. They weren't, and the marauders became bloody smears on the rock and ice of the slope below. Edric Ulfensbane wouldn't take such a cowardly course and presented his icicle-encrusted axes to Archaon. Sliding the steaming blade of *Terminus* in the drift, the Chaos warrior crunched along the crag towards him. Reading the northman like a hunter might the tracks of a wild animal, Archaon reared back and to the side, out of reach of Red Edric's wild and murderous swings.

'Drown me in snow, would you, northman?' Archaon seethed, before ducking beneath the arc of the Norscan's weapons and grabbing him by his furs. Throwing him down into the drift, Archaon proceeded to bury the man alive, drowning him as he might in a stream or river. Red Edric's arms and legs flailed as he choked on the snow, held there in Archaon's feverish grip. Leaving the northman's body to freeze, Archaon recovered *Terminus* and trudged past Dagobert and Giselle, who had watched from the wagon.

'That wretched book earned the trouble of its keeping today,' Archaon told him, pointing his crusader blade back up at the pass blocked with a small sea of settling snow. Dagobert nodded, shivering to think what it might have been like for them buried in the avalanche. 'Keep reading,' Archaon said. 'I wish to know more of the misfortunes that are to befall us... before they actually do, of course.'

'It doesn't work like that,' Dagobert said, a little harshly. Archaon turned on the priest. Dagobert's frost-rosy cheeks paled, while Giselle – chained to the wagon – wouldn't even look at the Chaos warrior. 'I mean, my lord,' Dagobert said, 'that much of the translation is educated guesswork and interpretation.'

'Then guess well, priest,' Archaon told him, walking on through the snow, 'lest we all die for the sake of secrets already in our possession.' Calling through the crystal cold air, Archaon ordered Zwei and Drei to find them an alternative route through the pass. On the way back down the mountainside, the warband and wagon encountered a frost-bitten Gorst, the flagellant, weighed down with his chains, only just having caught up to them.

Hieronymous Dagobert did as he was bade by his master. As the warband passed over the very spine of the world, the damned tome told Dagobert of death from the skies in the form of a flock of harpies, nesting in the north-eastern slopes, and the manflesh they intended to regurgitate for their screeching, cliff-bound young. It did not tell of the Skewered Skull hobgoblin clan that bounded out of the foothills of the Dark Lands at them on long-legged war mongrels. The foothills formed part of their slave grounds. Attempting to catch and imprison Archaon was more foolish than trying to kill him, however, as the hobgoblin half-khan and his clan discovered too late. The warband decimated the clan to the very last rider and gangling, lupine steed, wiping the Skewered Skull clan and its ruling khanate from the face of the Dark Lands forever.

Leaving the slave grounds for some other foetid breed of greenskin to assume, Dagobert steered Archaon from the different types of doom to be found at the fortress of Uzkulak with Hashut, Father of Darkness, and the contested dwarf stronghold of Karak Dum. *The Liber Caelestior* also suggested that the infamous Road of Skulls held nothing but foes unworthy of Archaon's blade and led out onto the Eastern Steppes, where men went mad for want of landmarks on the endless expanse of the horizon. So at Dagobert's word the warband braved the treacheries of the Shattered Shore, where land and ice were indistinguishable and the world looked as though it had been smashed by the fist of an angry god.

It was here, in the howling desolation of a desert of ice that Archaon began to truly feel as though he were drawing nearer to his goal. Here on the edge of doom, where the gloomy heavens were like no other and where the seas sat frozen and unnatural, he found a kind of peace. He discovered that the buzz of insanity on the air soothed the ever-present pain in his ruined eye. That the petty concerns of the Empire and its bordering nations were long behind him and that the world was opening up before him. The scale of the place was heart-stopping. On one side, a range of frost-shattered peaks reached into the heavens as though they owned them, with the cragginess of splintered obsidian. On the other, searing depths plummeted below a covering of broken bergs in a darkness that threatened to swallow the world. Between them, Archaon had only a sky in mourning and the ice-riven shore. He could feel the black heart of the lands beating beneath his boots, calling him on with every distant quake. Despite standing in a land barren and lifeless, the Chaos warrior had never felt such life. Such will. Such possibility. It lifted the darkness of his spirit and put him in a murder-happy mood.

'Tell me again, priest,' Archaon called through the freeze. The air almost shattered about his words. Dagobert was seated up front in the wagon, buried in a nest of thick, lice-infested furs. Giselle drove the wagon. She would rather have spat on Archaon or Dagobert than accept a kindness from either of them, but with the air around able to freeze the blood in her veins, the Sister of the Imperial Cross had no option but to take the offer of furs for her own trembling body. 'Tell me how I might achieve an end to eternity,' Archaon said with a laugh that echoed about the face-scalding wasteland of white. 'How might a mortal man end a world?'

Dagobert cleared his throat. Calling through the frost-threaded air was an effort.

'With a nature indomitable,' the priest said, 'like the land, at one with its savage calling. With a heart's desire deeper than the ocean depths. With steel, cold and true, my lord.' With every passing day, Hieronymous Dagobert read more of Necrodomo the Insane's twisted prophecies and with every day the priest sounded more like him. 'To earn the honour of ender of worlds, Lord Archaon, you must offer yourself as a weapon to be wielded by the very powers that would test you. You must become the Everchosen of the great gods of darkness. You must become an acolyte of the Waste's insanities, a disciple of the Ruinous Star like there has never been and doom to all who cross your path.'

Archaon thought on the warriors he was to meet. The warbands who had made the trek north like his own. The madmen who deceived themselves into the belief that they were worthy of ancient evil and its infernal sponsorship. The Chaos warrior smiled to himself. It almost cracked his frozen face. He felt a kind of savage pity for such victims of fate. Their journeys, their trials, their lives had all been in vain, for they were yet to meet their end. Their end had a name – and it was Archaon.

'They will join me or die,' Archaon spat, his words misting on the razored air. 'Tell me more, priest. For I long to hear of my saga again.'

'Words,' Dagobert said. 'Just words. Any fool can tell a story.'

'Then there is no better choice for my own,' Archaon replied harshly, 'than you.'

'Words are nothing without action,' Dagobert said. 'Words are but fantasy to the reality of the blade plunged through the heart or passed across the throat. You will have to kill more men alone than entire armies leave behind them on the battlefield, than the lives taken by sea and storm and the victims claimed by pox and plague. And that, just to get the attention of the dread pantheon.'

'I have their attention already,' the dark templar proclaimed. 'I am Archaon. Past and future ring with my name. I have been selected by fate and will soon be Everchosen of the Ruinous Powers. They want sacrifices. They shall have them. I'm no blood-blind barbarian. This is no madness or malaise. I'm no pawn to be played and I enjoy not what I do. Men will die because they have to. Because they stand between me and my destiny. These monstrous powers shall have the souls they demand…' The wind rose to howl about the warband and the wagon, dusting them with ice. 'Yes, you hear me you calamitous monsters. I will be your weapon – but no more than the sword or spear issued to the soldier of state in prosecution of his duties. I am no more your instrument in the great unknown workings of the world than you are mine. You desire the doom of men, which with your assistance, I can deliver. The gods need a champion no less than the champion needs their blessing. I will be the Everchosen of Chaos not because I beg for it. I will not utter a word in entreaty – I will be chosen as the champion of the Ruinous Star, bearing the favour of all darkness, because darkness will not have a choice in my choosing. Only I will succeed where others have failed. Only I will bring an end to all and plunge the world of men into a futureless abyss.'

'Master, please,' Dagobert pleaded, as a screeching ice storm whipped up about them. 'You offend your patrons. The entities of the Wastes.'

'Soil your robes alone, priest,' Archaon said. 'Your fear proceeds from a cowardly soul – as it does in all men. Well, I am more than man. I am mine enemy's failure incarnate. I am the morrow. I am the world's end to come. Hear me, Dark Gods: warn your warriors, your doomed champions, corpses-in-waiting. You tell them Archaon is coming and the inevitability of their death is coming with me.'

The ice storm died. Crystals rained slowly to the shore as Dagobert peered fearfully up into the heavens. Beyond the storm-stored miasma of white, the warband could hear the grumble of thunder, distant and fading.

'Dagobert,' Archaon called. 'What must I do beyond the ease of killing, to get the attention of these daemon deities? These dogs of damnation.' Again, Dagobert peered through the ice-blind for some thunderbolt of displeasure or daemonic punishment.

'Speak, curse it!' Archaon roared in jubilant fury. 'I would know what that monstrous tome has to say.'

'The translations are difficult, master,' Dagobert told him. 'Some sections require primers, references and keystone texts we don't have.'

'Then we shall find them,' Archaon said.

'Even the sections we can translate are vague and open to interpretation.'

'Then interpret...'

'The Everchosen of Chaos will be known by the six treasures of dread antiquity he carries,' the priest called. 'Six trials to be passed – six gifts of the Ruinous gods, my lord, to be earned and recovered from the Wastes and the servants of darkness.'

'They shall be mine,' Archaon said.

'They are spread to the perversity of the northern winds, my lord,' Dagobert said as Giselle crunched the wagon along the ice of the shore. 'Hidden. Lost. Claimed by others.'

'Others that aspire to be Everchosen?'

'Others who believe they are,' the priest said.

'Such pretenders would have my pity,' Archaon said, 'that they come so far for failure. Instead they shall get my blade, through their deluded skulls.'

'These treasures, lord, are separated by great distance and watched over by guardians of the gods – powerful and unknown.'

'Then what do we know?'

'Two must be earned and two must be stolen,' Dagobert told him. 'One must be found...'

'And the other?'

'Will find you.'

Archaon laughed, hard and harsh.

'The Ruinous Powers wish to play. We shall indulge them, for now. Where does this perverse game of the gods begin?' the dark templar demanded.

'As yet I have discovered the location of only one of the treasures, master,' Dagobert said.

'What is this gift of Chaos?' Archaon asked.

'I know not,' Dagobert said, 'but whatever dark thing it is, it resides in the Altar of Ultimate Darkness.'

Archaon nodded. 'Where does fate take us?'

'To the New World, my lord,' the priest told him. 'The land of murder. Where the Witch King rules in the name of gods with bloody hands.'

'You speak of one of the elder races,' Archaon said. The dark templar had had occasion to kill a number of the secretive forest folk in the Laurelorn – wood elves, as frightened villagers would call them. He had never seen their cousins from across the sea but knew, as many did, of the aid they had offered Magnus the Pious during the Great War against Chaos. Of those who lived further still across the icy oceans, Archaon had heard little. He certainly had not enjoyed an encounter with a member of their weakling race.

'I do, my lord,' Dagobert said.

'Speak on.'

'I know little more than you, my lord. Rumour and dread legend from across the seas.'

'Speak on, priest,' Archaon commanded.

'An outcast species, master,' Dagobert told him, reaching for details from the heretical texts it had been his duty to keep from the world. 'Turned from the light and long separated from their kin – ousted after civil war.'

'Turned from the light,' Archaon echoed, 'to darkness. Do these *dark elves* worship our gods?'

'They do not, master. They venerate the deathless embodiment of murder itself.'

'A race of assassins, perhaps,' Archaon acknowledged, 'but one blessed with losing wars and fleeing from them.'

'From what I have read they are not to be underestimated, lord,' Dagobert warned. 'Their kind infests the New World. They have held their kingdom of Naggaroth safe from the clutches of Chaos for thousands of years. Their watchtowers line the border where the Wastes meet the lands of murder. They benefit from the God of Murder's blessing and sorcerous servants, who will know of our approach before we make it.'

The icy haze about Archaon cleared, revealing once more the black and white immensity of the landscape about them. They were still on the Shattered Shore, with great bergs of ice creaking against one another in the frozen sea to the west and the colossal range of midnight mountains to the east.

Archaon knew that there was no east and west where he was heading. No maps or guides that could show the way. Only the whim of the Wastes and the will of his Ruinous patrons.

'It seems we shall need an army,' Archaon announced. 'Fortunately for us, our gods have seen fit to furnish us with one – for it has long been in the ramblings of heretics and madmen that the greatest concentration of fighting men in the world can be found in the dread lands that are our path. We shall cross the Wastes. We shall kill the weak, conquer the strong and build an army of our own from the very best our enemies have to offer. Our banner shall bear the Ruinous Star of Chaos in all its glory. We shall best, commandeer and welcome warriors of all Dark Gods and creeds beneath the folds of its foetid fabric. It will be an army without equal. The Wastes will never know its like again, unless the gods of Chaos themselves decree so. I shall lead this army into the land of murder, where these ancient watchtowers will fall. The secrets of this Altar of Ultimate Darkness shall be mine and my host shall be sacrificed to the Ruinous Powers in its taking. This I pledge to my daemon gods – as always – with the blackness of my lost soul.'

in their sleep and feast on the remains. They were not worthy of Archaon and so he ended them.

Even to the eye untrained in evil, the Wastes were a time and place at war with itself. A land of mournful madness. The bizarre weather; the sunless, starless skies; the rise and drop in temperature; the strange behaviour of water; the land itself – the rock, the earth and ice, almost a living thing, alien and aggressive. Features of apparent claw and tooth, landscapes of suggestive undulation and meagre thorn forests of twisted trunk and withered branch. Unforgiving ranges of mountains, freshly erupted from the ground. Volcanic peaks that glowered in the distance. Quakes and flash floods. Waterfalls that were anything but. Rivers that flowed uphill and backwards. Lakes and inland seas that just seemed to bleed up from the depths of the earth. Polar deserts of frosted grit and glacial wastes. The only things to eat slithered and crawled, while strange lights danced and poisonous gases brumed like glowing streams through the terrain. Storms were common. Wind. Rain. Sleet. Hail. Snow. Dust storms. Ice storms. Storms of energies strange and unnatural. The heavens would churn. The Dark Gods would grumble their nerve-shredding thunder and lightning would crash across the land, of every colour and intensity.

All these things Archaon took in his stride. The one quality of the Wastes that even the Chaos warrior found difficult to manage was the way in which time and distance seemed to have no meaning. With light of different oppressive hues finding its desperate way down through the tumultuous heavens, it was almost impossible to tell what time of day it was. On the occasions that the clouds did clear, the sky above was black and empty – like the dead, glassy inside of a shark's eye. The warband could ride for days and get nowhere. At other times, they were barely out of sight of their last camp before entering a landscape new and markedly different from the one they had just left.

Archaon turned to what he had brought to the Wastes, rather than the insanity he found there, for some kind of measurement. It would be easy to lose himself in a labyrinth of distractions. In the absence of sun, map or fixed mark on the ever-changing horizon, he needed a way to judge his progress. Something more than guesswork or the timeless ramblings of *The Liber Caelestior*. To know how far he had come and judge how far he might have to go. The answers to these questions were invariably 'too far' and 'as far as is needed', but it helped to have a system. Something concrete and not at the whim of change.

Ultimately he had to use Giselle and Dagobert as some kind of marker. Archaon could not trust the enhancements of his own form. As a dark templar of the Chaos Powers, his impossible existence leeching from their potency, he was faster, stronger and more resilient in body, mind and soul than he had ever been as a knight of the weakling God-King. Regardless of where the sun had gone to die in the sky, a day's worth of travel exhausted the pair. They were hungry. They were thirsty. They were tired. It was in these physical necessities that Archaon put his faith. Still, time was difficult to trust in the Wastes.

As Oberon's hooves kicked up the ice and dust and the rickety wagon meandered its way north, Archaon passed the false-witnessing hours in brooding silence. When he wasn't lost in some dark thought, some deep fury at his fate or a scorching recrimination of the soul, then he was killing the miserable wretches that crossed their path. Beastmen. Lunatics. Half-starved warriors looking for answers at the top of the world. They found their answers in the reflection of Archaon's blade, moments before its cleaving edge passed through their unworthy bodies. Occasional wretches would impress Archaon with their pluck – usually their insistence on not dying immediately – or the usefulness of their servitude. They fell into line behind the wagon, trudging after Archaon like the wounded soldiers of some massacre or battlefield defeat, following in the footsteps of an indefatigable general who would not let them die.

They were watched by Archaon's warrior-henchmen. His

Swords of Chaos. They rode silently in their blank bone helms. Occasionally stretching their wings, they rolled uneasily in the saddle, flanking both Archaon and the wandering mongrels he chose to add to the number of their growing warband. Ever mindful of their master. Ever watchful of the traitorous dogs that fell into line behind the warrior of Chaos. Marauders, beastmen and armoured warriors, eager to share in the spoils of Archaon's growing celebrity, like a pack of scavengers on the murderous scent of a lone predator, stripping the butchered remains left in its wake for scraps.

Casting his gaze behind, at the tainted path taking him north into destiny, Archaon found the others he had enslaved on the road to damnation. The Swords and the rag-tag cavalcade of recruited savagery that were already very much part of the damnation about them. Gorst, always a stumbling silhouette in the dust, dragging his chains and back-lashed carcass after Archaon as he had done after the distant memory that was Diederick Kastner. Giselle, who just stared back at Archaon from the wagon. Her face wore the weariness of horror and disgust. At first such horror had been laced with pity at what Archaon had become. She, better than most, knew that the darkness of the templar's future had not been of his choosing. Such sentiment was soon lost in the hatred of the hostage, but even that had faded. Gone was the childish futility of a foul mouth and violent outbursts. She was as unbreakable as she had ever been. Her strength lay now in the tautness of her lips, the censure of her eyes and the burning silence that met any words Archaon had for her. When Archaon looked to the girl, he found only fear and abhorrence. He was a thing to her now. A force of unnatural nature that could be denied no more than the howling wind or raging sea.

When not punishing himself or other warriors of the Wastes, Archaon would demand of Father Dagobert answers to dangerous questions.

'For years we were the caretakers of damned tomes and the tales of men who searched for evil of their own making. Did you ever think that it would be like this?'

Dagobert sent ripples of encouragement through the reins, prompting the beasts whose burden it was to drag the wagon on through the bleakness of the Shadowlands. The priest was still the kind-hearted scholar that Archaon had known and loved. Such a heart and the affection the priest bore for the boy who had been Little Diederick, the man who had been Sieur Kastner the Sigmarite Knight, now weighed him down like a millstone. Dagobert had decided to follow the boy that had been his charge and the man who had been his friend into damnation's embrace. Perhaps he could have saved him once. With every step that took them north, such a hope became a fading possibility. A good intention that had become a bitter hope – that had become a lunatic's fantasy. He answered his master's questions as best he could, calling upon a lifetime's study of combated darkness and the recorded untruths of Ruination.

'I suspect,' Dagobert said, 'that it's an intense, personal and inconstant state. As a punishment might match the crime for which it was devised. Reading of such things, by so many in so many different kinds of spiritual torment, I imagine that we share common miseries as we share common joys. The searing reality of any one man's damnation seems specific to him, my master. You and I are both here as far as the chill in my bones and our words clouding on the air can tell me, but we live very different definitions of dread and darkness.'

Archaon nodded in the saddle. For years he had hunted men whose desire it had been to find this bleak and unforgiving place. Others who had returned from it, their souls and desires twisted by the horror of what they had found in both the Wastes and within themselves as they traversed such lands of torment and blood.

Ruins dotted the landscape, mostly the smashed and burned out remnants of fortifications, built from the dark stone of the region. Towers. Keeps. Forts. Bastions. Even the isolated derelicts of half-built castles and buried citadels. The only other buildings the warband happened upon were the tents of hastily abandoned camps and rough temples honouring one dire god or another. The structures also appeared not to obey the passage of time. Despite their state of ruination, the stone of some seemed freshly carved, while the walls of others were weathered and cracked, infested with stunted mosses, lichens and withered roots.

Beyond that, there were the bodies. The dead and the dying. Corpses. Everywhere. The Wastes were a warzone. Some of the unfortunate warriors and champions had clearly died in battle. The butchered torsos. The headless. The limbless. The unrecognisable. The ground soaked with blood and decorated with trailing gut. Others had been the victims of ritual sacrifice, impaled on stakes, cut to pieces or burned as part of daemon-appeasing ceremonies. Like the derelict structures, the cadavers appeared to defy the days, months and years. Some were waxy and cold to the touch, slow to rot in the climate, while others became infested with fat maggots and spoiled to puddle and bone within days, for little obvious reason. The strangest sensation for Archaon was accidentally happening upon the same smouldering ruin days later, only to find the bodies carpeting the grit and ice to be in a better state than when he had initially left them. Bodies he may have put on the ground himself. Freshly butchered corpses, rather than the clouds of flies, stripped skulls and mounds of spoilage the dark templar had left days before.

Archaon never truly got used to the perversities of the Wastes. The strangeness of the land and the weather. Its unpredictable effects on things both living and dead. The Chaos warrior understood that this was very much the point of the Wastes' existence – if the land had such a thing as a point. Its very nature resisted definition and defied expectation. Its inhabitants could be anywhere, at any time. They could be alive. They could be dead. The Wastes could be a promised land – a paradise – or it could be some kind of eternal punishment. It was everything and it was nothing. To Archaon it was a means to an end. The dark templar's intentions extended beyond its borders – he ruled his ambitions, they did not rule him. He brought death to his enemies but was not there to feed his blood lust. His black heart sought satisfaction from the goal upon which it was set, but he didn't lose himself to indulgence – a prisoner in gratification's loose embrace. Neither did he become lost in the infectious malaise of the place. He would not forget himself and remain. He was there with purpose. His movement was ever forward. Even if the path he was on led to nowhere.

'And what of the gods of Ruination that call the top of the world their home, trading in dark deeds and the souls of lost men? I have fought their servants for what already seems like a lifetime. I have stood sentry over those they would claim with their myriad and wicked ways. I have frustrated their desires with word, deed and blade. Though they curse me with gifts unasked for and invite me to their realm with prophecies and deceit, I hate them with all my heart. As I hate the God-King and the feeble powers of this broken and decrepit world. I hate them, yet I feel that I know them not. How can a man hate nothingness?'

'The Ruinous Powers are all things to all men,' Dagobert said cryptically, drawing upon his careful studies of dark arts and the pledges men have made – their very souls for desires they thought denied to them. 'This land is not their home. They are the land and the land is an expression of them. They dwell in the dark corners of men's hearts. A place warm and ripe for corruption. They prey on the fickleness of fancy and the inescapability of need. We hide behind the stone walls of temples and the false hope of daily rituals, half-remembered history and symbols that jangle about our necks, but the truth is that we are defenceless against their predations.'

Men were feeble things, Archaon knew. Mostly spoiling meat and the selfish desires that drove inconsequential existence. It took nothing to twist the hearts of such beings. Desires of the flesh. The blood of one's enemy. The promise of alleviated suffering. The granting of paltry ambitions. It cost nothing for the dark powers of the world to build temples in the blackest reaches of such hearts. Nothing for such beings to draw the twilight from men's souls. Like the leech within, they infected their host with a little of their own filth, to keep the darkness flowing. Most men harboured such a covenant, many unknown to themselves, masked by ignorance and denial. For few could tolerate the knowledge that they are truly evil without the comfort of a path or purpose. For those men, the path always led north. Through the Wastes and the Shadowlands. To the insanity beyond. To darkness, pure and true.

Like the lodestone, the desires of those who would kill in the name of ancient evil took them to the top of the world. Archaon was set on a course not of murderous malice or self-glorification. He travelled not for unknown pleasures or the alleviation of torments past. He was at the top of the world simply because the route to Armaggedon led through the Ruinous Wastes. If that was where he would find the means to end a world, then so be it. Nothing could quell his appetite for annihilation. Oblivion beckoned.

And so, the Chaos Wastes. There mindless marauders, who had ravaged, robbed and butchered their way north, gathered. They knew not why. The road to damnation was a lonely one and perhaps, Archaon considered, it gave the doomed comfort. To know that there were those who shared their madness. In truth, they were there to fight the foes of their dread patrons, each other and themselves – since there was only so much pain and bloodshed a single man, even a man devoted to Chaos, could achieve. Marauders found each other on the path and gathered about the suggestions of greatness in their ranks. Warbands formed. Warbands joined together to create hordes and hosts about emerging warriors and sorcerers, whose worthiness was tested before the growing number of the damned.

Like hungry wolves they fought each other for the wretched right to lead others of their ill-breed. Some became dark beacons in the cold havoc of the north, attracting hordes of their battle-kin to their banner, bringing the souls of hundreds under the yoke of their dark celebrity. Such men might even earn the loyalty of beastmen and greenskins or the fallen of the elder races. Such dark light in the world might then snare the service of monsters and daemons. From such a melting pot of savagery, the champions of Chaos are crafted. Some received the kind of infernal gifts and sponsorship required to exalt them to infamy. Dark heroes to those in their service. They became names known by others, known by the names of other great warriors whose heads they had claimed and followers they had taken for their own. Some became Chaos lords and generals, commanding armies that would threaten to conquer the very Wastes themselves. Such was the dark path to damnation and greatness. The path that the man who had never been Diederick Kastner found himself upon. The path of the Ruinous Powers.

'What are these gods of havoc and darkness?' Archaon had put to Father Dagobert. 'What do they want with me?'

'There are as many creatures of dread haunting the Wastes and the corruption of men's souls as there are evil desires in the world, master,' the priest had told him. 'Of the Ruinous pantheon, most find themselves afflicted by the dark will of four. Four ancient misfortunes of existence. Like the four walls of a prison cell, holding the conflicting hopes and fears in men's hearts hostage. He who would war with all else – the spiller of blood, the flame that heats the ire in men's souls, causing it to bubble over into the world.'

'I have felt this torment...'

'As all men have,' Dagobert said, 'since the first fist or the first stone was lifted in violence.'

'Go on, priest.'

'He whose dark desires are the very nature of desire itself,' Dagobert said. 'He who lusts. He who thirsts. He who both tempts and is temptation.'

'You said there were four,' Archaon pushed.

'He who is the end of all,' the priest continued. 'The constancy of suffering and desperation – whose sign is seen the world over in the diseased and the gasping hopes of the dying.'

'And?'

'He who is the very storm of change,' Dagobert said. 'The volatility and vitality of a world ever in motion. The embodiment of men's appetite for... more.'

Archaon nodded.

'I have known all of these afflictions,' the dark templar said.

'And they have known you, my lord,' Dagobert told him. 'As they know all men.'

'How can one man serve such opposites?' Archaon asked, the desires as described to him seeming at odds with one another. 'How can a man be both desire and death that would end it? Constancy yet the drive of change.'

Dagobert considered. He thought back to fearful texts read by candle-light in the temple vaults and long forgotten.

'He must not be the pots that keep the paint separate,' Dagobert said. 'He must be the ever-darkening canvas, burdened with colour upon colour until he becomes a shade of ruin pleasing to all the Chaos Powers to look upon.'

Once again Archaon nodded, for once again the priest's words had cut through the confusion that burned in his mind. Digging his heels into Oberon's flanks, the Chaos warrior urged the steed onwards.

The daemon-haunted north was ever calling. There damnation exerted its great influence and the gifts of Ruination were showered on the fearless, the accepting and the doomed. The endless darkness of the unstable region about the pole was more dream than reality. It was where gateways to unearthly realms stood tall and the raw promise of Chaos bubbled up through the appearance of reality. It was where lie became truth, a never-beginning eternity where men could lose and find themselves a thousand times over. Where fantasy and nightmare bred realities anew and mortals could stand like mirrors in the soul-shattering presence of gods. It was not Archaon's destination, however. He was no pilgrim of darkness. He was not there to prostrate himself at the feet of his daemon overlords. He had not travelled across continents to jostle and squeal like a piglet before the bounty of a sow's belly, begging for blessings, with a bottomless appetite for attention and favour. That was a path to greatness unworthy of one who might call himself the Everchosen of Chaos. A calling beneath the Lord of the End Times. Archaon would not seek damnation. It would find him. He would not curry favour with his infernal patrons. They would come to him when the time was right. When he was needed. When he had earned their power.

Instead, Archaon went west. In reality, there was no such thing in the Wastes. There was only the instinct of west. A direction that most of the time was signified by a general trend in the warband's wanderings. Without open sky or elevation to believe in, there were only two seeming constants in the Wastes – and even they, on occasion, were playful in their perversity. Archaon trusted that, if he kept the berg-shattered coast on his left and the daemon darkness of the pole on his right, his progress should generally be west. Taking care that their exploration of the Wastes had not taken them too far into the twilight insanity of the polar interior, Archaon routinely meandered away from its agonising attraction and every few weeks would reach the frozen, storm-battered shore, before turning inland once more. In the gloomy hinterlands between, the ring of shadow that encompassed the continent's dark heart, Archaon used the winds of Chaos to guide his path.

Thus, the saga of Archaon – warrior of Chaos and champion of the Dark Gods – began. He was no northern marauder or tribal chieftain, leading his brothers in the perpetual darkness of murderous territoriality. He was no blood-baptised champion, looking for the way to become lost. He was no fool sorcerer, searching for secrets, only to become one. He was Archaon. He would achieve the horror of the entire world. He was a living legend. Great things were his to achieve – and to achieve them he would need great men.

The first of these great men, Archaon slayed. They were new arrivals, like the dark templar himself. Untried and untested, leading small bands that were equally so. Men of the Empire, haughty Bretons, grim Ungols and Gospodars, even the occasional southerner. Some bore Ruinous favour for the terrible evil already wrought in their homelands: claws, spines, venomous fangs, horns or some other type of deformative horror – acid-dribbling maws, an overpowering stench or scaly, armoured skin. A hundred different aberrations of the mind or body, received as blessings for terrors rendered. Their conception of their pantheon or patron powers was simple and savage. They had carved symbols into their faces and flesh, indulged affliction, wrath, vice or dread powers they did not understand. They honoured their gods with insanity and the weakness of wild abandon. They did not know what they had become or the part they had to play in the circus of delirium and death that was the Wastes. They thought of themselves as victors when in actual fact they were victims. Of folly. Of fate. Of Archaon's irresistible path. Souls caught in the slipstream of the dark templar's supremacy.

So many died. Some even of note. Fastred the Bold, veteran of the Field of Green; Baba Kosch, witch of the Grovod Wood; Herrick von Raukov, the sickly seventh son of Ostland; the Knight of Brass, who Archaon had always assumed was just the subject of ballads and tales; Hjalmar Deathstrider, the famed axe man of Vidarheim and some hulking, corpulent thing calling itself the Gutwrencher, which had dragged itself north from the Mountains of Mourn. Few had been worthy of Archaon's blade, despite their infamy. Even fewer were chosen to join his warband's number.

As Archaon worked his bloody way west, he cut a swathe through the tribal lands of the dark continent. Northerners who truly called the Wastes their home and whose clans and castes observed the will of their gods with breeding, bleeding their last and the vile existence inbetween. They knew nothing of the fine lands of the south but the unworthies that travelled from there in pilgrimage and spilt their sweet civilised blood in tribal territory. What the marauding nomads, savage hordes and horsemen called existence was life in its lowliest form. The choice between starving and eating your enemy. Between the solitude of victimhood or the brotherhood of darkness in your heart. Between being butchered as a weakling or fighting strong. Between living a life of murderous survival or not living at all. The tribes had no true lands to call their own. The Wastes were ever changing, ever moving beneath their feet and the hooves of their hardy steeds. There was only the way of their wanderings and wars on the move. Tribes would routinely clash over the ugly Shadowlands, daubing the clan symbols of their kind in blood on smouldering ruins, erecting totems to their favoured gods and leaving skinned victims on stakes as a warning to others. Sometimes hours later, two different hosts would gut and bludgeon each other to extinction for the same miserable valley, derelict temple or storm-racked plain. The insanity was unending but such existence bred harsh peoples, worthy of the dark lands about them.

Archaon came to know them across the blade, with their ragged corpses under his boot. The Norse: fur-clad raiders of hairy brawn, they were pale of flesh but dark of soul, dragging the dragon-prows of their clinker longships up the frozen shore to unleash the fury of their number on the Southern Wastes. The Hung: squat orientals born in the saddle, as swift and savage as the spear thrown and the shattered-glass winds at their backs. The Kurgan: swarthy-skinned warriors of the Eastern Steppes, most at home under the shadow of Chaos. Indomitable. Innumerable. A melting pot of competing cruelty, the tribe had the greatest presence amongst the armies of the Ruinous Powers and produced some of their hardiest heroes and enduring leaders.

Archaon fought his way through them all. The Kurgan Kul, the sons and grandsons of Asavar the Everchosen. Archaon taunted them with the failure of their Father in Darkness, savagely cutting them down in favour of his own worthy claim to the title. The Dolgans, whose gypsy queen used her sorceries to curse her tribe's enemies with foul fortune and the misstep of luck. Any who fought the Dolgans had to battle with the terrain and weather against them, as well as the witch's inbred army of lover-marauders roaring for their blood. Archaon did not require luck to win his battles. For the dark templar, belief, skill and cold steel won the day, and he broke the Dolgans like a spine across his own indomitable will.

The Hastlings and the Tahmaks, who Archaon and his Swords met as they battled each other at the leaning citadel of Karda Fell. The Hastlings, with their flowing raven hair and beards almost forming manes about the savagery of their dark faces, and the Tahmaks who armoured themselves with the inset bone and skulls of their fallen enemies, had both spawned mighty warrior chieftains – Drach-Mal the Black and Radzseekl of the Burning Plain. After Archaon had killed enough of their tribesmen and the Fell was flooded with blood, the dark templar fought them together, forcing the warring pair to join forces against him. Both died badly and it fell to Drach-Mal's brothers and Radzseekl of the Burning Plain to hastily agree a slash-palmed truce and pull their tribesmen out from under Archaon's gore-splashed sword while there were still warriors to withdraw.

The Gharhars of the Upper Shroudlands received Archaon with submission and reverence at first. Having lost their warlord to a flesh-melding pestilence that had claimed a full quarter of the tribe, however, the skin-sloughers resorted to treachery, attempting to sacrifice Archaon as a daemon offering to reverse the Gharhars' fortunes. Many Shroudlanders died for their underestimation of the knight and his Swords of Chaos. The far Kurganites, known as the Dark Arghols, conversely were openly hostile from the outset. The Arghol women fought alongside their men in battle, all famine-thin, body-painted and criss-crossed in strips of cured flesh-leather. They seemed not to notice the scalding cold of the climate or the losses Archaon and his knights inflicted on their tribe. Again and again they attacked the warband. They attacked at that nest of debauchery, the Maidenhead, on the killing fields of the Red Decimation and during a blizzard of ash and ice that reached inside the vast ruins of Caer Targul. On one occasion warrior women, she-devils of the Dark Arghol, attempted to drag a screaming Giselle off into the gloom and would have done so if it weren't for the chain connecting her to the wagon.

While the degenerate Kurgans plagued the Shadowlands through which Archaon's warband fought, the dark templar sought worthiness both poleward and out on the continent's blasted shore. Horn-helmed Vargs from the Kraken Coast, in the Norscan north, had been yoked under the brutal leadership of King Ingvar the Ravager. The Ravager's marauder fleet rode the berg-storms of the shattered coast, burning and slaughtering their way inland like a river of lava. After halting Ingvar's invasions the Ravager King personally led an incursion north into the Ruinous gloom with the oath-answering Baldrgrim of the Bloody Beard and the Norse dwarfs of the Hel Peaks. Ingvar had but one intention – to end the mysterious Chaos warrior known as Archaon. Ingvar and his marauder army found the dark templar and his Swords of Chaos between the unscalable heights of the Vagassa Pass. There Archaon and his Chaos knights held them with sword, shield and armoured wing, butchering the bearded Norscans, their dwarf allies and their battleaxe-wielding king, in mounds of their fallen.

The Graelings tribe, meanwhile, saw fit to unleash the Werekin of Fjirgard upon Archaon's warband. For weeks the lycanthropes dogged their progress, tracking the rank scent of Gorst as the flagellant followed the dark templar and his warband this way and that across the insanity of the Shadowlands.

In the stunted pines of a withering wood, the Werekin of Fjirgard came for them through the mist, their howls echoing ominously about the contorted landscape beyond. Archaon and his Swords fought their combined savagery amongst the wasted trees. They would have dined on priestflesh, however, if it hadn't been for Dagobert prising the rusty chain of a spiked flail from the skeletal hand of a long-dead warrior of Chaos and beating back the pack of shapeshifters – very much as he had done to their wolf-kin above Archaon's infant form years before.

Further into the frozen continent's interior, Archaon's warband found the misshapen Tong – easterners with hunched backs, sharp teeth and a talent for the dark arts. Their warlocks were all whiskers and squinting hatred, withstanding the deep cold of the Wastes with the warmth of their mammoth-hair coats, their charmed fires and hulking Kurgan slaves, unfortunates snatched from the lands of the Tokmar and Yusak and worked to death. When Archaon had sliced and stabbed through enough of their slave-stock, the warlocks came at the warband with enchanted incendiaries, urns that unleashed firestorms of green flame. As Archaon butchered Yusak bodyguards, whose bodies had been warped and mutilated enough by their Tong slave masters, working his way to the warlocks, the templar was surprised to find larger urns raining from the sky.

With the frosted wilderness and the obscene shapes of standing stones erupting with unnatural infernos, Archaon realised that he had been led into a trap. The warlocks thrashed in the green flame, apparently having been sacrificed by their own witchbreed brethren. With little choice, Archaon crunched through the ice and grit at a run. His Swords were pinned down and at any moment the wagon – with Giselle and Father Dagobert within it – could turn into a fiery, green wreck. His heavy footsteps took him through the sky-striving blossoms of green fire, as the larger urns dropped and hit the ground. As he saw the lobbed urns fall before him, the templar was forced to skid and scramble in the opposite direction to evade a fiery death. Charging through the dying blaze of a short fallen urn, Archaon arrived before a pair of ramshackle mangonels, manned and manoeuvred by Tokmar slaves. Tong warlocks were overseeing the trajectory and loading of the weapon from a rhinox-hauled cart of prepared urns, protecting the fur tents of an encampment beyond. Archaon made short work of the brutalised mangonel crews and their vicious warlock overseers, thundering on through the cold and into the camp. Slashing his way through the hide shelters, the dark templar conducted the massacre alone, hacking his way through the privacy of each tent in turn and slaying without ceremony the wicked old men, their hags and chained slaves within.

Upon returning to his own warband, drenched in the blood of the easterners, Archaon found that one of the Tong's projectile urns had indeed come close to destroying the wagon, torching the horse that dragged it instead. Ordering Vier and Fünf to retrieve the two-headed rhinox from the cart of urns and yoke it to the wagon, Archaon moved around to find Hieronymous Dagobert clutching *The Celestine Book of Divination* to his chest, ready to save the tome from the fires.

Meanwhile, Giselle hid stoic and silent in the wagon itself, giving Archaon the enmity of her eyes, knowing that if the enchanted fireball had hit the wagon there would have been no escape for her. Archaon thought on the Kurgan slaves that had attacked him in the encampment and the way he had found them chain-staked to the tent floor. Bringing up *Terminus*, the blade of the Sigmarite weapon still aflame with ghostly torment, the dark templar chopped down through the freezing chain, freeing the girl. The Sister of the Imperial Cross was shocked – as was Dagobert – but both said nothing.

That night Archaon had expected the girl Giselle to leave, but in reality, there was nowhere she could go. She was hundreds, possibly thousands of miles away from the nearest civilised land, where the sweet flesh of a Sister of the Imperial Cross would not be cooked and cannibalised as an offering to a dark god. Even if she could make it out of the Wastes alive – which was unthinkable – where could she go? Naggaroth? Norsca? The Troll Country? The Darklands? How would she navigate? How could she even get there? The perversity of the situation started to amuse the Chaos warrior as he scoured the Tong encampment with Zwei and Drei for useful supplies. Even without her chains, the sister was still a prisoner and it was with some dark satisfaction that he saw her still sitting at the reins of the wagon upon his return.

As Archaon rode on, leading the Swords and the wagon up the snaking valley, he began to think on the reasons he had brought the girl with them. The Swords were soulless, expert and unquestioning warriors – a valuable luxury in the Wastes. Father Dagobert – although priest of the God-King no more and almost feverish in the madness that was his devotion to *The Liber Caelestior* and his translations of its futures – was eminently useful. Like mighty Oberon and the stalwart blade *Terminus*, he was the only part of Archaon's past that the Chaos warrior was willing to keep around. Such reminders helped keep the dark templar in the present rather than becoming a slave to the Wastes' myriad distractions, like losing himself in wrath, obsession, temptation or hopelessness. Giselle Dantziger was something else. She was not really part of his past and although he searched for a reason to include her in his future he could not find one. As he rolled in the saddle, with ungainly scavengers screeching and flapping overhead, it started to bother the Chaos warrior.

At first, Archaon thought it was some dark manifestation of his new existence. The sadistic streak that was working its way through his very being. As a devout Sister of the Imperial Cross, who unlike the rest of the warband, had not lost her faith in the face of the Wastes' insanity, he considered that he might enjoy her suffering. Something pure and resilient burned inside her no less than the Sigmarite blade *Terminus* did in the dark templar's hands. Perhaps, Archaon considered, it was not a sadistic streak but a masochism that had wormed its way into his soul. It physically hurt to be near the sister. Her simple faith, the light she kept alive for the God-King within her, was like an inferno for the Chaos warrior. A soul-roasting agony to endure. Yet endure it he had. He had kept her alive. Despite her obvious hatred for everything he had become, Archaon had retained her as an unlikely member of the warband.

The dark templar's thoughts took refuge in the idea that his actions might have a more straightforward explanation. The effect she had on him was the same effect she had on every other wretched thing of the Wastes. Like *Terminus*, the girl was a useful weapon against the evil of the world – the evil that even as a warrior of the Ruinous Powers, Archaon spent much of his time battling. Then he thought that it might be lust, pure and simple. Archaon had never thought of the girl as particularly attractive. Now that her hair had grown out of the harsh style required by the temple, however, it framed a comely face, like that of a farmer's wife or innkeeper's daughter. The kind of young women Sieur Kastner had spent a lifetime visiting unintentional heirs upon. Plain. Pretty even, when not screwed up in perpetual disgust and detestation.

Such thoughts were not without peril for the Chaos warrior. They bordered dangerously close to mercy, a notion that ordinarily would have prompted the dark templar to turn Oberon around and execute the girl in the wilderness. A man like Archaon – a living embodiment of the end of the world – could afford no such sentimentality. He could spare lives because it served his needs or even for perversity's sake but not simply because his heart told him to. As a Sigmarite templar Archaon had long understood that good and evil were not absolutes. A man's actions in service to the devotion of his cause – whatever that might be – determined the degree to which he could be called good or bad, virtuous or evil, devout or corrupt. He had known thoroughly despicable men who claimed to be ardent Sigmarites. He had also known the fallen find their way to damnation through the virtues of their faith. Archaon knew that himself, only too well. He knew also that there was a small part of him, a scintilla of light in the darkness of his soul, which still yearned to end every evil thing in the world – including himself. A sliver of regret, like the beaten child that runs away from home but still wishes to return and feel the embrace of the parent that beat him.

Archaon knew this truth about himself. He knew that it was the lost love he had for his God-King that poisoned him as much as the shard of wyrdstone embedded in his skull, leaking its corruption into his mind. Rather than return home to the arms of a loving parent, Archaon wanted to burn down the house. The God-King and his servants would pay for his neglect and abuses. The tiny glimmer of stale hope that afflicted Archaon scared him. It scared him that it might be the reason he was keeping Giselle Dantziger alive. She represented a way back from the darkness. Escape from the shadow. Though it was a spiritual agony to be in her presence, perhaps she was keeping some part of Diederick Kastner alive.

Such dread concerns accompanied Archaon and his warband west. West through miserable moorlands and out into open country. A mountain-framed tundra that was home to the horse tribes of the mighty Mung. The Mung were known among the Wastes to possess the finest steeds of any tribe on account of the way their witch-doctors unlocked the simple animal souls of their horses to devils and evil spirits. The eyes of Mung mounts burned with the spectral fury of beasts possessed. They could run faster and for longer than any equivalent mount in the Wastes and with herds of the black beasts, the Mung's territories were wide and ever expanding. Unbeknownst to Archaon at the time, his warband had ridden into the territory of a brutal chieftain calling himself the Hu-Mung-us, a chariot-riding giant of a marauder, nearly twice as tall as his stunted Mung tribesman. Considering Archaon and his warband to be mercenaries brought in by the centigor herd of a nearby territory, which had defiled Mung steeds and fathered filth filthy offspring upon them, the Hu-Mung-us sent his fastest spirit-steeds and horseback-mounted archers to run them off. He sent them in their hundreds.

Caught out in the open, Archaon and the warband were at the mercy of the colossal war party. Mung horsemen swept down on them like a flock of birds, wheeling and swerving, attempting to cut them down with their wyrdstone edged blades. The rhinox-hauled wagon was never going to outrun the Mung horses and Archaon feared that Oberon and the steeds of the Swords would fare little better against the marauders' possessed mounts. With the tundra swarming with the Mung, Archaon ordered his warband to head for the mountains where speed counted for less and they could thin the horsemen's numbers. The escape turned into a running battle, however, with the Mung war party moving almost as one, slicing through Archaon's band at blazing speed before routinely withdrawing and turning the sky black with launched arrows. Shooting in unison from the saddle, the Mung appeared to be expert archers as well as riders and it became apparent to Archaon that they might all be skewered alive on the wyrdstone flint-tips of the arrows.

Pushing Oberon to his flesh-steaming limits and with his Swords riding alongside, their wings outstretched like shields to the sky, the warband just got out of range of the tundra-stabbing shafts. The Chaos warrior turned to find that the wagon had fared less well. The material of the bonnet had been punctured to ribbons. Dagobert and Giselle were hiding between the wheels, the wagon bed soaking up the swarm of arrows like a wooden target. The two-headed rhinox had gone down beneath the barrage, appearing more like some kind of giant porcupine with so many shafts buried in its shaggy flesh. The creature was not dead, however. It was too stupid and its hide too thick to succumb. At the site of each arrow-inflicted injury, the beast suffered the horror of a rapid transformation. It swiftly became a moaning mound of hairy mutation, spawning new appendages, tentacles and growths. With these new gifts it dragged its spiny form across the tundra towards the wagon and the pair taking refuge beneath it.

Archaon turned Oberon about and started to ride for the wagon.

'Target the horses,' the dark templar ordered, as the Swords followed on their own steeds. The Mung swept in again, like a shoal of fish darting in and out of its prey. Instead of turning aside their flint-edged blades of corruption, Archaon swung *Terminus* about him, turning the flaming blade in his wrist and cleaving down either side of him as the swarm of marauder steeds passed by either side. The horses were bedevilled and fast but they were also light and lacking in armour. The plain became a cacophony of equine shrieks as Archaon cut through legs, opened up throats and chopped entire heads from oncoming beasts. With the Swords of Chaos following suit with their own bone blades, the warband cut a bloody, screeching path through the stampede. Encouraged by the progress Archaon was making against their enemies, a herd of centigor rode down out of the mountains, spearing the unsaddled Mung with the long shafts of their wicked weapons.

With arrows shot awkwardly from the confusion on the ground glancing and splintering off his plate, Archaon leaned from one side of Oberon to the other, cleaving through the Mung mounts until finally he heard the sound of a chariot, rattling at tundra-tearing speed towards him, blades whooshing through the air as they spun with the turn of the wheel. The Hu-Mung-us drove on a pair of demented steeds, with archers either side of him, bows at the ready. Archaon roared Oberon into a charge. The Hu-Mung-us whipped at his horses with spiked reins and Archaon and the Mung chieftain blazed across the bloody field towards one another.

Holding *Terminus* out in front of him, Archaon angled the blade to turn aside the arrows flying from the chariot. With the blades swishing either side of it there was no way the Chaos warrior was going to get near enough to take the chieftain's head off his shoulders. Hauling at the reins, Archaon brought Oberon to a sudden stop, using the momentum to slip down out of the saddle and onto the frozen earth. The field was littered with the bodies of horses. Slapping Oberon away, Archaon advanced on foot as the Mung chieftain's chariot thundered down on him. The Hu-Mung-us clenched his teeth in rage as he drove the horses hauling the vehicle, who frothed at the mouth, directly at Archaon. Sliding down onto his side in the frozen mud, the dark templar slipped between the ferocious horses as their hooves pounded the earth either side of him. As Archaon heard the swooshing scythe pass, he struck out with his own blade, cleaving through the right wheel, smashing one side of it to pieces. Clambering awkwardly to his feet, Archaon watched as the broken wheel stabbed into the hard ground, anchoring one side of the chariot to the earth. The vehicle bucked and was thrown suddenly in confusion, the horses knocked senseless by the sudden stop and the archers thrown forward onto their hindquarters. Only the Hu-Mung-us seemed to have held himself in place, although the towering marauder was bleeding from a gash on his head.

'Come on!' Archaon bellowed, running at a slight crouch towards the ruined chariot, *Terminus* held out to one side in both of the Chaos warrior's gauntlets. The huge chieftain slid a colossal scimitar, serrated with wyrdstone flints, from the vehicle before abandoning it and moving to meet the dark templar. Archaon readied himself for the impact of the giant's mighty blows and the satisfaction of his crusader blade punching through the marauder's body. It was a satisfaction that never came, however. A centigor bounded up behind the Hu-Mung-us and launched its spear, slamming it straight into the Mung chieftain's back, straight down between the shoulder blades. The Hu-Mung-us took two more unsteady steps before letting his scimitar fall from his grasp and crash down onto his knees.

'No!' Archaon roared, denied of his victory. The centigor heard his furious challenge and a savage smile formed on its bestial face. Moments later it was gone. Along with the hybrid's head, which had been sliced clean off its muscular torso by a bone sword wielded by Eins who had ridden up behind it to defend his master. As the blood steamed off the tundra and both horse tribe and beasts scattered, Archaon had to content himself with the howls of the dying and the unearthly shrieks of the rhinox spawn, put out of its misery by two more of the knight's Swords.

When Archaon wasn't slaying the subjects of the Ruinous Powers, he was actively attempting to recruit them. As

Dagobert translated more of *The Liber Caelestior* and unlocked the secrets of Archaon's further damnation, it became obvious that an excursion into the chill lands of Naggaroth to access the so-called Altar of Ultimate Darkness would be impossible without a full incursion from the Wastes as a distraction.

'The Witch King's mother is a sorceress of great power,' Dagobert told his master.

'The Witch King's mother?'

'Yes, my lord,' Dagobert said. 'The head of a coven of sorcerous hags. They will see us coming, master. They will know our dark intent.'

'Then we shall hide it within an even darker intent,' Archaon had told the priest. 'We shall invade the kingdom of Naggaroth from the north at the head of an immense army.'

'Where shall we find such a force, my lord?' Dagobert said. 'Warriors worthy of your leadership.'

'Finding men willing to die for greatness is not the problem,' Archaon told him. 'Certainly not here in the Wastes, where nearly every marauder, warrior and fiend is determined to bring glory to his daemon patron in blood. Finding men to lead such slaves to darkness in my name… much more difficult.'

And it was.

On his journey north, Archaon had met men like him. The damned. The doomed. Men who thought themselves bound for legend. Men who thought they could catch the fleeting eye of an uncaring god. The dark templar had travelled their path; he had fought and he had killed such men. He became to such accursed hopefuls as much a part of the Wastes as the perversity of the land and the howling ruination that swept across it. He became the test the aspirant flotsam and jetsam that washed up along insanity's coast had to pass. The yardstick of worthiness. A touchstone of warrior skill, dogged ingenuity and will irrepressible. A question of faith. The longer he spent in the Wastes, the more of a test Archaon became. As he travelled and slaughtered his way poleward, the knight found warriors more worthy of his blade and the time spent slaying them. These were men who had been to the darkness and back. Who had fought their way to the heart of it and returned. They had survived. They had survived others like themselves. This was a credit to them and Archaon began to think that they could be a credit to him also.

Those unfortunate souls that had returned from the lands of midnight delirium in the continent core were different. They were changed. Like Archaon, their bodies and minds had acclimatised to the abnormality and lethality of their environment. The mind-bending rulelessness of the place, its stomach-churning grotesquery, the constant demands of defence and slaughter. In the Wastes, you were only safe if you were dead, and there was no guarantee even of that. Those that had returned from the Gatelands at the centre of the Wastes and had not completely lost their minds were physically altered. They were not just stronger in mind, will and body, not just faster in thought and reflex, like Archaon had become. The world had confused them with something else. Their skin was no longer their own. They were gifted with extra limbs, some of use and some anatomical studies in uselessness. They returned unmade, malformed and inconstant of flesh. Their minds also seemed similarly fragmented. Their sanity had been smashed by what they had seen and even been subjected to. They had picked up the shattered pieces and reassembled them as best they could. They had not just returned themselves. They had returned at the head of sometimes hundreds of others, attracted to their possibility like a dwarf to a vein of gold. Archaon would use these champions of the Chaos gods. They would be the battering ram he would use to smash his way into the realm of Naggaroth.

Archaon's Swords of Chaos were a beginning – but only that. The winged warriors had proved themselves over and again. They were his personal bodyguard, however – their bone swords and shielding wings were always where he needed them to be. Their first concern always seemed to be Archaon's person. They were not an army. They were the honour guard of a dark hero. An armed escort into eternity.

Despite their silent obedience and life-saving interventions, Archaon was still wary of his knights of Chaos. He found himself studying their fighting style, in case one day they turned assassin and he was forced to fight them himself. He still didn't know where they had come from or how they knew where to find him. They said nothing of their origins, although the wings on their armoured backs and the weapons of bone drawn from their own bodies testified to time spent in the Wastes and the damned interior of the dark continent. They said absolutely nothing. Nothing about their lives before their fall to Chaos. Nothing about their time in the Wastes. Nothing about who had sent them or their reasons for seeking out the dark templar as their master. In turn, *The Liber Caelestior* had little to say about them, apart from the fact that they were Archaon's constant companions. His Swords. His Swords of Chaos. Only the markings of their plate said anything about their past. The eight points of the Ruinous Star suggested that they honoured all gods of Chaos with equal reverence and disdain. Glyphs and designs woven into the black of their armour and even the bone of their skull-helms told of their subservience to former warrior overlords and daemon masters: Hordrak the Prodigal, Khardunn the Gloried, Engra Deathsword.

Archaon needed more than guardians and henchmen. It was time for him to do more than wage war. He had to become a warlord. Not just a warrior, but a general. He needed to show the gods that he could harness their dogs of differing allegiance and sworn enmity to one sled. The one that would carry Archaon to a greatness impossible to ignore. For that he needed loyal lieutenants, whose talents, warbands, tribes and hosts would combine to create the army of lost souls Archaon would need.

Some – despite their warped minds and bodily blessings – were deemed undeserving of such honour. Haarlax Shrike, despite his death-dealing prowess, would not leave the tower of skulls he was constructing to honour his Blood God to join Archaon's band. He had to die with his followers and his tower had to fall. Lord Mortriss and his Knights of Ruin had been wandering the Wastes so long in the service of Nurgle that they literally fell apart – rusted plate and bone – at the swing of Archaon's sword and the smash of his shield. The spindly sorcerer Zartas Uthezarn had impressed Archaon with his mastery of pink and blue flame that poured from horrific holes in his palms. Only days after Archaon recruited the Changer's servant to his cause, the sorcerer had been showered with infernal gifts and degenerated into a sickly spawn. Archaon might still have found use for the malformed horror but for the fact that Uthezarn, on some level truly knowing what he had become, set himself alight in a purple blaze.

There were others who travelled as part of Archaon's growing warband but did not prove to be up to the task. Slaug of the Twin-Axes went mad in the Shimmering Hills. One day his drool turned to froth and the Khornate warrior cut through Wernher Ichelheimer, Gismund the Mad, Durgrim Trollcleaver and his Longshanks before Archaon and his Swords could put him down. Archaon lost Nikitia Vang and her warriors of the Annointed to the decimation that was Ogvaldr the Aesling and his fiend-tempered sword *Snaga*. The dark templar lost his Bronze Company to the last man in his attempt to bring Ogvaldr to battle again in the great depression known as the *Odea-Ossis* or 'Arena of Bones'. By the time he met the Aeslinger's warband again it was a shadow of its former self. Many of his best had been immortalised in stone with a single glance of the cockatrice that haunted the Inconsolable Mountain. With some regret, Archaon ended Ogvaldr the Aesling on the Arga Floe and with even more watched the daemon blade *Snaga* lost to a bottomless crevasse in the ice. Archaon executed much of the dross that surrendered to him from the Ogvaldr's warband but took the scampering plague that was the giant rat-thing Stenomys. Even the monster proved more trouble than it was worth, the infestations making their home in its fur afflicting Archaon's Kvellig cult warriors. The hairless tribesmen and their shamans suffered a pox that turned them into a herd of shambling corpses that couldn't be shepherded and ultimately ended up walking into the Wastes in all directions.

The witch Grastlana le Faux had her uses. In unleashing her dark illusions to make Archaon's warband appear larger than it was at the time, she assisted the Chaos warrior in dissuading some of the Wastes' larger monstrosities from attacking them. Her spectral additions had also impressed the disdainful Prince Aleghast and his warrior-entourage enough to join the warband rather than fight Archaon for the blood-right to cross the Burning Bridge – the only crossing for hundreds of miles across the glowing channel of molten rock known as the River Sunder. Aleghast proved incapable of taking orders, and not long after Archaon allowed the prince and his entourage to be eaten by the Ravening – a nomadic band of barbaric Kurgans that worshipped, as an incarnation of Khorne, a huge ogre in Archaon's ranks called the Great Spleen. Grastlana le Faux herself had to be ended after Archaon discovered that she had been assuming the illusion of his form and issuing orders to his men that furthered the witch's own Tzeentchian undertakings.

The last of Archaon's failures to recruit able warriors to his growing host was Bhorgl the Obscene. Bhorgl – like his Prince of Pleasure worshipping warherd – was a beastman. He was a bald, fleshy thing of shaved fur, muscle, piercings, tattoos and looted jewellery. He came to Archaon willingly, professing with his thick goat's tongue that Slaanesh admired the beacon of pride and self-adulation that was the Chaos warrior Archaon. Archaon didn't believe the beast's praise and didn't like him either but had to admit that the extra muscle would be useful. Bhorgl proved popular in the warband. His brute warriors brought with them the secret of brewing fungus ale from the black mushrooms to be found about ruined buildings. A number of his warriors were also crude musicians, with their suggestive horn arrangements and rough voices. Their songs were coarse and invariably about relations with livestock.

While away with his Swords, reconnoitring a distant temple to some renegade god of the Chaos pantheon, an unnatural storm swept in that seemed to turn the world about, losing the dark templar and his warriors in the maelstrom. Archaon was unconcerned. He had left the warband with Iskavar Gan. Iskavar was a pale and capable Kurgan warrior, whose warband had been slain by Archaon's own. The Kurgan's spear arm had been something to behold, several of Archaon's warriors ending up with javelins through them from impossible distances away. Always dressed in the filth of furs and the spikes of his black armour and shield, the Kurgan had accepted a place at Archaon's side as a lieutenant. He was easy to like and used to show off his aim by launching javelins into the sky and spearing vultures as they circled. In the spirit of the evening, with the fire roaring, vermin crackling on the spit and drink being passed around, Iskavar Gan took of the potent ale.

As the storm intensified and the warband huddled about the fire, Bhorgl's musicians played. Meanwhile, their muscle-bound beastlord and two of his Slaaneshi gors found their way through the material of the wagon bonnet and inside, looking for what treasures of the Wastes and supplies Archaon secreted there. To his pleasure, Bhorgl the Obscene found Sister Giselle trying to sleep. His hoof falls on the wooden floor of the wagon had disturbed her. In truth, like everyone else in the Wastes, the girl barely slept at all and when she did it was with one eye open. Hieronymous Dagobert had been sheltering in the wagon also, studying *The Liber Caelestior* in the meagre light of a candle. Bhorgl the Obscene wasn't interested in ancient tomes. The beastman couldn't read anything beyond the fear in his victims' faces. Licking his thin lips with his thick tongue, Bhorgl instructed his gors to restrain the pair.

'What do you think you are doing?' the priest demanded, the gor manhandling him around. 'Gan!' Dagobert roared.

'Gan!' But Iskavar Gan wasn't coming. Any members of the wider warband that might have cared that an atrocity was about to take place in the wagon – and there were few – had their ears occupied with the roar of the fire, the storm and the cacophony of bestial pipehorns. Iskavar Gan, a canvas water satchel of ale lying empty beside him, was unconscious, like a wrestler out for the count.

Dagobert blustered his anger at the intrusion and hollow threats, while Giselle fought, her screams punctuated with vulgar insults. Bhorgl let slip a wet chuckle. There was the sudden glint of a thin, curved blade amongst the thrashing covers. Giselle always kept a surgical shiv – long stolen from the hospice wagon's depleted supplies – beneath her pillow. The girl hit out, passing the blade across the gor's pink throat. It split open like a ripe fruit. Giselle kicked the beast from the bunk. Clutching its gushing neck, it fell back out of the wagon. Giselle scrambled back against the wagon sideboards.

'Are we having fun yet?' the Sister of the Imperial Cross asked with a snarl, holding the razor-sharp shiv blade out before her. Bhorgl drew a bulbous billy club from his studded belt. It was the beast lord's weapon of choice for subduing his victims or rendering them unconscious.

'I've changed my mind,' Bhorgl told her. 'I won't touch your flesh.'

'You'd better believe it, milksop,' Giselle taunted, waving the scalpel.

'Your flesh shall touch the inside of my gullet as it goes down my throat,' Bhorgl promised. 'You'll still be alive, of course. Raw flesh tastes better off the bone. Warm and with screams.'

An armoured shape stepped up through the bonnet canvas behind Bhorgl the Obscene.

'I'll ask the Great Spleen and his Ravening horde,' Archaon said, snatching the billy club out of the Slaangor's fist and knocking him to the ground senseless with a single smash to the beastlord's horny skull. A bone sword slipped effortlessly through the wagon material and round in an arc, stopping just before the hairless throat of the gor pinning Father Dagobert to the bunk. The beastman glared its salacious hatred of Archaon. Eins came up behind his master. They were both frosted with the ash and ice of the tumultuous storm. 'Get their beast-compatriots. Take these reprobates out to whatever cave the Great Spleen has crawled into and feed them to Khorne's chosen. He'll like that.'

Archaon had the monster sleep away from their camp. The ogre was too dangerous to keep nearby. He might wake like a furious bear from hibernation and kill them all. His pilgrim-barbarians – the Kurgan degenerates that worshipped the Spleen as some representative of their god – slept like dogs nearby. Like the Great Spleen, it paid to keep the cannibals' bellies full.

As the Swords dragged the Slaangor away, it licked at Archaon with its fat tongue.

'Timely,' Father Dagobert said.

'We have you to thank for that,' Archaon told him. 'We were lost in the storm.'

'And?'

'You scream louder than she does, old man,' Archaon said. The priest raised his eyebrows and shrugged. When Archaon looked at Giselle, she still had the curved shiv pointed at them. Her eyes glistened with confusion and loathing. Eins moved in to take it from her. 'Leave it,' Archaon commanded. 'She's not a prisoner.'

'We're all prisoners in this place,' Giselle said.

It shocked Archaon. He hadn't heard her speak to him in a long time – and only then in hisses of hatred. Beneath the rags of her old order and the grime on her skin and in her tangled hair, she had grown up. Her voice had lost the annoying insistence of youth and ignorance. She was older and wiser. Her dread existence in the dark corners of the world had gifted her that at least. He found himself transfixed. She hurt to look upon. She had, impossibly, retained some essence of simple purity in the Wastes. Hiding in the wagon. Hiding beneath the blankets of her bunk. Exposing herself only to Dagobert's obsessions and growing insanity. It was an impressive achievement. She was something to be admired. Or destroyed. When she spoke again, the words, uttered with a savage belief, cut through him. 'A prison without walls. Serving a sentence without end. Shackled to your doom.'

'Leave…' Archaon said. His voice was but a whisper.

'I leave, I die,' Giselle said. 'Here, in the shadow of your great darkness – a warning to the terrible things of this place – my light at least shines on.'

'Your light…'

'My burning hatred for you, *my lord*,' Giselle said through clenched teeth. 'And I would not have it extinguished for all the world, you abomination. If here, in this enforced exile, this prison, this cell of shadow about you – if here is the only place I can abhor you then here I will be. Sigmar hears all prayers, even in this cursed place.'

Archaon nodded slowly. The God-King's name, said with such bitter reverence, stung his soul.

'But he does not answer them,' the Chaos warrior told her. Slipping the wavy blade of a kris dagger he had taken from the butchered body of a Khazag horse-chieftain from its sheath of petrified wood, Archaon tossed the blade onto Giselle's bunk. 'You need to defend yourself,' Archaon said. 'I can see that. I keep company with the damned and I won't always be there to protect you from them. Put your faith not in prayers to weakling gods. Put it – as I do – in cold steel. Put it in a will of the same, and have the courage to put the blade where it is most needed.' Archaon looked about the miserable interior of the wagon. 'Get some sleep.' With that the dark templar left.

But Giselle Dantziger couldn't sleep. She felt like she never slept. From the secluded cloisters of the Hammerfall, her life had now become a living nightmare. A nightmare from which she wanted to wake up. She saw *The Liber Caelestior* in Father Dagobert's sleeping embrace. She wondered if the tome held the secrets of what she planned to do next.

Such a notion took her out onto the freezing grit. The chill wind felt its way through her tattered robes like the hands of death. Above the sky was dark and heavy, although it was impossible to tell if it were truly night or not. Archaon's men were sleeping around the flames of the dying fire. Grunting through their own bad dreams. Snoring. Farting. She found one that was not. Iskavar Gan's hand reached out for her filthy skirt-tails. The Kurgan had been skewered into the ground on his own willowy javelins. Demotion, to be sure. Punishment for his lack of leadership, in the face of Bhorgl's little insurrection. Death with the coming dawn. Archaon liked the warrior, but as his lieutenant Iskavar Gan had failed him and an example had had to be made.

'Forgive…' the Chaos warrior said as the Sister of the Imperial Cross pulled her skirts from his bloody fingers.

Giselle tip-toed through the limbs of sleeping warriors and tribesmen, the cold and horror of the gloom beyond the fire's light requiring her to stay close. Who knew what daemon things lurked in the shadows beyond the fire, waiting to rend flesh and swallow souls. Beyond she could hear the Great Spleen, as the warband often did, disturbed from its hulking slumber by such a twilight fiend. She could imagine the bald, fat-bellied ogre snatching the devil from the shadows and smashing it with the Blood God's own wrath into the rocky landscape thereabouts – for the Great Spleen did not deign to use weapons beyond the huge hands that its god had gifted it with. The cannibal barbarians of the Ravening would eat well tonight, with both beastmen and daemonflesh in the offering.

Beyond the fire, Giselle found the mammoth-skin tent the Swords regularly had the warband's lesser servants erect for their master. Oberon stood nearby, nibbling at stunted black lichen and grasses that were trying to force their way up through the frozen soil. The stallion's flesh was matted with scars and fresh wounds. It should have died long ago but some infernal force kept it alive, serving its master. Archaon regularly had Dagobert stitch the horse's flesh, as he had the priest do with his own. Dagobert was a fumble-fingered seamstress but the ragged repairs were enough to close both the steed and its master up and allow their bodies to unnaturally heal.

At the entrance, the heavy hide of the malformed mammoth keeping the worst of the wind and cold out, the sister found Eins. The winged knight of Chaos stood impassive in its armour and skull helmet. It had its arms folded and regarded her with the silent menace of a vampire. Its bone swords were sheathed and its wings creaked as it spread them – blocking the girl's passage. The girl and the killer regarded one another.

'You are here for your master's protection,' Giselle told him. 'And you think he needs protecting from me?' The scorn of the girl's forced laughter had little effect on the Chaos knight. 'I think he might consider it an insult to suggest that the chosen of the Ruinous Powers would need such protection.' Giselle put up her hair, winding it into a messy bun, to demonstrate her true intentions to the deathly henchman. She steeled herself and reached out to touch the thing's black wing. Her intention was to move it aside, but Eins slowly retracted it from her reach, unwilling to let the Sister of the Imperial Cross scald it with her unpolluted touch. With that, Giselle pushed her way inside.

It was warm. There was a small fire, providing both heat and low light. Archaon's armour decorated a rack made from the skeletal frame of a withered and twisted shrub. His shield and the crusader sword *Terminus* sat there also, the Sigmarite blade shimmering in its afflicted agony. Spectral flame no longer danced across its comet-carved surface as it did when the dark templar held the weapon in his God-King hating hands. Archaon was wrapped in a mound of furs by the fire. Giselle approached. She felt not quite in charge of her own movements. She knelt. She drew the Khazag kris from its petrified scabbard and held it over the mound. The blade glimmered in the light from the fire, trembling in the girl's grip. The sister held her breath. Time and again she tried to force it down. Again and again the serpentine blade stopped at dimpling the furs. She exhaled with the effort and slammed the knife down beside the sleeping Chaos warrior.

'What am I doing?' Giselle hissed to herself. 'What am I becoming? Blessed Sigmar forgive. I don't know what is happening to me.'

Leaving the blade warming by the fire, she pulled the layers of furs aside to join Archaon beneath them. She found only more furs.

'Have you come to return that to me?'

Archaon's voice was everywhere. Giselle turned. She squinted. He was kneeling in the shadows of the tent, beyond the fire, where Giselle's eyes struggled to acquire him. 'Perhaps to slide it into my heart?'

Giselle turned, fearful. Her fingers slid down the furs and back towards the kris. Archaon reared to his full height in the murk of the tent. He was all doom-laden melancholy and physical prowess. He wore only his eye-patch. The dark templar's flesh was both ugly and impressive. Horrific bruising. Patchworks of old scars. Fresh wounds – some stitched, some cauterised, some yet to be dressed. A black web of corruption reaching out from his ruined eye in the eight-pointed star of his Dark Gods, running beneath the flesh of his face like some savage's tattoo. 'Why are you here, girl?' Archaon asked. 'To kiss me, or kill me?'

Giselle's anger and disgust returned to her in a cold rush. Archaon was so ghoulishly confident. Like everything else, she hated him for it.

'I've come to save you,' the Sister of the Imperial Cross said.

'I thought that was Father Dagobert's hope.'

'It is a shared honour, my lord.'

'My lord?' Archaon marvelled. 'Not Ruinous dog? Son of the Dark Gods? Scum of all the world?'

'Can a man not be more than one thing at once, master?' Giselle said.

The knight allowed himself a cruel chuckle.

'Pray what have you come to save me from?'

'Why yourself, of course,' the girl told him. 'And the world from the plague that is both of you.'

Archaon smiled. 'Go ahead, girl... Save me.'

The taunt was too much for the sister. The Khazag knife was in her hand. She pushed herself up at him, the slight weight of her malnourished body behind the tip of the blade. Archaon was predictably fast. Killers of all breeds of darkness tried to destroy him every day. His reflexes came from some unearthly place and the strength in his hands and arms was like cold iron. He brought around his hand and snatched the girl's wrist from between them. The blazing manoeuvre was shocking enough but Giselle let out a half-scream as Archaon came at her. He followed with some kind of combat roll, a choreographed tumble that took him over her and then she over him, the kris held between them. Giselle ended up in the furs, Archaon on top of her, both her wrist and the knife pinned above her head.

'Save me!' Archaon roared. The rawness of the command echoed about Giselle's heart. It was daring, barbed and bombastic in delivery – but behind the volume was a desperation. A pleading behind the words. An inviting vulnerability in the trailing last syllable. She felt Archaon's grip tighten about her wrist. Giselle got her fingers to the messy bun she had tied in her hair outside the tent. There she had secreted the surgical shiv she had used to slice the beastmen open. Within moments it was out and clutched in her white-knuckled fist.

She stabbed at Archaon's snarling face. The razor tip of the blade shot for the knight's good eye. For that second, the darkness of Archaon's eye became her world. The play of pupil and the beautiful colours about it, tinged to an unnatural hue. She saw the momentary surprise – the fear even. Then a terrifying acceptance. He said nothing. The searing intensity of his gaze did all the talking. He invited her into the darkness. The shiv lurched forward. Giselle Dantziger would change the world in the God-King's name. She would slay the chosen of the Dark Gods. And he would let her.

But she faltered. The strength died in her arms. Like a fire doused, the struggle left her. With his hand about her wrist, the dark templar slowly moved the blade aside and pinned her to the furs. He burned into her with his gaze. The fight suddenly returned but she was only half there. She spat at the Chaos warrior and bit at his face like some wild animal. He kissed her back. The bloodshed of the Wastes, the laughter of the Dark Gods and the appetite for apocalypse were washed away. The immaculate fire that burned on his lips and in his chest could not be ignored. Archaon's heart felt as if it were broiling in his own blood. It thumped against the inside of his ribcage, slowing. Slowing. Searing to a stop.

He pulled his lips from Giselle's. The dark templar's face was strained with a panic he had not known for a long time. A bugle horn that drowned out his racing thoughts and sounded the end of Archaon. The blood settled in his veins. His lips stung. His heart felt fit to burst.

Giselle squealed as Archaon's fists squeezed about her wrists, threatening to pulverise the bones in each. The kris knife and shiv tumbled from her grip and fell down the side of the furs. Archaon released her, grabbing at her ragged robes and tearing them. There, around her neck, Archaon found it. On a tarnished chain, he found Sigmar's hammer. It was only half there, the silver bearing the harsh marks of a file – probably taken, like the surgical shank, from the hospice wagon's supplies. In the light and with the girl already covered in the grime of the Wastes, Archaon hadn't noticed. He stared down at her in disbelief. She had smeared the sacred silver on her lips. The sister just looked back through him, watching the warrior of Chaos die. There were no taunting words to be had. No death-bed threats. No recriminations. A silence racked Archaon's body.

The dark templar's face contorted about a snarl. He would not be purified. He would not be burned in the fires of his God-King foe. He would not allow the world to go on without him. He was the end of existence, not the other way around.

Giselle watched the agonising battle rage on in the knight.

To be. To not be. The dark templar's forehead glistened with cold sweat. The muscles in his face were taut to the point where the sister thought they might break it. He suddenly thrust his left shoulder at her, as though popping back in a dislocated arm. They both heard it. The distant thunder of Archaon's heart – willed back to beating. It thumped rhythmically and insistently between them.

A chill terror crept through Giselle. She had tried to kill Archaon – chosen of the Chaos gods – and failed. She had tried to save him but instead had damned herself. She could not quite imagine what horrors awaited her. She lay there then, in the furs, expecting vengeance to come… but it did not. Archaon faltered. The presence of the God-King within him had weakened the Chaos warrior. He lowered himself slowly and lay his head against her chest. The pair lay there for a long time, the fire crackling beside them and the winds of the Wastes battering the heavy hide of the tent. Archaon held her. To the sister's surprise, she held him back. She felt his breathing slow. Archaon was asleep. As she drifted into oblivion herself – for the first time in a long time – Giselle Dantziger's thoughts were not on murder. She dreamed not of death, but of life. Of hope in the darkness. Of a fool's paradise in the hearts of doomed men. A place where the dying fire of noble gods might be stoked once again.

CHAPTER XII

*'Khaela Mensha Khaine, for hate's sake,
hear our petition – as blood answers
the throat slit. Keep the hearts of the
druchii cold and bitter, wherein the
murderous will of our survivor-civilisation
be preserved for all eternity. Bring death,
just and swift, to the weak. Daub the
revenger's blade with the blood of enemies
old. Watch over the inconstant north.
Grant the wild men and their wilderness
your darkness. Let blade and bolt bring
sacrifice to your altar. Bless the druchii,
ever your acolytes and assassins, with
murder in your name and victories as
certain as spite.'*

– Hellebron, the Hag Queen of Har Ganeth,
The Pact of the Pitiless

Eisarnagga Glacier
The Watchlands of Naggaroth
The Soul Harvest – First Blood (Druchii Remembrance)

The will of the Dark Gods took Archaon west. It did not matter that west was the direction the dark templar had chosen for himself – he was the chosen of the Ruinous Gods in all but name and a regular doom would not do for him. While other warriors and chieftains stumbled onwards into their doom, the incomprehension and darkness of the continent interior waiting for them, Archaon was reserved a greater fate. He would not be showered with gifts that ushered others through greatness and on into spawndom because he asked for none. He would not be a simple pleasure. A mind lost. A bloody fate. A soul to be played with. He would not be a pawn moving through a perpetual war or a player in a never-ending round of gladiatorial games. Not even for the gods' entertainment. Archaon's will burned bright in the maelstrom and like a gratification denied or a tasty morsel on the plate left for last, his journey would be savoured.

By the time he passed over the Anvil of the Gods, where dark heroes were forged and the mountainous ridges of Damnation's Teeth and the Arkhang Peaks fought for supremacy of the skies, Archaon commanded a considerable force. With a mighty army made up of champions of the Chaos gods, glory-hungry warriors, amalgamated warbands and tribesmen of the infernal north, Archaon crossed the impossibilities of the Abyssal Plain. He tested the mettle of his men at the great gathering known only as the *Wars of Omission* – fought between and within the colossal black walls of star-shaped ziggurats that pervaded the land and towered over the blood-soaked earth of the Wastes. His host was nearly burned alive in the deep freeze of the Kankgari Basin before facing the Golden Horde of the savage Chi-An, the Serpent Cults of the Tu-Kara and the fleshless warlords of the marauder Yin.

All Archaon did was give battle to the lesser existences of

the world – either as general or blade to bloodied blade – or sleep. He gave his everything to fighting his way across the warping landscape of the Wastes. When you knew not where you were, when you knew not the time of day – let alone the week, month or year – progress was everything. Archaon fought on. The madness of the Shadowlands was his mentor, and the murderous intentions of his myriad enemies his teachers. He learned much of combat and of death. As the knight of a weakling god, decked in protective plate, he was an expert with broadsword and shield, on horseback or face to faceplate. In the Wastes he had come to understand the limitations of such strength, such technique and practice. He learned more than he could have imagined in the Wastes – because he had to. He had learned to be deadly with bow and crossbow, and a confident thrower of javelin and spear. He made it his goal to become proficient with every exotic weapon used in failed attempts to end him and acquired the speed and agility necessary to evade attacks rather than trust their failure to his plate and shield. *Terminus* was his constant and tortured companion, but Archaon learned new ways to wield the weapon, unthinkable techniques and handling learned from the barbarian Kurgan, the warrior Hung and damned companions of the elder races.

Archaon even learned how to kill and defend himself without weapons – with the hand and mind, learning both eastern secrets of empty-handed death and manipulation of the strange energies of the Wastes about him in the form of basic wards and protections. He learned how to slay with effortless proficiency, not just the vulgarities of decapitation, the removal of limbs or the stabbing butchery he had acquired in the knightly orders. He came to know the precise vulnerabilities of man, his bestial aberration, the warriors of other races, the monster and the daemon.

When exhaustion or injury finally sent him to his bed his sleep was fitful and feverish. His flesh would roast or it would cool to ice. He would sometimes be out for days or on other occasions wake with a terrified roar, disturbing Giselle as she nestled next to him or others from their own nightmares about the camp. It was not unusual. In the Wastes – so close to the infernal darkness of the world – all dreamt of the dread things trying to find their way into their consciousness and feast on their souls.

For Archaon the nightmare was even more intense and had become increasingly so as they worked their way west. It wasn't a dream or some fanciful notion of vulnerability. It wasn't the work of a sorcerer or infernal servant of the Chaos Powers. It wasn't even the darkness that he had always carried, bubbling below the surface of his understanding. It wasn't subtle. It wasn't the exploratory thoughts of a dark intelligence. It was powerful. Overwhelming. It was something else. Something predatory was stalking his soul. Something unimaginably ancient. A thing of bottomless evil. Dead of colossal heart. Thunderous in the world-trembling rumble of an infernal throat. A thing of savage nature, at war with itself. Churning with change, yet always the same. Both sensing and insensible. Its presence seemed to press up against his own. Horribly, Archaon found himself within the monstrosity's consciousness as much as it had crashed through his own. It was always the same. He was trapped in something dangerous and alien. A womb-like darkness, like an abyss. The infernal fog that made him gag. The sensation of inhabiting a mind savage and primordial, warped to bestial distraction. The hiss of lethal things unseen, hunting him like murderous thoughts through the darkness. Sometimes they would find him and Archaon would roar himself conscious. At other times they would stalk him for days, through a clammy feverishness from which the Chaos warrior could not wake. The horrors of the Wastes, of malformed men, of monsters and daemons held little dread for Archaon compared with the thing waiting for him behind the patch and closing lid of his eyes.

Archaon woke. He breathed in sharply. He blinked the darkness from his eyes. The thud of a monstrous heartbeat faded to nothing and the rasp and rattle of his dark prison bled away. He was cool and clammy, despite the warmth of the fire in the tent. Dogs were barking.

'You were dreaming,' Giselle said. The girl was sitting at a makeshift table beyond the fire, wrapped in a fur. As usual, she couldn't look at him. The Sister of the Imperial Cross wore a mask of disgust and self-reproach. 'Making strange noises.'

'How long was I asleep?' Archaon asked.

'About a day,' Giselle said. 'Who can say out here?'

Archaon felt his neck. It was wet. There was blood from a tiny nick across his throat. He stood and walked about the fire.

'You tried again,' Archaon said. Giselle still had her kris in her hand. She was picking a symbol into the rough wood of the table. A twin-tailed comet. The comet heralding Sigmar's birth. Archaon bridled. The engraving sent a ghastly shiver through him.

'Tried,' the Sister of the Imperial Cross said. 'Failed.'

He reached for Giselle's chin, moving it up with his finger. She looked at him for a moment and then away. Lust – love even – drained from her face. Archaon was the doom of the entire world. His gaze seared with dark destinies to come. He would raze ancient lands. His hands would drip with the blood of entire races. He would drive gods to extinction. He was entrancing… and abhorrent. Giselle couldn't look at him. Archaon pushed her chin up. What remained of her hammer of Sigmar dangled about her neck. Archaon found himself forming a snarl at the sacred object. Above the chain, however – just like those across his own throat – the Chaos warrior found the nicks and slices of a blade danced lightly across the flesh.

'You tried again,' Archaon said, almost to himself. It was a little routine the pair had grown accustomed to. Now and then the girl would try to end the man whose fate it was to end everything else. Predictably, she failed and failure drove her to consider taking her own life. The fire and obstinacy of her youth had not quite abandoned her, however, and at the last moment – the moment before the kris did its worst – Giselle found the crestfallen strength to draw the blade from where it had sliced at her soft skin. Archaon knelt before her.

'Your God-King does this to you,' the dark templar said. 'You feel the hopelessness of his failure. Abandon him as he has abandoned you.'

'And pray to your dread gods?' Giselle said, glassy-eyed.

'No,' Archaon said. 'For I have none. Let the powers of darkness favour me if they will. Let them lend me their strength and draw strength from my victories, if that is their want. You will not see me kneel to them even as I kneel before you now. All gods are fickle. Don't trust in them. I don't. Believe as much as you need to or not at all. Ultimately, the only thing you can really believe in is yourself.'

'You serve the Chaos gods…'

'They serve themselves,' Archaon said. 'As do I. This world is not fit for man or god. The Empire and nations of old, the exotic lands beyond and even here – the cruel Wastes. All will fall and all will burn for me. I will be the Lord of the End Times. The harbinger of doom for all – man and god – for in a world of the slain, with no men, no savages, no ancients of the elder races to pray to them and erect their temples, what will become of these gods, their heroes and their daemons?'

Archaon saw Giselle nod, even if it was just a little. Archaon stood, grabbing the furs about the girl and drawing her to him. They kissed. It was gentle. Tender even. Then he pushed her, spinning her naked form out of the furs and back onto the bed. The playful movement drew from Giselle a laugh. It was stifled and forlorn but it was the first time he had heard honest joy from the girl's lips. In a world of vile threats, screams and thunder, it was pleasing to the ear. For a moment the pair of them could have been young lovers, a servant girl and a farm hand kissing in a barn or a woodcutter and his wife, enjoying a simple life of contentment. As Archaon gathered the furs about him, Giselle's laughter died and her smile faded. They were not young lovers or enjoyers of a simple life. They were the unimaginable horror such people feared. They were the end to such life. They were death to warmth, affection and love – the very things other people lived for.

Giselle's blood ran cold. Her heart felt like stone. She started to say something to Archaon, but the dark templar was gone.

Outside, it was brighter than usual. Archaon's army had been making their way south for weeks and the Chaos warrior had started to feel the intensity of the continent's dark interior ebb away. It took a moment for Archaon's eyes to adjust to the dazzle off the ice. The army was camped out on the Eisarnagga Glacier – an ice floe meandering out of the twisted landscape of the Wastes, reaching down into the northernmost watchlands of Naggaroth. Here the druchii – or dark elves, as those who lived through the misfortune of meeting their kind had described them – defended their malicious lands with a continent-spanning line of sky-piercing watchtowers. A day did not pass without a madman, warband or marauder tribe testing the unbreakable resolve of the elves. The druchii lived for murder, however. They were organised, fortified and unimpressed by the horrors that came out of the north. Not even the most determined of Chaos incursions – with the mountains of iron and spite awash with Ruinous degenerates – had succeeded in any lasting invasion of the Land of Chill. The curdled spirit of the dark elves and their twisted witch-masters would not allow it.

Fortunately for Archaon, he did not need to conquer Naggaroth – at least not yet, nor with the army under his present command. The dark elves' time would come. With half the world aflame and with Archaon commanding the legions of evil, the druchii lands would fall as all were destined to do. But not today. Today an excursion into their frosted realm was required rather than an incursion to conquer it.

Archaon's tents – shelters of shaggy mammoth tusk and hide – were mobile and set on a wooden platform. The platform sat on a set of carved wooden blades, like a sled or sleigh that cut through the ice and was dragged by a team of black woolly rhinox. The tents incorporated a number of chambers, including the general's own quarters, those belonging to Giselle and Father Dagobert respectively, a tusk-arched stable for Archaon's steed Oberon and a tabernacle for the gathering of his warlords. The tabernacle also included a small shrine to the Ruinous Star, though the dark templar didn't care for it, preferring to appease the daemon deities of the Wastes only when he had to and through the spilling of enemy blood.

The dogs were barking. Nearby Escoffier was feeding his hounds. The mad Bretonnian had a sack full of bones, the carcass of some beast he had murdered in the night. Escoffier kept the swarming pack of warhounds ravenous on purpose. He had no idea when Archaon would call on him and his emaciated monsters. He kept them ever hungry. Ever ready to tear Archaon's enemies – and sometimes his wayward allies – apart, at the warlord's command. Buried in a shaggy mound of flea-infested dog skins, which kept the cold from the Bretonnian's own bones, Escoffier moved through the pack. The skinny beasts were all claw, drawn lips and dribbling jaws and the packmaster had to beat them back with the bones with which he was feeding them. The dogs were noisy but Archaon had instructed Escoffier to stake them out close to his tent. More than once the hackle and snap of the voracious hounds had warned the Chaos warlord of uninvited visitors approaching the tent.

Archaon already had protection, however. Turning he saw Zwei and Drei, perched up amongst the tusk-tips of the shaggy hide tents like a pair of black raptors, stretching their wings and keeping watch over their master while he had slept. Fitch, a hunchbacked thing, spindled of limb, served both as skinner for the rhinox-train and ostler for beasts of burden, including Oberon. Having just milked the shaggy beast-cows and returning with a bucket of suspect-smelling produce, Fitch splashed the liquid into a wooden cup for Archaon.

'Master,' Fitch said, his eyes averted and head low. He extended his long arm and offered the cup to the Chaos warrior. Archaon took the drink, allowing Fitch to withdraw from his presence and go about his business with the wretched, whip-mauled animals. Archaon went to drink the milk but his nose told him that there was something wrong with it and he tossed it out onto the ice and slush. His army was camped about the shelter. As a pair of warriors in fur and spike walked by, they noticed their warlord standing at the bone rail that ran around the tabernacle platform.

They lowered their horned helms before walking on. This was more out of animal subservience than military etiquette. Archaon was a warlord of the north, a leader amongst leaders, a general of a sizeable Chaos host. He did not waste his time with drills or formalised expectations. His army was not a state troop of the Empire or even a free company of irregular militia. They were savages, maniacs and madmen. The vast majority of them amounted to little more than rabid dogs. You did not harness such strength with uniforms and codes of conduct. You put them on chains and released them when you needed to. Since chains themselves were impractical, warbands and tribesmen were kept in line by their own chosen and chieftains, some of whom Archaon controlled by adopting them as his lieutenants. Others served the Chaos warrior purely out of fearful respect. They were drawn to his singularity of purpose and the ruthlessness with which he prosecuted his will. He claimed to be the chosen of the Dark Gods and acted like it. The damned were lost and always looking for powerful forces to guide and orient themselves to in the insanity of the Wastes – and Archaon was indeed a powerful force. He had confidence and direction and these were all lesser men who needed to make the leap of faith necessary to join Archaon in his doomed quest.

There were, of course, some of Archaon's warriors that actually did require chains. The dark templar could see the Great Spleen like a small mountain of flesh, out on the floe, a little way distant of the camp. The gore-drenched ogre was a chosen of Khorne, an almost unstoppable bloody avalanche of bone-breaking destruction. He was staked out on four colossal chains that he barely noticed on account of the crushed flowers that were rubbed into the links and which acted as a soporific. Archaon's army had fallen foul of the strange flowers in an otherwise bleak, bone-filled basin that nearly claimed them. Many of Archaon's men had settled to sleep there amongst the skeletons of other unfortunates who had never woken. Before they had stumbled out of the depression, Archaon had ordered some of the flowers gathered, which then had been rubbed on the Great Spleen's restraints, in an effort to keep the frenzied brute from smashing through the camp. As it slept on the ice, the barbarous marauders known as the Ravening that followed in its huge footsteps and honoured the Great Spleen as a manifestation of the Blood God, conducted some primitive cannibal ceremony before the statuesque corpulence of the thing.

Corsair-Captain Vayne also favoured chains. Archaon had been searching for a champion from the south, a warrior that knew Naggaroth and could advise him on the enemy he would face. Vayne – as Archaon knew him – was a druchii slaver. A reaver, who while transporting a mysterious cargo for Morathi the Hag Queen across the Sea of Chaos, had lost both his floating fortress the *Citadel of Spite* and the cargo to an unnatural tempest. Washed up on the icy shore of the Wastes and guided by his witch lover Sularii, Vayne had taken the remainder of his corsair crew inland. His lover's visions of the mighty *Citadel of Spite* beached in the Shadowlands prompted Vayne to gather a small army of slaves. The Chaos god Slaanesh was merely toying with the sorceress, however, and the corsairs' wandering led them into the Prince of Pleasure's embrace.

Polluted, bereft of vessel, having lost the Hag Queen's mysterious prize and unable to return to their homelands, the druchii lovers had wandered the Wastes for the better part of two hundred years before Archaon found them and put the corsair-captain's Slaaneshi slave army and knowledge of Naggaroth to good use. Archaon could see Vayne's reaver-officers in their scale cloaks, walking up and down the lines of their slaves – desperate wretches, caught in the Wastes and shackled to the corsairs' colossal chain gang army. The Slaaneshi slaves were surprisingly little trouble under the expert thraldom of the druchii. What little food was allowed them was drugged to keep the dire creatures in a perverse state of shared delirium. With their irons loose and scavenged weapons handed out moments before battle, the slaves had little choice but to maintain formation and fight for their lives against the enemies of the corsair-captain and his witch lover.

Archaon's compact with the druchii pair was simple. Once the dark templar had done with the gathered depravity that made up his army, he had promised them as prisoners to Vayne and Sularii. Archaon didn't tell them that he expected the challenges with which he would present his host to fully decimate their number. The agreement was rendered further pointless by the fact that those necessary losses might very well include the dark elves themselves. Still, it was easier for both Vayne and Archaon to agree to such arrangement rather than have the inconvenience of killing one another in advance – and following the death of Iskavar Gan and the doomed attempts to replace him with Balduin the Blooded, the Chevalier Malraux, Xandressa Headtaker and Tangrul-Targ as the army's second-in-command, Vayne had made a capable and entertaining subordinate.

Archaon could not see Vayne and the sorceress Sularii amongst the druchii number. The dark templar finally spotted the dangerous pair approaching his tent, accompanied by an animated Father Dagobert, who was fingering through the pages of *The Liber Caelestior*. The three of them were matched in number by the Chaos knight Eins and his accompanying pair of winged Swords. Like a delegation they were making their way through the Tusker herd of the beastlord Gorghas Hornsqualor. Muscular and shaggy, Hornsqualor's beastmen were covered with fur of dour white, almost matching the ice of the glacier about them. Like the beastlord, the beastmen had each been blessed with a single horn, similar to a narwhal, making the herd appear grizzled, rearing unicorns.

From the slavers and beasts, Archaon's army spread out across the ice, enjoying the meagre comfort of small fires and the less-oppressive heavens. The largest contingent to have joined Archaon's army of Chaos was the celestial Hundun. Under their eastern warlord, Fengshen Ku, the Hundun marauder clan belonged to the Dreaded Wo tribe and were made up of mounted members of the respected sword clans and their retainers that formed hordes of pike-wielding supporters. With their black, lacquered armour, pairs of curved long swords and iron masks – forged in expressions of horror and dismay – Fengshen Ku and the sword clan of the Dreaded Wo were a dark and determined force. Archaon had been told by Vayne that the Hundun very much resembled the celestial warriors of the Dragon Kingdom, manning the empire-spanning wall of the Great Bastian, which kept the marauders of Chaos at bay.

Both Fengshen Ku and Gorghas Hornsqualor – in the latter's own primitive way – honoured the Chaos Powers equally, as Archaon professed to do. The army was infested with lone aspirants and Chaos warriors, claiming various infernal patrons and eager to prove themselves in the army of a Chaos general like Archaon. The daemonsmith Zorn and the dawi-zharr, called 'the Mechanicals', paid homage to their bull-headed Father in Darkness and the infernal entities by possessing the hellcannons *Tauriax* and *Wrath of Hashut*. The daemon Shzmodeous, who most of the time took the form of a living darkness, revered only itself. Beyond the Great Spleen, whose followers in the barbarian Ravening thought him the living embodiment of the Blood God and Dravik Vayne, who was firmly in the barbed clutches of the Prince of Pleasure, there were two others who had brought the worshippers of individual Ruinous Powers in any number under Archaon's leadership, in their own individual and disturbing ways.

The dark templar had found Mother Fecundus in the thawing mires of Al-Quagoon. The witch had given herself body and soul to the Plague Lord – or as she called her patron, Father Nurgle. Mother Fecundus was carried by her followers on a palanquin. She could not walk. She was too massive – a bloated breeder of men. Her palanquin was more of a birthing throne than a litter and from it her obscene, malformed body dropped large, writhing pupae. Mother Fecundus's army was made up of warriors birthed in this way, for like an insect queen, she only mothered males – a plague upon the world. Emerging from their disgusting cocoons, the fully-grown warriors had already received the blessings of their father in the form of chitinous plates that grew out of their bodies like armour. Many came forth too twisted for use but the vast majority of Mother Fecundus's plague of men took their place amongst the ranks of their dour brothers. Old souls taken by Father Nurgle and placed in rank new bodies.

No less disgusting were the Brothers Spasskov. Vladimir and Vladislav Spasskov had been aspiring ice mages in the court of Kattarin the Bloody. Eager to impress their Tsarina, the competitive desire of one brother to outdo the other took them further and further north, where the temperatures plummeted and the winds of Chaos that fuelled their enchantments were most powerful. Their rivalry took them into the Wastes, where finally the two brothers fought a terrible battle of hail and storm, cutting each other to shreds in a shard storm of ice. Attracted by the terrible war of enchantments, the Changer of Ways had the bloody blizzard reform and freeze. With a change in the weather, the patron-pleasing sculpture thawed and melted, to reveal that Tzeentch had cursed the rivals with a single body. The dark god had given Vladimir and Vladislav a leg each and both of their spell-casting arms, but their torsos and skulls had been fused back to back, to form a fraternal fusion of flesh, with twice the skill and power of a single sorcerer. This did not prevent the brothers trying to outcompete each other, using their powers, amongst other things, to craft the bodies of their enemies into god-pleasing spawn of ever-increasing horror and invention. Their macabre army of victims were called the Fleshstorm, an ever-changing scourge of spawn that could divide or join together like a single monstrosity.

Archaon cast his gaze across his Ruinous army of Chaos. They were battle-hardened by the butchery of the Wastes. They were harnessed in a single purpose and fearful of Archaon's wrath. They were assured that the dark templar was indeed chosen of the gods, needing to believe that their own path to immortality lay in his shadow. They were ready to be unleashed on the Land of Chill – as Archaon was ready, damnation-blessed by a bloody passage through the Wastes and the deaths of all foes that had put themselves between him and his objective. He had achieved the impossible in earning favour from the capricious Powers of the accursed north. It was time to demand their joint sponsorship. To yoke the dark pantheon to the unstoppable wagon train that was his destiny. Only the Everchosen of Chaos was granted the right to lead the infernal armies in their collective daemon glory across the burning surface of the world. Archaon had pledged on the blood in his veins and his empty soul that the title would be his. It was time to honour his gods in the passing of their perverse trials and tests. To collect the great treasures and artefacts of power that had marked his predecessors as Chaos-favoured of all. His search for such hidden treasures had driven Archaon, by force of will alone, to gather an army of the depraved and despoiling and mount an invasion of dread Naggaroth and the druchii lands of conquest.

'My lord,' Dagobert began, as the approaching group crunched up through the ice. 'I have great news. The Swords have located the resting place of the Altar of Ultimate Darkness. It was exactly where *The Liber Caelestior* said it would be.'

'And this surprised you, priest?' Archaon said with withering impatience. Dagobert was long used to such treatment from his Chaos overlord.

'It resides in a great war shrine to the south,' Dagobert

said. 'A dark citadel of black stone, towers tall and twisted architecture.'

'I will see the doom of our destination for myself,' the dark templar said, stepping down from the shelter and barefoot onto the ice. Pulling the furs of an all-encompassing cloak of shaggy mammoth hide about him, Archaon set off through the encampment. As he passed between the miserable fires his marauders, Chaos warriors and champions were warming themselves before, the considerable length of the furs trailed through the snow behind him. Many servants of evil rose in respect. Other warriors bowed. Some hammered fists into the Ruinous Star to be found in the madness of their tattoos, scarring or the inscriptions on their armour. Even the lowliest beastmen, slave or spawn acknowledged their general. The man in whose soul-crushing fist their fate resided. They snatched at the furs winding their way through the camp at his back and kissed them, they lowered their heads in primitive deference or simply withdrew before his glower like the beaten dogs they ultimately were.

'Master,' Dagobert continued behind him, 'the Dark Gods have truly favoured this venture.'

'Again,' Archaon growled, 'this surprises you?'

'This citadel is a blessing for both yourself and Corsair-Captain Vayne,' Dagobert informed him. Archaon slowed suspiciously. He turned to find Dravik Vayne smiling behind him. As usual the druchii was intoxicated on his favoured blood-mixed wine, some infusion, or a depraved and recent union. The sorceress Sularii was working her magic on him as Vayne and Archaon beheld one another, her tongue and a stream of indecent enchantments in his pointed ear.

'Service to the Dark Gods and their chosen should be blessing enough for the captain,' Archaon said dangerously. Dravik Vayne was easy to like. He was an incredibly useful lieutenant, the dark templar had to admit, and with his slick wit, intelligence and the convivial abandon of his leadership, always managed to keep the myriad factions of Archaon's army as one in the warlord's absence. He couldn't trust the druchii as far as he could spit, however.

'Why, Archaon,' Vayne slurred away blithely, 'whatever do you mean?' Sularii laughed at her lover's joke. Archaon gave his own savage smile. A warning before he turned and marched on through the encampment and across the open ice.

'Priest, an explanation – before I gut and bone this cur like a fish and feed him to his own slaves.'

'The citadel, my lord…'

'It's the *Citadel of Spite*,' Dravik Vayne interrupted. Archaon frowned.

'Your vessel?' the dark templar asked.

'The same,' Vayne insisted. 'The Prince of Excess has had his fill and has seen fit to return my *Spite* to me. Archaon, you must help me get it back.'

Archaon ignored the druchii and stomped on through the ice. The sorcerous twins, the Brothers Spasskov, were standing on the precipice of the ice. Each Tzeentchian brother held an identical staff of warped crystal, one tinged blue, the other pink. Beneath their feet, and under their elemental control, the Eisarnagga Glacier was growing. A moving wall of ice, it cracked, reached and froze its way south out of the Wastes. It shattered forests and pulverised rock beneath its accelerated and irresistible advance down through the dark valleys and evergreen expanse of Naggaroth. Using the sorcerer's ice magic had meant that Archaon's army had only needed to camp on the ice floe and allow a frozen tendril of the glacier to take them into enemy territory.

Archaon said nothing to the Chaos sorcerer. Both brothers had their eyes closed in concentration. Vayne shrugged Sularii off, allowing the sorceress to playfully hang her arms around the Brothers Spasskov with a mock pout instead. Vayne pointed the long nail of a slender finger. Some way distant, above the pinetops, between the crooked mountain peaks and through the winding valleys, Archaon could see a collection of jagged towers, lithe and leaning.

'There,' Vayne said. 'The *Spite*. My *Citadel of Spite*. I'd know those mast towers anywhere.'

'All right,' Archaon said. 'It's the *Spite*. What in the eight points is it doing here?'

'It was lost in a storm,' Vayne told him. 'Vast and unnatural, coming out of the north and across the Sea of Chaos. A storm that took my vessel.'

'And deposited it... here?'

The corsair-captain gave a pained smile. 'Come now, Archaon. The Chaos Powers are not without a sense of humour. You should know that better than anyone. Their nature is the very definition of irony.'

'While you wandered the timeless Wastes, looking for your floating fortress,' Archaon said, 'the Dark Gods had placed it here. In your ancestral homelands. In Naggaroth, where you were returning with your slaves and cargo.'

Vayne nodded. 'So it seems.'

'These beings we serve,' Archaon said, 'are truly twisted in their treatment of their subjects.'

'To Mathlann my course belonged, to Atharti my heart and to Khaine my soul,' Vayne admitted, taking a dusky bottle offered to him by Sularii and drinking deep. 'The Prince of Pleasure did not enjoy me until after I lost the *Spite*. Slaanesh saw me and like some trinket or bauble for sale, decided I must be his.'

'We may take more from them yet,' Archaon said, thinking of the End Times to come and the unforeseen consequences for all of the soul-trading gods of the world.

'What we should do is take the *Citadel of Spite* back,' Dravik Vayne said. 'Archaon, you must help me.'

'*Must* is not a word used to the chosen of the Ruinous Powers,' Archaon warned the dark elf.

'It is because you are the chosen, my lord,' Vayne said, such pleading an ill fit for his thin lips, 'that this is possible. Think, Archaon, my ship – but your flagship. Think what a glorious command she would make, bringing the wrath of the Dark Gods to the wine-dark seas. You have an army, chosen one – why not a floating fortress from which to plan and launch your reign of terror?'

Archaon considered. It was an appealing prospect but all too often the champions of Chaos lost their way to true greatness on side paths of distracting endeavours, calling to them like sirens on the breeze.

'You may lust for such glories, sybarite,' Archaon told him, 'but I live only for the treasure contained within your abominate vessel and the glory it may bring my cause. What was the nature of the cargo you were transporting for your Hag Queen?' Archaon looked from Vayne to his sorceress. The corsair-captain nodded.

'An archaeological find from the Wastes,' Sularii said. 'Recovered stone and architecture. A temple of some kind with a centrepiece.'

'A temple?' Archaon questioned her. She nodded.

'An altar?' Again the dark elf sorceress nodded.

'The gods are to be praised and cursed in equal measure. So it truly is here,' the dark templar said to himself.

'This is magnificent news, my lord,' Dagobert said. 'But I'm afraid that the Ruinous Powers have seen fit to set other obstacles before us for their entertainment.'

'Speak, priest.'

'The Swords report an engagement before the citadel of which you talk. A druchii warhost...'

'Likely the garrison of a local dreadlord or sorceress securing the polluted place,' Vayne offered.

'Or the Hag Queen's own spears, having claimed it for herself,' Sularii said.

'Some resistance was to be expected,'

'The Swords claim the druchii warhost to number in the thousands, lord,' Dagobert interjected. Archaon looked to Vayne, who shrugged.

'Either the Hag really wants your Ruinous treasure,' the dark elf said, 'or she wants to prevent others from claiming it.' Archaon's withering gaze didn't change. 'Really wants.' Vayne added with a smile. 'Plus, we have no idea how long it's been here. Time flows unnaturally in the Wastes.'

'That's not all, my lord,' Dagobert said. 'And you're not going to like it.'

'I already don't like what I'm hearing.'

'The Swords have sighted another force,' the priest said, 'coming out of the north-east. A force that currently lays siege to the druchii, the *Spite* war shrine and its contents.'

'Not...'

'Servants of the Gorequeen, my lord – and her monstrous consort, the Blood God himself.'

'Gorath...'

'And his Bloodsworn, master,' Dagobert said. A snarl crept across Archaon's face.

'Curse the gods for their childish games,' the dark templar said, 'their confluences and coincidences.'

Even Dravik Vayne didn't offer some blithe joke or doom-laden encouragement. The druchii out in force was understandable, expected even. Dark elves would have been assigned to cordon off and isolate the tainted fortress. Shields and spears in even greater number would have been sent from watchtowers to the east, west and those residing in the country. The Hag Queen's witch covens would certainly have seen the coming of Gorath's incursion into the Lands of Chill. Gorath the Ravager. Gorath the Decimate. Gorath the Slayer-Son of Valkia, daemon princess of Khorne. Gorath of the Skull Mountain. A knight like Archaon, of some foreign land and forgotten god. His star would have burned bright on the horizon. A warrior of Khorne without equal. A killer of legendary prowess in the Wastes. A lord of cold fury.

'His head shall be yours,' Vayne pledged solemnly.

'Or ours his,' Dagobert replied. 'More skulls for his mountain.'

The priest and the Champion of the Prince of Pleasure began to argue but Archaon silenced them with a hand. Dagobert was right. Archaon had faced Gorath and his army of Bloodsworn knights several times in the Shadowlands. The knight was an imposing sight in the red of his bronze, baroque armour. Not that Archaon would have known it was the Ravager. His knights were all armed and armoured the same. In their murderous wake, the Bloodsworn attracted all manner of gore-praising deviancy. Berserker Norscans. Shadowland savages. Bestial dog soldiers and their flesh-rending hounds. Daemon slayers. Each time the dark templar's warband had met the Bloodsworn in battle, Archaon's warriors had been forced to withdraw, savaged and broken by the Ravager and the implacable advance of his knights. Some claimed that they were not men at all, but things of infernal construction. That they were built of daemon-brass in the Blood God's forge. An army of clockwork knights – bronze warriors of cog and steam. Impassive. Unstoppable. Unbreakable. They would fight all day and all night in Gorath's name, as Gorath did in turn for his Blood God.

Archaon was silent for a moment. There had been others. Other champions of Chaos. Other chosen. Morbius the Unliving at the head of a thousand corpse-warriors that Nurgle had blessed with a diseased kind of life. Goldemar the Great. Theoderic Rageblade. The Newfangled. Kudren Drax, warlord of the north. Chosen of the gods. Favoured of the Ruinous Star. Those who would be Everchosen of Chaos. All had fallen before Archaon's blade. Gorath was different. Archaon was a legendary warrior. A strategist. A leader of dark and depraved men. He was admired by the dread pantheon for his ingenuity, his singularity of purpose and his many gifts. Gorath had but one gift. The ending of life. He was the blood-blessed chosen of Khorne. Archaon had barely escaped with his life and the remnants of a warband the last time they met. And the time before that. If their clashes had taught Archaon anything, it was that of all the dread warriors of the Wastes, it was the Gorequeen's champion that would probably end up standing over his corpse.

'I can't beat him... can I?' Archaon said. Vayne and Dagobert left the question hanging in the chill air. No one would dare tell Archaon what he could and could not do. Neither did the pair rush to foolish affirmations of a doomed battle with the Bloodsworn. Archaon hadn't been the only one to barely escape with his life. 'Dagobert?'

'My lord,' the priest said. 'The Ravager is of the Gorequeen's daemon blood. Khorne's chosen in these mighty affairs. Gorath and his Bloodsworn are here in the Land of Chill for one reason. They have been guided here by destiny – or some ill force – as we have. He means to claim the terrible treasure contained within the Altar of Ultimate Darkness. He means to usurp your fate, master. He means to become the Everchosen of the Chaos Powers.'

Sularii moved round behind Archaon and draped herself across his muscular shoulders. She nibbled at his ear and allowed her thin fingers to drift down across his chest.

'Archaon is the greatest champion the Wastes have ever produced,' the sorceress said playfully. 'That Gorath could kill us all in his sleep doesn't change that fact. If the Blood God's followers were truly unbeatable then the lands would already be theirs. Killing is undeniably Gorath's strength but that doesn't mean that he is without weaknesses. We have to find them and exploit them. What say you, my lord?'

Archaon looked out across the peaks and the twisted treetops to the crooked towers of the black citadel, Vayne's *Spite*. He thought of the death waiting for them in the valleys below. The armies of the Hag Queen securing their prize. The Gorequeen-favoured Gorath and his mechanical slayers. The horrors and trials of darkness waiting for him in the citadel itself. He thought on his own small army. His rising star about to be extinguished in an ocean of blood. That would not happen. He wouldn't allow it.

Sularii's hand dipped down through the furs, trailing down the scars on Archaon's chest. He grabbed the slender hand in his crushing grip and removed it from his flesh. He heard Sularii moan slightly. Archaon looked at the Slaaneshi's sorcerous hand. He stared down at the glacier ice that burned beneath his bare feet. And it came to him. A chuckle built deep within him, finding expression in a mirth that seemed to ill fit the certain death they were facing.

'My lord?' Dagobert asked. Vayne allowed himself a smirk of contagious madness. The Brothers Spasskov continued their mumbling incantations. The Swords – as usual – said nothing. Archaon shrugged Sularii from his shoulders and turned, marching back up through the ice and towards the camp.

'Ready our forces,' Archaon said. 'Get the army off the glacier and into the mountains. We shall attack both the druchii and the Bloodsworn from the forests on the higher ground.'

As the warlord walked away, Vayne looked to Dagobert.

'The Hag Queen's warriors will mount a determined defence,' the dark elf said. 'The Bloodsworn won't stop until they have their mountain of skulls. I hope he has more of a plan than attack from the high ground.'

Dagobert looked thoughtfully after his master.

'You cannot command the legions through bloodlust alone,' the priest said. 'That is why Gorath the Ravager will never become the Everchosen of Chaos. Such a title belongs to a man who is a living contradiction of both the strengths and weaknesses of the Ruinous Powers. Our master is such a man. Trust in that, druchii savage. You shall have your dread vessel and Archaon shall have his prize.'

'How can you know?' Dravik Vayne said. 'What does your tome say, priest?'

Dagobert hugged *The Celestine Book of Divination* to his belly. Dravik could see the insanity in the priest's eyes.

'It says that sometimes you just have to have faith.' With that, Hieronymous Dagobert turned in the slush and followed his master.

CHAPTER XIII

'All praise to the screaming darkness of the world
Receive these untimely ends as dread offering
May their blood-glory bring you calamitous concord
May their screams carry your names into forever
May their spirits lend you terrible strength
Bestow on this reaper of souls your dark blessings
Let him bear the Mark that burns eternal
And in him see the Ruinous wonder of the world'.

– Inscription, 'Ara Ultimesh Noxa'
(The Altar of Ultimate Darkness)

The Iron Mountains
The Watchlands of Naggaroth
The Soul Harvest – First Blood (Druchii Remembrance)

The battle was difficult to watch. Bringing his army down through the rust-tinged peaks of the Iron Mountains and the dark forests of twisted fir and pine, Archaon had his men observe the slaughter from the highlands. Over the jagged treetops, Archaon and his horsemen, his marauders, his monsters and slaves to darkness, waited in silence. Their warlord was in the saddle and silent. His Swords, his chieftains and champions remained the same, drawing from the army a dark calmness. Among their ranks there was dread, there was envy, there was mindless need. Archaon and his army watched as blood was spilt and man, elf and infernal machine died.

The druchii were savage warriors indeed. They were ice and they were fire. Their ranks were cold, determined and disciplined in the execution of their duties, while murderous glee danced across their faces as they licked their thin lips in the delicious taking of life. Stunted watchtowers – nowhere near the size of the skygrazers on the northern borders – had been constructed about the tainted citadel. They bore bulbous keeps in their tower-tops that glowed with a ghastly light like spectral lighthouses. The elegant parapets swarmed with rotations of druchii crossbows and bristled with bolt throwers that peeped over the jagged crenellations. Between the tower perimeters, formations of dark elves held their ground with beautiful choreography, locking their longshields for the enemy's impact before sliding their serrated spears over the top and into the opposing lines. Up to their boots in northern savages and berserker blood, the Hag Queen's murderers clearly took pleasure in their work but never did they lose themselves in the bloody moment, break formation or push on into the valley to build on their success. When their dreadlords called them back to their lines, the dark elves retreated, the plates of their slender armour rattling rhythmically with their return.

Archaon watched as black clouds of bolts drifted across the battlefield, cutting through Gorath's red-skinned beasts and dog soldiers. Small groups of swordsmen ran through the carnage with the grace of acrobats, finishing tribesmen and Khornate marauders with economical butchery. They then withdrew before the streaking death of tower-shot spears and the dark energies unleashed by the druchii witches. The flanks of the Ravager's army were savaged by dark elf riders, slashing through tribal horsemen with their serrated blades. Their cold-blooded, scaly steeds bounded up the lines on powerful legs, their tails stiff like rudders, guiding their fore-talons and jaws through the delicious horseflesh of the Khornate cavalry.

All the while the *Citadel of Spite* towered above the battlefield like a bad dream. Beyond the citadel towers of black stone and metal from which Dravik Vayne's corsair colours still flew like shredded rags, willowy mast-towers bore yards and furled black, leathery sails in great lateen configurations. Like much of druchii architectural deviancy, the fortress was both imposing and elegant – a midnight study in svelte stone fortification, storm-harnessing sailcraft and the macabre. Its stern was a mighty portcullis, while its prow was the tapering black skull of some twisted, abyssal behemoth. Like a talon, the *Spite's* cluster of towers seemed to reach out of a cragged berg of obsidian that was buried in the valley floor like a keel or colossal flint spear-tip. The rock was dangling with dead weed and riddled with caves, hollows and grottos.

The druchii were defending well. The dark garrison was drilled to perfection and their safeguarding of the Ruinous citadel, warped and tainted by its time spent in the stormy Wastes and on the Chaos seas, looked likely to hold. It seemed likely the *Spite* would remain in the Hag Queen's possession. As well as the willowy field pieces mounted on the sentry towers, the druchii had positioned deadly bolt throwers in the treelines. Gorath's approach had been direct, bold and merciless – as befitting a champion of the Blood God. His forces had ripped up the valley like an elemental force and had crashed straight into the dark elf defences. The druchii had positioned bolt throwers in the evergreen woodland growing out of the steep valley sides, and they were slamming spears into the marauder host's withering flanks. Archaon couldn't see them but druchii scouts were also amongst the trees, giving the thrower crews cover and cutting down axemen, enraged beasts and both Bloodsworn riders and their gore-splattered mounts as they attempted to rush the ballistas.

Leading his horde from the west, down the valley side and through the bleak woodland, Archaon knew that he too would have to face the same druchii defences. He had little desire to aid Gorath's assault but it would take nothing for the bolt throwers to turn back into the forest and skewer Archaon's men. Similarly, the dark elf scouts would cut his advancing forces to shreds with repeaters fired from their hiding places. This, Archaon could not allow. Signalling Escoffier, the mad Bretonnian, Archaon ordered his warhounds released. The mangy pack of whippets tore away from their chains, their skeletal frames and hunger carrying their throat-tearing maws through the forest at a scrabbling weave. Archaon waited. The warlord listened. Then he heard it. The shrill screams of elves being savaged and torn on the treeline below. He heard the carnage of the bolt throwers slow as their crews fought off the mindless beasts. For the druchii scouts there would be no hiding from the blood-hungry hounds. They would be torn from their crooks and hollows and ripped apart by the frenzied pack.

Fengshen Ku trotted forward on his steed. Archaon nodded to the marauder lord. Digging his leather boots into the horse's sides, the Hundun warlord led his mounted sword clansmen down the valleyside after the hounds. Retainers and pikemen of the Dreaded Wo followed on foot. It was the easterner's honour to finish what the hounds had begun. The throats of surviving druchii scouts and ballista crews were destined for the marauders' curved blades.

Undoubtedly the relief offered to the Bloodsworn's western flank would provide them with an advantage. Gorath wouldn't need it. Archaon had seen the Ravager at work before. He had suffered it before. Gorath the Ravager was a merciless servant of the Blood God. He thought little of the souls he sacrificed in the name of achieving his deity's dark will. Blood-blessed beastmen, Shadowland savages and Norscan berserkers were nothing to him. He granted them the mindless end they deserved. They slaughtered and were slaughtered in Khorne's booming name. Their skulls joined those of their victims on Gorath's growing mountain.

The dark elves enjoyed the distraction of marauder incursions. They broke up the weeks and months of miserable guard duty in the wintry watchlands. They had not, however, faced a champion of Chaos like Gorath the Ravager. A warlord of hate, who saw all – his enemies, his own warriors and the innocents often caught inbetween – as sacks of flesh to be butchered and blood to be spilled. He allowed the druchii their overconfidence. He sacrificed his front lines of barbarians and gors to their storms of bolt and spear, the serrated steel of their swordsmen and the cool discipline of their ranks.

Archaon watched and his warhost watched. The hope. The belief. Victory, certain in druchii minds and the sibilant orders of their captains and dreadlords. Then it came. The unleashing of Gorath's brazen Bloodsworn. His baroque army of clockwork knights, some on armoured clockwork steeds, punching up through their own ranks and advancing through the bloody haze with the unbreakable certitude of infernal machines. Hidden in their number was the Ravager himself, no less infernal in his slaughterous rampage. All died before his blood-hungry blade: beastmen, berserkers, reptilian monsters, dark warriors of the elder race. Horned daemons – red like the depths of that which had spawned them – moved through stomping ranks of knights like howling slipstreams of gore, leaving the drizzle of death in their wake. Archaon watched the tide turn. He watched the Khorne-worshipping warriors of doom sacrifice their own ranks in open celebration of the slaughter to come. Then, the thunder. The Ravager's irresistible advance. The unfolding storm of the Bloodsworn smashed their way through the blizzards of bolts and shield walls that so far had held the illusion of being unbreakable. With a stomach-turning realisation, the druchii began to die in horrible number.

Archaon could imagine his own army decimated before the unstoppable onslaught of the Ravager's ranks. All that he had fought for. All that he had created. Gone in mere moments of mindless rage. The glory of the Ruinous Star, followers of disparate gods fighting under one banner, one warlord, one cause, unified in the even greater glory of a single apocalyptic goal: all sacrificed to appease alone the Blood God's wrath. He could not allow such waste. The Dark Gods stood for more than just momentary spectacle – the soul-shattering scream or the fountain of blood. Their very best champions – their chosen – their Everchosen should be more than just slayers, regardless of their infamy and considerable skill. Such warriors and chieftains had their uses but they were both solution and problem. The wide world would not be conquered by such goremongers. The legions of darkness would be led by a man of darkness, not of blood. A warlord who saw victory through the twilight of black skies, devoid of hope and sun – through the gloom of the End Times to come, not a rage-red haze of blood.

'Will you be leading the attack, master?' Dravik Vayne put to Archaon.

'I will,' the Chaos warlord told his Slaaneshi lieutenant.

'Would you like my forces to secure the *Citadel*?' Vayne volunteered, eager to be both on board his vessel-fortress and out from under Gorath the Ravager's blade. Archaon allowed himself a smile.

'You will sound the retreat,' Archaon told him.

'My lord?'

'Have your forces hold position in the trees, above the snowline,' the dark templar said.

'Hold, sir?' Vayne asked, confused.

'I will take the horde down after the Hundun,' Archaon told him. 'I'll punch through the Ravager's flank with the witch's maggot-men and Hornsqualor's beastmen.' Archaon nodded to himself. He would need the staying power of the Plague Lord's afflicted and the gors to carry him through the Blood God's marauder madmen and on to the Ravager himself.

'My lord, you will need–'

'–you to do as you are ordered, druchii-swine,' Archaon barked back at him. 'Remain here and sound the retreat, Corsair-Captain Vayne.'

For a moment, words failed the slaver. He had never known Archaon to order a retreat – and certainly not before a battle had begun. 'Do you hear me, corsair-captain? Hold position here… I shall bring your floating fortress to you.'

Archaon dug his heels into Oberon's black, scaly flanks. The stallion moved on down the incline and through the snow-dusted forest.

'Now, my lord?' Dagobert said, the fat priest buried in the folds of robes and shaggy furs.

'Now…' Archaon said, his voice cutting through the thin mountain air. Dagobert signalled to a Hundun archer the priest had requested of Fengshen Ku from the ranks of the Dreaded Wo. The celestial dipped his signal arrow in pitch and had another marauder set it aflame. Aiming up high through the treeline, north, in the direction of the Eisarnagga Glacier and the Wastes, the Hundun archer pulled back on his ivory bow as far as the taut weapon would allow before releasing the flaming arrow into the Naggaroth sky.

As Archaon rolled in the saddle, Oberon stomping and skidding his way down through the woodland scree and snow, he could hear the sound of battle beyond. Druchii screeching their last. The whoosh of spears and bolts through the air. The rattle of armour and the march of Bloodsworn knights. The hack and slash of decapitation. The steam of hot blood on the glass-cut breeze.

Turning the stallion to one side, Archaon rode out onto the bare mountainside, where the pines were thin and roots could not cling. Though high above them, Archaon had broken the cover of the forest and was now in full view of bolt thrower crews on the dark elf tower keeps and the clash of druchii and Chaos warriors on the valley floor. About him his Swords of Chaos rode. The maggot-warriors of Mother Fecundus stormed down the slope in their thick, chitinous armour. Shaggy beastmen crushed grit beneath their hooves as they raged their way down towards the Ravager's forces. With his horde roaring down the mountainside after him and Fengshen Ku's sword clansmen standing aside amid the slaughter of druchii scouts, Archaon rode out across the blood-soaked dirt of the valley floor.

Within moments the cool air and the serenity of Oberon at full gallop was gone. It was like hitting a wall. Archaon didn't have to worry about spears and arrows from Gorath's horde. It was not the Khornate champion's style. His Bloodsworn lived for the judder of their blades through enemy torsos and the spray of hot gore across their furs and armour. As Oberon smashed through beasts and marauders, horribly trampling unfortunates under hoof, Archaon swung *Terminus* about him. The Blood God's rabid servants came at him. Cleaving through helm, horn and bone, Archaon hacked his way in through the ranks. Norscans. Khorngors. Skull-draped savages. All died as the Chaos warrior cut a path into the side of the Ravager's horde, his own marauders following in his bloody path. If Archaon was the spear-tip of the assault – deadly and irresistible – his Swords were the wedge that opened the foe-host's side like a grievous wound. Hacking and slashing from the saddle with their bone swords, the winged warriors followed Archaon into the chaos and confusion of the battle, leading Archaon's marauders into the bloody fight.

Archaon had only just got used to the brighter skies of the southern lands. When they disappeared, the warlord looked up into the sky to find a haze of repeater bolts blotting out the heavens.

'Shields!' Archaon roared back at his horde. Bringing his own body shield up and holding it to the sky, the Chaos warrior covered himself and his steed as best he could. The willowy shafts of crossbow bolts rained down on the valley. The druchii were hiding behind the distance created by their cowardly weapons. As the shield drummed with the pitter-patter of slender bolts, Archaon growled. About him the Swords of Chaos took cover behind the open expanse of their gargoylesque wings. Maggot-men hid behind their chitinous shields, while Hornsqualor's warriors did their best to weather the slaughter. Fengshen Ku's clansmen shielded themselves with the bodies of their enemies while Escoffier's warhounds were pinned to the valley floor like crucified mongrels.

The Ravager's horde was cut to ribbons but it didn't seem to bother the maniacs. Bloodshot of eye and foaming at the mouth, Gorath's marauders seemed not to care about the bone-grazing bolts embedded in their flesh. They fought on in their excruciating pain, intent on butchering their way to the craven druchii that had fired upon them. Oberon half-whinnied, half-growled as bolts found their way from the sky, past Archaon's shield and into the steed's flesh. As the shower of death died away, Archaon urged the beast on into the murderous fray.

Archaon stabbed and slashed down through Gorath's slayers with his templar blade. He caved in skulls with its gore-stained pommel. He punched berserkers away with its cross-guard. A northman's spear found its way under his pauldron and into the white-hotness of his skewered flesh. A warrior's axe cut at his side, exploiting the damage created in the wake of a previous injury and hacking at his scarred flesh. His shield was an arm-numbing nexus of furious blows. Every blood-thirsty lunatic in the Ravager's army wanted his steel through the Chaos warrior and it was only Archaon's desperate bladework and the positioning of his shield between him and such furious intent that kept both the dark templar and his steed alive in the sea of murder. If the Khornate horde's attentions had not been split between his attacking force and the wall of locked druchii shields barring their path to victory, Archaon was in such a position that he would have gone down under the deluge of wrath that perpetually threatened to crash over him.

The air was thick with the haze of blood. Archaon was there. In the chaos, in the havoc. Amongst the pushing and pulling. The crimson flash of blades. The hot agony of injuries sustained. The glory of inelegant violence visited upon others. There were shouts. Challenges. Screaming. There was death everywhere. The sky darkened to a doom-laden red. Black lightning stained the sky. Moments seemed to grind to a halt.

The horned head of the red-skinned beastman Archaon was about to end suddenly exploded. Skull fragments and what passed for the mindless brute's brain were spread across Archaon's breastplate. As the creature's muscle-bound body dropped, the brazen flash of an axe betrayed another warrior of Chaos. One of Gorath's Bloodsworn. One of the Ravager's infernal contraptions. The thing moved with clockwork assuredness, its plate barely containing the daemon-force that drove the mechanical nightmare. Its steed was the thick-set parody of a horse. A brimstone-snorting beast of cog, mail and clinkered plate.

Archaon should have been impressed. He wasn't. He had faced the Ravager's clockwork knights before. Flinging his battered shield around, Archaon smashed the knight's head from its shoulders in a shower of metal intricacies and ichor. The blood-cursed thing that possessed the suit of armour howled from its confinement with a forge-spitting fury. The knights were there, about him. They had hacked through their own to get to the Chaos warrior. Their steam-snorting steeds were suddenly everywhere, as were their axes. Archaon's Swords rode at the knights, smashing them aside with their own midnight steeds, engaging the warriors and preventing them from burying their master in blades.

Gorath the Ravager had decided that his prize could wait, however. He would honour both his Blood God and his Gorequeen with the death of a warrior equal. Smacking aside the rage of the knights' colossal axes, Archaon stabbed his greatsword straight through the breastplate of one – only to find that no heart resided behind it – and rent open the back of another as it passed on its daemon-fuelled mount.

Gorath the Ravager was ready for him. Smashing aside two more of his daemon knights, the champion of Khorne rode forth. Archaon knew this was his foe. Decked in gore-bathed brass and mounted on an infernal metal steed, Gorath was all but indistinguishable from his Bloodsworn knights. His armour did not glow with the same daemon radiance, however. His suit was more than just a prison for some daemon machine. Beneath his breastplate hammered something far more dangerous than cog or piston. Beneath it beat the heart of a thrice-cursed warrior. A man who had pledged his soul to the Lord of All Hate. A man who had promised his god a world drowning in blood. Like Archaon he was committed to a singular doom. His axeblades had never known defeat. His name threatened to burn itself into eternity.

Archaon got his shield between the first of the weapons and an axe-cleaved torso – but only just. The force took him from the saddle and into the bloody mire below. As Gorath turned his infernal steed, he ran down on Archaon again, smashing the shield and Archaon with it back into the ground. The Chaos warrior was barely back on his feet when he found the steed standing over him, the fury of its hooves smashing at the shield. Archaon backed from the onslaught, only to find that Gorath was no longer in the saddle. The Bloodsworn's serrated axes opened Archaon up, both his plate and the flesh beneath ragged with gouges and gashes. The dark templar's shield and greatsword rang with the pneumatic impact of the blows as they rained down one after another on the warrior of Chaos.

For a moment, Archaon came to believe the Blood God's champion unconquerable. Every time he rallied, every time he pushed back the rhythmic storm of axeblows and managed to plunge the tip of his blade into the monstrous warrior, he found little to suggest a man. Something that could be killed. Stabbing blows to the thigh, to the shoulder and Gorath's back only revealed the arcane working of infernal machinery. The Gorequeen's chosen did not slow. Did not stumble. Did not stop. It was all Archaon could do to withdraw *Terminus* from the screeching metal embrace of the damaged bronze to smash aside the Ravager's furious whirlwind of axeblows. Archaon's world became the seconds he snatched from death as the Khornate champion pushed him to his limits. Axe. Axe. Axe. Axe. Axe. Occasionally the Ravager would butt him with his extravagant helm or bury the chisel-tip of an armoured boot into Archaon's stomach. Mostly Archaon was just a moment's doom away from being hacked apart by the Ravager's relentless axes. Their barbed edges ripped through his plate where they managed to make contact, while the flat of the blade bludgeoned Archaon from side to side, sending the Chaos warrior tumbling into brawny marauders and druchii shields, necessitating swift kills before he was forced to face the flashing storm of the Ravager's blades once more.

As Archaon fell through the druchii shield wall again, he turned – battle-drunk – and took the head from a dark elf warrior. As he did, the bloody glower of the sky blinked darkness. Archaon readied himself for the Ravager's axes but suddenly they weren't there. Archaon looked to the Khornate champion to find that he too had noticed the brief darkness and was staring up into the sky. Concerned at the progress the combined marauder hosts were making through their bolt throwers, their hail of repeater bolts and ranks of spearmen, the druchii had despatched one of their great beasts to destroy them.

The drake was a youngling. Broad of wing but slender of black body. A reptilian nightmare, it was a thing of sinuous, serpentine beauty. Seated on its midnight shoulders, between its beating black wings sat a druchii sorceress. Guiding the young beast left and right with her thighs, the dragon witch screeched her intention to own the field of battle. Her skin was the white of ice, while behind her an impossible length of sable hair twisted and turned with the drake's sky-slithering manoeuvres.

Gorath the Ravager roared at both the battered Archaon and the dragon witch. The champion's voice seemed to proceed from deep within his infernal armour. It was the sound of roaring forge-fires and contorted steel. He would take them both for the glory of his Blood God.

As the sorceress directed her beast down at him, the drake spewed forth a stream of corrosive gas that turned a column of his Bloodsworn marauders to molten flesh and steaming bones. As both Gorath and Archaon had to roll away from one another and out of the drake's stream of corrosive horror, the dragon witch hauled the beast skyward and turned it around for another pass. Holding her willowy black staff high, the witch visited upon the battlefield a howling gale of phantom blades that cut those enveloped in its swirling course to strips of flesh. Again and again Archaon and the Ravager managed to evade the sorcerous storm, with their warriors dying about them. With every pass, the Blood God's champion roared his challenge to the witch but the only way the screeching druchii hag would oblige him was by bathing him in the blood of his mulched marauders.

With the valley floor a red mire about him, swallowing armour and bone that steamed as it sank, Archaon felt a quake beneath his slipping boots. A rumble that proceeded from the very ground itself. The herald of a doom he had arranged for all of them. It was time.

Looking up he saw Dravik Vayne on the valley side. Horns were being sounded. Several of his Swords looked up from the butchery they were committing in his name. They seemed loath to leave the field of battle as he had ordered.

'Go!' he roared. 'Get the host to high ground.'

With hesitation the winged warriors rode for the western slope, waving Archaon's army on with their bone blades. The marauder host were retreating back to the treeline at the corsair-captain's insistence, leaving their warlord alone amongst the enemy. There wasn't much time. Cleaving a nearby druchii warrior in two, Archaon watched the dragon witch bring her midnight drake down low across the carnage. Gorath was waiting for her, directing her on with his axes. Archaon had to act now. It had to be now. Slipping his gore-smeared blade into his back-scabbard and shouldering his mauled shield, the Chaos warrior ran at the Ravager. Stamping through sizzling bones and with pools of blood erupting about his footfalls, Archaon came at his enemy, his hands empty of weapons.

Looking from the foul drake as it swooped down on them to Archaon's madness, Gorath's mindless certainty abandoned him for a moment. Turning, the Ravager went to hack the defenceless Archaon in two but the dark templar dropped into a roll at the last moment. He rose as the champion's axe passed overhead, sinking his armoured digits into the baroque armour's busy design. Hauling the Ravager to him, Archaon threw Gorath's armoured form over his own and rolled the two of them through the slaughter-swamp. With Archaon sinking into the gore and Gorath the Ravager held on top of him, the Chaos warrior waited. The drake was coming straight at the pair. The dragon witch held her staff high and unleashed her bladestorm. The razor-gale sliced up the mire about them and tore up through the Ravager's back. Gorath roared with infernal insistence and hauled himself away from Archaon but the dark templar held his foe to him, using the brazen-armoured warrior as a shield against the dragon witch's stream of phantom blades. Archaon felt the druchii magic tear through Gorath. Through his ornate plate. Through his brass workings and the workings of his infernal enhancements. Then finally through what remained of the Ravager's hate-blessed flesh. As the remains of the Blood God's champion were torn from his grip by the bladestorm, Archaon felt the drake pass overhead.

Archaon lay there for a moment. Drenched in blood. His soul fired by murderous desire. He felt the Blood God's favour in his heart. His own blood boiled within his veins. The moment was mindlessly intoxicating.

'Get up...' Archaon told himself. Scrabbling out of the gore, the warrior of Chaos watched the dragon witch take her monster up into the sky. Staring about the havoc of the battlefield, Archaon found himself surrounded by the carnage of the decimated Bloodsworn. In the face of his own host's retreat back up the valley side, rallying druchii forces were rushing down on him with their slender spears and jagged blades. With the bolts of repeaters plucking at the marshy slaughter, Archaon ran for Oberon. The stallion was rearing and kicking out with its hooves at a pair of dark elf spearmen. Archaon came up behind and twisted one of the druchii's head from its shoulders. The second he grabbed from the back, drawing the spearman's own weapon across his face. Hauling the shaft of the spear towards him, Archaon felt the warrior's jaw break before he worked the weapon most of the way through his shearing skull. Tossing the body of the druchii aside, Archaon mounted Oberon and rode for the eastern slope of the valley. Like the west, through which Archaon had brought his host, it was sparsely wooded. Bolt throwers blasted spears down at him and scouts fired their repeaters from their hiding places. Weaving through the fired spears and with Oberon soaking up a number of wicked-tip bolts in his stallion-flesh, Archaon rode into the trees. He didn't wait to engage the ballista crews he passed, or scouts appearing from behind the rusty-brown trunks of evergreen giants with slender swords. Archaon knew what was coming. Knew what he had unleashed on the valley. He knew he had to get as far up the valley side as possible.

Behind him he heard the battlefield slaughter die away. Dreadlords would have ordered their weapons turned on the fleeing champion. Riders and their reptilian mounts would have clawed their way up the incline to engage him and Gorath's daemons would have hunted him through the trees. None of these things happened. Chaotic and druchii alike were transfixed by a spectacle so horrifying that they had even stopped slaying one another.

The tendrils of mountain mist feeling their way through the trees fled like scared spirits. A serpentine hiss descended upon the valley and the pines shook with a sudden gust of icy wind. Archaon's hair whipped about him. Everything felt cold. Then the valley echoed with the cataclysmic boom of the terrible things about to happen.

The freezing water crashed around the valley's meandering course, spuming and foaming up the slopes and mountainsides that guided its scalding wrath. It shattered the lower reaches of the highland forest, rending fir and splintering pine, leaving naught but smashed stumps as the waters cascaded back down into the raging advance of the thunderous flood. The deluge tore up the black soil of the valley floor and carried with it the collected debris of its destructive path and mighty bergs of ice.

Archaon patted his steed. The show was about to begin. An offering to the dark pantheon. Ruin. Havoc. Fear. Death. A gift worthy of a true champion of Chaos. Catastrophe. He was no butcher. No expert in the bloody arts like Gorath. He was a living expression of the apocalypse to come. He was Archaon. Herald of the End Times. He rode fate like a ship slicing through the waves. He would not be driven from his course. He would not sacrifice his destiny for blood, not for pleasures unimaginable or limitless power. He would not exchange it for immortality. It was his name that would echo through the ages, until there was no one left to hear it, to utter it, to fear it. Archaon looked down into the valley at his sacrifice. He saw the ice-waters smash into the Bloodsworn's rearguard. Furious bodies went everywhere. Backs were broken and brains bludgeoned from warrior skulls by huge chunks of ice. Weapons glinted uselessly in the coursing depths. The raging flood was an enemy even the chosen of Khorne could not fight. Archaon watched. Enjoyed. Like toy soldiers his enemies had their legs washed out from under them. They rose on the seething froth before disappearing into frozen waters. Their rag doll bodies were mangled in the tumbling logs, rocks and debris rolling across the valley floor and became part of the elemental force that smashed into their compatriots.

'Run, you bladeslaves,' Archaon said, his words hot on the breeze. 'Run.'

The Chaos warriors could not outrun their doom, however. Beastmen hammered into the ranks of Shadowland barbarians. Berserkers cannoned through Gorath's clockwork knights. Even the unearthly band of bloodletting daemons and mounted Bloodsworn riding at full speed couldn't evade the wrath of the valley-swallowing flood. A smile split the frozen mask that was Archaon's face as the Bloodsworn host – the infamous butcherers of Gorath the Ravager, the Rage-blessed of Khorne – were snatched, mechanical steeds and all, by the rising waters and dragged into the glacial maelstrom.

Archaon did not fool himself into thinking that the wall of furious water would be enough to kill all of the Blood God's champions. Gorath might be gone but the infernal Bloodsworn knights and the slayer daemons that haunted his warhost might stand a chance of surviving the watery doom. Being tossed about in the thrashing currents, buried in an ice-stabbing havoc of water, berg and black earth, might have given Gorath pause for thought. He might come to understand that there were others who coveted the treasures of Chaos. Others who might be Everchosen of the Dark Gods. Archaon's army was small but tempered in the relentless battle of the Wastes. They were not the Bloodsworn, however, and a champion – even a champion of such Ruinous patrons – needed to think of victories beyond the blade.

When Archaon had thought of his army at Gorath's boots, chunks of hacked flesh and puddles of gore, it was more than he could bear. It wasn't sentiment. It wasn't ownership. It wasn't pride. Every useless death represented a backward step on his dark path. He would sacrifice them all in a heartbeat if it advanced his interests – taking the world but one moment closer to Armageddon. The very blackness of his soul yearned for the doom of all the world. He was the instrument of the Dark Gods. Their key to dark and shackled futures. Hang mercy, loyalty and rank presumption. His appetite for the end was the irresistible force that kept him moving forwards. Fatewards. Determined to see the destruction of all. Blade, flame, flood or famine. Archaon didn't care – as long as there were fewer souls to plague the world than there had been moments before.

That had been the reason Archaon had instructed a retreat and saved his army from death. A swift and bloody death at the hands of Gorath the Ravager and his Bloodsworn. It had been the reason he'd had the Hundun archer signal the Brothers Spasskov. It had been the reason he had left orders with the Tzeentchian sorcerer to halt the creaking advance of the Eisarnagga Glacier and unleash the howling energies of change on the colossal ice floe. Like an unbroken stallion, free of chain and halter, the glacier had charged away. A seething wasteland of ice had crumbled to a thick, berg-clashing slush that in turn had given way to the scalding torrent that had swamped, flooded and crashed its inescapable way south through the gorges and valleys of the Iron Mountains.

Within several heart-stopping seconds, the tsunami of ice and dark water had smashed through both Gorath's army of hate and the druchii formations that were standing their ground against him. Thrashing dark elves and Bloodsworn warriors were carried away by the thunderous current. The Hag Queen's minion-soldiers at first thought to make for their stubby garrison towers but it swiftly became apparent that the fortifications – including the thorny crown of their keeps – were going to be under water. Some desperate druchii even contemplated climbing the tainted berg of dread rock upon which the *Citadel of Spite* sat. They were not given the chance to seal their doom in such a fashion, however, as the crashing meltwaters of the Eisarnagga snatched them from their purchase.

Archaon nodded. That was better. The battlefield was much transformed. It was no longer a field, for a start. It was a rising, coursing body of black water as wide as the wooded mountains either side would permit. Even above the waters sloshing and creeping up the mountainside, Archaon could feel the freeze coming off the crystal cold river of ice. Amongst the tessellation of smashed bergs and slush, Archaon watched druchii and Chaos marauders drowning. They were dragged to the depths by their armour. They were smashed senseless into ice, rock and each other. They swam past one another – oblivious now to the threat each other presented. Archaon had poured cold water on both the dark elves' murderous glee and the fiery rage that burned within the warrior-acolytes of the Blood God. Archaon allowed the water to do its worst. Druchii and marauder began to grasp for one another, pulling each other down below the surface of the black water. It wasn't murder or battle – it was survival. Too far from anything that might be described as a shore, those dark elves and Chaos warriors not bouncing along the valley bottom or smashed by the tumbling logs and debris were claimed by the cold.

Archaon slowed Oberon. The steed's flesh was steaming with the exertion of galloping up the mountainside. As the berg-crashing waters slushed rapidly up the slope, Archaon urged the horse on a little further at a slow trot, the Chaos warrior enjoying the carnage he had caused on the field of battle. He did not hear the druchii run up behind him. The silent assassin had trailed through the trees, up the mountainside, moments ahead of the rising waters. Archaon turned to find the athletic dark elf already behind him. He drew *Terminus* but by the time he had the druchii had cast his cloak aside and revealed the twisted blades of two longknives in his gloved hands. Leaping up onto Oberon's rump, the assassin was sitting behind the dark templar as he drove the knives down through Archaon's armour. With the twisted blades skewered down through his flesh, Archaon roared his pain and anger. Both *Terminus* and his shield fell from his grasp. With the assassin turning the cruel blades inside him, Archaon too was tumbled from the saddle.

Getting to his feet, Archaon could still feel the assassin on his back. Working his blades deeper into him. The druchii had no intention of letting go until the Chaos warrior had been well and truly skewered. Stumbling at a tree, Archaon ran at the trunk. Turning and smashing the assassin between him and the unforgiving wood, the dark templar bellowed his pain. He felt something crunch in the druchii, however, and the assassin allowed a gasp of his own agony to escape his slight frame. Again and again Archaon smashed the assassin into the ice-threaded bark until finally he felt the murderous dark elf slacken his hold. Reaching back, Archaon grasped for the assassin's wrist and wrenched it around in his gauntlet's grip. Bones splintered in the wrist. Turning the assassin's broken arm around he forced the druchii from his back and slammed him back against the tree. The assassin hissed his pain and intention to kill the Chaos warrior. Holding him against the tree by his throat, Archaon reached for one of the knives in his back. It was excruciating to withdraw the twisted blade. Once he had done so, he stabbed the longknife straight through the chest of its owner. The druchii gasped as the blade twisted straight through him and pinned him to the trunk. Extricating the second, Archaon stared into the assassin's eyes as he used it to cut the druchii's heart out and held the still-beating organ before him. Both warrior and assassin shared a moment of horrific understanding before the dark elf's head fell forward. Stumbling away from the dead assassin, Archaon roared as he held the heart up to the sky and crushed it in his fist. As gore dribbled from his fingers, black lightning split the heavens.

When he turned to find Oberon he found that the horse was still and stricken with fear. Hovering above the tree tops was the midnight drake and the druchii witch. She had destroyed Gorath the Ravager. Now she would kill Archaon. The dark templar looked back down the slope to where he had dropped *Terminus* and his shield.

Archaon looked from his bloody fist back up to the heavens, where the clouds had been rent asunder. From the swirling maelstrom above dropped a fireball that left a blood-murky trail of smoke. The witch lifted her staff. The drake's slender maw opened wide. Archaon instinctively lifted his arms in front of his face. Instead of corrosive breath or a bladestorm of dark magic, the fiery heat of daemon hate washed over him. The fireball struck the dragon and its rider, slamming them into the mountainside with explosive fury. An inferno roared about witch and her monster. Peering through the gaps between the digits of his gauntlet, Archaon watched as some furious infernal entity fought through the flames. A daemon princess, of a terrible martial beauty, had descended. In crimson armour forged in Khorne's own hate and bearing two great horns from her head, Archaon recognised the horrific creature as Valkia the Bloody – the Gorequeen sponsor of Gorath's atrocities. The daemon had descended in celebration of the slaughter wrought in the valley below and in honour of her champion's blood. Swinging a monstrous spear about her armoured form, she took the dragon witch's head off, allowing the shock of its pale face and its lustrous length of hair to bounce down the wooded slope past Archaon.

As the Gorequeen batted the drake's jaws aside with a daemonshield bearing the teeth of its own horrific maw, Archaon took Oberon's reins. Skidding down the slope, Archaon recovered *Terminus* and his shield. He left the doomed drake to the Gorequeen's wrath, knowing that the daemon princess would need no assistance in despatching even such a beast. Shouldering the shield and sliding his greatsword into its scabbard, Archaon mounted his steed. As he rode back down towards the rising shoreline, he cast a glance back at Khorne's dread consort. It was agony with the knife wounds in his shoulders but worth it to watch the monstrous daemon slice through the drake's throat and bury her spear in the beast. Watching her, Archaon wondered if he too might one day earn the infernal patronage of a daemon sponsor. Some dark thing from the beyond to further his interests in the apocalyptic times to come. Riding for the waters, Archaon found himself snarling. Unlike Gorath the Ravager, he did not need such Ruinous favour. He would fulfil his destiny and become the Everchosen of Chaos with or without the help of the gods and their wretched servants.

Still Archaon urged Oberon on. He did not want to be around when the Gorequeen looked for other challenges with which to slake her bottomless thirst for blood and battle.

As Archaon reached the rising fury of the frozen waters, he smiled to himself. The Ruinous Powers had never known a victory so devastating and complete. The dark templar promised them many more. At the water's edge Archaon found several Bloodsworn knights clawing their way out of the coursing glacial flood. They were bereft of their smashed, mechanical mounts. Their joints of infernal workings were frozen and riven with ice. The appearance of their Gorequeen on the field of battle had driven them on but there they stood, like statues, waiting for an end. Archaon granted their wish. Splashing down into the freezing shallows, he drew *Terminus* and cleaved helmets from Chaotic constructs. A rusty ichor that passed for blood dribbled down their breastplates and into the water, staining the shore brown.

Archaon slapped his stallion's scaly flanks with the flat of his smouldering sword, urging the beast on into the frozen waters. Clamping the saddle between his armoured thighs and taking the reins harshly with one gauntlet he swung *Terminus* about him with the other. Guiding the horse, who was now swimming through the black meltwater with his big, broad hooves, Archaon went with the current. As he headed for the rocky foundations of the *Citadel of Spite* – the Chaos war shrine now baptised in the rising waters that battered their way through the valley – the Chaos warrior slapped the water with scything sweeps of his blade. Each cut and thrust put flailing marauders and drowning druchii out of their ice-rimed misery.

Archaon dug his heels into Oberon, forcing the steed to swim for their lives towards the horrific outline of the *Spite*. The dark templar could feel the horse struggling with the temperature. Archaon's plate also had frosted and burned with cold through his leggings, numbing his limbs. Death kept them both busy. Screeching elves and current-fighting northmen swirled past them – an invitation to Archaon's smoking blade. He hacked the slender appendages from freezing dark elves and through the Norscan plaits and wild facial hair of hoar-frosted skulls. A biped reptilian steed, which had long thrown its druchii rider into the chaos of the crashing spume, suddenly reared out of the white waters churning along the *Spite*'s glistening bedrock. It snapped at Oberon, eager that Archaon and his steed not supplant the beast's precarious claw-tip purchase on the *Citadel*'s rocky hull. Oberon reared – whinnying his surprise and dipping Archaon waist-deep into the freeze. The dark templar smashed the reptile's jaws aside with the pommel of his greatsword but the thing's jaws snapped again with almost elastic insistence. Oberon instinctively leant away, nearly toppling Archaon into the rising waters that were racing away down the valley. Throwing himself back at the beast, Archaon sliced the reptile's scabby throat clean open. Working its jaw in gushing disbelief, the reptile scraped free of its purchase and was dragged down the valley by the coursing waters.

Sheathing *Terminus*, Archaon slapped the reins either side at Oberon's thick neck, urging the stallion on up the same outcrop of rock to which the reptilian beast had been clinging. The dark templar needed to get them both out of the water. Skidding and sliding up the wet rock, the steed managed to mount the outcrop and Archaon urged them into the dry hollow into which the rock shelf led. Climbing down, Archaon turned back and watched the glacial waters climb up the slopes of the valley side, swirling up through the pines and firs, bouncing mangled clusters of corpses along the forested shore. Looking up, Archaon could see the dark stone of the *Spite*'s walls and the towers grasping for the sky beyond. Had the Chaos warrior not spent what seemed like an immeasurable eternity in the impossibility of the Wastes, the vessel might seem strange. A citadel that floated on a bedrock-berg of cavern-riddled stone. A floating fortress that harnessed the wind in its colossal, tower-spanning sails and drifted across the oceans, guided by dark magics. Vayne had been right. The *Spite* would make him a mighty flagship. First he must make the corrupted shrine to Chaos his own. He must discover her secrets and claim the treasures she had held onto for so long. Treasures denied even to the inquisitive Hag Queen of Naggaroth.

Leading Oberon into the hollow, Archaon found his progress blocked by the rusty bars of a portcullis. Vayne had warned him about this. He had told the Chaos warrior that the dark elves enslaved all manner of deep-ocean beasts in the system of caves running through the fortress bedrock. Exterior gates allowed water in but imprisoned the creatures until they were unleashed on the druchii's enemies on the high seas. Archaon knew that all manner of aquatic horror lay between him and his prize. Horrors that were all the more so for being exposed to the corruptibility of the Wastes. Stepping down from his steed, the dark templar took *Terminus* in hand and advanced on the portcullis. The darkness beyond was thick and stank of the deep. There was no way to open the gate from the hollow. All the gates were controlled by capstans in the floating fortress. Resting his back against the bars, Archaon took one in each hand and heaved skyward. After an extended grunt of exertion, the dark templar forced the portcullis back up into rocky ceiling.

There was a hiss. Something beyond was stirring. Archaon turned to find it slithering down the tunnel towards him. The thing was horrible to behold. A colossal black eel, with huge glazed eyes and an extendible jaw of curved glass fangs, each the length of *Terminus*. Despite its large disc-like eyes, the creature snapped blindly at the portcullis that Archaon had raised a handspan from the floor. Its fangs clashed against the rusty metal as the famished monster battered its head against the gate in a frenzy. Archaon watched the horrid thing for a moment, feeling the simplicity of its dark purpose. He stepped forward to let it sense the satisfaction of the meal he would make. The beast went wild, smashing its head bloody against the portcullis. Archaon leaned back and then thrust *Terminus* forward. The blade passed through the bars and straight into the rubbery flesh of the sea monster's head. He held it there, the metal of the crusader sword sat in the thing's brain as death throes rippled repulsively down its length. When he withdrew the weapon, the monster fell still.

Forcing the portcullis up through its rusty workings, Archaon advanced up the creature's slimy length, leading Oberon into the darkness. The knight wouldn't ordinarily bring his horse into such a confined space, but with the waters rising up the bedrock of the *Citadel of Spite* and threatening to flood its labyrinth of caves and tunnels, Archaon had little choice but to allow the steed freedom to follow him.

As the daylight diminished behind him, Archaon's eyesight adjusted to his surroundings. It was a primordial blackness. The darkness of the deep. The druchii had imprisoned beasts of the ocean abyss. Then the warping powers of Chaos had crept in through the rock and shadow to re-craft the creatures into new horrors. Archaon could imagine few places more damning and desperate. Somewhere in this dread place he was to find the first treasures of his Ruinous masters. The Chaos warrior cursed them for their twisted games.

Desiccated weed hung from the rocky ceiling and the broad passage opened into a cavern. Archaon found himself smiling in the darkness. He could imagine how such a labyrinth might eat away at the nerve of those attempting to penetrate the depths of the lightless place. Even a lantern or torch would provide little illumination in such an environment. The rock was black. It soaked up the light, leaving nothing for the eye. At best a light source would simply show a foolhardy wanderer in the tunnels where next to place his boot. Tunnels would only be obvious to a traveller already within their craggy confines, while vast caverns and cave systems might pass totally unnoticed in the blanket of gloom.

That most natural of fears – the dread of that which you could not see – had little effect on Archaon. Like the monstrous beasts haunting the inky blackness, the Chaos warrior was part of that dread. Unlike many of his brothers of the damned, fighting their way through the insanity of the north, Archaon did not need to trust in light alone. He had been blessed with other ways of seeing. His soul was a blazing inferno of dark intent that cast all about him in the dreadlight of stinging shadow. Archaon's time in the northern murk of the Wastes had only enhanced his talent further. This place – that would rob the worthy of their senses and feel its way into their chest with the chill talon of fear – was nothing to the Chaos warrior. He crunched through the twisting tunnels of the caves, across vaulted caverns and through the foetid shallows of groundwater lakes. Monsters waited for him there. Ravenous. Feasting upon one another in the absence of their ocean feeding grounds until only the most deadly of creatures remained.

Taking *Terminus* – which struggled to summon even an anguished glow in a place of such degenerate evil – and the shield upon which he carried the Ruinous Star of his calling, Archaon slapped Oberon on the hindquarters with the flat of his blade. The horse whinnied and clopped off into the darkness. The steed did not need much persuading to leave the warlord. Its skittish sense told it what Archaon already knew. That starved beasts from throughout the subterranean realm had been drawn down on him, led to their doom by his fresh stench. Archaon made it easy for them. Clashing *Terminus* against his shield, he roared his dares into the darkness. Then he saw them. Crawling. Slithering. Skittering their way towards him. Monstrosities of the deep of every shape and size. The only similarity they shared was the growl of their bellies.

'Come on, you wretched things,' Archaon hissed through the gloom. 'Hungry? Come get some.'

The killing began. Chitinous nightmares migrated across the cavern roofs, withdrawing into their shells before dropping like cannonballs against the Chaos warrior's upheld shield. Twitching shrimp swarms clicked about him in the darkness, trying to get through his armour and burrow into his flesh. Giant, malformed crustaceans erupted from tight grottos – all spine and pincer – aiming to cut the dark templar in two. Lakes disappeared to reveal tentacular behemoths that glissaded across the cavern floor on their own slime, coming at the knight with glutinous feelers and blasting him with jets of stinking water streaming from blowholes in their octopod flesh. Coiled serpents launched at him, their trapjaw maws a pit of teeth framed with leathery frills that opened as they struck. Beasts that seemed all gulping mouth and stomach attempted to swallow him whole. Things that draped feathery tendrils about him from above burned both armour and flesh. Scaly monsters with shovel-shaped heads and clamping jaws that attempted to drag the Chaos warrior into their cave lairs.

Suddenly Archaon heard the shriek of his horse through the darkness. Taking the heads from humanoid things with snapping jaws and shells, Archaon scrambled across the slippery rock. Clipping tentacles and grasping appendages reaching from crevasses and grottos as he passed, Archaon slammed *Terminus* through the slimy skulls of serpents that slithered into his path. He saw the ghostly outline of his steed pinned to the cavern floor by some crustacean horror. The crab-beast was an armoured monstrosity of shell, chitinous legs and webbing between for the unholy creature's propulsion through the water. A nest of pearlescent eyes danced about on thick stalks while the beast went to work with the crushing pincers of its four muscular claws. Oberon shrieked its animal horror. The crab-beast had the horse clamped between the rocky floor and the bottom of its clickety body. The thing opened its chunk-claw above the terrified horse.

'No!' Archaon bawled, his announcement echoing about the caves.

Batting away one opportunistic claw with *Terminus*, Archaon ran at the beast, chopping the top half of a second pincer away with a savage flash of the broad blade. The thing reared horribly, allowing Oberon a hoof-scrabbling moment of hope, but the horse was still firmly held against the ground by the crab's shifting weight. A thick claw, as big as the Chaos warrior himself, swept in from behind, snatching his armoured form up in its crushing embrace. Archaon felt his plate buckle and mail split under the cleaving pressure. It was a second crab-beast, bigger than the first and intent on stealing the colossal crustacean's prize. Turning *Terminus* about in his gauntlets, Archaon smashed the blade down through the chitinous crux of the claw in which he was clamped. Twisting the blade through the meat and sinew of the claw's inner workings, the dark templar felt the beast release him. Dropping between the creatures, Archaon found his shrieking steed beside him. It was straining its neck to be free and Archaon laid a gauntlet on the horse's nose before turning his attentions back to the monstrosities battling pincer and claw above them.

Plunging his crusader blade into the second creature's exposed belly, Archaon sawed through the softer shell, opening the creature up from below. It was slow to react but when the beast realised that half of its innards were trailing across the craggy floor, it withdrew behind its snapping claws. As the tips of crushing pincers glanced off the dark templar's sword, Archaon worked his way within the beast's feverish grasp. With a sweep of the blade Archaon took the monster's eyes from their twitchy stalks, blinding the thing. *Terminus* crashed down through the chitin, breaching the shell. Another cleaving swing over the Chaos warrior's head broke through the thing's armour and mulched what passed for its primitive brain. Taking a moment to catch his breath, Archaon dragged the tip of his messy blade along the rocky floor of the cave. Oberon had stopped shrieking. The horse was dead. Its thick, muscular neck was now just a bloody stump. The stallion's magnificent head lay a little distance away. The crab-beast had sheared through its neck with one chunk-claw and discarded the animal's head.

Archaon felt the searing heat of fury run through his veins like lava. He charged the monster who had already started picking flesh from the carcass. Smashing two claws aside with his great sword he chopped an insistent third from an armoured appendage. Leaping up off the stallion's body and from one of the monstrosity's scuttling legs, Archaon heaved down on *Terminus*, his gauntlets hanging from the crossbars and his weight driving the broad blade down through the crab-beast's shell like a spear. The blade slid straight through the creature and Archaon hung there for a moment as the clicking stopped and the creature's limbs dropped and fell still.

Tearing *Terminus* from the butchered crustacean, Archaon settled down on one armoured knee beside the dead steed. His steed. Oberon had been there through it all. His training as a knight. His life as a templar. He had followed the Chaos warrior north to his doom and had survived the insanity of the Wastes. He laid a gauntlet on the horse's scarred flesh. Archaon felt a strange warmth wash through his chest. It was an alien sensation, feeling like some kind of illness or infirmity. A remembered weakness. He had killed so much and cared so little for so long that he had forgotten his affection for the stallion. It was hard to believe that the pair of them would never ride again.

Archaon moved his hand across the beast's still warm hide and through part of its midnight mane.

'Thanks for always being there,' Archaon managed. He looked up. He sensed hunger in the darkness. Creatures were closing in. They smelled carrion. Hot blood, freshly spilled and horseflesh. They would pay for their curiosity. The dark templar pushed himself to his feet. Oberon was dead but he was still alive. The killing had to continue.

Archaon cut, hacked, stabbed, sliced and smashed his way through the relentless onslaught of nightmares. Dripping with ichor and crunching through shattered shell and bone, Archaon fought them. He saw them slither and crawl at him, thinking he was blind to their advance, that he was easy prey. The emaciated creatures of the deep paid for their cruel instincts. Archaon cast their ugliness in the darklight of his being. He turned with speed and bloody assurance, cleaving claws, tentacles and wicked appendages from beasts who in turn were defenceless without them. The dark templar buried *Terminus* in the grim, fishy flesh of the sea monstrosities about him, opening the beasts up and filling the dank air with the foul odour of the depths. Soon Archaon was taking the fight to the beasts, slaying the warped, the scaly and the spined as they fed on the banquet of dead monstrosities about the Chaos warrior. Ravenous creatures feasting on each other's foetid flesh, allowing Archaon to move through them, indiscriminately ending beasts lost in their own gluttony.

Standing in the thick murk, his chestplate rising and falling with the efforts of dealing death, Archaon stopped. Salty gore dripped from his plate and chunks of gloopy flesh dribbled from *Terminus*. The shallows gathered about him as freezing glacial waters climbed the bedrock foundations of the floating fortress and flooded the cave systems that riddled its buoyant architecture. With the slaughter sinking into the freezing waters, the monstrosities retreated. Their element called to them – as did freedom – and they could smell the scent of easier prey flailing and bleeding in the waters outside the caverns. Washing the ichor from his armour and shield, Archaon sheathed and shouldered his weaponry and started to climb. He was certain his prize lay in the dark citadel above. Every crag, handhold and cutting purchase took him closer to it.

The agonising ascent took him up the rocky sides of midnight chambers, through the abandoned grottos of fled monsters and up an abyssal dropshaft that weaved its crooked way through other cave systems and the inky vastness of open caverns. The climb was murderous. The rock was like obsidian. All edges were sharp and surfaces greasy. The drops were dizzying – even in darkness – and the Chaos warrior had to risk heavy leaps of faith across razor-sharp chasms he could barely see.

As his body burned with the unending exertion of the climb, Archaon's hands felt the crumbling architecture of crafted stone. It was ancient and came apart in his fingers.

It lacked the twisted angularity of the cave rock below and before long the dark templar found himself in the pulverised foundations of the druchii citadel. Staring about the lightless environs and heaving himself onto a precarious ledge, Archaon found he was in a dungeon, out of which the bottom had fallen. The stones about the dungeon walls – the ones the knight was perched exhausted upon – were the only ones to remain. Something attracted Archaon's attention immediately. A door of black metal set in the opposite wall. It wasn't the mouldering metal of the ancient door or the shattered stone about it that held the Chaos warrior's gaze. Between the dungeon door and the floor, Archaon could see a darklight that was not his own. A powerful evil lay in the passageways and chambers beyond. One so potent and pervasive that its darkness reflected off the walls and about the corners of the labyrinth in which it sat like the light and heat of a blinding inferno.

Standing and edging carefully around the loose flagstones about the edge of the chamber, Archaon found himself before the entrance. He could feel the dark radiance through the metal of the door, even though the metal of the door itself was cool. Levelling his armoured shoulder against the ancient metal, Archaon heaved at the door. He would not be denied. Not this close to his prize. Not this close to the Altar of Ultimate Darkness. With some surprise, the dark templar went straight through the door. The dungeon door did not open. Its locks were firmer in their resolve than the door's constitution and the black metal disintegrated about the warrior.

Shrugging off the splintered shards of withered metal, Archaon brought up his gauntlet to shield his eyes. Even in a corridor of simple, black stone – like many that made up the dungeon vaults of the *Citadel of Spite* – Archaon found the brilliance of the darkness blinding. The walls were saturated with the sheer malevolence of the treasure the labyrinth contained. Its darklight shone off the floor, the stone and the walls. It burned to stare upon. He closed his eye but it made no difference. There was no blinding glare to block with a squinting lid. The socket of his other eye, covered in its black leather patch and within his helmet, could not be closed to such wonder. It saw the darkness of all the world. A truth that could not be seen to be believed. The shard of stone within his skull bled its warping potential throughout the Chaos warrior's mind. A growl erupted from the dark templar's chest. Something savage and animalistic. Like food, drink, physical gratification or to breathe, Archaon needed the evil beyond. It sang to him, blazing into his being with its scarring potency. He hungered for it. He lusted for it. He began to realise that he would simply die without it.

Blinded though he was, Archaon sensed movement in the oblivion. He grunted the barbaric acknowledgement of an enemy. Many enemies. The labyrinth was swarming with the hunchbacked, the flesh-smeared, the shambling, the fang-faced and formed that were impaled on their own bones. Here were the druchii. The slaves. The unfortunates taken with the *Spite* by the unnatural storm. The miserable army of wretches that Dravik Vayne had left behind. The soul-ravaged remnants of dark elf corsairs and the *Citadel*'s legion of slaves. They only knew allegiance to the altar now. The Altar of Ultimate Darkness that Vayne had recovered and transported across the ocean for his power-hungry Hag Queen. Its corrupting influence had spread throughout the dungeon decks, the caverns below and the crew towers above. It had drawn them all to it. It had made mindless acolytes of them, twisting their minds beyond depravity and into the unknowing savagery of oblivion. Naked in their barbarity, their skin bleached to transparency by the darkness, they knew only that an interloper had entered the labyrinth. That the interloper was a threat to their mind-scalding shrine. That the interloper had to be torn apart. Groaning where mouths would still allow, the troglodytes lurched and shambled into one another, choking the passageways with their malformed number.

Not unlike the army of unfortunates swarming about him, Archaon grunted with brute intention. He needed to kill.

They needed to die. It was agony to hold the simple sense it made in his head. Archaon drew *Terminus*. Any remaining essence of the God-King's intentions for the blade were gone. It had been forever polluted. Like Archaon, it was being re-forged in the fiery darklight. Like a furnace, the labyrinthine sanctum that housed the Altar of Ultimate Darkness – blazing with the abyssal radiance of immaculate evil – was remaking them both. The crusader blade burned no longer with the torment of its godly service. The sword was swathed in a bloody flame. It seethed in silence. It gave itself, its cleaving edge, the profanity of its pommel and the upturned smile of its cross-guard over to the darkness it had once fought. The blade had turned. Archaon smiled with his weapon. It spread to the insanity of a death-drunk grin.

The troglodytes chattered with their needle teeth. They drooled in the darkness. Bones broke as withered, claw-like limbs were brought to readiness. Archaon ran at them, his steps shattering the black stone beneath his boots. His roar sent great cracks and splits through the sanctum walls. He slammed into the freakish horde with his shield. No one troglodyte was his equal. Their twisted frames were lank and light. The passage was wall to wall with groaning bodies and the first few ranks of wretches were just smashed into oblivion by the sheer force. Skeletons shattered. Heads and malformed organs burst like ripe fruit. Archaon pushed at the mess. The floor became slick with blood and the dark templar skidded. There were simply too many troglodytes. Their obscene carcasses were crammed into the corridor and flesh and bone would give no more. Like a wave of misshapen flesh they rolled up behind the Chaos warrior. Within moments they were everywhere. Clawing, tearing finger-talons. Biting needle-jaws. Bludgeoning limbs that ended in bone growths. Emaciated arms and legs that stamped and strangled with a madman's strength. They were before him. They were behind him. Those Archaon put on the floor still ripped at his legs, eager to find flesh through the plate and mail. Others hooked their way up his back and tore at his face and helm. The dark templar became lost in the blinding evil, adrift in a sea of corrupted flesh.

He punched his blade through the horrid creatures and smashed them into the walls and floor with the unrelenting force of his shield. He smashed through skulls with the pommel of the greatsword and butted druchii malforms into a brain-splattered mess with his helmet. The dark templar pushed on through the labyrinth, feeling his way not only through the carnage but along the walls. Every junction was an agony. A wrong turn would mean minutes more of meaningless slaughter. The knight's darksight didn't abandon him, though. Although it was soul-razing to look upon, Archaon forced himself to stare into the blinding glare of doom reflected off the walls. Where the mind-scalding radiance was brightest, Archaon made his bloody path.

The sea of bodies kept rolling in like a tide. Archaon was unyielding but step by step, death by merciless death, the gibbering droves wore him down. The thrust of his arm wouldn't falter. His legs would stomp on through the meat at his feet. He would never surrender to the horde – even in their combined strength, tearing at him like a single creature of innumerable arms, claws and jaws. The troglodytes tore at the dark templar, their sharp nails like hooks in his armour and flesh. They wrenched pieces of plate from his body. They ripped his mail to shreds. The padding of his doublet became rags in their clutching, filthy claws. Archaon's shield – bearing the Ruinous Star of the Chaos pantheon united – was torn from his arm and *Terminus* was taken from his blood-slick grip by the unrelenting throng.

This did not stop the Chaos warrior. Fumble-fighting his way through the darkness, he was shrine-blind. He was without weapons, without armour, naked as a newborn and sliced to ribbons. But Archaon fought on. Dripping with blood – his own and everyone else's – he used his fists, his feet, his knees, his elbows and his head to beat the monstrosities about him to death. He wrestled the troglodytes for their lives, breaking necks and spines, tearing withered limbs from their sockets and wrenching deformed skulls from torsos. He screamed his sacrifice to the sanctum ceiling and punched through ribcages to rip feeble hearts from malformed chests. He didn't know where he was. Darkness had become his world and the blinding darklight of the altar was everywhere. Bodies carpeted the floor beneath his bare feet. The walls and surrounding architecture were wet with blood. Archaon became an infernal instrument of decimation. Some of the creatures he just broke to hear the chorus of their suffering. Others he killed quickly. Mindlessly. A number he played with, allowing them hope before cruelly finishing them. He savoured the rest, enjoying their victimhood and the last gasps of their worthless lives. His guiding star – his star of Ruination – was always the end of all. His limbs felt like lead. His mind was overcome with his dark purpose. His heart thundered beneath the sliced flesh of his chest.

Suddenly there were no more. There was nothing left to kill. It was a shock. Archaon grabbed out at the darkness – to make sure that there was nothing left hiding or cowering in the shadows. Archaon stumbled through the butchered bodies and fell against a stone column. The column was slick with spilled blood. On it Archaon's bruised fingertips traced a symbol carved into the stone. He stared at the column as hard as he could but blinded by the absolute blackness in which he sat and the darklight all about him he could make out nothing. All he had was what he could feel. The bloody steam rising from his aching body. The air thick with the stench of fresh death. The stone beneath his gore-stained fingers. He knew the symbol instantly. It had been worn with dark pride by those he had fought and killed in the Wastes and those that had joined him in the killing.

He stumbled across from the column and fell, almost braining himself on another. It bore the horror of another symbol. Another expression of another dark god, commanding followers in the Wastes and beyond. Archaon crawled through the bodies, eager to confirm the terrible picture he held in his mind. He found more columns and more symbols. Four larger pillars, each bearing the dread symbols of the gods of Chaos. The four Ruinous Powers of Chaos. The four horrific forces in the world to which the lost and damned pledged their souls – each holding the others in delicate balance. The obelisks formed the four points of a star, the four tips of a cross, the four corners of a square. Between each one Archaon found other columns, further out from the original four, which bore a multitude of other symbols – some the dark templar recognised and some he did not. Renegade entities, daemon princes of Chaos, Dark Gods masquerading as the barbarian deities of other races. Archaon had found it. One of the dark treasures of Chaos. The Altar of Ultimate Darkness. Holding one of the obelisks in his filthy hands, Archaon lowered his head in exhaustion and subservience. The darkness denied him the horror and beauty of the shrine. The Altar of Ultimate Darkness was not meant to be seen. It was meant to be experienced. It was a means by which a mortal might achieve communion with the gods. Its medium was darkness. And blood. About him Archaon heard the ooze and thick drip of blood from the bodies he had butchered. He had reconsecrated the dark altar without even realising it.

Archaon got unsteadily to his feet. He glowered into the blackness. He saw only darkness. He heard only blood. He waited but nothing happened. His glower dropped to a smile of madness that swiftly became a snarl.

'This unholy quest is complete,' Archaon announced to oblivion. 'Now give me what you owe me, you abominable wretches…'

Archaon was suddenly struck from all sides by powerful bolts of dark energy that seared from the tips of the columns. The experience was beyond pain. Beyond feeling. Archaon roared and thrust his fists at the ceiling. The energies crackled across his flesh, burning the hair from his head and his body. The darkness sizzled over his skin, cauterising gashes and open wounds. The bolts of energy lanced through his mind and met in the dark templar. He felt the shard of wyrdstone rattle horribly in his skull. He felt his scalp burn where the energies seared into him, creating an eight-point crown of pain and black-scarring around his hairless head. Archaon felt the presence of darkness within him. His soul howled at the centre of damnation's storm, being torn this way and that, but never straying from the serenity within the swirling havoc of dark voices, dreams and feelings that enveloped his being. He felt the darkness change him, as the height of the sun in the sky transformed the day into dusk and the dead of night into the dawn.

Then as quickly as it had begun, the magnificent ordeal was over. Archaon was on his knees surrounded by corpses. His flesh was the bronze of dried blood. His body ached with the agony of battle. He trembled with power and potential undreamt of. The gods of Chaos were with him. They had blessed the venture that was his life of death. They had scarred their union into him: eight black, ever-smouldering marks, charred around his head like a Ruinous crown.

Archaon pushed himself up and stumbled through the bodies. He fell from the Altar of Ultimate Darkness and clawed his way through the carnage to the wall. With his back to the overpowering evil of the blinding darklight of the shrine, he walked away with all the strength he could muster. He walked through the ruined sanctums, through the labyrinthine slave pits and the citadel underbarbicans. He felt his way along sharp passageways and through chambers of black stone. He met no opposition. He had killed all who had haunted the *Citadel of Spite*'s corrupted architecture.

Grasping the slender bars of a warped and wicked portcullis, Archaon flung it up into the stone of the gate it barred. He strode through the archway, feeling the bite of the cold night air on his naked flesh. At first the gloom coming off the surrounding mountains and the searing stars in the open sky dazzled him. As his eye adjusted from the absolute darkness of the floating fortress's inner sanctums to the twilight outside, he wandered across the stone deck. Towers reared above him, colossal and crooked, challenging the mountain peaks for supremacy. Beyond, Archaon could hear the slosh of water and the clash of ice. Beneath the soles of his feet he could feel the gentle sway of the floating fortress – ever so slightly. As the glacier had melted and rampaged through the valleys, building in strength and volume, the *Spite* had started to rise on its freezing waters. Between the natural buoyancy of the cavern-riddled foundations of the floating fortress and the dark magics re-awoken by its baptism in the calamitous body of water forming about it, the jagged keel-ridge of the floating fortress had almost cleared the valley floor.

Reaching the black stone battlements of the *Citadel*, Archaon looked down at the glossy, berg-choked waters that crashed along the druchii vessel. He then looked up the mountain slopes. The valley floor was gone. As were the bodies of the Hag Queen's druchii army and Gorath's Bloodsworn marauders. They had long been washed through the mountains and out towards the nearby western coast of Naggaroth. In the valley's place was the broad, flowing course of a meltwater river. It was black with depth and white with shattered ice. On the mountainside nearby, the forest was ablaze. Archaon could see his army camped out on the water's edge, above the snowline. Dravik Vayne had ordered the great pines and firs of the mountainside cut for huge bonfires. Even from the towering deck of the *Spite*, Archaon could see that victory over the druchii and the Bloodsworn had resulted in a celebratory mood. There was drinking, eating and the enjoyment of the fires. There was a union among Archaon's army of the apocalypse that the dark templar had never known.

He stood and watched for a minute before spotting Vayne, his sorceress and his corsairs down by the new shoreline. By the raging meltwater, Sularii and the Brothers Spasskov inspected the Tzeentchian's sorcerous handiwork. Further along the shore, Archaon could see a line of armoured figures, kneeling and frozen in the snow. The battered remnants of Gorath the Ravager's Bloodsworn knights – infernal warrior contraptions that had sunk in the glacial waters and slowly marched their way to shore to find their leader dead and their allegiance transferred. Archaon could see that Vayne was taking no chances with the clockwork knights and had them under his Slaaneshi guard. The corsair-captain himself paced the snowy shore, not taking his eyes off his beloved *Spite*. When he finally saw his warlord and master standing at the battlements and looking down upon the encampment, the dark elf's laughter echoed up and down the mountainsides. He clapped his hands in grinning approval before picking up Sularii and savagely kissing the sorceress.

'I told you he would do it,' Dravik Vayne laughed. He called up at Archaon. 'Permission to come aboard!'

As Vayne's carrying jubilation drew the eyes of the celebrating army to the *Spite*'s towering battlements, as marauders, beastmen and Chaos warriors saw their general's blood-drenched form, horns were sounded, swords and shields were clashed and a roar of supremacy rose to meet him.

'Permission granted,' the Chaos warlord told them.

CHAPTER XIV

'Always know that you know nothing…'
'The Way of the Kyu-Shinobi is the way of death unseen, proceeding from every darkness and shadow…'
'Even monkeys sometimes fall from the trees…'
'The arts of death did not fail you – know that it was not the art that failed – it was you…'
'Victory is ever in your grasp – even if you fail to achieve it…'
  – Dark Empress Shotoko of the Invisible Army,
    from The Nine Disciplines of the Kyu-Shinobi
(Trans: The Bloody Pool of Myriad Rivers Merging)

The Saturnine Sea
The Great Eastern Ocean
Vermintide

And so Archaon headed out across the expanse known as the Great Eastern Ocean. It rivalled the Wastes or the Steppes beyond the Worlds Edge Mountains for its mind-breaking endlessness. Dark, choppy seas gave way to glassy waters. Land was a rare treat.

The *Spite* kept no log. No records of where the floating fortress and its growing corsair flotilla had been or where it was going. The weather changed so regularly that there was little point in following its fickle nature in ink. The floating fortress crashed through intruding ice, struggled through furious squalls and cut across the crystal calm of sun-scorched seas. With the ocean so vast and open and the heavens so changeable, it became difficult to keep track of time. The sun did rise and set but the days ran into one another like paint on canvas.

Like Father Dagobert with his torturous translations of *The Liber Caelestior*, the floating fortress and its flotilla of captured vessels pushed on into the unknown. Brooding in his throne, atop the *Spite*'s tallest tower, scope in hand, Archaon would have the priest read the insanity to him. It didn't make much sense to the Chaos warrior. Dagobert – the portly priest wrapped up in his moth-eaten furs – was never without the damned tome. His wild, grey hair draped both his fat face and the book over which he was perpetually hunched, creating a private booth for his distractions. The mind-twisting translations had driven him to madness and back, at some times convincing the priest that he knew everything and at other times that he knew nothing. When Archaon's anger got the better of him – threatening to pitch both the tome that toyed with his existence and the priest translating it over the tower battlements – it took Giselle's entreaties and distractions to calm him. In less dangerous moods, Dagobert tried to placate the dark templar with analogies and comparisons. He told Archaon *The Celestine Book of Divination* was very much like the telescope through which he scanned oceans and his future the horizon. He insisted that the same spot in the distance might appear very different from different approaches or through the perversities of changing light and weather. This did not please the Chaos warlord any more.

Archaon's destiny ate away at him. He had achieved the first treasure of the Chaos gods and had been blessed with their Mark. As the years passed and he made the ocean his own, Archaon noticed the changes such a blessing had brought him. Like an animal, his senses had grown keen. He smelled the fear in those about him. His teeth had grown sharp and his tongue tasted his impending victories on the air. He could hear the blood gush through his enemies' veins. Staring hard enough, he could see through the very flesh of his opponents. He could see the horror of their innards and the exposed vulnerabilities their weakling bodies presented. He could see the cracks of former breakages in bone, the positions of organs hiding within cages of rib, hearts that beat like entrancing targets. His own muscle and sinew was taut – like a spring-loaded trap – making his attacks savage, blistering in speed and frenzied in execution.

Within, Archaon was like cold stone. His own doubts and fears were afterthoughts. Every action had the full commitment of body, mind and soul. Every stab and sweep of his sword was blessed with boldness. He believed he had overcome every failing, every challenge, every enemy and like wings that belief took him far. Between his blade and their secret doubts, his enemies undid themselves before him. Archaon would entertain no fantasies of death, no delusions of grand failure. He walked, thought and killed with the assurance of a god, though unlike many of his calling, he had no aspirations to be one. Such figments of fancy were a weakness – and Archaon believed he had none.

Other changes were more physically obvious. Networks of blue veins appeared through his pallid flesh, forming insane patterns across the surface of his body. Showing Dagobert, the priest did not seem to know the dialect but the Brothers Spasskov recognised it instantly, telling Archaon that he was bleeding the incantations of ancient magical wards through his skin like a tattoo that covered his body. The warlord was suspicious but the sorcerers told him that it was a blessing from the gods – the veins and letters forming an enchantment, like a suit of ringmail beneath the surface of his skin.

When Archaon had his sword, shield and crusader armour recovered by Vayne's corsairs from the caves below the *Citadel*, they were all a mess. His battered shield was covered in sucker marks from a great squid beast he had fought and the greatsword *Terminus* was stained with gore. His plate was scratched and his chainmail in shreds. Upon reassembling the mess, he discovered that the suit of armour had an infestation. A cloud of tiny black flies – so tiny, they were all but impossible to make out individually. All attempts to rid the rank plate of the infestation failed. When still, the flies settled and accumulated on the armour, making Archaon one with the darkness in poor light. When the Chaos warrior moved, the disturbed flies formed a haze drifting about him like a miasma or black mist. In combat Archaon found that the mist distracted his enemies and masked some of his movements and evasions. Over time, the dark templar's intentions to rid himself of the infestation faded, adapting his ducks and weaves to the mist's movements.

Such gifts and adaptations made Archaon only hunger more for the treasures and blessings of Chaos. He was the chosen of the Dark Gods but not the Everchosen. Not general of the daemonic legions, not herald of the End Times and the coming apocalypse. Unlike the Altar of Ultimate Darkness that the *Citadel of Spite* carried within its depths, Father Dagobert's heretical volume said little about the location of his next treasure. All the priest could tell him from the twisted translations was that it was an ancient relic of infernal significance. The priest gleaned that the artefact was to be found in a tomb, in an undiscovered land, somewhere in the Great Eastern Ocean. It had been the torment of such details that had driven Archaon to adopt the life of a buccaneer. For years he had had warriors and captains chasing every clue and scrap of information regarding the treasure's nature, location and existence. Many failed to return, while others returned to the *Spite* with little more than their lives. In some of the warlord's most desperate moments he deprived them even of those, but most he simply sent off again in pursuit of some new intelligence or possibility.

Archaon had sent his marauders to their deaths in the jungles of Pahaulaxa, to the south sea islands of cannibal giants, the Hinterlands of Khuresh and the Witch seas of Naggaroth. His warbands plundered lost cities, put entire islands and their primitive civilisations to the flame and fought savage southerners of similar ilk and madness from the bottom of the world. Those that did return carried with them innumerable tales of lost treasures, cursed artefacts and lands of the lost. There was little to narrow Archaon's miserable search. Poring over maps recovered with enemy ships, ancient scraps, charts and improvised scribblings, Archaon discovered nothing that would tell him of the treasure's location. The Chaos warrior thought he might go mad.

For a year or two, insanity did indeed prevail and the ocean ran red with the blood the warlord spilled in mortification. Every sign of civilisation sighted through the warlord's scope was destroyed. Coastlines were ravaged. Forests were torched. Ancient city-ports were turned to sunken rubble. Lone vessels, convoys and fleets were attacked on sight. Crews were butchered and ships blasted from the waves. Archaon's armada left thousands of bone-littered wrecks in its wandering wake. Portly merchantmen and greatships from the west; slavers, pirates, raiders and marauders; flotillas of oriental and druchii designation.

Archaon became the terror of the Eastern Ocean. The Dragon Emperor despatched fleets of mighty war junks to destroy Archaon's armada after Heyang was sacked and burned. The druchii corsair kings of the Broken Lands called him the Red Death. The Hobgobbla Khan slavehulks avoided the Chaos armada like a plague, while the actual plaguefleet of Papa Feste failed to bring the guns of his bloated galleons on Archaon on several occasions. Both the maritime empires of the Man-Chu marauders and the

Nipponese pirates of the Kironshima Wan swore blood oaths on Archaon's end. The cannibal civilisations of volcanic island chains in their skull-adorned catamarans and outriggers prayed to their fire gods for aid against Archaon's dread fleet while the lizard men of Hexoatl and the Emerald Empire sacrificed each other to Tzunki and their Old Ones to rid them of the raiding warlord.

Dravik Vayne and the armada's Chaos lieutenants knew they had lost their master to madness the day he left aboard a flotilla of recently recruited junk-raiders with their defecting Man-Chu crews for company. The *Spite* had sighted a clanfleet bearing the markings of the Eshin. Vayne had told Archaon it was a trap and that the skaven assassins of the Ind and the Lords of Decay had long plotted his downfall. This did not sway the mindless warrior, who sailed straight into the brown, stinking filth that was the Saturnine Sea and the fleet of fat, filthy dhows waiting there. The verminships were armed with cannons that projected unnatural flame that set many of Archaon's black junk-raiders ablaze. The dhows were also swarming with skaven decked in the black headdress and rag robes of warrior-assassins. Bare-pawed and armed with an assortment of curved sabres, cleaver falchions and kris-blades – each glazed with all manner of exotic poisons – the creatures were nimble and trained in the low arts of death. The clanships vomited forth skaven in such number – swimming, swinging and leaping from their fat vessels – that Archaon's flotilla of marauder junk-raiders was swiftly swamped with Eshin vermin.

Vayne knew better than to disobey his master's orders but when the flotilla didn't return, the corsair-captain set a course for the brown miasma that was the Saturnine Sea on the horizon. The effluent waters bobbed with the corpses of Man-Chu raiders and ratmen alike, many bearing the trademark butchery of the warlord, both enemy and ally. Vayne considered it unlikely that despite being new additions to the armada, the piratical raiders of the Man-Chu would turn on Archaon. Vayne had every flaming wreck and piece of wreckage searched. They found him in the belly of a verminship. The vessel was listing badly and still aflame. Within they discovered their lord amongst a tangled nest of dead assassins. The ratmen had been broken, smashed and gutted. Some of their death-smeared weapons had found their mark, however. Archaon had been cut and stabbed by the assassins but had fought his way to bloody victory. Vayne found him still smashing what remained of a skaven's skull into the hull of the verminship with groaning insistence – the victim of some murderous delirium.

'Secure the ship,' Vayne told Archaon's Swords as the grim sentinels stood over their crazed master. When Eins and Zwei didn't move, Vayne pushed, 'The master will want the wonder of the ratmen's cannons at his command. This hulk is going down. Have the vessel jury-rigged for return to the *Spite*'s drydocks in accordance with your overlord's wishes as well as his wellbeing.'

Taking a moment to demonstrate their displeasure, the silent Swords left the site of degenerate massacre and attended to the skaven ship. The sorceress Sularii watched them go, flanked by a pair of Vayne's druchii corsairs. As the winged warriors left, excitement cut through the mask of dour concern that sat on her sharp features.

'Are we going to do it?' the sorceress asked.

Vayne allowed himself a wolfish smile.

'There'll never be a better time,' the dark elf captain told her, stepping daintily through the carnage, limbs and dismembered bodies. He turned to the corsairs. 'Go. Watch the Swords. Ensure they are distracted with the doom of this vessel.'

The druchii nodded. The corsairs nodded and left to attend to their duties of subversion and sabotage. Archaon moaned as what remained of the skaven's skull disintegrated in his hands. He looked up at Vayne and his sorceress with an unseeing eye. He wasn't blood-drunk. This was no blessing or affliction of the Blood God. Quite the opposite. He was lost in a storm of sensual savagery. A storm of the corsair-captain's arrangement. The experience was more than a gift from the lieutenant and his Prince of Pleasure. It was a dreamy distraction. The air was muggy with death and the passion that had brought about such endings.

Vayne soaked up his master's ecstatic sufferings. He knelt down behind the warlord, laying his slender hands on the Chaos warrior's shoulders. He leant in to Archaon's ear. The chosen of Chaos seemed not to know he was there. His neck spasmed and his head twitched in some private heaven of his murderous making. Vayne kissed the brawn of Archaon's blood-speckled neck and nibbled at his master's ear.

'I wish I could be in there with you,' he hissed lasciviously. Turning his head, for a moment, it seemed that the warlord had understood him.

'Dravik...' Sularii warned, coming up behind the corsair-captain and needling the druchii's shoulders with her own dagger-sharp nails. The realisation that Archaon might not be as lost in his never-ending moment of bliss as first thought sent a thrill of horror through the dark elves. The Chaos warrior could snatch for his heretical blade – buried in the muscle-bound body of some rat monster half-breed – and end them for their treacheries. 'Dravik...' Sularii groaned, sensing the imminence of her end. Even the prospect of her death excited the dark elf sorceress. Archaon seemed to be fighting the deviancies he was experiencing. A snarl wrinkled its way through his lip. The warlord had been locked in the sensual sanctum of his own mind and Dravik Vayne had thrown away the key. Taking his face in the digits of his willowy fingers, the druchii leant in and kissed the chosen of darkness, the chosen of the Ruinous Powers and now the sole chosen of Slaanesh.

'Dravik...' Sularii moaned once more. The sorceress ached for her captain. It was his genius that had led them to this. To the darkness below the *Citadel* and a shrine of Chaos unseen. Blind to both the dangers of treason and the blood-drenched altar before which he kneeled, Dravik Vayne – champion-subject of Slaanesh – had run his fingers over the symbols and sigils crafted into the erotic suggestion of the shrine's stone. The Prince of Pleasure had promised him such raptures. Such satisfactions. Such sorrows. Gone were notions of fearful allegiance. The Ruinous Powers unified in one goal and behind one champion. The god-serpent that had him in the snaking, crushing coils of euphoria had whispered secrets to the dark elf's soul. That Archaon the Chosen was a false prophet of darkness. That Slaanesh did not share glory. Slaanesh the Selfish. Slaanesh the Craving. That the Hag Queen of all Naggaroth was but the Prince of Pleasure's concubine. That she would be Dravik Vayne's also and see him to the Witch King's throne.

'Dravik...'

The serpent promised him such wondrous things. Arousing within him appetites unknown. The depths of bottomless greed. Lust for absolute power. The serpent wounded him with taunts and accusations. It laughed through the echo of his excuses and passed water on his pride. The Prince of Chaos told him that above this Altar of Ultimate Darkness lay a vessel that was his to command alone and an army that awaited enslavement. Above lay a legend to be claimed, that Archaon's great accomplishments could become his own. That in a death claimed, the Chaos warlord and his infamy would become Vayne's own. Dravik Vayne – corsair, captain and champion of Slaanesh. Slayer of slayers. Averter of the World's End. The times would not be Archaon's to end – for without the endless pleasures of the world and time to enjoy them, there would be no need for a prince to champion them.

'Dravik...'

The bright rising star that was Archaon's soul would belong to Slaanesh. He would not be fought or brought to battle. Such delusions were suicide. Rather than face the certain slaughter of Archaon's sword, Vayne had used the blade against him. The corsair-captain had his sorceress – who was not without skill in outlandish potions and poisons – concoct an intoxicant of power and potency.

Without wanting to risk discovery in the poisoning of his overlord's meat or wine, or the swift death that would come of spilling even a single drop of his master's unholy blood with bane-smeared needle-knife or stiletto blade, Vayne decided on *Terminus* as the mode of deathly transmission. At opportunity and in secret, Vayne massaged the metal of the weapon with Sularii's intoxicant. A poison of the soul, it moved quickly through the blood. With every foe that fell beneath the blade, the intoxicant spread, entering the unfortunate victim on the sword and infecting their blood with an unthinking ecstasy. Each soul in such taking became the Prince of Pleasure's own. As Archaon finished his infected foes with skill and economic butchery, he breathed the blood of the fallen that hung on the air like a red mist in the warlord's murderous wake. Speck by speck, droplet by airborne droplet, Vayne found a way through the Chaos warrior's considerable defences without even having to lift a blade of his own. Day by day and death by death, Archaon fell into the Prince of Pleasure's embrace. He became a degenerate. A wanton savage. Moaning the incomprehension of what was happening to him. Insensible to everything but the murder-lust of his flesh's own fire, Archaon fell from the certitude of his apocalyptic path and into an exultant bliss.

Dravik Vayne had been an adoring follower of both Khaine and the Prince of Chaos. He was a lover rather than a fighter. He was not some bludgeoning champion of the Blood God or the Ruinous Star, mindlessly swinging his weapon like a woodcutter at the trunks of trees in a forest without end. His talents lay in the glories of murder. In the taking of a life before his foes knew that it had even been lost to them. So it was with his master Archaon.

'Dravik…'

And it was done. The corsair's wicked dagger had passed through Archaon's throat as though it were rancid butter. Blood gushed between them, splashing Vayne's neck and scale armour with the heat of his master's blood. The druchii pulled his lips from those of the warlord. The snarl was gone. Archaon didn't grab for the grievous wound or rise and stumble for help. He sat there in the gore of others, in gore of his own pooling about him. Allowing. Accepting. Enjoying. He grinned like a lust-drunk idiot. The Prince of Pleasure's glorious torments waited for him beyond a necessary death. Archaon willed it on. Waiting. Wanting. As Archaon died before them, Vayne and the sorceress became lost in their own pleasures. The Chaos warrior was barely aware of the pair as they rolled through the blood and carnage about him. He was lost in death-raptures of his own. The end was coming.

Perhaps I chose unwisely? There is time. There is time, before the end. To start again. To twist the destinies of men unborn and create calamities of my own making. Perhaps the failure is in my blood, forever to repeat itself. Ambition that is blind unto itself. Treachery. Murder. The service of the Ruinous Powers accomplished through the service of the self? The dark nectar of the gods. But in whose service is my pawn? My gods? My daemon need? Doom, plain and simple it seems. His own. And the doom of all else. What kind of corruption is this? What kind of perversity? Nothing I slipped into the ripe fruit of his soul. No blessing he was given by my abyssal overlords. Not my patrons. Not my princely foes. It is a kind of mortal madness. What kind of man lives not for the gifts of greed – for power, for supremacy and eternity? What kind of man exists only to end all other forms of existence? Cannot a man's future be corralled? Must it buck the saddle, the chains and halters of fate? This soul must be tamed. But not by me. As we all come to learn, the best lessons are those taught to us by our enemies.

CHAPTER XIV

'To be the hammer or the anvil. Destiny affords only these choices.'

– Khureshi proverb

The Hellespont
The Great Eastern Ocean
The Festival of Ghosts – Year of the Jackal

'You're awake.'

Archaon was. It was a statement, but in the accent sounded like a question. Through the haze of a befuddled mind, the Chaos warrior thought it sounded like a celestial or easterner. Archaon began to fade. A slap across the face brought him back to consciousness. He grabbed at the wrist to which the hand belonged and found it to be spindly and ancient, but possessing great strength for such a withered limb. He tore the wrist back from the Chaos warrior's grasp. 'You have slept enough,' the ancient told him.

Rubbing the crusty confusion from his eye, all Archaon

could see was a ghoulish blue light. It faded. Then there was movement. Bodies. Rippling skin. Writhing bodies. Archaon kicked back across the rocky floor and found that but for his eye-patch, he too was naked. His mind raced to catch up. He didn't know where he was or what was happening. Then, in the eerie blue light that illuminated the cave, he recognised the horrific mass. It was the Fleshstorm – the spawn that fought for the Brothers Spasskov, and by extension himself, when their disgusting talents were needed. Unfortunates of the Great Lord of Change, the Fleshstorm was a single morphing entity, made up of thousands of assimilated bodies. Bone creaked, snapped and fused into monstrous frames while the naked flesh of the spawn writhed and stretched, seamlessly melting into one another. Arms reached out for him, while faces pushed through the horror in silent screams. Some individual spawn managed to break free and slowly, painfully tried to crawl away. They were all mangled limb and insanity, however, and rarely got far before the Fleshstorm reclaimed and reabsorbed them.

Archaon's palms were suddenly wet. He had backed through something warm and slick on the cave floor. He turned and found his face splattered with the same disgusting residue. Archaon had been a slayer of men long enough to know the temperature and copper-tang of blood. Tearing flaps of dribbling flesh from his face and back, Archaon flung them back at the mound of flesh and innards he had backed through. In the blue light the pool of blood and butchery appeared purple and seemed to be dripping from the rocky ceiling above the mound. It appeared as though someone had exploded or been turned inside out.

'What in the Netherhell do you think you're doing?' the cracked, ancient voice complained. 'So surprised to see these monstrosities that fight in your name? Eh? These things of darkness you gather about you?'

Archaon grunted. He was not used to seeing their insides on display. He felt the bile rise up the back of his throat. The voice was intensely annoying – like a distant scream that would not end or a mosquito buzzing continuously beside the ear.

'Who are you?' Archaon demanded to know. 'Where are we? How did I get down here?'

'Questions,' the voice bounced about the cave. 'So many questions, Archaon – chosen of the Infernals, the Daemon-Emperors of the north, the greater darkness beyond the Great Bastion. Perhaps they gave their blessing too easily? Eh? Perhaps you were judged worthy before your time?'

'Show yourself!' Archaon roared, smearing blood from his eyes. He squinted into the intensity of the blue light. It seemed to be moving about the rocky chamber with an ungainly motion. Archaon walked straight into the blinding blueness and found the wizened silhouette of a hunchbacked old man. He grabbed the ancient by the neck, despite the intensity of the blue light emanating from his forehead. Lifting the man from his feet, one of which Archaon found to be scaly and clawed like the talon of a bird, he throttled the ancient, shaking him back and forth. The old man shrieked like a strangled hawk as his body bounced about like a bag of bones.

'Who are you?' Archaon demanded.

Suddenly the blinding blue light was gone, glowing and growing in another part of the cave. In his murderous grip Archaon held a thing of knotted bone, flesh stretched to transparency and multiple limbs like some kind of human spider. Of the ancient there was no sign. Archaon cursed. The ancient was some kind of sorcerer or magician. Tossing the useless spawn back into the mountain of morphing bodies, Archaon ran at the blue light. It was emanating from the wasted ancient, who was getting to his feet with difficulty after assuming the form of some misshapen thing that was crawling away from the Fleshstorm.

The multiple limbed horror shrivelled to the wizened torso and willowy arms and legs of the ancient. It was as though he had morphed into the unfortunate thing and assumed its flesh for his own form. He squawked in terror as Archaon kicked at him. Taking a second head clean off the spawn, the Chaos warrior snatched up a small boulder of black stone from the cave floor and heaved it above his head. The transformation now complete, Archaon beheld a shrivelled old man, squinting at him in fear from the floor. Like Archaon he was naked but for a brilliant blue jewel – an oval sapphire – that was embedded in the flesh of his forehead. Like a third eye, the jewel was shot through with a sliver of darkness at the heart of its blinding brilliance that made it appear like the eye of some great reptile or dragon. The sliver widened and the ghoulish glow from the gem dimmed while the ancient's wasted limbs waved out in front of him in panic. The old man was stuck – unable to roll away because of his hunched back.

'Who are you?' Archaon bellowed, the bludgeoning rock towering dangerously over the frail form of the old man. Disorientated and agitated like some tormented beast, Archaon was in no mood for games. He wanted answers or people would die.

'All right, all right, all right,' the ancient bleated. What was left of his long, grey hair and the lustrous strands of his moustache plastered his age-mottled skull. 'Help me.'

Archaon tossed the rock aside and took the old man by one gnarled and bony hand. The ancient dusted himself off, untangling his wrinkled head from his hair.

'Your name,' Archaon demanded.

'That is no way to treat your saviour,' the ancient told him, prompting Archaon to bring up his hand to strike the old man. 'All right, all right, all right.' The ancient bent down with difficulty to pick up a bone – a femur – from the floor. He scooped up some scraps of shredded clothing. Filthy rags littered the cave where the Fleshstorm had assimilated fresh unfortunates fed to it by the Brothers Spasskov. As he pulled the shredded Man-Chu robes over his mountainous hunch and his sharp bones, the femur grew in his hand to the length of a warped staff. Without effort, the blue sapphire simply popped from the ancient's forehead, without leaving a cavity or as much as a dimple in his flesh. Catching the glorious gem, he slotted the eye-gem into the crowning joint-crook of the bone. Archaon found the new dullness of its glow entrancing. The potent energy the jewel seemed to give off made him lightheaded.

'You are Sheerian...' Archaon said.

'I am Khezula Sheerian,' the ancient repeated.

Except he wasn't repeating anything. Archaon had the information moments before the sorcerer uttered it in his outlandish accent. The old man emphasised every syllable.

'Sheeriang,' Archaon said, but the ancient shook his head with swift anger and annoyance.

'I am Khezula Sheerian...' the sorcerer said. 'Not *Sheeriang*, you simpleton with your sharp teeth and bullock's tongue.'

'You are a daemon sorcerer...'

'I am daemon sorcerer of the Great Changer of Ways.'

The ancient's ugly squint proved even ghastlier with his attempt at a smile. 'Do not mind the Eye,' he said, shaking the glorious blue jewel in the head of the staff. 'It sometimes has that effect on the weak of mind. Like the spyglass, it sees far. Farther than you can possibly imagine. Like the spyglass up close, however, things can become distorted and disorientated.' Archaon was bewitched by the gem. Drawn to its unnatural power like a man to the spectral hopes and dreams for his future. Under Sheerian's control the gem dimmed further and the sorcerer knocked the tip of the staff – nestled jewel and all – against the Chaos warrior's head. Archaon blinked.

'Who are you?' Archaon demanded savagely. Sheerian shook his head and began mumbling curses in a language the dark templar did not understand. He walked away, leaning on the staff and dragging his bird's leg through the grit on the ground. He picked up some rags from the floor of the cave and threw them at the Chaos warrior.

'Cover yourself,' the ancient said, 'for the Great Changer's sake and the sake of his servants.'

'I mean,' Archaon said, anger at himself growing behind

his fumbled words. *'Who* are you? What are you doing here? What am I doing here? What is happening?'

Sheerian silenced the dark templar's questions with a scowl and a flap of his bony fingers.

'I have watched you, chosen one,' Sheerian said. 'From afar. The Eye showed me both your victories and your failures. You would be Everchosen – champion of the Daemon Lords of the Great Northern Darkness. You would be herald of the apocalypse. Master of the End Times of both man and god.'

Archaon stared at the ancient as he hobbled about the cave. He tied the rags about his waist like some Darklands barbarian.

'I am he,' Archaon said.

'Did you not think you would face others who would covet such a prize?' Sheerian put to him.

'I have put a bloody end to many who harboured such false hopes,' the Chaos warrior uttered with pride.

'On the battlefield, yes?' the ancient sorcerer said. 'You are a mighty warrior – the Infernals would not doubt it, Archaon of the Western Empire, but there are many mighty warriors from which the Dark Gods of the world may choose their champion. You think that they were all going to come at you head on? Head on, the way you would face them in return. On the field of battle, you look for weaknesses to explore in your enemies' approach, no? Unprotected flanks? Breaks in formation? Overconfidence in the attack? Did you ever think that the most dangerous of your foes – your competitors for the Ruinous blessings of eternity – might come at you sideways, eh? That they might drop on you from the sky? That they might rise from the deeps?'

'Speak plainly,' Archaon warned. 'My patience wears thin with your convolutions.'

'Always rushing on ahead,' Sheerian said. 'Eager to be part of a future you are creating for yourself. Never spending the time to take stock. To consolidate your position before pushing on into the dangers ahead. It is why you have not seen this coming. It is why you are betrayed by those you would trust to prosecute your will. Why the army you have worked so hard to build will tear itself apart above us.'

'You speak lunacy, sorcerer,' Archaon said, but his voice lacked its usual booming assuredness.

Sheerian squinted at the gem, moving the headpiece of the staff about him and the chamber like some kind of precious crystalline lens.

'The Eye shows only the truth as it comes to pass,' the sorcerer said. 'If its distant reach shows lunacy then the world must be afflicted with such.'

'Enough of this,' Archaon spat and turned to walk away.

'There you go again,' said Sheerian. 'Into an unknown that will end you and bury your path to greatness. Wait!' As the ancient's screeching syllables bounced about the environs of the cave, Archaon slowed to a stop. 'This feverish need of yours to forge on has its uses but sometimes we need to be calm. We need to be patient. Even the servants of the Dark Gods can achieve a kind of peace. It is a peace you have never known, Archaon. It is why,' Sheerian went on, 'your treasures elude you.'

Archaon turned.

'What know you of the treasures of Chaos?' he said. He walked back towards the sorcerer. 'Have you seen them? Can this Eye of yours show the way?'

The Chaos warrior went to grab the bone staff but the sorcerer clutched it back. 'Do you see a land undiscovered?' Archaon demanded.

'An island, yes,' the Chaos sorcerer said. 'A great island of daemon savagery, reaching out across the blood-dark seas for you, chosen one.'

Archaon fell to his knees, blooding them on the cave floor. 'I have searched. In the name of the Dark Gods I have searched. Tell me...' he begged. He had searched so hard and for so long that it hurt to know that another possessed information perversely denied to him. 'Tell me, Sheerian, tell me.'

The sorcerer scowled at him. 'Like your enemies, this land you seek is everywhere and nowhere. Like your enemies, you will find this island where you least expect to.'

'Where?' Archaon boomed.

'Beneath…'

'Beneath what?' Archaon asked, his mind both murk and maelstrom. 'The water?'

'It has been beneath the water but also beneath the land,' the Tzeentchian sorcerer told him. 'Now it sits only beneath the heavens.'

'Curse your riddles, daemon,' Archaon growled. 'I must know. No more searching. Give me a course.'

Sheerian considered the warlord's request.

'You will discover this realm on a Black Meridian,' the daemon sorcerer told him. 'That is your course. My lord will grant you no more at this time. He is of most help to those who help themselves. Besides, you do not stop to ask the way as an earthquake steals the ground from beneath your feet,' Sheerian told him. 'Your enemies have moved and continue to move against you.'

'What know you of my enemies?' Archaon said, getting off his knees. 'All the world is my enemy.'

'You are more right than you know, Archaon the Chosen,' Sheerian said.

'I swear, sorcerer,' Archaon told the ancient, 'that if you afflict me with one more riddle, you shall pay for it with your miserable existence.'

'You have been betrayed, Chaos warrior.'

'By whom?'

'By friends old and new,' Sheerian told him. 'By your dark lieutenants, Archaon. By those closest to your damned pursuits, who in turn pursue damnation for their own ends. By those who would have you fail so that their own prospects be furthered in the eyes of the Dark Gods.'

'I am favoured,' Archaon told the ancient. 'I bear the Mark of the Ruinous Powers that burns like a star eternal in my flesh. I earned the allegiance of the dark god's servants. Does their betrayal not anger their daemon patrons?'

'Allegiance… betrayal,' the sorcerer said. 'These terms don't apply to the Infernals and their wretched servants. How often have you given some miserable minion your word that you would spare him before striking him down at your second thought?'

Archaon gave Sheerian a glower.

'Have you not – Archaon, Chosen of the Chaos gods – plotted the end of such Powers and those they would sponsor? Is your quest not the destruction of us all and the end of the entire world? Mortals? Daemons? Gods?' Sheerian cackled his excitement. Archaon burned into the sorcerer with his gaze. For a moment the Chaos warrior considered ending Sheerian right where the ancient stood.

'If you know I have,' Archaon said, 'then why ask me, you game-playing fool?'

'My Lord Tzeentch revels in such games,' Sheerian told him. 'He is their patron. Even of yours, ender of worlds.'

'You talk of friends and enemies, sorcerer,' Archaon said, tiring of the games Sheerian spoke of and those of his lord. 'What are you? How do you come to be here? I have never admitted you into the ranks of my host.'

'Are you sure, Chaos warrior?' the ancient cackled. 'You have not been yourself of late.'

'I think I'd remember you, Sheerian.'

'I am memorable,' Sheerian admitted. 'Those already shackled to your doomed quest have freed themselves. The shrine that showed you favour now favours others also. It corrupts hearts of men as it does the very stone of the citadels and towers under which it sits. Your champions have made their pilgrimage to the darkness and the Ruinous masters of that darkness have shown them their own ways – their own paths to greatness.'

'I fight for these false gods, these inconstant things of shadow...'

'Then you fight for false gods,' Sheerian agreed, 'and inconstant things of shadow. Accept that such Powers cannot be trusted – any more than you or I.'

'How many of my men have betrayed me?'

'Many.'

'Who amongst my champions and warlords?' Archaon demanded, 'must now die for their lack of vision?'

'At this very moment,' the sorcerer told him, squinting horribly through his sorcerous Eye, 'your army is at war with itself.' Sheerian gestured to the bloody mound of flesh that Archaon had crawled through earlier, the gore and scraps of flesh still dripping from the rocky ceiling. 'Your arch sorcerers petitioned their lord and mine for ways to destroy you.'

'The Brothers Spasskov…'

'You harnessed their sorcerous rivalry, Archaon,' Sheerian said, 'but then claimed their victories for your own. Gorath the Ravager. The warrior titans of the Red Mountain. The island of the enchantress Thusula and her daemon daughters. Was it your blade that secured such achievements or the talents of your slave sorcerers? You think in the face of both your ignorance and success that the pair would not set aside their rivalries and remember their shared blood? The blood of brothers? Being of my lord's following, they were amongst the most capable of your lieutenants and you equipped them with the tools they required to overthrow you – wounded pride and the selfish ambition that infects such a wound. You gave them that. The rest was potential they already had.'

'Vladimir… Vladislav,' Archaon murmured, looking at the pile of ruined flesh. Then to the ancient, Archaon said, 'I have not been all that I could be.'

'No,' Sheerian agreed. 'You have not. You are a warrior, as brave and untrue as any that have already held the title Everchosen of the gods. But you are not ready to command the legions of darkness.' The sorcerer shook his brown-spotted head. 'No. Those daemons, those fiends would tear your soul to shreds.'

Archaon nodded slowly. The Chaos sorcerer's cackling accusations were an annoyance but a true one. The dark templar had fallen far and was paying for his shortcomings as a leader of darkness in the world.

'But I will be ready. One day. One day soon, sorcerer. These pretenders to my title will pay for their betrayal,' Archaon growled. 'As will the Dark Gods that sponsored them.'

Sheerian gibbered to himself. 'Yes, yes…'

'How were the brothers to usurp me?' Archaon asked, looking back to the mound of shredded flesh that was Vladimir and Vladislav Spasskov.

'Rituals and summonings,' the sorcerer said. 'They called upon my Lord Tzeentch to reveal to them the secrets of releasing the serpent spirit of the *Yien-Ya-Long* – a mighty beast of antiquity that once laid waste to Grand Cathay, riding the winds of change and visiting the fires of transfiguration on the simple people of the provinces. They asked my lord for the incantations to give such a monster form.'

'The *Yien-Ya*…'

'Don't hurt yourself, boy,' the sorcerer told him. 'The *Yien-Ya-Long* or "Flamefang" in your bullock-tongue.'

'Flamefang,' Archaon repeated, 'is a dragon?'

'Oh yes,' Sheerian confirmed. 'And not some young drake or winged serpent. Flamefang is a monstrous creature. Warped and ancient. Your sorcerer-twins were to summon the beast back from the beyond.'

'They failed?' Archaon put to the sorcerer.

'They succeeded in their petition,' Sheerian admitted. 'My Lord Tzeentch sent me with the incantations but my summoning… was not without difficulty.' The daemon sorcerer jabbed his staff at the remains of the Brothers Spasskov and the mountain of fused and writhing bodies that was their conjoined army of spawn. 'Your sorcerers had prepared one of these wretches for my flesh transference. Alas, my Lord is fickle – and the summoners' own form was chosen for my emergence.'

'Then I have your Lord Tzeentch to thank,' Archaon said, 'or right now I would be facing the spirit of some great beast.'

'My patron Power has taken a great interest in you, Archaon the Chosen,' Sheerian said. 'There are not many who would use the gifts of the Dark Gods to destroy them. Such bottomless aspiration is to be admired. Rewarded, even. As the pantheon turns its back to you, Archaon, my Lord would take pity on your plight. He would see you survive your present doom, overthrow your enemies and find new friends amongst the ranks of his daemon followers.' The ancient gave him a horrid smile that almost cracked his face.

'Your Lord Tzeentch empowers a pair of his sorcerous acolytes to kill me,' Archaon marvelled, 'while sending another one to save me?'

'He is the Changer of the Ways,' Sheerian said. 'Only he knows the truth of all things, while the rest of us drown in an ocean of confusion and contradiction.'

'You spoke of reward,' Archaon pushed.

'For my Lord Tzeentch,' the ancient went on, 'the greatest weapon he can bequeath is knowledge. He sent me here not for your paltry sorcerers but for you. There are great beasts to be unleashed, Archaon, and you are one of them. Unleashed on your true path. But, like you, I digress and there isn't much time. First, your enemies.'

'Tell me.'

'While the Brothers Spasskov visited the Altar of Ultimate Darkness and prayed to my master for the means to destroy you,' the sorcerer Sheerian told him, 'others were in attendance. You know the shrine. In such darkness it can be many things to many people. That barbarian hulk you dangerously keep in the dungeons…'

'The Great Spleen?'

'Did you and the druchii really think that you could control such a creature,' Sheerian continued, 'a monstrous manifestation of the Blood God's own wrath, and hold it captive in slumber? It visits the Altar of Ultimate Darkness in its savage dreams. Your friend Vayne…'

Archaon's hand went instinctively to his throat. He could still feel the slice of the corsair-captain's dagger through his flesh. But there was no gaping wound or even the suggestion of a scar to be found.

'Dravik Vayne is no friend of mine,' Archaon snarled.

'He and his druchii witch,' the ancient said, 'while trading in the potions, poisons and concoctions that laid you low, have been negligent in their attentions to other matters. With the fires of its rage stoked from within, and without the soporifics that would keep the drugged creature so, the Blood God's monster wakes, hungry and furious.'

'What of Vayne?' Archaon said, his words searing with hatred.

'He serves the Hag Queen of Naggaroth and the Prince of Pleasure,' Sheerian said. 'He and his sorceress always have. A course has already been set for the Land of Chill where they will deliver to their queen the Altar of Ultimate Darkness as they were originally charged to do. They have their orders from the altar. Take back the *Spite*. Have the corsair crew enslave your mighty army. Kill the chosen of the Dark Gods, the bearer of the Mark eternal – Archaon of the Western Empire.' The dark templar reached once more for his throat.

'Was I lost to a dream also?'

'Yes,' the sorcerer hissed. 'You chose well in Dravik Vayne. He is as devious and deceiving a druchii as any that have existed. You chose perhaps too well. He had his witch poison your own blade, which then you used to infect those you butchered – breathing back in the poison originally intended for you, little by little. Ingenious really. Almost worthy of my own lord. With every life you took, you were in fact taking your own. Your mind enslaved. Your throat vulnerable to the druchii's own blade. The *Spite* is back under Vayne's captaincy. The quiet and steady enslavement of your crew has been going on for months, with many of your loyalists imprisoned in the sanctum dungeons. And…'

'I was slain by Dravik Vayne,' Archaon said.

'You were,' Sheerian confirmed. The sorcerer bit at his gnarled lip. 'A soul as old as yours has known death many times.'

'I'm not interested in your celestial philosophies, sorcerer.'

'But not like this,' Sheerian said. 'Emboldened by the infernal influence of the Altar of Ultimate Darkness – with the lies and whispers of their patron Powers in their ears – your enemies moved against you. All at once. Unknown to you and unknown to each other. You were slain. This is true. By the Prince of Pleasure's druchii servants. But you were not you at the time of your slaying.'

'More riddles?' Archaon snarled.

'You have been replaced, warlord,' Sheerian told him. 'Many times. The Lord of Flies – sworn god-foe of my own daemon lord – blessed the womb of his witch with a plague of men.'

'Mother Fecundus?'

'While you put the witch's army of maggot-men to your own uses, she had uses for you. Sapping your soul like a disease or some thing that lays its eggs beneath the skin, she birthed mindless monstrosities in your semblance. Into one she implanted what she had drained of your being. It is this thing that has commanded your army for past months, was subject to the druchii's treacheries and had its throat slit by Dravik Vayne.'

'Then how did I come to be down here, in the lair of the Brothers Spasskov and their monstrosities?'

'The body is but a sack of flesh without the soul. What remained of you was secreted down here, under the *Citadel*, where the Brothers Spasskov kept their spawn. While the witch's maggot took your place in degenerate impersonation, your body was here, amongst this abomination of bodies. The witch is devious but I suspect that my Lord Tzeentch had a hand in it. There is something of his tangled elegance in the idea that his sorcerers toiled here – right here – in the arts of your destruction, mere footsteps from where your body lay defenceless.' Sheerian gestured to the Fleshstorm with his bone staff. 'Here, in this spawn, like the rockpool fish that sits in the anemone unstung.'

Archaon's fists were clenched at his side. His face was a mask of stone cold fury. His army was riddled with dissemblers, assassins and usurpers. The scale and beauty of the betrayal was breathtaking. His warmongering lieutenants had used him and cast him aside. His gods had abandoned him. Failure ran like lead through his veins. His heart thumped for vengeance, hammering inside his chest as though it were fit to burst.

'I am whole again?' the Chaos warrior asked, his words like the clearing of steel from the scabbard.

'As much as you ever were,' the sorcerer said. A smile began to spread across the ancient's shrivelled face.

'I will be the end of the gods,' Archaon told Sheerian. 'I will be the death of all the world. I will slay everything that walks or crawls – but it starts here with those that have failed me and tricked me into failing myself. They shall all die for this.'

'Yes, yes…' Sheerian hissed.

Archaon turned away, the blue light of the Eye washing across his scarred back as he strode into the shadows. The dark templar's bones ached for blood. He stretched his neck from side to side and crunched the knuckles of both fists. There was killing to be done. It was time to go to war with his own army. He had made them. The scourge of the Shadowlands. Warlords of the Northern Wastes. They had ridden disaster through the chill lands of Naggaroth. They had brought destruction to the shores of the Great Eastern Ocean, encapsulating the lands, waters and tempests in a ring of Ruinous fire. Indeed, Archaon had made them. Now he would break them.

'You are Archaon,' Sheerian announced to the gloom. 'Warlord of darkness, risen out of the west like the Ruinous Star. You have gathered about you the warriors and champions of doom. Men and beasts who themselves receive the blessings of their patrons for dark service in your name. How will you, one man – one great man, but one man alone – destroy an army of destroyers? Men and beasts who have already laid you low with steel and cunning? Do not dive head first into the waters of your doom. Think. Consider. Be at dark peace. How might such decimation be achieved?'

Archaon closed his eye. He breathed. His heart slowed to the stabbing rhythm of hate. He became one with the darkness. Then it came to him. The warlord smiled.

'Your master offers reward?' Archaon asked. He did not bother to turn to address the daemon sorcerer.

'Perhaps,' Sheerian said. Then thoughtfully, 'Archaon, give him something worthy of a reward. Some offering or suggestion that his interest in your fate is justified.'

'You were sent with secrets, sorcerer,' Archaon said, his voice bouncing ominously about the cave. 'Incantations. This Flamefang...'

'The savage spirit of a serpent ancient and long passed,' the sorcerer told him. 'A monster of fang and flame that no wall or great bastion would resist. The terror of Grand Cathay has afflicted the eastern empires for the best part of a thousand years. Know what you ask, Chaos warrior. You would have me visit Lord Tzeentch's storm of change upon the world once more?'

'I would,' Archaon told him with serene certainty before striding into the shadows.

'Yes,' Khezula Sheerian, Daemon sorcerer of Tzeentch hissed, both to the departing Archaon and himself. 'Yesssss...'

CHAPTER XV

*'The spawn of the north, ancient, from the clouds impending,
A thunderbolt in flesh from angry skies, like death descending,
Detested of claw, of jaw, of scale, of flame – it is nature's bane,
Hunting the lesser races, across ocean and waste, ever at change,
It is the very form of our darkest fears –
And like a nightmarish vision in the heavens – it appears...'*

– Khezula Sheerian, *Visions of the Fifth Tier,
Scaling the Impossible Fortress* and *Netherhell Bound*

The Black Meridian
The Great Eastern Ocean
The Festival of Ghosts – Year of the Jackal

Archaon could hear cannon fire. It had started. News of his apparent death had spread like a disease, infecting the minds of champions and madmen with fantasies of brief bloodshed and taking Archaon's place at the head of the Ruinous horde. Cut off from the influence of other champions, the warrior-captains of vessels making up Archaon's raiding flotilla were first to declare their explosive intentions for their patrons and for themselves. Months of uneasy peace and fearful unity went up like a barrel of gunpowder. War junks, marauders, pirate xebecs and slaveships were all firing upon one another in pre-emptive strikes, boarding and slaughtering crews that fought for enemy gods.

For Archaon, standing in Dravik Vayne's cabin, aboard the corsair-captain's elegant raider, nothing said coup d'état better than looking down on his own corpse. The maggot-man that Nurgle's witch had replaced him with was a ghoulish match. It filled the dark templar with disgust to know that there were others aboard the *Spite* that enjoyed muscle and reflexes tempered by decades of battle and their warlord's fearful features. The doppelganger wore a death mask now: a face from which the worries of command had been removed, from which the horror of an unexpected end had fallen. Vayne had opened his throat from ear to ear with his wicked blade and allowed gore to cascade down his victim's breastplate. The warrior's face was calm and untroubled. In death, Archaon seemed to know a peace he had never known in life. Even before renouncing his weakling God-King and accepting as his masters the capricious Chaos Powers.

He looted his own corpse. His infested plate and mail. His helmet. His boots and gauntlets. His shield. The polluted blade, *Terminus*. Tearing the Fleshstorm's shredded cast-offs from his hips, he slipped into his gore-stained arming doublet and armour sticky with blood. He shouldered the shield with a grunt. With darkness writhing and weaving about him and the weight of plate once more on his body, the Chaos warrior felt complete. Sliding his greatsword into a scabbard across his back, Archaon snatched druchii lanterns from the cabin and smashed them down on his deathly semblance. Within moments the maggot-man was a raging inferno of oil-fed flame that rapidly began spreading through the cabin.

He stared at his own funeral pyre. It was an end but also a beginning. He would start again. He would learn from his mistakes and be the herald the apocalypse truly deserved. The lieutenants, the beastmen and marauders that had betrayed him would pay with their lives. The wretches that had failed him did not deserve to live. There were only two of the hundreds and hundreds on board the floating fortress that he needed. That he wanted. That he cared to take on with him. The girl Giselle, who had once tried to save him from himself, and Father Dagobert, whose knowledge of both his past and unfolding prospect of his future made the priest indispensable. Besides, *The Liber Caelestior* was with them. Archaon would need the secret of his tomorrows, contained within the damned tome.

Taking a pair of crossed corsair cutlasses from where Vayne had them displayed on his wall, Archaon kicked open the door. He dispensed with the stealth he had used when entering the raider's cabin from the gothic maw of the rear window.

The sun had set on the Great Eastern Ocean. Morrslieb was yet to rise but great Mannslieb was low and heavy on the horizon, casting its bloody double on the dark waters that rolled beneath it. Archaon's breath clouded before him. It was cold. His search for the treasures of Chaos had taken the *Spite* to the farthest reaches of the southern seas. Beyond the Lost Isles. Beyond the continental capes of Lustria and Khuresh. Beyond the shipping lanes of the elder races and the reach of map and chart. The skies were crystal clear and the waters stabbing cold.

The druchii raider's sails were furled on their lateen gaffs. Above, dwarfing the tiny ship, was the mountainous silhouette of the *Citadel of Spite*, its crooked towers like a midnight claw reaching greedily for the heavens. The confusion of the corsairs on the raider's deck was mercilessly exploited by the Chaos warrior, who put the spiked knuckle guards of his cutlasses through the gaunt faces of the first two dark elves he met. The face-smashing cries of anguish drew corsairs and slave-crew to Archaon, who opened them up with brutal sweeps of his curved blades. One of Dravik Vayne's corsair-commanders got a cutlass straight through him and then became a shield of scale and black leather as Archaon ran at an assembling line of druchii dreadshards that punched a hail of willowy bolts from their repeater crossbows into the officer's cadaver. Throwing the bolt-mangled body at them, the dark templar slipped through their number, clipping off limbs, skewering helmed heads and carving through druchii flesh.

Leaving his cutlasses through a pair of staggering dreadshards, Archaon took their repeating crossbows from their agony-open fingers, one in each arm. As hastily armed slaves poured from their forecastle enclosures, screamed on by druchii officers, Archaon unleashed the crossbows at them. As bolts buried themselves in faces, throats and bare chests, the stream of slaves started to form a shrieking mound over which following thralls had to climb – straight into the path of Archaon's final quarrels. With both crossbows spent, the Chaos warrior allowed them to crash to the deck and snatched his cutlasses from the impaled dark elves staggering behind him. As their guts rained down on their boots, the druchii collapsed and Archaon continued his wolfish advance up the length of the vessel.

As he sliced through slaves and gutted their dark elf overlords, the Chaos warrior fired off loaded bolt throwers as he passed. Criss-crossing the raider's black deck as well as oncoming corsairs with his wicked blades, Archaon released the ballistas as he went. The corsairs called them *reapers* and their name was well-earned. As their ratchet-claws released the taut sinew of the bowstrings, the heavy trident-headed bolts shot away, smashing through the hull, rigging and druchii crew of a vessel sailing alongside Vayne's docked raider. Slamming individual reapers facing the *Spite* to maximum elevation before releasing their stone-spearing bolts, Archaon fooled the Chaos warriors crewing the floating fortress's mighty bolt throwers into thinking that they were under attack. As the dark templar took heads from Vayne's Slaaneshi elves and butchered the raider's slave-stock, he heard the buck of the colossal war machines in furious reply. Bolt shafts the size of tree trunks smashed down through the deck and screaming slaves. Archaon felt a quake pass through the ship as a third colossal bolt followed the second down through the ruin of the top decks and slammed through the bottom of the raider's hull. Skewered and in the throes of a savage fire sweeping up the ship, the druchii vessel began to take on water. Without the support of the surrounding deck, the foremast began to topple, taking the rigging, wreckage and topsails over the side with it.

Deciding that his work aboard the raider was done, Archaon ran at a throng of screeching corsairs. Skidding down onto the deck and between their boots, Archaon cleaved through the backs of their knees. A druchii officer was suddenly upon the prone templar with a pair of curved knives, but placing the soles of his boots against the leather of the corsair's chest, Archaon launched the officer back across the deck. Throwing one of his cutlasses at an oncoming druchii, the blade slamming into the middle of the dark elf's chest, Archaon plunged his other weapon into the gut of another corsair before the officer – with cat-like reflexes – was back on him. Archaon slapped the corsair back before smashing one knife from his enemy's hand with an armoured gauntlet. Again the officer came at him with the single knife. Allowing its tip to pass under his arm, Archaon grasped the druchii's slender hand in both of his own. Holding the knife in an iron grip, Archaon tore back the fingers of the corsair officer, breaking bones and ripping digits from their sockets. The Chaos warrior heard the dark elf squeal but silenced him with an armoured elbow to the face. Both knife and officer hit the deck.

Archaon heard agonised lines give and felt rigging whip over his head as the foremast started to drag the mainmast down. Scooping up the dark elf's knives from the ruined deck with their finger rings, Archaon ran at the officer, who buried both his helm and head beneath cowering arms. Springing off the corsair's back, Archaon's other boot found the ship's rail, from which he launched himself at the rope dragged upwards by the excruciating descent of the mainmast. Riding the momentum of the rope, Archaon allowed himself to be propelled upwards at the *Citadel*'s side. When the rope had nothing left to give him, the Chaos warrior stabbed out with the talon-tips of his knives, the wicked tips of the blades scoring down through the salt-dusted stone of the floating fortress's side. Scrabbling with his boots and hooking into the crooks and ridges of the black druchii stonework, Archaon's slide down the side of the floating fortress slowed to a gruelling stop. With the raider flooding and aflame in equal measure below, the dark templar had little intention of clinging to the wall like a bat above the devastation. Sticking the stone of the wall with alternate blade tips, Archaon made the muscle-roasting climb required to reach the lowest of the *Citadel of Spite*'s contorted battlements. Hauling himself over the serrated crenellations, Archaon took a moment to catch his breath before climbing on board his twisted flagship.

Beneath his boots Archaon felt the great vessel rock. Over the side he could hear furious agitation in the icy waters, an eruption of bubbles and turbulence that thrashed the surface of the sea to a white maelstrom. Peering over the fanged bulwark of the *Spite* and down its stone side, the dark templar could see light in the depths: pinks, blues and purples. Beneath the black waters Archaon fancied that he could see impossible flame and the crash of titanic bodies. Beasts were rising from the ocean. As they broke the surface, Archaon could see some of the floating fortress's monstrosities – creatures that the warlord had ordered set upon enemy hulks and flotillas – wrapped around some greater beast. Something Archaon hadn't seen before. Sea serpents and the tentacles of a giant-beaked kraken were coiled about the monster's form. The great beast rolled like a crocodile, tangling itself further in lengths of tendril and serpentine body. Archaon saw huge claws rend huge chunks of blubber and scale from its attackers. Jaws flashed and crunched serpents in two, while wings struggled to unfurl and beat through the water like monstrous fins. The kraken wanted to drag the beast down into the depths and drown it, but as the creature turned its colossal maw on the squid and its flesh-shearing beak, the kraken released it. Streams of purpurescent flame followed it into the darkness before the beast wriggled free of the last of the strangling serpents and beat its wings for the surface. Breaking through the bubbling foam rising from its own fiery breath, the gargantuan creature latched onto the side of the floating fortress with its massive claws. Once again, Archaon felt the *Spite* list to one side as the floating fortress took the extra weight of the beast on its starboard side.

There was something spellbinding about the thing. It was huge. It was obscenely ugly. It was climbing up the *Citadel of Spite* towards Archaon. The dark templar looked down on the beast. Flamefang. The curse Archaon had ordered Sheerian to unleash upon the *Spite*, upon his mutinous Chaos host, upon the world once more. All to be caught in the degenerate god Tzeentch's unfolding storm of change. The terror of Grand Cathay was flesh and doom once again – and what a horror it had become. It was a dragon – that was for sure. Its lithe body was long and serpentine, like some colossal serpent of the sky, simultaneously sinewy and powerful. Its spindly limbs supported scythe-like claws that could cut through the trunks of trees, while the beast's wings were colossal, sun-blacking shelters of gnarled bone and stretched flesh. The thick, whipping coils of its tail, which seemed simply a continuation of its snaking body, balanced the length of a slithering neck, in turn supporting a gargantuan head: an armoured skull of twisted horn, gavial jaws and twisted teeth.

The Chaos warrior had encountered nothing like it before, even in his wanderings through the Wastes. He had only seen its kind in pictorial form. Oriental dragons stitched into the flags of Cathayan vessels or carved into the lacquered breastplates of the Dreaded Wo. Its predacious size and presence was heart-stopping enough but as Archaon stared down at the ascending monstrosity he had unleashed, it somehow managed to exude a dread that was more than the threat of its savage power. At his command, Khezula Sheerian had brought into existence an otherworldly thing. A slinking beast of world-eating spirit, encased in the devastating form of its ancient terror. The creature's flesh was not its own, however. Like the daemon sorcerer who had summoned it, Flamefang had been forced to make do with the materials available. The dragon's ancient scale and primordial flesh was long gone. The small mountain of bodies that had been the Fleshstorm had found new form and purpose, stretched horrifically about the dragon's monstrous spirit. Archaon could see eyes, mouths and faces staring out from the melded beast-flesh. Its skin was pale and flesh-pink, thick with muscle and tendon, threaded with rib and bone. It was a creature crafted of the living. A howling, screaming, begging nightmare of borrowed flesh and suffering – stomach-churning to behold.

As he became entranced with the dragon, the dragon in turn became entranced with its prey. The marauders and beastmen on board the *Spite* and the surrounding flotilla were all damnation's children. They all had the whiff of destined greatness about them. The Dark Gods were fickle in the choosing of their champions. To the Chaos dragon, Archaon was a blinding light amongst a constellation of lesser stars. His power and potential burned to behold and the beast knew it must have him. Like a wild thing of impulse and darkness it would swallow the swarms of souls about it like an ocean behemoth might clouds of shrimp. It knew that Archaon was special, even if it couldn't possibly conceive how or why. It had his stink in its ghastly nostrils – the stench of destiny – and knew it must have him.

It saw him with the hundreds of eyes peering in horror from its form. Its twisted cage of dagger-teeth parted and from the bottomless blackness of its throat a glorious fountain of purple flame vomited forth. Throwing himself back behind the knife-edge of the bulwark, Archaon dived for the deck, allowing the unnatural inferno to roar past and reach for the skies. Scrabbling to his feet, Archaon lurched for the nearest cover. Flamefang was suddenly there, its serpentine neck carrying the Chaos dragon's monstrous head up to the stone deck. Again the jaws parted. The dark templar clambered awkwardly over a balustrade and dropped down onto the stone steps of a stairwell leading down onto a mezzanine deck. The sky disappeared beneath a blanket of flame. Archaon expected to hit the black stone of the steps. His fall was broken, however, by Gorghas Hornsqualor and a throng of his shaggy white warriors. The beastmen roared their fury at the Chaos warrior as they tumbled together down the stairs. In a brute rage the beastmen grabbed the warrior with their brawny arms and proceeded to kick dents into his plate with their hooves.

Archaon wasn't worried about Hornsqualor's troops. He felt the deck shift as Flamefang pulled its monstrous length up onto the *Citadel*'s deck. The beastmen were so involved in defeating the Chaos warrior that had fallen on them that they hadn't noticed the colossal beast that was now snaking its way through the *Spite*'s towers and architecture. Inbetween the hairy, white fists and the bloody hooves, Archaon caught glimpses of Flamefang's horrific body passing overhead. He could hear shrieks and screams as the monster cut marauders in half with the mindless snap of its jaws and buried entire warbands, crowded tents and warriors of the Ruinous Powers in flame. Archaon got his gauntlet to his brawny restrainer's single horn. With his arm around the beastman, he twisted and snapped the creature's neck with a horrible, bleating screech. He didn't have time to deal with Gorghas Hornsqualor and his bully gors and found himself crawling away. The beastmen chuckled their harsh derision, watching the Chaos warrior scramble behind the corner.

Their mirth was lost in the purple firestorm that enveloped the stone stairwell as the dragon slipped its long neck and open, elongated jaws down through the cruel druchii architecture and blasted them to fiery oblivion. Some monstrous, primordial urge to serve its Dark Master drove it on. It wanted forms to change and the souls that fled such abomination. It wanted Archaon. The blazing light of his significance drove the monster mad, flashing briefly and temptingly before becoming lost once more in the miasma of dark souls that lit up the floating fortress.

After the heat washed away and Archaon heard Flamefang slither monstrously away to create havoc towards the stern, Archaon turned to see what remained of the beastmen. Instead of a huddle of cremated beastmen, the Chaos warrior found that the dragon's breath had actually turned the brutes into small, fleshy mounds that were erupting in change. Like anemones turning themselves inside out, the creatures had been transformed into blossoming spawn by the form-altering power of the Tzeentchian monster's fire. Instead of a fiery death, Flamefang visited upon its victims the blessings of its infernal master, Lord Tzeentch.

'What you think?' came a voice. Archaon turned to find the sorcerer Sheerian hobbling around the corner, his bone staff tapping its way along the black stone. The ancient leant on the staff and Archaon was bathed in the azure glow of its gem headpiece. The jewel seemed to blink. 'What do you think of Lord Tzeentch's gift?' Archaon didn't give an answer and Sheerian didn't wait for one. 'Change is coming, Archaon. For you, for me, for the poor mongrels hereabouts,' the sorcerer said, gesturing to the chaos and confusion that swarmed the *Citadel*'s decks. 'For the world.' The ancient smacked the base of the staff down on the stone. 'Go then, chosen one. Ring the changes with your blade, with your vengeance. Bring my lord the souls of your enemies, Archaon. Sacrifice them on the altar of your ambition.'

Archaon got to his feet. He found the sorcerer intensely annoying and didn't relish the opportunity to serve his warped god as some kind of puppet executioner.

'That means you too, sorcerer,' Archaon told him with dark certainty. Khezula Sheerian smiled his ghastly smile. He rattled the jewel of the Eye in the setting of its bone staff.

'I die,' the daemon sorcerer told him, 'but not by your hand, you insatiable cur.'

Archaon grunted and turned. The great flesh-smeared belly of the Chaos dragon snaked its way above them. It was getting bigger. With every swallowed victim, the monstrosity grew in size and horror. Its victims became part of its slithering bulk. In its warped form Archaon could see faces staring down on him. He recognised them as members of his own army. Their mouths open and screaming. Flamefang was claiming his army for its own. It was harnessing the power of their flesh. The Chaos warrior wondered if he had done the right thing in having Sheerian unleash the creature once again on the world. Indeed, it was an exquisite punishment for his enemies and the followers that had failed him. It thwarted the designs of men and gods but Archaon had to wonder whether he too would be its victim. Whether he would find himself in the colossal creature's belly and swiftly assimilated into its dreadful form or bathed in its transformative flame. Archaon knew that he possessed no blade, no shield and no armour that would turn such a weapon aside.

He had no intention of fighting the beast, however. Like all of the servants of the Dark Gods, the dragon itself was a weapon to be wielded. A punishment to be delivered. That was all that mattered. The daemons, the princes and the Dark Gods would know that he was not their plaything – a slave to infernal destiny. His choices were his own, no matter how insane they seemed to others and indeed himself. He would feed Tzeentch's monstrous pet his unworthy army. In horrible death, the warriors and marauders that had failed to unify under his banner would be joined in their shared failure. There were a few amongst their number who deserved his special attention and walking away from the cackling sorcerer Sheerian, Archaon made good on the distracting carnage that Flamefang was creating at his flagship's stern and returned to the *Citadel*'s main deck.

Even before the arrival of the horrific dragon, the *Spite* had been in chaos. News of Archaon's death, brought by

Dravik Vayne and his sorceress, had initiated a full-blown mutiny. Chaos warriors who coveted command of the army for themselves went on murderous rampages, assassinating champions they considered to be their greatest competition. Weak-minded marauders and beasts flocked to the banners of such mad men, spreading the carnage, mindlessly changing allegiances as the dark warriors behind which they had thrown their brutal support were brained and butchered. Petty rivalries and long-standing hatreds – formerly kept in check by Archaon and his lieutenants through the threat of retribution – exploded in wanton murder and massacre. The case for every Chaos god was argued with the blade. Each champion and marauder fought for the prospects of his own patron or power in the bloody belief that the Blood God, the Lord of All, the Changer of Ways or the Prince of Chaos was worthy of the host's destructive potential.

Archaon drank deep in the havoc of it all. His hands trembled in expectation. His gauntlets rattled about them. He walked through the death and the destruction. Bolt throwers had been turned inwards and their spear-storms unleashed on the crowds of marauders fighting for control of the stone expanse of the *Citadel*'s blood-slick decks and wards. Punching through the bodies of five, six, sometimes seven Chaos warriors at a time, the wicked shafts tore men from their death dealing and skewered them like meat on a giant's spit. Other artillery pieces had been man-handled around in the chaos and fired into the riotous carnage. Druchii bolt throwers adorned the razor crenellations of the *Citadel of Spite*'s port and starboard sides at intervals, ready to slash through the sails of escaping enemy vessels or ensnaring them in barbed line-trailing grapnels. As well as these nightmares being turned on the Chaos host, the fevered hordes had to contend with the motley collection of other artillery pieces that the army had pilfered from captured vessels before scuttling or re-appropriating them – great cannons, mortars and carronades. Archaon blinked as the Hung marauders fighting amongst themselves before him turned to a thunderous drizzle of red. His armour was showered in their gore as the great muzzle of an ancient bronze carronade belched canister shot into the crowds, cutting a murderous swathe through the madness. A cannonball trailing some kind of enchanted fire whizzed over the warlord's head, while a corsair's crossbow bolt twanged, snapped and glanced off his armoured shoulder.

The stone deck was awash with blood and body parts, while barbarians, buccaneers and slave-warriors slaughtered each other before him. It was pure insanity. There was little room for manoeuvres amongst the throngs on the slippery deck, just grabbing and killing. The hands of the fallen grasped for Archaon's boots as he walked through the sweet butchery. Druchii corsairs, spike-furred Norsemen, clansmen and retainers of the Dreaded Wo. None of them recognised Archaon as he moved through the confusion and horror they had brought on themselves. Shaggy beastmen roared challenges at him as he moved through the mutinous massacre before being axed down by bearded berserkers of the dawi-zharr. Some madman had opened the stables and released rhinoxen and horses out onto the confusion of the deck. The animals ran about in panic, slipping in the blood and scrabbling their way through the carnage. Marauders were trampled and gored, while others saw the animals no differently to the other murderous shapes coming at them out of the pandemonium, slashing at them as they cannoned by or slaughtering the steeds and beasts of burden with pikes and spears.

Archaon saw several warriors of Chaos attempt to mount passing horses: Hrodgar Deathchosen and Orchan Varg, one of the Bloodsworn clockwork knights. They rose above the rabble and the death to ride and kill but their ascendency was short lived. The horses could not keep their footing on the rolling, blood-greased deck and swiftly both the steeds and the warriors were dragged back down into the butchery. Hands and claws grasped for them. Spear-points jabbed. Axes flashed. Within moments the mounted warriors were part of the mess on the deck.

Archaon came to a stop. He could smell the coppery sting of death on the air. He licked his lips. He could taste annihilation. He had spent so long attracting dark souls to his destiny like moths to a flame. So many years of his life building a horde of Chaos warriors, slayers and madmen. An army of such skill and number that could end a world and be worthy of the Ruinous Star. He had failed. Even as they hacked each other to pieces about him, he could not see in them the warriors, beastmen and daemons of his doom. They were a wretched assemblage. A rag-tag union of the lost and the damned. Slaves to darkness, blundering through their existence, savagely striking out like blinded animals. They had not been worthy of his apocalyptic fate but worse, he had not been worthy of them. The loyalties of maniacs, marauder tribesmen and altereds were held together with little more than the skein of a spider's web. They were a liars' alliance, lying to each other and themselves about their intentions. They were a monster of the deep, horribly devouring itself.

Standing on the stone deck, with the crooked mast-towers and sinister citadels stretching for the skies about him, Archaon took some comfort in the likelihood that this was the way it was meant to be. He was being tested. How could he lead these legions if he couldn't hold together an army of beastmen and Shadowland marauders? Archaon nodded to himself. His worthiness was to be found in the way he had achieved so much with so little. With a malingering horde of spawn, savages and back-stabbing lieutenants he had achieved much. A place in history, at least. He had swept across the Northern Wastes, besting with sword, stratagem or number all challengers who had stood in his irresistible path. He had smashed his way through icy Naggaroth before making the Great Eastern Ocean his own. They would not be the ones to accompany him into eternity. At his side they had indeed earned their squalid place in history – but Archaon was destined to destroy the world, a world without a future and in no need of a history.

The gods were cruel. They persecuted even those that

realised their prophecies and prosecuted their will. The Altar of Ultimate Darkness had been their gift. It had bequeathed on Archaon their Mark. The eight points of the Chaos Star – a Ruinous union of blood and treachery. The Chaos gods were monsters. Their gifts were invariably curses also. Like the spawn whose horrific form bequeaths strength and murderous abilities that the trapped soul within could barely have dreamed of in its former existence. Every favour of the Dark Gods was also a test or some sly part of a greater doom. Archaon only needed to look upon his flagship to know that. The *Spite* – whose banner-trailing, cloudscraping towers were a sight to strike distant captains and port governors stone dead with dread, whose flotilla trailing darkness had been the terror of an entire ocean – had been a lens through which the darklight of evil had been concentrated. The conflicting influence of the Ruinous Powers, reaching out from the Altar of Ultimate Darkness and into the souls of every great warrior, every witch and every wretched thing that fought in Archaon's name. It had promised them their heart's desire – whatever that had been – and perversely destroyed the beautiful confederacy that had united behind their chosen champion.

Dravik Vayne's *Citadel of Spite* had already been a devastating study in dark genius. The enchantments of its black stone, the lines of its serrations and crenellations, the crooked cruelty of its towering architecture. The *Spite* had indeed been a wonder. The Altar of Ultimate Darkness had sat within its depths, corrupting the simple evil of its black heart. The *Spite* had brought it to the floating fortress from which Archaon terrorised the high seas. Spreading its corruption like veins and arteries through the dark stone, it pumped its poison into the souls that called the *Spite* home. It almost became a living thing. Its catacombs were haunted by much more than nesting sea monsters. Its archways became toothed gateways to whispering oblivion. The tents and camps that sprawled across its stone decks and plazas sat upon glyphs and symbols that had wormed their way through the stone to demand sacrifice. The towers and citadels became secret temples to individual Powers, channelling the altar's dread influence. He could see that now. The warping stone and midnight metal of the *Citadel*'s architecture was not twisting into agonising new forms to honour the warlord Archaon and his victories. It was contorting with its hate for his endeavours. It was laughing at him. It was spitting in the face of his failures.

No more. No more.

Archaon looked up at the *Citadel* tower. The warlord knew where Dravik Vayne and his witch would be. Father Dagobert and Giselle would be with them, up in what had been Archaon's cabin chambers. He could feel the floating fortress turning in the water beneath his feet. The corsair would take the *Spite* back to Naggaroth. He would be changing course without delay. He would be setting that course atop the bulbous keep, crowning the main mast-tower, the tallest of the *Spite*'s towers. That was where Archaon would find him.

Between him and the tower, however, was a horde of his Dreaded Wo, arch-marauders that had terrorised Northern Cathay for as long as anyone could remember. Archaon passed through throngs of Dreaded Wo like shadow. In their lacquered armoured and horned helmets they came at their attacker. Archaon slipped their curved blades from their scabbards and drew their single edges across marauder throats. Turning his wrist and bringing the oriental blade back for the strike, the Chaos warlord cut through the Hundun sword clans with their own cursed weapons, burying steel in one warrior only to snatch a pike from another's retainer and hurl it into the chest of another. As they came at him with blade, boot and back of hand, their movements dark and graceful, Archaon broke them. He ducked beneath the discipline of their fists, scooped aside their dancing blades and killed with a messy efficiency the Hung marauders did not have within them. He turned and spun. He broke necks and twirled the vicious attacks of lesser warriors into one another, impaling tribal princes and their peasant servants on each other's weapons. Archaon stabbed and cut with the superior blades of the Dreaded Wo, slicing limbs and heads from marauder bodies, working his way across the madness of the stone deck.

The easterners became an archway of steel. Archaon worked his marauder sword, the dull glint of the wretched skies flashing off its arcs and crescents. Blood sprayed his way as throats were opened and wrists were slit. The grating hiss of razor-edges clashing filled the air, punctuated by the plunging of Archaon's blade through marauder torsos. Stabbing the weapon through the side of one unfortunate sword clansman's helm, the sword went straight through the skull and out the other side. Snatching a retainer's pike from his trembling hands, Archaon rested his boot on the marauder's lacquered breast plate and kicked the warrior away. Swinging the pike around by the tip of its shaft, the Chaos warrior opened up a throng of closing Dreaded Wo, the point of the pike blade tearing through the arms and chests of the marauders.

As the black-armoured warriors crumbled to the deck about him, Archaon heard it. The unmistakable roar of one of the Blood God's foetid servants. An unreasoning bellow of rage that shook the stone of the deck and made the littering corpses jig and dance. The Great Spleen had awoken. Dazed. Furious. Eager to appease its dread deity with sacrifices, the ogre was enraged. Like a gore-dipped statue it rose above the Hundun warriors, each bare footfall a stone-pulverising quake. Archaon saw its beady eyes – black with rage – peering over the tusk-snarled mess of its maw. He heard the rumble of the great metal links of an anchor and realised that the Great Spleen had one of the *Spite*'s colossal anchors in its possession. Throwing the cruel weight of the black, barbed thing into the air, the Great Spleen turned on its blood-slimy heel, swinging the anchor around on its length of chain. There was little Archaon could do to defend against such a weapon. Unlike the Dreaded Wo attempting to skewer him on their beautiful, curved blades, he could see the weapon coming. Dipping down into the gore, helmet pressed to the deck, the Chaos warrior heard the dreadful path of the anchor as it ploughed through the armoured bodies of the Hung marauders, dragging their smashed corpses along with it.

Archaon was up, pike ready in hand like a javelin, but the ogre heaved and the anchor hummed through the air, orbiting the corpulent mass of the Great Spleen and searing around for another pass. The anchor bounced and sparked off the deck, showering Archaon with shattered stone. Archaon went down again, allowing the deadly weight of the thing to pass over his helmet. Kneeling, Archaon launched the pike at the ogre, burying it between the slabs of pectoral fat that wobbled from its chest. The anchor came crashing down to the deck, smashing through the legs of Hung marauders and some of the Great Spleen's own blood-barbarians. The ogre snorted two streams of snot from its flat nose in fury before snatching the pike from its steaming flesh. Archaon was already up and on the run, stepping swiftly through the demolished corpses the Great Spleen's anchor had left behind, scooping up the pikes of retainers and the curved blades of Hundun sword clansmen. These came at the Blood God's champion like a shower of steel. Pikes sailed through the air, swords whirled hilt over blade at the monster. The Great Spleen roared as it feverishly removed the weapons from its belly. With all of his might, Archaon launched a pike at the ogre's head. The monster turned, just in time, allowing the pike to sink into its globed shoulder, the Great Spleen's muscle and fat soaking up the entire head of the weapon. The creature bawled its pain. Archaon had not killed the ogre – as he had hoped to – but he had reminded the Blood God's champion how to bleed and how to feel the agony of the flesh.

Archaon closed on the beast. Snatching a pair of bone axes from the deck, the Chaos warrior took the Great Spleen barbarians to task. The savages were beside themselves. They had never seen their god-monster bleed. It was impossible. It was blasphemy. Like Archaon's own, their weapons were roughly hewn from the bones of great beasts and sharpened to lethality. He hacked through the cultist barbarians, turning aside the savagery of their mindless attacks while ripping open bellies and the backs of skulls. While surrounded by the painted wildmen, Archaon heard the sound of hooves on the deck behind him. He expected to find beastmen attacking from the rear. Instead he found a recently recruited Chaos warrior called Horakrux Hearteater, mounted on a steed liberated from the deck-stables and riding down on his new master. Archaon could feel the champion's hunger for his end. Tearing a bone axe from a blood barbarian, Archaon hurled it at the rider but it glanced off the warrior's shield. The warlord need not have bothered. The Great Spleen's anchor passed straight through its own barbaric acolytes and smashed both horse and rider aside.

Before Archaon knew what was happening, the anchor had come around again. He jumped and the horrific inevitability of the thing passed beneath his boots. Again the Great Spleen swung the anchor around. Archaon tried to jump again but the anchor hooked the dark templar by the heel and sent him tumbling across the deck. Archaon felt his plate buckle and crack as he bounced off the stone deck and through the flesh-canvas tents adorning it. He hammered through a warherd of beastmen like a cannonball before smashing into the horde of foetid warriors the beasts were fighting. He came to a sudden stop.

Archaon's landing was cushioned by the throng of warriors about him. He tried to shake the confusion from his head. He slipped his helmet off and to his surprise found a hand offered to him. Not an axe coming for his head or a dagger in the gut but a hand. He took it and found himself pulled to his feet amongst a group of armoured warriors. As he blinked the daze from his eye, Archaon came to realise that they looked very much like him. Their armour was rough and chitinous but similar in style and colouring. It was not unusual for warriors to honour champions and warlords so, but the figures were eerie in their similarity, to each other and to Archaon. As several turned he saw their cold and clammy faces. A face he had seen before. And not just in a looking glass or mirror. He was amongst Mother Fecundus's maggot-men. Her birthed horrors. Her brood. The fruits of her sorcerous reproduction.

Archaon stood amongst the brood as they huddled, soaking up the bleating threats and abuse of the beastmen. Above him, on a stinking palanquin, raised upon the shoulders of ten mock-Archaons, the Chaos warrior saw Mother Fecundus, ordering her creations on. Drawing *Terminus* slowly from his scabbard and shrugging his shield from his shoulder, Archaon prepared himself. He was ready to face himself. Plunging the greatsword straight through the back of one of his doppelgangers, Archaon pulled the blade free to take the heads from two more. Mother Fecundus shrieked in maternal horror, directing her progeny to destroy the betraying son. Within moments the maggot-men had turned on Archaon. They didn't just look like him. They moved like him. They fought like him. After his initial element of surprise, the warlord suddenly found himself hard pushed, desperately trying to predict his own movements as great swords and shields clashed.

Suddenly the Great Spleen was there. The anchor came around on its colossal chain, smashing through maggot-men and the beasts fighting them. Archaon watched his own face crumple in horror as the anchor punched through bodies and dragged them away in a swirl of red. There would be little stopping the Blood God's maniac. Of that, Archaon was sure. The best the Chaos warrior could do was make the monster work for him. Stabbing the maggot-man behind him through the neck, Archaon ran up the mound of building corpses before the palanquin. He discovered Mother Fecundus in her birthing throne. Nurgle's witch gurgled her horror at Archaon. The Chaos warrior snarled up at the mountain of putrid flesh.

'You'll get no mercy from me, hag,' Archaon told her. He turned to show the Great Spleen that it was him but found the monster confused at the appearance of so many similar faces. 'Here!' Archaon called at the thing, immediately drawing the champion's attention. Archaon leapt. The anchor sailed around on its chain, the furious force of the improvised weapon smashing straight through the palanquin and birthing throne, turning Mother Fecundus into an amniotic explosion of rancid gore and fluids.

Landing and rolling across his shield, Archaon regained his footing. There was death and violence everywhere. The air was thick with the howls of vengeance and the stench of lives lost. The dragon's flames ran rampant across the decks and through the dark sanctums of the floating fortress's interior. The dragon itself had launched its slithering bulk from the *Citadel* and into the heavens. Rippling like a serpent of the skies, Flamefang weaved and banked on its great fleshy wings trying to acquire several winged warriors in flight. Nodding with admiration and approval, Archaon watched his Swords go head to head with the beast, on their own infernal wings. Diving and spinning, the Swords slashed at the monster's sides as they passed, but the creature would not be denied. Opening its narrow jaws wide, the dragon turned sharply and swallowed two of Archaon's bodyguards whole. Another landed on its back and proceeded to open the dragon up at the spine with one of his bone swords. The monster brought its wings in close and turned into a dizzying roll that threw the Sword from its flesh and sent him into a tumbling descent of his own. Before the Chaos warrior could regain control, the Chaos dragon had whipped its serpentine body around and blasted the falling warrior out of the sky with a stream of purple flame. Archaon watched the flailing spawn tumble from the heavens before thudding horribly against the stone deck of the *Spite*. It looked like it might have been Vier.

With a growing snarl on his face and his head held low, Archaon made for the main mast-tower. He could feel the pounding steps of the ogre behind him, crushing beasts and maggot-men underfoot. Cutting through Kurgan warriors on the deck as he ran, he smashed their weapons aside with *Terminus*. He left the marauders to the Great Spleen's wrath that unfolded about the monster like an unholy storm. Shouldering his shield and slipping the greatsword into his back-scabbard, Archaon weaved through the mutinous crowds. He ducked, weaved and slid out of the path of marauder blades, Norse axes and druchii crossbow bolts. As the Blood God's monster closed on him, dragging the chain and anchor across the stone deck behind him, the hordes parted ahead of Archaon. The ogre snatched up the champions of enemy gods with a colossal fist and chewed their heads clean off before tossing the armoured bodies aside and sweeping the deck for another victim.

On the final approach to the *Citadel* tower, Archaon had to rely on his bare hands alone. He turned blades around in the hands of others, popping shoulders, tearing tendons and breaking bones. He wrenched at limbs, prompting the most excruciating crunches from his passing enemies. Enemies who had been former allies. Marauders and warriors screamed as he hurt them with impunity. Several were swept by Archaon's leg but such movements were restricted by the dark templar's armour. He dallied long enough to kill two. One received a gauntleted fist in the throat while another had his neck broken in an elegant twisting motion that the warlord risked as he passed.

Leaping up at the mast-tower's willowy architecture, Archaon climbed for his life. Every wicked spur and toothed ledge was a blessing. Hauling his armoured form up the black stone of the *Citadel*, the Chaos warrior heard the Great Spleen thunder up behind. As his armoured digits clawed their way to handholds and Archaon began to climb the tower foundations he heard the whoosh of air through the thick chain and the sound of the wicked anchor cutting through the air. Archaon found that his face split with a smirk as the thing smashed through the stone beneath his dangling boot. The anchor came around. This time the Chaos warrior had to lift his knees to escape the Great Spleen's whirlwind attack. He felt the mast-tower shudder as the anchor went to work on the black stone foundations like a massive pick axe. Again and again the ogre swung its huge chain around, smashing through the stone, each time narrowly missing the dark templar.

'Come on, you beast!' Archaon called, enraging the monster further. 'Can't you hit me?' The warlord felt the *Citadel* tower foundations crumble under the ogre's relentless assault. Not that Archaon would want him to. The stone gave an ear-splitting crack from within. Like a lumberjack, the Great Spleen was felling the tower, with the temptation of Archaon's anchor-skewered body directing every swing. 'Harder, you mindless thing,' Archaon roared as he climbed. 'For the hate in your veins and your abominable god...'

Suddenly the anchor appeared beside him. The black metal of the thing was buried in the stone like a grapnel and the Great Spleen was attempting to heave its colossal blood-stained bulk up the tower after him. Archaon felt the *Citadel* quake. As the ogre hauled on the chain with its savage strength, something shattered in the stone foundations. Scrambling across the side of the tower, desperate for handholds, Archaon felt the tower go. The sound was excruciating. At first the mast-tower rocked. Then it started to lean and waver. Then it fell. Like an ancient tree it toppled, its foundations pulverising under its own weight. Rigging and the *Citadel*'s colossal sails began to fall.

Archaon dropped to the deck and scrabbled away. There was an almighty splash as the bulbous towertop struck the water. The air was thick with black dust and a teeth-grinding sound. Through the deck Archaon felt the *Spite* begin to lean to one side. Pushing himself to his feet and with the silhouettes of battling marauders all about him, Archaon climbed up onto the side of the tower. Beneath his feet he could feel the floating fortress listing. The colossal weight of the *Citadel* tower was dragging the *Spite* over onto her side, flooding her upper catacombs and lower decks. Archaon's flagship was going down. Beneath the tower base, the Chaos warrior saw what was left of the Great Spleen. The blood-mad ogre had heaved the tower over onto itself in its blind rage. The monster-champion's bulk had been crushed by the weight of the stone, so that now only a brawny arm and gore-stained fist was visible. The beast's barbarians stood before their fallen god, weeping tears of blood.

Archaon squinted through the dust along the length of the tower. The bulbous keep that crowned it was already in the water and flooding but the druchii and the degenerates that had made the tower their home were crawling out from windows and loop holes. Sliding *Terminus* from his back-scabbard and his shield from his shoulder, Archaon began to jog along the wall of the tower. As he met Chaos warriors and champions extricating themselves from the flooding tower he ended them. He briefly fought Kallidon the Dark before opening up the Kurgan warrior from the navel to the jaw. He butchered without a thought men and monsters who would formerly have given their miserable lives in his service. Archaon pushed on behind his shield as the bolts of corsair crossbows hammered into its surface. As he met them they drew their wicked cutlasses. He slammed them back, turning and cutting them down with blade-shattering sweeps of his own sword.

Beyond the corsair's cleaved corpses, Archaon found the druchii who led them: Sularii, Dravik Vayne's witch lover. *Terminus* came up to claim her but there was something in the dark elf's eyes… a gaze Archaon felt difficult to break. As she made her alluring way up the tower towards him, her dark eyes and coquettish smile becoming his world, Archaon found that he had sheathed his sword and shouldered his shield. The witch reached out for him and touched his face. She licked her lips with a forked tongue. A new blessing.

'Sularii!' Archaon heard the stabbing words of Dravik Vayne. 'Stop playing. Just kill him.'

The dark templar blinked the sorceress's bewitchments away. She was there, in front of him, but it was a curved dagger of black metal that caressed his cheek rather than the druchii's fingertips. Archaon looked down its length. The blade glistened with the witch's poisons. Further up the toppled tower Archaon could see Dravik Vayne, the corsair commander, seething with hatred. His pair of cutlasses dripped with deadliness also and their tapering points sat nestled in the back of his prisoners' skulls. Gorst and Fitch clutched each other nearby while before his blades, the servant of Slaanesh was walking Father Dagobert and Giselle down towards him.

'I'm sorry, master,' Dagobert said through his curtains of long, grey hair. The priest held the precious *Liber Caelestior* in his clawed grasp. Vayne not only had the priest prisoner but the ancient tome also. Giselle said nothing. She simply gave the Chaos warrior a stabbing glare. He watched as she slipped a stiletto knife from her sleeve, a knife she had used in attempts on his own life. Now she intended to use it on Vayne. Archaon gave the slightest shake of his head. He grabbed Sularii's wrist and brutally twisted it in his grasp, turning the poisonous blade between them and spinning the witch into his embrace. Holding the dark elf to him, Archaon put the blade in her hand to her own throat. Dravik Vayne's contorted face slackened to a smile.

'You're dead,' the druchii said, staring at the warlord.

'I'm many things,' Archaon said, 'but dead isn't one of them. You will not be able to say the same soon, you treacherous worm.'

'You have no army...'

'It wasn't worthy of my name,' Archaon told him. 'And its lieutenants were not worthy of it.' Dravik Vayne gave him a snide smile. Out of the corner of his eye, Archaon noticed movement.

'And you were not worthy of us,' the champion of Slaanesh told him.

'Perhaps,' Archaon agreed.

'You are not worthy of your gods,' Vayne continued. 'You are not worthy of your destiny.'

Like a dark thunderbolt, Eins dropped down beside him,

the black stone of the tower pulverising beneath its boots. Fünf landed beyond the dark elf corsair, on the sinking tower keep. The pair drew their bone swords from their wings and prepared to engage the druchii, prompting Vayne to turn and point his poisonous blades both ways. The Slaaneshi's face screwed up with hate.

'Back,' he warned Archaon's remaining Swords.

'I am worthy of a destiny of my own,' Archaon told him. The weaving movements drew closer. 'A fate of my choosing. Not some snaking, labyrinthine path that gods, daemons and traitors choose for me.'

'Then go,' Vayne seethed, moving his poisonous blade tips between Archaon's people. 'Seek out such a fate, if it exists. Leave me to my god and his desires. Leave me to my *Spite*.'

'Your floating fortress no longer floats, druchii,' Archaon told him. 'It's going to the depths. And it's taking you with it, you treacherous scum. The captain goes down with his vessel.'

'Kill her,' came a voice from behind. It was Khezula Sheerian. The ancient was hobbling up the tower behind the Chaos warrior, his bone staff tapping its way up the black stone. 'The priest, the girl,' Sheerian said, 'they're dead. Kill the witch.'

'What are you talking about?' Archaon demanded of the sorcerer.

'Do it,' Sheerian said. 'Do what you do best, Archaon. End her.'

'You'll doom us all,' the corsair-captain snarled.

Archaon nodded slowly to himself. 'I'm known for that.'

And it was decided. Sularii managed a half-scream as he cut the witch's head from her shoulders with her own blade. Tossing the dark elf's head into the ocean, Archaon felt the stone beneath his boots suddenly judder. The charms and incantations that kept the *Citadel* afloat were losing their battle with the depths. Water about the colossal vessel began to thrash and foam as the black stone and rocky foundations of the vessel started taking it down below the waves. Vayne watched with a lover's horror as Archaon allowed Sularii's body to fall into the white water. It was all there in the druchii's screwed-up face: his love for Sularii, his love for the *Spite*.

'You idiot,' Vayne spat, his dark charm and venomous smile gone. 'You'll put the Altar of Ultimate Darkness on the bottom of the ocean.'

'Where it belongs,' Archaon told him.

'It was a gift from the gods,' Vayne said, considering his own anger at his failure to reclaim the altar for his witch-queen.

'They give,' Archaon said, 'and they take away.'

'They do…' Vayne seethed. The corsair-commander turned and rolled back up the tower at the two Swords blocking his escape. He passed under the bone blades of Fünf and slashed the Chaos warrior with the poisoned metal of his own cutlass. The Sword shrieked as Archaon had never heard and fell to his armoured knees. The warlord couldn't tell whether it was a cry of pain or pleasure, enslavement or release. The poison's effects were swift and devastating. Fünf simply withered to nothing before Archaon's eyes.

'He's mine,' Archaon called as Eins went in to attack. Vayne turned and assumed a druchii fighting stance. Something dark, exotic and designed to catch Archaon off-guard. He only need nick or slice the Chaos warrior with his blades. He sneered his madness at Archaon who advanced without drawing his blade. The black stone of the tower cracked and shattered underneath them. Water foamed and fountained about as the *Spite* began its torturous descent into the depths. Beyond, Archaon's army of darkness tore itself to pieces, the gods delighting in the butchery and spectacle.

'Master!' Giselle screamed.

'We've got to get off this ship,' Father Dagobert called.

Archaon didn't have time to dance with Dravik Vayne. Dagobert was right. The *Spite* was going down fast. Without druchii magic to keep it afloat, the unimaginable weight of the black stone fortress and the bedrock it sat upon was pulling it swiftly down. Archaon had seconds before they would all be in the freezing water being dragged down with the

Citadel of Spite. As Dravik Vayne closed on him, his blades oozing their deadly poison, Archaon stopped and tore a piece of shattered black stone from the crumbling tower wall. Vayne ran at the Chaos warrior, eager for the advantage. Archaon hefted the small, jagged boulder up onto his armoured chest and then above his head. Throwing it down on his enemy with all his hate-fuelled might, Archaon's rock smashed through Vayne's offered blades and put the corsair's skull in. Dropping the cutlasses, the Slaaneshi's largely headless corpse stumbled about for a moment before dropping to its knees and slipping down into the foaming waters. Archaon spat after the corsair-captain and traitor.

He turned to Dagobert and Giselle, with Eins standing with them.

'Now we go–'

Sickening shock stole the words from the end of his sentence. The beast was there. Flamefang. The Chaos dragon, tearing up the water as it swooped in low and fast. It was flying for the toppled tower, intent on claiming the winged warrior that had evaded its sky-snapping pursuit.

'Down!' Archaon roared. But it was too late. It was natural for them to turn. To set their own eyes on the danger before they tried to evade it. Such split-second curiosity cost them, however. The lengths of the beast's fang-filled jaws were open. Its neck, its tail and its body were straight. Carried on a gargantuan flap of its wings, the horror came at them like a bolt from one of the druchii throwers. Gorst pushed Father Dagobert down through a tower window and into the flooded chamber within. Eins grabbed Giselle and tried to take off from the tower. Fitch stood in honest horror and soiled himself.

'No!' Archaon bawled as Giselle and Eins disappeared into the gaping trap of the dragon's maw, swiftly followed by Gorst and Fitch. 'No!' he roared again, but there was nothing to be done but save himself. He turned and ran back up the length of the tower. He found Khezula Sheerian standing there. The daemon sorcerer was clutching his bone staff, leaning against it with his misty eyes closed. The sorcerous gemstone that crowned the staff blazed blue. Sheerian had seen with his Eye his Lord Tzeentch's perversity. He had seen that as he had claimed the Brothers Spasskov in his summoning that the Chaos dragon would claim him as part of its own. Archaon leapt from the sinking, black stone of the tower. The great jaws of Flamefang missed him but took the daemon sorcerer a moment later.

Archaon felt it immediately. His armour and mail burned his skin with the deep cold of the water. The shock almost knocked the wind out of the dark templar. Within moments he had something else to worry about – the weight of his plate was dragging him down like an anchor. He clawed at the foaming water. Bubbles raged about him as the colossal *Spite* started its descent below the waves. The evacuating air and thrashing waters were about the only thing keeping the Chaos warrior from sinking. As his head broke the surface he heard the shouts and screams, the drowning boom of the sinking fortress. He saw Father Dagobert. The priest was still clutching *The Liber Caelestior* to his belly to protect it from the water. He was on his knees, precariously reaching out his pudgy hand for the struggling Archaon. The Chaos warrior went under again. Bubbles rushed past his sinking form and it took a clawing, thrashing effort to reach the surface again.

Dagobert was still there. He was shouting something to Archaon, his long, grey hair framing a face lined deeply with his concerns and fears. Dagobert never saw the Chaos dragon return for a second pass. This time flying up the length of the sinking tower, Flamefang streamed purple flame before it. Archaon looked at Dagobert. The priest looked back at him. He didn't even turn around. He knew what was coming. Archaon watched Dagobert disappear in a wall of unnatural flame. Archaon would have called out but he was already half drowning. All he could do was stare up through the shallows as Hieronymous Dagobert – his priest, his father, his friend and his conscience – was lost to the transformative horror of the dragon flame. In that one moment Archaon lost both his past and his future.

The Celestine Book of Divination, Necrodomo's predictions and the destined path he had seen for Archaon the Everchosen of Chaos was now gone. Burned. Warped to oblivion with its faithful translator. Mulched ink and parchment, sinking slowly to the bottom of the Great Eastern Ocean.

At the realisation, Archaon stopped struggling. The deadweight of his armour dragged him down towards the depths. He cared nothing for the men, beasts and daemons that had joined his ranks. To them in turn he personally was nothing. Merely a path to greatness. Hieronymous Dagobert had raised him like a son. Giselle had been ardent in both her love and hate for him. Like the girl and the priest, even Gorst had been with him at the beginning of his dark journey. In turn, the damned tome whose secrets had become both Dagobert's life and his own future was now lost. Forever. Like the Altar of Ultimate Darkness, it was on its way to the darkest depths where no champion of Chaos, no Everchosen of the Dark Gods might acquire it. He was lost and everything was lost to him. The Ruinous Powers had played their sick game. They had tricked him into thinking, feeling and believing that he was the one. They had tricked others into following such a doomed pursuit. They had done this for their own infernal entertainment. They had made Archaon a beacon of darkness. A living deathtrap – so that he might draw mighty souls to his cause before slaughtering them in the Dark Gods' names.

The *Citadel* thundered through the stormy depths. Archaon felt the weight of his armour and the irresistible pull of the sinking fortress take him down. Above, the light of the world was fading. Below there was only the cold invitation of darkness. Archaon allowed it to drag him down. He was done. He was finished with the world of men and gods. They had finished him. The remaining air in his lungs scorched his way through his chest. He wanted to let it go. He wanted the ice-stabbing cold of the blackness below to take him.

Then he saw it. Death from above. Framed in the dwindling twilight of the sea's surface, he saw the thing he had unleashed on the world. The serpentine outline of the monstrous Flamefang. The Chaos dragon had plunged below the waves, drawn down on the sinking doom that was Archaon. Its spindly claws and massive wings pushed it down through the raging bubbles, down through the crumbling masonry of the *Citadel* and down through a sea of bodies. Down to feast on the blinding darklight of the Chaos warrior's soul.

Archaon felt his body tense. The desire to breathe, to live and to fight shot through his frozen body like a lightning strike through a mountain top. *Terminus* came up in his grasp, the water and the deep cold a sluggish drag on his movements. He watched the growing silhouette slither through the water like a snake, its colossal jaws moving from side to side, the horror of its long serpent body cutting through the depths with an undulating ripple. Archaon tensed the remaining warmth in his body through his right arm, preparing for the strike. The Chaos warrior was ready. *Terminus* was ready.

Then he heard a single word echo about the addled, air-deprived rawness of his mind. That word was 'No…'

A 'No' of defiance? A 'No' of defeat?

The Chaos dragon's narrow jaws opened. The dagger-trap of its maw and the bottomless reaches of its throat beckoned. Archaon would never know. As *Terminus* slipped from his grasp and dropped quietly into the depths, Flamefang snapped its colossal jaws closed and plunged Archaon into a darkness he had never known.

'No…' was all he could hear.

'No…' said Archaon, though his lips spoke not. His tortured spirit ached for release.

'No,' said the Dark Master, his words echoing though eternity. 'You are a slave to shadow. You are the prince of calamity. You are the future, my son. You are my future.'

'I am an end to all futures,' Archaon roared at the reasoning darkness.

'Yes, you are…'

'*All* futures, thing of dread that stalks my soul,' Archaon told it. 'My will is my own. My destiny cannot be held in the pages of a damned tome. My soul will not be crushed in the claw of some daemon or dark god.'

'Whatever you need to tell yourself…'

'This flesh will never be yours,' Archaon told the darkness. 'This soul will rail against your bidding. You will come to regret the day you chose me, horror.'

'You were not chosen, Archaon,' the Dark Master raged, scorching him with every word. 'You were never chosen. You were sired on the world so that I might end it. And end it I shall, Archaon. End it I shall. Return to embrace your destiny.'

CHAPTER XV

*'I am settled, and throw all that I am,
Every corporeal desire and spiritual agent
at this hopeless feat.'*
– Dantalion Altieri, *From the Abyss*

*The Black Meridian – The Cliff of Beasts
The Southern Wastes
The Blazes – Dies Irae dies Illa*

'No…'

Just a word.

Archaon felt the scalding touch of plate against his skin. The weight of *Terminus* in his frozen fist. The darkness all about him. From the shimmering twilight above he saw the black shape of dread itself descending. The Chaos dragon, its narrow jaws stretched wide, its great talons and wings carrying its serpentine bulk down through the waters. 'No…' Archaon said, bubbles raging from his blue lips.

Instead of kicking away through the water or clawing

himself to the side and out of the path of the dagger-trap maw, Archaon surged straight at it. He felt the colossal jaw envelop him like a cave, with rows of twisted stalactites and stalagmites ready to stab straight through him. The dragon's mouth began to close but the Chaos warrior had some stabbing left to do of his own. Kicking up and away from the beast's eye-pimpled tongue and its mangled lower jaw, Archaon thrust upwards with his greatsword. Up at the grotesque roof of the dragon's mouth. Up through faces that stared back down at him from the soft, wet flesh in unspeakable horror. *Terminus* slipped straight through the assimilated patchwork of victims. Archaon put everything he had behind the blade, despite resistance from the icy water. The crusader blade passed through flesh, gristle and slammed through the bone of the monster's malformed skull. Archaon slammed the weapon all the way up to its jewelled crossguard, in the hope that the blade would pierce the abomination's warped brain and once again end Flamefang's reign of transformative terror.

The jaws suddenly spasmed open. The tongue assumed a choked rigidity and the water about Archaon clouded with regurgitated blood. The jaws closed and then jerked opened again. Archaon's gauntlet slipped from the sword's grip and the Chaos warrior found himself tumbling through the dark water as the creature's neck retracted the colossal set of jaws. *Terminus* had not sliced deep enough to kill the monstrous thing. With the length of crafted steel embedded in the back of its throat, the monster was finding it difficult to swallow. Archaon watched the snaking shape of the monstrosity beat its wings for the surface. Fading... fading until finally it broke the ocean surface and disappeared.

Archaon yearned for the weight of *Terminus* in his grip but the greatsword had gone with the dragon. The Chaos warrior had bigger problems. The air trapped in his lungs was roasting him from the inside out. The pressure was unbearable. It threatened to rip its way out of him. He instinctively tried to breathe deeper but there was nothing left of the desperate gasp he had taken on the surface and only the murk of salt water about him. He was deep. Deeper than he had thought possible and between the dragging force of the descending *Spite* and the deadweight of his own plate he was sinking further. With feverish hands he began to tear the mangled plate and shredded mail from his body. Armour sank from his thrashing form and with every piece the dark templar felt the grip the depths had on him loosen. As he tore the final few pieces away from his blood-sticky body he kicked for the surface. The Chaos dragon was gone from his thoughts. As was the loss of his blade. Armies and the destinies that went with them were unreachable in his thoughts. He had only one feeling. One desire. A need so overwhelming that all else fizzled to oblivion. Air. Archaon needed air. He felt his limbs weaken. He felt his mind slip. The Old World had not claimed him and neither had the New. He had survived the insanity of the Northern Wastes. He would be thrice-damned before he allowed the Great Eastern Ocean to claim him. He kicked. He clawed. He roared himself free of the freezing water's seductive grasp.

The sound echoed through the clear, chill skies above. There was splashing. There was coughing and spluttering. There was the sweet ecstasy of lungs filled to bursting with urgent air. Archaon kicked in the water to keep his head above the surface. For a moment he just breathed. He blinked the stinging salt water from his eye. He was there, in the frozen seas of the south. The unexplored seas near the bottom of the world – which no northerner had known – skirted even by the traders of the elder races. Into waters only the damned would dare to venture. Archaon was not alone, however. The *Citadel of Spite* had gone down, taking the Altar of Ultimate Darkness with it to the bottom of the cursed ocean. Wreckage floated about the site of the *Spite*'s sinking: canvas and cordage mostly. Vessels from Archaon's flotilla that had not blown each other to pieces had been flame-savaged by the Chaos dragon and were now making their escape. The water was crowded with bodies. Some had been dead before they hit the water, victims of the mutinous insanity that had swept through the *Spite*. Others had succumbed to the deep cold, as Archaon would if he couldn't find a way to get out of the water.

Marauders and Chaos warriors were screaming for help. With their last frosted breaths they called for compatriots and enemies to return in the fleeing vessels, but the ships were leaving. Archaon could tell by the angle of their masts that many were listing and wouldn't make it far anyway. Those that could make their escape did, on a northerly heading. They weren't coming back. Not for the scum of the world or the Chaos warrior that had led them. They were wise to do so. If they had returned, Archaon would have butchered them for their betrayal.

Archaon swam. It was the only thing he could do to retain what little warmth remained in his body. He felt the icy tendrils of doom creep through his body and stab through his mind. It was becoming difficult to think. Men and beasts died about him in the water, their fur frosting, their armour dragging them down. The dark templar sensed creatures in the water – monstrosities newly liberated from the caverns beneath the *Citadel* had surfaced to feed on the calamitous bounty. Warriors screamed for their lives as serpents and great-gulleted beasts took them. As an undulating monstrosity closed on Archaon, the Chaos warrior smacked his fist at the freezing waters. Sensing that the dark templar might be more trouble than he was worth, the sea monster followed its instincts and slithered at a nearby Hundun tribesman who let loose a gargling scream before being chomped below the waves.

Archaon knew he had little time. As he rolled with the motion of the waves he stared up at the empty sky. If the cold or sea creatures didn't get him then the returning Flamefang would. He could only hope that it had sought out havoc elsewhere. Spotting a tangled piece of floating wreckage, Archaon swam arm over exhausted arm across to it. It appeared to be some mangled spars and cordage from a sunken war-junk. Upon reaching the debris, Archaon discovered that the wreckage had already been claimed by three Kurgan warriors, huddled together and shivering. Archaon hauled himself up onto the bobbing spars, drawing from the marauders a storm of curses and warnings in their tribal tongue. Archaon – bare-chested and white with rime – climbed out of the water. The Kurgans drew their cruel weapons. Archaon gave them the slit of one eye. His mouth curled to a frozen snarl. For the first time the marauders saw the patch on his eye and the eternally burning Mark of Chaos that smouldered like a crown about his bare head.

'Leave,' Archaon growled. The Kurgan looked to one another for reassurance but there wasn't any. They looked to their weapons. 'Go on, get out of here,' the unarmed templar snapped as he moved towards them, prompting the marauders to jump into the deadly waters.

After the *Spite*, the collection of ropes and spars was a miserable command. That didn't stop rabid Chaos warriors from trying to climb aboard – like Archaon attempting to save themselves from the frozen waters. Taking a length of spar, the dark templar bludgeoned his former allies, caving in their helmets and heads before lashing their bodies to the wreckage for extra buoyancy. Stripped bodies of wet floating debris and mounds of corpses floated about him. What full-bellied sea monsters could not swallow, Archaon claimed for his raft. Some were almost frozen solid by the time he got to them, while others – in death – had started to rot and balloon with unnatural speed. As he rolled corpses in the water to get them into position, Archaon discovered that one of the ragged cadavers was a winged warrior of Chaos. It was one of his Swords. Vier. There was movement beneath the Sword's armour that Archaon took for breathing and the dark templar hauled the warrior up onto the raft.

Incredibly, Vier was alive. He had not only survived the dragon's flame but also the fall and brutal landing. Archaon swiftly discovered, however, that the movement wasn't breathing. Vier was suffering under the influence of the

Chaos dragon's breath. His form was undergoing grotesque changes that simply through force of will alone Vier was attempting to resist.

Archaon dragged Vier's mangled body into an upright position. Beyond having bone-shattered injuries, his back was hunched. At least one of his wings and an arm had been horribly fused to his body. Things writhed about within him wanting to be free, wanting to blossom into new forms, but the Chaos warrior groaned his way through them. The two of them sat and they shivered as the raft bobbed away from the floating collection of bodies and debris.

Without means to steer the raft, Archaon was at the perverse mercy of the currents that seemed to be dragging his macabre jury-rigged vessel further south into the darkness and temperatures that plunged further than Archaon could imagine.

Frosted in his scraps of armour and decorated in a motley collection of mismatched weaponry, Archaon appeared more like one of his miserable marauders or tribesmen than the warlord who had led them. Survival was his prime concern. Water. Food. Warmth. He licked the frost and rime routinely formed on the wood of the spars. He cut frozen meat from the mound of corpses that made up the raft. He established a small fire in a cooking pot, burning scalps and the fat cut from the better-fed of the cadavers. Enough to dry his furs and armour – scrap by painstaking scrap – and warm hands that felt as if they had already fallen off. Vier took nothing. The Sword just sat and suffered through his attempted transformations. Archaon found himself watching the Chaos warrior for signs of treachery, signs that he might have become something else. He was loath to dump his Sword of Chaos, however, and secretly welcomed the distraction.

It was a miserable existence but as the days turned to weeks, it was an existence – and to Archaon that was all that mattered. He spent his time searching both the seas and sky. Flamefang would make short work of the raft with its narrow jaws and streams of warping flame. He saw nothing of the dragon, however, and assumed that it had headed inland in search of more populous prey. The bleak horizon was equally empty. The waters were dark, the air cutting and the seas empty of sail. Mainly Archaon slept. Boredom, exhaustion and futility combined to drag him into wretched dreams. In some he was still a warlord, commanding champions and the legions of Chaos. In others he was haunted by a daemon darkness. The thing that watched him from the shadows and even now, in the stark emptiness of the polar seas, seemed to be with him. Murmuring the insanities of fevered sleep, Archaon wished it gone. Sometimes it stayed. Sometimes it seemed to leave. Sometimes it left others in its stead. Corpses that rose from the lashed cadavers to point, to accuse and berate with droning insistence. Father Dagobert, Giselle, Sheerian. Giselle in particular would scream at him, spit at him, slap him. Her furious strikes were too feeble to leave an impression on the Chaos warrior but were sometimes enough to snap him from his nightmares.

Shuddering to wakefulness, Archaon found that he was shaking. It was cold. Colder than before. The fire in the pot was out. Vier was groaning his agonies. The raft was rocking and the dark templar could hear a slushy creak. He had been asleep for some time. Rubbing some life back into the frozen mask of his face, Archaon got to his feet. The horizon had changed. It was not the mind-bending flat line stretching into eternity that it had been. It was angular and shattered. He had reached the seasonal ice of some southern land. Great bergs bobbed about him. The dark waters were gone. Ice lay before the raft and the skies were the broiling black of pitch. Far beyond, in the distance, Archaon could see the distant pinnacle glow of eruptions, betraying the presence of volcanoes dotted about the horizon.

It seemed that the raft had been drifting for some time through the outer extent of the ice. Its passage was demonstrated in the narrow channel of black water and slush it had cut south as it had drifted. Before the raft the ice had also cracked. The fracture extended south, as far as Archaon could see, funnelling the ramshackle raft on. It was like a long, black line extending into the distance.

Archaon's mind ached back through the slaughter, the devastation and the cold. Back to what Sheerian had told him. That the next treasure of Chaos to be discovered lay on a Black Meridian. The Chaos warrior's eyes followed the fracture south. A black line of water through the whiteness of the ice. A Black Meridian. A nasty chuckle escaped the dark templar's burning lips.

As the raft bounced and slushed its way through the fracture, the blackening skies plunged the frozen wilderness into darkness. With the volcanic brume churning above, lanced by strange lightning it became clear that these southern lands had never seen sun, moon or the blessing of a clear sky. There was something supernatural and potent about the place. The freezing air could not only graze the skin and stop the heart, it burned with the presence of the Dark Gods and their daemons. Far, far across the great oceans – at the bottom of the world – Archaon had discovered the Southern Wastes. A frozen hell like the one he had traversed in the north. As the cursed heavens raged and the darkness became absolute, drowning the meridian and turning the ice to a frosted obsidian, Archaon came to realise that these Southern Wastes were much, much worse.

The land seemed as if it was surrounded by the chill seas. It shared no border with the realms of men. There was no eternal battle to fight. No champions vying for the favour of Ruinous gods. This was a darker place – of abyssal soul and purpose. It was primordial. A land of chaos and havoc. A place of degenerate malevolence. As he drifted further into the savage lands, the temperature plummeted and the winds picked up. The darkness beyond the raft became a blurred stream of snow and howling elemental ferocity. The mountains of fire and fury drew closer. They stormed the explosive brilliance of magma into the inky skies above, raining ash into the maelstrom and trailing bifurcating rivers of lava that cut through the unnatural ice, giving the land what little light it enjoyed – the infernal glow of a dungeon or underworld.

In the light of the lava, the denizens of this desperate land were revealed to Archaon. Even in the blackness of the storm, Archaon could make out shapes in the darkness. The movement of beings. Hundreds of them. Thousands. He was in an undiscovered realm. The darklight of his own doom didn't extend very far in such a place. In the radiance of the crawling rivers of magma, however, Archaon saw that the bleak realm was overrun with monsters. In the depths of the darkness, in the shrieking swirl and the infernal cold, Archaon saw beastmen without number. These were not the weakling corruptions of man and beast he had encountered in the forests of the Empire, nor the savage tribes of animal fury he had yoked to his warmongering in the Shadowlands. These were daemonbreeds. Diabolical fusions of fiend, beast and god knows what else. These shaggy beasts were sculptures in midnight muscle, cloven of hoof and crowned with extravagant tangles of daemon horn. In the ember twilight, their gore-smeared snouts and bestial fang-faces were contorted with the base desires that ruled their monstrous kingdom. On those faces Archaon found his Dark Gods – rage and the barbaric tribal ambitions it served, the hang-dog suffering of such a wretched existence and the animal indulgences that were to alleviate the afflictions of both mind and the flesh. The ruinous drives of all living things were to be found in the swarming hordes of beasts that plagued the storm-scathed wilderness.

When a throng of monstrosities were drawn in on the thawing flesh of his corpse-raft, Archaon and Vier were forced to abandon the craft. Sinking into his scraps of fur and leather and tightening a belt heavy with recovered weapons, the dark templar set off on foot with the horribly transformed Vier limping behind. Despite a broken leg, hunched back and malformed limbs, the Sword of Chaos simply would not give up and die. Drawing a bone sword from his remaining wing he hobbled behind his master like a wretched sentinel, moaning his exertions.

The beastfiends about the raft had no weapons of their own – no blades to cut flesh or hack bone. Instead they just set upon the dead marauders with their clawed hands, tearing flesh and organs out of the cadavers with animal abandon. Archaon left them to sink their muzzles into the spoiling meat but as he crept away he could hear the creatures' fangs tearing and the pegs of their chisel-teeth working their way through the carcasses. Nothing would be wasted – of that Archaon was sure. The Chaos warrior didn't plan on being there when the meat ran out.

His footsteps in borrowed boots took him through the howling storm. For six days and six nights Archaon stumbled along the benighted path – although without sun or moon to tell one from the other it was almost impossible to tell. All Archaon knew was that his belly burned with hunger and his lips cracked for want of water. His legs fell to numbness with the torment of steps never-ending and his senses ached with the demands of constant vigilance. Beyond, Archaon could hear the infernal roaring of beastmen at war. Tribes of fiendbreeds fought for the miserable featureless territory about the meltwater darkness of their birthing pools on the obsidian ice. They snorted, wrangled and butchered each other without end, burdening the icy gales with the perpetual bellows of death and savage celebration. Those closest sniffed with suspicion at the advancing Chaos warrior. Their milky eyes saw little but opportunity and death but their sense of smell was daemonically acute. If Archaon had been anyone else, he was sure that he would have been torn to pieces in moments. He wasn't just anyone else. He was Archaon. Chosen of the Ruinous Powers and Herald of the End Times. None of the creatures would know his name or have heard of his deeds but the Chaos warrior had the stink of dark destiny on him. He was an evil they had never known and they were cautious of it. Occasionally beasts would charge from the darkness and rage at Archaon, prompting the dark templar's frost-scalded hands to slip down to the jangling nest of blades and axes that sat snug in his belt. They would not attack him and as soon as he had trudged out of the barren slush of their territory, they left him alone to pursue aggressions elsewhere.

As the black fissure in the ice turned to a river of inky meltwater and the channel in turn became a road of solidifying volcanic stone, Archaon saw other things in the storm-flashed hordes. The landscape was a colossal graveyard. The bleak, howling wilderness was littered with the monstrous bones and skeletons of legendary creatures. Things giant, warped and long dead. Like outposts or tribal hubs, the great bones and vaulted ribcages of these beasts formed shelters for the swarming beastfiends of the wilderness. There were daemons here – in profusion. The storms begat the infernal things – monsters springing forth from the momentary blindness of lightning strikes and billowing blizzards of ice and ash. The creatures of nightmare stalked Archaon and each other through the crowded forest of shaggy beastmen. Their outlandish forms and the horror of their fiendflesh and faces were pure terror to behold. They were the diabolical servants of the Dark Gods, crafted in their image and just about everything else. They knew Archaon not by his scent but the potency of his presence. The Chaos warrior burned with the darklight of fate. It drew them down on him and Archaon had to be constantly alert to their predations.

Every time a horror leapt from the storm or tore through a roaring sea of beasts at him, another suddenly emerged from its hiding place in the infernal gloom and horribly destroyed its devilkin. The daemons and fiend-princes of different Chaos gods played at the game of death and destruction about the dark templar's implacable advance, ripping each other apart in contestation for the Chaos warrior's soul. With the maelstrom swirling above his head, Archaon could almost imagine the Ruinous Powers looking down on him. Their eyes could be hungry for glory or full of disappointment and disapproval. Archaon could not know and he did not care. He had found the undiscovered realm and was on the Black Meridian. A mighty treasure of Chaos waited for him and nothing would put the warrior from his path.

Then he heard it. Not the roar of a beastman or a daemon shriek. It was the heaven-shattering thunder of dragoncall. Tzeentch's monstrous calamity. The *Yien-Ya-Long*. Flamefang. The terror of Grand Cathay and now the terror of the Southern Wastes. Denied its prize and still hungry for the warlord's soul, the creature was hunting him through the maelstrom. Archaon peered into the raging tempest about him and up into the spewing murk above. For a moment he thought he saw the winged monstrosity, beating its wings through the raging turmoil of the skies, but he couldn't be sure. The purple inferno that erupted some way distant into the hordes was unmistakable, however. Bathed in the violaceous glow of its own transformative flame, Archaon saw the thing. He dropped into a crouch, desperate not to be spotted by one of the many eyes that writhed in the smeared flesh of its supernatural hide. It was huge. Much bigger than when Sheerian had given the monster's spirit form on board the *Citadel of Spite* or when Archaon had fought it below the waves. As the Chaos dragon carpeted the bestial hordes with Lord Tzeentch's blessing, turning the beastfiend and the daemon, the torched and thrashing to spawn, Archaon could see why. Turning its head to one side and opening the colossal length of its narrow jaws wide, Flamefang funnelled the changelings down its gaping throat – their precious flesh to be assimilated into its own. With such an appetite, the Chaos dragon had decimated the east. Now, fuelled by fiendflesh and daemon souls, the gargantuan beast intended to make the Southern Wastes its own.

Archaon pushed on. Flamefang had been unleashed at his command. It had feasted on his failure but it would not claim him. The Chaos warrior nodded to himself. Greater things waited for him than a dragon's gullet. Keeping low, Archaon hurried on along his damned path. His Black Meridian. As the endless road of black volcanic rock approached one of the many black peaks that blighted the swarming ice, the Chaos warrior felt the soles of his boots warm. The stone was shot through with glowing cracks, betraying the melted rock beneath. The road was leading him right up to the volcano and had in fact been created by a channel of magma that had cascaded down the mountainside and slowly slurped its way impossibly straight and impossibly north towards the coast. Unusually, the volcano's summit was dark and dormant but for the slightest suggestion of a cooling glow. A crown of lesser cones reached out of the black scree-side of the central tor, each summit a furious pinnacle of dribbling ash and sky-scorching lava.

Stepping from the burning stone, Archaon trekked alongside the road, his path turning from black crust to the murky red of bubbling magma to the furious splashing yellow of liquid rock. The sputtering lava glowed with the diabolical heat of a daemon furnace and Archaon was forced further and further from its flaming shores as the channel grew wider. As he neared the volcano, with Vier hobbling behind, it became clear that a series of structures had been carved into the igneous rock. A small, craggy city of black stone, dusted with ash. The architecture was colossal and ancient. Massive pillars. Standing stone archways. Dark temples. Rough amphitheatres.

As Archaon and Vier moved through the damned structures on the rising slope of the volcano, it became clear that the city had been long abandoned. Beastfiends swarmed the ruins, assuming structures for themselves with territorial ferocity. They fought between themselves. They gorged themselves. They cannibalised their own. They slept. All the while, hunted through the ancient derelicts by predacious daemons.

Archaon and Vier moved up through the city-slope as quietly as they could. Progress was agonisingly slow, moving from building to shattered building. They hid behind fallen pillars and crumbling ruins. They moved through the darkness of collapsed temples and across the ash of forgotten arenas. They waited while hordes of beasts fought each other in the streets. They held still and silent while the victors crunched the bones of the fallen. They moved on only when the hordes passed on. Still, the Chaos warriors were forced to butcher many of the beastfiends. Grabbing the monsters. Strangling. Slitting throats. Stabbing through muscle and into hearts. Their murderous progress through the city was silent and bloody. They could not afford to bring a city of bestial monstrosities down on them.

As the ruins began to thin on the lower slopes of the volcano peak and the ascent became harsh, Archaon picked out standing stones at intervals about the mountainside. The stones bore a selection of runes and symbols, obviously infernal in nature but many the Chaos warrior didn't recognise. Even the storm seemed to grow to a respectful stillness about the mountain. Assuming the dark peak to have some corrupt spiritual significance, like a shrine or burial ground, the Chaos warrior strode on unmolested. Beastfiends and daemons seemed not to congregate in the craggy upper reaches, where the lava channels raged and the standing stones communicated silent significance.

Step by step Archaon began to loosen the rags, furs and shreds of armour that had provided feeble protection from the murderous cold and freezing temperatures of the Southern Wastes. As the rigid rags began to thaw, Archaon felt drenched to the marrow but a few minutes walking alongside the roasting river of molten stone dried and warmed the warrior's frozen bones. Holding a hand out against the glare and the intense heat, Archaon ascended the slope, jumping from burning boulder to igneous crag. The climb was harsh but welcome after the monotonous road leading to it through the dark wilderness and the slow progress through the ruined city. Above, Archaon could see that the channel was oozing its way from a ragged cave entrance in the side of the main tor. An entrance shaped like an eight-pointed star. The realisation put a crooked smile on the dark templar's lips and a surge in his step. He was close.

The first indication that there was anything wrong was the coolness on the back of his head. For a while now, Archaon had been baked in the unrelenting heat of the lava channel. Beads of sweat had rolled from his brow and down his bare head. The sensation of the breeze dancing across his skin was immediately pleasant and horrifying. Spinning around, Archaon caught the final moments of Flamefang's descent. Spotting him alone on the scree slope, the Chaos dragon had thundered from the black, billowing heavens, flapping its wings at the last moment to effect a landing on the volcano's side. Smashing into the mountainside, its talons sinking into the hot rock like anchors, the sheer size of the beast shook the ground beneath Archaon's boots.

Behind the creature, stone archways toppled and columns crumbled to the ground. The dragon's mighty arrival had sent a quake through the ruined city, sending the fragility of its structures into a succession of collapses that swallowed the city in a cloud of black dust. From below Archaon could hear the furious bellow of disturbed beastfiends and the howl of daemons. As Flamefang clawed its thunderous way up the side of the volcano, its tail whipped this way and that, cleaving through the structures behind it and laying fiend-swarming temples to waste. With every colossal movement, the Chaos dragon shook the ground.

Archaon lost his footing and began to skid down towards the monster. Boulders bounced down the slope, dislodged from above, and tumbled down at both Archaon and the dragon. Moving from side to side, the dark templar allowed the larger pieces of rock to plunge past him and shatter on the assimilated bulk of the Chaos dragon.

Flamefang too was struggling with its footing, its great claws tearing through the loose rock and scree of the slope. Sweeping its neck around, the monster reached up, snapping at Archaon with its gargantuan jaws. Archaon leapt from his purchase, sending the boulder he was standing on down towards the beast where it was pulverised in the trap-jaw tip of the dragon's maw instead of the Chaos warrior.

Flame washed up the mountainside, forcing Archaon to take cover behind a rocky outcrop, where he found the

Sword Vier similarly taking cover. Looking back up at the cave entrance, Archaon snarled. He would never make the climb up there with the Chaos dragon at his back.

Vier seemed to know exactly what his master was thinking. What his master needed. Painfully drawing his bone sword from one warped wing, the warrior bumped his mangled fist off Archaon's shoulder before moving out from the outcrop. Archaon nodded, peering out after the Sword of Chaos. He skidded down the scree-side at Flamefang, who was simultaneously distracted by the beastfiends swarming at it from the demolished section of ruinscape. As it snapped and streamed purple flame at the gathering hordes, Vier made his wretched approach, his vengeance intended to buy his master the time he needed to reach his prize.

Clawing with bloody fingers at the shattered rock, Archaon pulled himself up towards the cave entrance. His only chance was to get inside and put the mountainside between himself and the dragon. As the agony of the climb took hold, Archaon could hear the screeches of daemons and the savage futility of beastfiends snapped up in Flamefang's monstrous jaws. Soon Vier was lost to him, as was the crumbling city and its fell denizens as the demolishing of structures sent great clouds of ash and black dust skyward. The volcanic miasma was lit up by the purple flash of flame, as the Chaos dragon visited the transformative wrath of Tzeentch on the Infernals.

It was a gruelling climb. The ledges and handholds cut like glass and most of what Archaon placed his boots on came away from the cliff face. Below, the carnage had ended. Flamefang erupted out of the cloud of dust and destruction the undisputed victor, clawing its colossal way up the steep incline after Archaon. The beast of Tzeentch surged up the slope, several beats of its wings carrying it to its prey – the blazing soulfire of the Chaos warrior's irrepressible spirit leading it on. Once more the jaws opened. With nowhere to jump to, the dark templar was forced to allow his boot to skid down the slope. The dragon chomped at the side of the mountain, its twisted teeth dislodging chunks of black rock and a shower of gravel.

Climbing around the side of the volcano, Archaon attempted to take shelter behind one of the razor-sharp ridges running down the side of the mountain. He heard a horrible thunder build up within the creature's gigantic form and knew it was about to breathe its purple flame. The inferno torched the mountainside, blasting grit and loose rock from the volcano. Archaon managed to haul himself around the razor-sharp ridge in time, the black rock soaking up the worst of Flamefang's warpflame. With horror the dark templar realised that the purple flame had washed across the furs covering the back of his shoulder and two fingers of his left hand. The little finger and ring finger seared, as if they had been dipped in boiling oil. Archaon snarled through a cry of pain and tried to secure his purchase.

Suddenly he felt the burning furs draping one of his shoulders move. The warpflame had given them a new and horrible life. Feeling a morphing set of jaws sink into his shoulder, Archaon tore the rippling fur from his flesh and cast the mutating thing down the mountainside. Through the scalding sensation of his two fingers, Archaon felt his flesh rebel. Skin stretched. Flesh changed. Bone began to grow. Disgust washed through him. He thought of the unfortunate Vier and the horror he had both resisted and become. The fingers began to change and Archaon didn't want to know what they were to become. He certainly didn't want the flesh-warping effect to spread. Slipping a marauder's axe from his belt and placing his left hand against the warm rock of the mountainside, the Chaos warrior cleaved down with the axe and struck them off. As the two digits fell with the sparks from the stone, Archaon clutched the injured hand to him. He felt his own blood soak through the material to his chest.

Again, Flamefang's great gavial jaws came at him and with pain-fuelled fury, Archaon flung the axe at the beast. The weapon's rough blade buried itself in the creature's nostril-flaring snout, doing little to persuade the beast to leave him alone.

With one bloody fist clutched to his chest, Archaon climbed for his life. With the monster's jaws chewing through the scenery behind him, the Chaos warrior scrabbled his way up the scree slope, punching handholds into the igneous rubble. With the dragon's jaws just torso-sheering moments behind him, Archaon hauled himself up through the ragged star-shaped opening to the cave. The light. The heat. The radiance of the river of lava slowly coursing through the rough, black passage beyond was almost unbearable. Everything was bathed in a blinding infernal glow and flame danced from the shreds of clothing and armour that Archaon was wearing, just by being close to the channel of bubbling magma. Slapping out the flames and dragging himself along the course with one arm, the Chaos warrior kicked back through the gravel to safety.

Or so the dark templar thought. Suddenly the Chaos dragon's jaws were there. It had hauled itself up to the cave entrance and pushed the colossal length of its narrow jaws down into its depths. Archaon heard the tortured screams of the assimilated unfortunates whose stolen flesh charred and burned at such proximity to the molten rock.

'Burn, you monstrosity,' Archaon hissed back at the creature as the mournful roar of Flamefang itself joined the flesh-stolen of its form. The thing struggled with its purchase, the dragon tearing its claw-holds away and dashing itself with spatters of hide-scorching lava. Its jaws suddenly plunged down the length of the cave, the writhing dimensions of its head turning the star-shaped opening to rubble. Archaon kicked back through the grit. The blaze of the liquid rock roasted him from one side while Flamefang's mangled fangs attempted to snap up a scrabbling foot or leg and drag its soul-prey back into the open.

Archaon watched as the dragon's jaws opened. Bathed in the effulgence of the passage, the horror of the monster's maw was revealed. Within its depths Archaon saw another head – a blind, obscene set of jaws set within the first. The huge head shot out at the Chaos warrior, all malformed flesh and twisted fang. Archaon kicked back from the thing that seemed to extend on a horrid neck of its own. The jaws parted to reveal a third set of jaws within the second. Like a telescope the horrid appendage extended, snapping at Archaon with a savage, rhythmic abandon. The beast wanted his flesh and his soul so badly that Archaon could feel it in the feverish snap of the inset jaw. Archaon kicked back at the monster's reach, his right boot snagging on the monstrous fang-trap. The jaws retracted and dragged the dark templar a little way back through the grit before his boot came free. With nothing but a scavenged marauder boot for its agony and trouble, the furious Flamefang withdrew its narrow jaws from the cave entrance and took its lava-scorched screeches into the sky.

Archaon tried to spit after the beast but the chamber was too hot and his mouth was too dry. He had to get away from the infernal intensity of the lava flow. Limping with one boot through the razor-sharp volcanic shale, Archaon made his way up the searing passage. As it snaked through the blackness of the mountain's interior, the molten glow lighting his way, Archaon looked down to his bloodied hand, to his missing fingers. He had to do something about the injury. Crouching and reaching for the bubbling lava as close as he dared, he felt the searing agony flare up once again as the heat cauterised the wound. Retracting the hand and working his remaining fingers and thumb, he found them to be burned but serviceable. Tearing a scrap of clothing from his body he fashioned and tied off a swift bandage before lurching on through the brilliance of the cave.

The draining potency seemed to go on forever. The passage wormed its way through the roasting mountain, with Archaon stumbling along it, the half of his face and head turned towards the molten river scorched to redness. The Chaos warrior finally found some brief relief as the passage opened out and the channel widened. He rested for a moment against a crag of jagged black rock, cowering before the intense heat before drawing his gaze upwards. Only then did he realise that he had reached the end of the cursed Black Meridian. The journey was over. He had arrived.

CHAPTER XVI

'Unconquered.'
— Epitaph – The tomb of Morkar 'The Uniter',
First Everchosen of Chaos

Mount Ceno
The Southern Wastes
Horns Harrowing: The Season of Fire

Pulling his rags across his mouth, Archaon found it difficult to breathe. The opening chamber was a pit of heat and noxious gases. He found himself within the colossal cone of the volcano tor. The interior seemed dormant but for the bubbling lake of lava that dominated the chamber floor and lit the walls of the cone with a dungeon glow. Limping towards it, Archaon discovered that a series of stones – like stepping stones – led from the seething shore to an island of black rock that occupied the middle of the lake. Looking about him, Archaon found that the walls all about the cone interior were decorated with stone caskets. Resting on crags and spurs, equal in distance from one another and reaching up the dormant volcano interior, Archaon beheld thousands of sarcophagi, rough and carved of igneous rock. Hobbling over to the nearest, resting on jagged spurs in the rockface nearby, the dark templar saw that it bore the Ruinous Star of the Chaos Powers united. Putting his ear to the casket top, the Chaos warrior heard the strangest sound. Archaon would recognise it anywhere. It was the sound of battle. It was the sound of blades clashing, bawling war cries and men dying. The sound was distant. Like an echo of eternity. Archaon drew one of several short blades he was carrying – a Kurgan falchion. Using the flared tip of the poor blade, Archaon prised the lid off the sarcophagus and pushed it aside. Within, the sound of battle eternal died. The coffin was bare of bones. It contained only the rusted remnants of a Chaos blade. Listening through the lids of the next and the next, Archaon found the same. The distant cacophony of war. Different battles. Different voices calling out in triumph or death. In each Archaon found a mouldering weapon, some still bearing the stains of ancient slaughter.

The dark templar nodded to himself. He was standing in a tomb. Here, in the wickedness of the Southern Wastes, the exalted warriors of Chaos had been laid to rest – their bones recovered to wither in the noxious heart of this mountain, their souls to fight on for the glory of their deranged gods.

Tearing a rag from his torso, Archaon tied the material about his foot and strode on towards the molten lake. Once again the intense heat threatened to overwhelm him. Stepping out onto the first stone, Archaon felt assailed from all sides by the blinding fury of the lake. As he stepped from one stone to another, his will weakening and his knees faltering, the poisonous gases of the chamber filled his lungs and the heat scorched his skin. Everything sizzled, slurped and crackled. As he reached the final stone, the craggy footfall cracked and sheared away into the lava. Falling to a crouch, his hands clutching the small rock and his foot held over the searing surface of the lake, Archaon jumped. He landed on the island's shale shore and rolled through the shattered rock, cutting his back to ribbons. Pulling shards of stone from his flesh, the dark templar walked up the shore. Above him, the volcano opened out onto the broiling blackness of a doom-laden sky.

The island seemed to support a roughly hewn architecture. It was scorch-shattered and dusted with ash. The structure lay in ruins but Archaon recognised certain elements of its construction. There seemed to be a hearth and a firepot of molten rock. Hollows contained the solidified dregs of molten metal. Shapes and moulds that had been carved into the stone. Archaon even saw what was left of a hammer, buried in the dust. The Chaos warrior was fairly sure that he was standing in some infernal smithy or daemon forge. As he passed through the crumbling ruins and reached the heart of the forge tomb, his suspicions were confirmed.

Archaon fell down to his knees in the volcanic grit. He lowered his head in reverence and relief. Before him stood a stone dais bearing the assembled pieces of a suit of infernal armour. Archaon stared up at the ancient plate. Its design had a simple monstrosity to it. The work of the insane genius of some daemon craftsman. Both the metal plates and the mail upon which they were set were fashioned of some outlandish metal. The suit's bold cuirass and pauldrons suggested both fortitude and elegance, while the plates that covered both arms and legs appeared to overlap for extra protection, like the hull planks of a clinker-built vessel. Sturdy armoured boots and the intricate workings of plate gauntlets sat abandoned in the dust, while the reinforced expanse of a body shield bearing the riveted glory of an eight-pointed star and a central spike rested nearby. Bronzed skulls had been crafted seamlessly into the suit's fearful breastplate. They appeared to complement the leering, brazen skull that was the suit's fearful helmet. Extravagant eruptions of daemon horn adorned the sides of the helm while the sculpted eye sockets allowed the infernal light of the forge to probe its inner darkness.

Archaon rose before the ancient armour. He approached

the daemon design with the flutter of excitement and expectation in his chest. This was truly a treasure of Chaos. He took the skull-crafted breastplate from the stone dais and held it up for inspection. The metal was thick but unexpectedly light. Unlike the weapons within the caskets, the unusual metal of the suit's forging seemed untouched by the ravages of time or the decimating attentions of the environment. Turning the breastplate around, Archaon noticed that there was a bronze plate on the gorget interior bearing an inscription. It was an epitaph, like one might find on an ancient tomb. It simply said *'Unconquered'* and bore the name Morkar beneath.

Morkar. *Morkar*. Archaon knew the name. How could he not? It echoed about the Northern Wastes, carried on the curses of champions and the boasts of murderous marauders. Morkar was legend. Morkar – the Uniter. The beacon of Chaos whose dark light eclipsed the dawn of civilisation. The First Everchosen of the Ruinous Powers. Morkar – Ravager of the fledgling Empire of man. Slain by a false god two and a half thousand years before Archaon had been born. Archaon stared about the volcano interior at the thousands of sarcophagi lining the black walls. Morkar's United. The honoured warriors of Chaos who had fought at Morkar's side. Archaon nodded to himself with dark glee. The fabled armour of Morkar was his. How it came to be here so long after the Everchosen's defeat, Archaon could not tell. All he knew was that the Dark Gods had tested him. They had sent Archaon by way of insanity, betrayal and death but finally the path to damnation had led him to victory – to this infernal mountain and a Ruinous treasure of the Chaos Powers. The armour of Morkar was his reward. The second treasure by which the Everchosen and Lord of the End Times would be known.

A smile bled through the dark templar's cracked lips. He began tearing the rags and scraps of leather from his body. The armour was his and plate by damned plate, Archaon dressed his bruised and broken body with both its physical and infernal protections. Despite the heat of the surroundings, the armour felt cool on the Chaos warrior's skin. Volcanic dust showered from the ancient plate revealing the strange lustre of the metal beneath. Hefting the body shield onto his left arm, he snatched up the skull-helm by one great horn. He went to slip the helmet over his bare head – to plunge face first into the darkness within – but something caught his eye. Turning the helmet around and staring down at the leering skull Archaon noticed that between the horns and set in the brow between the crafted eye sockets, there was a depression. This the Chaos warrior found odd since the armour bore no other examples of damage. Scraping the depression with the finger of one gauntlet, the dust that caked it fell away, revealing its true shape and dimension. A shape and dimension that the dark templar had seen before and instantly recognised.

Crafted in the forehead of the helm was a distinctive socket – an eye-shaped socket – set to receive a decorative jewel of some kind. And Archaon knew which jewel. It was just the right size and shape to ensconce the Eye of Sheerian. The prophetic gem of Khezula Sheerian, the daemon sorcerer of Tzeentch.

Archaon looked up from the helm. Up the black rock of the mountain interior and up out of the caldera top. He stared up at the tumultuous black skies with wretched scorn and a face full of hate.

'You faithless gods,' he roared up at them. 'You monsters of the perverse. You givers and takers... Why?'

Archaon angled the helmet to see inside. The helm had been crafted to allow its owner to wear a band or crown. Morkar's armour was that of Ruinous royalty. The front of both the missing crown and the helm allowed the setting of the sorcerous jewel which had to be a further treasure of the Chaos Powers. A treasure both Archaon and the Dark Gods had conspired to put in the belly of the monstrous dragon, Flamefang. Both cold fury and futility flooded the Chaos warrior. Then, as he thought on such a treasure being so close to his feverish grasp, Archaon's god-cursing snarl dropped to a savage smile. As the Dark Gods had set Ruinous champion against Ruinous champion, Archaon would do the same with their hallowed treasures. With the enchanted armour of Morkar, perhaps Archaon could defeat the colossal Chaos dragon that hunted him like soul-prey across ocean and Southern Wastes. His fate decided, Archaon slipped the helm over his head and became one with the darkness within.

Staring about the inside of the helmet, Archaon knew only the deepest darkness. The slits of the skull-helm eye sockets admitted none of the evil glare of the lava lake. Holding his gauntlets out in front of him, Archaon could not see them. When he tried to take the helmet off, he discovered that it refused to be separated from the gorget and cuirass upon which it sat.

Then he heard a noise in the darkness. Distant. An ancient echo of slaughter long past. Building to a cacophonous crescendo. In the blackness of the helm he heard the sounds of battle. Blades. Shouts. Screams. Just like he had heard within the sarcophagi of Morkar's long dead warriors of Chaos.

'Worm...' a blistering voice ventured from the black oblivion. It sounded as old as time itself, like an antique blade honed on the events of a dark history to come. 'Scavenger... Robber of graves. This is blasphemy. That the pantheon would send such a miserable beggar to fall before their warlord, their prince. To fail so completely and to have his screams echo for always about the darkness of my tomb.'

As the potent presence spoke, Archaon felt the darkness within the armour wash over his skin. Like a man drowning in a lightless void, Archaon felt the darkness enter his ears, his nose and his roaring mouth. It gushed down his throat and soaked through his skin. It granted him oblivion. He was completely alone. Not even he was there. There was only the voice.

'You thought you could steal from me, worm?' the words proceeded, powerful and primordial. 'I wore this armour on the precipice of dark providence. It was baptised in the blood of a king who would become a god. It carried me to my doom. *My* doom – as it carries you to your own, pretender to the crown. This armour is mine.'

Morkar…

The impact was like nothing Archaon had ever felt. The Chaos warrior was not accustomed to being hit but occasionally it happened. When it did it felt nothing like the colossal blow that had just knocked him from his feet. He felt himself skid through the volcanic dust before coming to a stop. He was blind. He was trapped on an island of black stone at the heart of a molten lake. He was being attacked. Archaon tried to get up. The dreadful force had hammered him from the right. He instinctively brought up his shield. The same force suddenly smashed into him from the left. The Chaos warrior flew to the side, smashing straight through the igneous rock of the forge before rolling to a stop in the dust and shattered stone. Archaon tried to get up but he couldn't even find his way to the thought. The impact had smashed his mind into a stunned ache.

Pushing up out of the grit, another blow found him beneath the chin of his helm. Archaon flew backwards through the air before coming back down with a heart-stopping crash. Archaon clawed at the shale beneath his armoured fingertips. Volcanic shale. The Chaos warrior tried to find his way to a single thought. Shale. The shore. Archaon was locked in an abyssal darkness. The blows smashing him about the island were daemonic in their intensity, supernatural in their precisely applied force. Incredibly, these were not his biggest problem. His biggest problem was the likelihood that the next blow would send him flying off the shale shoreline and into the lake of molten rock. When the impact came, it was soul-shattering.

Suddenly, light. The blinding radiance of the day. A sun Archaon had not seen in what seemed like forever. Colours. Shapes. Trees. He was there. Back in the forests of the Empire. Smoke stung his nostrils. The smoke of destruction, utter and merciless. He could taste blood on his lips.

His own and that of barbarian tribesmen whose slaughter hung on the air like a bloody mist. There was a barbarian before him. A Reiklander. A small mountain of muscle, decked in forest furs, trailing the long, unkempt mane of a savage. He was not alone. He introduced Archaon to his companion. A dwarf hammer. A warhammer of haft, rune and gold. A warhammer whose enchanted and unstoppable head trailed blood and destiny. *Ghal Maraz*. Skull-splitter. And then Sigmar hit him.

Something broke deep within Archaon. His body smashed through the trees before bouncing off and around the thick trunks of Empire oaks and Reikland heartwoods. His armoured form spun like a discarded doll before coming to a stop in the leaves and the dirt. Archaon brought up his weapon, a sword that smoked with daemonic fury... but again Sigmar was there. The Unberogen had stormed through the forest at Archaon like a force of nature. *Ghal Maraz* smashed though the blade and it shattered like silver glass. The barbarian turned on his heel and brought the terrible weapon around and down.

When it hit Archaon it felt like an earthquake. The Chaos warrior was smashed down through the black forest earth, the stone and roots and into a hollow of his own making. Sigmar leapt into the pit, landing like a great cat. Like a wild lion, his face was contorted with noble savagery. Eyes narrow and teeth bared. He had confronted a thing of evil and now he was to destroy it. It was the end for Archaon. His God-King would destroy him.

His God-King. Archaon reached back. Back through the blood and treachery – back to a time of simple falsehoods. A God-King and the tales that were told about him. Tales that false priests and templars promoted as belief, venerated and worshipped. Archaon knew this tale. He knew how it ended.

Morkar the Uniter. Favoured of darkness. Everchosen of the Chaos gods – smashed and defeated – pushed his helm up off his head and looked up at Sigmar Heldenhammer. The man who would be a god. *Ghal Maraz* came up, for it was his destiny to end the evil that had ridden out of the north on a deluge of Ruinous warrior-savages.

'Brinnan utva lioht,' Sigmar spat – a curse of his barbarian ancestors. An Unberogen curse Archaon had come to know in his former calling. Not only as his God-King's holy words but also a Sigmarite templar's way of life. *Brinnan utva lioht. Burn by the light.*

'Brinnan utva lioht,' Archaon spat and brought the great hammer down on Morkar's head with such righteous force that rather than split the Everchosen's skull, he obliterated it, hammering blood and bone into the forest bedrock.

Archaon rose from the molten rock of the lake. Lava spilled down his glowing plate. Magma dribbled from his backplate and pauldrons. Through the socket-slits of his skull-helm and the haze of heat, Archaon could see. Liquid rock bubbled and spat about him like an infernal sea. He had been knocked into the lake of lava but the daemon runes and dark enchantments of Morkar's armour had saved him. Striding out of the magma and up the shale shore, Archaon shook the igneous globs of cooling stone from his shield. Within the plate it was as dark, cool and empty of vengeance as Archaon could wish it. Outside, the outlandish metal of the armour steamed and cooled.

Snatching up furs for his shoulders and the ragged cloak that had failed miserably to keep him warm out in the frozen wilderness of the Southern Wastes, Archaon moved with power and purpose across the stepping stones of the raging lake. Like the twin-tailed comet that heralded the Heldenhammer's coming – he would not be stopped. Like the world's wretched end – he would not be stopped. When he reached the wall of rugged, black stone that was the hollow interior of the volcano, Archaon started to climb. He hauled himself up the stone sarcophagi of Morkar's marauders and the razor-sharp jags and ledges. He climbed. Like a rising star of the Ruinous Powers he ascended. The mountain's height was nothing. The weight of his armour was nothing. The dark templar hauled himself up over the lip of the caldera, the lake of lava raging beneath him.

Hubris had put him from his path. It had made him blind to treachery. It had sent the army with which he was going to conquer the world to the bottom of the ocean. But he had come back from calamity. Another treasure of Chaos was his. And another would be also, if he could only find a way into the belly of the daemon-dragon that had swallowed it.

He did not have to wait long.

CHAPTER XVII

'So two titans of darkness met,
In sight of daemonlands undreamt.
One shook the world with titan's deeds,
The other to death was condemn…'
  – Necrodomo the Insane, *'The Liber Caelestior'*

The Hinterdark – The Obliviate Plain
The Southern Wastes
Horns Harrowing: Season of Fire

Out of the storm-swirling skies it came. The *Yien-Ya-Long*. Flamefang. Chaos dragon and terror of Grand Cathay. A thing crafted of stolen flesh. A great serpent slithering through the heavens, the beast beat its stretched skin and clawed its way into a banking turn. Mouths screamed in its sides, eyeballs writhed in the sockets set in its warped form – ever on the lookout for soul-prey. Within moments of emerging from the cavernous crater, Archaon knew it had him. It wheeled. It turned. It surged. It cut down through the howling gales and swooped in on the lone figure standing atop the glowering summit of the volcano. In the maelstrom, in the darkness, against the black rock of the mountain, Archaon would have been all but invisible – but to Tzeentch's monster, he was a beacon of soulfire calling the beast down on him.

'Come on,' Archaon grizzled, his boots crunching through the grit. 'Come on you ugly brute.'

And then it was there, a plume of purple flame raging before its mangled jaws. Archaon's instinct was to run, to take cover behind the boulders and crags of the mountaintop. The disgusting sensation of the warpflame's effects still remained with him. Through the searing agony that was his left hand, he fancied he could still feel his missing digits and their rebellion in flesh. The inferno washed across the peak, feeling its way about the rocks and ridges before it found its victim. Archaon stood like a statue, with the purple blaze raging about him. It filled his socket-slits with its blaze of change that danced across the surface of his plate. As the firestream abated, Archaon felt no scorching warmth through the armour. He felt no rebellion of the flesh as spawndom claimed him. Morkar's armour was impervious to the dragon's wrath. Slipping an axe from his belt the Chaos warrior threw the weapon at the passing beast, burying the blade in its morphing flesh.

Again the dragon came at him. And again. Each time its warped jaws were preceded by the fury of its transformative flame but again and again the dark templar emerged from the inferno unscathed and ready with a sword or axe to toss at the beast. Then suddenly the colossal creature was gone. It had vanished into the broiling, black heavens.

'No!' Archaon roared. 'I'm here you aberration. I'm here!'

He glared up at the firmament as it boiled like molten pitch above him. He peered through the swirling maelstrom that howled across the Southern Wastes. He stared at the darkness beyond the infernal glow of the volcano, at the savage hordes of beastfiends and daemons that were tearing each other to pieces in the madness of the storm.

He heard Flamefang before he saw it. He never actually saw it at all. As he turned, the great jaws of the Chaos dragon were already there, beckoning like the entrance of a cave. Archaon was knocked from his feet by the snapping force of the maw as it snatched him from the mountaintop. Then the dragon's mangled mouth clamped shut, trapping the Chaos warrior in a prison of fang and twisted tooth.

Archaon had seen Flamefang claim its victims before. Like a hungry hound it gorged itself, wolfing down its prey, sometimes using the length of its jaws like a trough to scoop screaming crowds of unfortunates into its gullet in eagerness to assimilate their flesh and forms. And with each victim the beast had grown. Not Archaon. The Chaos dragon reserved extra suffering for him. Crunching down on the dark templar, the monster intended to masticate him first. Crush him within its titanic jaw. Skewer him with fang. Shear him to miserable pieces within its mangled maw. The armour of Morkar would not allow such desecration. Ordinarily the victim would be blind to the gnashing horror within the beast's mouth but Lord Tzeentch's beast flooded its mouth with warping flame that lit up its maw and bathed Archaon in a purple blaze. To the dragon, Archaon mused, his armoured form must have felt like chewing on a musket ball.

Then, through the fires of change he saw it. The Imperial cross of the pommel. The modest twinkle of gems set in the crossguard. *Terminus*. The greatsword still sat in its scabbard of morphing flesh, buried in an outbreak of faces that peered down from the roof of the Chaos dragon's mouth like blisters. Archaon reached for the blade, but as he did the mouth was suddenly awash with a burning liquid that exuded from his monstrous surroundings. The stinking deluge preceded a swallowing action, and the telescopic jaws of its inner mouth and the one within that shot forward to snap shut about the Chaos warrior like a toothed cage of smeared flesh and bone. Pressing himself against the inside of the inner maw and reaching between the bars of its stabbing fangs, Archaon stretched. He reached. He snatched at the sword with his armoured fingertips. As he reached it, clamping the pommel between two fingers, the Chaos dragon ingurgitated. Dragging the sword free of its fleshy prison, Archaon held on to the blade as his armoured form was hauled to the back of the dragon's throat where he was swallowed again and began a horrible journey down through the beast's undulating gullet.

Archaon was filled with pure disgust. His plate was awash with the creature's assimilating slime. The stench inside the monster was an overwhelming, oblivion-inviting air the dark templar was forced to breathe. The creature was living horror. Archaon could feel the morphing, muscular movements in the flesh about him, taking him down the beast's snaking throat and into the cavernous lairs of its monstrous body. Spat and slinked through a series of gullet sphincters, Archaon found himself sliding further through a slurping passage in which the mouths of victims set in the walls bit at his armour and hands tore at the difficult to digest plate. The assimilated unfortunates did not succeed and within several horrid moments Archaon slid down into a larger chamber – some kind of pre-stomach or gizzard – and came to a stop in the digestive shallows of a small lake.

Clawing his way back up through the slime and the fleshly shoreline, Archaon turned to take in his surroundings. The walls had a flesh-smeared architecture – a horror all of their own. Within their trembling, ooze-exuding structure were bones, ribs and scraps of armour. It was here, in the prison of its own flesh that it kept its captured treasure. In amongst the gristle and sinew Archaon could see coin, precious stones and Ruinous artefacts. Assimilated victims reached out for him with arms that extended from the walls. Others screamed in perpetual agony, all merged mouths and torment. The pool from which he had hauled himself was alight with isolated tongues of transformative flame. The waters shifted from side to side, splashing up one side of the chamber and then the other as the great dragon banked and flew. The pool itself was drowning in part-assimilated bodies. From there, it seemed, the poor wretches would find themselves part of Flamefang. One with its flesh. Trapped in gibbets of twisted bone. Draped behind the stretching transparency of its skin. Doomed – until finally their horror would be complete as limbs and organs parted ways to serve the Chaos dragon's warped form. Archaon had never known such rancid disgust. He knew only that the colossal beast had to die.

Stomping through moaning shallows, with *Terminus* clamped in the vice-like grip of his gauntlet, Archaon advanced through the beast. Pushing through fleshy slits and serrated valves, Archaon traversed bloody, rippling chambers lined with shredding teeth. He pushed through forests of embedded limbs that clawed for his mercy. He marched through masticating orifices that threatened to smother and absorb him. Everywhere he searched for the sapphire glow of the daemon sorcerer's gem. The prophetic Eye of Sheerian. A Tzeentchian treasure that had blessed the endeavours of Morkar the Uniter and belonged in the setting of his mighty helm. As it had fostered the decimations of the first Everchosen of Chaos, it would do the same for the last. It did not deserve to furnish the fantasies of a senile sorcerer or slosh around the digestive pool of a damned abomination like Flamefang. It was destined for greater service. Without *The Celestine Book of Divination*, Archaon would need the enchanted jewel to show him the path ahead. To show him the Ruinous treasures that once reclaimed would mark him as the herald of Armageddon and Lord of the End Times.

As the Eye beheld Archaon, Archaon beheld the eye. Through the womb-like darkness of the dragon's warped innards, the Chaos warrior saw the slightest suggestion of the gemstone's ethereal glow. Hefting *Terminus*, the dark templar stabbed his way through the writhing flesh of the stomach wall and sawed his way to systems new. As he cut his way to an adjacent set of chambers, Archaon felt the dragon twist and contort about him. He was up to his knees in blood as the beast bled internally. It could feel the agonies its last meal was inflicting on it from within and was forced to land on the black ice of a midnight plain. Even from within, Archaon could hear the war cries of beastfiends attacking in number. He heard daemons leaping from the storm to sink their defiant talons into dragon flesh. They would tear it apart, Archaon knew, but as the stomach walls stiffened and bucked, Archaon knew that Flamefang was visiting the wrath of its transformative flame on the dark monstrosities of the Southern Wastes. Small lakes of assimilate slime erupted in purple flame as the Chaos dragon scorched the hordes about it to spawn.

Archaon stepped back. Swinging *Terminus* about him, Archaon hacked at the tendon and sinew that blocked his progress. It was butcher's work but as mouths in the flesh about him screamed and the Chaos dragon coughed and spluttered its torment, a mad grin spread across Archaon's face.

'Hurt, you abominable thing,' Archaon roared. 'I want you to feel this,' he spat, doused in blood and hacking through the thick flesh. 'I want you to feel it all.'

Tearing his way through its last sinewy resistance, Archaon stepped through into a different chamber. It was tighter. Darker. It even smelled differently. There were riches here. As well as the horror of flesh-smeared unfortunates embedded in the walls of the chamber there was coin, jewels and objects of precious metal. Archaon had entered some kind of inner lair, within the Chaos dragon itself, encrusted with swallowed wealth. The dark templar felt suddenly on edge. Something wasn't right. Moving around the twisting corners of a fleshy canal, Archaon saw it. A bright blue radiance that seemed to call out to him. His armoured boots slapped through the chamber's blood-threaded slime and he quickened his step.

There was a sudden cracking sound. Something the Chaos warrior hadn't heard before. He froze. The glowing gemstone shone. It twinkled. It blinked at the dark templar. Archaon almost had it in his grasp. But he was not alone in the canal chamber. He was being stalked by something from within the Chaos dragon's warped body. Archaon turned his head. He could hear more cracking. Peering through the gloom he saw movement. There were other riches here. The most precious of the lair's treasures. There were eggs set within the fleshy walls of the chamber. The lair was some kind of birthing canal. Archaon had no idea whether the Chaos dragon was male or female, some combination of the two or neither, but deep within its grotesque carcass it was harbouring the next generation of monstrous calamity, ready to inflict on the world.

Archaon's lip formed a snarl. He watched the shell of the egg before him fracture and crack. The internal agonies he had visited upon Flamefang had awoken the infant dragons. The stink of Archaon's fresh flesh and the prospect of a first meal now drew them from their shells. Archaon revolved his armoured wrist, turning *Terminus* around in the grip of his gauntlet.

'All right,' the dark templar announced to the chamber. 'Let's go.'

The dragon exploded from its shell. A sinewy gargoyle of half-formed flesh and fang. Flapping its slime-coated wings and tearing its way from one wall of the birthing canal to the other, the infant monstrosity came at him. Before the beast even leapt for the Chaos warrior, a second was on his back and a third hammered into his shield from the side. Archaon fell through the fleshy curtains of the chamber, his ears full of the metal-scraping cacophony of dragonclaw. The monsters were supernaturally strong. They were ravenous and prised at his infernal armour for the succulent flesh within. They snaggled his armoured limbs and one had the back of his skull-helm in the flesh-stripping fangs of its maw. Archaon rolled and the infant dragons rolled with him – grotesque sculptures crafted of misbegotten flesh. They tumbled and ploughed through the shell of a fourth egg, liberating another beast, the commotion drawing a fifth – some kind of malformed runt – from the sphincter of some side chamber.

Archaon was buried in dragonflesh, the beasts slithering

about him like a nest of strangling serpents. With the chamber moving about him with Flamefang's own movements, it was difficult for the Chaos warrior to find his bearings. He felt their plate-wrenching claws, the lengths of their gnashing jaws and the muscular constriction of their bodies test his armour. He had no idea how long it would take the supernatural spawn of the Chaos dragon to find a weakness and exploit it, burrowing into his torso with their twisted, narrow jaws. As their tumble came to a stop at the canal wall, the Chaos warrior found himself on top of one of the monsters. Bucking and landing on his shield with the full weight of his armour and all the force he could muster, Archaon slammed the shield's spike straight through the trapped beast, bursting what passed for its malformed heart. Pressing his advantage, Archaon worked his arm free and smashed the infant dragon that had him clamped in its maw across the snout with his greatsword's crossguard. Drawing *Terminus* back immediately, Archaon sliced the head of the dazed dragon from its warped shoulders.

As the infant dragons died, the faces set in the wall of the birthing canal screeched Flamefang's horror. The beasts' siblings hissed and hackled with reptilian hate. Two retreated momentarily to the walls, the monster that had come straight at him and its sibling runt, leaping from fleshy surface to surface, their savage senses driving them to find a weakness and exploit an opportunity. Archaon tried to get to his feet again but the dragon snaggling the back of his helm, his neck and his furs was anchored to his back. Tripping across an embedded ribcage and the grasping attentions of limbs snatching at his from the chamber floor, *Terminus* tumbled from Archaon's grasp and the Chaos warrior once more fell to the floor. With the birthling snapping and clawing at him, the dark templar took the ragged length of his slime-drenched cloak and wrapped it about the monster. It had him but now he had it. He felt the muscles in his arms burn as he heaved at the cloak-fashioned noose, watching it tighten about the creature's sinewy neck. Its larger sibling hissed at the Chaos warrior and leapt for his back but Archaon gave its surging snout an answer with his armoured elbow, batting the thing aside. With a roar, Archaon returned to the beast before him, heaving and strangling until finally he heard the bones within the monstrosity's neck break and a final breath rattle from its choking maw.

Shaking the impact from its warped skull, the larger sibling came back at Archaon but the Chaos warrior was done with the abomination. As he rolled over to meet it, he hammered the creature in the face with the unrelenting force of one armoured fist, sending it coiling and hissing back at the wall. As he got to his feet, picking up his shield, the runt leapt at Archaon through a leathery curtain of flesh. Smashing the creature aside with the shield, Archaon batted it back, again and again until it lay senseless before him. Holding the edge of the shield above the trembling monstrosity's head, Archaon watched it experience some kind of brain-dazed fit before bringing the shield down on the beast's skull and ending the horror.

Turning, Archaon beheld the final monster before him, holding itself low to the fleshy floor, snaking this way and that. Snatching *Terminus* up from where it had tumbled from his hand and buried its tip in the chamber floor, Archaon came for the creature. The beast retreated, no longer feeling the advantage. No longer on the attack. When he had backed it up to the wall, with nowhere left to go and no option other than to attack, Archaon waited. He waited for the beast to give him everything it had. It did not disappoint. With the savagery of its parent abomination, the dragon sprang forth. With wings held close and neck extended, the monster shot forward with its fang-filled maw. Side-stepping and lifting his shield, Archaon allowed it in under his arm. Grabbing the back of its ferocious skull with one gauntlet he swept *Terminus* down with the other. The gore-smeared blade cleaved the dragon's head from its shoulders, like a woodcutter's axe to a branch.

With the dark metal of his chestplate and pauldrons

rising and falling with the exertion of battle, Archaon took a moment before marching on through the birthing canal, towards the searing glow of the Eye of Sheerian. Around the next fleshy corner he found his treasure. The sorcerous jewel was embedded in the chamber wall, the burning inner darkness of its eye inviting Archaon to prise the artefact free. Bathed in its sapphire radiance, Archaon could feel the prophetic power of the artefact. He saw himself dig the gem from the wall of flesh and clean it with his cloak. Before the Chaos warrior knew what was happening, it was done. He saw himself slot the Ruinous treasure into the socket of his helm, feeling the potency of its predictive power close to his mind. And it was so. The Eye of Sheerian flooded him with possibility. He lived in the searing immediacy of the moment but also in the moments of others. As the dark eye of the jewel blinked, Archaon had other sights, other perspectives flash through his mind. With the eyes of so many victims embedded throughout the Chaos dragon's body, the experience was a sickening whirl of disorientation. Like the fear of a fall from tree or cliff, the visions that preceded each blink of the jewel filled Archaon with a heart-sinking rush. He was privy to the darkest recesses of the daemon-dragon's form: the suffering of half-assimilated unfortunates, the rage-tinged sights of slaughter-fuelled beastfiends and the preysight of daemons hunting Flamefang's wounded progress through the bestial hordes of the ice-wept plain. He even saw through the Chaos dragon's own eyes as it snapped up the monstrosities of the Southern Wastes in its mighty jaws and blasted the Dark God's predacious daemonkin to oblivion with terrible streams of its warpflame.

Finally his wandering gaze came to settle on himself. Archaon, dressed in the dark armour of the Everchosen of Chaos, the Ruinous Star of Chaos on his shield and the greatsword *Terminus* in his hand. The Eye of Sheerian blazing back at him from its resting place in the leering skull of his horned helm. Willing the potent jewel closed, the sapphire radiance that lit up the chamber with its ghoulish glow died, returning the birthing canal to a womb-like gloom. Stepping forward, the Chaos warrior saw the eyes through which he had seen himself. A face in the flesh-sculpted wall of the chamber that he recognised. The naked suggestion of limb and curve that he had known. That he had touched and felt for.

'Archaon…'

It stung to hear his name spoken by Giselle. Giselle Dantziger, the Sister of the Imperial Cross. Giselle Dantziger, who had shared his bed, had tried to save his soul, had failed. Archaon moved to her and knelt before her assimilated form. 'Archaon,' she begged. The Chaos warrior laid his gauntlet against the soft skin of her cheek. She begged him to perform the service she had failed to perform for him. She begged him to do what he did best. 'Archaon… kill me.'

Archaon stared at Giselle. The wretched hordes of Chaos, the beastmen, the murderous marauders, the treacherous champions of the Dark Gods. All who had betrayed him, as was their nature. They had deserved no fate better than the monstrous Flamefang had offered. The Swords. Hieronymous Dagobert. Gorst. Giselle. They had just been victims of the calamity Archaon had ordered the daemon sorcerer Sheerian to inflict on the world once more. He shook his head. Feelings, raw and unpleasant exploded in the Chaos warrior's chest. He didn't want to kill Giselle. He didn't want her to live like this either. All he really knew was that he wanted the Chaos dragon dead. Archaon quaked in the Everchosen's damned plate. He wanted to send its monstrous spirit howling back to its twisted master. He brought up *Terminus*. He would kill the beast of Tzeentch. He would kill it from the inside. Archaon plunged the greatsword into the ceiling of the fleshy lair. Tendons contorted and a ripple of agony passed down the length of the canal.

'Yes…' the warrior of Chaos hissed. He pulled the blade free and stabbed it through a nearby wall and into the organs beyond. He went mad, like a frenzied animal, skewering, gutting and stabbing any horrific thing inside the beast that looked important. Blood flooded the chamber and those beyond like a tide washing into a coastal cave. He buried *Terminus* in the assimilated wretches of lair walls and organs, releasing those that had betrayed him from their suffering. He sliced the dragon open, rending gashes in the beast's belly and sides, cutting his way through from the inside out. As the great Flamefang flew, it roared its torment, funnelling flame through the labyrinthine butchery of its insides. The Chaos dragon was attempting to repair itself as fast as Archaon was taking it apart. About him the great caverns of the monster's innards shook, as though the wounded beast had landed.

'No,' Archaon roared above the dragon's furies. He plunged *Terminus* as deep as the blade would go into the creature. Then he forced it further and further, piercing his way through the monster. The greatsword sliced through organs and sinewy flesh. Archaon climbed in after the weapon – almost swimming through the dragon's insides. He squirmed the blade onwards. About him he could hear the thunder of Flamefang's heart and the rhythmic pulse of its beating in the raw horror about him. 'You... have... to...' Archaon snarled as his exertions pushed the blade on. He suddenly felt it hit the tough resistance of muscle. He could feel the dragon's lifeforce quaking through the length of the blade. 'Die...'

Archaon thrust the templar blade ahead of him. He felt it pierce deep into the thunder of muscle. He felt the great organ burst and shred itself in the futility of beating. He felt the Chaos dragon spasm about the failing organ in the serpentine death throes of a legendary beast. The *Yien-Ya-Long* – Flamefang – the terror of Grand Cathay, had been felled by the Chaos warrior. As he waded through the blood and back to Giselle, he felt its flesh quiver horribly about him as the monster began to die. Mouths in the walls and muffled deep within the flesh began to scream. Giselle was out of her mind. Flamefang was dying and as part of the horrific fusion, she too felt the approaching end.

'I'll get you out of here,' he promised her. He meant it. But she was no sorcerer's jewel. She would not be plucked from the dragon's flesh. It was impossible to tell where her flesh began and that of other unfortunates emerged. He brought the gore-dripping *Terminus* up, producing from the girl a miserable sob. The sword dropped. He would kill her just trying to cut her out. The Chaos warrior looked about the chamber, powerless to act. Taking a life was simple. Saving one – one already taken by the Dark Gods for their entertainment and the feasting of souls – altogether impossible. Archaon thought on Father Dagobert, who had saved him more times than he cared to remember. Father Dagobert, who Archaon had been powerless to save. Archaon quaked with frustration. With rage. Then it came to him. A name.

'Sheerian!' Archaon roared, his fury echoing through the cavernous confines of the daemon-dragon. In the silence that followed, Archaon heard a grunt from the other side of the chamber. Cutting a leathery curtain out of his path, the dark templar found the sorcerer embedded in the flesh of the opposite wall. His age-mottled skull protruded from the slime-streaming wall of sinew, as well as the hobbling bird's foot blessing of his master Lord Tzeentch. His withered arms and bone staff were lost to the dragon's flesh and his mouth was covered by a film of stretched skin across his yellowing teeth. The daemon sorcerer watched him with his milky eyes. He couldn't take his gaze from the Eye that sat in Archaon's helm. The prophetic jewel that had been his.

'Sheerian,' Archaon said. 'You snake. You devil. Save me from the dagger in my back, would you? While having me sharpening one of your own.' Archaon gestured about him. 'Only a sorcerer of the Lord Tzeentch would make the instrument of my salvation the very instrument of my destruction. It seems that your thrice-duplicitous lord had a surprise for you also, daemon. Didn't expect to find yourself in the belly of the beast you unleashed, eh?' Archaon rested the blade tip of *Terminus* under the ancient's squirming chin. 'You work for me now, do you understand, daemon? I am Archaon, Everchosen of Chaos and Lord of the End Times. Your soul – like all others – belongs to me.'

Archaon watched the sorcerer blink his milky eyes slowly in acceptance.

'Your treacherous god gave you the incantations to give this monstrosity life and form,' Archaon spat. 'Can you take away what you have given it, sorcerer?' From behind his sinewy mask, Khezula Sheerian – sorcerer of Tzeentch – nodded from his prison of flesh. Drawing the blade tip of *Terminus* through the skin stretched across his mouth, Archaon tore away the obstruction. The sorcerer worked his ancient jaw and licked his cracked lips.

'Archaon…'

The dark templar was in no mood for the daemon sorcerer's cackling lies and entreaties.

'Incantations,' the Chaos warrior ordered. 'Now!'

Sheerian went to work mumbling the enchantments, invocations and bindings that had harnessed the raging soul of the mighty *Yien-Ya-Long* in the flesh of men. As the powerful magic, learned from the lips of Lord Tzeentch himself, began to take hold, Archaon waded back over to Giselle. He sheathed the mighty *Terminus* and shouldered his shield. The dark templar took hold of two fingers of one hand that protruded from the wall of smeared flesh. 'Hold on,' he told his lover. His saviour. 'Just hold on.'

The dying Flamefang instantly knew something was wrong. An agony that could not be felt nor described began to tear at its soul. It was a torment not known by man nor beast. It wasn't like the freezing maelstrom of the Southern Wastes or the scorching embrace of molten rock. It was nothing like the raging of beastfiend hordes or the sinking of daemonclaw into its inconstant flesh. It wasn't even the hot torture of armoured and indomitable souls upon which it had feasted, felt deep within. It was deeper even than that. Tzeentch was calling back its abomination. Archaon heard the Chaos dragon rage against its master. It roared across the icy plains, through the maelstrom and up into the black, boiling skies. The dragon's flesh began to melt. To fall away. To disintegrate. The thousands of unfortunates that made up the great beast's horrific form fell upon the creature, tearing it to pieces. Archaon looked about the chamber. The walls were alive, thrashing in their traumatic fury. Flesh dribbled from the ceiling and down the walls. Limbs emerged. Naked bodies. Howling victims, bereft of sanity. Men, women and beasts that had been through misery and back.

The floor of the birthing chamber began to give way. Archaon held onto Giselle, pulling the girl free of the shredding sinew and to him. As the dragon returned all that it had eaten, all it had consumed, Archaon stood atop a writhing mountain of bodies. There were screams of joy. Of pain. Of minds lost and never to return. Wrapping Giselle in the ragged length of his cloak, Archaon carried the girl in his arms. He stepped down through the bodies, out onto the icy expanse of the bestial swarming plain. As beastfiends set upon the victim mound, sinking their muzzles into fresh flesh, Archaon became aware of a commotion behind him. Turning to face the threat he discovered that throngs of beastmen were being slaughtered. The Chaos warrior saw the flash of bone swords and fountains of black blood erupt from the decapitated and limbless. From the brief butchery, Archaon watched his knights, his Ruinous honour guard, his Swords of Chaos emerge. Bereft of their armour, Eins, Zwei and Drei were a trio of dark angels. They were ashen of flesh, with gargoyle's wings. Limping up behind them was the misshapen Vier. Archaon was glad to see him, despite the horrors the dragon's flame had wrought on his form. Archaon nodded to himself as he came to realise that the bronzed bone that had grown about the heads of the Swords like helms matched his own helmet. Morkar's helmet. The helm of the Everchosen. As he moved on, the winged warriors cut down the few beastfiends drawn to members of Archaon's departing party rather than the feast-mound of defenceless victims before them. In silent subservience and with their wings enclosed about them against the bitter cold of the Southern Wastes, the Swords of Chaos followed their master.

As he passed Sheerian, the sorcerer was recovering his bone

staff and rolling the corpse of a butchered beastfiend chieftain out of furs that had been skinned from its tribal foes. As the ancient hobbled with his bird's foot and staff towards Archaon, his cloak of furs trailing through the ice and gore behind him, his milky eyes were downcast. He was no longer the daemon emissary of Lord Tzeentch. No longer the guardian of the Eye and surveyor of a thousand glorious sights. Like Archaon he had been betrayed by his gods. He was now slave-sorcerer to the Everchosen of Chaos, Lord of the End Times. The sorcerer usually had a lot to say for himself. But not today. He gestured to the mountain of tumbling bodies with his bone staff, the living, screaming corpse of the Chaos dragon.

'Master…'

'It will serve, sorcerer,' Archaon said simply and walked on. The warlord would no longer play at politics. Lieutenants were not to be flattered and promoted to positions of trust and authority. Archaon would rather be feared than respected for his powers of leadership. Those that followed the herald of the apocalypse would please him with their service or they would die – it was as simple as that.

As he led the Swords and his slave-sorcerer out into the stormy maelstrom of the Southern Wastes with the girl Giselle in his arms, Archaon found his progress unimpeded. The savage beastfiends through which he would have had to hack were swarming the bounty the warrior had left behind. He heard the crunch of bone on the wind, the slurp and flesh tearing of muzzles buried in bodies. He heard the screams of men and beasts being eaten alive. Archaon could think of no fate better for the champions of Chaos and marauder tribesmen that had failed him. In the swirling havoc ahead, Archaon sensed the predacious stalking of daemons in the furious darkness. He slowed to a stop.

'Don't,' he warned them, calling into the storm. 'Just don't.'

As Archaon walked on he could not know it, but the daemons of the Southern Wastes were parting. Parting to clear the Chaos warlord's dark path.

EPILOGUE

*'Who-e'er thou art these lines now
reading,
Think not this world your gaze receding
I wander on, my doom to lead
Through daemontide and deserts drear
With dry eye and heart bereft of bleeding
I commit myself to damnation's deeds
For them alone hath brought us here.'*
– Fliessbach, *Tales Untold*

*The Obliviate Plain – Skelter Delta
The Southern Wastes
Horns Harrowing: Season of Fire*

Archaon lay Giselle down on the warm volcanic rock. The Chaos warrior had made for an infernal glow on the horizon. It was the only light in the benighted place and drew Archaon and his miserable band of followers on like moths to a lonely candle. Skies of broiling pitch and storm-smeared gales of ash and ice closed in on them. The temperature plummeted to a brutal freeze and the depths of darkness hid things that lived fantasies of killing them. The light turned out to be a delta of crackling lava, a creeping channel of molten rock from a distant volcano denied to them by the storm. The river of glowing, red death had bifurcated into a delta on the approach to an abyssal escarpment. The separated lava flows dribbled down the cliff face, into a chasm the depths of which allowed no light to escape.

It was as good a place as any to make their miserable camp, Archaon had decided. With the bottomless chasm at their backs and the channels of slurping magma on all other sides of their position within the delta, they were unlikely to be rushed by the hordes of beastfiends they could hear beyond, in perpetual preoccupation of tribal slaughter. The glow of the molten rock would also show the daemons stalking them through the wilderness before they got too close. Most importantly, the delta had what they needed more than shelter, food or water. Warmth. The Southern Wastes didn't need its daemon denizens to kill them. The murderous drop in temperature alone would see to that.

Posting the silent Swords on the three corners of their wretched triangle of land to ensure nothing tried to leap the lava channels or climb up the abyssal cliff face at their backs, Archaon cut a length of Sheerian's foetid fur cloak and covered Giselle with it. He had the misshapen Vier stand over the girl as a personal sentry. Despite the improvised blanket and the lava-warmed rock upon which she lay, the girl was still shivering. Archaon suspected that it would take time to recover from the dreadful experience of being one with the daemon-dragon. Perhaps she never would. The Swords, the sorcerer Sheerian: they were already part of the infernal insanity that was the raw power of Chaos. The girl had no such expectations or defences. She had been dragged into damnation kicking and screaming. For that the warlord knew he would have to answer. The servants of Dark Gods volunteered for their sufferings. The pig-subjects of Sigmar and the worshippers of weakling gods everywhere had it coming. There were few who were truly innocent and undeserving of their doom but Archaon suspected that Giselle might be such a soul. It was what had compelled him to save her. He was simultaneously drawn to and repelled by her. No doubt, the Chaos warrior decided, this was some other perversity of the Dark Gods. They enjoyed their games and for now Archaon was saddled with his conflicted feelings for the girl. It was about the only other thing he felt beyond seething hatred for the Ruinous Powers he served and the bottomless need he had to bring an end to the world of their enemies.

Archaon joined Khezula Sheerian by the searing radiance of the lava channel, where the ancient was warming his bones. Sheerian leant against his staff and peered into the swirling storm beyond.

'One of yours?' the sorcerer asked, gesturing towards a figure working his way towards them. Archaon's gauntlet strayed for his greatsword but narrowing his eye he recognised the miserable wastrel approaching. With frosted rags and chains pulled about him and his head trapped in a cage, Archaon recognised Gorst. Somehow the flagellant had tracked them from the site of his soul-scarring liberation and followed them through the storm. Archaon grunted. Yet again, the flagellant had followed his master. Even here in the impossible lethality of the Wastes, Gorst had found them. It was like old times with the madman following him across all creation.

'One of mine,' Archaon admitted, indicating to the winged Eins that he should bring Gorst across the scorching channel. There were few to truly call themselves such and Gorst had more than earned it. Archaon had led and Gorst had, continued to follow. To where the warlord did not know.

'Where are we?' Archaon asked the daemon sorcerer.

'A dark realm of nowheres,' Sheerian told him.

'No riddles,' Archaon warned.

'There are no riddles to be had here, master,' the ancient said. 'We are in the Southern Wastes, a place of primordial evil. Where the Dark Gods are free to craft their servants from the storm. Where daemons rule and no men exist to bring sense to the dread pantheon's insanities. We are about as far from salvation as any mortal man has been, my lord. Where are we? All frequented have names but I have no idea what this blasted place is called. I cannot tell you where we have been or where we are – and only the Eye can show you where we are going.'

The sorcerer licked his thin lips. The skeletal fingers about his staff began to shake. He stared up at the jewel set in Archaon's skull-helm in the hope that the warlord might use the potent artefact before him so that the sorcerer might once again experience some suggestion of its power and radiance. The Eye opened. It blazed to life, blinking as Archaon cast his gaze across the horizon – its inner darkness seeing all.

Archaon stared into the Southern Wastes. The glorious, Byzantine brutality of it all. The thunder of beastfiend herds clashing in the darkness. Soul-starved daemons feasting on the wretched existence of such creatures. The abyssal cold. The deep darkness. The raging mountaintops that banished both in their volcanic brilliance. The god-furious approach of some decimating superstorm. Sheerian waited. Archaon said nothing for what seemed like an eternity. The wandering gaze of the Eye moved between the dread perspectives of the Waste's wicked denizens. Then, 'I see an infernal palace, distant and huge,' Archaon told the sorcerer. 'No. Many palaces. All colossal. Ever changing. Indescribable.'

'And, and?' the sorcerer feverishly prompted.

'Beyond them, the dark heart of the entire world,' Archaon told him.

'Yes?'

'Like the fallen sun,' Archaon said, 'as black as it was bright. Impossible. Irresistible. Blazing its darkness but drawing all into the depths of its brilliance.'

'As it draws your gaze, Archaon,' the sorcerer told him, 'and that of the all-powerful Eye.'

'What draws it?' Archaon demanded. 'I must know.'

'You fought your way across the Shadowlands of the north, yes?'

'Yes,' the Chaos warlord confirmed.

'But never the pole,' Sheerian pushed. 'Never the very top of the world. The Realm of Chaos itself.'

'No...'

'Where reality gives way and men may walk the path of the gods,' the sorcerer cackled in excitement.

'Then what is this oblivion into which I stare?' Archaon put to him.

'No man can guess,' Sheerian said. It was not the answer Archaon was looking for.

'But if a man,' Archaon said, 'in fear for his very existence had to guess?'

The daemonic glee on the sorcerer's face died a little.

'Some say the darkness at the top of the world is a gateway through which the dread of destiny pours. A broken gateway, ever open to an unknowable realm beyond. It infects all with its rank possibility.'

'And of this southern darkness?'

'A polar gateway the same, my lord,' Sheerian said. 'Bleeding the unknown into the world we know.'

'And a man who would walk the path of the gods would need to pass through such a gateway,' Archaon said. He was no longer asking. The daemon sorcerer nodded his agreement. 'And might enter one gateway only to leave through another...'

'Yes, master, yes!' the ancient cackled.

'Yes... Yes...' Archaon heard. The words burned to hear and echoed about the confines of his mortal mind. A voice. From the storm.

'Did you hear that?' Archaon asked.

'Hear what, my lord?' the venerable sorcerer asked, still living their previous glee.

There was something out there with them. Of that Archaon was sure. Unlike the monstrous creatures of the maelstrom, it was a familiar darkness. Something that had been with

Archaon his whole life. Always in the shadows. A lord of such burning obscurity. Using the searing power of the Eye, Archaon searched the blackness of the furious oblivion. His gaze settled on a monstrous form, hidden in the approaching tempest. An ancient evil. Dreadful... Potent...

'Do not see meeee...'

Gone.

'It will not be seen,' Archaon said. The ancient stared out into the maelstrom.

'The Eye sees all, master.'

'Well it does not see this,' Archaon rumbled.

'What was it, my lord?'

Archaon struggled for the words.

'Some daemon,' Archaon said. 'Some dark prince of oblivion. A beast eternal that wishes to stay in the shadows – as it always has. It stalks us. It stalks me and the doom that is my fate. What being could do such a thing? Hide itself from the Eye's gaze? Shield itself from a gift of the gods?'

It was the ancient's turn to struggle for words.

'Well...'

'Speak, sorcerer!' Archaon boomed. He drew the blade *Terminus* with sudden savagery. 'You counsel me in such matters of the damned. Without counsel, what use are you to me, daemon?'

Sheerian searched for an answer to please the Chaos lord.

'There is one,' the sorcerer croaked as Archaon's blade came up. 'A beast that led the legions at the dawn of time.'

'Speak on,' Archaon hissed, bringing *Terminus* down.

'He plunged the world into darkness but lit the abyss with his daemon arrogance,' Sheerian told the Chaos warrior. 'For that my master, the dark god Tzeentch – the Great Changer of Ways – punished him.'

'How?' Archaon demanded.

'He cursed the prince of daemons,' the sorcerer said, 'forcing him into infernal subservience, stripping him of absolute power and denying him permanent form.'

Archaon nodded slowly. 'He might escape the Eye's

almighty gaze,' Sheerian assured him, 'for if set on his daemon form there would be nothing for the Eye to see.'

Archaon stared at the nearing tempest, as it raged its unfolding darkness through the maelstrom towards them.

'I feel it near.'

'The daemon dooms of men are rarely far away,' Sheerian told him. 'They like to remain close. Observing first hand the havoc they have wrought. This thing has no form, which means he is free to assume any.'

Archaon looked hard at Sheerian and then cast his gaze across to the sleeping Giselle, his Swords of Chaos and finally Gorst, the miserable wretch who had followed him across the face of the world, without doubt and without question.

'This beast hides both in the shadows and plain sight. If this daemon prince is invested in you, my master,' Sheerian said, 'he could be any of us… at any time.'

'Does this thing of the abyss have a name?' Archaon asked.

'He has many names,' the daemon sorcerer told him, seeming not to want to call the daemon by its given name. 'The Harbinger, the Herald, the Bearer. In the frozen north, he is the Shadowlord. In the east and the west, the Dark Master.'

'And to your master?' Archaon snarled.

'To my Lord Tzeentch and the dread pantheon he is… Be'lakor.'

'Be'lakor.'

It was as though Archaon had known the name his whole life. Always on the tongue's tip or just beyond the reaches of recollection. No more. Archaon would drag this monstrous force of darkness into the light. He would know its dealings in his destiny. The daemon prince Be'lakor would answer to the Lord of the End Times or would share in the world's fate. Archaon would extinguish the darklight of this Be'lakor's existence and claim its dark dominion as his own.

For a while, the Chaos lord and the sorcerer said nothing. Sheerian settled into his furs. Even without the Eye, he could see the furious tempest sweeping in.

'There is a storm approaching.'

Archaon thought on all that had come to pass and the doom he had pledged on his very soul to the waiting world.

'I am already here.'

ARCHAON:
LORD OF CHAOS

'Thank the gods for their ignorance. For if the prayers of mortals were universally answered, there would be naught left living, since all pray for an end one to the other.'

– Ignatz van Offen, *Offered Truths*

VOLUME ONE
THE LORD OF ALL

*'And doom came decked in the flesh of man,
Death to all he didst devise,
No infernal could against him stand,
Twas thunder under brimstone skies.'*
– Daemonsong

PROLOGUE

'At the dawn of the world, wisdom – savage and untamed – was with the beasts. The Dark Gods did not speak to the weakling races. The ferals, the half-breeds and the children of Chaos were sent to show the monster man how to express himself through the beast. And we were forever repaid in blood and hate.'
– Great Bray Gorganhok of the Dark Tongue,
The Lore of the Wilds

Hyborphregor Ice Shelf
The Southern Wastes
Horns Harrowing: Season of Scars

The storm had come.

He was there. Among them. At one with the howling gales that swept up sinister shores, through the black spuming peaks and across the Wastes of everlasting ice. Like the rolling thunder of such unnatural tempests, Archaon had travelled far. From one side of the miserable world to the other, he had slain his way south. He had sought out the dark challenge of the Ruinous Powers. He had rescued the artefacts of Chaos from obscurity and the hands of enemies unworthy. All to become the Everchosen of the Dark Gods. The Lord of the End Times. Herald of inescapable Armageddon.

He had butchered those foolish enough to believe themselves chosen. Bestial warlords. Exalted warriors of daemon patronage, with lies bleeding from their poisoned ears. Sorcerers and witches, whose wretched powers could not save them from the cold judgement of Archaon's blade. He had been the end to monsters and slain what could not be slain. He had slaughtered entire armies, including his own, for their unworthiness. Only those worthy of the apocalypse would join Archaon, as he ushered in the End Times to come. And so here he was. As far to the daemon south as any of manflesh had ever been. Flayed raw by the infernal freeze. Courting madness with the boundless horizon. A willing slave to ceaseless slaughter.

Archaon trudged through the black snow. His armoured boots were wrapped in the furs of some barb-skinned beast, the bony spines of which gave the warrior purchase across the frost and ice. The skies raged away above him, spitting and swirling like a ghostly, maddened creature, chasing its own tail. The armour of Morkar, First Everchosen of Chaos scalded his skin with its raw embrace. Archaon could not feel such pain. He wouldn't allow it. The common miseries of existence were nothing to him now. With every step he took towards a doom of his own making, he became less of a man and more of an idea. An abstraction. A living misery for others to endure. He was not some character in a great tale told. He was the silence after the words. The covers of the tome slammed shut. The crackle of page and ink on the fire. He was the nevermore.

Holding his shield out before him, Archaon turned the worst of the storm's fury aside. Splinters of ice shattered against the eight-pointed star of Chaos. The Chaos warlord cut an indomitable figure, smeared in the relentless blizzard, his cloak, loinmail and the furs of shaggy beastfiends he had butchered streaming after him like the tail of a comet. He jangled with skulls on chains that produced a mournful moaning in the wind. A sad and bitter tune for the bodies Archaon left in his wake.

The Chaos warrior's trudging footsteps slowed. He felt something through the soles of his armoured boots. Through the furs and skins wrapped about them. Through the snow that crunched like charcoal and the obsidian ice that gleamed with darkness. A tremor. A quake. Archaon took several cautionary steps back. The ice was moving. It was rising. The frozen mask that was Archaon's face creaked its way to a stiff smile beneath his skull-helm. He had found it.

Skidding back down the slope of the buckling ice and cascading snow, he listened to the crack of the ice floe as it shattered beneath him. Like a pair of spearpoints thrusting up through the ice, two mighty pinnacles burst free of the frozen land. They were jagged and sharp, crafted roughly from some kind of volcanic rock. As Archaon stumbled away through an avalanche of snow and ice that threatened to engulfed him, a great palace erupted from the frozen Wastes. Half swimming away from the dark wonder, Archaon peered up at the infernal architecture of the daemon fortress. It allowed both for the perverse flourishes of a Ruinous palace and the jagged crenellations of a fortification. As the ice parted and crumbled, the mighty building shuddered skyward. The gloom of the heavens broiled above it. Strange lights rippled through the maelstrom and lightning cracked between the twin pinnacles and the firmament. It rent the sky asunder.

As the mountainous palace trembled to a stop and the billowing clouds of black snow began to clear, Archaon could make out the strange architecture of the monstrosity. Although it was hewn from sharp, black stone – jagged and irregular – the palace had been crafted in the likeness of a daemon form. The twin pinnacles were both towers and the thumb-claws of great folded wings that formed the building's mighty walls. A craggy head of infernal horror nestled between them, forming the palace dome, while the broad, muscular body, with its rugged arms, cloven-clawed legs and spiked tail had been crafted crouched as the formidable fortress foundations.

'I have you now, dissembler...' Archaon growled, each word a stream of white from his helm.

The Chaos warrior had chased the fortress across the Southern Wastes. For months now – years for all Archaon knew, for time moved with a perverse uncertainty at the bottom of the world – Archaon and his men had drunk the black snow and feasted on nothing but beastflesh.

The continent was overrun with monstrous half-breeds and beastfiends: savage tribes of creatures that were dread fusions of animal and daemon. Hordes that, like their damned brethren hiding in the forests of the Empire, were drawn to the most twisted, gifted and monstrous of their kind. Shamans and beastlords led their great tribes one against the other, for a miserable patch of black ice that they might call their own and the base glory of their fell gods. Archaon had roasted their flesh, worn their bones and daubed his armour with their steaming blood. He had used their hides for warmth and had yoked their barbarian strength as the warlord of united tribes, for the creatures prized victory and dominion above all things. In doing so, Archaon had brought battle to the daemons, monsters and fiend princes that ruled this frozen hell. This beast he had sought alone.

The Forsaken Fortress, it was held, could never be sought out. Never be found. Those who had seen it had simply happened upon its dread form towering out of the Wastes. By the time they had returned to show others their find, the monstrosity had gone. Sunk down once more, below the ice. Daemon palaces and the forts of black ice crafted by the tribal beastfiends could be found across the Wastes, especially in the continental interior. The Forsaken Fortress moved at whim, however. The stone of its construction had come from far below or beyond the ice and was cursed, like the daemon prince to whom it belonged, without permanent form. Be'lakor...

The Shadowlord. The Dark Master. First of the oblivion princes. Harbinger of the Ruinous Powers. Be'lakor, who had always been with him and stalked the Chaos warrior still across the Southern Wastes. Archaon would not be stalked, and resolved to hunt the dark power that hunted him. Perhaps then he might gain answers to his questions. He might learn the locations of treasures of Chaos he had yet to find. The attainment of such would prove his worth to the dread Powers of the world and grant him the title of Everchosen of the Chaos gods. He would be the Lord of End Times and the Herald of the coming apocalypse. Only then would he show man, beast and god the folly of their existence. He would plunge all, his patrons, his enemies and everyone else, into an everlasting darkness. A true oblivion. A place of neither good nor evil where nothing could be won or lost. An eternal nothingness. A kingdom devoid, where not even Archaon would rule.

The daemon prince Be'lakor and his Forsaken Fortress could not simply be found, since none knew where the damned palace would appear. Archaon had been forced to trust his wanderings to uncertainty. To the potion-fuelled ramblings of Bray Shaman, the interpretations of auroral ghostlights, the bargains of daemon princes, cursed with the telling of truths and the riddles of his wizened sorcerer Sheerian. Khezula Sheerian, who had served the Great Changer. Sheerian, whose advice had seen Archaon slaughter his own army and sent the Chaos warrior into the jaws of the Chaos dragon Flamefang. Whose reading of ghostlights, shamanic ramblings and infernal lies now sent Archaon into danger again. Into the lair of daemon royalty. Into the clutches of a creature that had watched them from afar with doom-hungry eyes.

Such miserable intelligence placed the Forsaken Fortress on the Hyborphregor Ice Shelf. The enchanted jewel, the Eye of Sheerian, confirmed its disappearance from where it had been last reported amongst the fiery peaks of the coast. With this, Archaon had set off for the daemon palace. Leaving his bestial army with Eins and his Swords of Chaos, with the storm-wracked skies making flight for the warriors impossible, Archaon had been forced to cross the midnight ice on tuskgor-dragged sleds and mounted on strange daemon steeds. He had killed them all, pushing the creatures with such unrelenting ferocity across the frozen wilderness. The final leg of the journey Archaon had trudged on his own, insisting on no less fortitude from himself than the beasts he had sent to an icy grave.

Now that he was standing before it, there didn't appear to be a way into the daemon palace. This made a perverse kind of sense to the Chaos warrior. What need such a creature for a gate, door or portcullis at the front of his palace? Why risk such a weakness in fortification, when monsters, roaring armies of bestial half-breeds or daemonic foes might happen upon the Forsaken Fortress and attack? Why not offer them the indomitability of solid rock?

Scrutinising the towering fortress, with the glass storm raging uselessly about it, Archaon saw that half way up the structure, below the daemon dome of the palace, was a great carving in the stone. The eight-pointed Ruinous Star of Be'lakor's calling, across the dread architecture of the daemon's chest. It was the same star that adorned Archaon's shield. Like the Chaos warrior, the daemon prince served doom in all its forms, not favouring one dark god over another. At the centre of the star, however, Archaon saw a sliver of light. A weakness. A crack in the stone, as though the mighty fortification had been breached. Within, the blue ghoulishness of unnatural light shone.

Archaon shouldered his shield and clawed his way up through the snowbank. He had come this far. The Forsaken Fortress would not forsake him. If the thing attempted to descend into the ice it would have to take him with it. Where the ice and palace foundations met the snow steamed. When he reached out to it, the stone felt strange against his gauntlets. It wasn't the searing cold he had come to expect. Through the metal of his fingertips, the fortification felt warm, as though heated by some infernal fire within. Hauling himself up the precipitous wall and using the crooks and crannies of the volcanic stone for finger and toeholds, Archaon climbed the daemon palace. With the architecture crafted to resemble the infernal prince himself, Archaon felt as if he were ascending the mountainous form of a titan or god.

Sidling along jagged ledges, dragging himself up by his fingertips and leaping for razor-edged purchase, Archaon climbed the stone perversion. When he reached the bottom point of the Ruinous Star, he hauled himself into the great arrowhead cut into the stone. From there he settled his armoured back against one side of the carved shaft forming the arrow and both his boots and gauntlets against the other. Braced between the rock, the Chaos warrior shimmied and scraped his way up the centre of the star, where he found the sliver of an opening. It did not appear to be part of the infernal design. If anything, it looked like damage. The fortress seemed to have been stabbed in the heart. Passing his shield through first and angling his horned helm, Archaon slid his backplate, breastplate and muscular torso through the cleft in the rock.

Within the daemon palace, the sound of the blizzard died to nothing and Archaon was bathed in a dull blue light. It was impossible to tell where the ghoulish illumination came from, since there were no brands or torches. The floor possibly, or the walls. These, unlike the rock-like architecture of the exterior, were smooth. The lines of the chamber flowed. Everything was rounded and organic, as though the ribs, bones and spikes of the daemon's skeleton had been reproduced within.

Taking the weight of his shield, Archaon drew *Terminus*. The templar blade smouldered in the gloom of the palace. The Sigmarite sword had travelled with its wielder to hell and back. It had sparked blade to blade with daemon swords and been buried in the corruption of the doubly-damned. Its metal and the carved iconography of the God-King had been stained by the slaying of thousands in the name of the Ruinous Powers… and still a little of its nobility remained. In the deep strength of the blade, the trueness of its cleaving edge and the ring of its metal off enemy steel, it still carried some of the calibre of its former calling. Despite this, and in some ways because of it, there was no blade Archaon would rather have between him and a foe. Indeed, to the daemon and the damned, the sword still stank of faith and burned the flesh with its cold virtue.

Leading the way with the faintly glowing blade, Archaon moved through the rib-lined chambers and rachidian passageways of the palace. He was focused. He was ready. Should any daemon servant proceed from the darkness or rush him from the strange architecture, the dark templar would cleave them in two. There was nothing, however. No horrors haunted the palace. No things waited for him in the shadow. The Forsaken Fortress seemed empty. Yet Archaon felt like he was being watched. The darkness that afflicted the lengths of bone-lined corridors was a mirror through which he could not see but could be seen.

You are far from home…

The voice was everywhere. The boom was bottomless, like the abyss, and the words seethed like hellish flame. It was a voice he had known his whole life yet had never heard… until now.

The Chaos warrior moved across a large chamber, looking about him. He slowly turned and swished *Terminus* all around. He peered into the dark recesses of alcoves. He crooked his neck to look back the way he had come, the path now lost to shadow. As he moved through the nightmarish interior of the palace, the murk receded to reveal a large figure in the centre of the chamber. Like the Forsaken Fortress, it was horned, cloven-clawed and broad of wing. To Archaon, it appeared to be a replica of the fortress in miniature.

At first, he took it for the daemon overlord of the palace itself, but as his shuffled steps and defensive turns took him closer, he saw the infernal figure for what it was. A throne. Crafted from the same rough stone as the palace in which it sat. The daemon prince's crouching legs formed the seat, its star-scarred chest the back and its clasped talons the arms. The horned horror that was the daemon's grotesque head formed a kind of crafted crown, while the leathery, outstretched wings, hewn from volcanic rock, gave the throne a hellish grandness. For all its imposing abomination, the throne was empty, like the palace.

'I am where I need to be, daemon,' Archaon answered back finally. His words returned to him with a strange quality, echoing through the torturous skeletal structure of the daemon palace.

That is more true than you can ever know. Though not many who have sought out the Forsaken Fortress have found it.

'I am Archaon,' the Chaos warrior spat, angling his helm about the dark entrances to the chamber. 'I am the chosen of the Dark Gods and the end to the entire world. Nothing is beyond me.'

I am beyond you, chosen one.

'And yet here I stand, *Be'lakor*,' Archaon spat. 'I have your name, daemon. I have all your names. Shadowlord. Dark Master. Cursed of the Ruinous Gods. You, who have watched me from oblivion, like the craven being you are. I stare back, abyssal thing. I see you now, daemon prince, though there be little or nothing to see. And here I stand, before your cursed throne within your cursed castle.' Archaon waved *Terminus* at the darkness in invitation. The blade smouldered with expectation. 'Time for us both to take a closer look, don't you think? If I'm lucky, as with your palace, I might get to see inside.'

As Archaon turned, his weapon ready, his good eye and the darksight of his ruined socket everywhere, he set his afflicted gaze once more on the mighty throne. In it, crafted in his own image, sat the insanity that was the daemon Be'lakor within a rocky palace that was the same.

'Daemon,' Archaon told it. 'You have an undue fascination with yourself.'

The beast laughed. It was horrible to hear. Like the deep torment of rock and earth, as the land quakes and continents heave.

And with you…

As the creature spoke, the blue inferno burning within him escaped his ugly maw.

'I'm here to put an end to that, creature,' the dark templar told it, moving slowly and steadily in on the thing in the throne. A great infernal blade of jagged black steel stood upright before the throne, held in place by the loosely clasped talon of the stone arm. The daemon prince's own claw rested on the pommel spike of the weapon.

Oh, you are, are you?

'But first you will give me the satisfaction of all that is unknown to me, but known to you,' the Chaos warrior threatened.

You want secrets…

'I want truths,' he told it. 'And I'll have them, even if I have to cut them out of you, dread thing.'

The living truth that is Archaon, chosen of the Chaos gods.

'Aye.'

Archaon moved in. The daemon prince reared from his throne of stone, dragging his colossal blade with him. The beast's wings spread and he thrust his ferocious daemon head forward, shaking the crown of horns as he spoke.

Well you can't have it, mortal, Be'lakor roared at him, his words searing with hellfire. *You impudent worm – bold of word but feeble of flesh.*

'I thought you might say that,' Archaon returned. As Be'lakor dragged the tip of his infernal blade across the floor of the throne room and turned it upright in his claws, the Chaos warrior did the opposite. Turning *Terminus* about in his gauntlets, he aimed the point of the crusader blade at the floor. 'See, you can't give what you don't have, daemon.'

Archaon stabbed his Sigmarite sword straight down into

the floor of the throne room. Instead of turning the blade tip aside like the smooth rock it appeared to be, the material admitted its length with a shower of sparks. The blade steamed with the honour of its past deeds in the name of the God-King. The stone about it began to bubble and churn. Be'lakor let out a roar that descended into a hideous shriek. The palace trembled about Archaon and the daemon. It shuddered. It quaked. The daemon prince clutched his chest and crashed to his knees. The Ruinous Star scarred into his flesh steamed also. The infernal blade tumbled from his grip, falling straight through the floor with a splatter of stone, as though it had been dropped into a lake.

Archaon turned his greatsword in the broiling stone of the wound. Be'lakor screeched. His wings flapped and his spine arched. His knees sank into the floor and his claws trailed stringy stone where he had splashed the morphing material in his infernal agonies.

'Now we're talking,' Archaon told the daemon. 'This is a language that both of us can understand.'

Be'lakor's claws tore at his daemon form. He was becoming one with his surroundings. In the throes of white-hot pain and the purity that still afflicted the crusader sword's steel, he was changing. The palace was also losing its consistency. Liquid rock glooped and streamed from the ceiling while the ribs and bones contorted within the structure. Be'lakor and palace were as one. Except neither were Be'lakor.

'Your name, daemon,' Archaon demanded as his sword burned in the monster's flesh. Its wings and features dribbled away. The creature sank into the floor. Into itself. It splashed like a flailing swimmer before thrashing beneath the surface of the stone. Its face rippled through the horrific visage of a thousand other diabolical things. Archaon pulled *Terminus* from the daemonflesh. For a moment everything was silent. The shrieking agony that shook the palace was gone. The Forsaken Fortress had melted to a ruptured, contorted mess.

Archaon lost his footing as the floor seemed to sink through the palace. The Chaos warrior turned the greatsword about in his grip, aiming its tip back at the floor at his feet. Like a corpse in a river, the daemon floated to the surface of the stone. It was a lesser thing now. A thing of arms and hidden form, lost within the twisting folds of a hooded shroud. As the colour of the stone bleached from it, the daemon began to move.

Archaon lifted *Terminus* higher, indicating his intention to bury the Sigmarite sword in the creature's extended form once more, but the walls liquefied about him. The palace cascaded around him towards the ice floe. The fingers of one puny arm begged him to desist. The razor gales of the Southern Wastes and blizzards of splintered ice once again intruded on the scene. Archaon was standing in a sea of stone. The sea retracted to a lake. Then the lake to a puddle about the daemon until finally the thing held only its own form. Archaon stepped forward, holding his shield before the maelstrom and *Terminus* high above his head.

'Enough of your tricks, dissembler,' the dark templar told it. 'Your name.'

'Long forgotten,' the creature managed. 'Along with the face that it belonged to.'

'Well, Changeling,' Archaon roared through the howling wind. 'It matters not that you are known. Only what you know.'

'You sought me out?'

'Yes, daemon,' Archaon said. 'It is said by the bestial shamans and diabolical creatures of this land that you are a deceiver and that you meddle in the great affairs of this dark world. That you hold a looking glass to both the damned and the damning and that you become what is seen.'

'I have my questionable gifts, Archaon,' the Changeling hissed, 'as the chosen of the Ruinous Powers must have his own.'

'Then you have held your glass to the infernal prince I seek,' Archaon said, circling the prostrate monstrosity with his sword as snowfall gathered about the daemon.

'I have studied him.'

'Why, darknid thing? Speak and live to hold your mirror again.'

'It pleases my master...' the Changeling told him. '...the great Lord Tzeentch, to have the Dark Master's ambitions frustrated.'

'And so you impersonate Be'lakor, his form, his fortress.'

'To god-pleasing perfection.'

'You are a twisted thing, Changeling,' Archaon told the daemon, 'on a crooked path to nowhere.'

'It is my fate,' it told him. 'It is the fate of all the Great Changer's servants.'

'So I was told by the monstrosities that led me to you,' Archaon said. 'Your damned journey, your twisted path, might not be any use to you, lost one. But it might be to me. Archaon, chosen of all the Dark Gods. Choose, Changeling. Assist me or accept that your journey ends here, with my sword as your grave marker, at some Byzantine crossroads on your lost path.'

Archaon grabbed the daemon by the lengths of its twisted shroud and dragged it over to a black snowbank that offered a little shelter from the storm. In the depths of the snowbank's shadow, the blizzard died to a whisper. Archaon stared at the daemon. About them the southern continent was a blasted winter wasteland of warped confusion. The shredding splinters of ice drifted to the ground and stopped. The snow began to creak and freeze about them as the temperature plummeted. Archaon's plate scorched his skin with the abyssal cold. He tensed as the daemon creature before him got to its feet in the snow. Subtle but horrific changes were taking place inside the depths of the thing's hooded shroud. Something more resilient to the benumbing surroundings.

'Don't test me, warped servant of Tzeentch.'

'As I said,' it told him, ever at change beneath the frosted folds, 'it pleases my master to frustrate the daemon prince you seek. How may I assist you, great Archaon?' The Chaos warrior nodded. Satisfied.

'You have studied Be'lakor?'

'As I have studied all whose flesh I assume,' the Changeling said. 'As I have studied you, Archaon, whose boundless ambition surpasses even your ageless father-in-shadow.'

'What did you say?'

'I say too much, perhaps,' the Changeling tittered. Archaon shook his helm slowly. The Chaos warrior had crossed the surface of the known world and had travelled to hell and back. His experiences – the dark truths, the betrayals and the slaughter – had long washed anything approaching sentimentality from his cursed bones. There were truths he must know, however, even about himself, if he were to proceed in his apocalyptic quest.

'You say what your Ruinous master wants you to say,' Archaon told the Tzeentchian monstrosity. 'You are a miserable messenger. No more. So, let us play your dark lord's game. You mentioned my father. To which I am supposed to reply, "I never knew my father". Or my mother, for that matter. I'm an orphan. Abandoned on the steps of an Imperial temple. A temple of the thrice-cursed God-King.'

'Your mother was a nothing,' the Changeling told Archaon. 'Baseborn. Simple. Unremarkable. Unclouded of heart in a way our foetid kind abhor. The kind of heart our masters revel in corrupting.'

Archaon burned into the Changeling with an unswerving gaze.

'But they never got the chance.'

'No,' the Changeling said. 'Her blood is on you, Archaon. She died in birth. In the labours of delivering the apocalypse to the world.'

Archaon's gauntlet creaked about the hilt of *Terminus*. The Tzeentchian servant was enjoying this.

'And my father?'

'You have had several, Archaon,' the creature told him. 'The wretch whose wife you took and then left to raise your youngling brothers.'

'I have brothers?'

'Half-brothers,' the Changeling cackled. 'But they are long dead, Archaon. You have outlived them, chosen one.'

'My father?'

'Is Be'lakor, of course,' the Changeling's cackle became a howling laugh. Archaon surged forwards and landed a heavy kick in the creature's midriff with an armoured boot. The impact smashed the daemon back, sending it tumbling through the black snow. Archaon stomped after it, standing over its broken form. The Changeling did not get up. It coughed. It wheezed. It choked and spat daemon blood from the recesses of its shroud. The blood sizzled on the ice.

'The passion of the present will not undo the painful truths of the past,' the Changeling told him.

'Be'lakor.'

'You are his, chosen one,' the thing coughed. 'Did you not question, not for once, what you have achieved and how you could have achieved it? Out of the thousands, nay *millions* of lowly creatures of this world that ache for the power to challenge their stars and change their fate, why should it have been you? Why should you have risen from obscurity? Why should you be the chosen, the Everchosen of Chaos? The Herald of the Apocalypse... the Lord of the End Times?'

'Then I am...'

'Nothing... something... everything,' the Changeling hissed from within its hood. 'Like me, like all who serve the powers of light and the powers of darkness, you will be what you are needed to be. Have no doubt, though, Archaon of the distant Empire. You are blessed with daemon lineage. You are the son of a prince, chosen one – which in some corners of this foetid world would make you a prince in your own right. You are special not just because of what you made of yourself and your circumstances. Look at you. You stand where no mortal man has stood before. You are undoubtedly an indomitable soul. You are also special because of what others made of you and the circumstances of their own. Principally, your father-in-shadow.'

Archaon leaned in. The tip of *Terminus* reached into the Changeling's hood. The daemon leaned back into the black slush.

'And what does my father want of me?' Archaon asked through clenched teeth. 'You have been him. You must know. Why does he stalk me? What does this thing of darkness want?'

'What he has always wanted,' the Changeling answered. 'From the dawn of time. What my master, the Great Changer denied him. To command the legions of hell. To be the master of the entire world again. To subvert my master's curse of eternal servitude and be the Everchosen of the Chaos gods.'

'What does that have to do with me?' Archaon growled.

'Everything, I suspect,' the Changeling said before the seething steel of Archaon's sword. 'But in truth, I do not know. Some daemon secrets are buried deep, beyond even my arch-powers of study and reproduction. You are wrong, Archaon. I deceive. I do not become. The infernal and almighty have a way of showing you everything, yet truly telling you nothing. Unlike my Ruinous master, I cannot be all and know all.'

'I don't believe you, deceiver,' Archaon told the daemon.

'That is irrelevant,' the wretched creature said. 'I have told you all I know. The rest you must ask of your father-in-shadow, himself. For only he knows.'

Archaon held the Changeling there. The deep freeze of the Southern Wastes crept up through their bones. 'I have done what you have asked, chosen of Chaos. Destroy me,' the daemon said finally. 'Or release me.'

Archaon considered.

'Before I make that decision,' the Chaos warrior said. 'One more thing. You must know Be'lakor's palace, to have reproduced it so faithfully. Where is it, Changeling?'

The daemon hissed its hatred at Archaon.

'The Forsaken Fortress appears and disappears at perverse whim,' the creature told him.

'This I know already.'

'Sometimes it remains for weeks,' the Changeling said, 'sometimes for seconds. Right now it sits on the Pustular Plain.'

'Never heard of it.'

'Tis a realm far to the west,' the Changeling said. 'Where the ice melts to a boggy tundra about a rash of volcanic peaks that suppurate and ooze with disease.'

'How might I reach such a damned place?' Archaon asked.

'By travelling south…'

'You said it was far to the west,' Archaon growled.

'You could never reach the Pustular Plain on foot,' the Changeling told him. 'And certainly not trailing an army of beastfiends. The journey is far and the geography between here and there challenging and ever changing. By wing, by sled, by exhausted step you could not make it in time.'

'Then what could?'

'In the south, close to the continental interior towards which you have waged war, you will find other daemon palaces.'

'About the Gate?'

'The Gatelands,' the Changeling said, 'Yes… there you will find the palace of the daemon lord Agrammon. He keeps an infamous menagerie in the palace grounds, housing every dread creature imaginable. His prize possession is Dorghar, daemonic Steed of the Apocalypse. You will need to gain entry to the palace, steal the beast and break it. For it is the only creature I know can make the journey to the Pustular Plain in the time you may or may not have.'

Archaon turned his helm to one side and peered down at the Changeling, attempting to penetrate the depths of its hooded shroud. With sudden violence the Chaos warrior stepped forwards, putting a boot on the daemon's chest and forcing it down into the black slush. He held *Terminus* above the creature.

'The Steed of the Apocalypse,' Archaon seethed.

'The fourth treasure of Chaos,' the Changeling cackled, the information forced from him.

Archaon marvelled for a dread moment. The fourth treasure of Chaos. He had been traversing obsidian and ice for longer than he could remember. Slaying daemons. Butchering beastfiends. Searching. Ever searching. It was one of the reasons he was seeking out Be'lakor, the oblivion prince. Answers. It seemed now he would have them. The eternally burning Mark of Chaos that he wore on his flesh. The fabled armour of Morkar that clad that flesh. The Eye of Sheerian, the sorcerous jewel retrieved from the Chaos dragon Flamefang, now safely ensconced in the skull-face of his battlehelm. All great artefacts of darkness that had belonged to former champions of evil. Those who had borne the blessing of the Ruinous Powers in equal measure. Those who had achieved the title 'Everchosen of Chaos'. The fourth was a steed worthy of such a warrior. A steed he would tame and who, in turn, would carry him across the Southern Wastes to the Forsaken Fortress.

'And you were going to tell me this when?' Archaon roared at the Changeling.

'You never asked,' the daemon said silkily. It was true. Archaon hadn't. The Chaos warrior grunted. Taking his boot from the creature's chest, he started to trudge back through the snow and rising storm. He had left his army of beastfiends many leagues distant. His winged Swords had been grounded in the storm and, although hardy and ferocious, the monstrous half-breeds that made up his horde were riotous and slow. It was the reason the Chaos warrior had set off alone in the first place. Archaon heard the daemon Changeling's harsh laughter on the frozen air.

'Beware, Archaon,' the Tzeentchian wretch said. 'The daemon lord Agrammon is a slaver. Take care you do not become part of his infernal collection.'

'To hell with you, daemon,' Archaon snarled, holding his shield once more before the shredding gales.

But they were already there.

*'Beyond the maps and charts of man,
where gold lies cold and unplundered,
there lies a bleak and hellish land,
of savage darkness and thunder.*

*No tree or forest ever grows
in this lightless realm of cold,
a land of ice and midnight snow –
scorched by storms of shrieking souls.*

*Through swarms of beasts and
frenzied fiends,
fights a man who has travelled far –
in him the end comes to these lands,
in search of signs and treasures dark.*

*A wretched place that knows no peace,
before his blade dread daemons fall –
to his banner flock bands of beasts:
a monstrous horde behind him forms.*

*He leads them through an ancient gate –
a raging portal overwhelmed –
through which his destiny awaits:
passage to an abyssal realm.'*

– Necrodomo the Insane, *The Liber Caelestior*
(The Celestine Book of Divination)

CHAPTER I

*'The Great Beast is the land's fury to vent,
Decimation for others to know.
He is the topless mountains' torment
And unending desolation's woe.'*
— The Cloven Tribal Chant

*The Haemorrhagia
The Southern Wastes
Horns Harrowing: Season of the Raw*

Archaon went south. Ever south. The ice froze to breaking beneath his boots and the air seethed with burning lethality. The wind howled its mournful goading and the heavens churned their black intention. The chosen of the Dark Gods pushed on through the midnight drifts, the skins and furs trailing about his plate crisp with the biting freeze. Behind him the Swords of Chaos trudged, their black wings held before them to deflect the worst of the snow carried on the burning gales. Decked out in a hotchpotch collection of plate and mail scavenged from daemonic foes felled in Archaon's path and furs skinned from shaggy half-breeds, they had the appearance of frosted gargoyles. Eins. Zwei. Drei. With the misshapen Vier, twisted to grotesquery, stomping up behind them. His malformed wings, now useless for flight, were extended about Giselle.

Giselle Dantziger. Former Sister of the Imperial Cross. Giselle, who had carried from the Hammerfall the *Liber Caelestior* – heavy with the secrets of Archaon's future and inescapable damnation – and changed the fate of all the world. The friend whom Archaon had made prisoner. The prisoner whom Archaon had taken as a lover. The girl who was in equal parts his death and salvation. Whose heart, even in this damned place, still beat with simple devotion to the God-King who had abandoned her touch. Whose touch was torment, burning with an indomitable purity. Whose touch Archaon could not seem to live without. She tripped and stumbled under the weight of the furs in which Archaon had buried her. Woolly hides that he had skinned from the shaggy beastfiends of the continental interior and that had formerly protected the half-breeds from the murderous cold.

With his other twisted wing, Vier did his best to protect Khezula Sheerian from the maelstrom. Sheerian, daemonic sorcerer of Tzeentch. To whom the third treasure of Chaos, the enchanted jewel, the Eye of Sheerian had belonged. The ancient carried himself with perpetual pain and the burden of a wizened body. Hunched and using his bone staff to drag the deformity of a bird's leg through the snow, his filthy robes were a patchwork of sinew-sewn skins and a cloak of heavy black fur. His age-mottled skull was bare to the broiling heavens and the lustrous strands of his moustache trailed behind him in the harsh wind.

Whereas Archaon found that he loved Giselle but in turn was hated by her, the Chaos warrior simply hated Sheerian. Despite his animosity towards the sorcerer, Archaon had found the daemon to be a useful guide. In the depths of the Southern Wastes, where the beast hordes, long-forgotten monstrosities and the dangerous daemons of Chaos held sway, Sheerian's survival depended as much on Archaon's sword arm and savage leadership as Archaon's depended upon the sorcerer's dark counsel. The sorcerer had his uses. As he hungered for his precious Eye, its intoxicating gift of farsight and the secrets of the world it revealed, Archaon ached for the further treasures of the Ruinous Gods. The artefacts of darkness through which Archaon would earn the dread title Everchosen of Chaos. Sheerian's cursed knowledge, sorceries and his interpretation of the Eye's enchanted sights had helped to keep them from harm.

He had guided his worldly master (for beyond Archaon, Sheerian served no other than the dreaded Tzeentch) on towards his destiny. He had revealed the Gore Glacier, the treachery of Algis-Kar and the dark secrets of the Winter King. It had been Sheerian who had revealed the treachery of the daemonic thing Archaon had come to know as the Changeling, and in doing so had not only learned the location of the oblivion prince Be'lakor, but had also betrayed a brother Tzeentchian. If the Great Changer hadn't been such a twisted entity of unfathomable evil, Sheerian might have feared an infernal retribution. As it was, Archaon half suspected the sorcerer would receive some warped gift or malformed blessing instead.

Thunder crashed across the skies. Lightning slashed the firmament in two, throwing Archaon's army into impossible shadow against the obsidian ice of the Southern Wastes. A wretched cavalcade of shaggy hide, horn and muscle. Archaon's horde was an army of beasts.

The Southern Wastes were all but unknown by the men of the east and west and avoided by the elder races. Only the daemon, the monster and the beastman swarmed its black ice floes and mountainous wilderness. Tribes of savage half-breeds fought for warmth in their bones, flesh in their bellies and territorial supremacy. Many were ice barbarians, who wore the frost-threaded furs of conquered enemies and wielded primitive weapons of bone and stone. With no 'men' in the Southern Wastes there were no true 'beastmen', such as Archaon had encountered everywhere else on his doomed travels. The creatures of the Southern Wastes were an eye-stinging fusion of beast and lesser daemon, the infernal entities that plagued the benighted wilderness with their malevolence. They were beastfiends, led by the foetid best of their kind. Brutes blessed with either dark cunning or murderous might. Shamans who read tribal destinies in blood-splatters on the snow, the distant serration of mountain peaks and the crooks of exotic lightning that afflicted the skies. Beastlords, tyrant-gors and infernal bulls of brazen horn and mountainous muscle. Some suffered the specific sponsorship of Ruinous Gods, with monstrous mongrels and daemon princes leading warherds of the warped, the diseased, the obscene or the blood-mad.

Archaon had united many of the beasts, as was his gift. He was an exalted champion of darkness and the children of Chaos could see that. When confronted with one chosen of the Ruinous Pantheon, they expressed themselves in varying ways. Many simply attacked, like the wild things they were. Deep in their tainted flesh they needed to test him or at least sacrifice their herdkin on the altar of his dark sovereignty. Others had been warned of his coming by shamans and dread prophets, and lent Archaon their horde-strength out of the perversion of spiritual sympathies. Others still saw the growing army coming out of the north, with Archaon at its head, and felt fear or admiration. They saw opportunities for savage communion with their dread deities in the wars to come. The slaughter that seemed to find the champion of Chaos. The unending brutality that stalked his benighted plate and the god-bane of his steel. The butchery that seemed forever in his path.

Some said in their beast tongue that he was uniting the tribes and warherds of the Southern Wastes under a single banner of eternal bloodshed. Some that he was leading them to greater glory about the infernal palaces of the pole – to the Great Gate and the oblivion beyond. To promised lands of fresh suffering and slaughter that they had never known. A few even whispered, with their thick tongues and fang-crowded jaws, that Archaon intended to end the world – and not just the world, but all the worlds that were and would ever be. And man, beast and god would come to know their end at his hand and the power of catastrophe he wielded with it. Whatever the truth, the half-breeds of the Southern Wastes fought, they failed and they fell in behind the droves of beastfiends, pack monsters, centigors and the caravans of herd-sleds that churned up the black snow in Archaon's wandering wake.

Behind the train of beastfiends, which hoof-trudged, snaggled, butted and roared at one another, shaking their primitive skull-cleavers and bellowing crude threats, another trampled through the snow. He wore only the skins that others had lain across his sharp shoulders and the penitent chains that had always cut into his emaciated form. About his gaunt features and the wild-eyed stare of madness and devotion, he wore a cranial cage. The kind favoured by zealots and flagellants. The kind favoured by Gorst, who had followed his master across both the known and unknown world, from long before he was the abominate Archaon.

Gorst still bore the sacred Hammer of Sigmar, inked into his flesh and hanging as pendants of faith from his rusted restraints. These drew spitting, savagery and monstrous threats from the slaves to darkness about him, as they always had. Beyond their disgust that had long soaked into his skins and the barging snorting and bare-blade threats issued to the mad man, the beastfiends seemed suspicious and uncertain of Gorst. There was something about the symbols of goodly faith, or perhaps the way the lunatic Gorst wore them, that prompted mongrels and infernal creatures to bellow and snort their derision before stomping away. Perhaps Gorst, the all but skeletal man-thing, soft and vulnerable, was simply not worth the trouble. Or perhaps it was because dashing out his brains with a butt or the bulbous head of a femur-club would be far too much trouble as Archaon, who favoured the wretch, would savagely end them for such an affront.

As Archaon slowed, peering through the maelstrom at the light on the horizon, the Chaos warrior gestured for the sorcerer Sheerian, Eins and the beastlord Moraq Half-Horn to come forward. Sheerian struggled with his hunch and his leg through the snow to catch his master up.

'My lord?' the ancient managed through the storm. Eins was with him, but as usual the winged warrior did not speak. Like a dark angel he simply drew level with Archaon and matched him step for step like a sentinel or shadow. Moraq Half-Horn dug his sharpened hooves into the sides of the woolly rhinox he was riding. Sitting behind the scrawny beast's shoulder-hump and with reins of sinew guiding the twin horns erupting from the creature's snout, Moraq joined them. Archaon's barbarian horde was made of beastfiends of all the fell tribes he had conquered and the warherds that had joined his number for the honour of the coming slaughter. Many beastlords and chieftains led this assortment of mongrel creatures, routinely fighting one another for the right to lead the horde in Archaon's name and to report to the Chaos warlord directly. This changed on an almost daily basis. Today it was Moraq Half-Horn.

Moraq urged his rhinox on. The animal was a shaggy, scabrous thing with a will of its own and it fought the beastfiend chieftain for control. Moraq shook his daemonic skull, with its single horn that erupted from one bony temple to curve beneath the creature's own snout like a crescent. He bellowed and savagely kicked at the beast until it settled.

'What is that?' Archaon put to them with brute impatience. Eins remained silent but Sheerian attempted to wrap his thin, cracked lips around the dark tongue spoken by the beastfiends. With no men to afflict their monstrous wilderness there had been no need or opportunity to learn the languages of men. Archaon had found it easier to have the sorcerer translate his demands through the beastfiend's own tribal tongue. This became more difficult still, given that the beast language of barbarian tribes and warherds were given to regional variations of their own across the continent. Archaon had been a scholar as well as a warrior in his previous calling as a templar of Sigmar, and over time had picked up the basics of the brute tongue. This did not stop him tormenting Sheerian with the duty of translation. Archaon listened to the sorcerer and the beastlord Moraq exchange savage, angry words through the cacophony of the storm.

'He says it's called the Haemorrhagia, my lord,' Sheerian told him. '"Tis a region of quakes and ruptures, where the land fights itself and the black blood of the earth bubbles up from the depths. 'Tis a birthing place of daemons, awash with pitch and flame.'

'A place to warm our bones and camp perhaps,' Archaon put to them. Again there was a furious jabbering between the two, replete with grunts, snarls and apparent cursing.

'He says that it is the territory of the Skullfest,' Sheerian explained. 'The bloodied gorfiends of Khorne. They celebrate their allegiance to the Blood God by taking the skulls of half-breeds from neighbouring tribes and daemons that crawl out of the birthing grounds.'

'And who leads this Skullfest?' Archaon demanded. Moraq told them.

'Ograx the Great,' Sheerian translated. 'Daemonkin of Z'rughl Ka'kadron'ath the Brassbound, Bloodthirster of Khorne.' Archaon nodded his helm. The Chaos warrior seemed satisfied. 'We could always go around, my lo–'

'No,' Archaon growled. 'My destiny will not wait on mongrels and skulltakers. We will go through these tormented lands. We will see how *great* this Ograx really is. We shall see if he lives up to his father's reputation. If he does not, it will be his skull honouring the Blood God and his lands.'

Archaon pulled away from the group once more, his boots crunching through the black snow. 'Ready the horde, Moraq.' As Archaon spoke, Sheerian translated his savage orders into beastspeak. 'And pass the word. No snow and scraps for your dark kindred. They feast on red meat tonight.'

The beastfiend bellowed its acknowledgement and hauled its monstrous steed around. Archaon looked back at the infernal glow rising from the dark horizon. 'Onwards,' the warlord commanded before pushing on through the snow. Each trudging step took him into the quake-tormented lands of the Haemorrhagia. The black blood of the earth oozed up through the ice, where it took to flame and brought warmth to the glacial darkness. The frozen insistence of the continent interior tried its best to douse the fires of the ruptured ice and land. Flames roared, guttered and hissed in blizzard and storm. The fury of the earth's hellish interior would not be denied, however. Soon great pits and raging fissures opened about them, forcing the horde cavalcade to slog, weave and sled through the fiery torment. Archaon began to sweat in his heavy furs and armour and, although it was a discomfort of a different kind, it was welcome. The chosen of Chaos and his army of half-breed wretches did not have long to enjoy it, however, for out of the fires' blinding glare their infernal foes came.

Archaon squinted through the pit-flares and eddies of flame. A snarling smile drew back his lips and his gauntlet snatched for *Terminus*. The consecrated steel was once again to burn through the bestial and the daemon.

Bovine brutes of blood-stained mane and twisted horn stomped out of the brightness at him. Scores of them, and each branded with the hate-scorched sigil of Khorne. Archaon turned aside axes of razored bone and blades of wicked flint. The Swords of Chaos were about him, shielding their warlord with their gargoyle wings and parrying sweeps of their bone swords. Archaon frustrated their attempts to play sentinel at every turn, hurling himself headlong into the barbarian numbers. He leant out of the reach of throat-slashing flint, rolled out from under the cleaving descent of axe-fashioned shoulder blades and feigned left before darting right, out of the stampeding path of Ograx's bullfiends. *Terminus* opened up their backflesh, took horns from heads and stabbed through all but impenetrable muscle and fused ribcage to find the rupturing vulnerabilities within. Half-breeds died and the pits spat forth flaming coals and sprays of cinder in celebration.

They were but the vanguard of Ograx the Great's beast-force. Directed on by Eins and the staff-shaking Sheerian, Archaon's bestial horde rushed forward into the fray. Archaon was soon lost in a sea of muscle, shaggy hide and snorting steam. The land trembled beneath the hooves of Archaon's army and lakes of black ooze bubbled up about them. Pits gaped open and the earth tore apart. Flame reached for the skies. The ground upon which Archaon stood bucked and shuddered upwards, and he roared as the thunderous outcrop reared. He clashed *Terminus* against the eight-pointed star of his shield. Beastfiends bellowed their infernal celebration. Wretched horns were sounded and rude weapons of bone, twine and stone rattled as they were shaken jubilantly at the skies. Suddenly a hiss rose above the spitting of flame and tearing of the earth – a sound Archaon knew well.

'Shields!' he called savagely across the crashing sea of muscle and fur. He brought up his own. The Swords of Chaos extended their wings and enveloped themselves in a bubble of battle-hardened leather. Vier's warped remnants sprang out horribly, like a storm-shattered tent, to offer protection to the ancient Sheerian and Sister Giselle. The half-breeds of Archaon's hordes brought up their own defences – hide shields of cured flesh and shaggy fur, mounted on frameworks of entwined ribs. Nothing was wasted in the Southern Wastes. With little in the way of ore and metal to work with, materials were torn from the carcasses of the innumerable beasts that swarmed the continent. Weapons and armour were fashioned from friend and slaughtered foe. Archaon smiled to himself as he held his shield above him. It was raining bone. Rib and fibula – straightened, sharpened, hardened and fashioned into arrows. Archaon waited. He listened to the splinter of bone off his steel and the thud of arrows into hide shields. As the storm passed, the Chaos warlord came out from behind his Ruinous Star.

'Do your worst!' Archaon roared. Below him it was as if

a dam had broken. The sea of muscle and horn he had been holding back had been released. The base instincts of his legion's brute nature took over. With Moraq Half-Horn leading the way and smashing his own beastfiends aside with the hammer-head of his saddled rhinox, the monstrous half-breeds of Archaon's army surged forth through the havoc. Huge shafts of ice and stone erupted from the ground and spouts of pitch fountained about them. Fires spread and turned such fountains into furious beacons of flame.

Archaon leapt from one rising outcrop to another as his savage horde clashed with the beastfiends of the Haemorrhagia. Within furious moments they were among their attackers. Brays of stunted horn and shaved chest twanged their arrows off bows of blood-stained bone and strings of sinew. Horns were blown and a cacophony of weakling warcries rose from chests of red flesh. As Archaon's brutes waded into the mobs of miserable half-breeds, the brays dropped their cowardly weapons in favour of crooked pikes bearing heads of crafted horn, splintered bone or razored flint. They hurled their wicked shafts at Archaon's oncoming host but his beastfiends would not be denied. Hoof-hobbling on, sometimes with jagged pikes embedded in furry legs, shoulders and chests, the warherd charged the brays.

There were hundreds and hundreds of the infernal creatures. As Moraq and his beasts cleaved their way through the mob, the darkness gave birth to endless multitudes of red bodies. The murk rumbled with the bestial braying of hundreds more, awaiting their turn to honour the Blood God. To stab and gouge. To skewer and twist their primitive pikes in the flesh of their tribal enemy. Leaping and dropping from rising outcrop to rising outcrop, Archaon could see why Ograx the Great had held the Haemorrhagia for so long. Long enough to become infamous among innumerable other savage chieftains.

The Haemorrhagia rumbled beneath ice and rock. Beneath the thunder of hoof the world split. The ground shook. Flaming pitch vomited for the sky. The hellish earth opened up to reveal its infernal secrets.

Archaon perched with the agility of a cat on a shuddering outcrop. He cast his gaze across the waves of red muscle and twisted horn, rolling in from the twilight of the Wastes. He leapt off the rocky shaft, with *Terminus* and shield held high. Crashing down through the horde of brays, Archaon cleaved a half-breed in two. He brained beastfiends with his star-emblazoned shield and broke monsters with an armoured boot. He turned. He slashed and smashed through beastmeat. Bone spears split against the metal of the shield and the Sigmarite blade seared through daemon-pledged flesh. About him great rents opened up in the Wastes, and snow steamed away as clefts and chasms swallowed beastfiends whole. The gaping rifts unleashed an infernal glow on the battlefield.

Both the creatures branded with Archaon's mark and that of the Blood God fell to a fiery doom, braying and bellowing away their misfortune. Archaon hopped across the parting fissures, cutting and cleaving through the blood-soaked brays as he went. He jumped the flaming crevasses that opened at his feet and butchered his way through beastfiends as he stormed across the trembling ice. Creatures thrust at him with unthinking savagery, stabbing and cutting, but the pikes sparked and splintered off the unhallowed armour of Morkar.

'Enough!' Archaon roared as he bludgeoned brays with his heavy blade. Blood leapt from the screeching beastfiends with every furious strike. 'I want the Great One!' Archaon shouted across the torment of the earth, the *whoosh* of flame and the suffering he had created in his wake. 'I want the champion of Z'rughl Ka'kadron'ath. The Brassbound's kindred. The bestial prince. Ograx of the Blood God – where are you?'

Archaon's words were hot but his mind cut through the chaos and confusion like cold steel. He wanted to draw out the monster – and it worked. The Haemorrhagia shook with the thunder of the half-daemon's roar. A great shaft of black rock erupted from the ground with an explosive shower of cinders, carrying the form of Ograx the Great high above the fray. Archaon felt his face contort into something halfway between a snarl and a smile. As another spur of ruptured earth rumbled skyward nearby, Archaon took the murderous steps and barbarian lives it took to reach it. As the rock took him above the steam, smoke and glare of the battlefield he saw his opposite. The bestial warlord Ograx.

He was big, even for one of the southern half-breeds. The light of the fires gleamed off the brazen surface of his shaggy legs and cloven hooves. They were living metal, like a sculpture that had achieved a life of its own. A belt of flayed flesh and fur scabbards sat on his hips, surrounding the nightmare creature in a nest of weaponry: flint-serrated swords of bone, pick axes of sabre teeth, scapula hatchets and short, broad blades of daemonic design. Ograx's broad chest was a wall of red muscle, from which hung shrunken skulls, furs that danced in the wind and scraps of armour torn from his infernal victims. His face was a glowering mess of scars and bovine madness, amongst a princely crown of bifurcating hell-horn. As the two warriors of Chaos were thrust up at the sky, Ograx pulled a mighty axe from where it had hung across his mane-trailing back. It was a primitive weapon of bone and blood-stained sinew, holding the colossal length of the axe-head in place. The haft was a twisted spine while the axe-head was an actual head. A previous victim. The cranial-crest and snaggle-toothed upper beak of some Tzeentchian daemon. Rancid flesh still clung to the prize.

'Now, creature!' Archaon called at the beast-champion. 'Your master has waited long enough for the skull of one of his own.' As the Chaos warrior was finding, Ograx was easy to provoke and manipulate. He was a living fortress of flesh and fury. Fury, however, could only take the monster so far. It had little trouble taking Ograx across the flaming gulf between them, however. With a daemonic roar the bestial prince was in the air, his skull-axe held high above him. There wasn't enough room for both of them on the rocky outcrop and the beast's hooves alone would crush him into the stone. At the last moment, Archaon leapt for a rocky shaft rising beside them. As his previous purchase crunched below the landing daemon prince, the Chaos warrior pushed himself immediately back.

Slamming Ograx with the star of his shield, Archaon knocked the bestial champion from his footing. With a bellow of raw frustration, the creature scraped down the side of the shaft with his hooves and the claw of a hand. Brazen hoof-tips and talons sparked down the rock as the monster heaved himself to a halt. The skull-axe swooped about, forcing Archaon onto one foot as the daemonic beak bit into the rock at his toe. Kicking the weapon away, Archaon swung *Terminus* below him, batting the skull-axe clear and cutting away crag and cranny from the rockface. As the furious Ograx was forced further down the shaft, the stone ledge upon which he was perched gave way and plunged the hulking half-breed down into the flaming pit that had opened about them.

Leaning out, Archaon peered down into the steaming glare, looking for some sign of Ruinous life. It came in the form of a scapula hatchet flung furiously from the inferno and nearly taking the Chaos warrior's head off. Pulling himself back to the trembling shaft of rock, Archaon swore. Another razored shoulder blade came spinning at him like a throwing-axe, and the dark templar shattered it with a cleaving blow from his heavy blade. Seeing the red eyes of the half-breed prince searing up at him from the murky glare of the pit, Archaon released his grip on the shuddering spur and dropped down at the beast.

It was a long drop. Archaon's boots found their way to an incline of trembling rock, but it was all he could do to not plunge face first into the flaming lake of pitch that sloshed, spat and fountained with explosive insistence about the roasted isle upon which he had landed. Skidding through the scree, the Chaos warrior skipped back into a regular step. Ograx was suddenly there. Out of the smoke. Out of the steam. More importantly it was the half-breed's skull-axe that came for him. Allowing himself to skid beneath the terrible arc of its daemonic beak, Archaon was forced to release *Terminus* and put both hands behind his shield. As the blade rattled along the surface of the hot stone, Ograx turned with merciless force and intention. His axe struck Archaon's shield and smashed the dark templar back. Rolling across his pauldron and furs Archaon brought the shield back up at a crouch but again the skull-axe was there, with the monster's bone-shuddering brawn behind it.

Archaon risked a glance behind him. *Terminus* had come to a stop at the burning shore. The greatsword had skidded and bounced its way across the pitch pools of bubble and flame and was slowly sinking, blade first, into the black slurp. Still at a crouch, Archaon began to work his way over to the weapon but Ograx had him. Again and again the skull-axe came for him. Archaon could feel the beast-prince's god-fuelled might behind each strike. Ograx wanted nothing more than to slam the beak straight through Archaon, armour and all. And between his infernal weapon and the brute strength in the mountain range of muscle that ran down his arms, Archaon had no doubt that he could do it.

Skidding. Kneeling. Shuffling. The dark templar watched his blade sink while his shield and his bones took the mindless and unrelenting onslaught of the creature. As the cross guard descended, Archaon threw himself into a messy roll, arm over arm, holding the shield close. Ograx was all over him. Stomping through the grit and pools of pitch with his hooves, the half-breed brought his axe down on Archaon with furious insistence. With each roll the Chaos warrior just managed to get the shield between him and the impaling beak. On the roasting shoreline Archaon reached out for the sinking *Terminus,* the fingertips of his gauntlet trapping the pommel as Ograx battered his shield – and the shield, in turn, battered Archaon into the ground.

Clawing *Terminus* up out of the boiling pitch, the Chaos warrior heaved back at the skull-axe with his shield and an exhausted arm. Archaon swung the weapon at the half-breed's legs. The edge of the greatsword sparked off the creature's brazen leg, failing to cut into the metal. The raw frustration of the strike took Ograx from his cloven hooves and put him on the burning rock. Archaon swung *Terminus* down at the half-breed's chest but the prone creature got the bone shaft of his axe between the blade's edge and its intended target. The insistence of the parry carried up the Chaos warrior's sword arm, jarring his shoulder. Boiling pitch flicked from the steel and scorched a line across Ograx's broad chest.

Archaon heaved *Terminus* down at the monster but the half-breed was incredibly strong and pressed the haft of his skull-axe back at the dark templar. For a long time the two warriors held each other there. Archaon adjusted his balance and the angle of the blade. The daemonic bone of the axe's spine would not break under the templar blade's cleaving edge, however, and the pair assumed the trembling stillness of a quake-tormented sculpture, Archaon matching his skill and indomitable will against the bestial savagery of the muscle-bound monster.

Archaon became aware of movement about them. From the bubble and slurp of the steaming pitch, the creatures of hell were emerging. Wretched daemons and winged horrors crawled forth from the depths. Slick and black with pitch, many of the gargoyles were aflame and climbed up the walls of the pit, their talons taking them up towards their prey. They dripped with the black blood of the earth and extended jaws and wings lazily, as though they had just been awoken from infernal slumber in the dark womb of the below. This changed things for both Archaon and Ograx. From the shrieks and screams above, the monstrous beings of the Haemorrhagia were indiscriminate in their slaying, with bodies of the warlords' beastfiends flying down into the hellish pit. As half-breeds of the Blood God and the eight-pointed star thrashed and boiled in pitch and flame, the creatures began to claw their way up the searing shore towards the two warriors.

Archaon risked a withdrawal. Leaning back he brought his blade off the axe haft, allowing Ograx to move. As the bestial prince brought his skull-axe around for a leg-smashing sweep, Archaon resisted the urge to bury *Terminus* in the prone half-breed and settled instead on smashing his heavy blade down on the skeletal weapon. The skull-axe was smashed from Ograx's clawed grip and bounced across the hot stone out of reach. Archaon brought *Terminus* up to finish the job. To bury the monstrous creature in bludgeoning blows with the blade. He had grown accustomed to such wretches – the bested in battle – begging for their miserable lives or at least hiding fearfully behind outstretched arms and faces fixed with dread. This was not the end Ograx the Great had promised himself. He arched his back, leaning into his death. A growl trailed off into a hiss of hate as the champion gave Archaon the full horror of his half-daemon visage and the infernal glow of his eyes. Ograx dared Archaon to end him. For his innumerable sins, Archaon hesitated.

The Chaos warrior was hit from the side. The world became a tumbling mess of rocky floor and leathery wing. Archaon had been tackled by several creatures that had hauled themselves up the shore. Bounding for him and taking the dark templar down, like some great cat of the plains might a horse or rhinox, the daemonic furies had him on the ground. Archaon became aware of tearing claws, snapping jaws and the slip and slide of pitch-slick flesh. There were four of them, he thought. They savaged him with primordial strength and speed, searching for the soul hiding within the inconvenience of flesh. Between the slap of wing and the snap of jaw, Archaon caught sight of Ograx. He had left the half-breed prince prone and without his daemonic weapon. The brute was swarming with furies. Archaon didn't know whether to be pleased or insulted – either the creatures had sensed in Ograx an easier kill or a more formidable threat. The Chaos warrior settled on the sting of the latter. The monsters would not have been the first to be fooled by the muscle and rage. They would pay for their primitive assumptions.

Archaon rolled, dashing the brains from a snapping fury. His gauntlet, clutched in a fist about the hilt of his templar blade, landed a snout-crunching blow on another before the

Chaos warrior rose from the hot stone and shook a third from his armoured back. The fiend received an elbow to its mangled maw, knocking it stumbling back into the pitch rolling up the shoreline.

'Meet *Terminus*,' Archaon snarled, turning the Sigmarite blade with a bend of his wrist. The things circled on all fours, wings held close to their backs, spitting and hissing like the creatures of hell they were. One lunged at him but he punched it aside with the star-blazoned surface of his shield. Another came for his throat but Archaon swiped it down with a flourish of his blade. The blessed steel burned through daemonflesh in a way the pitch had failed to, and the beast released an unearthly shriek of agony. Archaon suddenly felt pain of his own as the third monster latched onto his wrist with its crushing maw. Whirling into a savage turn Archaon dragged the beast around and sent it slamming into the creature he had just opened from the chops to the naval. Still dragging the monster, he thrust *Terminus* forward, taking the first daemon through the chest. It released its infernal claw-hold on reality and died right there on Sigmarite steel, leaving the dead meat of its horrid, worldly form skewered on the blade.

Death, right there before the fury's burning eyes, had persuaded the third brute to unclamp its twisted maw from Archaon's arm. The Chaos warrior turned on it and with a savage thrust of the head, smashed its face back into its skull with a butt of his skull-helm. A back slice with his greatsword cut the distracted monster all but in two, leaving Archaon facing one lone and uncertain beast.

'Come on, thing of darkness and flame, don't disappoint me now...'

With a predator's patience it paced back and forth before surging for him. Archaon moved, allowing the beast to pass by before bringing the flat of his heavy blade down on the creature's skull. There was a wet crunch that sent the daemon to the floor. Stalking up behind it, Archaon stamped down on the monster's head, crunching his heel against the burning rock beneath. He paused to soak up the havoc in which he found himself.

Above, a three-way battle had unfolded about the opening pit. The savages of his own warherd were taking the fight to the Blood God's beastfiends, while both were forced to defend themselves against the infernal horrors that were crawling up from cracks, flame-howling pits and fissures that were opening up across the lands of the Haemorrhagia. He saw Moraq Half-Horn, still fighting from the saddle of his slain mount. His Swords of Chaos, like lieutenants amongst the half-breed savages of Archaon's horde, slashing with boneswords and parrying with unfurled wings. The sorcerer Sheerian, mumbling incantations and tapping his staff on the flesh of passing brays, prompting limbs to erupt from bestial torsos that clawed and strangled the afflicted creatures. The misshapen Vier, keeping Sister Giselle beneath his own mangled wing – the girl holding her furs about her like a comforting embrace, her face inflicted with the blankness of a battlefield stare. Before him Ograx the Great was a nest of writhing daemons. Archaon could hear the bellow and roar of the mauled half-breed.

The Chaos warrior allowed a snarl to fall from his lips. Slipping *Terminus* into his back-scabbard and shouldering his shield, Archaon scooped up Ograx's weapon from the roasting stone. He hefted the axe, feeling the weight of the daemonic skull. Turning the spine in his gauntlets, he spun the beak and the skull-crest around. The grit crunched beneath his boots, flames roared from the pit and furies snapped and snarled with savagery. Within the mound of infernal flesh, Archaon could hear Ograx the Great bellow his pain and frustration. Archaon nodded to himself. It was decided.

Lifting the skull-axe above him like a woodcutter, Archaon brought it straight down on the nearest hellfiend. Like a pick into stone, the beak of the weapon thudded through the back of the fury, prompting the creature to screech its agony and surprise to the heavens. Archaon tore the creature off the Blood God's chosen, dragging it back across the hot stone. Resting a boot on its thrashing form – a frenzy of wing and claw – Archaon finished the monster with another heft of the daemonbone axe. He peeled the infernal beasts from Ograx. The skull-axe crunched through torsos and hooked heads from shoulders. Archaon battered monsters aside, allowing them to claw and skitter their way through the trembling grit, before slamming the axe-head into them and then the brutes into the stone.

Finally, Archaon saw the bestial prince, his face and broad chest further mangled by the claws of the furies. Ograx was drowning in winged daemons, both alive and dead. Many still had the beastfiend's assortment of flint blades and scapula axes buried in their infernal flesh. Archaon dragged the carcasses from him as the bestial prince held a fury's head before him, smashing its face with a clenched fist while its twisted jaws snapped for him. This had gone on long enough, Archaon decided, and heaved the skull-axe over one shoulder. He brought the bone weapon down with such force that its beak cleaved straight through the back of the fury's head and out through its face, drizzling Ograx with honouring gore from the Blood God.

The beastfiend heaved the daemon to one side, leaving it atop the mound of other corpses, and got unsteadily to his feet. The two warriors of Chaos regarded one another as the havoc of battle, firestorm and slaughter unfolded about them. There were few words suitable for such an encounter, even in the beastfiend's dark tongue, and Archaon did not deign to use them. Actions spoke louder in the cacophony of Haemorrhagia. Turning the gore-dribbling skull-head of Ograx's axe in his gauntlets, Archaon placed it in the hot grit at his feet and kicked it across to the bestial prince. Ograx watched the weapon bump and hiss through the grit to his hooves. As the monster slowly picked it up, Archaon found his own hand twitch. The muscles in his arm were tensed and ready to reach for *Terminus* from his back-scabbard. Ograx was a savage. A daemonic half-breed. A barbarian disciple of the Blood God. Anything might happen.

Ograx looked up about the edge of the pit. His brays were falling into the pitch and flame, forced back by the savage hordes of Archaon, where they were being torn apart and discarded by the furies of the Haermorrhagia, climbing up out of the fiery depths. Ograx pulled a horn from his furs and put it to his ugly lips. As he belted a lungful of air through the crude instrument, the very air about them trembled. The sound threatened to stop the heart and burst the ear. The brays of the Blood God knew the sound.

'Hold!' Archaon called, the boom of his voice amplified by the pit. At the signal of the two warlords, the bestial hordes slowed to the stillness of a standoff. Creatures stood obedient and uncertain. Even the ferocity of flame and tearing earth seemed to die away. Ograx called out orders in a bullish voice. Archaon had his own: 'Destroy the daemons that crawl from the depths,' he ordered his savages. Warcries and thunderous threats built in the chests of half-breeds as bestial kin found a brute camaraderie in the faces of their former foes. With the thoughtless compliance of a yoked animal, the creatures fell on the plague of winged monstrosities crawling from the pit, stabbing, bludgeoning and mauling the furies with a shared and monstrous rejoicing. The gods would have their grotesque games and Khorne would have skulls for his eternal throne.

Climbing up the side of the pit, slashing and skewering furies from his path as he did, Archaon hauled himself up over the edge. He turned to find Ograx the Great behind him. Archaon offered the bestial prince his gauntlet. After a moment's feral consideration, Ograx put his claw in Archaon's hand and allowed the Chaos warrior to help him up. The battle continued about them. The Haemorrhagia vomited forth all it had – firestorms, the rebellious earth and the scourge that was spawned from the bowels of the Wasteland interior.

Archaon directed his horde to take the battle to the very land itself. It was as if the Southern Wastes themselves were contesting his supremacy. Such winged monsters were the stuff of nightmares. Daemonic creatures of whim and monstrous fancy. They were no match for Archaon, the savage hordes of the dark templar and Ograx the Great combined. As the ire of the land died down, the flames faded and the boiling pitch drained away, the great rents in the landscape came together like healing wounds, and winged horrors that failed to crawl back into the dark womb of the earth were torn apart by bestial hordes beneath the flayed flesh of Archaon's banner.

The Chaos warrior walked through the carnage. The land was a carpet of daemonflesh, rotting away with supernatural speed. The Swords of Chaos stalked close by, ever watchful for treachery. Through the muscular silhouettes of beastfiends, Archaon caught sight of Giselle. The girl was shadowed by the misshapen Vier, whose twisted body towered over her. It had been Archaon's instruction that the winged marauder not leave her side. The girl for her part had not been the same since their encounter with the Chaos dragon Flamefang, and their unfortunate arrival on the damned shores of the dark, southern continent.

Giselle wandered as if in a horror-drunk daze. Her face was at once disgust and disbelief at the ghastliness she had endured, and the bleak acceptance of her fate to come. Archaon, who cared little for his own hardships and almost nothing for anyone else's, could barely look her in the eye. They had been intimate once but that had been a long time ago. The girl's remonstrations and Sigmarite curses had become a lost hope to save him. Such cares had become futility, infatuation and perhaps even love.

Archaon himself found little space in his heart for such sentiments, crowded out by the darkness and doom that he had become. He desired an end to all and yet, when it came to the girl, Giselle Dantziger, there was a part of him that desired existence. Not just the endless violence and burning desire for wars to be won and foes to be conquered. Another kind of existence. Fleeting moments of flesh against flesh and hearts that seemed to beat as one in the hollow emptiness of the world.

Perhaps he had indeed fallen for the girl, but he would never admit that to himself, let alone to Giselle herself. Besides, their time at the top of the world had passed. Archaon had fallen so much further since then. He had been lost, but now he was truly damned.

Yet still he kept the girl alive, rather than cast her aside as he had so many. Her hallowed touch was agony to him. Somehow, in this benighted place – or perhaps because of it – the girl's simple faith in a false god, a God-King, had not abandoned her. It had been a long time since he had known such agonies. Now her mere existence seemed to burn his soul. She was a little of what remained; in the stale echo of her original affections continued to live the man he had once been. It was a weakness, Archaon knew this, but he could not bring himself to end the half-felt, half-remembered scintilla of his former existence. A life the many dark deeds of his doom had eclipsed and he could barely remember. For Archaon it seemed to live on only in his consuming hatred for the world, the gods that plagued it and the mortal multitude that were the slaughter-in-waiting. Only in Giselle did he exist as anything else and, for some perverse reason, Archaon couldn't find it in himself to destroy that. So, Giselle Dantziger lived on. A ghost of a girl, buried in furs and surrounded by fiends who would die to protect her in the most lethal of lands, simply because Archaon, their dark lord and master, wished it so.

The sorcerer Sheerian approached, hobbling with his staff. Moraq Half-Horn was with him, dwarfing the ancient with his brute bulk. The half-breed, in turn, was buried in the shadow of Ograx the Great.

'A truce, my lord?' the Tzeentchian put to him. Like everything the sorcerer said, it was some kind of a subtle challenge.

'An assimilation,' Archaon settled upon.

'But how can we trust such a mindless animal?' Sheerian asked. Ograx snorted, the stinking mist engulfing the ancient. The sorcerer stumbled back a little but was undeterred. 'A servant of the Blood God, for whom any of our skulls might serve as tribute.'

'I'll trust a mindless animal over a Tzeentchian sorcerer any day,' Archaon told the ancient. 'A mindless animal can be loyal. This is more than I can say of the Great Changer and his duplicitous minions, for it is in their nature to cog, lie and deceive.'

'My lord,' Sheerian protested.

'It is done,' Archaon said. 'The bestial prince and I have reached an accord, at least for now. If my skull had been destined for the Blood God's throne then I don't doubt that Ograx here would have been the one to take it.' Archaon gave the hulking monster a slight nod, which the half-breed returned.

'Pray, sir…'

'Pray yourself,' Archaon said, 'and keep your foetid gods happy, for I don't get to choose, sorcerer. I am to be Everchosen of the Chaos gods, the Herald of Ruin in all its cursed forms, not just the Powers towards which I feel wretchedly inclined. Now, convey my words in the dark tongue of the beast. Inform Ograx here that his warherd will join my own and that together we shall travel south and bring the wrath of the half-breed to the Gatelands and the infernal kings who grow soft within their palace walls.'

Archaon watched the bestial prince carefully as Sheerian spoke his words in the guttural tongue of the beastfiends. He saw Ograx look down on Moraq Half-Horn and then back at Archaon. When he spoke, it was with savage pride.

'Well?' Archaon asked.

'Ograx the Great wonders for whom he fights,' Sheerian translated.

'Tell him he fights for the glory of his god,' Archaon said, 'and through him the glory of all the Ruinous Gods – for it is through them that the darkness of all the world will be realised. Tell him I am the instrument of that realisation – chosen of all gods as he is chosen of his – and as such he fights for me, as the best of all the half-breeds of the Southern Wastes do.'

Something seemed to trouble the creature.

'Or he can fight for his life…' Archaon warned. Ograx moved quickly for such a hulking beast. He was suddenly behind Moraq, his great, bulging arm around the half-breed's neck. He picked the creature up by the arm-lock and his infamous half-horn, the chieftain's back against the scarring of his broad chest. Moraq's flailing hooves and thrashing arms told of the incredible force behind Ograx's mighty frame. Suddenly it was over. Moraq Half-Horn's body fell like a rag doll at the bestial prince's brazen hooves, while the beast-fiend's head – replete with the shock on the unfortunate creature's face – remained in Ograx's grasp. The monster threw the head down at Archaon's boots.

The dark templar stared at the half-breed hulk. His Swords of Chaos had cleared their bone blades from their wing-sheathes and Sheerian had stumbled back into his master in shock at the sudden violence.

'Treachery, my lord,' the sorcerer screamed. 'Skulls for the Skull Throne of Khorne!'

'No…' Archaon decided. He didn't move. His muscles were tensed but he didn't want Ograx to know his display had startled him. 'A skull for me,' the dark templar informed him. 'The Blood God's diplomacy, if such a thing exists. An offering. A bargain to be made – but with conditions.' Archaon looked straight at Ograx. 'The half-breeds fight for you, correct?' Archaon put to the bestial prince. 'And with them, you for me.'

Ograx the Great nodded his ugly head slowly. Archaon nodded his agreement also.

'Ready the horde, mongrel prince,' Archaon said turning to leave. 'We march on the continental interior, the Gatelands, where daemons rule and worlds beyond our own wait to be discovered.'

CHAPTER II

*'Those that worship the Prince of Excess
are free to serve as slaves to darkness.'*
— Lothal the Lost (Flesh inscribed)

*The Scabyrinth
The Southern Wastes
Horns Harrowing: Season of the Raw*

The ragelands of the Haemorrhagia gave way once more to the howling freeze of the Southern Wastes. Archaon pushed his horde of half-breeds to their limit. Such creatures were used to the idle violence and wanton debauchery of holding territories. Even encroachments and invasions were laggardly, aimless affairs following whatever gorfiend or beastlord had indulged its aggressions that day. The beastfiends of the Southern Wastes were not used to hoof-marching and cavalcadery, where the inhospitable conditions and unnatural geography prohibited such madness.

This did not stop Archaon leading his ragged horde of

barbarians and bestial savages from the front, setting the pace for the miserable creatures as they trudged through snowstorms and black drifts, across lakes of ice in which entire armies of daemons were encased, and glaciers that oozed ichor and doom. He led them between ranges of serrated mountains and along rivers of lava that snaked and steamed through the frozen wilderness from the flare of distant peaks. All the while, the lunatic Gorst followed in the horde's hoofsteps, trailing his master – as he always had. Nothing could stop the wizened madman, jangling in his chains and head-cage. No drift of black snow was too deep, no frost-shattered maze of dagger peaks too towering for the flagellant. From time to time Archaon would inquire after the madman. Every time Gorst was taken for gone, however – lost in some unnatural storm, picked off by a monstrous predator of the Wastes or simply swallowed by the darkness – the lunatic would appear. How he achieved this, the Dark Gods only knew.

Archaon took each step with dogged assurance. Time and distance had little meaning in the insanity of the Southern Wastes. This he had long known and tended to measure the passing of both in the number of half-breeds crashed to the ice, dead from exhaustion and exposure. Ograx's blood-brays were particularly susceptible to the deep cold of the continental interior, having formerly made their herdlands in the warmth of the Haemorrhagia. Every so many deaths, Archaon would open the Eye – the blazing jewel he had taken from the sorcerer Sheerian and the Chaos dragon Flamefang.

Ensconced above the eye sockets of his helm's skull-face, Archaon engaged the Eye's supernatural abilities. The gem glowed with damned energies, allowing Archaon to see far beyond even his own enhanced senses. Great distance and the obstacles of rock and storm were nothing to the Eye. It brought Archaon, in gaze at least, from horizon to horizon and beyond. With the great artefact, one of the six treasures of Chaos that marked a man as Everchosen of the Ruinous Gods, the dark templar had plotted the course of his incursion into the Wastes at the bottom of the world. He hoped that one day he would unlock the sorcerous jewel's secrets further and learn to extend its view ahead in time, as well as space. He looked forward to the time he might see the prospects of the very next moment, hour, day or year in the same way that the Eye already allowed him to see beyond the limits of his earthly gaze – to see his future, his destiny, rather than simply aching for it in the unknown of the present.

His relentless trek through the lands of shadow, ice and insanity, trailing a mighty cavalcade of brute half-breeds, had taken him south. Further south than any man had ever been. The Eye had reached over the black horizon for him to reveal a great canyon, a crescent canyon that cut deep into the Wastes. It was colossal, and curved its crooked way into the darkness of the polar interior, the infernal whimlands of Chaos, where sanity and reality had no business. The sorcerer Sheerian told Archaon that the chasm was one of eight mighty tears in the fabric of the interior that had been created by the calamitous collapse of the great polar gate – the gargantuan portal that led from the mortal realm to that of the Chaos gods. The Eye showed Archaon the shattered remains of the gate and the amaranthine balelight that bled into the world, reaching up from the rift and into the broiling skies like a Ruinous dawn.

Huge fragments of midnight stone – warpstone that ate the very balelight about it – sat strewn across the infernal region, too massive for even the strange forces of the Gatelands to erode. About them the Eye revealed the sovereignties of the great entities of ruin and the earthly palaces of daemon lords and princes. Topless citadels. Nightmarish palaces. Colossal fortresses of paranoid madness. Such abominations, crafted in stone, metal, flesh and bone, reared from fossilised battlefields, the carcasslands of rotting daemonhood and vast ruins of ancient grandeur and dream-bastions yet to be built. A place where the manifest melted before the mind and the desires of darkness achieved a warped reality.

As Archaon's determined steps led the horde down into the opening of the crescent canyon, beastfiends gave rancid thanks to their gods for the respite. With craggy stone walls rising up either side of them and a winding path descending into the frozen hell-hole of the Wastes, the crescent canyon offered shelter from the cut-glass gales and heart-stopping temperatures. With every hoof-fall down into the canyon depths, the temperature rose. Heated by the volcanic activity in the bowels of the earth and hot springs, the rockface of the crevasse became warm to the touch. The lifelessness of the icescape above gave way to unnatural mosses and lichens. The petrified roots and branches of hardy shrubs and woody foliage reached out for the horde as they made their way along the canyon.

The half-breeds were all but dead on their hooves, stumbling along in a listless train of savages. Archaon did not slow as he reached the shelter of the crescent canyon. He did not camp as any other warlord or general might have. He increased the pace further, snowdrifts and the slippery surface of glaciers no longer slowing their progress down. Although he did not share his desires with the brutes and lieutenants of his exhausted army, he was intent on reaching the Forsaken Fortress of Be'lakor before it disappeared once more, forcing him to criss-cross the frozen continent in aimless futility. He would not have the Dark Master escape him and, to ensure that, he needed a daemonic steed fleet enough to catch him and his capricious castle. The Changeling had shown him where he might find such a mount, so on he trudged. Through the canyon's torturous twists and turns, through the brush of midnight foliage sprouting from the grit path and drooping from the overhanging rock.

As the canyon cut through the twilight wilderness of the Wastes, it bifurcated into a series of smaller, deep ravines. The single path became many as the canyon turned into a maze of tight gulches, gorges and gulleys. Above, the ice sheet had managed to bridge the narrow chasm tops, providing a vaulted roof to the canyon, through which the bleak glow of lightning storms passed as if through black crystal. Sheerian called it the Scabyrinth, though Archaon knew not where the sorcerer had heard the term. Where the canyon had split into a delta of smaller paths, the ice had managed to reassert its supremacy and cover the canyon, like a crusty scab across a festering wound. It rained within the ravine's depths as the warm rock melted the under-ice to produce an ink-blot drizzle that guttered half-breed torches of bone and fat-smeared hide.

The drizzle sustained all manner of strange plants and animals. The Scabyrinth was an oasis of warped life – lowly creatures in the main. Things of long leg, claw and boot-crunching body. Wet serpents and spiders as big as Archaon's shield made their home in the crags of the rockface. Warpwater crayfish scuttled about the black streams created by the perpetual drizzle in the squelching gravel of the ravine floor, while leeches dropping from the canyon walls and fat, chitinous flies attempted to feed on the warm blood in their veins. It was a while before the horde encountered actual warm-blooded creatures, but when they did it was in the form of twisted vermin and packs of vicious wolf-rats.

As Archaon led his warherd down through the Scabyrinth, his half-breeds feasted. The legs of monster arachnids and malformed shellfish eaten whole provided an army's bounty after the necessities of cannibalism on the lifeless Wastes. They soon encountered those who viewed the undercanyons similarly. Beastfiend hunting parties and migrating daemon-breeds, who favoured the warm passage of the Scabyrinth over the murderous cold of the hail-lashed wilderness above. The disturbing forms of god-cursed spawn that leapt at them from caves and hollows. Malformed monsters of great size and ferocity. Some were hibernating in the twists and turns of the Scabyrinth undercanyons. Word was passed down the ragged line for half-breeds to be silent and soft of hoof.

Other creatures treated the depths of the labyrinth like a game trail, feasting on the things that travelled back and forth along it. Archaon and his beastfiends were forced to slay such abominations, swarming the great creatures while hacking them with bone-axe and viciously stabbing them with spears. Such creatures also provided valuable sustenance. Archaon passed the word for half-breeds to cut strips of meat from the colossal carcasses and hang it from their belts for later. Archaon did not intend to stop. He needed his warherd strong. He needed them to keep eating so that they could keep marching and fighting.

'We're getting close,' Sheerian said, hobbling up behind Archaon. The Chaos warrior knew what it must have taken to do that, pushing through the pain of aching joints and dragging his bird's foot. It wasn't simply to be agreeable or indulge in idle conversation. Sheerian knew better than to indulge such pointlessness. Archaon suspected that he wanted to be close to the Eye. Surrendering the jewel had been difficult for the sorcerer – to be forced once again to see the world as others saw it, cursed with the limitations of common sight. Archaon couldn't trust the Tzeentchian as far as he could spit, and often suspected he was scheming some way to earn the mystical gem back. In the meantime, the best the Tzeentchian could expect was hobbling close to his master and bathing in the Eye's sorcerous power. On occasion, when their needs were shared, Archaon found the sorcerer's knowledge and advice tedious but useful. 'Look…'

Sheerian pointed up at the ice above their heads. The black crystal of the floe had started to glow a dark purple as the balelight of the polar rift reached through the ice. 'The Gatelands, my lord.'

'And the palaces of doomed daemons,' Archaon said.

'Powerful entities, master,' Sheerian added. 'They bear the favour of the Dark Gods to hold sovereignty in such lands. It is a great honour reserved for the most dangerous and twisted of their kind.'

'Do you have a point, sorcerer?' Archaon growled, crunching through the wet gravel beside a black stream. 'For, if you do, I would have you make it.'

'Only that,' Sheerian said, his bowed head mottled with age, 'it would be wise to exercise caution here. That's all.'

'Understood.'

As Sheerian fell back, unable to keep pace with his master's determined progress, Archaon reached a sharp corner in the canyon. Archaon could hear shouting, and the roar of a great beast bouncing about the twisted path of the labyrinthine ravine. It had been some hours since his sword had been baptised in daemonblood or nestled in the flesh of some monster or brute beastfiend. Drawing *Terminus*, Archaon came to a halt. Opening the Eye of Sheerian, the warlord peered up the torturous twists and turns of the canyon. He saw an engagement of some kind. A monstrous creature, tormented by scores of infernal gors. One carried a banner of some kind.

'Sorcerer,' Archaon called, prompting Sheerian to hobble up behind. The Swords of Chaos moved forward like sentinels, bone swords drawn and wings extended protectively about them like warrior-gargoyles. Archaon raised a fist, prompting Vier to lay a twisted gauntlet on Giselle's shoulder and bring the addled girl to a stop. Ograx the Great saw the signal also and slowed, settling his mighty skull-axe across his shoulders. Behind his hulking form the cavalcade of half-breeds and beastfiends slowed also.

'My lord?' Sheerian asked. Archaon drew him close, into the halo of light that the sorcerous Eye cast about the warlord when it was open, so that the Tzeentchian sorcerer might also be caught up in its dark potency and catch a glimpse or vague suggestion of what Archaon was seeing.

'What do you see, sorcerer?' Archaon demanded. 'The banner: what does it show?'

Archaon saw the ancient's shoulders gently fall as he once again sampled the gift of the Eye. When he was younger, Archaon remembered seeing Sieur Kastner doing something similar. He would similarly demonstrate such relief upon taking a swig from his flask. The relief of an addict. Sheerian took his time. 'Sorcerer,' Archaon demanded. 'What do you see?'

Sheerian almost cracked his ancient face with a horrible smile.

'We *are* near…' the sorcerer said absently.

'Sorcerer,' Archaon told him, 'I swear by your faithless lord, if you don't tell me what you see, I'll put out your greedy eyes.'

'The claw symbol of the daemon lord Agrammon, my lord,' the ancient told him. 'Daubed on skins, armour and a banner. A hunting party, sent out to trap the exotic beasts of the Wastes for the daemon lord's collection.'

Through the Eye's shimmering gaze, Archaon saw the crude symbol to which the sorcerer made reference. A claw or pincer, an emblem of infernal royalty. The mark of the daemon Agrammon. With it Archaon saw the sensual sigils of the Prince of Pleasure, the Ruinous Power Agrammon honoured with his bottomless greed, his indulgence and his monstrous menagerie. The symbols were splashed across the shaven chests of beastfiend trappers: creatures of sickening flesh, entwining horns and long tapering snouts. Their eyes were blank and white, while in their pincer-fingers they held twisted tridents of sinewy bone, and long whips that they cracked about the foul creature they had trapped against the canyon wall.

Archaon turned the Eye on the monstrosity they had cornered. A primeval horror of scale and warty skin – gnarled enough to turn aside a blade – it was some aberration of the Wastes: a toad-like dragon. Its webbed feet splashed about in the shallows of the meltwater stream, and it unleashed thunderous croaks from its huge rubbery maw as Agrammon's bestial trappers thrust their tridents at it and slashed their whips of sinew in the shallows. As one of the long-snouts splashed through the black waters at the toad dragon, forcing it back, the creature ballooned its bulbous throat and reared up. Opening its great maw the thing regurgitated its last meal upon the beastfiend. The vomit was a deluge of bloody bile and steaming bones. The trapper trumpeted a ghastly shriek from its long snout as the acidic contents of the toad dragon's stomach drenched it. As flesh began to dribble from its bones, the Slaaneshi trapper stumbled towards its compatriot beasts but the long-snouts backed away. Within moments the beastfiend had become a steaming mound of melted flesh, hissing and dissolving on the shoreline of the stream. The toad dragon hopped forward, croaking its monstrous desire to be left alone. The Slaaneshi beastfiends trumpeted their own fears as they skipped back through the waters on the tips of their hooves.

Through the dizzying vision presented to him by the enchanted Eye, Archaon could see movement in the shadows. Along the opposite wall of the canyon, he could see the spiny silhouettes of rude wagons and ramshackle cages, dragged along by bipedal beasts of daemonic burden. The bars of the cages were barbed and twisted and held all manner of captured quarry. Half-breed prisoners. Wasteland spawn. Monsters and daemons. Prizes of every shape and size for Agrammon's ever-expanding collection.

A great black shape reared from one of the wagons where it had been making a fuss of the yapping pack of horned hunting hounds, whose tapering snouts had tracked the hunting party to the foul toad dragon. Rearing to full height and striding from the shadow of the canyon wall, a malformed hulk looked upon the failure of the beastfiend trappers to contain the toad dragon with sneering contempt. It appeared to be an ogre of some kind, warped by the corrupting insistence of the Southern Wastes. It was a horror to behold. Its flesh was black like the charcoal of a fire, while its back was monstrously hunched and its belly huge. The rest of the creature's frame sported a kilt of roughly stitched skins and furs that covered the monster's loins, passed across its belly and then over its shoulder before being pinned to its hunch on great spines that protruded from the hump. The furs did not conceal the creature's blubbery chest, which Archaon assumed the ogre exposed in honour of its patron power. The monster sported a second face – a malformed twin of some kind. Its eyes were misted and a milky black poison leaked from its mouth and dribbled down the ogre's colossal belly. One of the monster's arms was short and atrophied, while the other was muscle-bound and as thick as a tree.

'What is that foul creature?' Archaon put to his dread sorcerer.

'The brute is called Jharkill,' Sheerian said. 'He is the best of Lord Agrammon's hunters and the tyrant-keeper of his royal menagerie.' Archaon nodded as they watched the monster from afar. As the creature stomped forward from the shadows it gave some kind of unintelligible instruction to its hunter half-breeds. Beastfiends on the canyon ledges above the toad dragon hauled down on staffs of monstrous bone, prising boulders off the canyon side that crashed down either side of the cornered creature. The boulders carried between them a rough net of sinew that trapped the toad dragon and pinned it to the shoreline.

The toad dragon would not submit, however. As it thunder-croaked its amphibious fury, the thing exuded a slimy pus from its warty skin that allowed it to squirm and slide out from under the weighted net. As it bounded forward, the monster's grapnel-like tongue shot out from its gaping maw. The sharp tongue speared its way through the back of a fleeing beastfiend and out through its chest. There the fleshy grapnel opened and the tongue retracted like a whip, dragging the unfortunate creature back into the rubbery mouth. A second and third half-breed died similarly, trumpeting their horror from their tapering snouts as they were dragged to an acidic doom.

Stomping forward as the Slaaneshi beastfiends ran, Jharkill produced a great bow carved from the tusk of some previous victim-monster. Taking a bone arrow from a fur quiver that formed the back of its kilt, the ogre wiped the barbed arrowhead against its belly, smearing it in the poison that leaked from the mouth of its assimilated twin. Confidently stringing the bow as the toad dragon leapt forwards, the ogre held the arrow and hooked the sinew of the string on the clawed fingers of its atrophied arm. With its other monstrous appendage it pushed the tusk bow away from it, building a colossal amount of power in the barbarian weapon. As the toad dragon's belly heaved and its bulbous throat filled with the rancid contents of its stomach, the ogre let fly, sending the length of the arrow hurtling at the monster. With a thud the arrow hammered through the creature's scales and into the rubbery flesh of its shoulder.

The monster croaked in anguish, its bounding charge veering into a stumble and a splashing flounder through the shallows. Within seconds the poison had taken effect and the toad dragon was lurching this way and that up the shore, its eyes dazed and rheumy. The thing finally crashed into the bank, its warty back rising and falling with the exertion of breathing. Its mouth fell slackly open, as though it were half-asleep, and sizzling vomit seeped out, collecting about the creature's head.

Archaon watched with interest as Jharkill approached the monster and gave his bow to a beastfiend that had trotted forth. Several other half-breeds approached, cautious of their master's fury in the face of their failure. The ogre slipped a length of sinewy string from his furs, upon which were strung tiny skulls, pendants of glyph-etched bone and crude effigies carved in horn and petrified wood. He handed the string to another beastfiend, who moved nimbly forward through the black waters of the stream to tie the savage charm about the toad dragon's neck. This done, the half-breed returned with one of the effigies – a small, primitive sculpture of some four-legged monster. This the half-breed gave to Jharkill, who had taken up the shaman's staff. The staff towered over even Jharkill and bore the ragged banner that had initially identified the hunting party as belonging to the daemon lord Agrammon. Above the Ruinous symbols of Dark Gods and fell masters, Archaon could see a cross bar upon which a plethora of primitive effigies hung. They were all shapes and sizes. Some were crafted to represent creatures that stood on two legs, while others were figurines of four-legged monsters, like the toad dragon. Others cut such strange shapes and figures that it was difficult to imagine what monstrosities they represented. The staff jangled as Jharkill brought it down and the half-breed tied the effigy to one of the many strings of dried sinew that hung from the cross bar.

To Archaon's amazement, the ogre cracked his staff on the rock of the canyon floor, causing the toad dragon to immediately haul its drowsy bulk from the shallows. Jangling the staff towards the wagons and wheeled cages that were lined up against the opposite wall of the canyon, Jharkill seemed to control the creature's impulses. The monster groaned, as if in some private torment inflicted by the staff, and hobbled between the jabbing tridents of Jharkill's long-snouts and the snarling of his horned hunting hounds. It dragged itself up into a large cage that had been crafted to accommodate such a creature and lay miserably down.

With the cage secured, Jharkill directed word to be passed for the hunting party's wagons to roll on up the canyon. Archaon nodded with approval. On into the Gatelands, towards Agrammon's palace with cages full of creatures damned and monstrous for his daemon lord's collection. As the wagons and wheeled cages trundled away, the beastfiends of the hunting party trotted alongside, forming an escort. Jharkill walked up to one of the half-breeds, and Archaon recognised it as the creature that had initially fled in the face of the toad dragon's wrath. The beastfiend realised at the last moment that he was now to suffer his master's displeasure and turned his trident on the ogre too late. Jharkill snatched the beastfiend up from behind, ending the long-snout's trumpeting alarm by biting the half-breed's head off and tossing the decapitated body into the stream.

'Seen enough?' the sorcerer Sheerian asked.

'Enough to tell me how I'm going to get into Lord Agrammon's palace undetected,' Archaon said, turning and walking back to where Ograx and the Swords of Chaos had brought Archaon's army to a halt. 'We seek a daemon lord,' Archaon told them, with Sheerian translating his command into dark tongue for the bestial prince. 'A daemon lord who has something that belongs to me. I mean to get it back. There is a hunting party ahead, returning to this wretched daemon's palace. I mean to go ahead alone and join it by the time it reaches its destination.'

'You are going to steal the Steed of the Apocalypse?' Sheerian asked.

'I am,' Archaon said with supreme confidence.

'How will you find it, my lord?'

'The Eye will guide me,' Archaon said.

'I fear on this occasion, master, the Eye will not be enough,' the ancient mewled. 'For the daemonic beast Dorghar has many forms. It is a creature of ill will and monstrous temperament. I fear it will be difficult to locate.'

Archaon considered. Sheerian was, of course, correct.

'I am told this creature is the most prized of all Lord Agrammon's foetid specimens.'

'Some say that's true, my lord.'

'Then it will no doubt take pride of place in the greatest of the menagerie's cages and enclosures,' Archaon said. Sheerian nodded slowly, for the sorcerer could not fault the warlord's logic.

'You go alone, my lord?' Sheerian interrupted once again.

'Yes,' Archaon rumbled.

'Take at least your Swords of Chaos,' the sorcerer said. 'Agrammon's palace will be crawling with half-breeds, daemonkind and infernals.'

'Lord Agrammon must not know of our presence,' Archaon told the ancient with cold certainty. 'Or else all is lost. The fewer of us that enter the palace, the fewer there will be to alert the daemon lord to our presence and intentions.' Eins, Zwei and Drei stood in silence, but the stillness of their wings and the way they looked down at the canyon floor told Archaon that they were no happier about the prospect of their warlord entering an enemy palace alone. He was their warlord, however, and the order was observed without contention. Ograx the Great wasn't about to disagree. If the warlord Archaon wished to sacrifice himself on the palace altar of the daemon lord Agrammon, all the better. The bestial prince would simply take Archaon's barbarian horde for his own. For that reason, Archaon knew he could count on Ograx to hold the army back. 'Track the hunting party,' Archaon told him as Sheerian translated his words. He jabbed two fingers at the eye sockets of his skull-helm and then the same two fingers down at the canyon floor. 'Follow, but at a distance. Make camp near the palace and wait.'

Ograx wrapped his fat tongue around some choice words. Sheerian looked uncertain.

'For how long?' the sorcerer translated.

Archaon grunted. He had no sun or moon to guide them by. The only thing he could count on was the rhythm of bodily needs. Thirst. Hunger. Sleep.

'When the last gor of the horde has risen from slumber, on the third of such risings, three days as the rest of the world knows them will have passed. If I am not returned by then with my prize, then storm Agrammon's palace with every half-breed at your disposal.'

Ograx the Great nodded his head, heavy as it was with its crown of horn. As Archaon went to leave, Sheerian piped up once more.

'This steed, my lord,' the sorcerer said. 'It is one of the treasures of Chaos, is it not? A trapping by which the Everchosen of the Chaos gods might be known.'

'And possibly much more,' Archaon said, turning his head to one side. 'I would not risk so much for anything less.'

Archaon turned his back on the sorcerer. Ograx turned away also, intent on savagely issuing Archaon's orders to the horde through a brutal hierarchy of bulls, gors and taurs. He could feel Sheerian and the Swords of Chaos watching him go. He didn't look back. They had their orders and would obey them or there would be literal hell to pay. As Archaon trudged up through the wet gravel of the stream, he saw Giselle and Vier. The girl had wandered beyond the vanguard of the horde, waiting for Archaon's orders. She stood absently, up to her ankles in the freezing, black waters, the musty furs in which she was buried trailing through the meltwater stream. Vier hovered nearby in his own agonies, uselessly stretching his malformed wings. Archaon nodded to the Chaos warrior, whom Archaon had assigned as Giselle's minder and bodyguard. Vier bowed his head with difficulty, a signal of silent obedience.

When Archaon's gaze passed across Giselle, he found to his surprise that she was looking back. It was still the blank stare of horror relived – the kind of fixed mask of distant pain that Archaon had seen in soldiers returning from slaughter. The pair looked at one another across the umbra of the canyon. The flash of perpetual storms glowered through the ice above them and cast the pair in a ghoulish light. Archaon slowed. Giselle stumbled about in the water, her gaze unbroken. Fat droplets of meltwater plunked about them like rain. He thought she gave him a *look*. A softening of the lines about the mouth. A hardening of the eyes. It was an accusation glared across the twilight. He was leaving again. Leaving her in the care of madmen and monsters. Leaving her in this godforsaken place. Simply leaving her. Off to slip steel into beastflesh. To bring daemons to their knees. To carve the name Archaon in misery across the surface of the unknown world.

Archaon felt the pang of something he'd thought forgotten. Something dull and heavy in his chest. Responsibility? Guilt? Love? These were feelings fraught and fragile: sentiments unbecoming of the Everchosen of Chaos. With a will that burned with resistance the dark templar turned away, striding into his future with determination and fury at the miserable world, at the gods – both those that were Ruinous and those that were simply untrue – and at himself.

With Giselle's gaze burning into his armoured back, Archaon marched south, following the black stream and the curving progress of the crescent canyon. The wagon tracks and the hoofprints of the Slaaneshi hunting party were clear to follow and before long the twists and turns of the Scabyrinth became one colossal cleft. He no longer walked with the waters of the stream but against them, and before long Archaon felt the canyon floor ascend, rising to meet the plateau of the continental interior, the Gatelands and the sovereign territories of infernal royalty. He stomped his boot prints into the grit, passed water against the canyon wall and broke the stems of petrified foliage as he passed, all to make it easy for Ograx and the horde to follow his progress and scent. He even left the messy corpses of marauding creatures he happened upon to leave no doubt.

With the progress of the wagons slowing and the cavalcade winding its way up the canyon side, Archaon decided to make his move. Shouldering his shield, the dark templar advanced on the servants of Slaanesh. Hugging the crags and clefts and moving rapidly between the cover offered by boulders and sparse, black foliage, Archaon crept up on Jharkill's wagon train. Darting out from between huge rocks that lined the zigzag ascent, Archaon made a heavy run uphill towards stragglers of the cavalcade rearguard. Grabbing beastfiends from behind by their horns and their snouts and savagely snapping them around, the dark templar despatched the creatures. With the rearmost cage wagon bumping its way up the incline, dragged by two bipedal steeds and a beastfiend skinner at the reins whipping the beasts of burden with delirious abandon, Archaon made his move.

Unbolting the cage, which seemed to have been fashioned from the bones of some great Wasteland beast, Archaon found himself face to face with some kind of sabre-toothed hellcat. The thing looked half starved but unleashed a heart-stopping roar. Archaon pushed his way into the cage, infuriating the beast further and prompting the hellcat to leap at him with its trap-jaw open. The Chaos warrior didn't have time to tangle with the creature and had to take care of it before the beastfiend skinner noticed the commotion in the back of the wagon.

Grabbing the hellcat by its sabre fangs, Archaon turned aside the creature's savage attack. Bringing the blood-matted fur of its mane under one arm, Archaon tightened his lock around the beast's neck. Scrabbling back with its cruel claws, the hellcat attempted to extricate itself from the Chaos warrior's stranglehold. Gritting his teeth and trying to keep the creature's struggles to a minimum, Archaon squeezed for all he was worth. The brute's snapping and snarling suddenly changed to a throttled whimper. Finally something felt like it was breaking within the creature's muscular neck. As the struggle subsided and Archaon lowered the hellcat's emaciated body to the cage floor, the dark templar released the beast.

Catching his breath, Archaon sagged. Around the hellcat's broken neck, Archaon found the sinew string that carried Jharkill's shamanistic skulls, glyph-pendants and carved effigies. Slipping it off the creature's great head and around it sabre teeth, Archaon hung the cursed thing about his own neck. Resting his pauldron against the dead beast, Archaon heaved its carcass across the floor of the cage and out of the rear door. As the hellcat's lifeless body rolled back down the incline and off the edge of the narrow, rocky trail, Archaon slid his shield off his shoulder and slipped *Terminus* from its scabbard. He found a suitable hiding place for both sword and shield between the wheels, in the mangle of bones and sinew that made up the underside of the wagon bed. He then proceeded to bolt the cage door closed and lock himself within it like the myriad other specimens Jharkill and his hunting party were returning to the palace menagerie.

Checking that the beastfiend skinner was still fully involved with driving the infernal beasts that were dragging the wagon up the meandering incline, Archaon sat back against the barbed bones of the cage. Resting his own aching bones, Archaon tried to relax. He jangled the charms and effigies hanging about his neck. He would play the role of the compliant prisoner. He watched through the bars as the Southern Wastes juddered by. After a torturous ascent up the canyon wall, the hunters' train of wagons set out across the nightmare lands that afflicted the continental interior. The sky was a churning tempest of eddies and whirling blackness, lanced by spidery bolts of unnatural lightning that seared across it like a web. Here the elemental ferocity of wind, ice and hail lost its potency.

Archaon couldn't count the number of times he had almost frozen to death out on the Southern Wastes or been burned alive in some fiery pit or river of lava. The Ruinous wilderness had thrown everything it could at the dark templar. The Gatelands existed at the pleasure of whim and dark fancy. The realities of the cold and harsh weather were not constants there and so as the wagon train creaked and squeaked across the blasted, hellish landscape Archaon was treated to all manner of atmospheric madness from above. Storms whose thunder only existed in the mind, as a skull-splitting ache of the head. Infernal lightning that struck the ground, creating birthing pits for savage entities. Pellets of lead that fell like musket balls from the tumultuous heavens. Clouds of soot and flame that seemed to consume one another like monsters battling for supremacy across the sky. Dew that settled on everything like spots of black ink. Glowing banks of mist that swept in to change the very landscape across which it drifted.

The land below the bone-jarring progress of the cage wagon was little better. The wheels crunched through shattered obsidian while the black clouds of dust, kicked up by the wagons and the beasts hauling them, willed change on everything it coated. Hellquakes thundered up from the depths of the Wastes – unforgotten echoes of the catastrophic collapse that destroyed the polar gate and spilled ruin and death into the world. With every moaning tremor and furious rumble, the architecture of derelict palaces – warped, grand and ancient – rained about them. The battlefields inbetween were landscapes of carnage. Infernal bodies upon bodies, mummified into the land and covered with slaughter anew. The wagon train weaved through the harsh terrain of corpse mounds, ridges created by the fossilised remains of toppled monstrosities and fields of rib and bone that made for a bumpy passage.

The wagon train halted several times. A mire of carcasses and ichor forced the cavalcade into a detour, while Jharkill and his beastfiends suffered the rabid assaults of infernal skirmishers, issuing forth from the palaces of the damned and fortresses of the mighty. Jharkill added their corpses to the surrounding slaughter before moving ever on. South. Towards the gate. Towards the palace of his royal master. Archaon sat against the barbed bone of the cage like a good prisoner. He wasn't exactly enjoying the ride but he had walked across so much of the dark southern continent that he enjoyed at least not trudging through some blizzard or snow drift.

Trumpeting calls of alarm from the Slaaneshi beastfiends alerted Archaon to an approaching problem. Grasping the bars with his gauntlets and peering about, the dark templar could see little. When the black outline of a distant ruin moved, Archaon couldn't quite believe what he was looking at. The black towers of the derelict palace suddenly reassumed their former baroque glory, almost as though the furious warpflame that had gutted it had never been. The towers bucked skyward slightly, leading Archaon to believe that the land beneath it had moved. And it had. As the gleaming towers of black stone and brass majesty collapsed in on themselves and the walls of the fortress-palace toppled, a giant cloud of dust and corruption reached up from the calamity and into the heavens. Resting his skull-helm against the bone bars of the cage, Archaon saw that there was a ripple of the past – or possibly the future – passing through the Wasteland itself. Like a rogue wave at sea, the landswell had moved beneath the palace, restoring it to its former glory, before rippling through its foundations and destroying it again.

Now it was surging across the Wastes, bringing brief life to the mummified, mangled and long-dead that were quietly rotting on the ancient battlefields where they were butchered. Thrown up into the air by the rippling force, the warrior daemons, beastfiends and spawn screeched the horror of their last moments, thrashing and snapping before falling back behind the swell and reassuming the entangled stillness of the grave. There was little Archaon could do but grab the bars of the cage and hold on. As the black earth rose beneath the wagon, Archaon was suddenly confronted by the horror of intermingled bodies. Rather than wood, the wagon and its cage was largely constructed of bone, horn and sinew – the dead being a plentiful resource in the Southern Wastes and trees sparse. The dead whose bones had been meshed and tied together to create the cage were brought back momentarily to terrible life. As the wagon tumbled it was as if Archaon had been trapped inside a shrieking spawn.

With the moment of horror passed and the bars of his cage age-browned bone once more, Archaon found himself on his back. The wagon had been knocked over onto its side, and as the dark templar picked himself up he could see the landswell bringing the abomination of life to the battlefields of the east. With Jharkill barking gruff orders and long-snouts moving along the wagon train to secure beasts and right wagons, Archaon waited. The beastfiends got behind the bars of his cage and pushed the rickety vehicle back onto the braced ribs of its bone wheels.

One of Jharkill's bestial underlings gave him the blankness of its white eyes, seeming not to remember placing him there. A tongue slithered out from its long snout and tasted the warp-curdled air. Jharkill had collected so many specimens for his infernal master – monsters, savage beasts, spawn and daemonkind – that it was impossible to keep track. Taking Archaon for some warrior-daemon in his hell-forged plate, the creature eventually moved on, trumpeting at skinners to get their beasts and wagons moving.

Archaon cast a glance down the corpse road behind the wagon. Somewhere down that road, Ograx the Great led Archaon's horde after him. Looking forward, beyond the beastfiend skinner and his pack-daemons, Archaon could see the dread that lay ahead. The Gatelands. The storming balelight of the beyond, blazing for the heavens where the polar portal used to be. The serrated silhouette of infernal palaces encircled the raging gateway like a black crown, and before long the wagon train found itself in the shadow of one of the largest.

The road up to the palace of the daemon lord Agrammon was a well-worn path in the mummified remains of those foolish enough to have attacked it. The track weaved its way between colossal fragments of black stone, half buried in the cursed earth. Their size and grandeur led Archaon to believe that they were fragments of the polar gate that used to tower over the dread lands of daemonic sovereignty. Other hunting parties had joined them on the approach, and Archaon got the impression that Agrammon's ever-expanding menagerie was an endless enterprise. No monstrous specimen would be so impressive, no daemon so infamous or spawn so exotically repulsive as to sate the daemon lord's appetites and complete his collection.

CHAPTER III

'...sits Agrammon, daemon lord of a palace proud, in the Gatelands of infernal sovereignty. A serpentine nightmare of slithering indulgence and grasping tentacle, it is the Cagelord, a turn-key for the Prince of Excess, a collector, an enslaver, a master of the hoard. Its madness is greed, but not for gems or metals precious, not for cravings sweet or more land than a daemon can use. He is a gatherer of the flesh, a presenter of prisoners, of creatures exotic, of beasts infernal and myriad, keeper of a menagerie monstrous, about his palace proud.'

– Horror-Scribes of the Endless Mountain,
Bestiarum Diabolika

The Gatelands
The Southern Wastes
Horns Harrowing: Season of the Raw

As the rickety wagons closed on the main gate, Archaon saw that the massive exterior wall was made of metal. This came as a surprise to the Chaos warrior, since he had seen precious little of it in the frozen Southern Wastes. He assumed that Agrammon had the ore mined from beneath the Gatelands and processed for his needs, although Archaon couldn't tell what kind of metal it was. The walls were a bold black and covered in sculpted barbs, wicked skewers, spikes, hooks and grapnels. All were sharpened to a flesh-snagging point and glistened with poisons that sent victims into spasms. Archaon knew this as he saw the beast-fiends and daemons that had impaled themselves on the wall and were dancing a jig of delight to their death.

Increasingly the Chaos warlord thought that he had made the right decision. The twisted wall alone was designed to shred any attacker desperate enough to scale it. A direct assault by his horde would have resulted in horrific casualties. If he were to be captured by the daemon lord Agrammon or fail in his objective then it still might. Archaon licked at his dry lips.

A single tower extended high above the palace walls, made of the same twisted metal. It was covered in downwards slanting spikes like an urchin, making a climb almost impossible. Looking up at the cloud-grazing height of the citadel, its bulbous bell tower and the pincer-shaped crescent that crowned the tower spire, Archaon thought such a climb would be suicide regardless. As the train of wagons and cages rattled in through the twisted gatehouse, Archaon saw Jharkill talking to a daemonette – one of many Archaon saw stationed about the palace, standing in armoured corsets and executioner's hoods. They clutched sickle-spears and walked up and down the menagerie thoroughfares.

The colossal courtyard between the palace wall and the

citadel was the metal of cages and the black stone in which the barbed and twisted bars were set. Cage had been built upon tangled cage, three, four, and sometimes five stories above the black gravel of the thoroughfare. They had been built around one another in all sizes and configurations. They were uniform only in that they were woefully insufficient to house the captive creatures inside. As the wheels of Archaon's wagon hissed through the gravel, he saw monstrosities undreamed of, daemonic abominations, god-cursed spawn and bestial slaves with exotic fur and extravagant horns, housed miserably together as a single collection. He saw things with wings, things all limb, beasts of claw and fang, creatures of scale, blubber and armoured skin, great monsters that slithered, malformed titans and packs of lesser infernals that hissed through the barbs and bars of their cages at the new arrivals. The menagerie was colossal and its number of deplorable specimens impossible to count.

What struck Archaon instantly was the stench. The ripe funk of thousands of creatures all eating, defecating, living and dying in close proximity. The cramped conditions were nothing less than wretched. Archaon gagged as the reek overwhelmed him. The noise too was unbearable, the bestial misery palpable. The Chaos warlord had never heard such a chorus of woe. The menagerie was a nest of caged suffering: a collection of creatures, sitting in their own filth, waiting to die. All wore Jharkill's shamanistic tokens of obedience about their necks, or at least what passed for necks on the more warped specimens. Long-snout menials moved between the cages ladling slop and throwing rancid meat between the bars, but Archaon suspected that the only thing keeping the creatures of the menagerie alive was the unnatural hardiness of their warped constitutions. What pleasure Lord Agrammon could derive from this, Archaon thought, the Ruinous Gods only knew.

The wagon train trundled around the exterior wall before the gravel thoroughfare started to work its way inwards in a concentric spiral, finally arriving, Archaon expected, at the centre citadel. It was an insane design. It was completely impractical, unless your objective was to slavishly admire every exhibit, in every cage, in the entire menagerie. It occurred to Archaon that Agrammon had designed the spiralling layout of the twisted collection with exactly that in mind.

Progress stopped and started along the wagon train as dead exhibits were dragged from the barbed nightmare of their cages and replaced with new captures. The monstrous cadavers were then loaded on the wagons for dumping on the Wastes. As the cavalcade worked its way inward, Archaon realised that his turn was coming. Clasping his gauntlets around one of the bars of his cage, he hauled on the bone – quietly but insistently – so that it snapped. Archaon left the broken bar in place. It was not the only thing he would be leaving with the wagon. His shield and the blade *Terminus* were hidden under the wagon bed, between the wheels. Upon re-earning his freedom, the Chaos warrior would need them and so had broken the bar as a means of identifying the wagon once more.

Finally, in the doom-laden shadow of the citadel, the wagon came to a stop. The long-snout skinner climbed down and proceeded to open the cage under the infernal gaze of three daemonettes that had moved in on the wagon. Razored wire spiralled through the abundance of their dread flesh while drool continually dribbled from mouths filled with needle-teeth, working its way down their voluptuousness like a river finding the path of least resistance. One of the daemonettes held several hounds on a spiked chain. The creatures had tapering muzzles like the beastfiends in Agrammon's dark service and snuffled the ground about Archaon's feet as he was led down from the wagon.

A second daemonette used the crescent claw at the end of her sickle-spear to motion the Chaos warrior on. She looked on him through the slits of her executioner's hood with a predatory fascination, pushing him towards a cage opening with the curved blade of the sickle headpiece. Archaon took a moment to hold his ground. He wanted to be sure that he hadn't indeed become one of Jharkill's slave specimens and a permanent exhibit in Lord Agrammon's menagerie. Whether it was because the shamanistic tokens about his neck had been intended for another captive or because the damned wards that weaved their way through his pallid flesh like a network of veins countered such primitive charms and enchantments, Archaon didn't care. All he needed to know was that he wasn't going to spend the rest of his days voluntarily stinking out a cage at the bottom of the world.

Archaon's reluctance only angered his infernal keepers. A third daemonette slashed at the gravel with a barbed whip, while her rank compatriot pushed Archaon harshly towards the cage with her sickle-spear. Nodding and raising a gauntlet, the Chaos warrior approached his twisted coop. Two long-snouts were carrying the rotting half-eaten remains of a beastfiend with two bovine heads and interlocking horns, an aberration that must have taken Lord Agrammon's fancy. Climbing up the thick bars of the enclosure below, Archaon hauled himself up through the opening of his own cage – the cage that the corruption-dribbling corpse of the half-breed had just vacated. The daemonette slapped the bars with a claw and said something suggestive and unintelligible before bolting the cage closed.

As the daemonettes, the long-snouts and the wagons moved on, Archaon took in the degradation of his surroundings. The twisted metal of his cage made up the walls, floor and ceiling of several others, for the enclosure itself was enclosed with but one set of bars facing the thoroughfare for observation. All manner of monstrosity and warp-sculpted deformity was present. Above Archaon the cage housed some kind of huge carrion bird – a thing rotten and spoiled in itself but impossibly alive. It pecked at the bars and itself with its great bone-crushing beak and let loose an almost constant stream of milky excrement through the bars into Archaon's enclosure. The Chaos warrior moved about the mess in the limited space he had, allowing the stinking ooze to splatter a nest of blind wyrms in the cage below. The obscene creatures didn't seem to mind at all, their bulbous heads only emerging from the rippling sheath of their squirming bodies to snap at the cage roof and Archaon's boots with their hook-toothed maws.

Casting his gaze through the forest of black bars, Archaon saw a pair of hairless giant rats, conjoined at the tail: one twin feeding on the flesh of the other. A feral spawn jabbered and threw itself mindlessly at its cage door, while stabbing at itself with great bone scythes that might once have been wings. An almost constant stream of mind-splitting screams emanated from a thing nearby that hung from the ceiling bars of its cage by a monstrous tail, while its pectoral wings dangled about it like the fins of some shark of the sky or ocean depths. Below it a daemon beast, some great steed or juggernaut, slowly rusted in a pool of its own ichor, groaning and moaning like a guttering forge. On the other side of his cage Archaon could see that one huge creature had given up entirely. Either out of monstrous habit or spite it had blighted its enclosure with a haze of silk, forming a web in which a pulsing cocoon still gave the impression of horrid life.

Of the things that had a face, from his cage Archaon could only see two. The first inhabited the darkness of a cage across the thoroughfare. It claw-stomped up and down the enclosure, rearing its emaciated body up on its hind legs. Even at skin and bone it was twice the size of Archaon and its flesh was red raw with sores and infection. Patches of worn fur swarmed with fat mites feeding off the creature and driving it to distraction. An infested mane hung about the creature's monstrous, fang-filled jaws and ran down its back between the shredded leathery stumps of two mite-eaten wings and down the length of a tail that was shot through with thagomizer spikes. The creature stopped, seeming to know that it was being watched, before grabbing the bars with its fore-claws and bringing its daemonic face forward with glowering malice. Like the rest of its body the flesh of its face was a mesh of scratches and dappled irritation, but within it and above the fixed snarl of its leonine muzzle, its eyes betrayed a feral sadness. A knowing. A suffering that betrayed an almost human intelligence.

The creature stared at Archaon and Archaon stared back. The Chaos warrior could feel the monster's hate across the open space. The druchii of the north called such beasts manticores: monsters crafted of the Wastes, of unrivalled ferocity and spite. They were also treated with reverence and respect, since they were among the most cunning of Ruinous predators. Archaon had heard that rudimentary speech had even been witnessed in some creatures, if only to scorn the attempts of druchii hunters to capture them. Jharkill had bagged his prize, however, enslaving the scabby beast with his shamanic charms and caging it for his master's pleasure.

'Don't worry about him,' a voice came through the bars in dark tongue. Looking around Archaon saw a legless horror hanging from the ceiling bars of the cage next to his own. The thing had gangly, long arms, black skin and appeared to be nothing more than a truncated torso and a squashed head. 'He just wants to be free, see?' The half-daemon gibbered to Archaon and itself. 'Thoughts. Thoughts,' the creature said, slapping its narrow skull with a ghoulishly long palm as it dangled from the bars on the other. 'Thoughts like that will kill you faster than the food around here. Hope. A dangerous thing is hope. It is Lord Agrammon's weapon of choice. Oh yes, yes, yes, yes, yes. He'll get you hoping all right. Craving the impossible. Giving you an appetite for a freedom that just can't be had. No, no, no, no, no. It's the only thing to give you an appetite in this food-forsaken place.'

Archaon said nothing, allowing the creature's sanity to unravel before him. The rising volume of the half-daemon's voice and the creature's captive excitability was drawing daemonette keepers towards them. That, Archaon did not need. Not if he were to effect a quiet escape from his confinement. The legless creature hung by one willowy arm. He jabbed a long finger at the manticore opposite. 'He knows,' the thing jabbered on to itself. 'He knows.' Then to a passing daemonette with three snuffling hounds on a spiked chain: 'She knows.' He blew the horror a kiss, producing from her both a seductive snarl and a stream of abuse, in an infernal language that Archaon did not understand. Hanging there the creature bowed his head and lowered his eyes, mumbling a theatrical apology. Archaon watched the daemonette pass. Even when out of sight he could hear the rhythmic echo of her spear rattling along the bars – waking and provoking.

Archaon turned. The daemonette's spear had disturbed the thing in the cocoon. The sickening sound of swarming emanated from the pulsing hub of the silken haze. Whatever monstrous creature lay within was long dead, Archaon realised. Its body had been eaten from the inside out by thousands of warped spiderlings: translucent creatures the size of a hand that scuttled on stabbing talons. Their mouths were framed with fat fangs and within their abdomens squirmed a single eyeball that stared about their new surroundings. Archaon watched as, drawn by some kind of collective vision, the creatures descended on threads and crawled towards unfortunates in the other cages.

Turning back towards the hanging torso swinging before him on its arms, Archaon found the thing was licking its lips as it watched the spiders biting and swarming their thrashing victims.

'We feast tonight!' it gibbered before swinging back and forth across its cage. Archaon casually brushed a baby arachnid off his pauldron that had silently drifted down from the cage above. He squelched the miniature monster under his boot. The half-daemon was back before the bars, spilling over with madness. 'Stay or leave. Leave or stay,' the thing repeated before jabbing a finger at the sky. 'There's nothing out there for us. Death. Destruction. A becoming of that which we are not. Do I stay because of this?' It rattled the string of shamanistic charms about its slender neck. 'No. I stay for the safety of a cage. I stay for the food. I have a purpose here. I exist to bring pleasure to others – if not myself. Hope for nothing more than a wretched captivity and you cannot be disappointed. Oh no. That's what our infested friend over there doesn't seem to understand,' the half-daemon said, swinging about its cage, bar to bar, with its long arms and spindly fingers. 'Am I right? I'm right, aren't I? Yes, yes, yes, yes, yes. Over there with only his fleas for company. He paces. Paces. Paces. I fall asleep, he's pacing. I wake, he's pacing. I rant, I rave, I kill the thing in the next cage, he's pacing. Do you know what they call him? The diseased one over there?'

Archaon shook his head slowly.

'Mange,' the half-daemon chuckled darkly, 'for it is not just the creature on show in the cage but also the wonderful collection of mites that feed on his monstrous flesh. Where do you think you're going monster?' the half-daemon called across. 'Perhaps he's dreaming. Dreaming of somewhere high. Somewhere desolate and lonely, where the prey is fleet and the company wanting. Somewhere a monstrosity can... just... be.'

Archaon looked over at the manticore in its miserable state, standing on its hind legs, clutching the bars with trembling claws and glaring with silent malice and suffering. The menagerie was crowded with mindless monsters, warplings, slaves to the darkness and the low creatures of the world. While they all suffered as part of Lord Agrammon's legendary collection, it was the prisoners of the mind and not just the body that suffered the most. Savage creatures and abominations simply endured. Some no differently in their cages than anywhere else. Those that thought. Those that felt. Those that hoped. They were doubly doomed. The half-daemon babbled insanely but it was right about that. Beyond the ravages of imprisonment and starvation suffered by the caged captives, hope broke the spirit. It had broken the half-daemon, who – for all Archaon knew – might have been an exhibit in the menagerie for as long as it had existed.

'It's never going to happen,' the half-daemon jeered across the thoroughfare. Again, Archaon became concerned over the noise and the attention it might garner. 'Accept it, beast.

You've soared over your last mountain. You've slain your last piece of prey. You'll never be alone again. You hear? You hear?' the mad thing called. 'Not so long as I'm here, creature of horizons lost.'

Archaon looked from the glowering manticore back to the half-daemon. The Chaos warrior had heard enough. Had waited long enough. Based upon the time it had taken to work its way around the concentric curve of the outer thoroughfare, Archaon estimated the wagon train would be closing once more on the inner thoroughfare. Several times he thought he had heard the movement of the cavalcade, the roar of beasts and the opening of cages, but with the babbling half-daemon pouring madness in his ears it was difficult to tell. Beyond the growing infestation of spiderlings, the half-daemon was dangling one grasping arm through the bars of Archaon's cage. Despite the disarming distraction of the daemon's blatant insanity, Archaon knew that it meant him harm and had probably been responsible for the death of the cage's previous occupant.

'Want to hear a secret?' the half-daemon whispered harshly. He motioned with a single long finger, his willowy arm extended all the way through Archaon's bars. The Chaos warrior approached.

'Want to be one?' Archaon put to the murderous half-daemon. He grabbed the monster's hideous hand in his gauntlets and heaved. The creature's head smashed into the twisted metal. It gibbered and screeched its surprise. Archaon hauled on the sinewy daemonflesh again, yanking the thing's head and wretched torso into the bars – again and again. The thing had no doubt meant to do the same to Archaon and feed on his carcass – the fate suffered by the previous occupant. Archaon heaved mercilessly, allowing the creature to pull itself back before the Chaos warrior hauled it once more into the bludgeoning metal. Something suddenly went *crack* and the creature's hold on the ceiling bars went slack. As the half-daemon became a broken mound on the cage floor, bloody and still, Archaon dropped its arm and walked to the door of his cage. He found the manticore staring intensely at him, the beast's eyes glistening with bestial satisfaction.

'I fear your view is much improved, monster,' Archaon said. The creature blinked the baleful yellow of its eyes at him. Looking up and down the thoroughfare that curved between the lines of cages, Archaon lifted his boot and stamped down on the cage door. The simple lock shattered – for it was not metal and mechanism that kept the creatures of Lord Agrammon's menagerie captive. As Archaon walked across the deserted gravel, the manticore leant out. A stringy drool began to cascade from the monster's maw. It tasted something. Archaon hoped that it was freedom rather than the prospect of fresh flesh. 'Or perhaps, creature of darkness, you would prefer a view clear of cage bars altogether.' Before the door of the manticore's barbed enclosure, Archaon slipped the sinew string of Jharkill's charms and effigies from over his head and dropped it on the ground. He stamped down on the cursed thing, crushing the tokens of glyph-scored bone and stone into the gravel. 'Before I give you back the skies, great beast,' Archaon told him. 'Might I trouble you for a diversion? A settling of scores perhaps with your jailers or simply an opportunity to sate your all-consuming hunger. You look like you could use a meal.'

The manticore hissed through its sabre teeth. The stench upon which the words wafted almost made the Chaos warrior gag. Archaon could feel the harm the monster meant him through the bars. The Chaos warrior realised that he could be the meal the manticore needed.

He shook his head.

'You don't look that stupid, beast,' Archaon said. 'The last hundred things that tried to eat me are dead. Besides,' the Chaos warrior told it, recalling his battle with the *Yien-Ya-Long*. 'I cause horrible indigestion.'

Archaon reached through the bars of the manticore's cage. The monster growled as the Chaos warrior's gauntlets felt through its infested mane. Slipping Jharkill's bridle of charms from the manticore's head, he let it fall to the cage floor by the creature's clawed feet. The manticore looked down at the thing of dark enchantments and then up at Archaon. The Chaos warrior watched the beast stamp down on the charms and crush them into the floor. Grabbing the bars, Archaon heaved at the cage door and tore it open.

'Beast,' the Chaos warrior said, 'you are free. Unleash yourself on those who would see you back behind these bars.'

As Archaon stepped aside, the manticore fell down onto four feet. The creature was disgustingly lithe – all claw, slavering jaw and ribcage with a spiked tail flowing after it. Launching from the cage – its new-found freedom firing wasted limbs and appetite – the manticore tore up the gravel thoroughfare and bounded off the barbed bars of the opposite cages. Watching the monster surge away, Archaon turned and climbed up the cageside.

The creatures within screeched and spat at the Chaos warrior as he hauled himself up the twisted bars. Atop the row of cages, with monstrosities roaring their displeasure below, Archaon could see the citadel in all of its serrated glory. The crescent crowning the tower pointed its talon-tips towards the broiling sky. Archaon could hear the shrieking trumpet calls of beastfiends and long-snouted hounds. Daemonettes were hiss-squealing. The manticore had bolted up the walkway and ripped through the first of Lord Agrammon's infernal servants it found.

Keeping himself chest-down on the cagetop, Archaon saw bloody bits of hound and beastfiend flying through the air. Suddenly Archaon heard the sound of claws on bars. Something was climbing up towards him. Moments later the horned head of a daemonette rose above the cage. The creature's wire-threaded face betrayed an infernal dread. Disgust flooded the Chaos warrior and he bent his armoured knee to kick the creature off. Then the daemonette's horrid face changed. From below, Archaon heard the roar of the monster Mange. The daemonette's pincers scraped across the bars as she was torn back down the cages and into the savagery below. With an echoing screech, the jailer was torn apart.

The wretched call of horns rose from the spiral-thoroughfare, drawing daemonettes and hounds down on the escaped monster. Archaon nodded his appreciation. Getting to his feet, the Chaos warrior padded across the top of the cages, perching on the edge and looking down into the next concentric thoroughfare. The train of caged wagons was there, where Archaon's ear had put it. Horrid beastfiends with tapering snouts and serpentine tongues were moving monstrosities, daemonkind and warped beasts from their bone cages to their twisted enclosures. The miserable creatures wanted nothing more than to visit their wrath on Lord Agrammon's keepers, like Mange was doing on the thoroughfare beyond, but Jharkill's primitive charms kept their monstrous natures in check. All they knew was suffering, despair and the need to obey. Archaon watched the cavalcade trundle along through the gravel under the watchful eyes of daemonettes, standing with their sickle-spears while snapping their arm-pincers at the beastfiends to move the caravan on.

Archaon noticed his cage wagon with the broken bar. Watching the daemonettes snap their claws and crack their barbed whips at the trumpeting beastfiends, Archaon dropped down onto the gravel. Keeping cages and their monstrous occupants between him and Lord Agrammon's watch-daemons, Archaon sprinted towards the wagon and grabbed the axle, skidding down between the curved bone of the wheels. Allowing the vehicle to crunch overhead, the Chaos warrior slipped his shield and the templar blade *Terminus* out from the crude workings of the ribs and sinew of the wagon underside.

Rolling aside before the wagons of the next train rumbled forth, Archaon slipped the blessed blade of Sigmar into its back-scabbard and loosened the buckles on the weighty shield, sitting the eight-pointed star over one shoulder like a dark penance. He ran at the cageside of the opposite enclosures, the impact and rattling ascent disturbing the slumber of some three-headed brute and rousing the restrained savagery of a chimeric nightmare overhead. As he hauled himself atop the cages he set a flock of blood-sucking imps to whirling about their foetid enclosure in a maelstrom of wing and screeching ugliness.

This process the Chaos warrior repeated: climbing cages, dropping into the concentric spiral of gravel thoroughfares and crossing the keeper-haunted pathways unseen. He did this in the spiked shadow of the citadel, thrown across the stinking menagerie of the daemon lord by the bright hellshine of the great Southern Gate – working his way ever inwards, through the hoarded misery that was Agrammon's ever-unfinished collection of exotic monstrosity. There the daemon lord kept his most prized exhibits.

CHAPTER IV

'Today we sighted land. A frozen coast of darkness and storm. The horizon burned with eruption and hellfire. On the wind we heard the sounds of suffering and rage. The crew were unsettled and I came to know how my ambitions had damned us all. To the glad hearts of all on board I ordered prayers said and sails set for the safety of the north. This cursed land is no place for god-fearing men. I know that now.'

– Rodrigo de Velasca, captain's log, *The Plutón*
(lost)

The Gatelands
The Southern Wastes
Horns Harrowing: Season of the Raw

From the cagetops of the inner thoroughfare and the curving promenade of the tower-approach, Archaon saw the twisted enclosures of barb and bar built up around the black-brick exterior wall of the citadel. In the cages he saw some of Agrammon's most prized specimens. Great daemons tethered to the tower wall with gargantuan chains of silver sat in an eternity of misery on floor-carved wards and bindings. Spawn of exquisite grotesqueness and warp-sculpted grandeur. Monsters of every size and shape – crafted of nightmare, savagery and world-withering hate.

The enclosures about the citadel were guarded by a small army of daemonettes. The creatures' black leather armour was sewn into their obscene flesh with razored wire. Their pincers constantly clicked and snapped, while filthy locks of midnight hair danced entrancingly about the depravity of their bodies in braids, tails and blankets of black. Their faces alternated between horrific masks of needle-toothed glee and ghoulish, shrieking displeasure as they slashed the black stone of the promenade with whips and jabbed their sickle-spears through the bars of enclosures.

As Archaon worked his way across the cagetops unseen, ignoring the suffering, rancour and pleading from below, he looked for his prize. The fourth treasure of Chaos that deviant destiny had seen fit to hide in such a benighted place. Dorghar, daemonic Steed of the Apocalypse. He could not see the monster, however. In the enclosure opposite was a gargantuan thing. A giant. A colossal savage long dead, its mummified flesh and brown bones sat wrapped in shredded furs and tattered skins. Its skull was a massive horned horror of empty sockets and tombstone teeth and its towering spine curved into a malformed hunch. The corpse giant sat in the enclosure, barely a fit for the twisted cage, in unliving despair and deathly stillness. Through the tatters of its clothing and the ribs of its barrel chest, Archaon could see the green curselight of sorcery that allowed the long-rotten twisted colossus to live beyond the grave.

Further around Archaon saw a great bird of fiery purple

feather and strange flame that writhed about its body like a living hell. The cage floor was carpeted in the ash of plucked feathers as the demented bird half pecked itself to death in its miserable captivity, only to rise again. In the vivid inferno about the dark phoenix Archaon could see the torched souls of the great bird's victims thrashing in torment and reaching out for bars of the cage.

A shovel-nosed dragon was curled up in the next cage, its armoured skin a nest of crystalline shards instead of scales. The tips were blackened with old blood and scraps of flesh where the creature had sidled past its last shredded victim. The creature trembled with some kind of affliction or distemper, making its razor-sharp shards rattle like glass against one another, creating a haunting cacophony.

Beyond the dragon was a brute of a monster, its armoured hide stained red with the slaughter it perpetually sought. Its head was a horn-crested nightmare within which snapped a crowded maw of fang and ferocity. A multitude of false eyes peered out from the abomination as its tree-trunk arms and the mountain of muscle that was its torso tore at its chains. Even wearing Jharkill's crude enchantments, the slaughterbrute seemed in a constant state of murderous agitation.

Then he saw it. In the enclosure next to the blood-drenched beast was a maelstrom of black and spectral flame. A furious miasma whose searing blaze and silky shadow could not settle on one midnight form or another. One moment it was a thing of slithering menace, the next a chitinous midnight horror. Its darknid form swirled from one shape to the next. A thing of leathery wings and serrated maw. An extravagantly horned head on a wall of steaming muscle. A monstrous pig of twisted tusk and hunched back. A blubbery creature of flipper and shaggy mane. A tentacular beast of bulbous head and innumerable eyes. A dark, reptilian monster of snapping jaws, powerful legs and whipping tail. A chimeric fusion of predators and their prey.

Looking this way and that, Archaon dropped down from the cage and rolled through the grit. His appearance in the thoroughfare drew a raucous response from the miserable beasts in the surrounding cages. Above Archaon, the citadel – spined like a great towering urchin reaching for the churning vortex of cloud and darkness above – blacked out the sickening glare spewing from the Southern Gate. Despite the welcome darkness, the Chaos warrior felt exposed. Lord Agrammon's prize beasts were roaring, moaning and screeching to the dread heavens and Archaon knew that the monstrosities guarding such wonders could see as well in the darkness as the Chaos warrior could see in the day – not that Archaon had seen the true light of day for a long time.

Thoroughfares beyond, he could hear Mange taking his revenge on such wretched custodians. Daemonettes squealed both their agony and joy as the monstrous manticore savaged them. Beastfiends trumpeted their alarm, calling more infernal sentries down on the escaped beast. Mange was not the only flesh-hungry predator bounding down on them on all fours, snarling heads from slender shoulders. Archaon pictured him rearing up like the beastfiends who sat about him in pieces. He could hear the manticore liberate other lethal monstrosities from cage and curse, adding their unleashed fury to his own.

Padding across the thoroughfare with the light crunch of a thief, Archaon walked past the twisted enclosures of Agrammon's most prized and deviant wonders. Stopping before the daemonic darkness that raged in ever-changing torment and flame, Archaon knew that he had found *his* prize. The fourth treasure of Chaos. Dorghar, Steed of the Apocalypse. Doomed to wretched captivity here, at the bottom of the world, kept at the pleasure of a hoarding daemon lord.

With the Chaos warrior standing before the enclosure gate, the swirling transformations seemed to slow. The fire and shadow drifted to a stop. The beast was a miasma of black that watched Archaon as an unbroken steed might the approach of a foolhardy rider. Archaon felt the daemon's hate. He had no doubt it meant him harm. As shadow bled into shadow and the darkness intensified, the creature settled on a form. Archaon stepped forward and gripped the warped bars of the enclosure gate. It was as though the infernal monstrosity had reached into his mind and selected its appearance from the foetid dungeon-depths of his memory. The darkness solidified into the shape of a huge, black stallion. A noble beast of glistening muscular flanks, shaggy hoof, midnight mane and tail.

'Oberon,' Archaon said with wonder. He remembered the black stallion of his youth. The horse that had served as his templar mount. The transformation was not complete, however. The flesh began to split with equine brawn, forming criss-cross scars that seemed to heal as fast as they formed. Spikes of sharpened bone erupted from black muscle and fur. As the creature snorted, its nostrils blazed with the fires of damnation, while what should have been a whinny was a howling, brain-aching roar of crackling, infernal fury. As the stallion closed its mouth and the glare of banelight faded, Archaon watched the black eyes of the beast flush to a Ruinous red.

'Let's do this,' Archaon said with relish. He took an armoured saddle, spiked stirrups and bridle-harness from a twisted post by the gate and entered the enclosure. He approached the infernal steed slowly. The creature seemed to settle into its new form. It stamped and snorted short bursts of hellfire. Archaon lifted the heavy saddle onto the dread stallion's back. Dorghar backed and bucked a little. Archaon held up a finger of his gauntlet as a warning. As the daemon shivered its caution and attempted to shake the saddle from its back, Archaon slapped the monster across its monstrous muzzle, causing the thing to flinch. It stamped back at him and got a savage backhand from Archaon's armoured hand. Dorghar stomped on, lowering its nose. Fire-threaded drool dribbled from between its tombstone teeth. Its nostrils blazed. The steed brought the raging damnation of its eyes level with the slits of Archaon's helm.

Dorghar moved forward, resting the flat of its head and the points of its muzzle-spikes against the Eye of Sheerian, and pushed at the Chaos warrior's helm. Warlord and steed pushed against one another, until finally Archaon stumbled back. He allowed the beast the moment's illusion that it had won the battle of wills before slipping the studded, spite-cured leather of the bridle over its thrusting head. As the Steed of the Apocalypse stamped and turned with animal fury, Archaon made swift work of belting both bridle and saddle to the monster's furious form. Hauling the wicked bit up between the chisel-like blades of its teeth, Archaon rested the thick reins over the pommel of the armoured saddle. He came back to the front of the stallion and found Jharkill's bone charms jangling before the creature's chest on a string of sinew. Archaon knew that he had to tame the beast himself. He could not rely upon the beastmaster's primitive enchantments.

'Let's see what you've got,' Archaon told the steed as he tore the charm from the solidified shadow of the daemon. As he tossed the bone trinket away, Archaon might have expected some kind of bestial gratitude, as he had found in Mange's cage. Dorghar had no intention of fulfilling such an expectation. It snorted smoke and glowing cinders at the Chaos warrior. Once. Twice. A third time. Within a blink, the monster came at Archaon.

It charged the Chaos warrior and slammed him into the twisted bars of the enclosure behind. By the time Archaon's armoured body was smashed into the unnatural and unrelenting metal of the cage, Dorghar had changed form. The first time its head hit him it was a thick nest of spiked, skull-fused antlers. Archaon felt the full weight of the beast behind the charge and the spikes of the twisted antlers smash him into the cage side. With barely a moment to recover, the daemon steed came at him again, this time assuming the monstrous hammer-head of an unspeakable daemon that butted Archaon's battered body back into the bars. Dragging himself up, the Chaos warlord found that Dorghar had changed yet again; now its head had assumed the armoured shape of some hellish juggernaut. It came at him again, and this time the infernal metal of its head struck Archaon on his faceplate and crunched him between the battering ram of the steed's metal head and the warped bars beyond.

Archaon clawed blindly at the rivets and plates of the monster's head. He held on as the creature retreated. Tearing its head upward, Dorghar sent Archaon's armoured form into the barred roof of the enclosure. As Archaon found himself back on the floor of the cage in a demolished heap he spat blood at the inside of his helm. He pushed himself to his feet but found that Dorghar had morphed once more into a black, bovine monstrosity that kicked back at the Chaos warrior with its hooves. Archaon struck the wall of the enclosure once more with the force of daemonic ferocity. As he tried to pick himself up he found the nightmare form of the black stallion once more before him. Rearing. Roaring balefire. Cycling its spiked forelegs and shaggy hooves like a pugilist before smashing Archaon back into the ground with a savage kick. And another. And another.

Archaon's world became the grit of the cage floor and the sense-smashing impact of hoof on helm. The Chaos warrior's own fury got the better of him and, pushing himself up, he lurched at the beast. Launching himself at the stamping and hiss of steam from scorched nostrils, the Chaos warrior stumbled through the open door of the cage and into the black murk into which Dorghar had dissipated. The darkness suddenly became the whirlwind maelstrom of a storm. The blackness howled about Archaon like a cyclone, dragging the Chaos warrior into the air and catapulting him into the cage wall. As the storm the steed had become screamed darkness and flame about the enclosure, Archaon was tumbled along the barbed bars, pinned to the outside of the cage.

As the storm died to a shadowy whisper, Archaon brought his helm up off the floor. Dorghar had once again assumed the shape of the stallion – an infernal perversion of Oberon's noble form. It scraped its hoof through the grit of the enclosure and snorted like a bull. Dragging his smashed body up off the floor, Archaon smacked his helm with a clutched metal fist in the hope that he might knock some sense into his skull. The steed suddenly tore away, spraying grit behind it. Archaon came unsteadily to his feet and slapped a gauntlet on the pommel of *Terminus*. It suddenly became apparent that the beast wasn't coming for him. Like a streaking shadow it was thundering for the gate. Without the enslaving sorcery of Jharkill's charms, the daemon steed wanted a taste of freedom. It would make short work of the enclosure gate.

Archaon knew he couldn't allow the monster to escape. Instead of heading for Dorghar, the Chaos warrior turned and sprinted for the gate. Drawing *Terminus*, he turned the blade about in his gauntlet, grasping the weapon by its crossguard. As the infernal beast drew level, Archaon shouldered the steed from its step before smashing its head aside with the pommel of his Sigmarite sword. Slugging the monster with the grasped hilt of the greatsword, Archaon turned the beast enough to send them both crashing into the bars beside the gate.

Smashing the creature again with the pommel of the weapon, Archaon dropped the sword and grabbed Dorghar by its black tail. Dragging the dazed creature from the buckled bars, Archaon leant back into a swing and hurled the steed around and into the unforgiving metal at the other end of the enclosure. Dorghar stumbled away from the warped bars like a new-born foal, its legs unsteady. Shaking its head and snorting a brief burst of flame, the beast turned – the monster's eyes were rageshot. Its hooves scraped the grit of the enclosure and it lowered the bone spikes on its head. Archaon scooped up *Terminus*. He knew what was coming.

Dorghar charged. The daemon was suddenly a blur. The streaking shadow came at the Chaos warrior. Archaon feinted one way with his great sword before side-stepping out of the steed's rocketing path. Leaping, he grabbed for the pommel of the beast's armoured saddle, allowing the creature's momentum to carry him up onto its back. Archaon was no sooner in the saddle than the daemon steed blasted straight through the enclosure gate. Within the blink of an eye it had blazed across the thoroughfare, leaving a flickering trail of dark flame behind it. Archaon braced himself as the beast struck the cages opposite. He roared as the steed turned and slammed both its brawny side and Archaon's armoured leg into the twisted bars.

Desperately clawing at the reins and thrusting his boots into the stirrups, Archaon slapped the beast's flank with the flat of his blade. The flesh of the beast seared and steamed on contact with the Sigmarite steel and the creature once again thundered off. Captive monsters hissed, spat and roared as Dorghar crashed along the side of the cages, dragging Archaon through the barbs and bars of the enclosures.

With Mange creating havoc in one section of the menagerie and Dorghar in the other, the attendant beastfiends and daemonette keepers were stretched. Between Jharkill's barbarian enchantments and the mangled labyrinth of cages, there was little to demand the attention of Lord Agrammon's servants, but this was something else. Monsters, mutants and daemons were howling in the cages while escaped exhibits tore infernal jailers to pieces and smashed their way to freedom.

Dragging itself away from the enclosures, Dorghar began to buck and kick with daemonic fury, snorting flame and roaring its infernal displeasure. Bouncing and sliding savagely in the saddle, Archaon dug in with his heels, hauled on the reins and slapped the beast's flanks with the flat of *Terminus*.

Finally the monster settled and steamed but the Chaos warrior's efforts had far from broken the beast. Both Archaon and the steed heard the crank of a twisted portcullis and the screeching call for weapons. As a spiked gate in the side of the citadel shot up into its stone frame like an opening maw, hordes of daemonettes spilled out of the tower and into the menagerie thoroughfares. They were monstrous shieldmaidens of obscene form. The creatures shrieked and squealed their delight as they raced out onto the thoroughfare with sickle-spears and spiked, black shields. Skulking between them were shaven beastfiends. The long-snouts were all sinew and scraps of leather and were battered between the bulks of the daemonettes as they trumpeted their alarm.

In Lord Agrammon's citadel guard, pouring out from the tower, Dorghar and Archaon found a common enemy. The daemon steed reared at the thrust of sickle-spears, kicking weapons out of clawed hands and heads from obscene bodies. Clutching the saddle with his thighs, Archaon held onto the reins with one hand while chopping down through rancid shieldmaidens and emaciated beastfiends with the other. Beneath him, the Chaos warlord suddenly felt the ripple of some shadow-spawned transformation. Archaon rose as the Steed of the Apocalypse grew in size. As saddlestraps and bridle cut into the beast's growing bulk, its horsehair sprouted to a shaggy black carpet of curls. An onyx horn and a colossal pair of curved tusks erupted from its changing face and Archaon found himself mounted on a daemonic thundertusk. Dorghar roared as it reared and stamped down on the infernal horde gathered about it. Mulching daemonettes and beastfiends into the floor, the steed shook the ground with its fury, knocking Slaaneshi deviants from their footing.

As slender beastfiends clawed their way up through the midnight tangle of the steed's shaggy hide, Archaon cut through their miserable bodies with stabs and backslashes of his blade. Dorghar, meanwhile, swept its mighty tusks from side to side, smashing through daemonettes and breaking beastfiends against the caged sides of enclosures. Roaring, Dorghar thundered up the thoroughfare, making a mess of the citadel guard rushing out from the tower. Beneath him Archaon felt the steed transform once more. Its shaggy fur began to shed and its mighty form shrank. Sinking down onto the back of some kind of hellish black panther with burning eyes and obsidian claws, Archaon held on to the reins and armoured saddle as the cat bounded from one miserable beastfiend to another. Filleting each victim as it landed, Dorghar leapt from victim to victim – bounding off the sides of rattled cages and across the thoroughfare with fearful feline grace.

Archaon sheathed *Terminus* and took the reins with both hands as the steed accelerated up towards a throng of daemonettes who were approaching with their sickle-spears raised. Scrabbling left and right as the monstrosities hurled the razor-crescent crowned weapons, Archaon held on for all he was worth. Ducking and leaning out to one side to avoid the spears, the Chaos warrior had the distinct feeling that Dorghar was attempting to put him in harm's way. Hauling the beast out of the path of further weapons hurled into the ground before them, Archaon prepared himself for a spine-jarring turn. The thing had daemonic reflexes and a lithe, muscular body to match. Dorghar pulled suddenly left. With Archaon holding on for his life, the steed leapt on and then suddenly off the bars of a nearby enclosure. Sailing over the daemonettes and the spiked shields, Dorghar landed on the obscene carcass of a spearless infernal. Savaging the daemonette with its claws, Dorghar finished it with the crystalline deathtrap of its obsidian jaws. Snapping the monstrosity's head clean off, Dorghar spat it at the gathering numbers of Lord Agrammon's citadel guard before leaping clean up into the air from a standing start.

Clutching the reins and surging for the sky, Archaon rode out the sudden manoeuvre. Dorghar landed on the enclosure cagetops before bounding impossibly again, up at the citadel wall. Landing with savage grace amongst the poison-sickly spikes, the cat leapt from one to another – working its way up the side of the citadel, avoiding slipping off. Holding his chestplate almost to the steed's back, Archaon clung on while the beast ascended. Sickle-spears sparked off the metal of the tower as the citadel guard below attempted to acquire them. As the spears and appendage-claws of the daemonettes guarding the tower thrust through narrow arrow slits in the citadel wall, Dorghar was forced to abandon its savage climb. Feeling his stomach lurch, Archaon held on as the panther leapt away from the tower. With the concentric insanity of the menagerie below them like a spiralling maze, Archaon gathered the reins in his gauntlets. A snarl tore at his top lip as Dorghar took them both to their doom.

Plunging back towards the menagerie, Archaon felt

the rupture of muscle and the crunch-transformation of bone below him. Once more Dorghar was changing. The dagger-clawed panther became a horrific bat creature of unfolding leathery wings, flea-infested fur and devilish flat-nosed face. Beating its great wings, Dorghar soared up – high over the menagerie that had been its prison. Archaon held on tight to the flying beast. The powerful motion of the creature's wings took the steed and its unwelcome rider over the forsaken Gatelands.

Far beneath them Archaon could see the ruins of fortresses and palaces built within the ruins of others. The land was black but not with ice. It moved like a carpet of insects. Peering down as the monstrous Dorghar banked, Archaon could see that the ruins, the contested borders, the warped Wastes of the Gatelands were swarming with beastfiends, daemons and other monstrosities. Dark things of savage ignorance, perpetually driven to spill blood in the name of their patron prince or daemonic power.

About the pole, Archaon spied the fortified residences of infernal royalty and the lords of damnation. Proud towers, festering battlements, brazen bastions and fortress monuments bleeding ruin into the air crowded the frozen lands about the blazing glare of the southern pole. They were built one on top of another, as though the palaces themselves – ever in a state of crooked enhancement – were vying for the most prestigious placement. A location commanding an unrivalled view of the blistering pole. A position closest to their Ruinous patrons. This created the silhouette of a dark, gargantuan crown about the shattered vortex of the long-demolished gate, through which the raw power of the beyond passed into the mortal world. Lord Agrammon's citadel and great menagerie was but one decorative piece of such dark reverence.

Again Archaon's stomach took a vertiginous tumble. Dorghar's banking roll became a plunge. As the monster turned, Archaon clamped his thighs around the armoured saddle and clutched onto the beast. Dorghar rolled wing over wretched wing, attempting to throw the Chaos warlord off, but Archaon had his prize. He had travelled across the Southern Wastes to acquire it and he would not let it go now. Beating its wings through the broiling skies, torn this way and that by the perversity of gales, updrafts and violent eddies, the Steed of the Apocalypse soared across the tower tops of the highest of the daemonic palaces. Archaon hauled at the creature's reins but Dorghar plunged straight at the howling maelstrom of light and horror erupting from the ruined gateway and bleeding into the world.

Moving between realities was a sickening shock. Physically. Mentally. Emotionally. As the creature glided through the state immaterial – the very rawness of Chaos – Archaon felt a wave of indescribable intensity come over him. It was as though he had hit a wall of pain, of pleasure, of possibility – but had passed through it. He fought for control of his body and soul. His mind cried out both for relief and for more. He felt lost and as if he did not know himself, yet had never known himself or his place in the world better. Tears began to roll down his cheeks. He struggled to control his bowels and choked back the necessity of vomiting in his helmet. Experiencing the crude power of ruin – uncrafted and without purpose – was a dreadful feeling that both excited and appalled his every sense and shattered the very core of his being. It felt like he had died.

If Dorghar had intended such an overwhelming experience to unsettle and ultimately unsaddle its rider, the dread beast was disappointed. Bathing the Chaos warlord in the searing certainty of the unknown had not broken him. Archaon did not clutch his helm in immaterial agony. He did not slip from the monster's back in a warped daze. He did not scream his sanity away. With his good eye, Archaon saw things that were not meant to be seen in the howling blaze of the polar gateway. Far below – if such a thing still existed for Archaon and the steed – predacious daemons, entities of the beyond and monstrous personifications, hungered for the fragility of his soul. They were a horror removed. Ever warping. Ever waiting. Ever wanting. Archaon understood how such sights could drive a man to madness and shatter his reason.

Archaon, however, was more than a man. He saw the impossibility of worlds connected like no one else. He could not only see what fear-feasting daemons and the Ruinous Powers of the otherworldly realm wanted him to see; with the darksight of his ruined eye he saw light where there was shadow. Perversities twisted themselves into a contorted sense. The burning certainty of his gaze lit the way to truths that commonplace dread refused to acknowledge. With the Eye of Sheerian he saw even more. The sorcerous gem burned bright in his helm, granting the Chaos warlord sights of dread wonder. The Eye revealed the daemons and their abyssal masters to be living corruptions. Realisations of the mortal condition. Self-determining entities, spawned and living out their unnatural existence in a stormy maelstrom of dark vision and emotion. They were the architecture of purest intention, draped in an otherworldy flesh formed of hope, of fear and of the unbearable, myriad states inbetween.

The wondrous prize not only revealed to Archaon the true nature of such infernal princes but also the principalities in which the horrors dwelled. Like a lens, the hellish haze of the pole magnified the powers of the sorcerous gem. Staring far to the north, directing his gaze towards the region the repulsive Changeling had indicated, Archaon could see the Forsaken Fortress. Like a great stone sculpture of a monstrous daemon crouching on the horizon, the palace taunted the Chaos warrior with its distant presence.

Archaon tore up on the reins and hauled Dorghar to the left, putting the Forsaken Fortress in their sights. The beast could not know that the palace was the Chaos warrior's objective and found itself swooping out of the blinding blaze. Beneath the saddle the creature was changing yet again. Dorghar had assumed the form of the black stallion. It favoured Archaon's memory of Oberon, only with the ragged wings of its previous incarnation. Beating through the stormy, dark skies of the polar maelstrom, the steed seared northward. Galloping through the churning heavens, swooping between the crash of the lightning and the plunge of thunder, Dorghar surged up through the broiling cloud and down at the Wasteland. The warped wilderness passed like a blur below. The Steed of the Apocalypse weaved between the sky piercing towers of daemonic palaces and crooked citadels. Colossal fragments of the polar gate littered the wilderness whipping by, and within moments the beast was passing over the crescent canyon.

Archaon felt the scream of a storm erupt about him as Dorghar blasted up out of the curving canyon depths and back up into the maelstrom. Beneath him the creature was transforming once more. Not into some other monstrous beast but into a furious, living blaze. Like a comet streaking across the night sky, Dorghar accelerated. With the dread armour of Morkar protecting him from the worst of the flames, Archaon held on tight as the supernatural flame roared and whipped about him. Tensing his thighs and locking his gauntlets grimly about the reins, the Chaos warlord drew his armoured chest to the steed's blazing back. As an unnatural fireball blasting through strange skies, Dorghar galloped. He beat his fiery wings. He soared up through the heavens on a path of flame.

The frozen insanity of the Southern Wastes fell away from both warlord and steed. The flesh-shattering temperatures. The scalding gales of stabbing ice and agony. The warherds of beastfiends that swarmed the midnight land like a sea of muscle, shaggy fur and hate. The black of the ice receded. With it narrowed the deep clefts and canyons that zigzagged their way through the guts of the pole, meeting at the rift that bored its way through the bottom of the world.

Through the roaring flames that raged about him, Archaon saw the Southern Wastes recede. Warrior and steed travelled far, protected from the sky-scorching inferno that Dorghar had become. The dark creature beat its fiery wings and banked left and right, up through the storm-racked clouds and down through the broiling maelstrom that blanketed the continent with its unnatural miasma. Archaon held on as he felt the beast buck and writhe beneath him.

The blasted lands of ruin and flesh-searing freeze passed beneath him in a sickening blur. Dunes of black ice migrated across the Wastes. A ghostly haze swirled across the monstrous expanse making it appear like the surface of a phantom ocean. Glaciers of living obsidian grew. Mountain ranges of serrated darkness reached up out of the icy plateau. Volcanoes blazed their unnatural, molten fury at the skies, bathing the howling bleakness about Archaon in a strange glow. Dorghar tried to pull away but Archaon kept the beast on course.

The rocketing monstrosity raged north before the Chaos warrior angled its searing progress west. Guided by the Eye of Sheerian set in his helm, Archaon's farsight extended across the continent faster than even Dorghar could carry him. It took him across dread lands that were but a blink of cruel peaks, shrieking winds and deep freeze – lands that were a streaming blur beneath the Steed of the Apocalypse. The sorcerous gem granted him a vision of the benighted kingdoms of the west, where innumerable warherds of innumerable beastfiends fought, butchered and ate one another, filling bellies and lending strength for the next day of rank slaughter. Not that days, months or years had much meaning in the midnight hell of the Southern Wastes.

Dorghar came in low across these killing fields of frozen blood, ice-mulched corpses and bestial swarms. Like a living carpet of murder and hate, the shaggy monsters fought one another with mindless abandon. Some were scarred, frost-blackened creatures of bare muscular chest, curved blades of bone, draped in skulls. Others were striped deviants dragging fiends separated off from their herds into hollows for last hours of perversion and horror. Hulking beasts of humped back, matted mountains of fur and filthy horns overcame fiend victims with a noxious stench so intense it could be seen, while shamans of fur and feather wielded staffs of crooked spine that they whipped about them, turning daemonflesh to a bloody gruel that was carried away on the icy gales. The beastfiends barely looked up from their savagery and slaughter as Dorghar blazed its path above them.

Archaon gritted his teeth as the steed coursed upwards through the moaning maelstrom of cloud, punching up through the obscurity and into the searing silence of a world above the world. A darkness of crystal cold where the sickly stars shone once more. The Chaos warrior fancied that he could see the great curve of the world and the shattered lands of ice and berg that formed the western limits of the dark continent like an unfinished mosaic. Holding on and turning back, Archaon could see the distant Gatelands behind, with the wailing insanity of the collapsed polar gate roaring a hole through the cloud, revealing only the raging abyss of an existence beyond his own. A pit into which reality fell, was devoured by eternity, marinated in the impossible, before being churned up and vomited spectacularly back into the world.

Suddenly something changed and Archaon was forced to turn back around. Dorghar's fiery progress seared to whiteness. The flames intensified, becoming nothing more than an agony felt but not seen. The Wastes – that had rushed by like a bleak blur – now became a mind-scalding instant. The moment was a screaming flash, a raw elemental power coursing through Archaon's being. An unstoppable surge of blinding pain that sizzled through his plate, flowed through his paralysed limbs, stabbed his heart to a stop and blanked his mind.

When his eye fluttered open, Archaon saw only smoke. Through the slit of his helm he saw black steam swirling through oily smoke. His nostrils stung with the burned air. His ears rang with a mighty crack that still seared through his mind. Morkar's plate felt buckled about him. Archaon patted his cursed armour down to find that whatever had hit them had not breached the damned plate of the first Everchosen. Archaon's bones hurt within flesh that was still flush with a ghostly burn.

He pushed himself unsteadily to his feet and stamped out a small fire that had taken on the bottom edge of his furs and cloak. As the steam and smoke cleared the Chaos warrior found himself in a pit. A crater. About him was black ice that had been scorched to dribble. Black water began to pool about his boots. Beneath them he found rock – shattered but unyielding. Only then did Archaon realise what had happened. They had not been hit. They had been the ones that had done the hitting. Dorghar – the beast of a thousand transformations – had turned from steed to fireball and fireball to a stream of dark lightning that had thunderbolted for the ground. The creature's elemental power had burned through Archaon. Its sky-splitting speed had smashed both of them into the Wastes. Neither the searing blaze nor the murderous impact had killed the Chaos warrior. No bones had been broken and his heart continued to beat. The steed had succeeded in unseating its rider, however. It would have escaped Archaon – denied the chosen of Chaos his prize and made him chase the monstrous wonder across the world – but for the fact that he found it stumbling to its own feet. The thing had been equally dazed by the impact and drained by its efforts to rid itself of Archaon.

Now before him it was a black stallion once more, its midnight flesh ruptured with spikes of bone and its eyes alight with infernal fire. Archaon grasped for the hilt of *Terminus*, which he found to his relief was still sitting snug in its fur scabbard. He ran at the beast as it stumbled this way and that. Slamming his pauldron into the mount's muscular side he toppled it. Dorghar went crashing back down into the inky meltwater, with the Chaos warrior on top of it. Archaon grabbed the monster by the scruff of the mane and drew his templar blade. Resting the tip of the great sword against the side of the creature's throat, Archaon watched the blessed steel sizzle and burn against daemonflesh. The steed kicked out with its hind legs and tried to right itself but Archaon leaned in with the weight of his armour – the blade ready to skewer the beast.

'Yield!' Archaon roared at the Steed of the Apocalypse. 'Yield!'

The beast roared like a furnace at him through its daggered maw. It kicked. It bucked. It made ready for transformation but Archaon wouldn't let it. Turning the sword around he smashed its horse skull into the ground again and again, causing meltwater to splash about them. He turned the blade once more to the creature. With its gleaming point worming its way dangerously through smoking flesh, Archaon bawled, 'You will yield to me, daemon. For I am to be the Everchosen of Chaos, the Harbinger of Ruin and the Lord of the End Times: by dark right, you are to be my steed, monster. A daemonic beast of burden fit to carry me into the annals of history before I see fit to send the past, present and future of this miserable world into oblivion. Yield, creature of Chaos, or I will send you on ahead.' *Terminus* rattled with Archaon's rage and rested on the creature's neck. Gradually, the steed's struggles died away. It turned, searing its black flesh against the Sigmarite blade, angling its long face towards the Chaos warrior. Oberon's face.

Suddenly it spoke. The creature had an infernal voice that burned through the furnace-roar glowing through its sharp teeth. Archaon had no idea what the beast had said. It was in an unspeakable tongue that Archaon did not know and proceeded from deep within the beast. Staring at one another, actions seemed to speak louder than hellish words, and Archaon edged his sword away and the weight of his armour off the beast. Rolling to its hoofed feet, Dorghar shook its head, passing a brawny shiver down its flanks. It snorted steam at the meltwater. Archaon still held his greatsword out, his broad blade ready to chop down through the beast's neck. The daemon steed did not move, however. It stood waiting to receive its rider. Archaon nodded slowly to the beast and himself. The fourth treasure of Chaos – the Steed of the Apocalypse – was finally his. He would have rejoiced but for the searing ache in his bones from their thunderbolting descent and impact.

Slipping *Terminus* back into its scabbard, Archaon mounted the steed, settling back into the armoured saddle that seemed as much the beast as the sharp bone and midnight flesh. Taking the reins, Archaon motioned Dorghar gently on. Stabbing spiked hooves through the slush and into the icy sides of the pit, the steed climbed out of the crater. Casting the sorcerous sight of Sheerian's Eye through the still darkness of the icy plateau, Archaon found what he was looking for. Dorghar turned its head to one side. Its eye burned with an internal blaze and the roar of the furnace poured from its daemonic maw. There were no words this time. Archaon didn't need any to understand.

'West, Dorghar,' the Chaos warrior said. 'West, beast. Just a little further. We call on my father-in-shadow tonight. Somehow I feel we shall not be well received.'

CHAPTER V

'When we are not ourselves but we are no one else – who are we?'
— Khardunn the Gloried, *Kurgan Bead-Belt*

The Pustular Plain
The Southern Wastes
Horns Harrowing: Season of the Raw

The unrelenting blackness of ice gave way to the oily sheen of meltwater lakes and deltas of steaming slush. Here, in the western reaches of the dark continent, a miserable kind of life eked out rancid existence. Earth, rocky and ice-threaded, sat stinking and water-logged like a tundrous bog. The wetlands were ancient in their corruption and ravenous for flesh. The mire was an undulating sea of bestial bones, choked with hardy brown grasses and islands of fungal growth. Things sloshed about in the foetid lakes of glassy blackness as a rash of volcanic peaks oozed steaming pus, curdling the churning tundra with its diseased filth. This was the Pustular Plain, where swarms of black flies bled beastfiends alive and the dark chuckle of the Great Lord of Decay could be heard in bubbles that rose from the dark water depths and broke the surface in a continuous, stinking chug.

As Dorghar came in low, the beat of his gargoyle's wings created a wake in the dark waters, disturbing a miasma of feeding flies. The Steed of the Apocalypse glided in over trains of beastfiends working their way across the mire in single file columns. The creatures were horribly afflicted with growths, plagues and deformities that made movement a challenge and the thigh deep trudge through the bog-tundra an agonising trial. The bone staffs they used to traverse the freezing muck were crowned with a trio of thuribles in which burned peat. As well as lighting the creatures' way, the headpieces offered warmth and praise to their Plague Lord in the skyward mockery of the unholy symbol created in the darkness.

As Dorghar back beat its wings to bring the beast and Archaon to a halt, the Chaos warrior peered down at the mire. The monster's hooves creaked and splayed, ensuring both the steed and its master didn't sink. Slipping down out of the saddle, Archaon couldn't boast the same transformative powers and his boots oozed into the slurping freeze. The Forsaken Fortress had experienced the same problem. The architectural abomination loomed over Archaon – a palace constructed in the dread form of its monstrous master – but its wing-towers and horn-spires leant crookedly to one side where the palace was sinking. Wading through the muck, Archaon led the steed up to the smooth black stone of the fortress. Draping the reins over the razored protrusions at the base of the stonework, Archaon shouldered his shield and once again began the treacherous climb. There would be no door or gate. The palace boasted no barbican because the Forsaken Fortress did not admit visitors. The only unfortunates allowed inside the damned structure were those brought there by the daemon Be'lakor itself. Strangely, Archaon thought he qualified. Regardless, the Changeling had shown him the weakness in the palace fortifications. In the dread thing's faithful reproduction of both the Dark Master and his palace, the rival entity had revealed a breach. As he began to climb, Archaon began to wonder if a similar vulnerability existed on his father-in-shadow's own star-scorched chest.

Below him, Dorghar snorted and steamed, padding the marshy earth with its splayed hooves. Archaon reached. He jumped. He hauled himself up through the wretched wonder of the daemon prince's form. Though fraught with perverse dangers and a sloping angle of ascent, it was an easier climb second time around. Here where the volcanic peaks warmed the gelid bog and even the raging gales slowed to a stagnant stillness, it was much warmer than the continental interior and the structure was not caked in ice.

Archaon aimed for the heart – as he did in all things. The fingertips of his gauntlets hooked into the colossal symbol of the eight-pointed star scored into the midnight stone. He dragged himself up through the Ruinous iconography – the symbol of those that damned themselves equally to all the dread powers of darkness in the world. It was his guiding star, as it had been for his father-in-shadow and the doomed creatures that followed them both, as well as many more into which Archaon had thrust his blade. The eight-pointed star knew no middle ground. When it was on the rise, the servants of Chaos – from the most infamous warlords to the lowliest spawn – followed it or died. And Archaon's star was on the rise. It was time his father-in-shadow came to know this also.

Archaon found the fracture in the stone where he had before. A cleft in the wall over the palace's daemonic heart. The Changeling's wretched mimicry had indeed been a dark wonder to behold. Passing his shield through first, the Chaos warrior slipped through the breach in the defences and entered the Forsaken Fortress.

Inside, Archaon felt immediately vulnerable. It was an alien feeling for the warlord. He had travelled the world and killed just about everything that walked, talked and breathed. It would not have been an idle boast to call himself one of the deadliest warriors in the known world. He had the patronage of Dark Gods and seemed destined for a dread greatness. Still, in the darkness of the palace, with its smooth, flowing, almost organic architecture, Archaon felt trapped. Not like he had felt in manacle and chain. Not as a captured specimen, caged for display in Lord Agrammon's sick menagerie. The Forsaken Fortress held more dread for Archaon than doors of oak, bars of steel and cells of stone. Its phantasmic walls could fade at any moment. It was there and it was not. The palace could vanish from the Pustular Plain like a ghost, to reappear somewhere else in the Southern Wastes or, for all Archaon knew, the world. The Forsaken Fortress haunted the realms of men and beasts – and the Dark Master himself haunted the halls of his own palace. If it were to disappear now, it would take him hostage.

Stalking the fortress passages and halls that wove through the palace like the cascading innards of so many of Archaon's foes, the Chaos warrior's armour jangled lightly. The palace interior was lightless, but Archaon's darksight seared through the abyssal blackness. The Forsaken Fortress blazed with the fearful ruin of its construction. Its walls and floors – in their ornate wonder and madness – bled the raw essence of Chaos. Every speck of dust in the place burned with ancient evil and Archaon had eyes for such raging malevolence. In the darkness of the palace everything was reversed. The black oblivion burned bright with dreamy damnations and the wan brilliance of competing realities. It revealed to him a palace that was both there and not. Like a shadow, the Forsaken Fortress existed in so much as it was a semi-corporeal absence of something else. Purity. Mercy. Hope. Archaon's boots scuffed the midnight marble of the floor and his furs rippled with the ghostly breeze. He held his shield aloft – in part to be ready for anything that the fortress had to throw at him, in part to present the eight-pointed glory of the Chaos Star to potential foes. A simple sign of Archaon's allegiance to the Ruinous Powers in all their unified majesty.

Then he heard it. The single beat of a heart.

The Chaos warrior's boots scraped to stillness. He looked this way and that through the blazing darkness. About the strange, flowing architecture that represented the prince of daemon princes both inside and out, the sound was like a tiny peal of thunder in the midnight madness. Then again. And again. Archaon pulled his shield closer and slipped *Terminus* from its fur back-scabbard with a steely hiss.

The grotesque beating continued. Blinking through the radiant oblivion, Archaon thought he saw movement. The Chaos warrior suddenly realised that he had wandered into the throne chamber. At its far end he could make out the monstrous form of a daemon cast in cold stone. The infernal form of a muscular body. Clawed hands and feet. Horns and wings. It looked just like a miniature version of the palace itself. Before it Archaon saw the wisp and twirl of shadow – congealing, intensifying, solidifying into the blackness of flesh. A monstrous heart beat before the throne. It was a twisted thing of large daemonflesh – strangled by bitterness and belligerence – thundering through the contorted muscularity of its obscene form with an otherworldly will to exist that would not be denied.

Archaon licked at his lips. It was painful to even be in the presence of such a realisation. The warlord knew that he could not let this moment pass. The heart beat like a dare in the silent darkness of the throne room. Willing himself on, Archaon's gauntlet tightened about his Sigmarite sword. The blessed steel scorched the very air of the dark palace. One boot scuffed the marble floor ahead of the other. A hesitant stumble became the urgent steps of a walk. Moments later such steps became a plate-jangling run up the darkened length of the throne room. *Terminus* came up. Archaon's hand tightened. He would cleave the monstrous heart in two.

There was suddenly more movement in the shadows. Shapes emerged from behind the throne, sweeping up on either side to surround the great pulsing heart. Some slipped silkily from behind pillars while others erupted from the blackness of archways. Archaon skidded to a stop, his plate rattling to stillness and his blade up, its point aimed over the top of his shield. The Chaos warrior turned, ready for an attack or ten such attacks but the shadowy forms also grew still. Their weapons were not presented. They were simply placing themselves between Archaon and the daemonic heart.

Each was a living silhouette. A shadowy outline of a Chaos warrior. Shadow churned within each one, holding its form and giving the impression of plate, of horned helms, of furs, of aberration and weapons in scabbards or slung across backs. Archaon thought he could make out the shape of northmen, Kurgan warlords, damned kings, Kislevites in spike and fur, shadow-pledged marauders, bestial chieftains and warrior half-daemons. Men, women and monsters, long in their leaving of the world and now cast in shadow like statues of living darkness. Each seemed doomed to haunt the palace, cursed by their undying devotion to their Dark Master. Each still bore the mark of the daemon prince across their chest – centred on their black hearts. Be'lakor's Ruinous Star of darkness united and powers undivided. The sign of the Bearer. The Herald. The Harbinger. The star was scorched in a cruel light that cut through the shadowy form of each otherworldly warrior of Chaos.

Archaon turned with sword raised and shield held out before him. He was ready for the sentinels in shadow but the things merely assumed their positions about the throne and throne room. They waited as black veins sprouted from the monstrous heart in a horrific, labyrinthine network that finally began to assume a daemonic shape. Thick arteries carried the pumped ichor of the thing through a torso and long limbs. A spider web of black capillaries spread from these throughout wings and the rest of the body. The vessels' steam and smoked shadow assumed the form of spouting muscle and black bones. About the dark bloom of a brain, housing Ruinous thoughts and unimaginable power, grew a midnight skull. Horns sprouted from the nightmare, before the haze of shadowy steam around the daemon suddenly congealed about its monstrous form like an instantaneous frost. The infernal beast was now clothed in its blacker-than-black skin. Hooks, chains, skulls and scraps of hell-forged mail dribbled from its muscular flesh. The realisation was complete. Within the design of the Forsaken Fortress, sat the daemon-sculpted shape of the prince's throne – on that sat the daemon itself: the Dark Master, Be'lakor.

The abomination wore its infernal royalty like a cankered soul. Its horrific visage was an obsidian mask of the unreadable and unknowable. All at once Archaon thought he saw disdain in the thing's abyssal eyes, and pride and horror and glee. Mostly it just seemed bitter and irritated to be in his presence. Archaon stared at the loathsome creature. With his one good eye he beheld it. With his darksight gift he beheld it. With the sorcerous Eye of Sheerian he beheld it. It was there – in the infernal flesh. The Chaos warrior lowered his Sigmarite sword and his shield.

'I see you, dread thing,' Archaon told it.

Only because I wish it, mortal, Be'lakor told him. The daemon prince's voice was in everything. Heard. Felt. Archaon could even taste the bitter hatred coming off the thing. *You have wandered far off your course, chosen of the Chaos gods.*

'The Everchosen of Chaos,' Archaon told it.

You have not earned that title yet, mortal, the Dark Master reminded him. *The Everchosen of Chaos is known by his treasures and there are two yet to be found.*

'That is only a matter of time,' Archaon assured the creature. 'Is it not, daemon? Are not my moments, my months, my years – the very lives I might have lived – but playthings to a creature like you? Like skeins of wool about your claws – to cut, to let loose or to wrap about your finger?' Be'lakor glowered at Archaon with a withering intensity but said nothing. 'I look to the north, the south, the east and the west, and you are there, Shadow, hidden on the horizon. I try to remember my past and there you are, haunting my memories. I have dark hopes for the future – but you afflict even those with your potential presence.'

Is that why you are here, mortal? To whine, carp and plead.

'You know why I'm here, daemon-filth,' Archaon told it. 'Let's not play childish games. I have travelled far and found he who would not be found.'

You are here for answers…

'We will leave guesswork to idle philosophers,' Archaon said. 'I would know what you would have with me, creature. From your own faithless lips. Or I shall cut the truth out of your infernal carcass.'

Answers?

'Speak daemon, while you still can,' Archaon warned.

You have the very world on its knees before you and you came to find me… for answers?

Archaon felt the bottomless depths of the creature's scorn. Its mockery burned to hear.

'Are you going deaf?' Archaon shot back. 'My demands have not changed since the last time I asked. Yes, monster – answers. To questions. I ask a question and you answer it. That's how this works. Don't make me ask you again.'

What I would have with you? Be'lakor seethed. *I would have you realise your destiny… my son-in-shadow.*

Archaon bit at his bottom lip. The sound of his daemonic father admitting as much was like icewater in his ears.

'And who does my destiny serve?' Archaon asked.

We all serve those greater than ourselves.

'Be'lakor,' Archaon hissed. 'Daemon prince. Dark Master. Some say you are the crown-bearer of the Chaos gods. Nothing more than a slave. Others that you serve only yourself and your insatiable ambition.'

A mere pastime, Be'lakor said. *Some embroider. Some whittle. I craft the future in flesh and blood. Who does your destiny serve? It serves me, you miserable cur. You are a doll with which to be played and left abandoned on the floor. You are the piece of the game taken and placed to one side of the board. You are a living afterthought, Archaon of the North – like all my servants. Nothing more.*

'And yet here I am,' Archaon rumbled back. 'I'm not on the

floor. I'm here, where no man nor daemon thought I would be. I stand before the lowly Be'lakor – dung stain of the gods – in the armour of the Everchosen, carried here on the Steed of the Apocalypse, bearing the treasures of Chaos and the ever burning Mark of the Ruinous Powers in my flesh.'

You think you are the first to bear such dark honours? Be'lakor asked, the question like a scorpion's sting. *You are a nothing. Born of nothing. The hollow fruit of an empty womb. All that you are I put in there. But think not that I afford you any affection for that. My half-breeds roam the world. Thousands more serve me not in flesh but in deed. They carry my mark. They live for my favour. They know their place. They do not carp and question. They serve the darkness of this world through the darkness they find in themselves. They serve their father-in-shadow – the darkness that is Be'lakor, you worthless wretch. As you should.*

'And yet I am not without worth, it seems,' Archaon told the abomination. 'I am the dark hope of the Ruinous Gods. The same gods that laugh at you, my father-in-shadow, and scorn your wretched efforts. Be'lakor the Bearer. Slave to circumstance. Doomed to carry crowns but not to wear them. Doomed to choose but not be chosen. Granted eternity but denied form. You call me a nothing. You call me worthless. You are a prince without a kingdom to inherit. Nothing could be more worthless than that.'

Archaon turned his head and angled the tip of *Terminus* at one of his father's shadow sentinels. The silhouettes behind him had edged closer. 'Back off, darkling,' Archaon warned, 'or you will see the light – and it won't be pretty.' After a moment's otherworldly hesitation, the things drifted back.

'You can bring your bastards into the world,' Archaon continued, fixing his monstrous father with a hateful gaze. 'You can inspire the low and the faithless. You can keep company with shadows. What you cannot do is be what you were. The Great Changer cursed you, Be'lakor. You cannot be crowned while conducting dark coronations for others. As you will do for me, daemon. With you or without you – it is my destiny. I am chosen of the Dark Gods and I will be the Everchosen of Chaos. You will meddle no further in my future. I am not yours to be manipulated or mastered. I will destroy you, creature of darkness.'

The palace boomed with the daemon's laughter. It was a horrible sound that bounced about the strange chambers of the palace and through the twists and turns of labyrinthine passageways. It was everywhere and felt like a chorus of monsters laughing at Archaon.

You? Destroy me? You are less than worthless if you believe that. Perhaps, Archaon of the North, you are my biggest disappointment.

'Surely nothing could disappoint you more than yourself, daemon?' Archaon said. 'Destroy you? My blade will send you back to whatever deviant plane you came from. It is my deeds that will destroy you, monster. The Everchosen of Chaos is known by his treasures, but the Lord of the End Times – he is known by his aftermath. By the oblivion that follows in his wake and the endings he brings. An end to all things. To the mortal races and their foetid beliefs. To the gods – both of law and of ruin – who are sustained by such patronage. An end to you, daemon.'

Be'lakor's horrific features contorted further around an infernal snarl.

You have the soul-sucking gall to talk to me of ends, Archaon of the North, the monster seethed. *Let me show you what I know of ends...*

With the sibilance still on the daemon's wretched lips, the Chaos warrior turned. The shadow behind him had barely registered its Dark Master's instruction to act. Archaon slashed *Terminus* across the being's throat, opening up a ragged gash of blinding light in the sentinel. The other shadows retreated as the thing blazed in its death throes, screaming away its existence in a nimbus of palace-scalding brightness. With the Sigmarite sword still held overhead, Archaon stabbed forth and plunged the blade through the chest of the second. Expertly retracting the weapon and resting the flat of the blade on top of his shield, Archaon slowly turned. The second shadow screeched horribly as the blazing puncture wound in its chest became a vortex of light, churning the shadow of the warrior thing about like a whirlpool before devouring the entity.

Destroy the interloper! Be'lakor commanded, pointing one of his cruel, black claws at Archaon. The throne room was suddenly a cradle of darkness – every pillar, nook, archway and alcove became the birthplace of shadows. Warriors rushed Archaon from every direction. The living silhouettes bore the shapes of the things they had been. Some seemed to wear plate; others were shaggy shapes in fur; some were spiked like urchins while others were the muscular outlines of marauder savages and barbarians. Stained in a deeper darkness over each of their hearts was the Ruinous Star. The star of darkness united. Be'lakor's star. Archaon was caught in a maelstrom of rushing shadow. The solidified darkness of weaponry came at him. As the Chaos warrior smashed it furiously aside with shield and sword, it felt real enough. Real enough to carve a cleft of darkness through the warlord or stab howling shadow through his chest. As *Terminus* turned axe, spear and sword aside, there was the bright flash of an impact. With every axe blade and spear-head Archaon lopped from the weapons, every head he took and gaping hole he stabbed through their shadowy forms, a blaze of light erupted from the keen edge of the Sigmarite blade. His predicament worsened because with every flash of light, the orientation of shadows in the throne room changed. Sentinels disappeared from one place only to erupt from another, forcing him to fight twice as hard.

Very quickly Archaon came to realise that these were the shadow forms of past Chaos warlords – the blackness of their hearts pledged to Be'lakor – or perhaps even the aspirant Everchosen of Chaos like Archaon himself. Their axe strikes were too murderous, the spear thrusts too assured and bladework too masterful for rank and file butchers. Be'lakor had surrounded himself with failures – like himself. The shadows of exalted champions who had led hordes to war and whose blades had been altars upon which sacrifices to the Dark Gods had been made.

Archaon brought up his shield and was almost knocked back by the impact of a spear that bled shadow across the chamber, before its flight path sent it hammering into the Chaos star adorning the shield's surface. Archaon went to slice the spear shaft away but there was nothing there but the black haze of the weapon that had been. Moving between pillars and ducking back through archways, Archaon evaded the avalanche of presented weaponry. The palace interior was disorientating enough, but bathed as it was in a sea of shadows and punctuated by the blinding deaths of the sentinels, Archaon soon lost track of where he was. There was the silky smoothness of marble stairs – he almost broke his neck falling down them. There was also some kind of gallery, and he made a balcony-clearing hop and drop out of the path of a shadow-streaming battle axe. It was wielded by some mountainous barbarian of the Steppe with as much insane abandon in Be'lakor's dark service as it had in its former life. He was no longer in the throne room. Sentinels were already waiting for him in the large chamber into which he had dropped. Everything was the flowing architecture of the chamber and the trailing blackness of shadowy blades.

'Come on!' Archaon roared, splitting the silhouette of a northman in two before hammering a marauder aside with his shield. He brought *Terminus* back up above his helm and rotated the blade with his wrist. Suddenly accelerating the turn he sent blessed steel through the throat of a Kurgan warlord before lopping the head off the shape of a shaggy Norscan champion. As an axe half bit into his shoulder and a spear tip glanced off his armoured thigh, Archaon bellowed at the champions of shadow. Chopping down through what Archaon assumed to be an easterner, from the outline of his armour, before cleaving back and forth through a spear, Archaon slammed the darkness of an axeman into a pillar with his shield. Thrusting the Sigmarite blade through the gut of a Chaos knight with an ornately-shaped helmet, Archaon turned and smashed his fist into the featureless face of the axeman pinned to the pillar. Archaon hammered him again and again with his shadow-stained gauntlet before the warrior's axe dropped away to drifting darkness and Archaon's armoured knuckles found stone. Snatching the hilt of *Terminus* back and withdrawing the blade, Archaon unleashed a howling radiance that ate the Chaos knight alive.

Enough…

Be'lakor's voice echoed through the chambers and passageways of his empty palace. It wasn't enough to save the horned silhouette of a bestial chieftain that Archaon cleaved in two, or the shadow of the caped Kislevite champion in spiked plate who received the stabbing Sigmarite blade straight through the darkness of his helm's faceplate. In the blaze of their deaths, the sentinels became one with the palace shadows once more. Casting a quick glance about his surroundings, Archaon found himself in the vaulted expanse of some great feasting hall – all pillars and black tables. The Chaos warlord doubted very much that anyone had ever actually eaten in there.

Archaon saw Be'lakor. The daemon prince strode through a magnificent archway that led into the cavernous hall. The Dark Master's talons chewed up the black marble at his feet while his wings stretched and extended in the same way a pugilist might stretch his neck before a fight. Archaon didn't need such preparation. He had already fought his way back through half the palace and an army of shadows. As the sentinels dissipated, Archaon turned to present himself to his father-in-shadow.

'Enough?' The Chaos warrior repeated, his words echoing unnaturally about the chamber. 'Not nearly enough. In fact, I was just warming up.'

Be'lakor stopped. From the darkness of the vaulted chamber roof dropped a colossal blade. Ancient. Notched. Streaming with shadow, the blade stabbed down into the black marble floor of the chamber with an impact Archaon could feel through his boots. The Chaos warrior shivered. He had been standing there mere moments before. The blade quivered before its master, its crossguard great serrated spikes that were part of the blade. The pommel was similarly a great spike, making every part of the cursed, colossal weapon a death-dealing point. Be'lakor wrenched the infernal blade from the stone. It was broad and almost as long as the monster was tall. The Dark Master passed it between his claws, turning the weapon experimentally with his wrist. The massive blade trailed smoky shadow as its weight and cleaving edge moved through the air. It was as though it had been some time since the daemon prince had personally had the pleasure of despatching a foe with the blade. The fang-filled snarl of satisfaction that afflicted the creature's face told Archaon that the expectation of such pleasure was starting to return.

I was your beginning, Be'lakor told him... *I will be your end.*

'Then you will be an end unto yourself,' Archaon spat back, gesturing his impatience with *Terminus*.

Be'lakor's daemonic maw opened wide and the creature bent over as it released a stone trembling roar. Tables tumbled before the force of the infernal bellow, rolling across the marble floor and smashing into one another. Archaon chopped this way and that, cutting the furniture in two and bludgeoning it into splinters. Before long the Chaos warrior was buried in a mountain of long tables and benches. With its path cleared, the daemon prince stomped up the length of the hall, wings back and its great shadow sword held above it. Sweeping in, the blade was like a dark force of nature, smashing huge drifts of furnishings aside and carving stone-shattered furrows into the marble floor. Holding its colossal blade high, the daemon prince sniffed at the air. Shrugging off shattered tables, Archaon roared atop the height of wreckage and leapt through the air at the monstrous daemon. Bringing his shadow sword up and holding it hilt and tip, Be'lakor absorbed the murderous, cleaving action that drew dark sparks from both blades. Twisting his torso and heaving immediately back, the daemon prince pushed Archaon away, using the force of his leaping attack to throw him into a pillar. The marble was unforgiving and as the Chaos warrior hit the stone, his armour jangled over the sound of a sickening thud. Half bouncing, half dropping to the floor in his buckled plate, Archaon stumbled and slipped among the shower of pulverised marble.

The daemon was suddenly there above him. Archaon pushed himself to his feet, but was forced almost immediately back to the floor as the shadow blade cleaved straight through the pillar. Archaon rolled across his shield to evade the avalanche of black stone thundering from the chamber ceiling. Be'lakor shrugged the debris from his great arched wings, swinging on with dark, daemonic fury. Archaon rolled again. And then back again, his shield scraping through the grit. The shadow sword plunged down though the floor, cleaving the marble into craterous gashes. Archaon was up – and just in time. Like a monstrous black guillotine, the daemon's blade *whooshed* down towards him. Slipping *Terminus* across the surface of his shield, Archaon awaited the impact. He knew that the supernatural force of such a blow would sunder the shield and his arm in two. As Be'lakor brought his infernal strength down on Archaon, the Chaos warrior felt the force of his daemon might through sword, through shield, flesh and bone, and the soles of his boots that shattered marble about them.

Snarling behind the skull-fashioned faceplate of the Everchosen's helm, Archaon pushed back with all the power he could muster. Straightening his legs and arms, the Chaos warrior batted back the daemon with a thrust of his shield and drew a shower of black sparks from Be'lakor's blade as *Terminus* swept it aside. Archaon came straight in with a withering thrust of his sword – a manoeuvre that had every right to skewer a boar. Be'lakor had backed, however, and had brought his black blade around to knock the Sigmarite sword aside. Archaon spun around, his shield ready to receive the flashing glance of the shadow sword on its surface before following with another deadly thrust. This one found its mark and the tip of *Terminus* slid straight into the darkness of the daemon's midriff. Archaon felt no resistance through the shaft of the blade. The weapon had hit nothing but silky shadow. As Be'lakor stomped to one side – the thunder of his footsteps feeling real enough through the floor – he brought his blade down on Archaon. As the weight of the weapon crashed off the surface of his shield, Archaon decided that the monstrosity was once more flesh and bad blood.

Denied permanent form by the Great Changer, the daemon prince had found a way to turn his curse into a gift. Every time Archaon's blessed blade nicked, stabbed or sliced through the abomination's flesh it was the emptiness of shadow. Whenever Be'lakor's huge blade came down at the Chaos warrior, however, the daemon prince momentarily assumed all the monstrous brawn and infernal ire of his physical form. How Archaon could defeat such a creature – that was at once everything and nothing – he did not know. While his mind reeled with the futility of the task, his father-in-shadow proceeded to press his diabolical advantage. While Archaon ducked, weaved and deflected with sword and shield, the daemon prince's shadow sword sheared through the black stone of the palace interior. The Dark Master roared as he pulled down columns at the Chaos warrior, forcing Archaon one way, only to stomp one of his mighty claws down in his path. The blade landed blows on Archaon's shield with such searing force that it sent him skidding left and then right across the marble floor.

When Archaon countered with his own blade, in readiness for a renewed attack, often *Terminus* passed straight through the shadow that was the daemon's weapon. Lurching forward, Archaon found the bludgeoning force of the blade become real once more as Be'lakor attempted to cleave the Chaos warrior through the back. Each time Archaon got his buckled shield between himself and the blade's furious judgement. Each time the shadow sword came that little bit closer to cutting him in half. Knocked to the side by one such shield-crumpling blow, Archaon felt the flat of the blade descend. The Chaos warrior brought up his Sigmarite sword but the daemon's weapon passed straight through it. The notched broadness of the black blade solidified as it smashed Archaon into the stone floor. Forced down on one knee, Archaon got his shield up to deflect the second and third merciless blows. He rode out the earth-shattering fury of each daemon strike, preparing to bring *Terminus* savagely up into Be'lakor's gut. As he came out from behind the shield, templar blade at the ready, the daemon prince's great taloned foot was waiting for him.

Grabbing Archaon by the torso like a bird of prey with a tiny, tortured mammal, Be'lakor kicked out, sending the Chaos warrior straight through the chamber wall. From toe to temple, the impact was a sickening agony. There was the rumble of collapsing architecture, the pitter-patter of falling grit and the hiss of masonry dust on the air. Archaon found himself in another chamber, buried in a small mound of shattered rock. It took a moment to get back to his senses. The Chaos warrior coughed up blood, spitting it at the inside of his helm. Morkar's armour had saved him from the worst the wall had to offer but still, several things felt broken. Something deep inside his chest scraped at his every twist and turn. His left arm also throbbed with a dull ache that would not be ignored. At least his back had not been broken. Then, like a spooked raven flying away, Archaon felt a flutter of panic pass through him. Scanning the darkness he found his shattered shield nearby, but the Sigmarite sword *Terminus* was half buried in debris some distance away. Archaon felt the thunder of the daemon prince's steps approach.

Hooking his thumbs beneath a section of demolished wall, Archaon heaved the shattered section off him and scrambled through the grit to his feet. He was an equal distance from both his sword and the new entrance he had made in the chamber wall. He saw the shape of the approaching Be'lakor framed in the ragged opening. Archaon surged for the creature. As the monstrosity put his grotesque, horned head through the hole, Archaon grabbed a large piece of shattered masonry from the floor and heaved it up towards his chest. As Be'lakor turned his head, Archaon smashed the thing across the jaw with the stone. Not having expected such an attack, the beast retracted his horns from the ragged hole, spitting dust and ichor. Just as Archaon ran for his weaponry, the wall exploded. Be'lakor's mighty blade had demolished it in a single swing. With broken ribs shearing the flesh inside him, Archaon rolled, picking up his shield as he did so. Be'lakor stood there in the swirling dust and raining stone.

The Chaos warrior ran at Be'lakor. Archaon was without sword but the daemon was not. Lifting the shadow blade high above his head, Be'lakor brought the Ruinous weapon down on his son-in-shadow. Although it was agony to do so, Archaon leapt at the beast, meeting the cleaving action before it had time to reach its full speed and fury. Still, the strike pounded Archon and his shield straight back at the ground. As Archaon had planned. As the savage force of the blow took him back towards the floor, Archaon angled the edge of the shield. It smashed into the daemon prince's foot, shattering the bones of his taloned toes and shearing away a single, bloody claw. The creature wailed; not expecting such a swift reply to the attack it had not reached its shadow form in time. Rearing from the floor, Archaon back-slashed the ruined shield across the daemon's wailing maw. Burning with the agony of a fracture, Archaon took the daemon with a left hook, his shield smashing the monstrosity's face back the other way.

Having unbalanced the beast, Archaon ran back towards his Sigmarite blade. He skidded down through the grit and fragments of stone, his gauntlet reaching the hilt of the buried blade. Tearing it from its scabbard of stone, Archaon pushed himself up and flew back at the injured Be'lakor. The Chaos warrior was bursting with hope against dark hope; a need for the daemon prince's pain and fury to anchor him in reality. For the monster's appetite for revenge to keep him where Archaon could kill him. Perhaps, the Chaos warrior hoped, some choice words would keep the fires of Be'lakor's fury burning bright.

'You will not destroy me!' Archaon roared at his

father-in-shadow. 'You need me…' He spat as his rabid steps took him surging through the demolished architecture of the chamber – on towards the twisted creature that was the bane of his molested existence. 'I, however, have no need for you!'

Indeed, the Chaos warrior had stoked the fires of his father's daemonic fury. More than he could know – for seconds later the colossal shadow sword passed straight through him in a murderous arc of darkness and gore. The armour of the Everchosen remained untouched by the blade that had simply solidified as it had cut Archaon in two within his plate. The Chaos warrior's legs took two more stumbling steps before collapsing beneath him. In a cacophonous clatter, Archaon reached the floor, coming to a stop on his side. With his final, dust-choked breaths he watched the hulking abomination that was Be'lakor tower over him, the muscular black flesh of his chest rising and falling with effort and a father's regret.

You think you are the first?

Blood of my infernal blood? Flesh of my damned flesh? You think you are the first fool to challenge me? I was slaughtering turncoats and traitors at the dawn of time, you miserable cur.

I am Be'lakor. First of the daemon princes. A monster given form before histories were written and the degenerate races of this world came to know their capabilities. I was a warlord like no other. Primitive. Powerful. Pure of dark purpose. Before your rat-warren cities and delusions of civilisation. Before your mongrel God-King and the fall of his hammer, the tribes of men looked to the greatest of their mortal kind to lead them. To unite the barbarian and the savage. To conquer. To kill. To create.

The degenerate legions of man were spoiling fruit in my claw. They erected great monuments to my majesty – primitive stone structures of insanity and slavish ambition. With numbers beyond counting, the base and bloodthirsty rallied to my banners of flayed skin. They butchered their own in my honour – the weak of mind, of faith and flesh – and brought death and destruction to the lesser races.

Those that hid in the great forests of the world, those that took to the depths and those who thought themselves safe in far lands beyond broad oceans. The world was mine – as it will be again. Under my leadership – nay, my sponsorship – champions rose from the raging deluge of barbaric butchery that was my horde. Swine like you, Archaon of the North. Living weapons I honed to a razor's edge. Minds to which I had introduced pride, belief and ambition. Men of traitorous heart, in whose veins treachery ran free.

Some say this was my own doing. My mistake alone. That I had underestimated how deep the rot ran in men's souls. That with my dark example, I had inspired a generation of chieftains and champions. Dread warriors of growing skill, supremacy and influence, who came to be known to the gods.

Those that know better lay blame at the feet of the Changer of Ways. The foetid god, Tzeentch, all supreme in his understanding of the world, its people and princes. Patron of the ascended. Plague of the prideful.

The horror of mortal hope and fear. It was from him that such aspirant warlords and warriors learned of their power. From him they learned the arts of conspiracy and how to catch the eye of a god. Tzeentch, the betrayer. Tzeentch, the great wheel of the world that turns. Tzeentch, the bane of all existence – but one of many. Tzeentch, the doom of Be'lakor.

He saw the Dark Pantheon's faith diluted. Their trust spread between my dark champions and chieftains of their individual choosing. Soon I was a prince among many. The first among equals. I hunted down and slaughtered those that had betrayed me or intended to do so. Their appetite for power rivalled my own. So many hungered for a dominion of their own. So many followed such fools into oblivion. I was abandoned by my hordes. Robbed of my gifts. Drained of the power fed by our dread faith.

I see the same in you, Archaon of the North, as I see the Great Changer's hand in this. His poison drips from your ear. His lies guide your hand and the blade within it. Archaon – blood of my infernal blood, flesh of my damned flesh, living legend of my dark craft – you will not be the Great Changer's puppet. You will not be the double edged sword that wounds he who wields it. You will be Archaon, Everchosen of Chaos – blood of Be'lakor's blood and flesh of Be'lakor's flesh – or you will be destroyed. Destroyed. A thousand times, destroyed.

CHAPTER V

*'To swords, shields and armour blind,
Foes to forever darkness consigned.'*
– Inscription, *The Blade of Shadows*

*The Forsaken Fortress
The Southern Wastes
Horns Harrowing: Season of the Raw*

The daemon prince hobbled back through the demolished wall, snorting its otherworldly agony from the flaring slits of its nostrils. Archaon got up from the ground. Slow. Confident. He had wounded the monstrous beast. His father-in-shadow, who had come to know pain at his hand. Archaon scooped up the wretched, black claw from the marble floor. Ichor dribbled from its cleaved root. It was a foul thing to hold. A razor-sharp thing of daemonic dread, sharpened on the souls of the faithless to a searing point. It drizzled darkness into the air. Archaon slipped it into his belt like a prize.

'They say daemons are more than the sum of their parts,'

Archaon scorned. 'We shall see. I'll take you piece by piece if necessary.'

You will know no peace, shadow-son of mine. Not so long as I live, Be'lakor told him.

Archaon pulled *Terminus* from a mound of rubble and blew dust from its blessed blade.

'Let's see if we can do something about that,' the Chaos warrior told him.

Archaon advanced. Daemon and warrior circled one another. Be'lakor hobbled. The Dark Master worked his bruised jaw and gashed lip. Ichor dribbled down the eight-pointed star carved into the flesh of his chest. Archaon watched for a weakness. An opportunity. The daemon did the same. The shattered shield rattled ever so slightly in the warrior's grasp, as though it were an effort to hold up. He bent slightly over to one side, protecting an internal affliction.

Then it happened. Like a crack of lightning or a peel of thunder, father and son were locked in savage combat of the most desperate and merciless kind. Blades clashed in the darkness of the palace. Archaon and the daemon prince moved back and forth through the flowing chambers, sable sparks showered about them as the Sigmarite sword and shadow blade sang horribly off one another. *Terminus* was a thing of hallowed beauty. Anathema to the foetid things of the Wastes. Its steel was cold certainty whose weight could be felt in the hand and whose keen edge could be felt passing through the flesh. Be'lakor's sword of shadow was an unearthly weapon of notched darkness that raged in and out of reality at its wielder's whim. It smashed the blessed burn of the Sigmarite sword aside and blazed shadow through the air, threatening to cleave the Chaos warrior in half. It mauled Archaon's shield and knocked the warrior skidding across chambers. In the daemon prince's grip its colossal length was a swirling and black storm of impending doom, the shadow of death mere seconds away.

Gritting his teeth and with rivulets of effort working their way down his face within the mugginess of his helm, Archaon began to feel the rhythm of his opponent's manoeuvres. He got a sense for the daemon's movements. The predictability even of its unpredictability. The tireless sweeps of the massive sword that carved up stone and demolished architecture, searing back at the Chaos warrior just that little bit faster before some feigning strike or new movement. The twitch of its wings before it lunged the great blade at him. Even the horrific blade seemed to have a pattern. A time to cut down through reality with all the weight and sundering inevitability Be'lakor could bring to bear. A time to bleed away to nothing like oil on water, allowing *Terminus* to pass straight through. Clash by titanic clash, Archaon tried to learn his father-in-shadow's preferences, the diabolical tells that gave away his intentions and the style of the daemon's death-dealing bladework, all the while, moments from the shadow blade's decapitating path. Be'lakor clearly knew a thousand ways to kill a man but, like all warriors, favoured a certain approach. For the daemon, the length of his cursed blade was the fury of a black tempest to be visited upon its opponent. A savage style learned at the beginning of time that had remained with the daemon prince from the murderous dawn of the world. The massive blade was something to be swung with force and unrelenting devastation at a foe until the daemon's opponent lay in bludgeoned pieces scattered about the monster.

Archaon pressed the creature. Chopping. Stabbing. Countering with savagery and brute bladework. Hair's breadth evasions snapped back into furious lunges. Sparking deflections with the mauled shield rolled into pivoting slashes, the desperation of parries carried through into bellowing ripostes. Archaon drew on every murderous instinct: the technical excellence of his templar training, the exotic elegance of Hung swordsmanship and the barbarian bludgeonry of bestial slaughter. He threw all at the daemon prince, exploiting every weakness and forcing the monster into the unfamiliarity of defensive manoeuvres. Archaon's muscles ached with the relentless speed and power of his attacks while his mind seared with the split-second strategies of the choreographed assault. About the pair, the flowing chambers of the Forsaken Fortress lay in blade smashed ruin. The daemon prince's infernal weapon had carved a path of destruction through the midnight stone of the palace, leaving rubble, smashed balustrades and derelict stairwells in his ferocious wake. All the while, Archaon was pushed back through the chambers by the blade's black fury and the storm of shattered stone unfolding before him.

An inventive combination of hacks, slashes and shield-battering took the Chaos warrior within the shadow blade's arc of streaming darkness. Archaon felt his father-in-shadow's sudden caution. The conservative urgency of his movements. The great black blade was a poor weapon for close work and while *Terminus* was by no means a small sword, it gave Archaon the advantage in tight quarters. The shadow sword worked back and forth to turn aside the templar blade's onslaught. Several times in the manic blur of the battle, the sacred steel of the Sigmarite blade almost grazed the daemon prince's royal flesh. Be'lakor roared at even the suggestion of such success, and within moments Archaon and the monster were locked crossguard to crossguard. Between the thwarted blades father and son leaned in. The daemon prince roared the gargoylesque horror of his face while the muffled thunder of Archaon's bellowing rage came back through the leering skull of his faceplate.

'No...' Be'lakor hissed and heaved the Chaos warrior back. The blades parted and Archaon skidded back through the grit on the marble floor. As he did so, his arms came out with sword and shield to retain his balance. Be'lakor was suddenly in the air, the prince's wings outstretched and his colossal blade bleeding darkness down towards Archaon. The Chaos warrior felt the blade's terrible presence rip down through flesh, muscle and bone. Solidifying to a cleaving edge, the weapon had cut down through Archaon's sword arm and passed with ghostly insistence back out through the unhallowed armour of the Everchosen. The shadow blade was real once more as it hacked straight down into the marble to the side of Archaon's boot. *Terminus* fell from his non-existent grip and rang mournfully as it hit the marble. Heaving the shadow sword free of the cleft it had created in the stone, Be'lakor backed away, scraping the black tip of the sword along the floor with him.

Archaon stumbled back. He could taste blood and bile in the back of his throat. Time seemed to slow as shock wrestled for control of his senses. His arm had been sheared from his body at the shoulder. The dead weight of a limb hung uselessly in the plate, the armour down one side of his body dribbling with the blood gushing within. Archaon could imagine the stricken horror of his face and for a moment that became all he could think about. As his ruined shield dropped from his other arm and clattered noisily to the floor, the Chaos warrior shuffled around. He bent down with horrible difficulty, scraping at the floor with the armoured digits of his gauntlet as he tried to pick up the sword in the other hand. Turning, Archaon presented himself. He would fight on for as long as he could.

Through the eye slits of his helm he found only Be'lakor's back. The daemon prince was leaving the destruction of his ruined palace. His thunderous steps took him through the mounds of rubble, the collapsed walls and past the demolished pillars. Archaon tried to get his taut lips around a challenge. He shook the templar blade and stood in a growing pool of his own blood. Be'lakor did not turn, however. He merely brought the bleak darkness of his massive blade up and chopped through the last of the thick marble pillars holding up the ceiling and the palace floor above. Archaon watched his father-in-shadow disappear as the creaking stonework gave and thousands of tonnes of crafted stone descended. Crushed. Pulverised. Broken like a child's doll. Archaon waited for death. With the harsh rumble of collapsing architecture all around, the Chaos warrior did not have to wait lo–

There is no life for you, my son-in-shadow. No existence to call your own. No flicker of hope, like the flame of a guttering candle before a storm. I brought you into wretched existence. Your flesh is mine to do with as I will. To desecrate with claw, steel or flame, if I choose. To extinguish or exalt. You can be Archaon of the North. A doom of my creation. Kill. Raze. Destroy. All in the name of shadow. Enjoy the power I have given you. Relish the corporal delights of the flesh while it is still yours. Blood. Greed. Lust. Women to carry new life. Men to suffer at your command. Men to die at your hand. Collect the dark treasures of our calling. Inspire the strong to fight at our side – for only they are worthy of the End Times to come. Thin our ranks of the weak and undeserving – let your wrath be their judge. Swell the horde and the bellies of harlots with our future. Sons on a dark path, champions in the making, loyal lieutenants to fight at my side.

There are others. There will always be others. Sons whose hearts beat beneath my rising star. Ruinous champions of our purpose if not our blood. They will see this done if you will not, shadow-son of mine. On with your dark quest. North, Archaon. North. The

Southern Wastes have given up their treasures. For the last two – the two that will mark you as the Everchosen of the Chaos gods and Lord of the End Times to come – you must return to the top of the world. Hear me, son of shadow. Let my words be remembered. Let them guide your black heart. Let them stay with your sorry soul. To return to the top of the world you must walk in the shadow of the gods themselves, along a path with no bearing that winds through a world beyond your own. It is a mad man's path and you would have to be insane to take it – but take it you must.

The End Times are coming and we are their Harbinger. Go up by going down… out by going in… north by going south. As far south as south will go. There you will find the gateway to our darkest dreams. Whatever is left of you, Archaon, shall pass through a north no mortal man has known. Beyond that is the north that tempered your Ruinous flesh and beyond that the north that will be no more. There you will find what you seek and in doing so you will realise both our destinies. You shall wear the Crown of Domination as I shall wear you. Your form shall become mine. Your soul will be but a dimming bauble in the howling darkness of your being. A memory of our time together. No man nor god shall stop me. The legions of hell shall answer to my call and the world will be mine to destroy once again. This you will do for me, Archaon of the North, for you have… no… choice.

CHAPTER V

'A wise man knows that he cannot escape his shadow. It is the stain he leaves on the world and it follows him everywhere. It was there at his birth and will be with him until his last breath. When a man changes, so does his shadow. It grows with him and expands to reflect the darkness of his presence. A shadow knows no fear. It cannot be reasoned with. It simply is. A wise man also knows that the only way to escape his shadow is to cast none in the first place – but to do that, a man must truly fall from the light.'

– Al-Malik Abyssyn, *The Book of Shadows*

The Forsaken Fortress
The Southern Wastes
Horns Harrowing: Season of the Raw

...*choice*.

Choice?

'There is always a choice,' Archaon told the daemon prince before leaping at him. *Terminus* came down with righteous force, its sacred steel sizzling in the doomed darkness of the palace. Be'lakor turned the attack aside with an arc of raging shadow. Archaon hit the marble and rolled the rest of his momentum away, the soles of his boots the beat of a gnat's wings beneath a furious backslash of the shadow sword. Up right away, Archaon feinted and then feinted again, forcing the daemon to place the colossal length of the sword where he needed it. The creature was supernaturally swift for a monstrosity of his size, and brought the heavy blade back with the whipping insistence of a rapier. Archaon skewered, slashed and batted his way through Be'lakor's defences, forcing the beast back through an archway not quite tall enough to admit the monster's dimensions. As marble and rock dust rained down between them, Archaon dashed for an adjacent arch, skidding his way through before resuming the relentless clash of blades that filled the halls of the Forsaken Fortress.

Archaon's body burned with a desire to stop, for an end to the mind-numbing combinations and the muscle-tearing efforts to strike the monstrous daemon. As the pair moved through the collapsing stairwells, sword-smashed balconies and toppling walls, the hatred between them crackled. Their moves became bolder, the arcs grew wider and the force with which cleaving blows landed, ever more devastating. The chambers of the palace were benighted no more. The darklight of black sparks rained from the ringing blades. Father-in-shadow. Son, the doom of all. Archaon roared his need to end this abomination. Be'lakor roared the frustration of a daemon will thwarted.

Archaon swung for all he was worth, pledging with taut lips before gritted teeth everything he was to whatever foetid god or power would grant him the daemon's death. As the tip of *Terminus* grazed Be'lakor's star-scarred chest and nicked the black flesh of an arm, the Chaos warrior thought that his dark prayers had been answered. The blessed blade came into contact with Be'lakor's form; the wretched skin steamed away to shadow, drawing a stifled cry from the beast. Instead of withdrawing, the monster came back at Archaon with the full fury of his diabolical will. He, Be'lakor – first of the daemon princes – would not be bested by a mortal, a thing of mere flesh and blood, even if that blood was his own.

Be'lakor brought his huge, leathery wings in tight and spun around with all the devastating grace his dread form would allow. As the monster's blade seared around with him, it solidified to a great cleaving edge of streaming shadow. Archaon saw the manoeuvre but could do little to counter its devastating progress. Be'lakor was not of the world. He was a creature of the beyond and as such he moved. Archaon just got his shield up in time. He felt the blade cleave across the mauled shield's breadth and the force of the blow through his whole body. With the tips of his boots scraping the marble floor, Archaon felt himself smashed into a nearby wall. He hit it, shattering the stone about his cursed plate, before dropping into a clattering pile.

Coughing up blood, Archaon smacked the cross guard of *Terminus* against his helm to bring him back to his senses. He felt the quake of the daemon's furious approach and got shakily to his feet. He held the mangled shield out before him. The metal was offering next to no protection now. Archaon could only hope the eight-pointed star that adorned it and the diabolical sponsors it represented still offered some protection. The monstrous blow came. Archaon went through the weakened wall this time, sliding across the marble floor of the adjacent chamber with chunks of stone debris. Be'lakor stepped through the opening he had made, his broad shoulders and wings tearing further stone down about them. He was the fury and fear of a midnight storm. The dazed Archaon scrabbled mindlessly to his feet. Vanquished from his thoughts were the impulses and justifications for seeking out his father-in-shadow. There was only room in the stone- and sword-smacked skull for ghostly notions of survival.

Archaon was up but Be'lakor was before him. Once again he was in the terrible path of Be'lakor's blade. The tip of the sword trailed a smear of shadow like a black comet. A bad omen for Archaon. The Chaos warrior got his weapon between him and the blur of the daemon's blade. The impact smashed *Terminus* from Archaon's gauntleted grip, sending the greatsword clanging off into the darkness. Instinctively Archaon brought up his shield but it was smacked aside by a backslash full of infernal spite. The daemon followed through on his turn, bringing the muscular weight of his tail around. The force of the blow sent Archaon straight through the body of a marble pillar, sending the Chaos warrior to the ground once more in a cloud of dust and pulverised stone.

Something had broken. Even the armour of Morkar had failed to protect him from the brute force of his father's fury. The bones of his right arm were shattered. He could feel the sharp ache grow to a burning uselessness. He groaned. He crawled. He got to his feet and put his armoured back to another thick pillar. The column exploded above him, showering the Chaos warrior with rock and grit. Be'lakor was there. Tearing the Forsaken Fortress apart. Smashing through every balcony, stairwell and pillar with his sword of shadow. The daemon's bellow shook the vaulted chamber, drawing further falling stone from the ceiling. Archaon moved from pillar to fat pillar. His arm raged. His stomach felt sick with the cowardly necessities of survival and empty with the realities of reason: he could not realise his true destiny if he were dead. Archaon suspected that few, if any, could have lasted as long against the First Daemon Prince of Chaos. It gave him the coldest of comforts for, as the Chaos warrior worked his way through the chamber, weaving between pillars and negotiating spaces, he came to understand that he had failed. He would not learn the secrets of his father-in-shadow's black heart. He could not compel the creature to act against his own interests by leaving him alone, and he had failed in destroying the abomination.

His hand ached – not only from the torments of shattered

bones – but also for his sword. It felt something less than a limb without it. As the shadow storm of his father's rage swept through the chamber, Archaon tried to concentrate. His sight was useless in the inky twilight of the palace. The darksight of his ruined eye gave him an impression of his surroundings. All about him was stone saturated with evil and, in the presence of such material, Archaon's own darkness cast less of a shadow. This made making out anything beyond his immediate surroundings all but impossible. Unencumbered by such concerns, the Eye of Sheerian – set in the faceplate of his helm – found *Terminus* for him. Like an image surfacing slowly from the dark depths, Archaon could make out the shape of the blade at the foot of a flight of black steps. With nothing to reflect in the lightless environs of the palace, all Archaon could make out was the spiritual torment of the blade, bleeding from the steel, as it lay on the cursed stone of the floor. Then he noticed it. The silence. The absence of fury and thunder.

You cannot hide from me, shadow-son of mine, Be'lakor's voice rumbled through the darkness. *Not here in my palace.* The voice was everywhere, bouncing about the perverse, flowing architecture of the Forsaken Fortress. *Not anywhere. There is not a place on this mortal-infested ball of rock that I will not find you, Archaon. I am Be'lakor. First prince of the...*

A shiver snaked its way down Archaon's spine. The voice was everywhere but Be'lakor was towering right behind him. Wings outstretched. Arms up. Sword of shadow ready to come down.

Archaon grunted before accelerating away. Step by step, the Chaos warrior urged himself on across the chamber, towards the steps and his sword before them. He felt the marble give way behind him as Be'lakor's downward strike stove in the floor. Leaping the hole, the daemon snarled. A beat of its colossal wings took it surging on after the Chaos warrior, each of its massive strides effortlessly outpacing Archaon's own. Archaon jumped – a decapitating swipe of the shadow blade streaming just above his head.

Hitting the floor was painful – shockwaves of agony pulsing through his broken arm. Skidding through the grit on his breastplate, Archaon slid across the marble floor, left arm outstretched for the hilt of *Terminus*. Crunching to a stop a grasping finger's length from the blade, Archaon reached out. The shattered shield was heavy on his arm and the fingertips of his gauntlet clawed desperately at the floor. Dust and grit swirled about him as he felt the daemon's wings beat above. Be'lakor had leapt also, his wings slowing his descent and the great claws of his feet anchoring into the stone floor either side of Archaon's prone form. Again the sword of shadow reared.

Rolling round to see the daemon prince, Archaon flung around his arm and sent the shattered shield spinning up at the monster's groin. Archaon had no idea what the creature kept under the loincloth of black mail and had no desire to know. The daemon grunted as the shield hit him and doubled, abandoning the swing. Archaon rolled back the other way, bringing the flat of his boot around to catch the daemon in the jaw. It was satisfying but did little to stop the furious Be'lakor who reared once more, hatred churning furiously in his eyes. Archaon rolled. There was little else he could do. The colossal length of the sword smashed down through the marble creating a crater. As the weapon descended – like a black thunderbolt tossed down from the heavens – Archaon reached desperately once more for *Terminus*. But the templar sword was gone. Rolling out of the devastating path of Be'lakor's blade, Archaon followed his sword down into the crater, only to find that the sword had smashed straight through both the floor and the ceiling of the chamber below.

It was a long drop. It seemed longer still in the tumbling darkness. With a sickening thud the Chaos warrior hit stone. He was getting used to the skull-cracking sensation. With an involuntary moan, he brought up his head and began clawing for *Terminus* in the descending debris. Stamping down through the weakened stone, Be'lakor had dropped down on outstretched wings. The floor shook as he hit it, producing a bounce and a jangle from *Terminus* that brought the metal digits of Archaon's left hand to it. Getting shakily to his feet, Archaon slouched around, holding his broken sword arm in close and offering the trembling blade of *Terminus* in the other.

Why do you bring such torment to both of us? Be'lakor asked, striding across the chamber and readying his huge, black blade for the killing blow. *Why not just simply stay down and end this suffering? Why not simply die?*

'Never...' Archaon told the daemon prince. He gestured with the Sigmarite blade in his left hand. It felt awkward and unnatural.' ...and never.'

Then you give me no choice, Be'lakor thundered, his dread voice a darkness all of its own. Be'lakor brought up his blade. Archaon brought up his own, prepared to receive the full force of the strike on *Terminus* and his left arm. Suddenly Archaon was flying back through the air. The sword strike never came. Instead, the daemon's great clawed foot kicked him in his armoured stomach. Again the sickening slam of stone passed through his body. It was uncompromising. It was agony. It was over. Archaon fell. A great deal further than a floor of the palace or a stairwell. Archaon suddenly realised that he was outside again. That Be'lakor had kicked him straight through the palace wall and back out into the chill mire of the Pustular Plain. When he hit the ground it was mercifully soft. He felt the cold, dank waters of the slush-logged tundra explore his plate for a point of entry. The stinking waters spilled in through the eyeslits of his helm as he struggled to keep his head above the rank surface. He fought to stabilise himself in the mire. As he did so, Archaon found the light from the surrounding rash of volcanic peaks almost blinding after the absolute darkness of the Forsaken Fortress. With his helm just above the surface of the ice-threaded bog, Archaon slowed his movements. He knew that thrashing about in the primordial mulch would only drag him deeper. The Chaos warrior grunted. He was in deep enough already.

Above him the towering dread of the Forsaken Fortress loomed higher than ever. The nightmare lines of its design and construction cut a diabolical shape from the volcanic haze beyond. Archaon could see the ragged hole his exit had made in the smooth black marble of the palace. From the darkness within the darkness, Archaon saw a pair of daemonic eyes fixed on him. Be'lakor. His tormentor. His soul-sworn foe. His father-in-shadow.

Archaon…

'Dark Master…'

Archaon of the North… Be'lakor's dread words burned like a numbing cold through his mind. *It is time to return home, my son. Three Ruinous treasures, the Southern Wastes had to offer the Everchosen of Chaos. Three treasures you have claimed. You already bear the eternally burning Mark of Chaos – but now you must prove yourself worthy of it.*

'Do not lecture me on worthiness, monster,' Archaon snarled. 'I will achieve what has been *eternally* denied to you – the favour of the Dark Gods.'

The final two treasures will test you as none before have.

'As I will be your test, creature of darkness,' Archaon told his father-in-shadow, 'if you attempt to take from me what is mine by Ruinous right. A test you will lose, Be'lakor.'

The wind picked up. Sheltered within the marble confines of the infernal palace, Archaon had all but forgotten the glacial bite of the Wasteland wind. Even here it frosted the volcano sides and scorched the percolating tundra of any reed or shrub foolish enough to reach up out of the mire. Archaon sensed something strange about the building gale. It seemed heavy with the cursed power that leaked perpetually from the pole – as though it were burdened with some fell purpose. As it moaned about the contours of the Forsaken Fortress, Archaon noticed that the palace was bleeding away on the breeze. Speck by black speck of dust and darkness, the monstrous building was being carried away. Fading to nothing, Be'lakor and his palace would ride the perverse winds of the dark continent, to accrete elsewhere – appearing at random from the frozen maelstrom.

Up to his neck in the mire, with his cursed plate dragging him down, Archaon knew there was nothing he could do. Even if he could crawl his way back to the palace and begin again his doomed ascent, the Chaos warrior feared that there was little left to lay his hands on. The Forsaken Fortress and its Dark Master were now but a fading, phantasmic vision in this haunted realm. The swiftest of steeds and cold steel alone had failed to bring his father-in-shadow to account. The daemon Be'lakor would not relinquish his puppet strings. Archaon would have to find some other way of cutting himself free of destiny's tangled web.

The north, Archaon…

Be'lakor's words trailed away with the streaming shadow of his palace. The Forsaken Fortress was gone.

'Aye, the north, you ruthless thing,' Archaon rumbled, 'but sooner than you think.'

As the wind died down, Archaon saw the monstrous form of Dorghar approach. The Steed of the Apocalypse trudged warily through the mire towards him, its hooves splayed like webbed feet to spread the stallion's weight on the sinking surface of the frozen bog. The reins that Archaon had hooked over the dread architecture of the palace now hung loose from the steed's steaming snout. Venturing as far as it dared, Dorghar whipped its head back and forth, casting the reins out across the stinking space between it and the sinking Chaos warrior. Resting *Terminus* on the bubbling surface, Archaon reached out with his gauntlet, snatching at the rotting mulch of the marshy tundra. When he finally had the reins in his grasp, Archaon held on as the daemonic mount stamped back through the mire, hauling him from the vice-like embrace of the bog. Dragging him to solid ground, Dorghar snorted its infernal derision as the Chaos warrior got back his breath – not only from his efforts in the swamp but also the titanic battle that had preceded it.

Tearing *Terminus* from the mire, Archaon sat up and regarded the blade. It reeked like he did and was filth-splattered like his armour. The Chaos warrior sat quietly with the dull ache of his arm and his dark thoughts for a moment. He finally turned to Dorghar, who was snorting beside him. The glassy inferno of the steed's daemon eyes fixed on the Chaos warrior. Archaon gave it back a baleful glare of his own.

'What the hell… are you looking at?' Archaon put to the creature, but steam simply streamed from the steed's snout. Getting up and sliding the filthy blade into its fur scabbard, Archaon mounted the steed, clutching his broken arm to his side. The monstrous mount seemed to wait for instructions. Archaon grunted. It would be a long way back.

'On, you darknid thing,' Archaon told it, digging gently at its flanks with the heels of his boots. 'Back to the Gatelands. To the pole, where – darkness willing – we shall re-join the horde. Then north… as my father says, to march on fresh insanities at the top of the world.'

CHAPTER VI

*'Agrammon – Slave-Lord and Daemon
Lord of Slaanesh. Caged within his own
menagerie – the captive of greed. One of
the many horrors on show.'*

– Ledger Bestiarie

*The Gatelands
The Southern Wastes
Horns Harrowing: Season of the Ravening*

It took Dorghar longer to reach the polar Gatelands than it had to reach the Pustular Plains. In part the daemonic creature had all but spent itself – first in its efforts to rid itself of its unwelcome rider and secondly under Archaon's insistence that they reach the Forsaken Fortress before it moved on. Broken by the Chaos warrior, the daemon steed would not subject its master to the dangers of its swiftest forms. While the agonies of bolt and flame had taken Archaon from the continental interior, it was a relatively tranquil journey back.

Sitting astride the back of a huge bat-like monstrosity with a colossal wing-span, effortless beats of Dorghar's wings took Archaon for leagues across the thermals of volcanic ranges and above the ice storms below. Using the sorcerous power of the Eye of Sheerian, Archaon guided Dorghar towards the howling vortex at the pole.

Coming in low across bleeding glaciers, horrific frost-shattered landscapes and rolling oceans of black snow, Dorghar descended. The crooked spires and fortified ruins of infernal palaces and daemonic redoubts crowded the lands about the shattered gate. Their tower tops and dereliction created a serrated horizon, beyond which the horrific radiance spewed into the world. Between the rancid structures – forming as they did skyward sigils in their layout and decorated with bones, flayed skin and rotting bodies – were battlefields both old and new. Armies of household beast-fiends clashed with infernal royalty in the mulch of past massacres. Daemon princes fought flocks of furies, while spawn-warriors – blessed in their monstrosity – savaged hordes of infernal horrors. Archaon felt the gaze of gods on such conflicts, as creatures slaughtered their foes with dark oaths and the death spray of ichor.

Then Archaon saw it. His own horde of bestial savages. The army had taken to the field both in the spiked shadow of Lord Agrammon's tower palace and in advance of the orders Archaon had left with them. They were hacking their way through Slaaneshi fiends, daemonettes and all manner of liberated monstrosity – creatures of Chaos who, upon achieving their freedom, had set upon the first prey they had found outside the metal walls of the menagerie.

Beating its leathery wings as it came in to land, Dorghar cleared an area of Lord Agrammon's palace guard. Sliding down off the flea-eaten back of the monstrous bat, Archaon drew *Terminus* with his left hand. His right hung numb, shattered and painful at his side. As taper-snouted beast-fiends dragged themselves back to their hooves – the low creatures having been knocked down by Dorghar's flapping descent – they experienced the dubious welcome of the Sigmarite sword's filth-encrusted steel. Like many knights, Archaon favoured his right hand for such a heavy blade. His movements betrayed a subtle awkwardness – a sluggish jarring in the shoulder and wrist that many years of practice and the comfort of unthinking preference had fashioned into a deft, fluid set of movements that almost achieved the status of reflex. The great sword still sat in the grip of a seasoned warrior, however. It was wielded with discipline, skill and a savage strength born of a knight's righteous prosecution of his duties. Such duties may have changed for Archaon, but his templar training served him well. As Archaon strode through Slaaneshi deviants, he whipped the heavy blade from side to side, cleaving beastfiends back into earth baked with the unnatural energies pouring from the shattered gate.

Beastfiends of his own horde came at him and the monstrous Dorghar with rough axes consisting of serrated shoulder blades and tusk-embedded femurs. As the daemon mount transformed and Archaon strode towards them they recognised their warlord. The shaggy monsters lowered both their rude, blood-stained weapons and their horned heads.

'Ograx?' Archaon called, cutting down a pair of Slaaneshi fiends as they attempted to rush the distracted half-breeds. The beasts began to gabble in their dark tongue and jab filthy claws ahead. Leading Dorghar on through the havoc of bestial battle – the creature having reassumed its form as a nightmarish stallion – Archaon slashed at fleeing fiends and finished foes that still clutched miserably to life in the blood-soaked earth. Walking up through the ruins of a small fortress constructed from tusks, fangs and the broken bones of a daemonic behemoth, Archaon slew with wanton abandon, his heavy blade batting aside spears and thudding down through enemy bodies. Lord Agrammon's army of bestial slaves jangled with flesh-piercing rings and the hooked chains of their captivity. Armed with barbed spears and crescent shields, their shaven flesh was muscular and oiled, while all they wore were ragged loin cloths and obscene leather masks from which their long snouts protruded. Agrammon's creatures trumpeted their fearful delight as the soul-scorching torment of Archaon's blessed steel passed through their flesh.

When Archaon found Ograx, the beast-prince was atop a pile of butchered Slanneshi corpses, blood-drenched in his skins and shrunken skulls. Surrounded by a mob of his hulking southern beasts, the beastfiend champion wheeled about with his skull-head axe, chopping and pounding Lord Agrammon's slave breeds into the ground. Bipedal nightmares with whipping tongues and hook-taloned claws came at them only for Ograx and his infernal herdkin to knock skulls from snaking heads and screeching predators back into one another. Sweeping this way and that with *Terminus*, Archaon took the legs out from under one, before lopping the slashing tail from another. Burying the blade in the side of another before Ograx's axe could reach it, the bestial prince took a moment to shake the blood lust from his horned head and recognise his master. As one of the Slaaneshi seekers tried to raise its head from a butchered mess on the ground, Ograx stepped forward and kicked the skull clean off the daemon with his hooves.

'Your orders were not to attack until the third day,' Archaon bawled across the din of battle, turning away just long enough to casually slash a fleeing beastfiend across its shaven back. It trumpeted a screech as its muscular flesh parted like butter. 'Yet I find my horde fully engaged in an attack on the palace. Why, mongrel prince?'

The hulking half-breed proceeded to wrap his thick, bovine lips around what Archaon assumed to be an explanation, breaking off only to mercilessly butcher and smash the squealing slaves of Lord Agrammon's palace guard. While Archaon could pick up a little of what Ograx the Great was saying, between the snorting, grunting, garbled words, dark tongue and wanton murder, it was almost impossible to make out what the creature was conveying. Archaon decided to use a language that they both understood well. Bringing

Terminus between them, the Sigmarite blade bubbling and spitting with Slaneeshi gore, Archaon rested the blade tip on the slab of one of the prince's pectoral muscles. 'Why attack?' the Chaos warrior put to the creature once more, as simply as he could.

Archaon now realised the danger of having left the horde in Prince Ograx's clawed hands for as long as he had. One of the monstrous warrior's bestial brothers stepped forward, rumbling some kind of bare-toothed threat as a bone ring bounced about in his wet snout. A snout that Archaon broke with the pommel of *Terminus*. As the beastfiend bent over double, clutching its smashed face, Archaon drifted the blade tip of *Terminus* back down onto the wall of muscle that was Ograx's chest. The half-breed looked down at the filthy steel and then up at Archaon with the dead eyes of a beast of burden. While Archaon and Ograx stared at one another down the length of the Chaos warrior's blade, the southern beast with the broken face was set upon by a fiend that dragged the half-breed off to cut up with its claws in another part of the derelict bone palace. More words dribbled from Prince Ograx's lips. Slow. Thoughtful. Measured. No more comprehensible to the Chaos warrior than those that had proceeded them. Tiring of such activity, Archaon looked about. Hordes of his beastfiends were taking the fight to Agrammon's slave soldiers and the daemonic horrors that flanked them. Blood and infernal ichor flew. Heads rolled. Beasts were broken.

'Where's Sheerian?' Archaon demanded, looking back at Ograx. 'Where is that sorcerous wretch?' Archaon would much rather have the Tzeentchian ancient translate his fury for him. This time the half-breed prince favoured a simple gesture. Bringing his meaty fist up slowly, he moved Archaon's blade away and extended a single finger, pointing towards the urchin-like outline of Lord Agrammon's tower palace. 'In there?' Archaon put to the creature. Ograx the Great nodded with a barely suppressed snarl. 'Where are my Swords of Chaos? Where is Giselle?' Archaon pushed. Ograx kept his finger directed at the palace before moving it down to one of the butchered slaves at the Chaos warrior's feet. Archaon jabbed his sword at the slave and then offered up his wrists. 'Prisoner?' he asked the half-breed. Ograx the Great nodded.

Archaon swore under his breath. It became clear why his horde were fighting. They had not attacked the palace. They had been attacked. A retaliatory action for a perceived assault on the menagerie. Thinking that Archaon's camped host was responsible for the chaos Archaon alone had visited upon Agrammon's foetid collection, the daemon lord had despatched his own creatures to deal with the threat. With Sheerian, the Swords and Giselle taken, Ograx was only marching on the palace in order to get them back. Archaon nodded to himself. Unfortunately, Ograx had no idea what to expect upon reaching the inside of the palace's metal outer wall – how Agrammon's daemonettes would cut the horde to pieces in the spiralling gauntlet of the menagerie. This would require a different approach, Archaon decided. He would need access to the palace faster than the days and lives it would take for the horde to slaughter its way in. With the main body of Lord Agrammon's palace guard still within the walls, Ograx and the bestial horde had their part to play in strategically drawing them out.

As the glistening muscular form of a Slaaneshi slave soldier came at them, Archaon turned, cleaving the beastfiend's head and tapering snout from its shoulders in a left-handed back swing. Sheathing the bloody blade, Archaon picked up the creature's head, the shock of its sudden death still fixed on its face. Tossing it to Ograx, Archaon pointed to the palace as the great beast had.

'So many skulls, prince,' Archaon said, allowing the words to sink in. Even in Archaon's tongue the hulking half-breed knew the word 'Skull'. 'I want them. Take them for me.'

Something approaching a brute smile pulled at the monster's thick lips. It turned, holding the Slaaneshi beastfiend's head in one claw and its skull-axe in the other. It roared Archaon's orders in dark tongue to the high heavens, the horde and the Blood God itself. Archaon felt the effect of such a rallying call. Agrammon's slave soldiers died faster, heads flew further and gore fountained higher about them.

Leading Dorghar away, Archaon heard the mount snort its derision. The entity was clearly unimpressed. The Chaos warrior patted the steed on the spiked ridge of its snout, knowing the daemon would hate such treatment.

'We are going in there,' Archaon told it, indicating the spiky outline of the palace.

The daemon mount snorted its refusal. The Steed of the Apocalypse had been liberated from Lord Agrammon's horrific menagerie. It had no intention of returning to captivity. Archaon stroked his gauntlet down the creature's sable back. 'Show a little backbone, beast. My intention is to free captives, not become one. I have no more appetite for that than you.'

Hauling himself up into the saddle, Archaon dug his heels into the creature's flanks. Standing still, the steed would not move. 'Move, damn you,' the Chaos warrior ordered. Still the daemon remained still. Archaon felt the beast transform beneath him. Its skin hardened and creaked. Sliding off, Archaon found himself standing before a gargoylesque statue of the mount. Tall. Proud. Terrifying. Made of stone. For the first time, Archaon considered how this might look to both friend and foe. 'You are embarrassing yourself and what's more, creature, you are embarrassing me.' The statue of the steed seemed unmoved by Archaon's entreaties. 'We don't have time for this,' Archaon told the monster finally, before looking down at the bodies carpeting the crooked courtyard of the bone palace.

Spotting a stone hammer in the clutches of one of his dead beastfiends, Archaon casually knelt down and slipped the rough weapon from its owner's death grip. Archaon stood up. Still the daemon steed remained resolute, the dark stone of its construction soaking up the balelight of the demolished gate beyond. 'Last chance,' Archaon told the mount, his back to it. As a statue, Dorghar offered no kind of response. Not a snort. Not one of its furnace-like hisses. Suddenly swinging the rude hammer around with his left hand, Archaon smashed through the statue's stony teeth. Before the Chaos warrior's punishment, the mount's mouth had been a small cave of sharp stalactites and stalagmites – a daemonic maw crowded with stabbing fangs. As rock sprayed from the steed's mouth, the stone hide of the creature creaked back to daemonflesh. There was hissing and snorting now. The steed bucked and kicked, its empty mouth chomping feverishly at the air.

Archaon threw the hammer to one side but as he did, the daemon Dorghar stomped through the bodies and bloody earth at him. Stopping just before its master, it leaned in, touching the bone barbs that formed the ridge of its muzzle against Archaon's helm. Dorghar's eyes raged like a pair of hellish suns while the infernal fires within the beast hissed, spat and roared from the creature's mouth. As they did, the light of such fires glowed from the depths of both mouth and nostrils. Silhouetted against such brilliance were new fangs, growing into place and turning the monster's mouth into a nest of dagger-like teeth. Longer. Sharper. More lethal than before. With the steed's head against his own, Archaon watched the features of the stallion grow in horror. Skin ruptured to admit bone spikes, the hairs of its mane snaked with a serpent-like ripple while the monster's brawn bulged, tearing its own black flesh with ugly scars and raw splits. Archaon's gauntlet was already clasped around *Terminus*. It would be an awkward draw but the Chaos warrior was confident that he could have the daemon's stallion-head from its thick neck. 'Just get me in,' Archaon offered. 'Me alone.'

Dorghar seemed to consider. The roar of its furnace-like fires died a little and finally the bone spikes on its head came away from the Chaos warrior's helm. Releasing his Sigmarite sword, Archaon once more mounted the Steed of the Apocalypse and once more the monster seemed to stall.

'Don't,' Archaon told it, holding his broken arm in close and sending a ripple through the reins using his left hand.

Dorghar turned its head to one side and snorted its derision. As it surged away, Archaon nearly left the armoured saddle. The steed might have taken on the form of a black stallion but the power and reflexes beneath Archaon were those of a daemonic monstrosity.

Clutching the saddle between his thighs, Archaon pulled on the reins and drew himself closer to Dorghar's steaming flesh. At such speed, it was Archaon's instinct to hold his body down close to the creature's own, breastplate to back. He had experienced enough of the daemon's speed on their journey to the Forsaken Fortress and might have punished Dorghar further, but for the fact that he had told the monster that time was a factor. Dorghar weaved in and out of murderous throngs, leaping over tusk-lined palisades and straight through the mess of bone-weave walls.

With ribs and splintered spine raining about them, Archaon and Dorghar thundered across the field of battle. As bloody pools splashed up about the steed's hoof falls, the half-breeds of Archaon's horde roared their bestial jubilation. Trampling Slaaneshi slave soldiers and braining beastfiends with its hooves as it leapt and landed, the mount was unstoppable. It batted crescent shields and beastfiends behind them out of its path and into the ranks of compatriot creatures nearby. Spears came at them with savage surprise. It was the first thing Lord Agrammon's beasts could think to do upon seeing an armoured Chaos warrior and a daemon mount where seconds before brother beasts had been standing. The slave soldiers were not much for pelting such weapons and most went wide or high. The wicked tips of several of the spears glanced off Archaon's filthy plate while those that did thud into Dorghar's daemonflesh were soon shaken loose by the creature's thunderous advance. Moments later they were snapped and splintered beneath its raging hooves.

As Dorghar surged on through the Slaaneshi horde, beastfiends began to part for the daemon's thunderbolt progress. Trumpeting through their elongated snouts, the half-breeds clutched their crescent shields in close and stepped back behind the presented points of their cruel spears. Guiding the steed this way and that, Archaon pushed Dorghar on across the mulchlands of daemonic decay, through the hollowed nightmare of great palaces in ruin and about the colossal chunks of strange stone that littered the contested lands about the southern polar gate. The once mighty gateway to the beyond, now lying demolished in massive warp-shattered pieces, some long buried beneath the perpetual carnage that raged about the breached portal, some protruding from the twisted landscape, cracked, ancient and encrusted. Some sat in fresh craters like polished, steaming obsidian – unblemished by gore, filth or age – as if they had crashed just moments before. Weaving through the gargantuan wreckage of the Chaos gate, the pieces like standing stones that had toppled and smashed, Dorghar raced on. The steed's hooves churned up the mud, old blood and bones of the Gatelands in its midnight wake.

The palace of the daemon lord Agrammon grew before them, a towering, serrated silhouette against grim radiance bleed-streaming into the world from the ruptured gateway. The shaven beastfiends of the palace had their own predicaments here. Having freed one of Agrammon's prize exhibits, Archaon had rocketed into the north on the hunt for his father-in-shadow. The Chaos warrior had not spared a thought for the havoc he had wreaked, thinking – like the daemon Dorghar – never to return to the dread palace and its caged suffering. The stinking menagerie had been Agrammon's collection of exotic, monstrous freakery for thousands of years. Never before had the silent misery of the inmates been so afflicted by hope. The creatures that Archaon had set free had liberated other monsters. Freeing compatriot specimens from bars, chains and sorcerous charms or simply charging through cages and twisted enclosures in unbridled rage, the beasts had set in motion a chain reaction of escapes. Keeper daemonettes had failed to contain the spreading havoc and now, out on the bone-strewn Wastes upon which Agrammon's beastfiends marched, all manner of monstrosity was charging to freedom.

Here Archaon found that the beastfiends had little interest in a foe storming towards them. The slave soldiers were running for their lives from chaotic predators that pounced on their fresh flesh. Sickening spawn-things seized them from behind with tentacle, claw and scything limb. Sky-screeching horrors that stretched their ragged wings and fell on the beast guard from great heights with talon and maw. Suddenly the throng of beastfiends parted before the galloping Dorghar's furious advance, screaming into the broiling heavens as they were swept aside in a tsunami of ichor-slick earth. Some former exhibit of the menagerie – a malformed titan whose hunchbacked torso was afflicted by a multitude of monstrous limbs – shook the ground with the panicked footfalls of its escape. Swinging clubbed fists and the warped deformity of colossal limbs before it, the giant cleared small armies of its former guards and tormentors out of its path. Broken beastfiends flew through the air this way and that before the mindless passage of the terrified brute.

Archaon hauled on the reins. The Chaos warrior had no intention of being smashed to oblivion by the small mountain of twisted flesh and bone. Dorghar would not be stopped, however. The steed increased its speed, turning a palace-storming gallop into a furrow-cutting streak through the Gatelands that left hoof prints of flame behind it. As the giant's mighty flesh clubs pulverised the shrieking beastfiends before them, Archaon resisted the urge to grab for his sword. Doing so would have taken his hand from the reins and, at this speed, the Chaos warrior thought such an action suicide. Dorghar and Archaon were suddenly hit by the physical force of the malformed giant's fearful roar. Thinking that it was being attacked, the titan swung back with the bone-spiked boulder of one of its club fists. Archaon felt himself hold onto his breath, waiting for impact. The force of the giant's fury would likely smash both him and his daemon steed into a skyward stream of gore. The Chaos warrior braced for the horrifying impact – an impact that never came.

Archaon felt the Steed of the Apocalypse change beneath

him. No longer was the armoured saddle sitting on the back of a nightmare, black stallion. There was no snorting nor thunder of hooves. Archaon, sitting squarely in the saddle, sailed on a swarm of screeching imps. Dorghar had changed once more, this time assuming the form of a flock of tiny, black furies. A storm of tiny wings, lithe bodies and razored claws, the throng spread out as the giant's gargantuan fist smashed through the warp-baked earth. As the giant stormed on, grit and congealed ichor raining down about it, the monstrosity had no idea that it had failed to destroy the rider and his steed. Screeching together once more, the imps swarmed beneath the Chaos warrior. Those slave soldiers that had somehow survived the giant's destructive passage had Dorghar to look forward to. While Archaon sat astride the flock of tiny, shrieking monsters they shredded through Agrammon's Slaaneshi soldiers.

Within moments the palace gate was before them. The barbican was a smashed mess of twisted metal. Within the palace walls, a stampede of liberated monstrosities had grown and grown as it was corralled along the spiralling, concentric pathway that led through the menagerie. Great horned beasts, things of tusk and monstrous bulk tore through the bars of adjacent cages in the raging hope of escape and the terror of being recaptured. Creatures and captives from such cages were swept up in the stampede, swelling its force and number as charms were torn from their necks and the hold of Jharkill's primitive magic broken. As Dorghar swept Archaon up and over the palace walls, the Chaos warrior could see the monstrous horde of former exhibits pouring through the breached barbican with many helplessly impaled on the metal spikes that faced both inward and out from the metal wall.

Sweeping from side to side with the flock, the screeching swarm took him over the devastation of the menagerie. The broken bars of cages lined the gravel walkways. The long cavalcade that had brought Archaon in previously was now just ivory splinters stomped into the earth. Daemonettes had been stamped to death and crushed against the bars of the cages they had formerly patrolled. While many creatures had fled the palace menagerie at their first, terrified opportunity, the more savage and intelligent had remained. Predacious monsters stalked the walkways and demolished enclosures, their freedom – both from their cages and the sorcerous charms that enslaved them – allowing old instincts to return.

Creatures of claw, fang and sabre-tooth savaged their former keepers, tearing apart shrieking daemonettes between them like packs of voracious wolves and feasting on the carcasses. Long-snouted hounds ran for their lives, cowering in the demolished cages they had formerly been charged with guarding, as chimeric predators hunted them down and savaged the infernal watch dogs. Half-breeds, daemonkin and warrior spawn snatched broken bars, bones and abandoned weaponry, moving between cages to free further monsters and setting upon daemonic keepers whose slashing whips and shrill warnings did little to keep them from slaughtering Lord Agrammon's sultry servants.

Like a flock of bats, Dorghar began a circle of the tower palace. The inner enclosures had suffered the worst of the damage. Now that the daemon lord's most prized exhibits were free they visited their dangerous abilities on the tower and the structures about it. A glowing blaze danced about the ruined enclosures and scorched the spiked side of the metal tower, as a dread phoenix-like monster of feather, flame and flesh-shearing beak flapped about the structures, fanning the destruction. A shovel-nosed dragon waddled straight through the enclosures, the mighty crystal spines that covered its body dripping with the blood and torn flesh of shredded daemons. An octopoid monstrosity tore itself into pieces as the colossal beast attempted to haul the spiked tower down at its base.

Multi-limbed spawn gibbered and climbed like tree-top mammals, desperate to find a way inside, while carnivorous splice-creatures scrambled up through the twisted forest of poison-tip spikes with grapnel-like claws. The undead colossus, the green curselight burning bright within the towering rot of its carcass, tore the twisted mess of tangled enclosures up in its great mummified hands and smashed at the side of the palace citadel. At the huge entrance to the tower was the crumpled metal of a thick door. The unleashed fury of the abominate slaughterbrute smashed at the door. Horns, crushing jaws, hooves, clawed fists, the chitinous armour of spiked shoulders: the blood-crazed monstrosity could smell prey inside the tower and would not be denied deaths and the wanton destruction that was its only reason for being. It would pound the great metal door of the palace tower down or pound itself to a messy, god-honouring death in its attempt to do so.

As the shrieking flock of imps banked and circled the tower, Archaon could see the structure shake under the assault. The huge, cloud-scraping crescent that sat atop the bell spire honouring Lord Agrammon's patron power wobbled, toppled and tumbled down the side of the building. It fell down the considerable height of the citadel before bouncing off the downward angled spikes of the tower, spinning and smashing into the flame-racked menagerie. As he circled, the Chaos warrior would have liked to have seen the tortured exhibits and former captives tear down the tower of the daemon but with Giselle, the sorcerer Sheerian and the Swords of Chaos trapped within he could not risk such wanton havoc. He needed to do what every other former exhibit of Lord Agrammon's was failing to achieve. He needed to get inside.

From within, watch-daemons were blowing their horns to call reinforcements back from the Wastes outside the palace, not knowing that Ograx the Great and Archaon's bestial horde were keeping them busy with their deaths. From the inner part, the huge and bulbous bell tower crowned the spiked shape of the citadel, and the Chaos warrior could hear the ecstatic moan of the bell there. With his slave soldiers and daemonettes trapped inside, caught up in the chaos of the menagerie or being slaughtered outside the palace walls, Agrammon had become desperate. The groaning boom of the bell could mean only one thing as its peeling madness rolled through the Gatelands and the dread palaces crowding the ruin-spewing portal set in the bottom of the world. The daemon lord was appealing to other servants of Slaanesh, infernal royalty and infernal overlords also pledged to the Prince of Pleasure. For all Archaon knew, he was calling for assistance from the daemon lords in service to other Chaos Powers, in the perverse hope that they might assist him for their own diabolical reasons. That, Archaon could not allow.

Spiralling up and around the tower, Archaon guided the shrieking flock of tiny furies up towards the churning clouds above. The heights were featureless and devoid of windows, openings or even arrow slits. It was a barbed nightmare of black, otherworldy metal all the way to the top, glistening with all manner of deviant toxins designed to inflict pleasure, madness and death – in that order. Only the twisted columns of the metal belfry seemed to allow any admittance, with the bombastic boom of the citadel bell allowed to travel unhindered by thick metal wall or nest of spikes. Dorghar seemed to know what Archaon was planning to do and swooped straight in on the bell tower. The Chaos warrior thought he might leap to the structure but the Steed of the Apocalypse had other ideas, the flock screeching straight through the belfry. Archaon turned his helm, expecting to hit the unforgiving metal of the bell tower or even the bell itself.

As the tiny, winged monsters shrieked and streamed through the columns, Archaon found his boots reach the belfry floor. Grabbing out for the twisted metal of the structure, Archaon steadied himself. He slid down onto his knees, poked his head between the columns and stared down the serrated lethality of the citadel. With the bell tower buffeted by the perverse gales and tinged by the broiling clouds about the Southern Gate, it appeared to be one hell of a drop. To make matters worse, the monstrous assault being mounted at the base of the tower caused the structure to sway with a sickening motion. The Chaos warrior watched the swarm of furies weave, spiral and surge away. Turning, he found one of the imps clutching to a twisted metal column beside him.

'Never,' Archaon told it, catching his breath, 'never, do that again.'

The imp chittered cheekily to itself before flapping its wings and swooping off after the rest of the flock. Getting once more to his feet, Archaon found himself in the presence of the tower's great bell. Everything about its daemonic craftsmanship seemed darkly suggestive, and even the rapturous moan of its peeling was a soul-splitting sound that passed straight through the Chaos warrior and his plate in its attempt to stir him.

Looking under the bell and down through the tower interior, Archaon found it to be surprisingly devoid of structures. He had expected to fight his way through well-guarded chambers and twisting stairwells. Instead, he found a largely open space within the metal walls of the citadel – a colossal, vaulted single throne chamber housed within the soaring monstrosity of the palace tower. Archaon flared his nostrils. The twilight within was lit with torches dribbling with the fat of skinned half-breeds while the stench of the interior smelled like a torture chamber.

As he peered down through the darkness and distance of the tower interior, Archaon had to rely not only upon the sight of his good eye but also his darksight, and the piercing visions granted to him by the Eye of Sheerian. The wretched light of the torches danced their dull radiance off the expanse of metal below. Tower-spanning blades. Spear-tipped poles. A twisted nest of razor-edge shafts, serrated beams and inward pointing spikes. There were bodies everywhere. Things that had shafts of metal straight through them. Things hanging from hooks and sharpened spines. Things in a state of perpetual disembowelment. Things suspended from spikes running through limbs, hearts and skulls. Exotic half-breeds. Daemonforms that could barely be looked upon. Monstrosities of every variety – chimeric fusions, warped titans, spawn tortured by their many godly gifts. A personal collection and private pleasure. Something Lord Agrammon reserved for himself. The throne room was a twisted cage turned inside out – one in which the captives were impaled on the very bars that imprisoned them and through some warped damnation, were never allowed to perish. Archaon listened to the doomed specimens groan their agonies and ecstasies away, reaching out for one another with hands, claws and deformed appendages that trembled with the torture of the effort.

With a snarl of distaste curling his lip, Archaon climbed through, under the booming bell and down through the twisted nest of blades and spikes. The crowded criss-crossing of black metal shafts made the descent a long but easy one – even with the use of only one arm. As he moved down through the spider's web of lethal skewers, the Chaos warrior took care to avoid the grasping bodies of the impaled and the myriad spines, hooks and spikes that seemed designed to find their way in through his armour. He did his best to negotiate shafts and poles that were slick with the never-ending drizzle of blood, sweat and tears that fell down through the twisted nest of the afflicted like rain. Some spikes glistened with painted poisons or potions that would visit upon bare flesh only the Prince of Pleasure knew what. Other shafts were supernaturally sharp blades designed to shear off hand or foot. It was a death trap like no other Archaon had encountered.

As he descended, Archaon could see the throne room proper below him. The nest of skewering death merely existed as a private exhibit to be enjoyed at any time, the falling drizzle of bodily fluids helping to feed the shallows that flooded the floor of the chamber. The cacophony of the assault drowned out even the distant peeling of the bell, which Archaon now saw was being rung by some kind of daemonic herald – a child-like daemonette wearing its horns like a twisted crown. The herald hauled on a razored chain that ran the distance between the huge ground floor chamber and the bell tower. Meanwhile outside, the slaughterbrute and a growing number of other monstrosities were fighting their way into the tower. Pounding at the metal walls and door. Tearing, scratching and biting. Bathing the tower base in flame, the glow of which could be seen even inside the chamber.

Peering down through the dungeon twilight of the chamber, the miserable drizzle and the bars, Archaon looked for Giselle and the others. It did not take him long to find them. Even below the nest of skewers and blades in which he was perched, the interior walls of the throne room were carpeted with smaller spikes and hooks. Spread out around the chamber, Archaon could see that Agrammon had ordered the newly taken prisoners cruelly hung from such adornments. He saw Eins, Zwei and Drei hanging limply from a nest of piercing spines, their impaled hands and wings spread out so that the warriors could not reach their precious bone swords. Archaon could see the ancient sorcerer Sheerian hanging from a single wicked hook by his hunch, while the misshapen Vier was suspended nearby.

Then he saw her. Giselle, still draped in skins and furs, her head drooping to one side within her shaggy hood, and her body hanging from wicked barbs embedded cleanly through her delicate hands. Sheerian and the Swords had been hooked at intervals about the wall, with Giselle situated at the rear of the throne room.

As he stared at her, Archaon didn't quite know what was happening inside him. His chest fluttered with something approaching genuine feeling. Something that wasn't anger, scorn or some dark expression of his black heart. It felt light but stung deep, like a stiletto blade so sharp that it had passed unknowingly through the flesh to stab the organs within. Archaon knew he wasn't feeling the burning need for revenge – although he understood that would come. It wasn't that the daemon lord had taken something precious from Archaon and had to pay. That notion too would come to pass.

It was the ghost of some kind of responsibility that haunted Archaon. Something the doomed warrior thought he was long past. Something that he feared was unacceptable weakness in a champion of the Ruinous Powers, in he who would be the Everchosen of Chaos. Archaon knew it was more than just a fear. He looked about the nest of daemons he had crept into. If it were not for Giselle, he probably wouldn't have risked such a suicidal endeavour. Sheerian and the Swords had sold their souls to the Dark Gods – whatever their fate was, Archaon was confident that the Tzeentchian sorcerer and the winged warriors of Chaos had it coming. The lost and the damned that followed in Archaon's exalted footsteps only respected strength. In time they would rally to the banner of some other dark champion or worse butcher than Archaon for the Ruinous treasures he possessed. It had happened before, and the Chaos warrior had every intention of those lost souls losing their lives in his dread service long before they entertained such an inclination.

Kneeling above their bodies, their blood leaking down the walls and into the shallows, Archaon did come to wonder why he had kept the Swords and Sheerian around so long. The sorcerer certainly had his uses and the Swords had appointed themselves his bodyguards long before he knew who he really was. While damnation had cost him almost everything – a damned soul and a cold heart to go with it – he still felt some strange attachment to Giselle. Long after he had given himself to his dark fate and the necessities of his search for the treasures of Chaos, he had hardened to the afflictions of common men. He had loved the God-King and his service to Sigmar as a templar knight. Such love had been swallowed by the flames of his anger. A soul-scarring sense of betrayal so powerful that it had sent Archaon into the service of Dark Gods. In serving himself, he would destroy the cold majesty of all those foolish enough to call themselves god.

He had loved Dagobert – the priest who had raised him like a father. Frozen to an agonising numbness on the Southern Wastes, Archaon had felt little or nothing at the priest's death. A man who had loved him so much his loyalty had endured through heresy and madness, loved him so much that he had followed him on a doomed crusade to the other side of the world. Had tried to save him from his dark fate, from himself and the *Yien-Ya-Long* – and the only flame Archaon could keep stoked in the icy wilderness of the Wastes and his own heart was the burning desire to realise his dark and all-dominating destiny. Archaon could not save Dagobert from the abominate dragon, however, and although he made the monstrosity pay the price with its own life, he simply filled the emptiness Dagobert had left behind with his indomitable will to survive, to succeed and to see the dark days of the End Times silence man and god alike.

Giselle. Giselle. Had he come to love Giselle? To truly love her? From a young and foolish Sister of the Imperial Cross – and she had barely been that when he first saved her from the forest beastmen – she had become his prisoner. Like Dagobert she had tried to save him and save the world from his fate. She had poisoned him with the pure silver of her god. She had repeatedly tried to slip steel into his flesh. She had failed, but for all Archaon knew she still intended to do so. In the cold, dark insanity of the Northern Wastes, with nought but death to keep a traveller company, they had found one another. An unspoken need – at first physical – sprung from their shared hate.

To Giselle, Archaon was an abomination. A man tainted by fate, whose bottomless detestation for all the world would be the end of it. A man who hated his sponsors as much as his enemies and would stop at nothing to realise his destiny. To Archaon, Giselle was anathema. It was an exquisite agony to press his lips to her. To touch her. To share her bed. Her professed faith in her God-King had burned impossibly bright in the darkness at the top of the world. Of all those who shared Archaon's journey, she alone seemed to have kept her sanity. The corruptive influence of the Shadowlands seemed to have no effect upon her. While all else in Archaon's horde grew uglier and more unsightly with the passing years, their ageing flesh a patchwork of scars new over old and the gifts of darkness changing them from the inside out, Giselle had remained as pure and young as the day Archaon had met her. He had thought of her as plain at first and perhaps even tedious in the blindness of her beliefs. In the hideousness of the Wastes, however, he had come to truly see her beauty. Her devotion to the God-King that had formerly been an object of sour derision and hatred had become a wonder to Archaon. A faith held with such indomitable conviction that it buried even his own in its shadow.

He knew he should have killed her long ago, for it would have been a mercy. He knew he should have cut her loose, but like *Terminus* he could not bear to be parted from his past. Saving Giselle had been the last truly noble thing Archaon had done in the world. This need was a small, toxic part of himself that he was unwilling to let go. Giselle had become part of that. Archaon had to confront the possibility that in keeping her with him, some scintilla of his soul desired saving and that deep down, under the darkness, hate and the weight of dread expectation, he reserved a kind of hope that might one day lead the way to redemption. Perhaps Giselle Dantziger might save him still. Perhaps that was the reason Archaon had kept her close. So very close. Did he love her? He didn't know if after all the terrible things he had done and would do, he was capable of such a feeling. He knew he couldn't be without her. He knew, in dragging her to the other side of the world in the company of Ruinous and evil men, that despite her simple faith she had changed. While her skin was as soft as ever, her eyes were hard. Since coming to the bottom of the world, since the horror of the *Yien-Ya-Long*, she had changed. Her affections were not so much cold as absent. She walked through the frozen nightmare of the Wastes among beasts and daemons in a silent daze. Like her soft fingertips across his doomed flesh, Archaon had enjoyed her scorn, her challenges and their little war of words. She had said little in the months spent traversing the Southern Wastes. Like his Swords of Chaos, she had become silent.

The firebrand that Archaon had come to appreciate amongst his horde of sycophantic savagery had steamed away to nothing in the ice and snow. Her sufferings had sapped her of everything but a miserable determination to go on. Now here, in the palace of a daemon lord, at the very bottom of the known world, she suffered still. No more. No more.

In the booming cacophony of the infernal throne room, Archaon searched for threats. Foes that would come to know the Chaos warrior's cold steel. Daemonettes stood in the shallows. Armoured in spiked plate fashioned from the same strange metal as the tower, they carried the broad serrated blades of sickle swords and crescent shields bearing the sigil of their daemon lord, set within the Ruinous emblem of the Prince of Pleasure. Only parts of their chests were left exposed by curving chestplates – to honour their Lord Agrammon's infernal sponsor. The daemonettes knelt in the shallows, horned heads down, the gauntlets of the left hands extended to cover their sister's daemon breast in a formation of throne-honouring supplication. These were not keepers of the royal menagerie but Agrammon's palace guard. The elite of his daemonic horde. Should the beasts outside gain entrance to the tower it would fall to them to be Lord Agrammon's last line of defence. They would have to face Archaon first – as would their monstrous master.

Lord Agrammon was a monstrous creature indeed: a gangly, serpentine thing of desirous daemonflesh and dark appetite. Up close, Archaon appreciated that Agrammon was neither a he nor a she but a towering it.

A hermaphrodite horror, the daemon's long face held an unspeakable beauty that trailed into two sweeping horns and a cranial nest of long tentacles that drooped down behind the nightmare creature. The appendages oozed and slithered about the daemon's body, keeping it sickly and slick like an eel. The monster's upper body clicked with chitinous claws and pincers that continually nipped at the thing's smooth flesh, opening ichor-dribbling wounds that almost immediately healed in a perpetual frenzy of regenerative affliction. Its arms were slender but taut with the daemonic strength required to lift the spindly nightmare off its colossal talons.

Each one presented a clawed hand, within a clawed hand, within a clawed hand. Its chest and torso bled some different kind of noxious poison or infernal potion. These ran the length of Agrammon's serpent body, the slime-exuding coils of which ran around and around the sensual suggestion of the daemon's throne. The Slaaneshi horror wore no clothes or armour but simply jangled with the studs, spikes and decorative rings that were hooked through its infernal flesh.

Shimmying along one of the poles that spanned the tower, Archaon reached the back wall of the chamber. Slowly... silently... Archaon began the careful climb down, using the filthy hooks and poison-smeared spikes that decorated it. Taking great care not to impale himself on the lethal points and even greater care not to attract the attention of Agrammon and the daemonettes in the throne room, Archaon descended through the murky twilight.

Between the obscene throne, the dungeon glow of the torches and the haze of drizzle falling from the unfortunates above, Archaon was largely hidden from view. With the thunder of the assault on the palace door drowning out the scrapes of boot and the exertions of climbing down with one arm, Archaon risked a little more speed. It was ill-advised and the Chaos warrior slipped from a curved barb and fell the rest of the way, splashing into the shallows. By the time the foetid spray of gloop had fallen about him, Archaon had already cleared *Terminus* from its fur scabbard. He expected to be set upon by Agrammon's daemonette elite but the noise had attracted little attention. The daemonette herald continued to ring the tower bell. The booming assault on the door continued. The lesser daemons that made up Lord Agrammon's personal guard kept their formation before the throne. Agrammon itself was distracted by another matter.

From the shadows nearby, Archaon heard the jangle of chains. Being careful of the spikes, Archaon backed to the wall, as though impaled there himself beside the hanging Giselle. Four long-snouts brought forth a hulking prisoner. The beastfiends each held the end of a chain attached to a single metal collar around the prisoner's fat neck. Hauling at the chains, the long-snouts dragged the stumbling creature until he was presented before the throne. With the throne's back to him, Archaon couldn't see Agrammon's reaction to the prisoner but noted that the nest of tentacles snaking down the throne's back became twitchy and aggravated as though the daemon were displeased.

Looking back to the prisoner, Archaon instantly recognised him. He was looking at Jharkill, Agrammon's hunter of rare and freakish specimens for its caged collection. The long-snouts – former members of Jharkill's own team of handlers – pulled on the chains to bring the malformed ogre crashing down onto his knees in the shallows. One long-snout held the shaman's crossbar staff, jangling the useless charms that dangled from it. Another held Jharkill's great ivory bow. Both were tossed into the stinking slime before Agrammon's throne. Jharkill's skins were ragged and torn, his flesh a criss-cross of ribbons where he had suffered the barbed lash for his failures. Archaon pursed his cracked lips. He had brought the mighty Jharkill to this. He had slipped into the menagerie. He had started liberating exhibits. He had stolen one of Agrammon's prized specimens and escaped with the Steed of the Apocalypse. Now the menagerie was in chaos and the daemon lord's palace besieged by things that had been for so long imprisoned at Agrammon's pleasure – to feed the daemon's bottomless need to possess the rare, the abominable and the monstrous.

The daemon lord spoke. Its voice was the sound of a thousand souls in rapture. It was both chilling and thrilling to hear. Agrammon spoke in a damned language that Archaon did not understand. It was like crushed glass in the ear, but all the Chaos warrior needed to do was watch them speak with their bodies. Agrammon was demanding some kind of explanation for Jharkill's failure – that much was clear. The monstrous daemon moved between the indulgent excess of slick fury, spoken with the voices of its thousand swallowed souls, to sultry invitations and encouragements that drew delight from the gathered audience of supplicating daemonettes. It seemed that even in the midst of calamity, enduring the sting of disappointment, the Prince of Pleasure's daemon would still find something to enjoy. There were the myriad pleasures of new alliances to consider, with bell-drawn servants of darkness from nearby daemon palaces; a menagerie and collection to re-build – bigger, more exotic and ever more miserable that the first; delicious punishments to be issued among Agrammon's own wretched servants for their disastrous failure.

The long-snouts hauled at the chains, bringing Jharkill's head up before his daemonic master. It seemed to Archaon that the monstrous ogre wasn't much for begging or supplication and looked on Agrammon's obscene form with eyes shimmering with pain and dull hatred. The creature knew it was dead. Daemon lords did not make forgiving masters. The Slaaneshi abomination would find all manner of deviant uses for the monster's flesh, however, before it allowed him to perish in its dark god's honour.

Archaon watched as Jharkill's silence was rewarded with sorcerous words spoken from Agrammon's wet lips. Jharkill thrashed to one side as a malicious word from the daemon lord sliced his flesh across his belly and face in a single invisible stroke. The ogre's blubbery hide gaped where the daemon had cut him. Jharkill remained silent. Again and again, Lord Agrammon spoke the words, slashing the monster once more across his mangled face and across the hunch of his back. Thrusting his chest forward, the hulk's form rose and fell with the exertion of breathing and the relief of the unseen assault's respite. Still he would not speak, simply glowering up at the perverse form of his former master.

New words issued forth from the throne and Jharkill bent over, clutching his barrel chest as though he was suffering some kind of internal torment. The ogre huntsman's face contorted about his agony and the throne room echoed with a single, wretched scream. Once more the monster was allowed the Prince of Pleasure's blessing and could not help a crooked smile of relief crack his contorted features. The pain was over. The smile died on Jharkill's ugly face. Pulling his ragged skins and furs aside, Archaon could see a death mask of agony fixed in the flesh of the ogre's chest. With a single fell word, Lord Agrammon had murdered Jharkill's malformed twin – his brother abomination and sharer of his flesh. Jharkill's roar shook the throne room, sending ripples through the murky shallows of sweat and blood.

Archaon knew that he had to make the most of the distraction. Grabbing Giselle by the chin he lifted her head level with his own. The girl's face was strangely serene for someone who had hung for hours – perhaps days – from spikes erupting from the palms of her hands. Her eyelids fluttered before the blank white of her eyes.

'Giselle,' the Chaos warrior said softly. 'Giselle, it's me.'

The girl's thin eyebrows rose for a moment in recognition before her face screwed up in a moment of pain. Archaon felt her head fall as she lapsed back into unconsciousness. Lowering it he took the first of her hands and eased it as gently as he could off the filthy spike. There was blood. It leaked down the wall and dripped into the shallows, clouding the already murky water red. The metal at the spike point seemed discoloured, as though something had been smeared on it. As her hand juddered along the shaft of the spike, the girl stirred. Drawing his left hand back he smothered the scream of pain about to erupt from her mouth with his gauntlet. 'Giselle, listen to me,' Archaon told her, leaning the skull faceplate of his helm in close. 'We're in danger. No sound.'

The girl's head suddenly came up as though woken from a dream. Her eyes opened and while bleary were still blank white. Her dirty face and the mask of agony into which it had tightened suddenly relaxed. She smiled even, which Archaon thought strange, until he remembered the variety of potions and poisons dribbled, painted and smeared onto every blade, point and surface in the palace. Giselle groaned. It was a warm intimate sound. The kind that she had made with him before.

'Giselle, wake up.'

As he got the first hand off the spike and leant her body against his, he told her: 'Listen girl, wake up. I need you on your feet if we're going to make it out of here.' Giselle moaned again, reaching out for Archaon with her mess of a hand. 'No,' Archaon said, holding her with difficulty and trying to get her other hand off the spike. There was more blood. The Chaos warrior assumed that the movement must have been agony but the girl let out a half-stifled whoop of delight. Whatever monstrous concoction was smeared on the spike was poisoning the girl's mind, clouding it with reversals. In the palace of the Slaaneshi daemon lord, Giselle was experiencing pain as pleasure. With the girl leaning against his plate, Archaon could only hope such chemical enchantments worked the other way. Grabbing his helm by one of its great horns, Archaon pulled the helmet from his face and leaned in to kiss Giselle. The Chaos warrior knew instantly that he was right as the dreamy look was driven from the girl's face. She reacted as though her lips had touched molten metal and drew her head back. Her expression fluttered through the tautness of pain, through wide-eyed shock and confusion. Her eyes were no longer the blank white of euphoria. She saw him and whimpered.

'Archaon…' she managed, bringing her exhausted arms limply up and wiping the ghostly burn from her lips. All she managed to do, however, was smear blood across the bottom half of her face. The Chaos warrior allowed her to look upon the dread fortitude of his face. His pale skin, shot through with networks of blue veins that coursed with unnatural power. His hairless head, scarred with marks from a thousand battles. His cracked lips, broken nose and the patch he wore over his ruined eye – in the socket of which was still the shard of wyrdstone that had given him his darksight and allowed him to see the monstrous truth of the world. He allowed the helm of Morkar to fall once more. He had to get her out of here. With any good fortune he might be able to recover the sorcerer Sheerian, Eins, Drei, Zwei and

Vier from a similar fate. Giselle held on to him. He needed her to walk but she remained frozen to the spot. 'Archaon,' she said again, her voice a strangled whisper.

The Chaos warrior rotated. He had no good fortune and it seemed never would have. Holding Giselle to him in her furs, Archaon turned. With the cacophony at the thick metal door to the palace filling the throne room, Archaon had not noticed that the child-herald had stopped ringing the tower bell. That Jharkill was no longer roaring his fraternal fury. That the daemon lord Agrammon had stopped parting flesh with cutting words from his lips. He found Agrammon and his daemon court there, watching them both. The herald wore a deranged smile in expectation of the horror to come. The daemonettes were still in formation but had come forth, serrated swords presented, giving the Chaos warrior stabbing glares of predacious intent. The daemon Agrammon had simply heaved on the serpentine coils circling the dais and turned the metal obscenity of the throne around to face Archaon and Giselle.

Archaon decided that there was really only one thing to do and drew *Terminus* from its scabbard. The Sigmarite sword hissed as it cleared the fur. Holding the blade out in front of him, Archaon moved in front of Giselle, who was now standing bolt upright. Archaon was furious. Mostly at himself. The Slaaneshi daemon lord and its attendant monstrosities might not have heard the slip of his boot or the splash of his descent, but their unnatural senses were keenly sensitive to even the slightest moan of pleasure. That was undoubtedly why the holding spikes were coated with foul unguents and concoctions.

Agrammon said nothing at first. It merely watched him. His presence seemed to give the creature some sense of unearthly satisfaction. Once again, the daemon seemed unconcerned by the threat presented by such developments, instead reacting with the perversity of a ghastly smile. Perhaps it was impressed that the Chaos warrior had managed to breach the palace walls to rescue the prisoners. Perhaps it was looking forward to the rapture of old torments visited upon fresh victims. Perhaps the creature was ecstatic that the being responsible for the delight of its current woes had delivered himself before the daemon lord.

Archaon backed through the shallows and moved to the side, his footsteps sloshing through the bodily fluids. Daemonettes hissed at him. They licked their lips with forked tongues and stomped through the waters about him.

Agrammon nodded. Two of the daemonettes came at him. Archaon snarled. He was to be tested. The daemonettes' movements were fast. They moved with a slick lethality – like predators striking. Their swordplay was exotic and the serrated sickle swords were wielded with a combination of diabolical confidence, skill and strength. The Chaos warrior did not have time for such games, however. He could not afford to be separated from Giselle – who was his, once again – or manoeuvred around into a more vulnerable position. He saw no point in concealing his own lethality, however, and despite being bereft of his shield and fighting with his left hand, put the daemonettes down brutally. Within moments, one creature's head had been cleaved in two, while another lost a leg and was casually stabbed through both its hell-forged plate and its ample chest as it thrashed about uselessly in the shallows.

Another nod from Agrammon and three of its daemonic elite splashed through the waters at him. Archaon decided that if they were going to play the daemon lord's game, he would at least try to work his way around to the door. The three daemonettes died faster and easier than their infernal sisters, the blessed steel of *Terminus* sizzling through the throat of the first, then after side-stepping the serrated bite of a sickle sword, the second, before messily braining the third with the broad flat of the templar blade. Keeping their backs to the spiked wall of the chamber, Archaon worked his way around to the door, despatching a group of four daemonettes with little more trouble than the corpses in the shallows, already bearing witness to his brute skill.

By the time Agrammon sent five of its lesser daemon elite to slaughter him for its entertainment and insanity, there were black hell-forged blades everywhere, sparking off *Terminus*, threatening to sink their teeth through his plate, open his throat with arcs of curved death or cut him clean in half with the otherworldly strength behind the weapons. Archaon had begun to tire. Whereas the daemonettes could expect their sisters' blades to parry and block for them, Archaon only had a single sword. A sword that more often than not was being turned aside by the crescent shields of the infernal elite and needed to be whipped back to turn away the exotic stabs and sweeps of other daemons. With its length and heavy blade, the greatsword was simply not designed for such lightning work – even in the gauntlet of one such as Archaon.

The Chaos warrior half hacked the first and stove in the head of a second, but they were desperate manoeuvres and less than satisfactory kills. He paid for such clumsiness by allowing a serrated blade through and having the hooked teeth of the murderous weapon find its way between his helm and breastplate to slice at his neck. Without a shield of his own and his broken arm aching uselessly at his side, Archaon had no choice but to work around with glancing parries and darting deflections. Exhausted, and with Giselle squealing and moving about his armoured form to avoid the spiteful swipes and thrusts of daemonettes behind them, Archaon knew that it was only a matter of time before he was bested.

A tired lunge, combined with the fervour of frustration, sent the length of *Terminus* searing through the daemon-crafted plate of another creature. As the daemonette crashed into the shallows, her corpse refused to surrender the templar blade. Letting go and retracting his arm, Archaon narrowly avoided losing it to a murderous downward swing that ended up sending bodily fluids from the shallows fountaining upwards. Stumbling back but trying to keep the shrieking Giselle behind him and out of the path of blades swung with venomous force, Archaon was without weapon. With a daemonette either side of him, this was an intolerable position to remain in. Trying to rush one lesser daemon to reach *Terminus*, lodged in the corpse behind, only resulted in a serrated blade clanging off the side of his helm, cleaving a groove in the workmanship. An attempt to lurch forward and snatch a sickle sword from the claw-gauntlet of a dead daemonette was partially successful, but without the hilt of the unfamiliar weapon firmly in his grasp, the blade was struck from his grip by the whipping slash of one of his cornering tormentors.

Stamping a wall of water at one as a distraction, Archaon feigned going for the lost blade again. He knew he had to leave Giselle's side – it was the only way to save them both. Instead of actually going for the blade, Archaon lowered the horns on his helmet and charged. Crashing into the unprepared daemonette, he smashed her back, burying the pauldron of his broken arm in the plate of her belly. He could feel the lesser daemon smashing the pommel of her sickle sword into his back but Archaon charged on like a deranged rhinox, slamming the horrific creature into the chamber wall and impaling her on a set of wicked spikes. Tearing the sickle sword from her dying grasp, Archaon spun around, the gag-inducing waters splashing up about him. Hurling the lighter curved sword, blade over pommel, he buried it in the form of the final daemonette, who had been racing through the shallows at the unarmed Giselle. The wretched creature would have sliced the girl in two if it were not for the flying blade that thudded into her back. The daemon crashed down into the waters before the Sister of Sigmar, who simply stared, stunned, at Archaon. Tearing *Terminus* from the carcass of the Slaaneshi daemon, Archaon put himself between Giselle and Agrammon's horrific horde.

Infernal plate clattered as daemonettes clawed at each other to get to the Chaos warrior and his prize. The daemon Agrammon spoke. Its words sizzled on the air. Archaon didn't understand them but they sounded like a command.

The daemonettes parted as their overlord slithered off its throne and wound its way between the creatures. Archaon held out *Terminus* before him. He ached to wield the weapon with his right arm but the hot agony of the broken limb wouldn't answer.

'Come and get it, thing of darkness,' Archaon told the daemon. 'I'll tear through you as I have your wretched handmaidens.'

Agrammon did something horrible with its face that the Chaos warrior took for a smile. Shaking its horns and sending a ripple through its twitching, tentacular appendages, Agrammon reared. Archaon prepared himself for some kind of serpentine attack. He felt Giselle's slender body against the back of his plate. He flicked his gaze from the horrific daemon lord slithering to full height before him to the waiting horde of daemonettes – monstrosities he knew could destroy both him and Giselle if they abandoned the perversity of their games and rushed them in one go. From the flesh-hungry horde of daemonettes he risked a glance at Jharkill. Jharkill the huntsman. Jharkill the shaman. Jharkill, former keeper of Lord Agrammon's infernal menagerie. The malformed ogre was now on his knees, held down by chains that had formerly been his to shackle, by long-snout beastfiends that had formerly been his to command. The monster's hunched back rose and fell with his suffering. As Agrammon towered over him, Archaon grunted. He would have to fight. Only steel would settle this.

Archaon heard a hiss. Fat droplets splattered against his plate. They were not the sticky drizzle that coated everything in the throne room. The armour of Morkar smoked and sizzled at their acidic impact. Archaon took a step back but the daemon Agrammon had spurted a stream of unholy filth from its rearing serpentine form. Archaon was not the intended target of the disgusting attack. The liquid coursed down the blade of the offered *Terminus*. The liquid spat and steamed as it rolled down the blessed steel of the Sigmarite sword.

'No...' Archaon found himself cry out. In a life long forgotten, the blade had belonged to his templar master, Sieur Kastner. It had secured Archaon's own false future in the hallowed ranks of the Knight of the Twin-Tailed Orb. Through the horror and adventure of his dark quests, the blade had stayed with him – ever faithful to its original calling. In the damned Archaon's hands, it had destroyed more evil that it could ever have hoped by sitting in Sieur Kastner's rusty scabbard. Its blessed steel had been a boon in Archaon's battles against fell warriors, beasts and daemonic monstrosities pledged to the same dark path. Its edge had remained keen and the twin-tailed comet carved into its blade had burned bright as Archaon had fought his way across the globe. It should have been the blade's honour to cut through the flesh of daemons like Agrammon. Instead the metal of the blade began to dribble and run.

The acidic unguent that Agrammon had sprayed down on the steel was melting it in Archaon's very grip. As the length of the greatsword dribbled down to a silver stump in the Chaos warrior's hand, Archaon could hear the daemon lord's sickly laughter. The daemonettes joined in about their infernal overlord, followed by the unliving exhibits skewered on the bars above. Before long the vaulted throne chamber was filled with the infectious scorn of the diabolical creatures. The silver of liquefied steel swirled in the sickly waters about Archaon's boots. The Chaos warrior held onto his sword, the sword he had wielded for so long in the service of different gods: so long that it almost felt like a part of him. With a snarl that threatened to break his face, Archaon allowed the sizzling cross guard, hilt and pommel to tumble into the steely waters. It sploshed and hissed to its wretched end. So much of a life lived long ago was gone. Oberon. Dagobert. The Sigmarite sword *Terminus*. Archaon felt furiously compelled to defend what little remained.

He backed through the grim waters. Through the stinking drizzle. Through the laughter of daemons. Giselle stumbled and grabbed out for him, drawing further diabolical mirth from the monsters. Archaon looked around. Agrammon. The daemonettes. The defeated Jharkill. The thick metal of the hell-forged palace door that would see the monstrosities outside smash themselves to death before it admitted them.

'Want to make these wretched things pay for what they have done?' Archaon called across to the ogre huntsman. The daemons laughed harder about them, amused by the prospect of Jharkill, sagging in his shredded flesh, and the unarmed Archaon posing any kind of threat. 'Monster!' Archaon roared across at Jharkill, finally drawing the corner of an eye from the defeated creature. 'This is only over if you want it to be.' Archaon cast a glance at the huge, metal door that was the entrance to the palace and the thunder behind it.

Agrammon slithered down at Archaon. The daemon was done with the interloper and his delusions. Sharp words slipped from the daemon lord's lips and a shower of sparks lit the thick gloom of the chamber. An unseen force had slashed up across Archaon's breastplate and right pauldron, drawing a fountain of light from the metal. Archaon stumbled back and Giselle with him as the girl let out a sudden scream. Archaon held up his good arm and a further blinding flash flared from it. Another sparking surge rained fire from an invisible backslash across Archaon's chest. Giselle went down in the water and Archaon skidded back through the shallows. The armour of Morkar – First Everchosen of Chaos – would not be breached by the daemon lord's sorceries.

Agrammon's face clouded over like the sudden and perverse storms of the Southern Wastes that seemed to come from nowhere. Archaon instinctively knew that the monstrous daemon had finished playing with them. That within dark moments they would be dead. Jharkill, Sheerian and his Swords of Chaos too. In desperation, Archaon used the only weapon he had left. He turned to Giselle and grabbed her arm to help her up.

'I'm sorry,' he said as he turned and launched the girl at the daemon Agrammon. The infernal creature caught Giselle in its arms. There was an immediate hiss. Daemonflesh steamed from Agrammon's disgusting form. Like a hand pulling a piece of steel fresh from the furnace, the daemon burned at the girl's touch. Giselle, who still stung with belief. Who, impossibly, in this benighted place, had hung onto her faith. Whose soul belonged to the God-King and whose flesh was a sacred vessel. Agrammon screamed. The daemon had not known such exquisite torture in this doomed place. The sound of the daemon's torment howled up through the palace tower. Its coils contracted in agony and then bliss. It dropped Giselle and once more the girl found herself in the water.

Agrammon hissed its frenzied delight at Giselle as her head broke the surface of the shallows. Like an angry snake that had been tormented with a lit torch, Agrammon turned its serpentine horror on Archaon. But Archaon was gone. The Chaos warrior had turned and was running through the shallows, his steps spraying fountains of liquid skyward. The daemonettes between him and the mighty palace door had been as surprised as their infernal master. Many had rushed to their daemon lord's aid, drawn to the vision of pleasure and pain as Agrammon's soul came to know the anathema of a believer's touch. Several nightmarish swordmaidens in their spiked plate tried to check the Chaos warrior's advance. Archaon ran at them, smashing through their crescent shields. Ducking and weaving between the singing death of their sickle swords, Archaon wrangled with one monstrous maiden, only to grab her wrist and force her blade into turning aside another. An armoured elbow to the fanged face of the creature allowed Archaon the remaining steps he needed to reach the door.

Jharkill, meanwhile, had responded to the Chaos warrior's cue. Rearing from the shallows and raining the foetid waters from his hulking form, the malformed ogre dragged his neck chains with him, tearing beastfiends from their hooves. Gargantuan steps sent the crests of waves at the startled daemons, drenching their spiked plate. Several swordmaidens attempted to stop the rampaging ogre but found their armoured forms smashed across the throne room or stamped into the shallows.

The palace was suddenly a place of shrieking havoc. Between the sweet agony that was Giselle, the unstoppable force that was Jharkill and Archaon's slippery escape, the daemon Agrammon was seething. Spitting curses from its black lips, Agrammon slashed deep wounds across the mountainous hunch of Jharkill's already shredded back. Jharkill roared and fell against the colossal doors. The metal rang with the impact. Archaon felt it through the structure. He got his arm and pauldron under the massive bar sitting across the width of the entrance. Heaving. Pushing. Straining. Archaon fought gravity and the weight of the massive bar. With a final effort – a roar escaping the Chaos warrior's lungs – Archaon pushed the great bar from its brackets and sent it crashing into the water behind. The booming assault beyond the door had stopped. The monstrosities behind it had felt the impact and had heard the watery clang. With a bellow of pain rather than effort, Jharkill heaved at the metal doors. Falling to his knees, the ogre pushed them open.

A moment passed where nothing seemed to happen. It was almost as though the powerful forces screaming from the breach of the Southern Gate had sunk their claws into reality and dragged time to a stop. The daemonettes gasped in dread and expectation of the horror yet to come. Giselle gagged and whimpered as she knelt in the foul waters, with the swirling maelstrom of the daemon Agrammon's serpentine body slithering to a stop about her. Dread curses dropped from the creature's lips in languages dark and ancient. The daemon knew what was going to happen and yet still could not resist breathing in the sweet sting of relief that rolled in through the palace doors. Monstrosities, freaks and prisoners who had spent an eternity suffering the lash at Agrammon's command and caged for the daemon lord's pleasure now had the palace in their grasp. The expectation of violence and suffering to come was like a silent storm that rushed in through the open doors. The Slaaneshi daemons groaned and sank down into the water.

Archaon stumbled through the shallows. The horde of creatures outside were as shocked at the door's opening as the daemons inside. It took a moment for even the most mindless and savage of them to process what was happening. Like Agrammon and its savage kind, Archaon knew what was coming. Running across the entrance, the Chaos warrior leapt at Jharkill, using the momentum of his landing to turn the ogre onto its knees so that the hunched monster collapsed to one side of the entrance, its back against the barbed wall. Archaon was just in time. While the Prince of Pleasure's daemons were drunk on the sweet wine of retribution, the Blood God's eye had been drawn to the base, animal fury that drove such creatures to enact such revenge. Feeding the horde of monstrous creatures with mind-splitting ire, it had been the Blood God who had driven such creatures to throw themselves, broken and bloody, at the thick metal of the palace doors. They would not be stopped now. The fury had to find expression in the roaring that followed. In the pulse of violent intent through sinew and muscle and in the coppery taste of blood at the back of the throat.

Archaon ran through the shallows. Through the daemonettes, who stood there like a spiked forest of enraptured statues. Like an avalanche of black rage the monstrosities charged. Things of claw. Predacious fusions of beast and daemon. Spawn, raging with transformative power. Armoured titans of tusk and elemental ferocity. It was mayhem. Archaon dare not spend the seconds to look back. The unstoppable force of the escaped exhibits pushed the draining waters of the throne room before them, driving a stinking surge that caught Archaon in its rolling power.

There were terrible screams. Daemonettes and long-snouts were dying in the most brutal and horrific ways. While the Slaaneshi deviants had enjoyed the expectation, the storm of monstrosities, fired by the presence of the Blood God in their hearts and burning through their veins, had no intention of drawing out their revenge. The beasts found satisfaction only in death – as other escapees had done in the spiralling thoroughfares of the menagerie, savaging their lash-wielding keepers and the trumpeting beastfiends that patrolled their cages. Rank indulgence was soon replaced with the raw richness of blood and death. Behind him Archaon could hear the frenzied tearing of flesh, the snap of backs and bones, skulls crunching and the bellow of monsters raging their way through the butchered ranks. Above, the monstrous exhibits skewered on their bars had stopped moaning. Infested by the rush of retaliatory violence that had swept into the throne room like a crimson deluge, the unliving things were roaring, screeching and hissing their jubilation. As Archaon half waded, half stumbled through waters that were rapidly clouding black and red, his ears burned with the suddenly silenced screams of daemons ended brutally about him.

Skidding down through the blood, sweat and slime, Archaon snatched a sickle sword from a dead daemonette. The vanguard of the furious invasion had caught him. A splashing stampede rolled over him like a force of unnatural nature. Bony limbs and monstrous hooves trampled him down into the waters. As his head came up he felt an infernal radiance pass overhead, like a fireball, and Archaon had to duck back down under the foetid surface to avoid the flames of the dark phoenix that flapped about the throne room, seemingly setting fire to everything.

When Archaon pushed himself up out of the water he found some savage chimeric creature on his armoured back, snapping, clawing and stabbing at him with blade-bone appendages. Another leapt on him from the side, almost knocking him over. The Chaos warrior would have fallen if it wasn't for some great crested rhinox charging by with its array of twisted horns, knocking him back. One of the beasts was torn away, having been skewered on the rhinox's horns, while a third suddenly emerged from the shallows, surging at the Chaos warrior's groin with its skin-flayed maw.

The sickle sword was no replacement for *Terminus*. While its razored curve had been hell-forged and its twisted serrations designed to inflict horrific damage, it lacked the weight of a truly devastating weapon. Lifting it above his head, Archaon brought his left arm down with all the power he could manage – forced to compensate brute strength for the lacking weight of the blade. The chimera died messily enough, the barbed sickle dragging the creature's entrails from it as Archaon laid into the beast with a second mulching strike.

Archaon didn't have to worry about the remaining creature. Agrammon had finally come to its diabolical senses and was slithering its coiled length about its throne and spitting the venom of sorcerous words. A water-whipping maelstrom of laceration circled the daemon lord like a whirlwind of unseen blades. Warped predators bounding through the shallows were torn to shreds by the invisible wall, while ungainly titans were skinned alive and had flesh sheared from their bones. The dark phoenix was shredded in a steaming blaze of unnatural flame. The chimera was ripped from Archaon's back, where it had been savaging his armoured neck. The Chaos warrior, meanwhile, became a staggering fountain of sparks as the flesh-raking force clashed once more with Archaon's cursed plate.

Through the sparks and the wall of gore circling the daemon Agrammon, Archaon saw Giselle. Agrammon had her inside the fat coils of its serpentine form, while the whip-like tip of its serpentine tail was actually snaked around the girl. The daemon's flesh was black and steaming where it was in contact with Giselle, but despite the delicious torture of the soul-scorching experience, the monstrous daemon would not be denied its prize.

Forcing himself on, step after desperate step, the armour of Morkar suffering the wrath of the daemon's powers, Archaon sizzled with the sparks raining from his plate and down into the waters below. Punching through, Archaon ran up out of the shallows, stomping his way up the dais upon which Agrammon and its throne was supported. Swinging down with furious force, Archaon opened up one of the daemon's fat coils with the sickle sword, tearing through daemonflesh and spraying himself with ichor.

'Agrammon!' Archaon roared at the monstrous being. 'Your tower will fall. Your twisted palace will howl empty with the southern winds. The cages of your legendary menagerie will rust – legend no more. While so many have served you, you will now serve me: the chosen of the Chaos gods.'

Archaon had hoped to draw the daemon lord's attention with his bold taunts. Agrammon – ever the slave to temptation – fell this time for the Chaos warrior's trap.

'I serve only at the pleasure of my god, mortal,' the daemon seethed, its words like barbed ecstasies exploding in Archaon's mind. 'The Prince of such Pleasures.'

Agrammon, overcome with an infernal desire to see the architect of its woes ended, swept forwards with its gigantic, spindly claws.

'Then you can serve him in oblivion,' Archaon promised the daemon lord.

Ducking and weaving, Archaon evaded the daemonic talons, turning them away with savage flourishes of his sickle sword. At every opportunity, between the grasping and stabbing of the giant finger-blades, Archaon sank the serrated blade into the meaty daemonflesh of the creature's coils. All the while, Archaon felt the quake of a monstrosity approach. The abominate creature of chitinous plate, fang-fiend face and colossal horns that Archaon had seen both raging in its enclosure and furiously beating dents into the thick metal of the palace doors was storming its way through the throne room. The slaughterbrute was an unthinking monster already blessed by the Blood God with an appetite for decimation. It lived to crush with its colossal claws, stamp with its mighty hooves and gore with its freakish arrangement of blood-stained horns. Its torso and arms rippled with the muscular fortitude of a thing that never stopped killing, while its maw was a deathtrap designed for tearing heads from prey.

The abomination thundered through the vaulted throne

room, mindlessly crushing, smashing and killing anything in its path. Daemonettes became twisted mounds of spiked scrap through which the ichor leaked into the stinking waters of the palace. Monsters who, like the slaughterbrute, had suffered in Agrammon's royal menagerie, became showers of gore and ragged limbs that rained in the abomination's bloody wake.

Distracted by Archaon, the daemon lord was no longer protected by its flesh-shearing maelstrom. As soon as the abomination saw the daemon, it thundered towards it, stamping a fleeing long-snout into the shallows and beating a winged nightmare out of its path and into the spiked wall with bone-shattering force. Perhaps it was Agrammon's size or a daemonic threat the serpentine thing so obviously posed. Perhaps the abomination remembered and knew its captor when it saw it. As the abominate monster charged, Agrammon's coils tightened about the slaughterbrute, bleeding a powerful mixture of potions and poisons from it into the monster's flesh. Agrammon brought up a colossal claw to back slice the creature to ribbons, but Archaon knew that such defences would not be enough. Clambering over the clamminess of sickly-sweet flesh, Archaon almost became trapped in the moving coils of the creature.

'Giselle!' Archaon called out, but the girl didn't seem to hear him. Giselle was no damsel in a tale of old to be saved. She would not call out for help. She stared coldly into space, oblivious to the havoc about her. 'Giselle!'

As he got to her the Chaos warrior tore at the steaming tail of the daemon. The thing resisted his efforts and coiled tighter about the Sister of the Imperial Cross. Flashing a glance at the oncoming slaughterbrute, Archaon brought his sickle sword down on the tail. Again. Again. The sword's serrated edge sheared flesh from the thrashing horror but wasn't heavy enough to cleave through bone. He roared, cutting at the daemon. Finally, the bone shattered under the frenzied onslaught, caught between one of the sword's many barbs and the stone of the throne dais. Seconds later the thick coils slithering tighter about them suddenly unravelled. The bloody stump that Archaon had left was whipped away, trailing black gore. As the slaughterbrute and the daemon Agrammon collided, Archaon grabbed Giselle and ran for the wall.

The abominate beast knocked Agrammon from its throne. As the daemon's snake-like body wrapped itself around the monstrous force of the slaughterbrute, the pair of them smashed through the chamber. The creature alternated between the unrelenting force of its fist and the gouging slash of its thick claws. It savaged Agrammon with its dagger-toothed maw and gored it with its monstrous horns. Purple lightning enveloped them both, streaming from the spindly claws of the daemon, setting the slaughterbrute alight.

Archaon dragged the dumbfounded Giselle after him. The daemon's dead tail fell away in scorched cinders as the pair of them ran. The titanic battle crashed through the throne room with the daemon screeching its life away as the abominable monster mauled and smashed it into the floor of its own palace.

'Help me,' Archaon said to the stunned Giselle, as he tried to help Sheerian and the Swords of Chaos from where they had been hooked into the wall. Like Giselle, they all moaned the pure pleasure of their agonies as Archaon and the girl tried to prise them from the spikes on the wall. As the thunder from the other side of the chamber subsided, Archaon turned to present his sickle sword. If the slaughterbrute had finished with the daemon lord, the Chaos warrior knew that it wouldn't stop. The thing existed to bludgeon lesser creatures into oblivion, mindlessly honouring the Blood God that fuelled its fury and monstrous power. It knew only killing and Archaon and his people would look as good a murderous prospect as any.

'Get them up,' Archaon told Giselle as Vier's knees buckled underneath him, sending the winged marauder into the shallows. As the girl helped the warped warrior back to its unsteady feet, Archaon readied himself for the abominate monster that had turned from the lifeless tremblings and slitherings of Agrammon. The monster roared, shaking the very foundations of the tower, and levelled its nest of colossal horns at Archaon. The beast flared its armoured nostrils. It was as if the thing could smell a threat: Archaon.

'What's happening?' Archaon heard a disorientated Sheerian say.

An unsteady Eins appeared next to its master, its wings a punctured mess and one of its freshly drawn bone swords held in a hand dribbling with blood.

'Get them out of here,' Archaon commanded. The Sword of Chaos hesitated its protestation. 'Do it...' Archaon said, his voice sharp and grim.

As the Swords gathered their wits and shook off the Slaaneshi potion smeared on the spikes, they led Giselle and Sheerian towards the door. As the colossal slaughter-brute sniffed in the direction of the sorcerer and the girl, Archaon waved his sickle sword above him. 'Here, monster,' he called across the throne room. 'Here.'

With the Swords of Chaos cutting their way through chimeric beasts, spawn creatures and wild-eyed beastfiends, Archaon felt the floor shake and the foetid waters about his boots slosh and recede. The abominate monster was charging down on him. Turning the sickle sword about with his wrist, Archaon readied himself, although he knew not what for. An undercut to some softer part on the creature's belly? Did the monster have any softer parts? Perhaps he could get his blade past an armoured eyelid and into the beast's brain. The thing was monstrous brawn beneath thick chitinous plates that served the beast as a kind of natural armour. Beyond that there was the skewering forest of horn, fang and claw to worry about. The abomination roared. Archaon stood his ground but beneath his plate the sound shook his very bones. With the monster all but on top of him, Archaon still didn't know what he was going to do.

Something shot past Archaon, through the murk and

drizzle. It thudded into the brawn of the creature's neck. It was the size of a spear but Archaon recognised it as an arrow. One of Jharkill's arrows. The slaughterbrute took several more thunderous steps before crashing to one side. Archaon winced but stood his ground as the beast collapsed about him, scraping its way to a stop along the spiked wall of the palace. Opening his eye, Archaon turned to see that the malformed ogre was standing nearby. He was a mess, blood leaking from gaping slashes in his deformed flesh. His twin was dead, the thing's mouth gaping open and leaking the horrible substance Jharkill used to poison his arrows. He had recovered his ivory tusk bow and quiver from before the throne and, selecting another arrow, smeared it in the blood and poison dripping down his belly before putting it in the abomination – ensuring that the uncontrollable thing had been put to sleep. Archaon nodded with obvious approval. The ogre's marksmanship and knowledge of his quarry's vulnerabilities were impressive – and these were the least impressive of the monster's capabilities. He had indeed made Agrammon a fine servant and in time might do the same for Archaon.

Padding through the shallows and across the throne room while Jharkill picked off the menagerie's escaped monstrosities one by one, Archaon found the mess that the Blood God's abomination had made of the daemon lord Agrammon. The serpentine daemon had been smashed. It had been broken. It had been torn into colossal, twitching pieces. Archaon found the daemon lord's torso separated from the nightmare lengths of its body. The slaughterbrute had splattered Agrammon into the palace floor. Dragging its daemon entrails through the shallows, one of its spindly claws a broken mess, Archaon discovered that half of its chest had been crushed. Its array of horns were a shattered remnant and its tentacular appendages reached out for a body that was no longer there.

Archaon stepped across the creature, its back to him, and grabbed the shattered stump of a horn. Hauling the daemon lord's head up out of the shallows, where it had been gagging and spuming, Archaon brought the blade of the sickle sword to Agrammon's throat. Decimated though it was, he couldn't risk the daemon using its regenerative powers or spoken sorceries. Holding it there, Archaon only found the dreamy smile of a Slaaneshi deviant enjoying the agonies of its last moments. Archaon grunted.

'Your monsters,' Archaon hissed in the daemon's ear, 'are now my monsters. Do you hear that daemon? This is for *Terminus*. An end for an end.' Archaon drew the serrated sword edge across the daemon lord's throat, the barbed teeth of the weapon tearing it out. Dropping the infernal creature's heavy head into the ichor-clouding shallows, Archaon spat at the daemon. 'Welcome to oblivion…' he told it, before walking away.

CHAPTER VII

'Daemons rise and daemons fall – and in their falling, come ever to rise again. It is both our gift and our curse.'
– Necromagne the Dark Muse

The Gatelands
The Southern Wastes
Horns Harrowing: Season of the Ravening

Archaon left the palace of the daemon lord Agrammon behind. The barbed tower and twisted metal walls of the nightmare writhed with unnatural flame, fanned by the winds of the continental interior. As the palace raged behind them, lighting up the broiling black skies, the Chaos warlord ordered his horde assembled for a march on the palaces closer to the howling radiance of warping realities that spewed into the world from the demolished Chaos gate. Ograx the Great had led Archaon's savage warherd to victory out on the bone-tangled Wastes and had arrived outside the palace as Archaon was leaving. The beastfiends had stripped the daemonic stronghold of anything useful – weapons, armour and wagons. Archaon allowed a few hours for the creatures of his horde to quench their thirst with Slaaneshi blood and quell the rumble of their bellies with the flesh of the fallen. The Swords of Chaos took their place once more at the warlord's side. At Archaon's insistence the savage shamans of his bestial army looked to Sheerian and Giselle's wounds.

Archaon sat on the back of a bone-cage wagon that he had ordered covered in the skins of their foes. The Chaos warlord had the wagon furnished with a mound of furs for a bed. He had the lowly creatures of his horde attend with the freshest water they could find and cooked meat stripped from beasts of magnificent burden who had been found still in their menagerie cages. This he reserved for Giselle, with two more of the incredible beasts hauling the wagon and the twisted Vier at the reins. Giselle just crawled into the furs, holding herself like a child, staring deep into nothingness.

'Giselle, I…' Archaon began, but the words wouldn't come. Once again, he had failed to protect her. Once again, some monstrosity of the Southern Wastes had visited torments upon her precious flesh. Once more, Archaon had made such things pay with their existence – but that was little consolation to those who had already paid for Archaon's mistakes.

He wanted to tell her that he was sorry. That he had failed in his confrontation with his father-in-shadow and that he should have been at the head of the horde instead. The daemon Agrammon wouldn't have got its spindly claws on Giselle, on his Swords of Chaos and even ancient Sheerian if Archaon had been there. The Chaos warrior was sure of that. At one time he had found it easier to talk to Giselle. They fought, they spat their threats and even found their way to laughing the woes of the world away. Their lips craved the taste of each other's damnation. Their fingers burned across the purity and pollution of each other's flesh. Now Giselle pulled away from Archaon like every other dread thing in this benighted world. He had once again become a thing feared, untrusted and unloved.

As Giselle's lips parted, Archaon's heart – that sat heavy like a shard of obsidian in his chest – leapt. He leant in. His gauntlet moved for the mound of her body beneath the furs. Giselle's bloodshot eyes were dry and distant with tears that would not come. Her bandage-bound hand reached out for the cold metal of the gauntlet. A mumble became a forlorn hiss. Archaon leant in closer.

'Why... won't... you... die?' the Sigmarite sister said, her words stinging with the blank-face bitterness of betrayal. She pushed the gauntlet from her trembling body. Archaon felt cracks creep deep through the obsidian agony in his chest and bit back a snarl. The anger was not directed at the girl but at himself. The contortions behind the faceplate of his horned helm fell away to a slow nod.

'Aye,' he told Giselle. 'That's the question.'

Turning away, Archaon found Sheerian and the twisted shaman that had been tending to both the sorcerer and Giselle's wounds. Across the bonfire of bones that warmed the warlord through his cursed plate, Archaon saw the small mountain range that was the silhouettes of Ograx the Great and the huntsman, Jharkill. The beastfiend champion and the malformed ogre waited on the edge of the fearful distance left clear about Archaon's wagon. The stinking shaman approached but Archaon angled his helm at the thing, the warlord's silent gaze enough to stop it in its hoof tracks. The shaman had been busy in the camp with its filthy dressings, its wound-cleansing flame and the curved bone-shard of its wound-closing needle. Several times the shaman had tried to tend to its warlord's wounds and afflictions but every time Archaon had shaken the beastfiend's clawed fingers from his plate.

'My lord,' Sheerian said, risking Archaon's ire, 'if I may be so bold. If you ever want to swing a sword with that arm again, you need to have it bound in place. So it will heal, my lord.'

Archaon had all but forgotten the dull agony of his broken arm. He had grown accustomed to visiting savage butchery with his left, while the arm that his father-in-shadow had shattered dangled armoured and helpless at his side.

'My sword is gone…' Archaon said, his words taken by the doom-laden breeze.

'There will be other swords, master,' the ancient told him. 'Let there be the strength of an arm, the turn of a wrist and the belief of a clenched fist to guide their death-dealing path.'

Archaon hated the Tzeentchian sorcerer but he knew he was right. While Archaon was no ordinary man, with his fate-cursed bones and flesh blessed of ruin, he could not allow the unnatural healing of his body to fix the mangled limb in place. Such a limb would be next to useless and a liability in the monstrous battles the Chaos warlord was sure were yet to come. Archaon nodded and Sheerian pushed the shaman to approach with its splint and the black fur of a sling.

As the beastfiend went to work on the shattered limb, fresh agonies arcing through the warlord's being, Archaon instructed Sheerian to have Ograx and Jharkill come before him. As the beastfiend champion and the monstrous ogre stepped forth, Archaon felt Eins, Zwei and Drei close in slightly. Like gargoyles protecting some cathedral from evil spirits, the Swords of Chaos stood sentinel and silent about the wagon, their wings in tatters, but their bone swords intact and but a swift hand grasp away.

Archaon regarded Ograx the Great. The beastfiend was a blood-drenched vision of horn and muscle. The creature had its brain-splattered skull-axe by its side and about its waist the champion wore so many skulls dangling from its fur belts that the clinking arrangement almost constituted a skirt or kilt.

'Sorcerer,' Archaon commanded, 'ask this creature why he moved my horde into battle before my order to do so.'

Sheerian translated Archaon's words into the dark tongue of the Southern Wastes and Ograx replied dangerously in kind, the infernal beastliness of its jaws going to work at a snarling explanation.

'He says that he camped near the palace as you instructed, but that this monster,' the ancient said, indicating the malformed ogre, 'captured and caged those that the herdmaster would keep close.'

'Perhaps Ograx the Great might have lived up to its name,' Archaon replied, 'and kept those the herdmaster would keep close, close to himself.' When Sheerian hesitated, Archaon urged, 'Tell him.'

'Has there not been enough blood spilled, my dark lord?' the Tzeentchian wheezed.

'There certainly won't have been if you don't issue my wishes, my instructions, nay my *commands* to this brute.'

At Sheerian's words, Ograx roared his protestations. Beyond the fire, horns turned and the ears of beastfiends twitched at the confrontation. The hands of the Swords of Chaos edged closer to the wing-sheathes of their weapons. Sheerian held out his skeletal hands to calm the beast.

'He, he,' the sorcerer stammered, 'he says he attacked the palace to reclaim what belonged to Archaon, chosen of the Chaos gods but that if Archaon, chosen of the Chaos gods, had not wandered into the Wastes, hordeless and without words, then perhaps his harlot and her attendants would have been safe.'

Archaon savagely shrugged off the shaman, his broken arm splinted across the plate of his chest, the black fur of a tight sling holding it in place.

'Harlot?' Archaon barked at the Blood God's champion. 'I should have left her in charge. I think you are right, Great One. They were not safe with you at the head of this horde, your heifer's mind addled with the lust for blood.'

As Sheerian translated his master's fury, Ograx stepped forward, its hooves scratching at the frozen dirt. The beast could barely wrap its thick tongue about its ire.

'Or yours,' the aged sorcerer told Archaon, translating the best he could, 'buried in the fell flesh of that heretic woman.'

Ograx the Great spat at Archaon's feet. The warlord watched the head of the skull-axe come up. The strain of daemongut and the creak of ivory cut through the confrontation. Beside Ograx, the huntsman Jharkill had drawn its colossal tusk bow and held the spear-like length of an arrow to the bestial champion's horned head. The whisper of bone blades being torn from wing-sheathes followed.

'If he does that again,' Archaon commanded darkly, 'shoot him.'

Ograx quaked. The beaten plate strapped across his chest rose and fell with the exertion of keeping the creature's fury in check. About it, the ogre's arrow trembled, the Swords of Chaos closed with their blades of bone and Archaon glowered – injured, unarmed and uncaring, confident that he could kill the beastfiend champion with a single bare hand, if required. Worst of all, the warlord's cutting words had lit wildfires of doubt that would spread through the horde. Hulking beastfiends and warrior half-breeds who had brought dark honour to the Ruinous Powers in battle under Ograx's savage command now reared to full height. Where before such monsters would have fought for the Great One, now they smelled blood and the chance to lead Archaon's horde for themselves. The bestial prince lowered his horned head. It was as much of an acknowledgement or apology as Archaon was going to get.

'Great One,' Archaon said, his words translated into dark tongue by Sheerian, 'you lead the horde in my name still.' Archaon grunted; with the fires of possibility and greed stoked in the savage hearts of the beastfiend horde, he knew not for how long. Ograx nodded his brute understanding and lowered his horned head further in furious appreciation. As he turned to leave, Archaon's barbed words stopped the creature. 'However, beastling prince, think not to be left in sole command of my dread army again.'

Ograx the Great fought back his fury and with difficulty turned, as though Archaon's words were holding him there. He looked up the colossal shaft of the arrow at Jharkill, who with some hesitation of his own, began to lower his weapon. With that the beastfiend champion's hooves stomped away. Away from the burn of remonstration and through the barging shoulders and silent, standing hostility of a warherd that, moments before, he had commanded without question.

Archaon turned his attention to the monstrous ogre, who lowered his brute bow and unstrung his arrow. The thing's dead twin still sat in his chest, its face fixed in a mask of death and the oily, black poison that Jharkill used on his arrowheads still leaking down the ogre's huge belly. Archaon snapped the tinny fingers of his gauntlet and Sheerian brought forth the heavy shaman's staff that the huntsman used to control the monsters of the menagerie. It jangled with the charms hanging from its cross bar as the sorcerer laid it down on the ground before Archaon. Jharkill came forth, holding his tusk bow in the hand of his huge, muscle-bound arm while its atrophied opposite stroked the face of the dead twin. Kneeling before Archaon, Jharkill lowered his head.

'I am Archaon,' the Chaos warlord told the malformed ogre. As he spoke, Sheerian translated his words into another dialect of dark tongue. Something still savage but more sophisticated than the beastspeak of Ograx the Great and his half-breeds. 'Chosen of the Ruinous Gods, bearer of their gifts and taker of their treasures. Darkness willing, I shall be the Everchosen of Chaos. Lord of the End Times. Herald of the Apocalypse. In my expanding horde the weak are sacrificed and the strong are spared – to sacrifice themselves to my will. That is why the beastlord you had in your sights still lives. His strength is my strength. His talents enhance my own. I would ask no less of you, Jharkill of the Gatelands. Serve me as you served your last master.'

Jharkill's words rumbled up from inside him like an earthquake and Sheerian translated them.

'I am yours, Chosen one,' Jharkill said. 'For I have seen with my own eyes the favour bestowed on you by the Dark Gods of this land. How may I serve your dreadship?'

Archaon nodded slowly.

'I would ask of you no more than your previous daemon lord,' Archaon said simply.

'You wish to collect beasts?'

'I do.'

'But you freed the monsters of my lord's menagerie,' Jharkill said, confused. He was a skilled hunter and gifted in the primitive arts of charmongery. He was not much of a thinker. Archaon forgave him this failing. The warlord didn't need thinkers. Warriors who spent their time in thought rather than in slaughterous service were not to be trusted. Archaon had fallen foul of such dangers before.

'You mistake me, huntsman,' Archaon told him. 'Your master was a despicable tyrant who revelled in the suffering of his caged slaves. I have no such ambitions. I require no palace or menagerie to encircle it. I am no liberator either. The monstrous things of the world should not be kept in cages and captives should have their freedom. Freedom has its price, master huntsman, as you yourself know; these monstrosities you catch and enslave to your will should be free to serve me. They should be free to exercise their devastating talents – to butcher and destroy as they were born to do – and they should do it as part of my growing horde of beasts.'

'You wish me to catch the creatures you set free?' the malformed ogre rumbled.

'And bind them to your will, as you charmed them before,' Archaon told him, 'so that such monsters can rain down destruction on my enemies at my command. Can you do this for me, huntsman?'

Jharkill shouldered his huge bow and picked up his shaman's staff, rearing to his full hunchbacked height.

'As I am,' the creature said, 'they shall be. Yours, my master.'

Archaon smiled behind the leering skull of his horned helm.

'Good…' he hissed.

'It will take some time, my master,' Jharkill warned him. With Lord Agrammon's palace aflame and the menagerie a twisted ruin, the monsters of the daemon's collection had fled across the Gatelands to their freedom.

'I want only the strongest,' Archaon instructed, 'the most savage and talented of their kind. My horde is no place for the weak – even if they are born to monstrosity. I need things that can march with my bestial army, fly above it or range ahead of it to report dangers to come. I need giants, the scaled serpents of the sky, things fleet of foot that track and savage, daemonbreeds and destroyers, like the abominate thing that did for your former master.'

'They shall be yours to command,' Jharkill assured him.

'Hand pick prisoner long-snouts and half-breeds from my horde for your work,' Archaon told it, 'and take as many wagons as you need. I tire of this dread place. My army marches once more for the top of the world.'

'We are heading north, my lord?' Sheerian asked as Jharkill backed respectfully away from his new master. The sorcerer's cracked voice betrayed a relief that was difficult to mask. Archaon knew that the Tzeentchian longed for the complexity and sophistication of more civilised lands. Compared to the frozen, barbarian darkness of the southern continent, storm-racked and swarming with beastfiends, daemons and monsters, the Northern Wastes were positively urbane. The Shadowlands at the top of the world were ruled by men and their weak-minded desires. Warring tribes. God-pledged marauders. Soul-selling sorcerers. Warbands without number, fighting for Chaos warriors – the greatest of which led vast armies of the lost and damned at the pleasure of the Ruinous Powers. It was a place of possibility, where the servants of the Great Changer could fully deploy their talents.

'We are heading south,' Archaon told the sorcerer.

'But, my lord–' Sheerian began.

'The horde will march on the Gatelands and the daemons who built their palaces on the rim of their great master's otherworldly realm. We shall take the fight to these infernal princes and swell our ranks with recruits from the unslain.

Jharkill will bring me monsters and you will be our guide as we pass through what is left of the Great Gate.'

Archaon felt the heads turn across the camp, ears prick and hearts leap. A shocked Sheerian tried to find the words.

'My lord, I–'

'Serve at the pleasure of Archaon, Chosen of the gods?' the Chaos warlord said.

'Of course, but the Gate–'

'It is open, this Gate, is it not?'

'Yes, my lord,' the sorcerer said. 'It floods the world with madness and power, spilling unchecked and unfiltered from the monstrous beyond.'

'And I mean to take my horde through that gate and into–' Archaon began.

'You mean to enter the Realm of Chaos?' Sheerian marvelled with horror.

'I do, sorcerer,' Archaon said. 'And you shall guide me.'

'To where, master?' Sheerian asked.

'To the top of the world,' Archaon said. 'There was a Great Gate here. There was a Great Gate there. Would it not be madness for two such gateways – the only ones of their demolished kind – not to be connected?'

'It would be madness, master,' Khezula Sheerian said, but the sorcerer was no longer talking about dark realms and the portals that led to them. 'My lord, I'm not sure I can be of service to you in this matter.'

'You have been to this place, sorcerer,' Archaon put to him, 'this realm, this otherworldly plane where dreams are reality, the Dark Gods cower and monstrous forces shape the madness about them. Before you were summoned to this wretched flesh, you knew this nightmare realm.'

'I did, my lord,' Sheerian said, 'and I would not recommend a return. This place you speak of is less a place than a feeling, a knowing – fear, if fear had a shape. It is a stormy silence or the darkness of the depths. A thing to be experienced. A horror to be lived. A hell of ever-changing torments. A claustrophobic vastness. An endless intimacy, shared with your nightmares. Great intelligences exist in this void, things that came into being at the heart of soul-driven storms. Things born of dreads and desires. Things that long for a form of flesh in which to experience this world beyond their own.'

'Things like you,' Archaon accused.

'Things like the *Yien-Ya-Long*,' Sheerian warned, 'like Agrammon and Be'lakor – the shadow that haunts you here already. Like the Powers of ruin you scorn and serve.'

'When these things,' Archaon pressed the sorcerer, 'things like *you*, enter my world – the world that is mine to destroy – you assume the mortality and weakness of flesh. Does it not stand to reason…'

'The Realm of Chaos is no place to demand of reason, my lord,' Sheerian said fearfully.

'…that our mortality and the fell souls that drive us will assume a similar form on this benighted plane? Something temporary. Something else.'

'The place you speak of is a thing beyond words – beyond expectations. Your pledges and promises will have no meaning in an existence beyond your own,' Sheerian said.

'I am the cold fire that burns about my soul,' Archaon said. 'I suspect the dark radiance of such dark need will light our path – whatever form it might take – in this dread realm. The fires of my ambition will light our way, sorcerer, and you will guide us by that light.'

'My lord, I implore you,' Sheerian begged, 'I do not know the way. I know not if such a way exists. There are no *ways* through the Realm of Chaos. No one has ever done this before.'

'Then we shall be both the first,' Archaon told the sorcerer, 'and the last. This Realm of Chaos and the monstrous things that inhabit it – fed by the otherworldly presence of our hopes, dreams and fears – will be no more. I am Archaon, Lord of the End Times. An end to all. An end to everything that deigns to exist – in this world or any other. You will guide me and my horde through this inconstant realm, sorcerer, to the remains of the Great Gate at the top of the world, or you will find us wretched beings from that plane of damnations who can. Do you understand?'

'I do, my lord,' Sheerian told his master, and the sorcerer slunk away to dwell on their doom.

As he left, Archaon noticed another miserable creature. Gorst had finally caught up with the horde. The flagellant jangled in his chains, his charms and his head-cage, edging towards the nearby fire and the raucous beastfiends gathered about it like some emaciated scavenger, hoping to snatch some scrap of roasted meat or the marrow from an abandoned bone. Archaon grunted. Gorst would have, indeed had followed him to the ends of the world. He wondered if the mad man would be so ready to do so if he had any conception of where they were going.

Archaon got up from the wagon, leaving Giselle to horrors relived in the darkness both beneath her furs and behind the closing of her eyes. The daemon Dorghar trotted forth and Archaon climbed up into the armoured saddle. Eins came forward to receive his master's instructions.

'Have Prince Ograx get the horde on the move,' Archaon told the Sword of Chaos. 'Our doom awaits beyond the infernal palaces of the mighty.' Archaon turned Dorghar about. The Chaos warlord intended to lead the monstrous army from the front. He pointed at Gorst. 'And make sure that wretch eats his fill before we move on.' Eins nodded in silent obedience and Dorghar raced off to the south. South towards the Gatelands. Towards the crowded ring of crooked towers, palaces and daemonic fortresses that the bottom of the world wore like a crown about the amaranthine blaze of the collapsed Chaos gate. Towards the Chaos warlord's destiny and doom.

CHAPTER VIII

'This is the first of the tellings. The first narrative. It was the time of before. Before the plagues of vermin and the warm-bloods. When the world was young and the creators held the realms in order. It was an age of promise and great works. The creators drew their power from a realm impossible. A spiritual plane in defiance of reason. A darkling sea through which they walked, a path unknown in a beyond not of their making. This realm was troubled by malign beings and the creators' passage through that realm became troubled also. The pathways crumbled, and the gateways connecting this existence and that collapsed. The known and the unknown merged. The true paths became poisoned by the presence of things undreamed of. Abyssal forces. False *creators. New-born calamities. Fears given shape.'*

– Astromancer Tempac-Zhul,
*The Annal-Inscriptions
of the Great Catastrophe*

*The Gatelands
The Southern Wastes
Horns Harrowing: Season of the Ravening*

Archaon could not claim to have brought war to the Gatelands. There daemonic armies clashed, slaughters were undertaken and things died for their rancid masters with perpetual fervour. The palaces of infernal royalty were in a constant state of being ransacked and rebuilt. Fortresses had been under siege for centuries, while towers toppled only for others to rise like colossal stone weeds from the churning earth. Every kind of infernal aberration possible seemed to hold a miserable patch of aethyr-baked ground. Greater daemons of the Chaos Powers had been questionably rewarded for their eternal service. Daemon lords kept mad court in palatial grandeur, while dark princes fought from dread fortresses, forever pledged to destruction to earn their infernal heritage. Creatures of every description and perversity haunted the smoking ruins of the Gatelands, while otherworldy beasts, half-breeds and armies of lesser daemons fought battles without end in efforts to earn their masters' attentions.

So close to the collapsed gate and the roaring torrent of unreality blasting forth from the existential breach, the very nature of normality was under constant threat. The land beneath the boot, the stone and metal of infernal palaces and the maelstrom of the heavens was in a state of monstrous flux. What could be seen, heard, smelt, tasted and touched could not be trusted. The warped landscape about the polar rift, and the nightmarish architectural achievements sprouting busily about it, smeared into one another. Daemons, their fortresses and the spawn hordes that fought for them dreamed away to spectral shades. Ghostly palaces overlapped, existing over one another in the crowded madness of the Gateland interior. Daemon lords and hellbound princes existing in the same place at different times, the wraith-like lambency of their presence like an infernal afterthought. Bathed in the perpetual blaze of the beyond, fires of flux and flame whipped through the competing canopy of roofs, domes and towers. Warpquakes shook the lands about the dread gate, opening up glowing fissures, swallowing armies, shaking fortresses to their crumbling foundations and collapsing towers in sky-rocketing plumes of dust.

Archaon rode into the insanity of the Gatelands at the head of his growing horde. His bestial ranks had been swelled by Lord Agrammon's surrendering Slaaneshi long-snouts, while Jharkill was as good as his barbarian word in rapidly recapturing many savage Chaos creatures and monsters formerly housed in the daemonic menagerie. Tracking them through the tumultuous Gatelands, shooting them, drugging them with his evil unguents and enslaving them to his will with primitive charms and shamanic bindings, Jharkill had freakish titans, monstrous spawn, winged and warped serpents, chimeric predators and exotic abominations obediently fall into line.

Before the rotting wreck of Papa Gallows's palace of suffering, the stonework squirming with monstrous maggots and larval daemons, Archaon and Jharkill the huntsman happened upon one of their escaped monstrosities. It was a predatory fusion of beasts standing over the carcass of some bloated fury it had snatched out of the sky. The stubs of its wings flapped with the pure joy of the kill, while its ragged mane and sabred jaws dripped with the blue-black ichor of the downed fury.

Archaon heard the creak of Jharkill's tusk bow as the ogre hooked the string and the colossal shaft of the poison-smeared arrow with his atrophied limb, while heaving the bow away from his barrel chest. Archaon marvelled as the huntsman aimed up at the broiling sky and the distance from which the malformed ogre was attempting the shot. As Archaon watched the predator tear its daemonic prey apart, he recognised the beast. It was a manticore. It was Mange, the creature that had so effectively provided the havoc in Lord Agrammon's menagerie that enabled Archaon's escape. Archaon liked the idea of having such a savage creature as part of his host, but as he remembered the creature's misery in the cage and soaked up the flesh-tearing abandon of the wild beast, he felt an intervention creep down one arm. The barbed blade of Archaon's sickle sword came down to rest on the arrow shaft reaching out from the bow. Pushing on the arrow, Archaon motioned Jharkill's bow down. The ogre wrapped the contorted ugliness of his face around a squint of confusion.

'This one roams free,' Archaon said. The decision hadn't been prompted by sympathy or even a sense of loyalty born of the creature's original sacrifice. It was dark whim. The same whim that warped the landscape about them. The same whim that had created the Chaos creature in the first place. Or at least that is what Archaon told himself. Jharkill grunted his understanding and unstrung his arrow before the huntsman stomped on in search of further targets.

Digging his heels into Dorghar, Archaon motioned the daemon steed on. With his horde of tribal half-breeds united behind the flayed flesh of his banner, a growing mob of abominate monstrosities and a cavalcade of beast-hauled wagons and bone-crafted siege engines trailing the colossal host, Archaon slaughtered his way through the lands and palaces of the infernal mighty.

At the Brass Citadel Archaon led his army to a bloodbath of a victory against Kruor'gor of the Brazen Horde – a greater daemon in the service of mighty Khorne. Forced to kill the daemon's bloodletter battlehost to the very last infernal berserker, the assault on the Brass Citadel trapped Kruor'gor in his own palace. Archaon frustrated the Blood God's abominate servant. Unusually for the Chaos warlord, he would not meet the Skulltaker in single combat. Pummelling the greater daemon with monstrous attacks from his own horde and siege fire from his bone engines of war, Archaon stoked the greater daemon's bottomless ire to such a degree that the dread creature raged into the form of a hell-fed inferno: a titan of fury and flame. The Brass Citadel melted about the creature, drowning the great Kruor'gor in an insolent lake of liquid metal.

Before the cloud-piercing tower of the Roost, Archaon's horde was set upon by the Cerulean Brood – a flock of savage Tzeentchian daemons whose colossal wings rode the currents of raw magical power bleeding from the polar portal and into the world. Skewering and snapping up beastfiends from the ground with their twisted, snaggle-toothed beaks, the daemons dropped egg-like orbs of dark and explosive enchantment on Archaon's horde, the effect of each being whimsically different. Sometimes victims in the vicinity of the sorcerous orb's impact would erupt in the blossoming horror of spawndom, while at others violaceous flames tore through the ranks of the half-breeds. Archaon himself would have succumbed to a heaven-plummeting orb that turned the ground at Dorghar's feet into a tentacled maw of abyssal appetite, but the daemon steed's reflexes were faster than the appendages shooting out for the stallion's nightmare form.

While Archaon had his own winged monstrosities take to the sky and torch the feathered daemons, he charged a ghoulish giant of withered flesh, protruding bones and ancient animations laying its great, withered back against the foot of the Roost and toppling the Tzeentchian tower. Archaon let Ograx and his beastfiends do the rest, mobbing downed daemons and butchering the sorcerer infernals that worked the libraries of the Roost and fought with the cowardly craft of the witchbreed.

The Filth Fortress of Mortiphidus the Cankered slowed Archaon's horde down considerably. The colossal rotting carcass of the Cankered One sat atop its fat, pyramidal palace like a throne. The booming laugh of the daemon was everywhere and sickened Archaon's half-breeds to the bottom of their stomachs, producing in the creatures of the herd a phased biliousness and vomiting that did not make for ideal, vanguard warriors. Oozing, spilling, leaking and excreting from every orifice and stomach-gaping sore, the stinking essence of Mortiphidus made its way slowly down the palace tiers like lava from a volcano. Disease-ridden daemons bathed, played, splashed and frolicked in the seeping terrace shallows and rivers of rotten muck that proceeded from the great unclean daemon of Nurgle. The tiers seemed to indicate some kind of hierarchy, with infestations of miniature Cankered Ones evolving out of the rolling detritus.

Archaon's bestial horde found fighting in the palace gardens – a sickly swamp that had grown up out of the faecal flood plain surrounding the fortress – all but impossible. Noxious gases rising from the rotting marsh asphyxiated, poisoned and infected Archaon's half-breeds in equal measure, those returning from Mortiphidus's gardens carrying all manner of diseases and horrific afflictions. Others were overcome by the swarms of tiny, fat imps that rose from the swamp like bubbles in churning maelstroms of disgust.

Archaon and his Swords were forced to lead an attack on the Filth Fortress after successive assaults by Ograx the Great failed. In the sinking gardens at the foot of the palace – lost in a stunted forest of petrified fungi and the mind-splitting stench – Archaon was confronted with daemonic knights emerging from the depths. As the Chaos warlord and his horde pushed on, up to their waists in rancid muck, the swamp spewed forth long-lost warriors, clad in rust-encrusted armour that hundreds of years before might have seen the inside of some hellish forge. The knights advanced slowly in their bloat-bent plate and emitted a horrible, droning shriek.

As Archaon crashed his sickle sword through the infernal warriors and took encrusted helms from shoulders in showers of red particles, he was surprised to find no daemons inside. Instead, the rusted knights were writhing with maggots, fat on daemonflesh and black swarms of bloated infernal flies. It became suddenly clear where the droning shriek proceeded from as Archaon, his Swords of Chaos and beastfiends of the horde not only had to battle the enduring, sorcerous spirits of the daemonic knights but also a plague of flies intent on eating them alive. Between the haunted suits of hell-forged armour, the blood-sucking hurricane of flies and the swamp vomiting forth a never-ending garrison of rusted warriors, even Archaon ordered a retreat. Slurping back through the unbreathable stench, Archaon waded past the sinking bodies of blood-drained beastfiends sprouting the fruits of a fast-acting plague. Upon returning to his camp in an obsidian keep he had captured from a pantheon-honouring daemon prince, Archaon only had two words for his horde.

'Burn it...'

Wielding bone torches taken from serpent-lit bonfires of plague-ridden bodies, Archaon's half-breeds spread out about the Filth Fortress and its gardens. They didn't have to advance far before marsh gases from the rising rot – the same gases that had made it almost impossible to breath – spectacularly caught light. From the obsidian keep, Archaon watched as the oily discharge floating on the swamp surface spread the inferno through the gardens and fungal forest, before spreading through the tiers of the palace, up the rivers of rich muck and putrefaction. Archaon soaked up the suffering as the fires spread through the army of daemon followers flailing and screaming on the pyramidal palace terraces. Finally the flames spread to Mortiphidus itself, the colossal carcass of the great unclean beast giving the fires plenty of fuel. The flame writhed up about the great daemon of Nurgle. Lighting up the sky, the monstrosity's booming laughter still filled the air – riding on the crackle and hiss of the daemon's roasting rot. It was still there hours later, making his half-breeds feel sick, as Archaon ordered the horde on from the obsidian keep.

The further Archaon's army pushed into the Gateland interior, the more insanity they encountered. Warped daemonic furies swarmed through the cloudless blackness of a sky in which the moiling heavens had been burned dry by the elation roaring up through the collapse of the mighty Chaos gate. The creatures circled endlessly about the blaze of otherworldly energies spewing into the world. The spaces between the palaces grew tighter, making moving the horde, its accompanying monsters and the cavalcade of wagons and siege engines difficult. The fortress walls of the infernal palaces grew taller and grander in their obscene veneration of the Ruinous Powers. Colossal, crafted symbols reached into the silent madness of the skies, casting shadows down on enemy courtyards, honouring the most powerful of Chaos gods, as well as pantheon-praising eight-point stars of ruin and the rarer sigils of lesser known powers and daemon princes.

Archaon and his army found continual slaughter and butchery in the killing fields and thoroughfares that twisted between vaulting palaces, monstrous citadels and smoking fortress ruins. Bones crunched beneath boots everywhere they went, like an ivory gravel squelching in a bloody mire. Corpses swung from the razored crenellations of walls. Body parts and horned heads sat on forests of decorative spikes. Thoroughfares, that were almost rivers of gore, dammed by corpse walls and massacres.

Fighting his way over the concentric, polygonal walls of a star-shaped fort that through its eight-point layout revered the glory of the Ruinous Powers united, Archaon and his monstrous mob of mongrels laid siege to Kastaghar the Adulant. Kastaghar was a newly ascended prince, worshipped by daemonic disciples who were worshipped by other infernal creatures who, in turn, were worshipped by hundreds of other hell-born servants. The daemons of the Adulant indulged a monastic existence and lived as masons, castle custodians and worshippers of their fellow dark kindred, with only the dread Kastaghar allowed to venerate the gods of Chaos directly. With their pallid daemonflesh, and dressed identically in their midnight skull helms, black foil skirts, urchin-spiked pauldrons and hook-knuckled gauntlets, the dark brotherhood of the Adulant left their scarred chests and backs on show. Archaon found the fraternity to be staid and disciplined warriors, holding their fort and their own against the wild butchery of his half-breeds.

Face to face, Archaon found Kastaghar to be much like himself. The Chaos gods had been subtle in their gifts, with neither the warlord nor the daemon prince monstrous in appearance. They were intelligent, potent warriors who, unlike many savage creatures of Chaos, were not without dark humour or civility.

Even the multiple walls of the black fort could not stand up to the decimation wreaked upon their stone surfaces by Archaon's abominates. Giants and monsters smashed through, allowing Ograx and his beastfiends to flood the fort. Archaon was impressed with the reverence and discipline of Kastaghar's brotherhood, each daemonic acolyte fighting expertly for the leading disciple they worshipped. Though Archaon's losses were grievous, the brotherhood were simply driven back before the deluge of horn and muscle that streamed in through the fort wall breeches.

Even as the Adulant and Archaon circled one another within the star-shaped walls of the inner temple ward, the pair shared some dark pleasantries.

'What happened to your arm?' Kastaghar asked.

Archaon saw no point in lying. His right arm was strapped across his chest.

'It's broken,' the warlord said, 'so I will be destroying you with my left today. Forgive me – I hope you are not insulted.'

'On the contrary,' the Adulant said. 'In conscience, I cannot kill a warrior sporting such an injury.' Kastaghar stretched the pale flesh of his brawny neck from side to side before straining his back and bare chest. His face was handsome for an infernal prince but screwed up with exertion and sickening pain. Finally something popped horribly in his chest and his right arm fell uselessly by his side. Archaon found that he had laughed, his mirth echoing about the walls of the fort. Kastaghar the Adulant had dislocated his shoulder for the battle.

'Now we can both fight with honour,' he told Archaon. A member of the brotherhood threw his master a staff bearing leaf-shaped blades of black on both ends. Kastaghar twirled the weapon expertly in the fingers of his left hand for show. Archaon nodded.

'I find honour overrated, dark prince,' Archaon told him. 'But I thank you for both the gesture and the amusement I did not think to find in this place.'

'Perhaps I can entertain you further with a wager?'

'I like you, prince,' Archaon told him. It was refreshing to find a creature of regard and wit in the mindless violence and horror of the Southern Wastes. 'What do you have in mind?'

'A trial by blade, of course,' Kastaghar said.

'What else?' Archaon agreed. 'This is the Gatelands – the Dark Gods are watching.'

Now it was the Adulant's turn to laugh.

'I like you too, interloper,' Kastaghar said. 'Despite what you have done to the walls of my temple, a temple to honour all Dark Gods. You think little of honour, but you could have had your monsters level this unhallowed place and yet you have not. Your creatures met my brotherhood blade to blade – as you have met me.'

'Is there a point coming soon?' Archaon teased.

'Indeed, my dark brother,' Kastaghar said, laughing once more. 'Single combat: you and I – no champions. If I succeed in offering your soul to our gods, then your champion shall lead your host from this unholy place and leave my brotherhood to continue in their dark prayers.'

'You care for these underling wretches?' Archaon marvelled.

'I care for their devotions,' the daemon prince told him, 'and the devotions they will inspire in others. For without such dread faith and the spreading of dark truths, the Ruinous Powers would be no more.'

'I see your point,' Archaon said, once more smiling beneath his helm. He imagined himself riding through a world of cinder and bone, with no one left to worship gods dark or otherwise. He imagined the faith-starved gods of

Chaos, their emaciate energies sustained only by the atrocities of one fell warrior: Archaon, Lord of the End Times. Everchosen of Chaos. Destroyer of the Dark Gods. In the glorious taking of his own life – the last mortal to walk the apocalyptic ruin of the world – he would snuff out the dread Powers like guttering candles in the breeze. He would need more than bestial savages and monsters to achieve such a feat. Perhaps it was plain perversity. Perhaps he truly had come to like the dark prince – but in that moment Archaon decided not to kill Kastaghar the Adulant.

'I counter your offer,' Archaon said, drawing the barbed blade of his sickle sword. 'First blood settles the victor. If the blood is mine, you keep your fortress-temple and the creatures who would carry out their devotions within it.'

'And if the blood is mine, interloper?' Kastaghar said.

'Then you abandon this damned place,' Archaon said.

'To you?' the Adulant asked.

'To the elements,' Archaon told him, 'unnatural though they may be. You and your brotherhood join me and my horde. You can bring your devotions with you. I could once more use a man of faith at my side.'

Kastaghar the Adulant cast a gaze across the ranks of his surviving brotherhood, corralled as they were by Archaon's horde, within the walls of the inner temple ward.

'I choose life over death,' the dark prince announced, walking forth. 'Belief over oblivion. A brother's love over loss. Let's fight.'

Kastaghar came forth with his bladed spear, turning it with his wrist. Archaon tapped the cracked, black stone of the temple ward with the toothed tip of his sickle sword and advanced to meet the daemon prince. Kastaghar's spear spun at Archaon with sudden speed and savagery, the rotating blades threatening to cut the warlord in two. Archaon side-stepped the display, but Kastaghar countered immediately by spinning the spear before him like a wheel. Archaon used his sickle sword to turn the weapon aside. Then again. And again. The rotating blur of the spear stopped suddenly and became a thrusting menace, stabbing forth with murderous force and discipline. Archaon lurched back, swiping the spear-point from its path towards his chest, his groin and his skull faceplate.

Archaon was impressed with the dark prince's technique. He seemed fluid and graceful, backed up by infernal strength and fearlessness. The weapon too was a lightweight thing of craft and killing ability. Even in Kastaghar's left hand, the dark prince turned it, back-slashed and jabbed with it as though it were barely there. Its twin blades were leaf-shaped and equal to the tasks of cutting with their curved edge or piercing with their black points. The brotherhood had gathered around to show their support. They prayed for their master and sported further weaponry for him in the event that his spear should fail. As Archaon whipped about, turned and smashed the relentless spin of the spear he saw the blur of his own gathered half-breeds, who were roaring, snorting and calling thick-tongued obscenities, insults and threats at Kastaghar.

He saw Ograx the Great bellowing his fury, great streams of drool whipping from his shaking jaws. The Swords of Chaos waited obediently as part of the forming circle, anticipating further orders. Ready with hands on the hilts of bone swords, ready to be pulled from the sheaths of folded wings. Khezula Sheerian watched nearby, an almost perpetual concern etched into the ancient's features. Then – with great surprise – he saw the misshapen Vier, standing with Giselle. The girl had left the solitude of her wagon and furs. She had walked through the wreckage of the fortress walls and had joined the circle to watch Archaon fight. Her face was a sour void of blank disappointment.

Such surprise almost cost Archaon as the spear seared down at him once more. Archaon turned around, allowing the toothed curvature of the sickle sword to glance round, absorbing the clash of the spearheads. Archaon whipped his cloak and furs about him but by the time he had turned, ready to wheel the sickle sword at Kastaghar, the dark prince was once again thrusting for him. Leaning out of a throat jabbing stroke, Archaon lurched immediately at Kastaghar. As the Adulant brought the spear in close, twirling it over his head and then about his twisting body, Archaon dived into a heavy roll beneath it. With his plate jangling about him, Archaon swept the barbed blade of the sickle sword through Kastaghar's knees, but the dark prince had jumped up out of its path. As Archaon's sickle sword came up, Kastaghar's spinning spear smashed into the toothed weapon, tearing it from Archaon's grip. Archaon grunted as the hell-forged weapon, inferior in weight and craftsmanship, skittered across the stone floor of the fortress-temple nearby.

Kastaghar seemed to hesitate. He brought the spear blade down with all the force his left arm could muster. Archaon wasn't there by the time the blade sparked off the stone and was racing across the circle. Ducking beneath an opportunistic backslash of the spear, Archaon slid down onto his armoured side and snatched up the sickle sword as he skidded by across the smooth stone. Kastaghar was there almost immediately – the daemon prince not only moving with infernal grace and speed but also unencumbered by a full suit of plate. Again, Archaon felt the Adulant hesitate. This time Kastaghar didn't thrust or spin his spear at all but waited honourably while Archaon got to his feet. The dark prince wouldn't blood his opponent as he scrabbled about on his temple floor.

Shaking out his plate and turning the sickle sword in his own wrist, Archaon nodded his appreciation to the Adulant, who nodded back. The blistering attack that followed was nothing short of a sword storm, fuelled by Archaon's scorched pride. Bringing the serrated blade back and forth, around and surging up in a curved, gut-punching thrust, Archaon followed with a rhythmic succession of hacks and slashes, each manoeuvre sending the lighter blade at Kastaghar with all the belligerent force his arm and inner turmoil could draw upon. Kastaghar's defences were no less graceful than his attacks, using his twisting wrist and single arm to negate Archaon's furious assault.

Clutching the spear shaft along his forearm to turn aside the cleaving motion of Archaon's blade, the daemon prince twirled the spear around and about, the bladed ends clashing the sickle sword's relentless attentions away. Archaon fought on. As the Chaos warlord lurched forward with attack after murderous attack, Kastaghar was forced to weave, retreat, flip back acrobatically and twirl the spear before him in a whirling circle of death. Archaon's blade simply would not be stopped, however, and with a force that drew a roar from the warlord, Archaon chopped the spear in half.

Startled by the ferocity of the counter attack and the splintering crack of the spear, Kastaghar took several swift steps back. Archaon did not follow, however, allowing the daemon prince a moment to catch his breath. Dropping the demolished weapon, Kastaghar called for another and caught the chain of a flail that had been cast to him across the circle by one of the brotherhood. He clutched the handle and allowed the black chain of the flail to fall. Archaon could see that it sported a modest metal ball with eight spiked points, forming the shape of the Ruinous Star of their calling. Kastaghar nodded, returning his appreciation, before stepping forward.

As Archaon closed once more, moving about the dark prince, he worked the serrated blade around with slow turns of the wrist – like a scorpion ready to strike. Kastaghar had started to work his flail with his left hand, expertly sending the spiked ball about him, occasionally swinging the length of the weapon out at Archaon's head or sword. The two warriors of Chaos seemed to have the same idea at the same time. Closing suddenly, Archaon's serrated sword came up. Kastaghar's flail shot out. There was the excruciating sound of metal being tangled as the teeth of Archaon's sickle sword caught in the links of the black chain and both spiked ball and the curved edge of the serrated blade became a knotted mess.

Both Archaon and Kastaghar abandoned their weapons simultaneously, surging for one another with their gauntlets. The brotherhood and Archaon's Swords stood by to throw their masters fresh weaponry, but the pair did not seem interested. Latching onto one another with their armoured fists, the warlord and the daemon prince dragged each other in close. As they did so, their helms almost clashed. With a grunt, and still holding his enemy close, Archaon brought up his leg and rested the sole of his boot on the Adulant's chest. Archaon kicked Kastaghar away with such force that the dark prince went stumbling back at the ranks of Archaon's own followers.

Then the warlord realised his mistake.

While Kastaghar had held Archaon with his gauntlets, he had snagged him with one of his knuckle-hooks, the sharpened point of one hook finding its way between the plates of his cursed armour and pinching at Archaon's flesh. As Archaon kicked him away, he felt the hook tear away and the warmth of blood dribble down his chest. It was the most minor of wounds but the daemon prince had indeed drawn first blood on Archaon.

Archaon stood there and lowered his gauntlets, while Kastaghar tumbled through the inner ranks of the circle. He regained his balance at the edge of the ring, his chest rising and falling. He looked to Archaon. The dark prince knew that he had blooded Archaon but with the scratch hidden from view beneath the armour of Morkar, no one else but Archaon knew this to be the case. The two champions regarded one another. Archaon's lips formed about a concession but then he saw Giselle. The girl was standing in the circle immediately behind Kastaghar. Archaon's heart leapt at the danger the girl was in, standing so close to the Adulant with his clawed gauntlets – especially if Archaon failed to honour the wound the daemon prince had inflicted. Without a muscle on her face moving, Giselle reached to one side and pulled a bone dagger from a sheath in one of Vier's broken wings. The misshapen Sword of Chaos was as surprised at the movement as Archaon and tried to reach for the girl's arm, but failed. Grabbing the oblivious Kastaghar from behind, the girl drew the razored edge of the bone blade across the Adulant's throat.

With a single slice, Archaon's hope of assimilating Kastaghar and his brotherhood into the ranks of the horde died. They died with Kastaghar the Adulant himself. As the dark prince fell slowly to his knees and the bone blade tumbled from Giselle's bloody red hand, the circle was silent. Kastaghar's knees hit the floor of the fortress-temple before the daemon prince crashed face forward into the stone. Behind him, Giselle had a withering gaze of blank venom for Archaon before turning into the ranks of his horde.

Archaon knew he had to act fast. He bit back a snarl. Whether it was madness, some kind of petty revenge or some love-spawned hatred, it didn't matter! The girl had cost him. There would be violence. The brotherhood would attack, intending to avenge their beloved master of the deadly gods in the world. Archaon's own horde might tear Giselle to pieces in shocked fury, knowing that the girl defied their master, and her own, in such a cowardly action. Archaon raised an armoured finger and aimed it at the brotherhood who were beginning to break ranks with weapons and tears.

'Destroy them!' he roared.

Any enmity among the half-breed horde for Giselle evaporated as Ograx the Great and the vanguard of the bestial mob bellowed and ran at the acolytes of the fortress-temple. Within moments every beastfiend at Archaon's command was surging through the demolished walls, intent on blood-eyed butchery. As Archaon stood unarmed in the centre of both the fortress and the havoc of battle, he watched Giselle walk away. Shadowed by an uncertain Vier, the girl left the inner ward and climbed up through the rubble of the smashed wall, intent on returning to her wagon. Archaon stood motionless as the massacre unfolded. The remaining brotherhood fought with skill, discipline and dark love for their fallen master – who had fought with the same himself – but they were no match for the unleashed savagery of Archaon's barbarian horde.

With Eins, Zwei and Drei forming a triangle about him with their bone blades drawn, Archaon felt the death about him. Lifeblood gushed at the sky. Heads rolled across black stone. Soon the inner ward was puddled in red, with body parts, scraps of flesh and shredded armour littering the floor. Archaon looked at the purple blaze that roared up at the heavens from the breached polar portal, the dread radiance in which they were all bathed. A stone cold inferno that hid an open gateway to the gods. He turned to see Khezula Sheerian looking at him. The sorcerer's face was unreadable but Archaon had no doubt that Sheerian's twisted patron would have found the grim spectacle that had unfolded in the fort amusing.

CHAPTER IX

'There is beyond this eternity another. An existence all of its own. It is dark as the mortal mind is dark, deep as the mortal heart is deep. This realm is sustained by the self. It is a spiritual plane made up of the thoughts and feelings, needs and beliefs of all the knowing races – the highborn and the low things that walk the world, with aims of it being their own. It gives back in the form of energies that leak into our world and are harnessed by the gifted in the form of magic and its many refractions. Entities beyond understanding inhabit this dark realm of spiritual energy, this sea of soulfire. They are the behemoths and great monsters of the depths, although our seven seas together are but a teardrop in the dry, dark ocean of the beyond. There they endure, drunk on power, bitter

*with impotence – curdling in the malefic
nightmare of their own existence.'*
– Caledor Dragontamer, *Prophecies of Despair*

*The Gatelands
The Southern Wastes
Horns Harrowing: Season of the Raw*

Although Archaon's army was only blazing a single trail of destruction through the crowded citadels and infernal palaces surrounding the collapsed Chaos gate, daemon lords and princes throughout the Gatelands knew of his presence. It had been many hundreds of years since a half-breed host had unified in such numbers in the darkness of the Wastes to attack the dread palaces of the mighty, in the Gatelands of infernal royalty, where some of the greatest daemons of the Chaos gods ruled. When they learned that it was a man-thing from the north at the head of the bestial horde, rather than one of their own savage kind, this interested the denizens of the Gatelands even more. Not an immortal, an infernal or diabolical being crafted of the gods – but a weakling mortal; nothing more than a plaything of the gods.

First came challenges. Territorial warnings. Assassination attempts by creatures that had been dreamcrafted of murderous desire, singular of lethal purpose. The unleashing of titans that strode across walls and stomped their monstrous way through the castle courtyards and palace grounds of their daemonic foes. The mobilisation of infernal hosts, swarming through the wretched narrows and bone-jutting trails weaving between the vaulting walls of infernal palaces. Lank-limbed horrors and fountains of warping flesh that filled cramped walkways with lurid flame. Great fanged slugs that rotted their way through fortress walls on carpets of plague-ridden slime. Soul-thirsty slayers of red flesh and twisted horn. Packs of flightless shrikes, hunting, tearing and savaging on all fours, wearing spiked collars in the fashion of eight-pointed stars.

When Archaon and his horde weren't fighting their way through monstrosities between the royal residences of daemon princes and hellish dukes, they were mounting assaults on the palaces themselves. The palace of Sybarith the Forgotten had walls that seemed never-ending. When Archaon ordered an assault on the palace he almost lost half of his host to the endless debaucheries inside. Forgetting themselves, and the Chaos warlord they fought for, half-breeds – intoxicated by what they saw – had to be dragged away. Sybarith seemed unaware of Archaon as he stood over the profane creature and even as it was slain would not abandon the delights of daemonflesh.

Its sibling, Cybriss, ruled from the palace beyond. The palace architecture flowed with the curve and suggestion of beautiful bodies, while the walls had been mortared with the undying bodies of the daemon's victims. Limbs reaching out suggestively stroked the stone surface of the wall while faces stared out from their rocky prisons in horror. Mouths were contorted about shrill screams but what proceeded from the slave chorus was so horrifically beautiful that even Archaon felt compelled to enter the open gates of the lip-lined barbican. Just as he was about to step inside, the Chaos warlord – having no desire to battle his own bodily needs to slay another daemonic hedonist – brought his infernal mount to a stop and directed his curious horde around the monstrous palace instead.

Their journey took them into forge-forts of iron that glowed with furnace-light and cloaked the area with the smoke of infernal production. These were the daemon smithies of Hak'grorfane of the Black Flame – crafter of monstrous weaponry for his brother thirsters of blood. Lumbering juggers proceeded forth from the forges in which they had been created: hulks of black brass and spike on two legs, bearing mighty blade-horns on their armoured snouts and chimneys that belched smoke from the daemonic fires driving the metal monsters. When enough of Archaon's beastfiends had been trampled before the juggers' implacable advance and brutal forge hammers, the Chaos warlord unleashed his other monsters, who smashed the creations of Hak'grorfane and his infernal smithies to smoking scrap. Archaon found Hak'grorfane itself – a many-armed beast of metal horns, chain and forge-scorched flesh – to be lacking in the death-dealing arts of his brother daemons. It seemed that the Blood God had bestowed favour on the mighty fiend not for the skulls taken by Hak'grorfane personally but for those taken collectively by the brute craftsmanship of his hell-crafted weaponry.

After a gargantuan battle in which Archaon's sickle sword broke and Hak'grorfane wielded every weapon the daemon could lay its many clawed hands upon, Archaon fought him all the way back to the edge of the smith's hellish forge pit. Ducking beneath the swinging onslaught of a number of blades in a number of clenched claws, Archaon managed to unbalance the raging hellsmith and knock it into the liquid metal of its own forge. While the daemon still thrashed, roared and reached up out of the glowing, black steel, Archaon ransacked the smashed forge, taking for himself a selection of swords, axes, spears and hell-crafted daggers, which he draped from Dorghar's saddle in armoured scabbards and sheaths. The rest he left to the pillaging claws of his half-breed horde as they moved through the forge-forts and on towards the blazing rift roaring up from the collapsed polar warp gate.

Beyond forts filled with riches and reptilian temptresses of golden scale were palace-labyrinths that led to nothing. Fat, tower-crowded citadels floated above the serrated skyline on colossal ray-like behemoths that drifted through the Gateland skies. Beneath, there were monstrous fortresses that seemed alive, shaking the warp-infused ground with their demolishing movements and cannibalising the surrounding palaces with gate-shaped maws and portcullis teeth. Similarly to be avoided, even by Archaon's great bestial horde, were the black towers of the daemon Mardagg, the shadows of which drained years from the lives of beastfiends falling beneath them, turning some into white-furred withered husks, others into browned bones and others still into dust on the wind.

Archaon found, upon mounting a determined assault on a mirror-plated palace near the rim of the polar rift, that his horde had been fighting themselves for days – and winning. Beyond the illusory nightmares of Tzeentchian prince-fiends, Archaon discovered that the palaces of infernal royalty could not be touched – let alone conquered. The inner citadels and fortresses were but ghostly mirages of warped castles and towers that existed in neither one place nor another. They belonged to the world of flesh and stone. They belonged to warp-tortured oblivion. They belonged to the nothingness of nowhere.

As Dorghar cantered on, with Archaon riding high in the saddle, the Chosen of the Chaos gods became suddenly aware that there were no daemonic palaces and fortifications – ethereal or otherwise – before them. There were only the eternal fires of ruin, blazing high into the sky, all but blinding the eye and warping the flesh. What had been a brilliant radiance, up close had an indescribable absence of colour. It was not mind-scalding white, nor soul-devouring black. It refused to be any colour inbetween.

Archaon tried to hold its gaze but failed, for as the Chaos warlord stared into the fierce depths of the beyond, a thousand beyonds stared back. His eye stung with its woeful inability. His darksight was next to useless – the malevolence and smouldering doom that was Archaon was nothing in the presence of the raw effervescent abomination of Chaos spilling unfiltered and unstoppable into the victim world. Only the Eye of Sheerian gave Archaon any sense of a bearing – the sorcerous jewel's abilities being more powerful than ever, fed by the unnatural energies that bathed all who stood before the blazing flux of oblivion. Overwhelmed by such Ruinous brilliance, its sorcerous gaze seared to a narrow beam through the tumultuous clash of realities beyond. Even with the powerful artefact – one of the treasures of Chaos, no less – Archaon still felt as if he were standing in a midnight desert, trying to light a starless sky with a single candle.

Archaon didn't know how long he had stared into the dread depths of loathsome eternity. His plate felt warm on his skin, despite the fact that the warping radiance gave off no heat. Similarly, his blood ran hot in his veins and his mind felt slow, as if he were drunk on what he had seen and bottomless with curiosity for what he had not. Shaking his horned helm and some sense through the melting thoughts of his mind, Archaon willed Dorghar around.

It seemed as though he must have been standing before the rupture gateway for some time, since he found the horned multitudes of his half-breed horde stretching back towards the palaces of hellish royalty. They too were unnaturally calm. There was no roaring, butting or the shaking of primitive weaponry at the skies. The beastfiends stared as their warlord had, with thunderstruck horror and heart-pounding possibility at the unnatural wonder before them. Ograx the Great was no different. Jharkill the monstrous huntsman – who had lived several lifetimes in the light of the world's doom – had never been this close and he too was glazed of eye. The abominations that he had hunted and enslaved to Archaon's will had grown to a stillness, towering above the horde and watching from their cages.

The Swords of Chaos stood before their master, the punctured mess of their wings held in close, while the sorcerer, Khezula Sheerian – the only one of them to have experienced the soul-shattering realm beyond – looked fearfully on at the prospect of what his master was about to say. Only Giselle was missing, but Archaon saw the twisted Vier sitting at the reins of her bone wagon, pulled as it was by a pair of monstrous elkbeasts, midnight of hairless flesh and warped of antler. Reaching out with the beating storm in his chest, he felt her terror – felt the girl hiding from the silent expectation of some terrible thing beneath her furs, the stabbing flutter of her own heart like rolling thunder in his ears. It would not stop him. Not the coward beasts of his horde. Not the uneasiness of the sorcerer. Not the dread of a pure soul he was about to plunge into the raging depths of abominate corruption. Nothing would. Nothing could.

'We stand at the precipice of possibility,' Archaon called across the horde. As he did so, Sheerian turned and obediently squawked the beastspeak of his words at the half-breeds. Archaon could see the fear and uncertainty cutting into their bestial faces. The Chaos warlord prompted Dorghar into a spirited trot up and down the front line of half-breeds, allowing the unspeakable fires of damnation to cast him in a shimmering silhouette. Such words did not come easily to the Chaos warlord. He led by example. He held the horde together with fear. He was not given to speeches – especially delivered to wretched half-breeds, the monstrous issue of beast and daemon. For the first time in their dread union, the creatures of the horde were confronted by something that filled them with more fear than their dread warlord and master. Before them blazed the beyond. A colossal wall of warping flame raging up through the broiling heavens, scalding away the clouds, the sky and stars. A rift that blasted its way out through the bottom of the world and threatened to drag them screaming their miserable lives away to any number of hellish eternities. Their mongrel hearts might have pumped the blood of daemons about their bodies but their half-souls were a cowardly afterthought, filled with animal panic and sensory suspicion. Archaon understood that they needed a little more than idle threats, and they were idle, since once he was through the collapsed gateway and had become one with the howling infinitude, beyond there was no guarantee that he would ever return. This was not a possibility he shared with the horde.

'Our destiny awaits,' he roared at them. 'Many of you dread things have followed me across the frozen Wastes of your homeland. A homeland vast – carried on the backs of mountains, racked by storm and honed to a razor's edge by the frozen winds that carve through its wildness. You are part of that wildness – but like all savage things you cannot be kept prisoner...'

Archaon turned Dorghar about and cantered in the other direction. He thought of the creatures he had freed from Lord

Agrammon's menagerie and the irony of his own position as slave-master of such monstrosities.

'You cannot be held hostage – not even by this great, daemon-haunted land. Not by the frozen expanse of its mighty glaciers nor its raging ranges of frost-shattered peaks and volcanoes. Certainly not by the deep darkness of the ocean that surrounds it, washing up on its icy shores. An ocean I crossed to be here with you, to face the trials of the Dark Gods together and earn their Ruinous rewards. For I come from a land made up of many lands. A place far, far away. Forests, villages, cities that you could barely imagine, all begging for the flame. Kingdoms ripe for destruction. Empires unworthy of their existence, awaiting our savage dominion. Weakling races – of succulent, soft flesh – who think themselves safe in their civilisation.

'They will learn they are not safe. They will learn of suffering. They will learn of death. You will teach them and I will lead us all into the embrace of doom. A time of ending, a place of ash and darkness. There your Dark Gods will be waiting – to receive and reward you. To reach such a place – such a time – you must follow me across another dark ocean. Through a realm undreamed of far beyond the limits of blood and bone. Where only the thunder of the heart and the monstrous thoughts of the mind hold sway.

'In truth, I cannot tell you what to expect on this journey. Some experiences defy description. I can only tell you that it must be done, that I will venture first and lead us through this darkness and uncertainty, but I expect every single one of you to be at my back – as you have been thus far. It is a trial that must be endured – like the endless expanse of the land beneath your hooves or the frost that bites the flesh and numbs the spirit.

'Before the dawn there is the long darkness of night. Before the sweetness of victory there is the bitterness of battle, long fought.' Archaon hauled at the reins and leaned back in the saddle, drawing Dorghar's spiked hooves up as the creature reared before the horde. 'I will be watching you,' Archaon told his half-breeds. 'Your Dark Gods will be watching you, as they have never before. Disappoint us not and follow your master into eternity. For he is the Lord of the End Times and Everchosen of the Chaos gods. He cannot fail...'

Archaon turned Dorghar about and dug his heels into the daemon steed's flanks. The mount thunderbolted away from the horde, accelerating into a gallop at the Ruinous inferno roaring up from the collapsed polar warp gate. Behind him Archaon could hear the roar of the horde. He could hear the stampede of hooves, the bone-creak of wagon wheels and the ground-shaking trudge of enslaved monsters.

As he closed on the screaming oblivion of phantasmic flame, Archaon felt the world flux and warp about him. He too, from his bones, from the flutter of doubt in his chest to the indomitable will that saturated his entire being, all bent about the ferocious, unnatural force of raging unreality. The path Dorghar was hammering out with its hooves stretched before them, reaching out for eternity. The world of before smeared into a new form of existence. What Archaon knew bled away. His arm knew no pain. His flesh no cold. His lungs no air. His heart no fear. All he knew was that he was screaming. The shrieking soulfire of the Gate had him.

Oblivion had swallowed him whole. The flames of white-hot nothing writhed about him, purging him of doubt. The tempest howled up through him, the Ruinous force of the beyond stripping plate from his body. It dragged his bones free of his flesh before shattering what was left of his corporal presence into dust and cinders. Only the raw darkness that was Archaon remained – streaming, warping and fluxing like a shadow caught in an otherworldly hurricane. Colossal fragments of stone, the black of soul-eating darkness, rocketed skyward with him. Grit, shards and rubble seared up through the absent flame in an eternal experience of the Great Gate's explosive demise: the warp-saturated dereliction of the abominate architecture caught in the calamitous moment of its destruction.

Up became down and nothing became everything as

Archaon's monstrous essence – the curdled umbra of the soul, shot through with the liquid obsidian of apocalyptic ambition – was suddenly engulfed by the unknowing agony of the rift. Like the plummeting fragments of the Gate, reliving the horror of its reality-rending collapse. Swallowed by one of a million maelstrom-swirling maws through which the beyond screamed into the certainties of other realms, Archaon knew that the world was no more. The Gate was no more. He was no more.

Then… thought that… ended… When… experienced… as… he could experience… reduced… nothing more… dark smear… underbelly of existence… realms… horror… eternal… Why… hurts, the gods it…! No… no…

CHAPTER X

VOLUME TWO
PRINCE OF CHAOS

'Roads. Lives. Tales. To all things an end and a beginning.'

– Anonymous

'Riding hard through eternity,
the doom of all the world came forth.
Bloodthirsty and armed to the teeth,
his monstrous host, ready for war.

At the frozen top of the world
he found men of fate like himself –
for whom life was a bloody blur:
an unthinking, murderous hell.

Foe. Barbarian. Invader.
He came at the kingdoms of men –
from north, south, east and west: danger.
Testing resolve, gathering strength.

With the treasures of Chaos found –
their infernal promise assumed,
he was to be chosen and crowned –
and all hell to be broken loose.

'Twas the dark daemon Be'lakor's
damnable calling to perform –
a dread obligation abhorred –
a despised duty nevermore.'

– Necrodomo the Insane, *The Liber Caelestior*
(The Celestine Book of Divination)

CHAPTER XI

*'Taste of oblivion, Everchosen of the
Ruinous Gods. Experience your doom
through daemon eyes and come to know
the limitless light of the darkness you
would extinguish.'*

– Be'lakor – the Dark Master,
First Daemon of Chaos,
The Liber Caelestior, margin inscription

The Long, Dark Night of the All Souls
The Realms of Chaos
Eternitude

A dream. Just like a dream. Archaon found himself walking. He could hear the soft clatter of his plate. The jangle of Dorghar's halter chains as he led the daemon steed on. He reached for a weapon and found the hilts of several hell-forged blades in his belt, as well as the shaft of a hand axe and a sheathed dagger. He brought his right arm up before him. The tatters of a sling still hung about his neck. His arm seemed as new. He extended the fingers of his gauntlet and then clenched them in a fist. How long had he been in this place?

The dull agony of broken bones was gone. In fact, he felt nothing. His legs, striding through the darkness – perhaps for an eternity – were insensible to strain or fatigue. He pulled at a finger. Twisted it. Bent it back. Nothing. No pain. No discomfort. This truly was a dream, Archaon decided. A nightmare in which he knew he was trapped but could not, through will alone, wake from.

He remembered the Southern Wastes. The Gatelands. The horde. Then nothing. The warping, fluxing, roaring perversities of this realm had passed through him. Stripped him of bodily afflictions, his weakness of the flesh. Reducing him down to his essence: a streaming darkness, passing like an undercurrent through an ocean of others. A boundless sea within a sea within a sea within a sea. A bottomless abyss as wide as it was deep, dark with the energies that swirled, spumed and crashed through it. A spiritual storm through which schools of savage entities swam, predatory consciousnesses lay in wait and the colossal intensities of intelligences ancient trawled, drawn down on desperate souls. Archaon came to understand himself as part of such a maelstrom, a primordial darkness that was to the mortal world as the glassy facet of a pool. It reflected the world in dark imperfection but remained suggestive of something unknown but ever present beneath. The surface separated two different elements. Two different experiences of the same world – one the distorted mirror image of the other. It rippled at the insistence of both, those above and below. It invited those souls and entities so inclined to pass through the reflective illusion of a barrier between such realms, drawing the monstrous from the depths and the doomed to sink into the darkness.

Archaon knew he was nothing more than streaming shadow, coursing through darkness. At the mercy of prevailing tides. Surging before stormy fronts. Dragged along with rapidities. Whirled into the gyres and miniature maelstroms of raging tempests. Twisting and soaring through the streaming presence of other beings – aethyric evils, exalted essences and the searing passage of pure daemonic will – Archaon found the dark fire of his soul mauled. It had been torn this way and that by currents of raw knowing, streams of suffering, the downwellings of doom and the countercurrents of crackling ambition and false hope. Rings, eddies, traps, vortices and roiling embodiments – all threatening to put him from his endless course. His passage through the formlessness of the chaotic abyss.

Archaon felt familiar horrors in the swirling shadow. Things drawn down on him, following the rising star of the Chaos warlord's soul. Infernal creatures he had crossed. Daemons he had slain. Depraved intelligences like the beast Agrammon that slithered and streamed about the crowded constellation of souls that was Archaon and his horde. Monstrous forces of warping, elemental destruction, like the dread presence of the *Yien-Ya-Long*, that stalked the soulfire trail of Archaon and his army through oblivion like a great predator might hunt a migrating herd. These seething entities, who wanted nothing more than to avenge themselves from the beyond, ultimately kept their distance. They seemed cautious, as though other great forces in the hellish stormscape of the aethyr had already laid claim to Archaon's soul and were keeping watch over their property. Archaon felt the warp-scorching presence of such primordial and Ruinous entities. Of things impossible. Of dread power. Of myriad malevolence. Of promises eternal. Of fears indescribable. Like oblivions all of their very own, the Ruinous Powers burned like great dark stars, exerting an influence on every damned presence and victim-soul about them. Drawing them in. Sometimes they would stabilise the paths of the mighty. They would hold the exalted on their course to greatness and damnation, extending their monstrous reach and infinite influence to establish a temporary equilibrium between the irresistible forces of their realm-warping presence. Sometimes they would tear lives apart between them and, like behemoths of the deep, filter the soul-carnage left in the wake of slaughter, suffering and the meteoric rise of servant champions.

Several times, Archaon felt the blaze of their direct attentions. To be beheld by such beings through the looking glass stillness of storm centres all but scorched Archaon out of existence. He felt his fate flux and warp at their gaze. It was simultaneously the most wonderful and the most dreadful thing Archaon had ever experienced. He burned in the incomprehension of their interest. In the existential chill of their ignorance, Archaon felt predatory entities close back in. Even there he was not alone. Ever present in the havoc, in the dread and the darkness, Archaon felt the calamitous force of his father. The First Daemon of Chaos. Watching. Waiting. Wanting. The bitter vortex of his otherworldly presence was a warp-curdled and crushing darkness of his own making and Archaon could feel the distant pull of his aeonian desires.

Although Archaon knew from the scorching fleshlessness of his soul that he was not walking through the empty blackness in his plate, with weapons heavy on his belt and Dorghar snorting alongside him, it felt hauntingly real. He understood that it was simply the way his being could experience the impossibilities of the beyond – the mind-stabbing, flesh-shearing unrealities of this monstrous realm.

As he looked about, all Archaon could see was the darkness of his soul reflected back at him. It was a gaze-devouring nothingness. The lethality of the place saturated him. Looking up was the horror of a never-ending tumble into an abyss. Looking down was the deepest of dreads – like treading water in an ocean of predatory creatures that could bite you in half at any moment or drag you to oblivion to tear you flesh from chunk of flesh. Looking behind him carried with it the same spine-twisting, sickening expectation of some horrid thing waiting for him to turn before it struck. Everywhere else was moment by moment, heart-hammering horror and the dread of seeing something that could not be unseen – visions of mindless terror that could not be blinked from the eye. Fearful aspects that were ever present, even when they were not.

Archaon's tongue sizzled with the cold bitterness of the void while his nostrils stung with the coppery rawness of his flesh – wherever it was – being freshly flayed, over and over again. His ears bled with Ruinous whispers of dark things bargaining for his soul. Their temptations burned to resist. Their eternal entreaties tore at him like hooks and lines disappearing into the benightment. The shrieking. The screaming. The befriending and the begging. He listened to every word, his nerves the strings of some fearfully abused instrument. He fought their lies and the fragilities of his own soul, unruly parts of himself that desired acquiescence and an end to all torments.

There were those daemonic entities prowling the blackness that did not cog, whisper and deceive but attacked like ambush predators – frenziedly seizing upon the soulfire of the unclaimed, that burned like a beacon in the void. Things that punched through Archaon like an unstoppable evil, and wrestled him for his soul. Entities that struck with fang and force, to paralyse the spirit and poison the present. Abyssal creatures that feasted on the indomitability of his will, spreading rancid corruptions of the spirit through his resolve, infecting him with the plague of doubt. Infernal enigmas that forced Archaon back through the labyrinthine madness of choices yet to be made as they roasted his resolutions in the warpflame of their unbearable presence. Other horrors simply launched themselves from the darkness, goring without horn, tearing without claw and snapping without jaw. Such battles for the soul lasted a castle-crumbling age – and like a castle under siege, Archaon's defences began to crack and tremble under constant onslaught. He could not know that he had been fighting such ravenous beings for a lifetime. In the slave-pit of the soul, Archaon had fought for the survival of everything that he was and ever would be. Such infernal battles shook the very fabric of his being. Approaching it like any other form of combat or martial discipline, he had grown adept at such inner conflicts. He drove daemonic essences, who fought to inhabit his own, before him. Sending one after another back to the darkness and the dread, enjoying the solitude of several more lonely steps before some other monstrous aberration surged forth with infernal optimism and bottomless greed.

Archaon risked a glance behind him. He narrowed the gaze of an eye he knew wasn't there. He blinked the mind-scalding glare of the realm's tumultuous blackness from his darksight. Concentrating through the cacophony of distractions and the sense that not one, but a hundred different dread intelligences were in turn watching him through the darkness, Archaon saw his horde. The Eye of Sheerian, glowing with the intensity of the otherworldy energies all about it, helped Archaon see through the infernal void.

Casting a gaze down the spiked flanks of the daemon steed Dorghar, Archaon could see Khezula Sheerian, his furs gathered about him and eyes cloudy with a Ruinous glaze. The Swords of Chaos marched beside him, the scarred membranes of their wings long healed. The still figure of Vier held the reins of the bone wagon behind them, the vehicle dragged along by a pair of monstrous black elks. Within the wagon, Archaon could only guess the torments or invulnerabilities being endured by Giselle – her faith making her either an anathema to the spirit stalkers of the realm or a soulprize over which to be fought. Ograx the Great led the colossal, winding cavalcade of beastfiends that made up Archaon's half-breed horde, as well as wagons and beast-dragged siege engines crafted from bone.

Beyond the bestial multitudes, Archaon saw Jharkill the huntsman, the hunchbacked ogre still clutching his shaman's staff that jangled with his primitive charms. Following obediently in line were the caged chimeric predators that Archaon favoured releasing as a first wave attack, and the twisted titans and lumbering abominates that he saved as shock troops to break opposing armies. Peering further still, alone in the darkness some way behind the last of Jharkill's miserable monsters, Archaon could see Gorst, stumbling through the oblivion. The flagellant dragged his chains behind him and stared like a wide-eyed lunatic out through the bars of his head-cage. All in the train were silent as the grave, from beast-fiend to monstrosity to madman. No one wanted to attract any more attention from the abyssal murk than the light from their wretched half-souls was already doing. The sorcerer was quietest of all. Slowing – or at least what Archaon thought was slowing – the Chaos warlord and his steed drifted in line with the mottled ancient. How many times before he had done the self same thing asking the same questions, Archaon could not know. Something felt hauntingly familiar about the impulse and it occurred to Archaon, as it had occurred to him the thousands of times before, that the pair were routinely carrying out the same insanity over and over again.

'Sorcerer,' Archaon said, drawing the twitch of a response from the daemon. 'Where are we? Your master speaks.'

Sheerian didn't answer at first, the sorcerer seeming to overcome – like Archaon – some monstrous attempt to steal his soul.

'My master never stops speaking,' the Tzeentchian cackled cryptically. 'Where are we? Where your damned path has taken us, my lord. The invisible empire. To the depths of hells everlasting. To the cradle of darkness – the birthplace of daemons and the storm-racked sovereignty of the Dark Gods. Everywhere. Nowhere. Anywhere.'

'Speak sanity, sorcerer,' Archaon said. He was barely holding onto his own.

'You seek sanity,' Sheerian marvelled maniacally, '...in... this... place?'

'I seek the Great Northern Gate,' Archaon told him, his bold words sounding hollow as they were swallowed by the dark, abyssal emptiness about them. 'I seek the mortal realm to which we belong. I seek a way out of this infernal place. You are a thing of this darkness. Guide us.'

'Here,' babbled the ancient, 'there, neverwhere. How can

a daemon of this world or the next claim to have been anywhere in a place with no landmarks or features? Can a man who has stood on the sandy shore know his way across the deserts of the ocean bottom? Does feeling the breeze on his face equip him to find his way through all storms? We are lost and we are damned, my lord. We are slaves to the darkness. Accept it and allow yourself to become one with the madness of this place. Eternity will find some use for you – eventually – as it did me.'

The sorcerer's uselessness appalled Archaon and the Chaos warlord found himself reaching for the hilt of his sword. Khezula Sheerian heard the hiss of a weapon being drawn but the sorcerer didn't even turn to face his lord.

'Steel is not steel, in this place,' the sorcerer told him.

Archaon found himself looking down at the blade he had drawn. Sheerian was right. Killing him would not achieve anything – even if he could. He looked at his reflection in the dull steel of the hell-forged blade. He wasn't even surprised when he found none. Instead the blade saw straight through him to show Archaon the ghastly entities that had emerged from the oblivion behind him. Angling the blade around, Archaon saw that by slowing and calling out demands of his sorcerer he had drawn hundreds, perhaps thousands of soul-famished entities down on himself. As he turned the blade, his heart thudded at the monstrous abominations emerging from the darkness. Things of indescribable horror and abyssal appetite.

Archaon thought on the madness the sorcerer had spoken. His inability to guide them and his insistence that Archaon allow himself to become one with the madness of the realm. The Chosen of the Chaos gods knew that he had to do something. For all he knew they had been wandering the aethyric expanse of oblivion forever. The damned cycle had to be broken. He had to escape this limitless prison and cast off the chains of eternal damnation. He knew he could not do it alone but to call upon assistance from his Ruinous sponsors would prove his unsuitability to be their champion. He would be the Everchosen of Chaos exactly because he hadn't ever begged of their mercy. Archaon would still need a guide to find his way free of their diabolical realm.

Lifting up his gauntlet and sword, Archaon presented himself to the horde of daemonic entities swirling and swarming about him in the darkness.

'A share of my soul,' Archaon roared at them, the passion and fury of his announcement blazing like a distant city aflame through the daemon-haunted infernity, 'to the fell thing that can show me – and those that belong to me – the hell out of this dread place.'

'Master, no...' Sheerian said. Eins, Zwei and Drei surged forward, reaching for bone blades.

Archaon braced himself but some horrid thing shot out of the swarming shadows with such violent force that it surprised even him. Like a comet of churning hatred, the entity trailed a bloody miasma as it blasted into the Chaos warlord. This time Archaon didn't fight it. He didn't resist. He allowed the thing to be one with him.

For a moment he felt paralysed. His gauntlet opened and his sword dropped from his hand, falling through the darkness at his feet. He remained in that position for a few moments more, with his arms outstretched and chest braced, as though lightning were passing down his spine. Archaon's plate burned across his chest where the monstrous entity had hit him. Finally, looking down, he found Morkar's armour frosted with otherworldly crystals. As he relaxed he scraped at the sizzling residue with an armoured finger.

'My lord?' Sheerian asked fearfully. The Swords of Chaos had surrounded him, their weapons facing inwards. No one knew quite what to do.

Archaon slid down onto his knees and hunched over. It was the most awful sensation. An existence that was not all his own. A wretched intimacy of thought. A heart beat horribly, filling Archaon with darkness and desires not just of his own but also of those belonging to a denizen of the deep. The core of his being was suddenly flooded with violence.

A fury, hot and pure filled him. A primordial need to inflict harm. Other entities were flying at him. The daemon that had beaten them to his soul was fighting the monstrous evils to protect its prize. Beings that hungered for him tried to tear the entity from Archaon's living essence but the savage being that had him in its talons would not give up its infernal territory. Like a pack of wild dogs over a carcass, the daemons fought, roaring, hissing and spitting until one by one the monstrosities relented and sunk back into the darkness.

Finally alone with the entity that now wore his soul like a mantle, Archaon tried to slow the hammering of his heart. The beast that breathed with him was a storm that would not be calmed. Archaon roared as he had never done before. His pain was beyond the flesh. The creature tore at his very soul. His existential agony echoed through the raging void, taking with it flocks of scavenger daemons who fed on the rich honesty of his torment. He felt the withering corruption of the thing spread through what was left of his being. The daemon's maleficence twisted through him, turning his veins to ragged black roots and filling them with a liquid obsidian filth that passed for blood. As it reached his chest, the ichor strangled his heart with constricting rage. It scorched to blackness within his body, searing and spitting with the furious heat of the daemon inside him.

Archaon's roar narrowed to a scream.

Monstrous claws grew through his boots, while the black bone of stabbing dagger-like talons thrust out of the tips of his gauntlets. Spikes erupted from his spine, tearing up through his plate, furs and cloak like the dorsal fins of an ocean predator. Red spines ruptured up out of his armour, the cracks working their way between them filled with molten brass bled from beneath. The cooling metal steamed, forming the damned sigils of the Blood God. Legs snapped horribly beneath him as his knees assumed the digitigrade orientation of a daemon monstrosity. Pushing his helm from his head, Archaon's shrieking trailed off. Screaming didn't seem enough to express the agony afflicting his imagined body and soul. Since he was no longer solely in control of the lungs that had been filling the void with his suffering, there was little he could do.

The Swords of Chaos brought up their weapons in unison, while the sorcerer Sheerian came forward and picked up Archaon's helmet. Sheerian and Eins exchanged a glance of helpless alarm.

'My lord?' Sheerian asked, but the transformation was not complete.

Throwing his head forward, Archaon endured the bone-cracking agony of a skull growing out of the back of his own. As his head elongated, two monstrous horns erupted from his temples, willowing to blackness. When Archaon brought his face up it was a mess. Spikes puncturing through the flesh had carved his face up into an infernal mask. Blood from the wounds had stained it a Ruinous red and a nest of fangs had worked their way out of his jaw to create a monstrous maw. Above it his eyes burned to cruel brilliance.

'Archaon!' the sorcerer Sheerian called, fearing that he had lost his master to some hideous daemon of the abyss. Archaon tried to stand on his new legs, but heaved. Vomiting forth a stream of gore into the darkness at his clawed feet, the torrent was followed by a black, blood-slick tongue that flopped out of the daggered maw like a dead serpent. The malign presence looked out from the Chaos warlord's afflicted flesh. It stared at the Swords of Chaos with their bone swords ready, and the sorcerer clutching the helm of his master.

Archaon? the thing seethed through the oblivion. *There is no one of that name here.*

'Do you have a name, monster? Thing that corrupts my flesh and pollutes my soul with its bloody darkness.'

I... am... Z'guhl.

'Z'guhl?'

Z'guhl, the Skullreaper. Z'guhl of the Brazen Brethren. Z'guhl, the Left Fist of Khorne. Z'guhl, Blessed of Blood. Z'guhl, the Crimson Doom. Z'guhl the Deathbringer. Z'guhl, the Herald of All Hate.

'You have altogether too many titles, daemon.'

And you none at all, man-thing.

'Not for long, daemon.'

An eternity, if I so choose – slave-soul of mine.

'The Blood God's servants prize the present moment. They have not the patience for eternities. I promised you a share of my soul, you double-dealing fiend. I'll torment you from what I have left, blood beast of the void. How do you feel about sharing eternity with me, Z'guhl of the Hesitant Heart? Z'guhl of the Mortal Stain? Z'guhl the Soul Plagued? Ask yourself this, monster, are you in possession of my soul or am I in possession of yours?'

Enough…

'Enough?'

Enough.

'Like I said – no patience.'

Watch your words, mortal.

'My name is Archaon and I am Chosen of the Dark Gods – your Almighty Lord of Wrath included.'

I know what you are. You are he who would be Everchosen. You wear his plate and his treasures. You ride his steed and bear his Mark. You do not, however, carry the Everchosen's blade.

'His blade… You know of this blade?'

Intimately, weakling mortal. Intimately.

'Tell me warpling, on the blood that ever drips from your dark lord's axe, where can I find such a blade?'

Not here, Archaon. Archaon the Lost. Archaon, the Everbroken. Archaon, Lord of Nothing.

'Tell me, Crimson Doom, or I will be yours. I shall tear you apart, from the inside out. Your spine shall be my sceptre, your black heart shall be my orb and I shall wear your monstrous skull as my crown. Hear me, goremonger. Hear me!'

Hear you… or help you?

'Help me break free of this place. This doom of everlastings. This otherworldly night of the soul. This prison eternity. The havoc. The pain. The possibility. Help me or be destroyed, wretched thing of a thousand deaths. The choice is that simple.'

...Perhaps. Perhaps we could help each other. I have sought you out, Archaon. I have stalked your soul across eternity's expanse and through storms of damnation's ire. I claim your soul in so much as I might set it free.

'What do you mean, daemon?'

I mean to guide you from this dread realm, Archaon. I mean to take you to the Gate you seek, where mortals butcher one another for our pleasure in the Battle Everlasting.

'The Great Northern Gate, at the top of the world...'

Top. Bottom. Up. Down. North. South. These terms have no meaning here. The Gate glows with a lightshow of souls. That is all I know. Mortals gloriously bringing darkness to their fellow doomed. The brief spark of their passing and the insignificance of their offering attracting the Powers of darkness, who feed both off the faith of the fallen and the act of the offering.

'How can I trust the mercy of a blood-slaked fiend, freely given?'

Nothing is freely given, Archaon. All indulgences have their cost. I ask for a return in iron.

'In iron? You want me to slay for your fell god?'

All men do, although they know it not. No, Archaon. I would put the sword you seek in your hand, as my Ruinous lord's bloody blessing on your endeavour. The blade is called the Slayer of Kings *and shares its name with the dread entity bound within its daemonic steel.*

'An acquaintance of yours, creature?'

U'zuhl the Skulltaker. U'zuhl the Blooded Wanderer. U'zuhl the Right Fist of Khorne...

'Aye, a brother infernal.'

I am bound by blood covenants, lies exchanged in the Blood God's name and oaths black and ancient, to see my brass-borne brother free. Sorceries hold him, his infernal insanity and his fury in a prison of hell-forged steel. Bound there by the coward Vangel – Vangel the Everchosen – the second to bear such a name. Assume the same blood-sworn oaths and covenants as I, Archaon. I shall send you to the Slayer of Kings *and you shall send back my brother. You shall promise to free U'zuhl the Slayer from madness and his steel thralldom. So that he might kill for the mighty Khorne once more. To taste the blood he spills rather than watch it drip tauntingly down the walls of his steel prison. To wield and not be wielded. To take skulls and not be the mere instrument of their taking. Agree to this on blood that will once more be yours and I will take you to the gate of your choosing.*

'You will teach me the daemonic bindings of such a weapon?'

I will teach you the sorcery that binds daemon to blade, so that you might undo it and set U'zuhl the Skulltaker free.

'Then I swear on the darkness in my blood, to set your infernal brother at liberty. So, Z'guhl the Skullreaper, the Crimson Doom, the Herald of all Hate and sharer of my soul… lead on.'

CHAPTER XII

*'Doomed pilgrims conquer both foes and
their fears Fighting north, hearts cursed
with unhallowed joy –
'Til they hear the Battle Eternal near and
for Dark Gods kill, butcher and destroy.'*
– Xortan Freg, *Liber Malefic*

*The Battle Eternal
The Northern Wastes
Date Unknown*

The fiery flux of damnation reached up around Archaon. The tongues of warp-fuelled flame licked at his plate and the flanks of the daemon steed Dorghar. As the mount trudged through the hellish inferno of the Northern Gate, Archaon turned in the saddle. What once had been tortured thoughts and the dark desire to be free of the daemon-haunted hellstorm was once again flesh. Archaon felt the contraction of muscle as he turned. He felt the strength of his bones and the steady thud of an indomitable heart in his chest, pumping doom-laden blood through his veins. Even the shard of wyrdstone still remained in the socket of his ruined eye with the curse of darksight that went with it. His skin felt the cold of his plate and his once shattered arm now pulsed with the dark need to draw a weapon. Archaon didn't know whether it had been the warping energies of damnation or simply the length of time they had spent in the Realm of Chaos, but his arm felt long healed. Scooping up the tattered remains of the sling from about his body, the Chaos warlord tossed the shredded material away.

Behind him he found the horde emerging from the hellfires that raged between one dark plane and another. The Swords of Chaos walked closely behind, with the ancient sorcerer Sheerian hobbling nearby. Vier and Giselle's wagon heralded a train of others, as well as the bone nightmares of siege engines. Beyond them, through the otherworldy inferno, the Eye of Sheerian allowed Archaon to see Ograx the Great and the half-breed horde of southern beastfiends marching behind their chieftain. Jharkill and the great shadows of his charm-slaved beasts, giants and monstrosities could be seen striding through the gate behind them. It was hard to believe that before passing through the maelstrom-racked portal, Archaon and the trailing multitudes of his bestial army were merely a torrent of darkness, weaving, flowing and streaming through the abominate wraithscape of Chaos and through energies of the world unknown.

Turning back, Archaon caught sight of the monstrous Z'guhl. The thing was all horn, red daemonflesh and hate-dripping maw. Its eyes burned with lust for the blood that had started to flow through the creatures passing it. It was indeed an abominate thing and Archaon's reclaimed flesh crawled at the thought of how such a murderous, malevolent force had been ensnared in his soul. As the fiery pits of its eyes met Archaon, the Chaos warlord felt the ghostly intrusion of the daemon's thoughts once more.

Keep your dark word, manprey – as I have kept mine – or the legions of hell will not be able to save you from the Blood God's fury.

The promise burned on the surface of Archaon's tongue like the touch of a daemonic brand. Archaon gave Z'guhl a slow nod of his horned helm, before seeing the blood-letting daemon spit and stamp its claws at the passing sorcerer Sheerian. The ancient hurried on, unwilling to be the walking slab of meat that the daemon chose to sate its blood-hunger on. In reality, Z'guhl the Skullreaper had no dread desire to leave the Ruinous realm he haunted and ventured no further out of the gateway than he had already reached. Sending Archaon to achieve the almost impossible had been enough for Z'guhl to honour his own blood oaths and covenants to U'zuhl the Skulltaker, gore-favoured Herald of Khorne.

Like the hellish grandeur of its southern counterpart, the Great Northern Gate wasn't in fact a gate at all. Demolished in the same cataclysmic event, the black stone and structure of both colossal edifices had been blasted to oblivion. Instead, there was only the open, gaping wound of a rift between the two realms. The flames of oblivion roared at the northern skies, which about the Shadowlands of the Wastes were no less seething, roiling and storm-shot than those at the bottom of the world. The impossible colours that danced about Archaon and his emerging horde combined to form a violacious inferno that lit up the Shadowland and cast the silhouette of the frozen landscapes beyond in an amaranthine gloom.

Archaon felt the land flux, warp and tremble about the insane power pouring out of the demolished gate. The Chaos warlord had dreamed his way from flesh to the streaming shadow of soulfire and back to flesh again. The Northern and Southern Wastes had been long bathed in the intense radiance of ruin and were heavily polluted with warpdust and tainted debris from the devastated gates. Travel through them carried the constant danger of contamination and mutation. With strange similarity, the lands and even the abyssal realm beyond the gates maintained an equilibrium all of their own. Archaon found that it was the tumultuous instability inbetween that carried the most danger of reward; the shimmering mutability of one existence intruding upon another unleashed warping potential and the dark blessings of the Chaos gods on Archaon and his horde. Passing from the Gatelands and into the gate, there had been no time to comprehend the changes wrought on both body and mind. Marching out of the warping flux of the Great Northern Gate and into the Shadowlands, the Chaos warlord and his army of bestial creatures came to acknowledge the price of their passage through the Realm of Chaos.

There were many minor mutations and betrayals of the flesh across the horde that went largely unnoticed. Growths that blossomed across the skin, some becoming the buds of isolated spikes and spines of bone. Rampancies that spread through the body, blooms of gristle about bones and harmless corruptions that reached through the innards. Some limbs withered while others received grotesque enhancements, like arms that ruptured with the chitinous blades of new claws or crippled fists that sprouted bludgeoning nodules of bone. Other arms fell off entirely or spawned new appendages like shoulder-snapping jaws and nests of slithering tentacles. Muscular third and sometimes fourth arms now reached from globed shoulders to hold extra weaponry. Backs grew hunched and patches of skin erupted with all manner of affliction: scales, spines, chitinous shell, false eyes, bark-like encrustations and seeping sores.

Other changes inflicted by the horde's time in the Realm of Chaos were more dramatic. The perverse, warping effects of their immersion had stripped the half-breeds of their bestial natures. Snouts had receded, horns had willowed and thick fur had fallen out. While they were still daemon-sired fiends, their animal appetites, thick tongues and the dullness of their brute minds were gone. These were beasts who had transformed into men. Manfiends, who while still small mountains of barbaric muscle, were now things of human cunning and infernal spite – quick of mind and fleet of hoof. Ograx the Great was still an imposing wall of brawn, wielding his fearful skull-axe, but like the horde he led, the creature had forgotten the foetid savagery of a former life in the Southern Wastes. While the lower half of his body was living brass, his powerful legs were engraved with Ruinous symbols, fretwork and decoration. His infernal features and crown of horns might now have been described as darkly handsome and were truly those of a prince.

It was sometimes difficult to tell how the chimeric fusions and monstrosities of the horde had changed, since they were already warped carcasses of abominate affliction. Jharkill the huntsman, however, no longer carried his shaman's staff, with its cross bar and dangling charms. A huge rack of black antlers had sprouted from the ogre's head, proud and twisted like those that might belong to a monstrous stag. The charms and tokens that held the titans, predatory creatures and chaotic abominations of Archaon's horde in check now swung from the forest of snags on the ogre's antlers.

The Swords of Chaos had changed also. Their ragged wings had long healed but the darkness of the realm through which they had travelled had blessed them with a horrifying mutuality. While still flesh and blood, Eins, Zwei, Drei and even the misshapen Vier, were now terrifying wraiths of flickering shadow, both gangling and ghastly. Khezula Sheerian's transformation had been simultaneously striking and yet the most subtle. While still dragging his bird's foot and bearing the burden of a hunch, the ancient had bled away the years. His features were sharp, his eyes crackled with sorcerous power and lustrous lengths of straight, black hair cascaded from his formerly threadbare scalp.

Archaon's own blessings were not as physically obvious as those belonging to his horde or his henchmen. Even rolling in the armoured saddle of the daemon steed Dorghar – whose own afflictions were masked by the natural horror of its existing transformative powers – Archaon felt heavier. While blood roared through his veins and his heart thundered within the cursed plate of Morkar, Archaon felt a resilience and solidity beneath the flesh that was new. The shard of wyrdstone that was lodged in the socket of his ruined eye had spread while bathed in the warping influence of oblivion. The warpstone had threaded its darkness and endurance through Archaon's skull and bones.

Archaon found that the affliction also had a secondary effect. Like some kind of ancient menhir or a standing stone at the centre of some dread stone circle, Archaon's mere presence seemed to affect the environment about him. Wherever he went, the skies darkened. Thunder rolled and cloud broiled. Lighting storms flashed within the apocalyptic oppression of a storm ever breaking and bathed the land with an infernal glow. Indeed, Archaon had brought a little of hell back with him from the brink of oblivion. The wind streamed dust and ice about him. As the gloom darkened, the heavens rumbled and forks of hellish lightning stabbed down from the sky, Archaon nodded to himself. He was a living announcement of his own doom – a fitting misfortune for the Everchosen of Chaos and the Lord of the End Times to come.

There was suddenly commotion behind him. Turning Dorghar, Archaon found that Giselle's wagon had stopped. The girl had jumped down from the vehicle and was running this way and that. Vier had heaved the monstrous beasts of burden that hauled the wagon to a stop and had climbed down to assist the girl. At first Archaon thought that the Sigmarite sister was trying to escape. Now that they had returned to the north, perhaps she had delusions of fleeing and making her way home. Her movements seemed panicked, however, as she silently ran from half-breed to half-breed in the horde's front rank and even clawed at the chest of Ograx the Great.

The manfiends laughed with the cruelty of their new-found sensibilities, while Ograx tried to push the girl away. She tore at the fur straps of his small breastplate – a horned daemonic skull that sat strapped in the centre of the prince's chest. Archaon watched with interest as the girl collapsed before the hooves of

Ograx the Great, clawing away his breastplate. Pulling the straps and skull back, Ograx lifted his hand to backslap the girl, who seemed to be lost in a mad fever. Lowering his meaty hand as a mounted Archaon approached, he simply shrugged Giselle off, who got up and half collapsed again while careening straight into the flickering, black arms of the wraith-like Vier.

As Archaon slid down out of the saddle he found Ograx laughing with his manfiend kindred and strapping the skull back across his broad chest. As Giselle pushed away from the misshapen Vier, she stumbled, her fingers scratching at her face. She fell into Archaon's arms and the Chaos warlord turned her around.

Giselle's face was a stricken mask of panic. Her eyes were rolling back white. She was as young and beautiful as Archaon had ever found her but she had awoken in her wagon to discover that the Realm of Chaos had left her with a gift also. Her faith could not protect her from the Ruinous Power of hell. Where once there had been thin but inviting lips – that at one time or another had been employed in the whisper of prayer, curled in sadness and disappointment, tenderly kissing Archaon's own or even wrapped around the rarity of an occasional smile – now there was only flesh. While narrow nostrils flared and closed with panic and horror of discovery, the girl's jaw went to work opening a mouth that simply wasn't there any more. There would be no more prayer uttered in praise of the God-King. There would be no more smiles, sadness or the forlorn burn of meeting lips for Archaon. The curse seemed cruel, even for the Dark Gods, and Archaon heard their otherworldly mirth in the laughter of Ograx and his brute manfiends.

Archaon slid down onto his knees and held Giselle to him. The girl had awoken, terrified at the change. She had clawed at her face, running from the wagon and begging for help that she could not articulate and would not come. She had panicked and, thinking that she could not breathe, had all but blacked out. Archaon slipped his horned helm from his head and looked down upon her.

He tried to calm Giselle, soothing her and holding her. With the whisper of dark steel, Archaon drew the curved blade of a kris from his belt. He allowed the point of the blade to drift across Giselle's body and up to her face. Archaon didn't know what he was going to do. Use the knife like a butcher on her face, to give her back what was taken from her? Archaon's own lips fixed in a snarl. What kind of mutilated existence would that be? If he didn't, then Giselle would almost certainly starve to death. Archaon cursed the Dark Gods – the monstrous Powers who had not only taken from the Sister of the Imperial Cross the comfort of her uttered prayers but also, from Archaon, the delicate distraction of her lips and the words that might proceed from them.

Archaon felt the weight of the stone in his bones, dragging the blade down. He moved it across her. Over the pale flesh of her neck. Across the soot and grime of her chest and down over her heart. It was time to end it, Archaon decided. Quick. Easy. To remove from them both a further affliction. Giselle had endured enough horror, pain and madness to fill a hundred lifetimes. It was time to release her and bring the only one she'd had to an end. The kris knife trembled in the Chaos warlord's grasp. Anger built in his chest. At himself. At damnation. At the perverse Powers who would see them suffer so. He had killed countless things that walked and crawled but he could not bring himself to deliver mercy to one that he loved. A dark, twisted love that seemed to be coiled about his heart like a serpent, but love all the same. Something precious and all but forgotten in the living nightmare of Archaon's existence.

'Do it...' Ograx the Great told him. Archaon looked about. While the Swords of Chaos haunted the ground about them with their blistering darkness and the sorcerer Sheerian gave him an unreadable glare on sharp, uncaring features, Ograx was almost foaming at the mouth with his Blood God's lust for slaughter. Although the fiendish prince was staring at Archaon holding the knife over Giselle's heart, what he was living – over and over – was the plunge of the kris into the gory exposure of a blade-mulched chest.

Archaon's trembling blade began to rattle in his gauntlet. Injustice filled him with the dark promise of fury. He turned the blade suddenly about and pointed it at Ograx the Great – manfiend, butcherer and southern prince.

'I think to save my steel for you,' he told Ograx, before tossing the blade into the frozen earth, where it thudded up to its hilt. Archaon pulled Giselle to him and instead of laying a kiss where none could be received, tried to save her. Enclosing her tiny nose with his mouth, he breathed for her – filling her panic-stricken lungs with air the mindless horror of the experience had denied her. Pulling away, the Chaos warlord felt her breathe for herself. Her nostrils flared and contracted to slits as she breathed. Rising chest by rising chest she calmed, the nightmarish disappearance of her mouth accepted, along with the reality that she could breathe. The girl could only speak with her eyes. They had returned and were wet with dread, accusation and relief. 'I know,' Archaon mumbled. He leant forward and kissed her on the forehead. 'We'll work it out. All is possible. We have already proved that.'

Picking her up, Archaon barged past a glowering Ograx before settling Giselle back to sleep in her wagon. Ordering Khezula Sheerian to stay with her, he climbed back up into the saddle, prompting Vier to do the same with his wagon. The daemon steed Dorghar snorted, no more impressed by the spectacle than Ograx had been. Savagely jabbing the heels of his boots into the creature's infernal flesh, Archaon urged the beast on and led his monstrous horde out of the Northern Gate and into the slaughter of the Shadowlands beyond.

As the glare of the riftflame subsided, Archaon was granted his first clear sight of the Northern Wastes. It had been many years since he had first set foot there. Fleeing towards his fate, he had left the civilised lands of the Empire and his life as a templar of Sigmar behind. He had exchanged a life half lived, an unloving god and a world strangled by corruption and contradiction for the dire freedom of the north. He had embraced gods who cared even less so that he might destroy

them, and lived his life as a savage – a warrior of the Wastes –
so that he might one day return to the glowing ashes of the
Empire the architect of the world's end. In all of his time as
a wandering madman, a marauder and warrior of Chaos –
leading bands of other souls into damnation – he had never
travelled this far north. He had never crossed the Shadowlands. He had never bathed in the balelight of the ruptured
gate, the fires of doom that crowned the world.

The Shadowlands about the gate were everything he had
imagined them to be. The Northern Wastes were not as savage as the southern lands from which he had departed. The
southern continent was swarming with bestial barbarians.
It was haunted by daemons and fiends. Its storms rent both
land and ice apart while the limb-shearing cold, which would
descend on a monstrous whim, could kill in seconds. The
Northern Wastes were no less lethal, but Archaon admired
their subtlety. Beasts and lowly daemons lacked the imagination to influence the primordial chaos of the landscape
about them. The Northern Wastes were the hellish domain
of lost men, however. Doomed individuals who were not
lacking in the desires, perversions and needs required to feed
the afflicted land with suggestion – to inspire the warping
currents that swept south from the ruined gate with their
bloodlust, ambition and deviance. Here the land was a
law unto itself, dreaming itself up into a frenzy of forever
changing forms. Storms were everything and nothing – with
gales that might howl sweet visions through your being one
moment and then coat you in rancid acid the next. The cold
lacked the savage elemental punch of the southern continent
but was just as likely to creep into your furs like a serpent
and stop your heart, as claim frostbitten fingers and toes.

Here, in the wine-stained gloom of the Shadowlands,
Archaon found himself before the Battle Eternal. A cycle of
never-ending death and destruction. The doom at the top
of the world. Archaon had known warriors of Chaos who
had searched a lifetime to find the Battle Eternal. Pilgrims
of dark faith who had become lost in the madness of the

Wastes and had never breached the inner nightmare of the Shadowlands. Exalted warlords, with small armies of fell followers, who had been showered with the warping gifts of the Dark Gods but for whom spawndom waited. Whereas the Ruinous whisper of the Chaos Wastes drew man, beast and the lost of the elder races north with the promise of more, those that braved the murder and madness eventually came to seek some higher form of realisation. For Archaon that path had already been laid, as similar paths had extended before all of the Everchosen champions of Chaos who preceded him. For those unblessed with apocalyptic destiny or some other cursed fate, the Battle Eternal called. An irresistible force pulling at all who had been on the road to damnation long enough or who had impressed their dread patrons with rare deeds of darkness. Marauder chieftains. Bestial warlords. Truthseeking witchbreeds. Knights of ruin. The exalted warriors of Chaos, seeking solace in slaughter.

Those chosen to find the Battle Eternal – those that did not lose their way to blade or abstraction – all found the same. In the mutable madness of the Wastes, the Battle Eternal remained a constant. For the dark trials, the struggle, slaughter and fury were forever. Stumbling, half mad from the storm and perversity of the Shadowlands, the warriors of Chaos, clad in their blood-stained plate, feasted their eyes on a vision from their darkest dreams. Thousands upon thousands upon thousands of monstrous men, like themselves – fighting for the glory of their patron Power, fighting for the Ruinous Pantheon, fighting for themselves. Hacking. Skewering. Skull-cracking. Piercing with arrow and bow. Burning with the cold energies drawn from an otherwordly realm. Bludgeoning with club, rock or hand. Savaging, with mouth and claw.

They desired the decimating attentions of their Dark Gods. They knew they were watching. Drawing their weapons they became part of the perpetual havoc of the place – as all others had before. Sacrifices were demanded. The warriors of Chaos offered themselves and as many souls as they could steal from enemy Powers, carving the path to a glorious death on the battlefield of all battlefields. They did this in a kind of hope. Hope that their Ruinous Patron would see such a sacrifice. Hope that they may be rewarded for the darkness they had brought to the world. Hope that they might serve on – in daemonhood – and become more than they had ever been. Archaon grunted. These men, these beasts, these twisted souls were fools. Damned and deluded fools.

The daemon steed Dorghar stepped out into the slush. The battlefield stretched as far as the eye could see. The slaughter was like an amorphous blob of clattering plate, singing blades and fountaining gore. It was pure, cacophonous havoc. Helms bobbing and weaving. Banners held high. The blades of swords cutting through the gelid air of the north. The shafts of spears reared. Shields shattering before the devastating onslaught of hate-heaved weaponry. The light-smear of torches clutched in the gloom. The clouds of exertion, misting away on the wind. Warcries screamed to the sky. Roaring determinations. The cries of the wounded. The shrieks of the soon to be dead.

The ice was a filth-percolating slush, stained red with the incessant slaughter, body parts and constant corpses splashing down into the steaming sludge. In places hollows had formed that pooled with blood, in which the warriors of Chaos fought, thigh deep. Where the heat of gathering gore, blood and fresh death wasn't melting the ice, the white of the freeze was besmirched with rust from the veritable carpet of plate and armour. Armour belonging to Chaos warriors whose journey to daemonic ascension had ended in the rabid, scrambling slaughter of the Battle Eternal. There were bodies also. The butchered. The unworthy. The warrior victims, whose ice-white cadavers stared up through the ice or whose creaking limbs were frozen in place, reaching out of the corpse-stomped slush, mummified by the deep cold.

It was across this macabre, blood-logged plain, clambering over the frosted mounds and ridges of the freshly fallen that the bloodshed and desperation unfolded. Warriors of

Chaos stabbed, smashed and decapitated, only to turn and find another armoured foe, lurching out of a similar victory. Both would in time lay slain in the wake of some greater champion – a man bearing greater favour and determination until he too would fall to the lucky strike or back-stabbing cowardice of some nothing of a man. The insanity went on, as it always had.

'Banner,' Archaon called. A manfiend came forward. A comely youth that had once been a long-snout in the employ of the daemon lord Agrammon – muscular and bearing the buds of small horns. He held the banner proudly to the sky, pronouncing his warlord's intention to join the battle. The flayed flesh flapped in the wind. Archaon had no actual intention of joining the Battle Eternal. Its leagues of madness, surrounding the polar gate as it did, were simply in his way. Unlike every other Ruinous warrior on the battlefield, Archaon's destiny was taking him south.

'Protect the wagons,' he called back savagely, his orders relayed through the ranks of the horde. 'Defend the siege engines. Make sure you don't get bogged down or isolated. Scavenge what you can: armour, shields, weaponry. Exchange fur for plate, bone for steel – for this is the armoury of all the world. Pass the word. Have Jharkill unleash his beasts to clear us a path. His monsters to create calamity at our flanks. To the horde the rest!'

Archaon heard the thunderous cheer of bloodthirsty manfiends. Trapped in the wraithscape of the beyond for what could have been a wretched eternity, Archaon's horde could not wait to be part of the horror of battle once more. The top of the world would certainly afford them such an opportunity, Archaon mused. As the jubilant roar of slaughter-happy fiends shattered the still air of the battlefield, helms were turned. Chaos warriors who had spent many exhausted hours fighting their way through the morass of bodies and clashing plate were now confronted with a new challenge. Having slaughtered their way through a sea of Ruinous warriors, warbands, tribal hordes and small armies, the exalted warriors of darkness now faced the prospect of fighting an entirely new host. A monstrous horde that was marching through the fires of doom and straight out of the gates of hell at them.

'We are not here in search of favour. We are not here in search of reward. We have been blessed by the darkness and we fight as one. Death to the weak. New purpose and a place in our ranks to the strong.' Archaon pulled a broad-bladed axe of hell-forged craftsmanship from his belt and raised the heavy weapon. 'I am Archaon,' the Chaos warlord announced to the carnage and confusion of the Battle Eternal. 'Chosen of the Chaos gods. Walker of worlds. Herald of the End. And I bring you your doom.'

The ice either side of Archaon suddenly became a blur. Jharkill had opened the cages and unleashed the horde's pack of chimeric beasts. Like a torrent of fur, wing and snapping jaws, the emaciated fusions of monstrous beasts surged past. The stream of savagery smashed straight into the shocked warriors on the battlefield, who – exhausted and barely able to raise their weapons to defend themselves against similarly spent foes – were now barrelled to the ground by misshapen predators. The creatures clawed plate from savaged scarred bodies, before thrashing the rag doll corpses of the unfortunate warriors from side to side. Dropping the dead, the chimeric nightmares leapt at their next victim. With the surging advance of the emaciated predators slowed by such shredding butchery, the winged nightmares of Archaon's horde swooped over the Ruinous warlord's head.

Cutting down through the streaming ice and gloom, beasts of scale, feather and skin stretched between twisted bone beat their wings. Coming in low over the chimeric killers and their carnage, the airborne monstrosities plucked armoured warlords from stumbling steeds. They skewered Chaos warriors from the ice on single tusks and twisted horns before shooting for the skies to devour their prey. They streamed flame at the clashing mobs, turning columns of doom-pledged pilgrims into thrashing infernos, who shrieked through the battlefield confusion, setting alight the furs and cloaks of nearby champions.

As the horde's complement of warp-spawned creatures carved a path through the havoc, Archaon urged Dorghar on, the daemon steed ambling through the carnage. As well as the savaged slaves to darkness that the chimera pack left in its wake, tight throngs of blood-splattered warriors stumbled through the slush and away from the beasts, clearing the way for Archaon's horde. Rolling in the armoured saddle, however, the monstrous magnificence of his mount, the infernal craftsmanship of his ancient plate and the banner that bobbed above his head drew the Ruinous champions down on Archaon. Veteran warriors of Chaos, who had spent the lost and bloody years of their lives seeking out foes who fought for enemy gods so that they might draw some favour from their own miserable deity. The more deadly and infamous the opponent, the greater the glory in the eyes of the Dark Gods. It was a simple and merciless constant in the Wastes, which purged the unworthy and forged from the dross of damnation the most devastating of warriors. Marauder savages, beastlords, altereds, twisted sorcerers and exalted champions dressed from head to toe in foetid, baroque finery. All surged for Archaon from the flanks of the chimeric slaughter. Stumbling over the freshly savaged, doomed warriors were drawn to Archaon like moths to the furious flame of a torch in the darkness.

Riding tall on his daemonic beast – cruel, supremely confident and reeking of infernal favour – Archaon was a Ruinous altar of flesh and hell-forged steel upon which lesser men sacrificed themselves. With the frost of oblivion still sparkling on the battered brilliance of his dun plate, the veteran doomed of the Battle Eternal saw both blessed release and infernal salvations in the dark wonder that was Archaon. Riding out of the gates of hell with an abominate horde at his back, decked in the filth-treasures of Chaos, he immediately struck them as worthy. Worthy of their death. Worthy of a life, given in service of the doom Archaon promised to bring to the world.

As Archaon leaned left and right, hauling the daemon

Dorghar around, he felled the great warriors of Chaos about him with single, mangling strikes of his axe. Smashing straight through battle-brittle shields and blades, Archaon cleaved down through his armoured opponents, his axe crashing down through fell-hearted rivals and spinning gore-spiralling heads from damned shoulders. He was a dread sight to behold. With savage beasts consecrating the frozen ground before him with slaughter, a battle-hungry horde of scavenging manfiends butchering in his wake and monstrosities creating blood-misting carnage at his flanks, Archaon's progress through the warriors, warbands and unhallowed armies of the Battle Eternal became irresistible. Like a great ship ploughing through a sea of ice and bobbing bodies, Archaon drove the warrior multitudes before him, the swell of admiration and fear parting a path through the massacre.

'Archaon!' he roared to the skies. 'Archaon!'

It was an announcement. It was a warning. It was a challenge.

Then it happened. Dark-armoured warriors – some draped in filthy furs, some jangling with skulls and chains, some wearing great horned helms and others sporting plate of blood-stained spike – turned from the advancing horde. Whether it was a form of primordial submission, the dark inspiration of men still devoted to a doomed path or the mind-shearing whisper of Dark Gods, Archaon heard his name erupt from foes who were moments from the welcome of his axe.

'Archaon!'

His name spread like a plague through the blood, thunder and fatigue of the Battle Eternal. Men and beasts who moments before had swung their notched weaponry in exhaustion and their own belief, turned to hack warrior unfortunates out of Archaon's path.

'Archaon!'
'Archaon!'
'Archaon!'

His name became a rallying call, uttered in a plethora

of accents, for dread warriors whose plate and the banners bobbing above their warband advertised their allegiance to daemon princes and the different gods of the Chaos Pantheon. Some, like Archaon, fought for the pantheon in all its glory. Some fought for lies. Some fought solely for themselves and the corruption of calamities that had transformed the nobility of former lives. Others still bore the symbols of dark entities that even Archaon – having slaughtered his way across the globe – could not identify. They turned in advance of the crest of gore rolling before Archaon's axe. Before the bone-shattering, body-breaking carnage of his monsters and the fury of his fiend followers, who step by scavenging step, looted the battlefield dead.

No more was the horde a rabble of southern bare-chested barbarians, clad in cannibal furs and skins, wielding the sharpened bones of the conquered. The fiends baptised their manflesh with cold steel, plucked from the dead and the slush: scraps of mail, battered breastplates, spiked pauldrons, Ruinous Star-bearing shields, the clinker-plate of armoured boots, helms of horn and fearsome faceplate. Their gore-splattered claws were drawn to the wonder of forged weaponry that lay chill, blood-stained and rusting in the slush. Some were drawn to the savage ostentation of brute equivalents to their own bludgeoning weaponry: great serrated axes, pikes, spiked flails and the heft of monstrous hammers. Others couldn't resist the relative craftsmanship of blades that had found their way there from all corners of the world. In the hands of the horde, all killed with equal prejudice and indiscriminate butchery.

'Archaon!'
'Archaon!'
'Archaon!'
'Archaon!'
'Archaon!'

The Chaos warlord heard the chorus of his name move through the carnage of battle. It rose above the screams of the slaughtered and the ringing clash of desperate blades. For every ten unworthy tribal champions, altered hulks, sorcery-streaming witch-warriors and dark knights of doom felled, Archaon added an armoured axeman, some black-hearted bestial chieftain or broadsword swinging lord of Chaos to his number. Like a line of reapers moving through a field of wheat, Archaon and his growing horde felled the unworthy. Only the strongest, the most committed and doom-hungry of the gods' champions survived the onslaught of Archaon's horde. Men and monsters who had stridden through flame streaming from the skies. Who had survived chimeric predators launching themselves from freshly savaged foes. Who had walked away from the apocalyptic devastation of flesh-smeared giants. Who had fought clear of Prince Ograx's fiend mob and had slain their way through other warriors of Chaos who had achieved the same.

The Battle Eternal was a hellish vision of violence and brutality. The sound of clashing blades, death cries and bombast rang in the ear. The sting of the cold made way for the stench of old rot. On his lips Archaon could taste copper from the mist of blood in the air. His mind and muscles ached with the urgency of murder, carried out with bone-aching force and determination. All Archaon could see was the blur of furious attacks streaming by as he urged Dorghar back to the forefront of the battle-parting assault, where Chaos warriors pledged to Archaon's flayed banner only minutes before were making progress.

As he led his army through the havoc – killing the weak and recruiting the strong to his banner – Archaon was granted a view of what he had achieved. His darksight was merely a scramble of wretched souls clashing for miles around, while his good eye struggled to peer through the storm-streaming gloom ahead or the intense blaze of the Northern Gate, which threw everything before it into an amorphous silhouette. The Eye of Sheerian burned above the socket-slits of his helm, however, revealing to Archaon the devastation he had caused. Like a colossal wedge, Archaon's horde had charged out of the Ruinous fires of the Great Gate and into the havoc of never-ending battle.

Behind, Archaon could see the steaming, bloody expanse of fast-freezing bodies Prince Ograx's manfiends had left behind. Clad in real mail and plate, while wielding forged weaponry of steel and strength, the horde had proved more devastating than ever. Archaon watched broken corpses sail across the heads of the manfiends. Abominate giants and warped titans under Jharkill's influence swept and smashed enemies into the air with colossal bone clubs and the flick of monstrous horn-crowned heads.

The airborne nightmares of the horde tore Chaos warriors from their mounting assault on the flanks, beating their wings for the sky before dropping the armoured champions to their deaths. Winged serpents and mutant monstrosities soared along the same flanks, laying down streams of flame that cooked blood-sworn knights in their plate as the ice beneath their boots turned to shallows that swallowed their splashing bodies. Those warriors of Chaos that did reach the manfiends beyond the meltwater and the flames had other things to worry about. As they carved into Archaon's half-breeds, the chimeras, warhounds and emaciated predators that had been unleashed from the cages now prowled the crowded flanks – their lithe, skeletal bodies held close to the ground. The only evidence that they were even present on the field of battle were the unmanly shrieks and sudden disappearances of beastmen and marauders who, moments before, were there fighting next to their Ruinous lords and who, moments after, were gore-splatters in the snow.

Archaon had achieved more than just the slaying of enemy warlords and the Ruinous followers that fought for them. That was the purpose in every *other* servant of the Chaos Pantheon fighting before the Northern Gate. The Eye of Sheerian showed him that the wedge of Archaon's horde – including the freshly recruited and growing army of Chaos warriors and doom-destined champions that fought with him at the driving point of the path-carving assault – had actually disrupted the Battle Eternal. It was breaking up.

Archaon allowed himself a crooked smile and a grunt of derision. Truly only the Everchosen of Chaos could cause such a wonder. Only the Lord of the End Times could bring the greatest Ruinous warriors in the world, partaking in the greatest battle in the world, under his banner as one.

Archaon suddenly cursed – his daemon steed and himself – as Dorghar lurched around, nearly knocking him from the saddle. Like a stupefied fool he had allowed himself to be distracted in the middle of the battle he was threatening to end.

Dorghar reared and snorted. Dun-armoured knights who had been splashing through the red slush to rally behind Archaon now parted to reveal the wielder of a monstrous mace.

An abominate champion of Nurgle stomped forwards, making fountains of curdling meltwater splatter up about the dimensions of its grotesque form. Like a small mountain of rancid fat, its bare pox-riddled belly poked out from its filthy leper's shawls. The rusted plate that barely fitted around the trunks of its legs squealed for oil like a tortured child. The corroded shells of pauldrons sat on its great globed shoulders, while a tiny head sat inside the beaked, metal mask of a plague doctor. The crude instruments of the champion's former calling – saws, pincers and lancets – jangled on the belt of its brown mail skirts. The boils on its belly grew to horrid fruition. Bursting. Splattering. Dribbling their pus-streaked corruptions into the slushy shallows and mixing with the slick of rust that followed the Great Lord of Decay's champion. New boils erupted almost immediately from the afflicted flesh in a continuous celebration of rot and renewal. Worse than that, Archaon could see a growing army of the afflicted, shuffling in the champion's rank footsteps. The rust, pus and plague, the effluent corruption the champion had trailed behind it on its journey north, now clouded its way through the meltwaters of the Battle Eternal.

Archaon saw that upon coming into contact with the corruption, it was now spreading. Bestial champions, marauders and altereds who stumbled through the muck-infected slush were afflicted almost immediately by a septicity that felt its way up their pus-streaked and blistering legs. Dark knights and Chaos warriors decked head to toe in hell-forged plate were struck down by a living corrosion that crept up their greaves, turning their suits into rust-fused incubators of virulent plague. Champions of the Dark Gods, who stared on in horror as the supernatural contagion worked its way up through their bodies began to violently empty their stomachs, erupt with pox and bleed pus from their eyes, ears and nose. This spread the virulence further. Souls curdled by the Great Lord of Decay. Such warriors joined the growing horde of plague-riddled followers, stumbling in infected agony after the man-mountain of pus that stood before Archaon.

This was to be his challenge. As fast as Archaon was recruiting the warriors of Chaos to his doomed cause, the grotesque champion of Nurgle would be infecting them to his own. In their infinite, twisted perversity, the Ruinous Powers had inflicted two game changing warlords of Chaos on the Battle Eternal at the same time. Archaon, who minutes before had been so impressed with himself for bringing a fresh kind of havoc to a place that was nothing, came to understand that the Dark Gods would not be denied their cruel amusement. There would be a battle within the battle. A clash of two mighty hosts, one pouring from the decimated gates of hell and the other from the bleak insanity of the Shadowlands – each laying claim to the malevolent talent on display in the rampant, never-ending butchery of the Battle Eternal.

Turning Dorghar about with a twist of his torso and thighs, Archaon snatched the barbed length of a broad-bladed partisan from where it was standing upright in the petrified body of a Slaaneshi warlord. As Archaon rode around, through the savage clashes of champions who had been fighting through the Battle Eternal, he held up his weapon as a signal to his horde.

'Archaon!' he roared to the stormy tumult of the skies.

'ARCHAON!' the growing insanity of his horde called back.

Archaon turned to face the monstrous sack of disease-carrying putridity that was his opponent.

'Gangrysssss...' the Plague Lord's champion managed through the beak of its mask. 'Chosen of the Godsssss.' To this his blight-afflicted followers simply echoed with the cacophonous misery of a moan that might or might not have been the champion's dread name. Like a brain-fevered bull, Gangryss threw its disease-swollen bulk into a charge. It swung its monstrous mace through brute marauder warriors, mangling them out of its path.

Archaon's face drew back into a malevolent snarl. The Chaos warlord had competition for the gifts of the Dark Gods. Holding the reins with the arm upon which his shield sat, Archaon prompted Dorghar into a charge of its own.

Archaon leaned back in the rolling saddle. He narrowed his good eye in the darkness of his helm. He peered at the blazing mound of diseased ruin with his darksight. He stared straight through the plague-promised hulk with the Eye of Sheerian, the sorcerous jewel granting him a vision of the champion's rotten heart, thunder-pumping pus and spoilage about the monster's great body. Archaon's arm snapped forward like the string on a ballista, launching the shaft of the partisan through the air. It sailed through the northern freeze, rising, wobbling and irresistibly drifting downwards towards its target. Nurgle's great beast of a champion did not stop and did not care. When the partisan hammered into the meat of its rancid carcass, the monster missed its splashing step. Skewered on the barbed shaft, its mighty heart a barb-shredded mess, the champion lurched forwards before crashing down onto its armoured knees in the slush. It slid through the blood, snow and bones creating a crimson wave before coming to a stop. It still clutched the monstrous mace in one greening hand, the spikes of the crowning ball acting like an anchor in the ice.

The ruin of its chest rose and fell once more, pus streaming down into the waters about it, then the Great Lord of Decay's champion was no more. Archaon hauled up on Dorghar's reins – approaching the defeated champion slowly – and the Chaos warriors splashed to a slowing stop at his command.

Archaon took a deep breath of the freezing air. In the presence of the diseased hulk he thought better of taking another. He feared no opponent and had faced his fair share of Ruinous monstrosities, but there was a part of him that was glad he didn't have to face the champion of the plague-ridden.

Then he saw the partisan. The shaft of the barbed weapon had, moments before, been the sheen of midnight metal. Now it was browning, mottled and eaten through with emerging rust. Where the shaft sat in the champion's chest, pus seeped and corruption spumed. A few seconds more saw the partisan cascade to the ice in a shower of rusted flakes. Gone.

Even where he was sitting, Archaon heard the ugly beat of Gangryss's mighty heart thud back to diseased life. With a suddenness that shot a bolt of panic through Archaon's own, the creature was on its feet. It turned with a leper's grace, the spoilage of hidden strength in its arms brought to bear as the rusted ball of the mace came up and around, scraps of rotten flesh stuck on its spikes. Once again the shield, with its pantheon-blessed boss, took the brunt of the potent attack.

Spikes punctured the shield and the heavy head of the mace smashed the surface into a crumpled mess. The force behind the impact was devastating and took Archaon clean from his saddle. The armoured warrior hit the ice some distance away, rolled and clattered to a stop in a corpse-crowded pool of meltwater and gore. Gangryss was no daemon, like Archaon's father Be'lakor, but the monstrous champion had god-given gifts of its own. Its rotten resilience. Its otherworldly contagion. Its troll-like powers of regeneration. Its nerve-dead muscles, tendons and bones that didn't have to feel the torturous forces required to knock a foe like Archaon clean from his mount. Gangryss had been rewarded well indeed for the horror and havoc it had spread.

Gangryss was not the only one with gifts. The hulk's devastating blow would have broken any of a thousand dark champions. Not Archaon. Not any more.

Not that Gangryss felt anything. As Archaon scrambled arm over arm for the frozen edge of the pool, he saw the monstrous champion swing its great mace back around and up before bringing it down on the daemon steed Dorghar with unearthly force and power. Red slush and diseased meltwater surged for the sky as the mace came down. The hulk's corrupted lungs uttered a roar of jubilant determination. It didn't knock the steed unconscious. It didn't break its back. It hammered the beast down into the ice. Smashed into a shattered mess and into its own hollow beneath the surface of the battlefield, Dorghar was gone.

Archaon was surprised at the rage he felt, the presence of the Blood God's wrath in his heart. Perhaps it felt like losing Oberon all over again or perhaps he had grown to value and even like the sneering daemon steed. Conversely, it might simply have been the destruction of one of Archaon's dark treasures: the infernal steed destined to carry him into the bleak oblivion of the End Times. It might simply have been that the Chaos warlord felt that Gangryss had plagued the world long enough.

Archaon rose from the shallows, foetid water raining from his plate, as Gangryss turned to see that the champion-thing he had broken still lived and moved. Turning, Nurgle's hulk stomped through the icy graveyard at Archaon. Stabbing the shield upright into the bloody snow, the Chaos warlord reached down into the burn of the freezing waters. Prising a battle axe from the mummified fingers of its former owner, Archaon lifted the weapon above him. Its axe-head was made up of a huge and hollow blade, crafted in the design of the unhallowed eight-point star. He jabbed the head of the battle axe at the thunderous approach of Gangryss.

'End them!' Archaon roared to his army. 'End them all…'

Archaon's Chaos warriors and the plague slaves of Gangryss surged at one another. The clang of blades was soon followed by the cries of the wounded and the roaring defiance of the dying.

Archaon feinted right and then rolled left across his furs and pauldrons. Dripping with slush, the Chaos warlord allowed the champion's ice-mulching mace to smash into the ground, sending meltwater towards the sky. Archaon spun round, bringing the star-shaped blade of his battle axe about him. The axe tore through the stinking flesh of Nurgle's hulk at the side. Ducking the spiked head of the mace as it was swung around, Archaon felt the savage movement of air through his helm. Chopping down with the axe, Archaon smashed through the rusted plate of one leg before dragging the serrated spikes of the steel star back across the joint behind the knee of the other leg. The armour just crumbled there and the axe bit through flesh and tendon down to the rancid bone. Ripping through slabs of flesh on the champion's back, Archaon risked an economical hack at the thing's diseased paunch. As the axe thudded into the belly of Gangryss, Archaon ensured that he was out of the path of the spurting boils and gushing contagion.

Tearing the battle axe out of the champion, Archaon spun back on himself to wrong foot his opponent. Burying the battle axe in the hulk's meaty shoulder, Archaon shattered the rusted pauldron that covered it. As shards of brown metal rained about him, Archaon heaved his weapon out of the blubber of the monster's globed shoulder. He dare not leave the blade in his enemy for too long for fear that it would rot to nothing. As he stared at the horrific, muscle-shearing gash that his battle axe had left in Gangryss's spoiling shoulder, he was struck by a symbol burned into the champion's flesh. A symbol the axe had cleaved in two but a symbol that Archaon recognised. The monstrous warrior was an ever living example of the Plague Lord's patronage, yet the eight-point star seared into his shoulder supported his claim that Gangryss himself, at least, thought of himself as the Chosen of the Chaos gods. A festering champion of the Great Lord of Decay, drawing the eye and admiration of the Dark Pantheon with his ability to join all warriors of Chaos under a communal suffering, yoking the joint power of his collective horde with a single plague.

Archaon knew he had seen the symbol before. Then it came to him. In the Forsaken Fortress. His father's palace. He was staring at no ordinary Ruinous Star – the kind cut into the flesh of a thousand pantheon-pledged warriors of darkness or carved into the surface of countless shields. It was Be'lakor's star. The Mark of the First Daemon of Chaos. The Mark of the Bearer. The Herald. The same burned into the darkness of his shadowy champions. The same dread sigil that burned across the daemon prince's own heart and chest. Archaon was not the only mortal champion in search of the treasures of Chaos. Be'lakor had other pieces moving across the game board of the world. Gangryss was one of them. Gangryss and how many more, Archaon wondered? How many promised the power and the position of being Everchosen of Chaos – only to be a soul-in-waiting for Be'lakor to possess and flesh for the daemon prince to wear?

The shock of the discovery had cost him. Seconds had bled away with his racing thoughts and now Gangryss – who couldn't have cared less about the healing flesh of his shoulder and his patron's monstrous mark – all but had him. Narrowly leaning his helm out of a brutal backswing with the monstrous mace, Archaon began to understand how Gangryss could be at the head of such a host. As fast as Archaon was opening him up – revealing bone, ripping up muscle and allowing a nest of rotten intestines to follow his retracted axe out of the champion's belly – the monster's regenerative powers were healing him. Gangryss couldn't feel the pain of such injuries; he barely knew he had them before flesh knitted back together and innards slurped back inside his putrid carcass. Worse, the more damage Archaon inflicted, the more pus-streaked blood and contagion stained the slush through which Archaon was slipping and sliding.

Looking down, Archaon found that he was barely keeping a foothold on the edge of a hulk-stamped hollow brimming with bloody meltwater and doom. As his balance wavered and his armoured boot slid down, Archaon had visions of being rust-entombed in his ancient armour and living out the rest of his days in the putrescence of a plague-filled metal coffin. Instead of committing his footwork to another brutal axe swing through the champion's maggot-squirming corpulence, Archaon held his ground. Movement meant infection. Remaining still meant allowing Gangryss to land the bone-ringing blow he had been attempting to execute. Holding the battle axe under its star-shaped head and at its haft, nothing could prepare him for the mind-numbing impact of the brute's mace against the presented axe. Archaon was batted away from his foe and the deadly pool of corruption, rolling, flailing and skidding into a rank of the champion's plague slaves.

Again, Archaon's stone-laced skeleton had saved him. Blinking himself back to the moment, with the clash of steel around him slowed to a dreary metallic din, he pushed himself up and lifted his helm. The Swords of Chaos had raced into battle behind him. While Zwei and Drei leapt at the champion of Nurgle with acrobatic flaps of their wings, the wraith-warriors cutting the monster up with their bone swords, Eins was racing across the ice towards his master. Archaon felt the footsteps of the infected padding through the shallows about him.

Archaon rose and scooped up the axe that had been knocked from his grip. When Gangryss saw that Archaon still lived and was walking through the Battle Eternal towards him, it bellowed a lung-shredding challenge to the stormy skies.

'Come get me,' Archaon roared back, 'you sack of spoiling meat.'

Stomping through the pus-swirling pool, Gangryss forced his fat legs on, batting champions both pledged to Archaon's banner and his own aside with murderous sweeps of his mace.

Turning the battle axe about in his gauntlet, swinging the

blade about his body to the left and then the right, Archaon marched across the red ice. He would have to destroy this plague champion once and for all or surrender all of his dark treasures to the monster – stripped from his frozen corpse one by one.

As the determination of a slip-shod march became a slush-splattering run, Archaon spied a kind of hope. Narrowing his eye he swooped under the mottled steel of rust-riddled blades and lurched out of the clumsy arcs of flails and hammers brown with old blood. Holding his battle axe beneath its star-shaped blade, he despatched those servants of Nurgle who he could not avoid, mercilessly sinking the steel points of his weapon into their skulls. Tearing the axe blade out he allowed plague slaves to drop beside his footprints before economically skull-hooking another unfortunate.

'Youuuuuu...' the hulk seethed, the deep rasp both an accusation and a challenge issued. Archaon didn't need an invitation. He had invited himself to the monstrous warrior's doom. As the champion of Nurgle brought his mace over his beaked mask, his intention to smash his opponent into the Chaos Wastes clear, Archaon stomped at speed through the slush. As he held his own weapon close, Archaon leapt from the ice. Gangryss turned the beak of his mask in confusion, since the Chaos warlord was too far away to effect an attack. The grotesque hulk was wrong. So very wrong.

Archaon curled into an axe-hugging dive. Hitting the ice with a half-accomplished roll, Archaon tumbled across his shoulders and the furs mounted on his back. Stamping his armoured heels into the freeze, Archaon brought himself to an abrupt halt – transferring the dreadful momentum of the manoeuvre to the battle axe that he launched from his clutched gauntlets. He sent the weapon off with a roar of effort, watching the battle axe spin haft over the star-shaped steel of its razor-sharp blade. The speed, cutting hiss and ugly revolution of the weapon was a sickening wonder to behold. Within moments that seemed like a sickening age, the battle axe landed in the head of the Great Lord of Decay's champion, splitting his beak mask down the middle and cleaving through the front of Gangryss's demolished skull.

Blood, pus and brains slurped down the champion's chest in a slow but insistent cascade. The small mountain of fat and spoilage tottered, his armoured feet slapping backwards through the slush. His gargantuan mace tumbled from his plump, twitching fingers and his hands began to blindly grasp for the battle axe firmly buried between his eyes.

Archaon knew this would not stop Gangryss, with its god-blessed regenerative powers. The Chaos warlord had already resumed his charge. Ice and brittle bones crunched beneath his furious footsteps. Meltwater splattered behind him, while his cloak twisted and turned in his wake. Archaon closed on the skull-split Gangryss. Snatching his cloak with his right gauntlet, the Chaos warlord pulled it around in front of him like a cape. Holding the material out like some kind of shield, Archaon left the ice once more. This time he embraced the momentum of the charge and smashed into the wall of rot-threaded blubber that was Gangryss. Striking Nurgle's champion like a cannon ball at a castle wall, Archaon felt the splatter of pus from the bubbling boils on the monster's belly, his presented cloak keeping his armour from the worst of the corrosive corruption.

As Archaon went down in the slush and bloody meltwater, the champion stumbled backwards. Gangryss suddenly disappeared into the depths of a hollow Archaon had spotted behind it. The gruesome tentacles of a monstrous spawn slapped, grasped and seized victims from the edge of its crater. Some thrice-blessed champion or creature of the Battle Eternal, rewarded for its fortitude and butchery with transforming gifts that turned it from devout servant of the Chaos gods into a mindless, tentacular maw buried in the ice. A thing of horrid darkness that served on by dragging the weak and unworthy of the Battle Eternal into the thrashing teeth of its horrific jaws.

As Archaon crawled arm over arm towards the abomination,

he heard the burst of Gangryss's gas-bloated belly. He heard the excruciating crunch of bone and rusted steel in the beast's masticating maw. He heard the horror of a death from which Gangryss – champion of the Plague Lord, Chosen of the Ruinous Gods and servant of the Dark Master – could not survive. As Archaon neared the edge of the hollow he could hear the groans, bubblings and rumblings of the spawn-monster's cavernous stomach. Then suddenly a magnificent fountain of blood, pus and macerated bone rocketed up towards the heavens in a steaming stream.

'Heal that,' Archaon dared the monstrous champion of Chaos. The Chaos warlord heard a familiar sound. It was the whooshing revolution of the battle axe. With its star-shaped blade spinning over its haft, the weapon had been vomited up out of the pit with the rest of the rancid champion. As it descended, Archaon lowered his head. As it thudded blade first into the ice, like a wood axe in a block of firewood, the warrior grunted.

Archaon heard something within the hollow and envisioned that he might be the next mighty champion of Chaos to sate the appetite of the monstrous spawn. Snatching up the battle axe from the ice, Archaon ran forward, intending to chop snaking tendrils or loathsome tentacles reaching out for him and hell-bent on dragging his armoured form down into the pit and a waiting maw. As the squelch of his footfalls took him closer, however, he found no such abominate appendages feeling their way towards him. Instead he was confronted by the nightmarish form of a midnight stallion, climbing out of the hollow. Upon crossing the lip of the ice crater with its spiked hooves, the steed shook itself from snout to tail, rattling the armoured saddle that sat on its back. The daemon Dorghar's eyes burned with the infernal fire of its transformative powers. Snorting the last of Gangryss's repugnance from its nostrils, the daemon steed once again spoke. Its words were unknown to Archaon but the furnace-hiss of otherworldly scorn that accompanied them was unmistakable.

'Yes,' Archaon told Dorghar simply. 'Quite.'

Grabbing the reins and slipping an armoured boot into a spiked stirrup, Archaon hauled himself up into the saddle. In the desperation and drama of Gangryss's end, Archaon had not noticed the haunting silence of the battlefield. The freezing wind moaned about the armoured forms of Chaos warriors who had slowed to stillness. Through the statuesque wonder of warriors and monstrous talent, only one figure moved. An emaciated wretch in rags and chains, his head forever trapped in a cage with no key. The flagellant Gorst. Gorst who had followed Archaon unharmed across the Southern Wastes. Who had survived with him the dread dangers of the dark Realms of Chaos. Who now walked unmolested – and unlike the rest of Archaon's horde, unchanged – through the Battlefield Eternal. Gorst dragged his trailing chains through the bones, bloody slush and still bodies before coming to a stop himself and staring up at his master.

About them, dread serenity swept through the carnage, bringing the Battle Eternal to a halt never witnessed before. Foes lowered their weapons. Banners drifted to the bloody ground. The din of battle died.

'I was one of you,' Archaon called across the frozen silence, his voice carried on the shearing wind. 'A puppet in a sick show – like this. Dancing for my dark masters. I dance no more. And neither should you. The gifts of the gods are no such thing. Let us not seek reward. Let us not ask for power. Let us not wait on that which is given. Let us take what is ours. Darkness is ours. Ruin is ours. The world turns beneath our feet for the taking. Real power resides not with gods or any following but with those who take it from them. I am Archaon, doom to my enemies, doom to all the world, doom to the gods invested in that world. Come with me. Why earn the treasures of Chaos when you can steal them? Why kill for Ruinous patrons when you can kill for yourself? Why sell your souls so cheaply, when you can make the worlds of gods and men pay for your miseries?

'I might be Chosen of the Dark Gods – but I did not

choose them. I will be Everchosen of Chaos, whether the dread Powers and their daemons wish it for me or not. The legions of hell will be ours to command and we shall use them to demonstrate true power. The power to choose. To be or not to. To drag the sick perversity of this daemon-haunted existence kicking and screaming into a time of Ending. To end the world, the gods that torment it and ourselves. That is real power and I ask you to seize it with me. With he who is one of you: lost, damned even, but a slave to darkness no more. With Archaon…'

The infernal fires of the collapsed gate blazed, like flames upon which gunpowder had been dashed. The balelight of the beyond burned ferociously at Archaon's god-thwarting words. Archaon couldn't tell whether the brilliance raged in warning or celebration of his wondrous achievement.

'Archaon!' a voice boomed across the killing fields. A skull-axe thrust up at the sky, above the heads of countless warriors. It was Ograx the Great, the half-breed prince who was beast no more. The former bestial champion of the Blood God, whose army of manfiends had smashed through the havoc of the Battle Eternal, collecting before its example an ever growing vanguard of Chaos warriors. He knew precious few words in his master's tongue but he knew the glory of his name. With his chest heaving, Ograx roared the warlord's name to the storm-crashing heavens.

'Archaon, Archaon… Archaon!' the daemonbreed chanted.

'Archaon!'

'Archaon!'

'Archaon!'

Once more the battlefield rang with the thunder of his name, uttered like a dark oath from thousands of doom-lifted hearts. Warriors of Chaos, fighting for every Ruinous Power and daemonic master, united as one dark, apocalyptic force behind the dread syllables of his name.

'ARCHAON!'

'ARCHAON!'

The warlord turned his daemon steed about to soak up

the power and possibility of his intoxicating achievement. The ground trembled. The fires of hell roared forth from the gate of oblivion. Thunder tore through the sky and lightning shattered the gloom.

'ARCHAON!'

He held up his battle axe, the steel blade of the Ruinous Star rising. He lifted it above the chanting thousands. The dark star of a Chaos undivided. United. As one. The chanting echoed to nothing on the chill air.

'Let us be the storm that rolls south!' Archaon bellowed back at them, levelling his battle axe towards a world awaiting its end. It was all the monstrous horde needed to hear.

CHAPTER XIII

*'There is a mountain of shadow thrown,
The only feature the Wasteland knows.
The mountain waits;
The mountain slumbers;
The mountain quakes;
The mountain thunders.
A mountain more than storm or place –
The Black King of an ancient race.'*
– The Mad Minstrel, excerpt, *Chimerica*

*The Chimera Plain
The Northern Wastes
Date Unknown*

Archaon would not make the same mistakes again. There would be no repeated disasters. You could not be betrayed by those you did not trust – and Archaon trusted no one. The only betrayals the horde suffered would be his own.

Archaon's colossal host marched south. Through the

Shadowlands. His vast Ruinous army contained representation from every marauder tribe fighting for god-fearful territory in the Wastes. Northmen from the mountainous lands of Norsca. Berserker Bjornlings. Warring Aeslings and Sarls. Werekin. Expeditionary raiders from the Kraken Sea and Varg reavers. From the cruel lands of the Kurgan and the Eastern Steppes he had Yusak warlords, centigor nomads of the Endless Land, savage horsemen of the Tokmar and Skull-landers of the dread Kul. Of the mighty Hung, Archaon's host boasted masterless warriors of the Man-Chu, Weijin invaders and terrors of the Great Bastion, pirate clans of the Yin and even fallen hordes of the unstoppable Ungol.

Where Archaon's marauders happened across territorial hosts of their parent tribes, the Chaos warlord gave instructions that such savages be assimilated into his army or be utterly wiped out. Bestial hordes needed little convincing of Archaon's strength when stunt-horned scouts reported back his army's expanse and growing number. Only Clovak Moonhoof and Truskag the Red denied Archaon the brutality of their beasts. The coward Clovak Moonhoof and his half-breeds fled Archaon's outriders and were lost in one of the Shadowlands' soul-swallowing storms. The blood-crazed Truskag the Red, conversely, gave Archaon's expeditionary champions a sample of their talents by leading his warherd into sacrificial annihilation, in honour of his gorethirsty god.

The bulk of the horde's continual supply of recruits were small hosts, warbands and lone champions wandering the Wastes. Chaos warriors and dread sorcerers, devoted to different Ruinous paths and honouring different barbarous gods and aspects of the Dark Pantheon. These warriors had found themselves on the path to darkness from innumerable lands, both civilised and savage lands. Many heralded from Archaon's homeland – the doom-ripe principalities of the Empire. His horde also boasted twisted knights of Bretonnia, raven-haired warriors of the southern states, who felt the chill of the Wastes worse than most, man-eating hulks of the Ogre Kingdoms, who had wandered too far north in search of slaves, and hardened Kislevites, fallen veterans of the border wars against Chaos invaders.

Confronted with the fearful number of Archaon's Chaos army and the potent determination of their purpose, most warriors from these far off lands and their motley warbands of afflicted oddities came to see the darkness from Archaon's unique and incontrovertible perspective. Whether delivered in person or through the champions he honoured with temporary command of despatched hosts, the offer was always the same. The dark warriors and their bedraggled followers could continue their service to the Ruinous Powers or single unholy god under Archaon's banner of the Ruinous Star – bringing honour to Chaos in all its contradiction and undivided glory – or be sacrificed by Archaon's horde to the self same cause.

Most had been wandering victims of the Wastes and its perversities for some time. In Archaon's great host they saw food, water and even protection from predatory daemons, competing warbands or the insanity of the environment itself. Some champions felt they had lost purposes of their own, if they ever had them, and felt the pull of Archaon's fate and the prosecution of his personal mission to find the legendary treasures of Chaos. Some simply gave him their blood fealty based upon some measure of supremacy. His warrior prowess. The wonder of his accomplishments. The leadership of his loyal masses – the example of warriors like themselves, who rode with Archaon and fought for him.

There were of course those who refused his dark offer. Upstarts, newly arrived in the Wastes and wrapped up in delusions of their own invincibility. Madmen who didn't seem to understand that they were courting certain death or whose minds had been so warped that they didn't care. Then, of course, there were the pretenders. Exalted warriors of Chaos, dark lords and monstrous sorcerers who had been deceived by their patron Powers or had lied to themselves: champions who called themselves the Chosen of Chaos and boasted of their fearful ambitions. Death was the only cure for their predicament and Archaon granted such warriors the swift mercy of his battle axe for such Ruinous blasphemies, before assimilating their warbands into the dark magnificence of his horde.

As the colossal horde wound its way through the warping landscape of the Shadowlands it drank polluted rivers dry. Archaon had charged Jharkill with the training of mounted hunting parties to track and kill herds of twisted beasts that roamed the gloomy wilderness. Many parties disappeared – no doubt eaten by something they in turn had been stalking – but those that returned did so dragging the warped carcasses of rhinox, roaming sauria, thundertusk and razorgor hogs, ready for skinning. Jharkill himself Archaon kept busy with the hunting and enslaving of further monstrosities to add to their abominate collection of calamities. Chimeric predators. Skulking daemons. Flocks of flesh-feasting harpies. All fell to the huntsman's eye, his poison-smeared arrows and the brute range of his tusk bow. It had been Jharkill who had found the Chimera Plain.

Intent on finding the *Slayer of Kings* as soon as possible, Archaon had entrusted small hosts of his greater horde to four champions of Chaos who had proved themselves worthy lieutenants. Having his colossal horde make camp in a fang-lined impact crater called the Whispermaw, where champions of Chaos were supposed to hear the land give up its secrets, Archaon sent his four champions off in search of the lonely mountain. All set off in different directions, the mounted champions and their contingents swallowed up by the gloom of the Shadowlands.

Casimir Ghislaine returned first. The Bretonnian knight wore his exquisite suffering like he wore his suit of immaculate armour. His dark plate was riven with barbs and spikes on the inside as well as on its polished surface and enclosed the Pleasure Lord's champion like an Iron Maiden. His steed's armour and Ghislaine's saddle were similarly a nest of spikes to suffer upon. Archaon was furious with the Slaaneshi knight for returning so swiftly but Ghislaine insisted that he and his host had been gone for months. He hadn't found the mountain Archaon was seeking but had discovered another called the Thunderhead, at the foot of which he had discovered the age-browned bones and rotting armour of the past champion simply known as Deng. Deng had been a hulking easterner, a former worshipper of Tzeentch, the Great Changer, who had been a silent but deadly warrior-lieutenant in Archaon's horde. His lacquered armour was very distinctive, however, sporting a daemon-mask helmet through which Deng's strange blue eyes used to blaze. It was unlikely that Ghislaine had found the armour of another such champion and Archaon reasoned that Deng and his host must have been caught in some kind of storm at the Thunderhead, trapping them in some horrific version of the past.

Lothar Bott made his way back some weeks later at the head of his slave-swarm of mange-eaten beastmen, also unsuccessful in his quest to find the lonely mountain. The Nurglite was a stinking sorcerer with three heads, grotesquely conjoined at the temple and jaw in the same orientation as the Great Lord of Decay's sigil. Carrying a scythe-staff and riding a skeletal steed, Bott was an unimaginative, if capable lieutenant who carried out his master's orders and no more.

Ulfen Schorsch was the last to return. A champion of the Blood God, Schorsch was a ghoulish sight in the red and black of his armour, trimmed as it was with spikes and draped with blood-soaked furs. Worst of all was his patron's gift of a fleshless face. Sparse muscles and tendons were still visible about his blood-stained skull, as well as a pair of piercing eyes that never closed and peered out from hooded sockets. A pair of gleaming brass fangs framed his jaw and marked him out as a warrior-parasite. A cannibal. He commanded a contingent of similar warriors, who bore the same curse of fleshlessness and blood-hunger, which he called the Crimson Company. Many of the Crimson Company were merciless warriors of Chaos in their own right and acted as Schorsch's own lieutenants.

At first, Archaon thought that the fleshless-faced champion had news for him. Instead, Ulfen Schorsch only had news of a running conflict the Crimson Company had become involved with along the banks of a river of eel-teaming mist. After an unsuccessful ambush, a furious Schorsch had committed his host to hunting down their attackers in a labyrinth of razor-sharp canyons. Stalking and slaughtering their foes to the last urchin-armoured warrior of Chaos, Schorsch boasted to his master of a battle to the god-honouring death with Kormac Graw and the bloodfeast that followed. With fang-lisped insolence, Schorsch told Archaon that Graw was a celebrated champion of the Ruinous Star, very much like the warlord himself. Archaon was furious with Schorsch, berating the bloodthirsty champion not only for failing in his mission but also for wastefully sating his personal appetites on potential recruits for the horde.

When Jharkill returned from a hunting trip a day later, however, he soothed Archaon's anger with news that he had sighted the mountain his champions were searching for. Leaving Casimir Ghislaine in charge of the crater camp and Khezula Sheerian with a secret responsibility for watching over the twisted Slaaneshi, Archaon took charge of a scouting party himself. With the ogre huntsman tracking for them through the changeable landscape of the Northern Wastes and taking the Swords of Chaos as a Ruinous escort, Archaon also selected Ograx the Great as extra muscle. If there was blood to be spilt, then who better than a champion of the Blood God to perform the duty? With the half-daemon, Archaon also ordered Ulfen Schorsch and his Crimson Company along, to demonstrate his displeasure with the Chaos champion and his butchers.

With Jharkill's broad strides taking the monstrous huntsman at a pace through shimmering highlands on the border of the Shadowlands and the wider Wastes, Archaon had little trouble keeping up on the back of Dorghar. The members of his wraith-warrior escort also made short work of the frost-baked terrain, for Eins, Zwei and Drei now seemed less and less part of Archaon's world of blood and muscle. Day by day they continued a transformation they had begun in the Realm of Chaos, assuming the terrifying form of solidifying shadows. The servants of the Blood God enjoyed the pace less, however. At least Ograx had the benefit of having walked half way across the world in the footsteps of his master. Ulfen Schorsch and the leeches of the Crimson Company were attempting to keep up in full plate and weighed down with their butchers' weapons. By the time the highlands dropped down into a desolate wilderness, the skull-faced Schorsch was in no doubt that he and his men were being punished.

As Jharkill tracked for them across the featureless Wasteland, the ground as hard as iron below their feet and the clouds the colour of iron above them, the malformed ogre pointed out the mountain to his master. Following the line of the huntsman's tusk bow, Archaon sat up in the saddle and picked out a distant peak rearing out of the cold haze of the wilderness. Using the Eye of Sheerian, the jewel glowing eerily in its setting, Archaon brought the sight of the mountain streaming closer.

The mountain looked as unnatural as any other feature of the Chaos Wastes. Thrusting up out of the plain, it was a fat peak, nestling in scree and boulders. Its lazy inclines were thick with dust and grit, which had given purchase to isolated patches of wretched vegetation. Sitting in the broad peak was a hollow, like the crater of a dormant volcano, despite the fact that it was clearly a mountain. As Archaon stared at it, something bothered the Chaos warlord about its shape and the strange, sweeping lines of its ascent. Something he could not quite explain. Like much of the warped Wastes, it seemed dreadfully suggestive of a land that was living. A track swirled its way about the mountain's odd dimensions, up to the rim of the hollow peak in which Archaon was confident he would find his prize.

Riding across a chill plain of stunted grasses and spidery patterns of burned soil, where lightning had showered down on the expanse, the scout party was accompanied by small twisters of dust and ice. Even on the desolation of the plain, Archaon and his warriors of Chaos were not alone. The Wastes wouldn't allow it. The very perversity of the land itself seemed to take pleasure in rising and falling – allowing paths of least resistance to drift wanderers into bloody converges and encounters. Here, out on the haze of the plain, the fat mountain – the only feature for many miles – drew travellers towards it. The mountain harboured no obvious draws, like a settlement in its foothills or the refreshment of a waterfall cascading from its heights. On the insanity-inducing endlessness of the plain, it offered the reassurance of something different. A break in the dry, cold monotony of the wilderness and its eye-stinging haze. A feature that invited curiosity on the horizon.

For a time Archaon's small host seemed on course to meet a larger warband led by a warrior-shaman. The Mung Savage was on horseback and trailed a train of wretched spawn tied one to another like a chain gang of criminals. Archaon suspected this was done to ensure the horrors did not wander off on their own. The shaman changed course suddenly, however, leading his band of unfortunates away from both Archaon and the mountain. Believing that the warrior-shaman had had some kind of prophetic indication of the danger ahead and had turned to avoid Archaon and the doom he represented, the Chaos warlord held his own heading, despite entreaties from Ulfen Schorsch and his Crimson Company to hunt down and slaughter the shaman and his spawn.

Not long after, a lone knight in black, burnished plate approached the party from some distance away, making his meandering way towards them. Upon taking off his helm, the knight introduced himself as Sieur Wenzel, grinning inanely through the tangled curtains of his long, unkempt hair. Slipping a dagger from his belt, Sieur Wenzel prompted the Swords of Chaos to reach for the bone swords in their wing-sheathes – ever in defence of their master. The mad knight only meant harm to himself, however, opening up his throat in front of Archaon and his Chaos warriors, before crashing face first into the hard ground.

The body attracted predators, chimera and chaotic fusions that stalked the scouting party. The monsters were blessed with the same chameleonic hides, which rippled with the dun colours and textures of the plain, hiding the danger of their numbers in the haze. Ograx the Great smelled the danger first. Dorghar seemed unconcerned and it was only a matter of time before the huntsman's eye spotted their stalkers. When Jharkill warned his master of the imminence of their attack, Archaon slipped his battle axe from where it sat in one of his armoured saddle's many holsters, hooks, sheaths and scabbards. Lifting his body shield up onto one arm, the Chaos warlord waited for the attack. The beasts were as fast as the lightning storms that burst above the desolation of the plain. They appeared suddenly from the haze, their surging movements revealing their positions.

Chimera swarmed the scout party, cannonballing members of the Crimson Company over and turning the savage tumbles into the desperation of clattering plate, claws and jaws. Thrice-breeds and abominate fusions leapt at Archaon, while others surged into the sky only to swoop back down at the hunting party. The air was thick with the roars, hissing and shriek-bleating of the monsters' myriad heads, as well as the whoosh of their bat-like wings and the seething snap of their serpent tails. One of the beasts sank its claws into the body of Sieur Wenzel before surging up into the heavens, while others seemed unwisely preoccupied with Dorghar and the feast its midnight flesh would make.

As the chimera swept in, emboldened by hunger and twisted of predatory instinct, Eins, Zwei and Drei kept their closing number back with shadow-smeared flourishes of their bone blades. A surging opportunist left the ground and beat its wings, sending its drool-trailing jaws at Archaon and his mount. While Dorghar casually kicked the skulking forms of snapping chimera senseless with its spiked hooves, Archaon smashed the airborne monster aside with a swing of his shield. As the beast hit the ground nearby, it shook comprehension back to its three heads. It needn't have bothered. Rearing, Dorghar brought its huge hooves brutally down on two of its skulls before kicking the snapping head of a malformed lion clean off its body.

The attack was over swiftly enough. With half of the number dead, the pack of chimeric monsters broke off, either beating their wings for the sky or slinking back into the haze that had formerly hidden them. Whereas the kills of Archaon and his Swords of Chaos were modest enough – including even Dorghar's brutal contributions – the pack suffered most at the hands of the rest of the scouting party. Jharkill's bow hammered monstrous fusions into the iron-hard ground and pinned them there, impaled on the great bone shafts. Ograx the Great hadn't even bothered to slip his skull-axe from his back. As a beast warped into the barbaric flesh of a man, Ograx was a wall of brawn and daemonic strength. When he wasn't wrestling the chimeric monsters with his bare, muscle-bound arms – breaking necks and spines – he was stoving in ribcages with his hooves or lifting beasts above his head to gore on his infernal horns. Ulfen Schorsch and his Crimson Company, however, attacked the closing chimera with as much frenzied ferocity as the beasts themselves exhibited, hacking creatures apart with serrated axe and sword, painting the plain red with the excesses of their butchery.

As the ogre huntsman recovered his arrows, Archaon urged the scouting party on, pulling the Crimson Company from their favoured ritual of draining their enemies of polluted blood. Archaon's orders were edged with distaste, having little time for the appetites of the fanged warriors, who looked like animals feeding on animals amongst the slaughtered chimera.

Step by step, the fat mountain rose above them. Closer, it was clear that the chimera pack had made their home in the caves, hollows and on the gentle bone-strewn slopes of the peak. Slipping between boulders and openings, the predators' chameleon-like abilities could not hide their silhouettes creeping up and down the mountainside. At the foot of the narrow slope leading up the mountain's broadness, Archaon brought Dorghar's clopping hooves to a halt. Jharkill grasped the daemon steed by the chains and waited on his master. Archaon turned his helm. The Swords of Chaos stood behind him like statuesque shadows. Ulfen Schorsch and the Crimson Company crunched to a stop in the grit and scree with Ograx the Great bringing up the rear of the scouting party.

'This is as good a place as any,' Archaon announced, prompting Ulfen Schorsch to ask if they were heading up the mountain.

'Some of us are,' the Chaos warlord told him from the saddle. 'For some, this journey has come to an end.'

Ograx the Great was suddenly behind the fleshless-faced warrior. Wrapping the muscular vice of his arm around the neck of the Blood God's champion, the prince of fiends tore at his grotesque head. Schorsch's clawed gauntlets scratched at the irresistible force of the arm and he sank his leech's fangs into Ograx's flesh. As his feet left the ground, the armoured warrior kicked out, clattering furiously in his plate. The struggle was over as fast as it had begun, however, as – with an excruciating crunch – Ograx tore the fleshless skull of the warrior from his suddenly flaccid body.

Realising that they were being betrayed, the Crimson Company ripped the barbed blades of their swords and axes from their belts, rallying to the commands of one of Ulfen Schorsch's own lieutenants. This was one of the reasons that Archaon had ordered them killed. He was the only dread authority in the vast horde and the only one permitted to empower subordinates. The Crimson Company might have pledged allegiance to Archaon but Schorsch's band of cannibals still harboured loyalties of and to their own kind.

Spinning around, their bone blades already whispered from their wing-sheathes, the Swords of Chaos decimated the front rank of Crimson Company warriors with a single coordinated strike. The decapitating slash sent skulls sailing through the air, the gloom glinting off their brass fangs.

With weapons in each hand, the Swords swept the blades of the Blood God's warriors to one side and stabbed the tips of their shadowy swords through the bared bone of skulls. Retracting in unison, Archaon's henchmen worked their way methodically through the Crimson Company, who were caught between the merciless bladework of the Swords and Prince Ograx's skull-axe, being used to smash skulls from spines in showers of brain-mulched fragments.

It was not in the nature of the Blood God's servants to flee and the Crimson Company did not disappoint, forcing Ograx to murder each warrior where he stood, smashing the armoured leeches into a mess against the hard earth of the plain.

Archaon looked down on the carnage. What others might have called brainfever or a murderous madness of the Wastes, Archaon considered pruning. Hordes, like shrubs and bushes, were at their healthiest when trimmed to ensure guided growth. Archaon needed warriors of character to lead the contingents of his monstrous horde into battle – a horde that assimilated more and more Wasteland wandering dross every day. What he did not need was the loyalty of those contingents in the hands of conspirators and dissenters, who might be tempted to secretly build an army within Archaon's own, secure the future loyalties of other lieutenants and murder Archaon for his great treasures. This was not warp-baked paranoia. It had happened to Archaon before. He had lost an entire host through the machinations of pretenders to his titles to come and had barely escaped with his life. To ensure that never happened again, that the wild and wayward forces at work within the monstrous legion at his command were kept in check, Archaon routinely slaughtered his own. Issuing charismatic warriors, defiant savages and overly successful lieutenants acting on their own initiative with tasks and missions that took them and their loyal followers away from the horde, Archaon would have them secretly butchered. If he had any evidence of their plotting against him, Archaon would even end them himself. That had not been the case with Ulfen Schorsch and the Crimson Company, however. Archaon simply had an instinct for those overreaching individuals whom he felt would disappoint him. Such assassinations always happened in secret but there was a general suspicion amongst the horde's wretched multitude that such a practice went on, and this also helped to subdue would-be challengers. In a land of madness, leading a dark army of the vile, the bloodthirsty and the daemonic, it sometimes paid to advertise a little darkness of your own.

'Burn the remains,' Archaon told Jharkill, stepping down from Dorghar. 'With anything you can find.'

Archaon's boot crunched in the grit next to Schorsch's decapitated head. The warrior's eyes still stared up at Archaon in searing, uncloseable accusation, while his fanged jaws snapped unconsciously in the dirt. Leeches were notoriously difficult to kill and Archaon wanted to ensure the fiery end of the vampiric Crimson Company. The monstrous ogre nodded his understanding, keeping hold of Dorghar. 'Stay with Jharkill and my steed,' Archaon told Zwei, who was cleaning off one of his bone blades. Like the ogre, the wraith-warrior nodded silently. 'You two,' Archaon told the others, 'prince, with me.'

As Archaon set off up the winding incline, Eins and Drei flanked their master, while Ograx the Great, flicking gore from the skull of his daemon-headed axe, followed, his brazen hooves pulverising the grit of the trail. As they ascended, the wind picked up. The dizzying expanse of the endless plain glowered about the mountain, stretching off into the gloom in all directions. The fat mountain, meanwhile, wound its ridge-lined track up and around its odd bulk, working up towards the lip of the hollow above. Unlike the cold dirt of the plain, where only stunted grasses managed to grow, the stone of the mountain was warm underfoot and even provided shelter enough in crooks and clefts for twisted shrubs and the occasional petrified tree. As Archaon advanced, he saw chimera take to the wing from the heights ahead and swarms of monstrous eyes blinking malevolence from the darkness of caves. The predators did not seem to want a re-match and instead withdrew or fled to the safety of the skies.

As they hiked up the sweeping incline, winding up the fat mountain like a serpent, Archaon started to notice stains in the dirt. They were a reddish brown, and at first the Chaos warlord took them for the sites of recent kills by chimera on the mountainside. Upon closer inspection he found it to be rust blotching the mountain trail. Sporadic patches of corrosion that had stained the grit and stone. Looking about, Archaon saw that the stains were everywhere, covering the mountain like a rash. He considered the possibility of surface iron deposits or perhaps the abandoned weapons of the chimera pack victims. He knew this couldn't be the case when he came across his first blade, stabbed into the mountainside and sitting straight up in the rock.

Kneeling down, Archaon inspected the weapon, an ancient blade almost black with rust and age, eaten to a ragged shadow of its former glory and design. Walking from patch to rust-red patch, Archaon found more weaponry, also corroded and ancient. Spearheads bearing the stumps of broken shafts. Brute axes buried almost up to their withered hafts. Blades – stone-cleaving broadswords, the tapering elegance of longswords, serrated scimitars cleaved into the rock, ensorcelled swords of dark magics long dead, rusting daggers stabbed almost up to the hilt. As Archaon trudged up the trail and around, he found himself in a graveyard of such weapons. The mouldering steel of primitive butchery, bejewelled craftsmanship and hell-forged lethality.

As the incline steepened and Archaon's strides pushed him up the mountain path with greater urgency and insistence, he found other weapons buried in the mountain. Amongst the stunted forest of blades, Archaon found hundreds of metal arrow shafts, rust-shattered and buried in the rock. He also discovered the pitted surface of great cannon balls sitting half buried in the mountainside. The countless swords that sat like the grave markers of soldiers in the stone were broken up by the occasional monument – great rotting weaponry of gargantuan size that had been smashed deep into the rocky surface. Monstrous axes, hammers and the huge spiked balls of chain-trailing flails – the kinds of gargantuan weaponry that could only be wielded in the huge hands of giants, great daemons and titanic abominations. Even they had done little but crack their way into the surface of the indestructible mountain.

Archaon's mind whirled with dark thoughts. Perhaps the peak had been the site of a colossal battle? The Chaos warlord discounted the idea. The blades had not been abandoned there in the hands of rotting champions. They were embedded in the dirt and rock. Perhaps the mountain was some kind of unholy site or colossal tor? Archaon could see some brutal deity like the Blood God honoured with steel in such a way, but he couldn't find any evidence that the mountain was dedicated to an infernal patron or marked by a daemonic sigil. The mystery ate away at him as he ascended. Behind, Eins and Drei followed their master in unquestioning silence, their own blades ready to behead some hidden attacker or emboldened chimera leaping out from a cave entrance. Prince Ograx simply chewed up the mountain path with stabbing steps of his hooves, yawning with boredom.

As they approached the crowning lip of the hollow peak, Archaon became increasingly agitated. The mystery no longer occupied his thoughts. In such a sea of rust-eaten steel and myriad swords, Archaon began to worry that he would miss what he had come to the mountain to find. Vangel's daemonblade – the *Slayer of Kings*. Sword of the second Everchosen of Chaos. The steel prison in which the abominate entity U'zuhl the Skulltaker was trapped. How many of the magnificent weapons, half buried in brown-stained stone, could the *Slayer of Kings* be? As he rounded the hollow peak, Archaon's progress slowed, the Chaos warlord moving from weapon to great weapon and inspecting the rusted ruin of each blade.

With no blade matching the specific description the daemon Z'guhl had given of the *Slayer of Kings*, Archaon reached the end of the mountain trail. He felt the hollow peak above him like a dare. Without stopping for breath, the Chaos warlord mounted the rocky wall. Like the rest of the mountain, the approach to the peak was littered with embedded blades, sunk in rust-stained blotches of stone. It was as though the mountain had been attacked by some great army. He hauled himself up through the weapons. They made for excellent purchase, with the exception of age-corrupted hilts and axe hafts that simply disintegrated in the hand or under boot, showering the climber below in brown flakes. Nothing would stop Archaon, however. He felt close. He knew that the *Slayer of Kings* was on the mountain. That the treasure of Chaos was there for the taking. Ever impatient, Archaon started to leap from blade to rusted blade, heaving himself up through the forest of weapons at speed – even in his cursed plate. As his ragged cloak flapped in the rising wind like a banner or flag, Ograx the Great and the two Swords of Chaos followed. Ograx the Great found the climb a test but Eins and Drei, helped by occasional flaps of the wing, had little difficulty making the kind of ambitious jumps to which Archaon was committing himself. Moving across as well as skyward, Archaon swiftly inspected swords of particular magnificence, blades that could possibly have matched the description of the *Slayer of Kings*.

With no luck in locating the daemonblade, Archaon pulled himself up and over the precarious lip of the crater peak. Standing on the edge of a mighty hollow that ran deep down inside the fat mountain, Archaon's black heart sank. Eins, Drei and the fiend prince were beside him, dusting off their hands. The mountain was no volcano. Not even a dormant one. It was hollowed out at the core, however. It reached down through smooth lines and a mountain trail that spiralled into the depths like the one leading up the rocky exterior. Just like the exterior, the inside was covered in a rash of rusted blotches and protruding from each one was an ancient blade, axe, spear or other kind of weapon, rearing up from the stone at crooked angles. The swarm of blades gave the hollow the appearance of some great mouth, brimming with needle-like teeth.

Peering into the depths, past the madness of the swords, the chimera-haunted caves and dark crevices, Archaon's darksight picked out a light in the darkness. Although the mountain itself was no more corrupted than the endlessness of the surrounding plain, and a number of ancient swords glowed with the malevolence of time long served to the Ruinous Powers and their champions, there was but one that burned with radiance reserved for a dark blade, a daemonsword – a weapon worthy of the Everchosen of Chaos. A blade that seemed to take pride of place at the bottom of the sword-stabbed pit.

Archaon dare not wait. He was so close. He didn't even bother with the spiralling trail. Skidding down the steepness of the hollow wall, grasping the mouldering hilts of swords and crumbling hafts of axes, Archaon made his descent. Scree and grit shifted beneath his boots, making the descent a skid and slide as much as a weapon-weaving trudge. Disturbed rocks and small boulders started to bounce beside and from behind the Chaos warlord as Eins, Drei and Prince Ograx followed in their master's footsteps.

As a large rock over which Archaon had climbed became dislodged, the Chaos warlord skidded to one side – grabbing a pair of swords to stabilise his position on the steep gradient of the descent. The boulder rolled, tumbled, pranged off and over the rusted blades afflicting its path. Accelerating and bouncing, the large rock smashed into the bottom of the pit near the burning balelight of the dread blade.

Archaon felt it immediately. Building beneath his boot. A rumble. A tremble. A tremor. A quake. Soon the entire hollow was shaking with a monstrous force from deep within the mountain. Dust billowed down into the crater. Carpets of dirt, grit and loose rock shifted beneath his feet and flowed like a flood through the fixed forest of blades. Archaon tried to grab the rust-eaten shaft of a spear that protruded from the rock like the skeletal trunk of a petrified tree.

The ancient metal of the weapon just disintegrated in his gauntlets, however, and Archaon felt himself lose his footing. Skidding. Grasping. Falling. Tumbling down through the corroded weaponry that was like a spiked wall. Many blades succumbed, becoming clouds of red dust and showering fragments. Some of the finer crafted weapons were age-ravaged to blackness on the surface but still boasted good, strong steel within. These blades surprised Archaon with their resilience. The savagery of their limb-smashing, gut-wrenching impacts. Their insistent refusal to break as Archaon's armoured form clattered through them.

Hitting the bottom of the pit with a crash of plate, Archaon felt the dying rumble of the quake through his gauntlets. As it died away to a rising silence, grit and dirt still hissed down the slopes and through the blades. Small rocks and boulders bounced off the sword-barbed nest of the hollow, several thudding and shattering against Archaon. Grunting, the Chaos warlord pushed himself up. The rock had become still beneath him. The hollow was a swirling, dust-choked miasma. Behind Archaon, Prince Ograx and his Swords of Chaos completed their messy descent. Archaon held up a finger. He wanted silence. Something wasn't quite right.

He turned, grit scraping under his boot. There was movement in the murk. Chimeric predators and monstrous fusions were scrambling from their caves. Some clawed their way up and out of the hollow. Others took to the skies with the urgent beating of leathery wings. Archaon looked about. He took in the contours of the mountain hollow. The pit bottom beneath his feet. The strange quaking that had rippled through the rock. As the dust cleared, Archaon felt the bile of a bad feeling climb the back of his throat.

'This is no mountain,' he announced to the grit-skittering silence of the hollow.

As he did so, what Archaon had formerly taken for the cragginess of a hooded cave opening suddenly flickered to life. As dirt and dislodged scree rained from it, an armoured lid rose like the great stone door of an ancient temple and

Archaon and his hench-warriors were suddenly caught in the gold maelstrom of a colossal, reptilian eye. At its heart was a chasmic sliver of black – the pupil of the eye unfocused and unseeing. The Chaos warriors froze as they were bathed in golden doom, remaining still as the craggy lid made its dozy descent.

Archaon risked another glance about the hollow. Much of the centuries-accumulated dust and claw-scraped rock that had sat atop the colossal creature had fallen away in the rumbling quake of the titanic creature's disturbed movements. It was still difficult to make out through the fog of dust and the fact that Archaon was standing right in the middle of this madness. He could make out the half-buried features of a gargantuan and monstrous face. A single tusk rising like a peak of its own from a cavern-closed mouth. The winding, hollow-hugging twist of a head-sprouting horn.

The thing was impossibly huge – even for the Wastes. Like a sleeping god-monster, the fat mountain that the Chaos warriors had climbed was the abomination's slumber-curled body – its form buried in the dust and corruption of the Wastes, whipped up about it on the backs of perverse winds, twisters and Gate-flowing gales. Like some animal, it had scraped itself a colossal hollow in the rock and earth of the storm-plagued plain, raining the warp-baked material down on itself as it settled, curling itself up in the shape of a fat mountain. The hollow or crater in which Archaon and his hench-warriors were standing was the pit created at the heart of the curled beast.

The stone seemed half fossilised to the colossal creature's skin. Clefts and hollows created by the titan's curled body created the caves and shelter overhangs of which the chimera of the plain had made such good use. Archaon could now see the true flesh of the beast. A ridge running across the monstrosity's half-hidden face was in fact one of its colossal legs. What Archaon had taken for the smooth surface of a great boulder, was in fact a gargantuan claw resting across the beast's nose. The talon-foot to which the scything claw belonged had shaken loose the encrusted dust, dirt and petrified rock that had encased it to reveal the gargantuan scales, like those of a dragon. This was no dragon, however. The horns, the tusk, the scales and the dark face of the monster reminded Archaon of creatures he had fought the last time he had crossed the Wastes. Ancient abominations that were a ground-shaking, storm-bathing fusion of dragon and ogre. Mountainous titans of muscle and darkness-pledged savagery from the waist up, curse-blessed with the legs, bodies and tails of dragons.

The oldest, largest and most monstrous of their kind were called shaggoths, and Archaon had faced one such monster during the lost years of his wanderings – as a marauding warrior of Chaos – when the Wastes still had the making of him. The beast had carved up the landscape with its colossal storm-forged axes, decimating a full half of Archaon's warband and the warbands of scores of other warriors similarly fighting for their survival. The creature had almost been the end of him, but Archaon had prevailed. This monster was something else. Impossibly huge. God-tremblingly powerful. Something beyond ancient. Perhaps one of the forefathers of the abominate race. Archaon looked about at the midnight sheen of scale and the storm-scorched skin of the monstrosity's face… Krakanrok the Black.

Archaon looked across the rust-stained surface of the hollow. Krakanrok the Black. Unimaginably old and huge. All but immortal. A mountain of lightning-lashed flesh, pierced with the blades of a thousand dead warriors – the rusting steel such an insignificance to the monster that each one was like a speck of dust on a knight's suit of armour. Krakanrok did not care… But Archaon did. Stabbed into the petrified rock and sable flesh of the monstrosity's face was an ancient blade that through Archaon's eyes burned with the dark light of ruin. The benighted orb of its pommel. The age-tarnished upturns of its crossguard, giving the stone-sheathed sword the appearance of hate-bared fangs. The Chaos half-star in which the broadness of the blade was set. The eternity-encrusted rakes and sweeping gullets of the sword's warped serrations. This was the *Slayer of Kings* – of that Archaon had no doubt. It sat an abomination-blinding distance below the monster's closed eye, almost covered by the claw of the creature's taloned foot that rested across its nose.

Archaon couldn't believe what he was going to do. He could not defeat such an abominate ancient of the world with steel alone. It would be like trying to destroy a mountain, which Krakanrok had almost become. Archaon had fought for every treasure of Chaos he had so far claimed. This was not a test of steel, he decided. This was a test of nerve. Like the shimmering shadows of the Swords and Prince Ograx, snarling in silence, Archaon stood transfixed by the heart-stabbing shock of their doomed predicament. Swallowing down his dread with the bile burning the back of his throat, Archaon willed his limbs to move.

Treading lightly on the gravel, Archaon approached the impossible monster. He turned to the wraith-warriors behind him but he dare not speak for fear of waking the beast and attracting its apocalyptic attentions. Archaon pointed at the sky. Eins nodded and the two shadow-smeared warriors unfolded their wings. If Krakanrok the Black did wake, Archaon intended the winged warriors to get them off the mountain as soon as possible. To Prince Ograx, Archaon gestured towards the colossal claw, indicating with an upward motion of his armoured palms that they gently lift the thing.

The half-breed was all muscle and living metal. He stretched his neck from side to side to indicate that he was ready, but the expression of his fiend's face was one of horror and uncertainty. He may have been a daemonbreed. He may have conquered the bestial hordes of the southern continent and walked the Realms of Chaos with Archaon, his master. He had never faced something so unimaginably colossal, its mountainous flesh quaking with raw power and calamitous possibility.

As the pair slid their hands beneath the claw and slowly – so slowly – lifted it from the abominate's face, Archaon felt his arms burn. He felt his bones groan. His cursed plate rattled with the effort. Ograx fared better. The prince was built like a horned barbarian from the waist up, while his cloven feet and the brazen brawn of his legs solidified below him into the unbreakable stillness of a statue. The Blood God's indomitability burned up through his veins, while the daemonic strength of his father gifted Ograx with the ability to take the titanic weight of the claw alone. Whether in service to his master or driven by the monstrous pride of the prince – an advertisement of his power and an unsubtle warning to Archaon – Ograx lifted the claw off the Chaos warlord's gauntlets. The mounds upon mounds of muscle that globed on the prince's arms began to tremble. The fruits of exertion began to bead about his horns and drip from his cheeks.

Archaon nodded to Prince Ograx and the half-breed nodded back his insistence that he could hold up the claw. Archaon was about to venture forth when he saw that lifting the weight above his head and the muscle-rippling demands of the task had burst one of the flayed-flesh straps holding Ograx's bronzed breastplate in place. The primitive piece of plate bore the rough-carved sigil of the Blood God and was more for decoration than anything else, swamped as it was by the wall of brawn that was the half-breed's chest. As the plate dangled away from the trembling demands of the prince's flesh, Archaon could see that there was another symbol burned into the flesh beneath. A searing star that seemed to scar eternal. A symbol that Archaon had seen before. On the unkillable champion at the top of the world. On the living shadows of warrior-servants long past that Archaon had fought in the Forsaken Fortress. On the Dark Master's own monstrous chest. The Ruinous Star of the Herald. The Dark Star of Be'lakor.

Archaon stopped and stared at the betrayal that burned in his champion's flesh. A creature whose bestial nature and infernal heritage Archaon had long despised. A half-breed who had disappointed and impressed him in equal measure.

A warrior that Archaon had placed at the head of his horde all the same and employed as his brutal enforcer. Prince Ograx – a shadow placed pawn of the Dark Master. A blunt tool with a deft purpose. The creature's mindless violence putting it beyond the shadowy veil of suspicion. A traitor-beast slipped unsuspectingly into Archaon's brutal trust.

Perhaps Ograx had been Be'lakor's long before they met on the field of battle. Perhaps the daemon had worked the prince's infernal father or claimed Ograx in the eternity of madness between the Chaos Gates. Perhaps the Dark Master had recruited Ograx to his cause the day before they set off for the mountain. Archaon would never know.

The glazed quiver of the prince's own eyes came down from the claw he was holding above his head. Archaon had not moved and this had attracted the half-fiend's attention, knowing not how long he could bear the weight on his own. When he found Archaon staring at the exposed sigil on his chest, Ograx glared at him. The fiend's face was a mask of contortions. Archaon didn't care. Whether Ograx had been placed by Be'lakor to ensure success in Archaon's quest or whether the prince was waiting for the right time to murder him and claim his dark treasures for himself was irrelevant. He would have been or would be the Dark Master's willing puppet.

Archaon knew he had a battle coming. Another desperate fight against the monstrous Ograx, this time to the death. At that moment, standing on the cusp of calamity, there was nothing to be done: no words or blows to be exchanged. They were caught in the dire nature of their circumstances.

Archaon took several steps towards the abominate face of Krakanrok the Black. Watching the craggy lid for any signs that it might rise on the golden sun of the titan's gaze, the Chaos warlord reached out his gauntlet. The huge blade had spent a Waste-warped eternity buried in the fearful flesh of living catastrophe. It hungered to be held once more. To be wielded by one who could end the world with its talents. Dust fell from its two-handed hilt. Its crossguard rattled.

Spidery cracks felt their way through the petrification of its pommel-orb. Its broad blade seemed to shift slightly in its sheath of flesh and stone, edging fitfully towards Archaon's outstretched fingers.

As Archaon felt the ghost of a quake beneath his boots, he grabbed hold of the blade's hilt. Like some kind of horrific infant, the weapon seemed to be soothed by the action and the rattling subsided. With it the monstrous intention of movement died in the flesh upon which Archaon was standing. While the daemonblade seemed soothed by the black-hearted touch of a warrior of Chaos such as Archaon and the dread violence he intended with the weapon, Archaon felt something himself in the ancient blade. The horrific thing seemed to grip back – as though the sword wielded him as much as he intended to wield it. Archaon closed his eyes for a moment and enjoyed the bloody passions that raced through his heart. He fell through visions of slaughter. Tidal waves of blood crashed over him. Death and its dealing became his only desire.

Gripping the sword, Archaon's gauntlet creaked about the age-ravaged hilt. He felt as if he could pulverise the ancient metal in his hand. Archaon forced his eyes open. He breathed deep and wished a cold calm down through his being. The monstrous being in the blade would not have its bloody way with his soul. The *Slayer of Kings* would be his, not him the goreslave of U'zuhl the Skulltaker. With a snarl, the danger of his circumstances returned. Krakanrok the Black. Prince Ograx. The fifth treasure of Chaos.

Tensing his arm, Archaon pulled the daemonblade from where it had sat for centuries – buried in rock and abominate flesh. The stone sheath refused to release its prize at first but with some teeth-gritted insistence, Archaon felt the blade rumble from its resting place. With a murderous thrill that shot through his soul like a battlefield victory, Archaon held the *Slayer of Kings* up to the sky. To his relief, there had been no reaction from the monster-mountain upon which he was standing. The ancient wound inflicted by such a weapon – even a daemonblade – would have been nothing to the father of the dragon ogre race, whose flesh and scale were as ageless as they were immortal, whose mighty soul would have been a lightning storm eternal.

Archaon admired the blade. It was encrusted with age, like a thing fossilised and primordial. Even through the petrified rock and solidified wyrdstone, Archaon could feel its power. They would forge a mighty partnership. He would feed the blade what it desired – the soulfire of warrior victims, taken from them in the hot doom of defeat. The *Slayer of Kings*, in turn, would serve the Everchosen of Chaos once more. It would be Archaon's ambassador of darkness. The everlasting darkness he would bring to foes defeated and the apocalyptic end he would visit upon the world. As he held the crooks and crags of the magnificent blade to the sky and considered the horrific daemonic force enslaved in steel, he thought of his soul-pledged promise to Z'guhl, the Skullreaper, the Herald of Hate, the Crimson Doom. How Archaon had promised to set the blade's daemon free not only to honour his compact with Z'guhl but also so Z'guhl could honour his compact with his infernal brother. Archaon smiled behind the skull-plate of his helm.

'I will set you free, mighty daemon,' Archaon said, half to himself. 'Slayer in steel. Spiller of blood. Feaster of souls. Fury of the razor's edge… But not today.'

The sword's reaction was instantaneous. Like a rage building, the hilt grew hot through Archaon's gauntlet. It trembled in his grip. Cracks felt their way through the petrified stone and encrustation before suddenly – with a forge flash and the whoosh of a freshly stoked furnace – the material exploded. Archaon turned his helm and was showered with shards of wyrdstone and fragments of rock that pranged off his plate. When he turned back, he found the wonder of the daemonblade in his hand. The *Slayer of Kings*. The rage that coursed through the steel prison of the blade bathed Archaon in its hellish radiance. The barbs and curves of the blade's cutting edge glowed almost to transparency, while the Chaos half-star crackled furiously with the infernal energies and bindings that held U'zuhl, the Skulltaker of Khorne in service to the blade and the blade in service to the warrior brave enough to inflict its rage upon the world. The steel fangs of the crossguard, thirsting for blood. The hilt that burned in the hand. The pommel-orb, whose smooth, dark crystal writhed with the baleful yellow fury of U'zuhl's eye, looking down on Archaon with abyssal hatred. Then he heard it. Like a blade ringing off another, Archaon heard the daemonsword's steel sing. He felt the sword throb and its blade resonate. The terrible sound built, filling Archaon's heart with a ghostly dread and turning his stomach. As the daemon's sufferings built to a steel shriek – its eternal thirst for blood, its bottomless hunger for souls, its infernal fury to be free – Archaon understood the danger that they were all in.

Looking from the dread magnificence of the screaming blade to the cragged eyelid of Krakanrok the Black, the Chaos warlord realised what the daemonblade was doing. If Archaon would not set U'zuhl free then he would be destroyed – and since U'zuhl could not turn the service of the blade upon he that it served, the daemon would need to stoke the thunderous wrath of an awoken titan. Archaon watched as the rock-encrusted lid rose once more, flickering before the golden sun of a single eye behind. He felt the mountain beneath him stir. Tremble. Quake.

At first, Archaon did not know what to do. The dire magnitude of their circumstance was overwhelming. The daemon in the blade would shriek its fury and hunger until the gargantuan father of dragon ogres, awoken from an aeons-long slumber, effortlessly destroyed them all in his thunder-fuelled anger. The bloody solution was accomplished before Archaon had barely thought it through. With the daemonsword bleeding its wrath into Archaon through the warm metal of his gauntlet, his mind burned with necessity while his arm seethed with bloodthirsty action. Ograx the Great, visibly shaking under the weight of Krakanrok the Black's colossal claw, knew the problem's solution a mere second before it was brutally carried out. Leaning forward under his monstrous burden, Prince Ograx roared his defiance, that of his daemonic father and that of his bloody god. Archaon whipped the *Slayer of Kings* around to present it like the tail of a scorpion. Fury smoked from the blade, burning on the air and making the weight of the broad blade a nothing in Archaon's hand.

Thrusting the daemonblade forward with merciless force, Archaon rammed the *Slayer of Kings* into Ograx's open mouth, down his throat and into the monstrously muscular torso of the half-breed. With the blade up to the fanged crossguard in its scabbard of butchered flesh, the shrieking of the imprisoned daemon died on the wind. The hate-hot blade bubbled in the bloody ruin of Ograx the Great's body, while the entity U'zuhl feasted on the soulfire of the Blood God's champion – the rich brutality of his death and the countless deaths for which the half-breed was responsible. Ograx might not have been a king, but he was a prince, and the slaughter-filled barbarity of his existence seemed to satisfy the steel of the Slayer.

As Ograx faltered, Archaon was there to take the burden of Krakanrok's mighty claw. Eins joined him, while Drei grabbed the toppling half-breed before he crashed to the ground. The half-breed was dead. Far from displeasing Khorne, his sudden and violent death honoured the Blood God. His crashing corpse or the dislodging of the daemonblade might have cost them still in waking the father of dragon ogres, however, had the wraith-warrior not reached Ograx in time. Combined, Archaon and Eins did not have the strength of the Blood God's champion and juddered down to their knees under the weight, before laying the claw back across Krakanrok's abominate face with as much arm-trembling care as they could manage.

From the rocky floor, Archaon watched the lid of the monstrous eye droop back down, eclipsing the golden sun behind it. After a few heart-thumping twitches, the abhorrent creature returned to its eternal slumber. Archaon's pauldrons slumped. The Chaos warlord shook his head slowly from side to side. The shimmering shadows of Eins and Drei simply waited on their master's instruction. As Archaon got to his feet, he looked down at the corpse of Ograx – his face fixed in an expression of pure horror, mouth agape and brimming with the blood in which the *Slayer of Kings* snugly sat. Archaon wouldn't risk unsheathing the sword from its cadaver-scabbard until he was very far from the lonely mountain. Walking past the Swords of Chaos he nodded at Prince Ograx. Eins and Drei clasped the corpse, one under each arm, intending to drag the daemon prince between them, the crossguard, hilt and pommel-orb protruding from the half-breed's open mouth and skewered head.

'Let's get the hell out of here,' Archaon announced, walking on ahead. As Eins and Drei dragged Prince Ograx and the daemonsword behind their master, Archaon said, 'All of us.'

CHAPTER XIV

*'Now shall ye assay, he said unto Alderiq.
And anon young Alderiq fought for all he
was worth, therewithal the knight emerged
victorious, presenting the head of the
invader beast, for he loved this land, its
kingdom and its people highborn and low
and would not see it polluted by things
unfit for existence.'*

– Roland Rancourt – *Le Morte D'Alderiq*,
Chapter IV: Of the First War and
how King Alderiq won the field

The Marches of Brilloinne
The Bretonnian Coast
Jour de Roi IC 2518

Archaon felt the galleon roll with the storm. He had given up the cavernous darkness of the great cabin to Giselle but found himself returning there often. To be alone with his thoughts. With the accusatory silence. To be alone with her.

The world had indeed turned. The years had passed and taken their inevitable toll. Even the warlords of Chaos suffered the ravaging attentions of time. The girl was little more than an emaciated bag of bones now. A wasted, skeletal wight of a girl, whose soft skin was stretched to transparency across the sharpness of her bones. A horror to behold, rippling with ribs and spine. She had not the miserable strength to lift herself from the bunk and furs. She was a cursed invalid that Archaon kept alive for his own selfish reasons. Without a mouth, the girl could not even scream away her sufferings. Most of the time she simply lay there, still, like a cadaver in an ancient tomb. The lanterns that swung and creaked with the pitch of the vessel were kept low and the windows of the great cabin boarded up. For Archaon it was a ghoulish retreat.

Like a flagellant – like Gorst – returning to the chain or whip for purification and self-remonstration, he would stand before Giselle to remind himself of what he had done. He had lived a long life of blood, fear and darkness. His victims. His dire acts. His dread and unsung achievements. His world-shaking atrocities. These all seemed lost to a life half remembered. It was in the girl that he found the true horror of his Ruinous existence. It was a daily test. A punishment he subjected himself to for his many failures. His failure of an innocent young girl. The failure of the abyssal love that even now he somehow felt for her. The failure of his dark quest to find the final treasure of Chaos – the Crown of Domination – and end the living nightmare all the faster.

The years of his life had ebbed away in search of a treasure it had taken longer to find than all of the others combined – and every day he returned to Giselle to look upon her terrible beauty. She was like a mirror in which Archaon saw the terrible things he had done. He had brought a terror to the world. He had massacred with indifference. In the wretched suffering of this girl eternal, this memory of his past that would not die – when he had been a better man – Archaon came to know the true measure of his darkness.

He lay with her nightly. Archaon didn't sleep. Not any more. He just sat there on the bunk, amid perfumed silks and rich furs stripped from the palaces of the mighty and the dead. Holding her. Holding her to him. Holding the blade of a dagger to her throat. He felt her willing him on. Begging him without words to do what he had failed to do many years before. When they had shared a bed and each other it had been Giselle's turn to fail him. Fail to slide the dagger across his throat. Fail to release him from the suffering of a dark existence as he nightly failed her.

He knew it wasn't love that stayed his hand. The obsidian of his heart, that sat heavy and useless in his chest, was beyond such things. Giselle had been his prisoner. A slave to his physical needs and her own in the long, dark night at the top of the world. He had inflicted upon her the unspeakable perversions of his foes, enemies who wished to wound him through her. He had visited upon her the savagery of the Southern Wastes, the madness of the Northern Wastes and the living hell that was the Realm of Chaos inbetween – where daemons stalked your soul and Dark Gods all but destroyed you with their obliterate gaze. And now, an endless search through faraway lands for treasures that refused to give themselves up. She was a slave again. Slave to a need he had for her that was beyond words or physical expression. Prisoner within the agonies of skin, bone and withered muscle that would not obey. When Archaon looked on Giselle, he knew he was a monster.

He heard the rattle of his plate. He watched the shimmering glint of the lantern's low and ghoulish light off the dagger's blade. His face was a wretched snarl behind the skull of his helm. Black tears of will defied had left the stain of their progress down one side of his face. He sat behind her on the bunk, amid the mound of furs. He had Giselle's horror in his armoured embrace. His blade was at her throat. It would take nothing. Nothing. He heard the slightest of murmurs issue from the misery of the girl's form. The slightest of movements as Giselle's skeletal touch pulled at the cold metal of his arm. He wanted to release her from torment. To give her what she desired. What *she* needed. The dark will wasn't there, however. A roar built within Archaon's chest. A fury that wracked his being as he leant his head and horned helm back to bellow his withering rage to the cabin ceiling. To the storm-churned sky. To gods that would not listen and did not care.

The blade drifted from Giselle's throat. Archaon let it tumble into the furs. Pushing her gently away, he got up off the bunk and walked away, becoming one with the darkness of the cabin. Giselle slipped back into the furs, tears of her own glistening across eyes that caught the lantern light. She had not even the strength to turn over and bury her head in the covers. From the shadows he watched the girl. Her suffering and torment as she tried to tremble the emaciated horror of a hand down the furs towards the knife. To pick it up and to use the blade... on herself. Archaon's heart thumped its encouragement. He wished she could do it. Save herself. As the skeletal fingers plucked gently at the dagger, he saw the hand shake and then fall. Giselle could barely life the hand, let alone the blade she intended to clasp within it. Archaon turned away. He could bear to look on her no more.

Closing the archway door to the great cabin behind him he found Zwei and Drei standing silent, like sentries, either side of the entrance. In the chart room, Archaon spread the fingers of his gauntlets and leant against the dark altar. It was covered with Ruinous symbols and the implacable illustrations of daemons. Over these were laid maps, charts and twisted instruments. Ancient books and dusty grimoires were stacked about the room, while a lantern swung above the altar, throwing the chart room in a fiendish light.

There was a lifetime of study in the chart room and the Chaos warlord had spent many lost hours searching history, the quill-scratched ramblings of mad men, ancient stone tablets and mythical maps for clues to the location of the final treasure of Chaos.

On the shattered coast of the Northern Wastes, Archaon's colossal army had searched for vessels to transport their number. For months the horde camped out on the storm-lashed coast, taking raiders and Norscan longships where they could. These Archaon despatched with false word of a thousand slaves stranded on the coast following a shipwreck of a slaver fleet.

The Chaos seas spat out a number of greedy opportunists, which Archaon's hidden horde enslaved since the number of their vessels were unsuitable to their needs. A month later, the ocean offered up a legend. Captain Kurdogoli Darghouth. The Devil of Araby. The Dread of the Infidels. The Cloven Captain of Kalabad. Darghouth had come a long way since his days as a merciless slaver and then brutal corsair on the Pirate Coast. Some said his appetite for human flesh extended beyond trading and stealing such cargoes and that he would select the finest specimens to be roasted for his table. Estalians. Tileans. Even the occasional dwarf. As wealth lost its appeal and the dread of victim-nations became Darghouth's guiding star, the pirate gave up the harsh strictures of his one god for the freedom of a pantheon of Ruinous admirers. Plying the coasts of Estalia, Tilea, the Pirate Principality and the Border Princes, the Cloven Captain amassed a fleet of gun-toting galleons, as well as carracks and caravels loaded with cannibal crew.

Some he took with ease on trade routes he knew all too well. Others were warships sent to deal with the piratical threat he presented. All failed. Darghouth's attack fleet was heralded by a swarm of smaller craft, including lanteen-masted cogs and armed pinnaces. Behind these trailed hulks that carried victims by the hundreds – to be traded, eaten or sacrificed to the Dark Gods at Kurdogoli Darghouth's bestial whim.

His hunger for suffering and destruction took him into cooler climes where he found new prey in Bretonnian shipping and the great ships of the Empire. Farther north he found the Chaos seas replete with raiders, madmen and warriors of the Dark Gods. In Archaon, the Cloven Captain met his match. Playing the part of the stranded slaves, Archaon allowed himself and his horde to be transported over to the pirate captain's fleet before staging a bloodbath of a mutiny. Sparing Kurdogoli Darghouth and some of his most gifted cannibal captains, Archaon had offered them continued service to the Dark Gods in his name or the fate of being fed to his monstrosities. Darghouth and his captains had chosen life over death. To confirm that they had made the correct choice, Archaon gave them as their first responsibility the transport of Archaon's monsters and abominations over to the fleet's hulks with the horde's mounts, wagons and siege engines.

With a Chaos fleet once more at his command, Archaon left the execution of his orders to trusted lieutenants spread throughout the armada, which sailed like a black plague south from the berg-clashing coast of the Wastes. Navigation, the running of the flagship and communication through the fleet he left to the Cloven Captain. Archaon, in turn, divided his time between study on the long ocean voyages and savagery upon reaching his destinations. Each one was either a possible resting place of the Ruinous Crown of Domination, or of other illuminating treasures, ancient texts or individuals that delivered to Archaon with their dying breath further clues to the crown's location. Months. Years. Decades came and went in fruitless search for the treasure. What felt like a doomed quest to some of Darghouth's cannibal captains and crew, captured from vessels and flotillas that ran foul of Archaon's dark armada, was nothing to Archaon and his horde, who had endured eternities in the Realm of Chaos.

There were mutinies, of course, shore-sent forces that failed to return. Splinter flotillas that attempted to leave the fleet. Archaon had learned much since the last time he had commanded idle warriors on the high seas. He trusted almost no one and although he was infrequently seen, his authority was felt in the brutal recapture, horrific torture, execution and macabre decoration of his vessels with the bones and body parts of those that lacked the fear, dark faith and common sense to be loyal.

For almost a century, Archaon held the world quivering in the palm of his gauntlet as his vast fleet and the thousands upon thousands of Chaos warriors under his monstrous leadership circumslaughtered the globe. In the Kraken Sea the longships and raiders that tormented the north were decimated by Archaon's fleet – so much so that the mist-shrouded kingdom of Albion and the Sea of Claws saw no Norscan raids or invasions for a year. For months Archaon's ships haunted chill Naggaroth, razing the coastline of the Sea of Malice and destroying swarms of druchii reavers. For the inscriptions on the mighty monoliths that stood ancient and untouched in the east of Naggaroth, Archaon brought blood and fire to the dreadlords of the Witch-King's coastal strongholds.

Sailing east, Archaon's fleet met the miserable flotillas of other damned souls out in the desolation of the endless Great Ocean. Plaguefleets of the low races and the hellships of Chaos captains, who wished – like Archaon – to bring terror to the world. Some, like the Bloodships of Bjornvar the Berserker, went to the bottom of the ocean with their lack of reason. Others – upon sighting a horizon blotched with the black sails of the dark armada – fell into formation behind the flagship with signalled obedience. No shots were fired and no lives were lost. Souls were another matter entirely.

Rounding the squall-lashed cape of the Southlands, Archaon almost lost half of his fleet to the cyclonic fury of an unnatural storm that swept up out of the Southern Wastes. The Sea of Dread, conversely, killed with calmness as for months the fleet saw not a breath of wind. Archaon's army suffered under the blaze of the unrelenting sun and were forced to resort to blood-letting slaves to survive the ravages and madness of thirst. When they did reach land, the horrors of disease waited for their number on the foetid Mangrove Coast. Seeing virtue in a violent distraction, Archaon visited the frustrations of his followers and the wrath of his fleet on the stilt cities of Clan Festerlingus. The skaven of the south with their sun-bleached fur and savagery poured from the swamps and swarmed the shallows, while verminships and coastal clanfleets of neighbouring infestations – to which word had been sent – hit Archaon's anchored armada from both the north and the south. With a fleet becalmed and an army weakened by equatorial fevers and rat-bred pestilence, Archaon eventually ordered his armada north, leaving the skaven with their stinking mangrove kingdoms.

Plundering the city ruins in the Lands of the Dead, Archaon honoured the Dark Gods at several Chaos shrines half swallowed by the sands. Going in search of ancient scrolls and the Crown of Domination itself, Archaon was disappointed, as he had been a hundred times before, to find that the Straits of Nagash and skeletal civilisations that plagued the bordering lands with their unlife did not hold the secrets to his lost treasure.

Negotiating the clashing cliffs of the Gates of Calith, where the ancient Hinterlands of Khuresh threatened to reach out and touch the polluted lands of the southern continent, Archaon took his fleet to the legendary Lost Isles, hoping to learn more of the Crown of Domination. There his army laid siege to the ancient High Elf fortress colony of Tor Elithis, only to find that it had long succumbed to daemons of the Southern Wastes who held it as their own.

As they travelled, Archaon discovered that he was being hunted. The Dragon Emperor of Grand Cathay had heard of Archaon's coming. Spies had reported the warlord's decimation of coastal kingdoms of the Ind and the emperor had been advised to have his own amassed armada of celestial vessels meet Archaon in battle out on the Far Sea, away from the Cathayan coast. It was a colossal battle, fought on the sun-blushed emptiness of open water. Archaon never got the chance to meet the Dragon Emperor's admiral, although he wished he had. Fighting for days, through the equatorial heat of the sun and the star-lit depths of night, both fleets eventually broke off the engagement. Although Archaon's hordes and airborne monstrosities claimed many celestial sons and war-junks of the enemy fleet, the impregnable turtleships of the armada smashed through Archaon's formations and celestial sorcery claimed many Ruinous warriors. A change in the wind made further engagement difficult and while Archaon hunted for the Dragon Emperor's fleet, he never saw their exotic vessels again.

Re-fitting his fleet in the shattered lands off the coast of the New World, Archaon's fleet rounded Lustria to sack the scaled civilisations of the Fire Islands, not for their gold but for the treasure of their ancient knowledge. Finding himself once more on the expanse of the Great Ocean, Archaon decided upon returning to the Old World, with its delusions of enlightenment and the sweet taint of ancient corruption. He became convinced that finding the treasures of Chaos everywhere but the Old World meant that it was almost certain to be nestling somewhere on the edge of civilised darkness. Having spent decades bringing hell to the other side of the world, Archaon found himself strangely pulled towards his homeland and its neighbouring nations. His blade ached for the blood of pompous fools and the crushed will of the underclasses upon which they had always ridden high. Dark dreams drew him north. The taunts of daemons and sorcerous whisperings.

It had been lifetimes since he had set foot in such a land. He had left the Empire a formidable warrior. His time in the Wastes and the abyssal realm had crafted him into an almighty champion of darkness, exalted to demi-godhood by the Ruinous treasures in his possession. The decades on the far side of the world had done more than temper the living weapon he had become. With age, study and experience had come the rewards of merciless leadership. He was not just a dark warrior at the head of a fractious mob, the first among equals. He was not a brutal conqueror leading a bestial horde into bloodshed. He was a warlord of consummate skill. He had held a great Chaos host together – which ordinarily would have torn itself apart along divisions of Ruinous worship and individual allegiance – through strategy, cold supremacy and the ruthless force of his dread will. He had become a worthy leader of the dark things of the world, commanding the corrupt hearts of mortal monstrosities and inspiring in his champions and lieutenants a reverence usually reserved for their daemonic overlords. His armada was doom sweeping in from the darkness of the open ocean. His army of pantheon-pledged champions and veteran Chaos warriors had been hewn from calamity into a force of darkness undivided. An abominate army of ruin that shook the world.

As he sailed north to his destiny, Archaon's fleet met strange ironclad vessels that belched smoke and fire in the waters of the Black Gulf and made the seaport beardlings of Barak Varr pay in torture-sought knowledge and blood. Archaon's dark armada all but wiped out the pirate fleets of Sartosa and sacked Tilean cities, ransacking libraries and private collections of antiquities in search of answers to dread questions. He burned an Estalian armada of carracks and caravels at anchor at Magritta before lighting up the coastal kingdoms of the west. An attempt to make back out to sea was frustrated by storms that swallowed the dark warlord's own and succeeded in smashing the armada up along the shores of Bretonnia. The bad weather held his great swarm of black ships to the coastline along the Sea of Claws. With his monstrous armada barely holding off the rocky shores and the glowering moonlight of Morrslieb dusting the distant Marches of Couronne with its dread attentions, Archaon became suddenly aware of an intrusion in his dark thoughts.

Archaon…

The warlord looked up from the altar, with its maps and scrolls.

Archaon… Chosen of the Ruinous Gods. Pawn of the Harbinger. Hear me.

As Archaon left the chart room, he hauled himself up the companionway ladder with his cloak trailing him. Zwei and Drei followed like shadowy sentinels.

Brother darkness. We are bearers of his mark both…

'Lord Master on the deck,' a Chaos warrior called from

his sentry position on the ladder archway. Archaon looked back to see Eins – the wraith-warrior was standing against the poop deck rail, his wings globed to protect him from the storm. Archaon always had Eins on deck when he wasn't. He might have left command of the flagship and coordination of the armada and its captains to Kurdogoli Darghouth, but Archaon left Eins as his trusted eyes on the deck. The Sword of Chaos nodded his head at Archaon who strode out towards the helm.

The great black deck of the galleon rolled with the churn of the seas. Above, the clouds billowed and flashed with the shore-smashing storm. Rain and salty droplets from waves crashing about the flagship's tall, port-sealed sides pattered across Archaon's dark plate. The storm ruffled his furs and tugged at his cloak.

The flagship had been a captured Estalian battle galleon that the Cloven Captain had re-named the *Perdición* in honour of his new master. Kurdogoli Darghouth had confided to Archaon that it was considered, even among his own wretches, bad luck to re-name a ship but the warlord had told him that where they were going, bad luck was the least of their worries. Archaon had added that they would be bad luck indeed to any vessel falling within the scope of their spyglasses.

The Cloven Captain was where Archaon always found him – at the Ruinous Star of the *Perdición*'s great wheel. A dark-skinned southerner stood aside at the rhythmic rattle of Archaon's approach and bowed. The buds of horns ruined the shiny perfection of his blade-shaved head, while his face jangled with hoops, jewellery and gold. His chest was tattooed with maps of his many journeys and his bulging arms bore the mangled flesh of scar tallies. He had been one of Darghouth's former slavers, now serving as the captain's enforcer and boatswain on board the flagship. On the rare occasions Kurdogoli Darghouth left the wheel of his dark ship, he also doubled as helmsman. For now his great hands were employed in holding the Cloven Captain's spyglass and sack of spiced wine.

Kurdogoli Darghouth was a breed apart, even for the cannibal wretches that crewed his vessels. Magnificent of black beard and moustache, the Kalabadian tied the lustrous lengths of his midnight mane in a turban. A boat cloak rolled off his powerful shoulders and down the length of his stallion's back, having the torso of a man but the body, legs and tail of a horse. The Cloven Captain's hooves clopped on the deck as he re-aligned himself to the pitch of the *Perdición* – although having four legs instead of two, the Ruin-blessed Darghouth coped with this better than most. Archaon caught the glint of the captain's mighty scimitar – the broad curve of its monstrous blade half sheathed to the side of the Cloven Captain's muscular flank.

Darghouth said nothing as Archaon approached the wheel, too busy with keeping the *Perdición* and Archaon's dark armada off the Bretonnian rocks. Snatching the spyglass out of the southerner's hand and slipping it in his belt, Archaon stepped up on the rail and leapt for the rigging. Scrambling up for the lines, Archaon hauled himself up through the shrouds and ratlines as bonnets and sails buffeted about the towering main mast. The effort tore at old injuries and the tenderness of muscle. Stone-laced bones ached with the jarring ascent. Archaon might have benefitted from the gifts of the Dark Gods – an enhanced body, an ever-keen mind and an indomitable will. He might have lived beyond his years, the warping powers of Chaos helping him to resist the ravages of old age. He hurt like any other warrior of half his age, however. Bones grated in their sockets. Muscles burned for the youth they had once known.

The higher Archaon climbed, the greater the forces threatening to tear his armoured form from its purchase. The wind dragged him back and forth with a terrible will, while his gauntlets slipped on the wet, swollen ropes of the rigging.

Archaon's mind ached with the intrusion once more.

You have come far, exalted one. Now come to me and learn what the Dark Master wants for us.

With a snarl, Archaon leapt for the highest of the main mast's yards and hauled himself up. Holding on to the tapering trunk of the mainmast, Archaon felt the ship move below him, rolling through the storm-whipped waves and leaning over into the wind. He suddenly realised that he was not alone. In the bone basket of the crow's nest, Archaon saw Gorst's wretched form, quietly rusting away in his chains and head-cage. The flagellant had exchanged the whip for the lash of the wind and the freezing rain.

Anchoring himself to the shuddering mast with a leg and an arm, Archaon aimed the spyglass about the battle galleon. Behind the flagship, with the Ruinous Star of its shredded pennant whipping with the wind, Archaon could see the countless ships of his fleet rounding the long shore spit of the curving Bretonnian coastline. Vessels of every exotic designation sailed in the fleet. In the main, the Cloven Captain favoured Old World designs over equatorial craft, the complexities of vessels sailed by the elder races or indeed the war-dhows, xebecs and galliots of his own pirate coast. Bone-lined carracks and spiked caravels swarmed with smaller cogs and storm-battered pinnaces, while towering galleons of black sail and fat hulks formed the trailing backbone of the armada.

Swinging slowly about the wet wood of the mast, Archaon turned the spyglass south, in the direction the fleet was heading. Squinting through the storm, Archaon could see the torches of distant Marienburg and the lantern-lights of fat merchant vessels moving hurriedly into the colossal port and out of the storm. Lightning flashed above the city, giving Archaon the momentary impression of a forest of masts belonging to the anchored fleets and vessels of the port, poking up above the tile and thatch of roofs.

Archaon edged around. As he did Gorst reached out for the warlord, fearful of his master falling. The voice was suddenly there again. A powerful presence that cut through his thoughts and echoed about his mind.

The history of days to come knows Archaon as the Everchosen of

Chaos. It knows me as the Curseling. As the Twisted Twin. I offer you the most twisted of all things, chosen one. I offer you the truth.

Archaon scanned the rocky cliffs of the Bretonnian coastline. A benighted realm, cast by the storm and the balelight of Morrslieb breaking periodically through the cloud, in different shades of glowering darkness. Then he saw it. A figure on the cliffs. A tall figure standing in the haze of a thick mist. Under Morrslieb's gaze and with the spuming mist lit by sporadic flashes of lightning, the ghostly shape assumed the eerie appearance of some twisted phantom.

Pulling the spyglass away from his good eye, Archaon drew upon the Eye of Sheerian set in his helm. Cutting through the mist, the tendrils of which swirled about the cliff like the serpentine embrace of a hydra, the Eye granted Archaon a vision of the figure. It was the Curseling from his dreams. The Twisted Twin that had spoken to him through some sorcerous means.

A Tzeentchian fusion, the warrior-twin wore the gleaming plate and scalemail of his calling. His armour ached with sigils sacred to the Great Changer. An ensorcelled blade sat in a scabbard on his hip, while the spiked length of a flail hung from a chain on his belt. A matching cloak snaked about the brute warrior, held in place by a colossal shoulder spike. The other arm, bereft of plate, bulged with muscle and pulled the cloak tight about it. Sprouting from the same shoulder was the horror of the sorcerer twin. A thing of squirming, worm-like horridness. No eyes. No ears. Nothing but a needle-toothed mouth that whispered into the helm of its warrior-twin. A mane of feathers ran down its back, while in one long-fingered hand of a spindly arm, the sorcerer thing held a staff. The headpiece of the staff was a Tzeentchian eye, but within that burned the Ruinous Star of Be'lakor, the Dark Master. Archaon's lip curled. Unlike the hulk Gangryss, unlike Ograx the Great, the Curseling was not hiding his allegiance. The headpiece dribbled a strange, sorcerous smoke that writhed about the Curseling, settling into a haze that washed over the cliff edge.

Archaon thought on the sorcerer's invitation. His memory of him from dark dreams and his dramatic appearance on the cliff. Here. Now.

'All stop!' Archaon roared down from the crosstrees. As the Chaos warlord began to clamber down through the rigging, Gorst watching him as he went, he felt the *Perdición* answer. 'Drop anchor!' Archaon added as he snatched a line and leapt from the shrouds, the weight of his stone-laced bones and cursed plate taking him swiftly to the black deck.

'All stop, master,' Kurdogoli Darghouth told him, his hooves clattering on the deck as he twisted and turned at the wheel, giving orders for signal flags to be hauled up, ordering the dark armada to fall into position and hold a storm-battered station on the cliff. It was not an ideal location for such a request but neither Darghouth nor any of his Ruinous captains were going to argue with an order issued from Archaon's own lips. 'Lower the launch,' Archaon barked. 'I'm going ashore.'

'Lower the launch, aye,' the Cloven Captain echoed, before adding a snort and a rattle of the lips. Archaon threw the dark-skinned boatswain his spyglass before the Ruinous thug went off to whip a crew together for the launch and have the boat lowered down the towering side of the galleon.

'Going ashore. In this?' a cracked voice barely managed above the storm. Archaon saw the daemon sorcerer Sheerian hobble with difficulty across the pitching deck on his bone staff. His gift of youth regained had been spent in the service of Archaon and so he was a spot-livered ancient once more.

'I'm not afraid of a little water,' Archaon told him.

'That's not a little water,' Sheerian returned. 'It's a lot of water. But that's not what bothers me.'

'The sorcerer on the cliff,' Archaon agreed. 'The Curseling.'

'His name is Vilitch,' Sheerian told his master. 'He's blessed by the Great Changer. A very powerful sorcerer. His brother unfortunate is Thomin. He's no beginner with a blade either. Do not underestimate the Twisted Twin.'

'Am I not to be underestimated?' Archaon said as the

launch was swung over the side and Zwei and Drei climbed in with the crew of slave-strongbacks and spawn.

'Of course, master,' the ancient said, 'but Vilitch is no fool. He knows this of you and invites you anyway.'

'U'zuhl thirsts,' Archaon told Sheerian, slapping his gauntlet against *Slayer of Kings*, the daemonblade sitting in a black, baroque scabbard across the Chaos warlord's back. 'He groans for the blood of weakling sorcerers. Should I feed him your soul instead?'

'What I'm saying, my most mighty lord,' Sheerian said, 'is that you are almost certainly walking into a trap.'

'I'm counting on it,' Archaon told the sorcerer, as he climbed over the bulwark and into the launch. 'The Curseling honours the Great Changer with his powers and deceit but wears the mark of the Dark Master. Perhaps his god-blessed ambition has the better of him. Like Ograx and that monstrosity at the top of the world, the Curseling seeks to serve Be'lakor through the wider pantheon and become the Everchosen of All Chaos.'

'And perhaps his hearts beat with allegiance to the Great Changer still,' Sheerian said amid the boatswain's rough calls and the launch began its juddering descent. 'There is no love lost between my Byzantine god and the Dark Master. This could be more than a trap. It could be a double cross.'

'Yes,' Archaon agreed, seeming to enjoy the prospect of action on dry land after such a long, storm-battered journey up the Bretonnian coast. 'But for whom?

Zwei sat at the front of the launch, like some kind of gargoylesque figurehead, flapping his wings at the boat's coxswain to help the strongbacks and spawn keep time with their oars. The slaves and god-blessed unfortunates had been selected for their physical strength and the powerful heaving of their arms on the oars sent the launch cutting through the stormy waves and rock-churned surf. Drei sat in the back of the launch with his master, wings outstretched like a ghoulish parasol, to protect Archaon from the worst of the weather.

As the boat crunched up on the gravel of the nearby

landing, the strongbacks and spawn hauled the launch ashore. Ordering the slaves and spawn to wait on the exposed landing, amid the crashing waves, Archaon threw himself at the wet rock of the cliff. Zwei and Drei were obliged to follow suit, the wraith-warriors batting their wings to give them the extra lift required to get their first handholds. Clawing his gauntlets at wet handholds and moss-greasy ledges like grapnels, Archaon powered up the cliffside. Jumping for purchase on the summit overhang, the Chaos warlord dangled dangerously for a few moments, his plate and the stone laced through his bones threatening to drag him to his death. Hauling his armoured form up and over the edge, Archaon allowed the insistence of an offshore breeze to ruffle through his cloak and clear the grit from where it had fallen onto his plate.

With Zwei and Drei shimmering their shadow forms into a flanking formation, Archaon marched towards the Curseling. A glow of mist swirled about its cloaked form, the crackling haze seemingly separate from the weather around it. The ghoulish flesh of the Twisted Twin made Archaon's own crawl under his plate. The warrior stood impassive, like a statue, seemingly unaware of the monstrous twin sprouting from its shoulder. All the armoured warrior knew were the sickly whisperings of his monstrous brother. Like a blind worm, Vilitch twisted and turned, its needle-like teeth gnashing at silent sorceries. When the Twisted Twin did speak, it spoke through the helm of the blank-minded warrior-twin.

'Welcome to Bretonnia, Archaon.'

'To hell with your welcome, Curseling,' Archaon told him. He gestured to the raging storm above. 'This is your doing?'

'Change is mine to wield like a sculptor his clay or artist his brush,' the Curseling said. 'A ship-enslaving storm is child's play. You should see what I can do with light and the very darkness that crafts it. Or flesh and the thoughts that drive it.'

'You Tzeentchians are all the same,' Archaon scorned. 'So in love with your sorcerous powers and fiendish intrigue. Dropping clues of doom to come into the poisonous tedium, you force me to listen to before coming to an actual point. I have scores of such sorcerers at my command. You don't impress me, creature of unnatural arts – and neither will what you have planned for me. Besides, I've never met a sorcerer I couldn't kill. Despite your talents, you all share the same weakness. My steel in your twisted flesh.'

The Curseling chuckled but Vilitch's mirth sounded stilted, proceeding as it did from the warrior-twin.

'You don't disappoint, Archaon.'

'You do,' the Chaos warlord told the sorcerer. 'You wear both the iconography of the Great Changer and Be'lakor, the Dark Master. Is it not inappropriate to wear the sigils of sworn enemies? Neither daemonic power will thank you for that, Curseling.'

'Like you, Archaon,' Vilitch said, 'I serve the interests of all Dark Powers, through reverence of the pantheon.'

'You serve only your own ambitions,' Archaon accused. 'Like all who bear the Dark Master's mark, you are driven to madness with your desire for what I already have. The treasures of Chaos.'

'All but one of the treasures, Archaon…'

'And there it is,' the Chaos warlord said. 'The bait in the trap you already close about me.' Archaon sniffed at the glowing mist that rolled and twisted about them. 'A sorcerous trap.'

'You are indeed a treat,' Vilitch told him. 'I didn't expect the dark, driven, indomitable warrior of folk songs and stories to be so entertaining.'

'A twisted mind, desirous of such treasures without earning them,' Archaon continued, 'might seek to acquire them through the promise of the last.'

'Very good, Archaon. Very good,' the Curseling said, the toothed worm-mouth of the sorcerer managing a horrid grin. 'And how might Vilitch achieve such a thing?'

'You would engage me in some fool's errand,' Archaon said. 'Some cause of common darkness which necessitates me and the might of my army. Something to put all under your sorcerous spell. Something to stack the odds firmly in your favour, since neither you nor any of your tested minions could hope to stand before me blade to blade.'

'Excellent!' the Curseling cackled, each sound seeming forced and affected through the lips of another. 'Truly, the Great Changer smiles upon you, Archaon. Now, the details.'

'Do they even matter?' Archaon said.

'Always,' the Curseling said. 'I see that I still have a little to teach you, mighty Archaon. 'A great lie – the kind that takes the lives of men, their futures, their very souls – is predicated upon the foundation of seeming truths. These truths rely on details that are an antidote to incredulity – as a life-saving potion might be to a poison – incredulity that would destroy the lie.'

'Being in your mere presence is an education, Curseling,' Archaon told the Tzeentchian. 'A repulsive one, but an education all the same.'

'Why thank you, Archaon,' the sorcerer returned, 'and I hope that when I have done with you, the pantheon will descend upon the self-importance of your soul and tear it to infinite shreds for eternity. So, the details.'

Archaon looked about the mist-swathed coastline and the darkness of the storm above.

'These are Lucus lands,' Archaon said, his half-remembered truths fielding the lie Vilitch needed him to believe. 'The coastal Marches. If my charts are correct, Brilloinne Castle is not far inland. Baron Lucus was a famous knight of legend, even when I was a child. As part of his questing he recovered many cursed items, trinkets and dark artefacts of sorcerous power, securing them in the chapel about which he built his mighty castle. I assume you want access to this chapel.'

'I couldn't have put it better myself,' the Curseling said. 'Baron Lucus is long dead but the lands belong to his grandson. While he is not half the man his grandfather was, he is wealthy and his fortifications are well maintained. He also commands the allegiance of those still loyal to his grandfather's memory, including an army of pilgrims devoted to protecting the sealed chapel's secrets.'

'You have attacked Brilloinne Castle already then?' Archaon asked.

'I led a horde of spawn – all honouring the Great Changer with their gifts,' the Curseling told him, 'but they lacked the discipline of your monstrous army as I lack your warmongering leadership, Archaon. I lost my unfortunates before the castle walls to Baron Lucus and his attendant knights.'

'So the baron is already alerted to your intentions,' Archaon stated, 'and no doubt has sent riders with word to neighbouring lords, knights oath-honoured to protect his grandfather's legacy and pilgrims sworn to secure his chapel and its dark secrets.'

'Yes…'

'And why would I do this?'

'You tell me, Archaon: why would you do this?' the Curseling asked.

'For one thing,' Archaon said, 'and one thing only. The location of the final treasure of Chaos. The Crown of Domination. But you know this already, sorcerer.'

'Let me trade you truth for truth,' Vilitch said. 'I know not where the crown you seek is, but I know one that does. Take Brilloinne Castle and its secrets for me and I will tell you where he can be found.'

'And then I shall have to gut you, I expect,' Archaon told the sorcerer, 'as you try to spring whatever feeble trap you have intended for me.'

The worm-like sorcerer's mouth formed a horrid smile.

'We are going to make such a good team,' the Twisted Twin said, 'you and I.'

CHAPTER XV

*'Where'er my eye roams
Whate'er I fail to see.
My thoughts untravell'd
Shall ever return to thee.'*

– Jouffroy, *The Pale Sisters*

*Brilloinne Castle
The Bretonnian Coast
La Fête du Lac IC 2518*

Archaon walked the battlefield in a daze. About him tendrils of glowing mist reached through the ranks of dying men. The fields of Brilloinne were red and silver with the bloodied plate of the fallen. Men of noble birth. Knights with honourable histories. The lords of the Marches. Now they suffered like their lowly subjects. In the mud. In pain. Shown no mercy. Horses got up from where the smashed bodies of their owners lay before running off through the havoc of battle. Squires screamed, going down under axe and blade as swiftly as the knightly standards they humped through the butchery. Lances shattered against hell-forged plate. Steeds shrieked and reared with sword-cleaved legs, tumbling feathered paladins from the saddle.

It was havoc.

Like the land, Archaon's mind was a mist-shrouded realm. He fought, though he knew not why. He killed out of instinct but the will wasn't truly there. The *Slayer of Kings* cut through the sorcerous fog and the crisp air of the Bretonnian morn, reflecting an infernal radiance off the silvered plate of knightly warriors about to die and armoured chargers moments from being cut in half. Swinging the fat curves and serration of the daemonic weapon about him, Archaon cleaved through the colourful shields of men-at-arms hiding behind them and the bloody gush of pilgrim mobs that seemed to run straight into the orbiting path of the blade.

Archaon's mind rang with doubts and questions. He was not some gore-clouded champion of the Blood God or some Slaaneshi deviant, living the moment by moment drive of their desires. He was Archaon. He thought for himself. And yet he could not find his way to answers. He was slaughtering. He was issuing orders. He was mounting a siege but he knew not truly why. It seemed a battle without purpose. He fought for the acquisition of knowledge, of dark treasure, to realise his destiny: he did not attack without reason like Chaos raiders sailing south in their longships. He was Archaon. He was Archaon.

Above him the walls of Brilloinne Castle reached for the dark, stormy skies of a long-fought day. The brick, beautiful in craft and pattern, formed high walls, towers and turrets. The castle was a statement of angular elegance, streaming with colourful banners and pennants, its colossal drawbridge closed before a red moat, choked with bodies. From within, Archaon could hear the agonising release of trebuchets. Gargantuan pieces of shattered masonry and castle wall were launched up into the dark sky, growing smaller, smaller, until rapidly they grew big, black and unavoidable. Hammering into the battlefield like vengeance issued from the heavens, the boulders created bloody craters of mangled flesh and armour before tumbling off through the ranks of Chaos warriors and mud-splattered knights. Ruinous armour and the polished silver plate of Bretonnian lords were equally unimpressive against such obliteration.

Archaon had ensured that his own siege engines, crafted of daemonbone, tusk and sinew gave an equally devastating account of themselves against the castle walls. For hours now, the eastern wall of Brilloinne Castle had soaked up the most appalling onslaught, with smashed sections raining dust and brick under each merciless impact. Archaon had fought his way forward through a sea of shields, spears and pot-helmed men-at-arms, leading the spiked silhouettes of Ruinous champions and dark-armoured warriors of Chaos to the castle walls precisely because he expected them to fall at any time now.

Archaon heard the crank of the drawbridge. Seeing a way into the castle, Archaon swung the *Slayer of Kings* about him. The daemon U'zuhl glowed with blood-slaked fury as Archaon scythed heads from Bretonnian shoulders, like a reaper in a field. The bodies of men-at-arms, yeomen and squires thudded to the ground, allowing Archaon to lead his Chaos warriors, his fiends, his marauders and bestial hordes on through the ranks of silver knights. Progress was slow along the banks of the body-choked moat, and was slowed further at the sudden whoosh of arrows unleashed by ranks of longbowmen firing from the castle walls. Archaon brought up the Ruinous Star of his shield defiantly towards the heavens. Zwei and Drei were with him, globing the black shadow of their wings about their master, creating with the shield a barrier that thudded and pranged with the shattered shafts of arrows.

The drawbridge boomed the rest of the way down as the castle gate vomited forth another resplendent stream of knightly riders. Surging forth with lances and shields, the silver armoured warriors urged their huge steeds on, their heraldry and surcoats a blur of colour. It was a bold move to be carried out in isolation. Lifting the shield higher above his helm and with arrows still hammering into its metal surface, Archaon cast his gaze across the battlefield. Reinforcements had arrived. A column of knights riding out of the north, fresh, immaculate and trailing banners of eye-stinging colour – no doubt despatched by lords of the Northern Marches, fearful that an invasion force might be headed their way. Turning south, Archaon saw nothing. Then, blotching out of the heavens, he saw armoured knights swooping down out of the sky. Beautiful warriors on winged pegasi, come to inspire the knights and the base-bred of Brilloinne with hope. Come to defend the dark secrets of the castle's chapel against those who would steal them.

Archaon grunted. He struck the silver helm from a knight who ran at him with a broadsword before stamping back another, crumpling his breastplate and sending the nobleman surging back into the brick-shattered castle wall. He turned to Zwei.

'Give the signal,' the Chaos warlord said. 'Bring forth *my* knights.'

Zwei launched himself into the sky to carry out his master's order. With arrows raining down about him, Archaon exchanged blows with a fat, aged knight who roared at him through his grey-threaded beard. The enchantments of the knight's glorious blade sparked off the *Slayer of Kings*. With a roar of his own, Archaon smashed down through the ancient sword with his daemonblade. As the knight looked down at the ancestral weapon, with its ensorcelled blade shattered, Archaon brought the *Slayer of Kings* back with savage force, thrusting it straight through the Bretonnian knight. As the fangs of his crossguard scraped the demolished breastplate, Archaon tore the daemonblade out of his foe, allowing the horror-stricken knight to topple forwards onto his armoured knees before taking his head.

'Jharkill!' Archaon bellowed, mulching the knight's gaunt squire and his bannerman with the flat of his irregular blade.

The malformed huntsman was not far behind. He smashed men-at-arms into muddy graves, wielding his thick tusk bow like a club before stringing the brute weapon with the length of a colossal arrow and firing it at marauder-swamped knights. As skewered steeds crashed to the ground, Chaos marauders descended upon the armoured warriors, beating them to death in their plate. 'Jharkill!' Archaon roared again, Bretonnian arrows cutting through the air about him. 'Unleash your monsters – bring this fortress down into its foundations.'

As the ogre snatched his shaman's staff from an attendant half-fiend, Archaon pushed on through the mud and clashing bodies. Killing. Decapitating. Plunging his daemonsword through armoured foes. He desperately wanted to reach the drawbridge, but it was already rising. A manfiend and a marauder savage clung to the shuddering oak of its ascending form but Archaon knew it would take more than a pair of pantheon-pledged wretches to grant his army access to the castle.

Like a force of nature, the knights riding from the castle smashed into the throngs swarming the besieged fortress. Everything was suddenly broken bones. The shrieks of the impaled. The screams of the trampled. Horses dying. Trains of bodies shot past, skewered on the lengths of lances. Walls of horseflesh, armour and colourful caparisons blurred by. Bretonnian knights were hammered from their saddles by the plate-piercing spikes of maces and flails. Presented spears and pikes went home before snapping in the hands of the infernal warriors clutching them, and both knights and their Ruinous foes went down under an avalanche of faltering steed. Chaos warriors in suits of hell-forged armour suddenly disappeared before Archaon in a cacophony of demolished plate. Blood. Metal. Everywhere.

Archaon turned to present his body shield to a magnificent knight thundering down on him with the merciless length of his lance. As the weapon punched the metal surface of the shield, Archaon locked his shoulder and pushed back. His boots skidded back through mud and bodies as the Ruinous shield, the cursed plate of Morkar and the warlord's stone-laced bones soaked up the impact. The lance began to shear, split and shatter, showering the area with splinters. As Archaon's boots ground to a half-buried halt, he felt the steed slam into the shield. Archaon surged back through the throngs of clashing warriors, barrelling dark knights and their Bretonnian opponents out of his path. When he came to a stop once more, Archaon felt the armoured rider leave the saddle and sail over his head. Pushing the steed back, Archaon came out from behind the shield to see that the spike in its centre had gored the warhorse. Going up on its hind legs, a ragged puncture wound in its chest, the beast gave one last whinny and a kick of its legs before toppling over and burying a fleeing yeoman.

Archaon whirled around to see the unsaddled knight some distance away, trying to scrabble to his feet, struggling in both crumpled plate and the mud. Archaon ran forward as the knight attempted to tear his sword from the gaudy decoration of its scabbard. As the blade cleared its sheath, Archaon booted the knight in the midriff, half lifting him from where he was on all fours in the battlefield mire. The sword slipped from the knight's hand and he landed on his chest. Putting a boot on the back of the knight's helm, Archaon put his weight down on the knight's head. The helm sank under the mud, water flooding in through the faceplate eyeslits and breathing holes. As he held him there, the knight bucked and kicked out in his heavy plate. Men-at-arms and a deranged squire came at Archaon but the *Slayer of Kings* tore through them. Arrows from the castle walls sang off his plate, with two finding their way between his pauldron and backplate. Archaon wouldn't move, however, until the knight's thrashings slowly ceased.

Reaching back, Archaon tore the arrows from his plate before turning around. The knights of Brilloinne continued to smash their way through the ranks of his armoured warriors, his half-breeds, his manfiends and marauders. Exalted champions of Chaos in their benighted plate, bearing the gifts and cursed weaponry of the Dark Gods, rode in through the murderous malaise to meet them, while wretched sorcerers unleashed their dread powers on the silver-suited knights.

Archaon heard a monstrous clash to the north. Peering through the forest of blades, the fountaining brain and falling banners, Archaon could see that the castle's knightly reinforcements had been turned aside by Archaon's own arriving dark knights. Warriors in black plate riding possessed mounts. Slaaneshi horsemen on spiked steeds. Columns of knights in rusted plate, riding skeletal horses. The Blood God's chosen astride mounts of metal and thunder. As the silver stream of riders were diverted by a wall of armoured steeds and mounted warriors, plate clashed, horses shrieked and weapons sang off one another. The Chaos knights, bearing ghastly shields and the armour-shearing blades of axes and serrated swords, smashed the knights of the Marches out of formation. By the time the noblemen had dropped their useless lances and drawn their swords, many had lost their heads or had the teeth of barbed axeblades buried in their breastplates and chests.

Screams brought Archaon's attention back around as knights swooping from the sky on their winged mounts soared across the battlefield. Some skewered dark warriors on their lances, tearing them from the battlefield in a screech of plate and flailing limb. Others leaned out and beheaded ruin-blessed champions from the sky with surging swipes of their glorious blades. Heads and helms dropped to the battlefield in the wake of beaten wings and spurting blood.

Pulling his shield in close and tightening his grip around the hilt of his daemonsword, Archaon bent his knee. As a shadow passed overhead, Archaon leapt for the creature. Swinging his sword overhead, Archaon cut through the throat of the pegasus. As he hit the ground, the winged horse dribbled gore across the battlefield before crashing messily into a throng of yeomen spear-stabbing a manfiend. Another leap only succeeded in turning a wavering lance aside, while a short run into a third sent the tip of the *Slayer of Kings* through the soft underbelly of another flying steed, splatter-spilling its entrails over the polished plate of Bretonnian knights. Archaon was so preoccupied with savagely ending the two noblemen that he didn't see where the disembowelled beast landed or the lance of the mounted warrior that followed. Swooping in on his beautiful white winged beast, the knight aimed his lance squarely at Archaon's horned helm.

Everything went dark for a moment. Archaon felt a crack of thunder pass through his faceplate, his skull and out the back of his head. The world tumbled. Then there was the slip-shod landing on his back, bloody mud oozing about him. He saw the pegasus knight pass overhead but also saw Drei beating his leathery wings in hot pursuit. Within moments, the wraith-warrior had mounted the beast behind the knight and slit his throat with one of his bone blades. As the throat-clutching knight slid from his saddle, down into the havoc of the battle, Archaon saw the sky close up above him.

His world, as disorientated as it had briefly become, was now the feverish smash of weapons and gritted teeth through mud-smeared faces. Men-at-arms bounced morning stars off his plate, while squires attempted to earn plate of their own by twisting the points of spears into his midriff. Suddenly there was a grizzled knight, helmless and sporting a leathery old scar that split his face in two. A greatsword seethed through the sky overhead and came down at the Chaos warlord. It appeared as though it might take off an arm or even Archaon's head. It would have done if he hadn't torn his shield back from the clawing attentions of two warrior pilgrims. Archaon felt the greatsword smack down across the surface of the shield. He knew another steel-splitting blow was coming.

Meanwhile, the Chaos warlord's world continued to darken as more and more rabid baseborns and legacy-hungry paladins swept in to destroy him. His shield boomed with the desperate desire to see him dead. Snarling beneath his faceplate, which was miraculously still intact, Archaon kicked out, sweeping the grizzled knight's legs out from under him. Swinging his daemonsword in a tight arc, the Chaos warrior chopped through leather boot and bone, felling his circle of attackers like trees. Sliding around in the mud, he continued to hack his attackers to a growing mound of screeching bodies, until finally – with a swish of his mud-slick cloak – Archaon was back on his feet. The face-split knight had also managed to haul his armoured form up and held the glittering sword above his head. He got no further. Archaon saw the surprise cross his face. Then the horror as the tip of one of Drei's bone blades poked out of his throat, having entered from the back of his neck. As it slipped out and then disappeared, the knight dropped his heavy sword and crashed to the ground, revealing the shimmering shadow of Archaon's bodyguard.

The formation of pegasus knights had banked and were swooping in for another skewering pass. Archaon readied himself for another sky-searing attack but he didn't have to. Bolts of unnatural energy struck a crooked path up from the battlefield, striking the pegasi and their knightly riders. It was Vilitch the Curseling, striding up through the destruction of Archaon's progress. The warrior-twin slashed men-at-arms out of his path with his sorcery-searing blade, while the twisting worm-like thing growing out of his shoulder directed his staff at the sky. As the Curseling's bolts struck the pegasus knights, both mount and rider were transformed into sacks of leathery flesh that fell from the heavens. The disgusting fusions of flesh splattered into the battlefield before sprouting tentacles, claws and exotic appendages that reached out for nearby unfortunates. Whip-winding tendrils about the boots of fleeing squires, the spawn dragged the boys back through the mud and into the abomination's absorbing fleshiness.

While sorcerous bolts streaked up from the battlefield, streams of flame blasted down from above. Knights aflame fell from the sky while pegasi kicked, flapped and bucked their agonies as they tumbled like balls of fire. Knightly riders were torn from their saddles by monstrous airborne predators, throwing and tearing the paladins to pieces between them, while their mounts were set upon in mid-air by winged serpents who savaged the wondrous steeds.

Archaon felt the ground quaking beneath him. Jharkill had unleashed his monstrosities as Archaon had commanded. As well as airborne monsters and the chimeric predators bounding, pouncing and mauling their way through the battlefield, the abominate titans of Archaon's army had been committed to siege. Everything fell into shadow as the monstrous giant Archaon had freed from Lord Agrammon's menageries stomped up behind. The giant was a small mountain of bone, withered flesh and the light of some malevolent life beyond life. Its bones had been etched with pantheon-pleasing symbols and its exposed ribs used as banner poles from which to hang Ruinous flags and standards. It picked up a colossal piece of masonry that had been launched from the castle and heaved it over the enormous dimensions of its deformed skull.

Archaon heard the tortured release of the castle trebuchets fire once more. Massive boulders hurtled skyward before tumbling towards the battlefield. Archaon gripped his shield. The Chaos warrior knew, however, that it could not save him from such an impact.

Things died horribly nearby. An irregular-shaped boulder smashed a throng of battling knights to nothingness before rolling bludgeonry through Bretonnians and the servants of darkness alike. Another managed to hit nothing for several mud-splattering impacts until burying one of Archaon's deadly sorcerers under a ton of rock. A third dropped straight down on the corpse giant, shattering the monster's malformed skull before landing behind it and tumbling away. Archaon stepped backwards as the bone colossus lurched. The ancient sorcery that gave the monstrosity life died to musty darkness and the giant toppled forward, its colossal masonry missile falling ahead of it. As the monster shattered to a small mountain of ancient bones, the falling piece of masonry cleaved down through the top of the castle wall. Its brick-pulverising path continued, cutting a narrow trench down through the side of the castle-exterior defences. As the dust settled and the excruciating noise of the impact subsided, Archaon watched tendrils of the glowing mist that cloaked the battlefield creep in through the narrow opening.

'To me!' Archaon roared, breaking into a plate-jangling run for the breach. Batting aside Bretonnian knights who were stumbling through the chaos with his shield, Archaon slashed apart men-at-arms that bravely barred his way with his daemonsword. Like a torrent of darkness, dread champions, Chaos warriors, Ruinous knights, manfiends, bestial half-breeds and marauders broke off from their desperate engagements and formed a rampaging column behind their warlord.

Inside the castle walls there was panic. The courtyard beyond was dominated by trebuchets, but upon seeing Archaon emerge from the breach in the castle walls and the hordes of Chaos pour through behind him, they abandoned their machines. Men-at-arms, charged with defending the fortress, poured from stairwells and archways, led by battle-scarred sergeants, while the remaining knights of Brilloinne brought their steeds back under control and rode for the besiegers.

With his dark horde a mist-swirling silhouette of spiked armour, horned helms and blades behind him, Archaon ran across the courtyard at his enemies. Smashing his shield about him with one hand – goring, bludgeoning and dashing – Archaon held the fierce fury of the daemon U'zuhl in the other, burning within the monstrous blade. Melting straight through the steel of lesser weapons, Archaon hacked the raging inferno of the daemonsword through the armoured forms of knights, through screaming squires and the unfortunate steeds that carried them. As Archaon stabbed, cleaved, brained and butchered a path through the crowded courtyard, the stench of sorcery and bloodshed stung his nostrils. He knew where he was heading.

As soon as he had entered the courtyard, he had seen it. The tiny chapel, rough compared to the surrounding architecture that had been built by Baron Lucus. The stained-glass windows were covered by stout oak shutters and lengths of chain, while the archway door was barred by three thick lengths of oak and criss-crossed with tarnished silver chains. It was unmistakable: the chapel Baron Lucus had constructed to house the dark treasures Vilitch the Curseling demanded.

As trailing splatters of blood flew through the air about Archaon, with hacked limbs and blades that had been seared in half, he was filled with loathing for the cowardly grandson of the mighty Baron Lucus – the hero Lucus, whose stories had even reached Archaon as a boy in the far Empire.

'Where is the baron?' Archaon roared, his words bouncing about the courtyard walls. 'The coward that hides behind his coin and his walls while boys and baseborns die for him?'

'Kill him!' Archaon heard from the castle walls. Looking about the castle Archaon found his foe. While longbowmen turned their weapons down into the courtyard, Baron Lucus the younger prowled the relative safety of the ramparts in polished plate of silver and gold. The plumage of his helm was colourful and extravagant, while the exotic saddled beast upon which he rode looked like one of the finest steeds Bretonnian coin could buy: a hippogryph, an elegant creature that boasted the back legs and body of a stallion and the wings, talons and beaked head of a monstrous eagle. The longbowmen seemed uncertain. 'Do as your lord commands,' Lucus shouted through the faceplate of his beautiful helm. Archaon swallowed back the bile rising up the back of his throat. He could hear the edge of cowardice along the cutting edge of the baron's words. Here was a man deserving of death. A fool that thought that money and status could save him from a man like Archaon.

The courtyard whooshed with the flight of arrows loosed from the castle walls. While several arrows shattered and split off Archaon's cursed plate – the Chaos warlord not even bothering to raise his shield – most ended up embedded in surrounding men-at-arms and the dirt of the courtyard floor.

'Still hiding, baron?' Archaon called up at Lucus. 'Your men are dying and your castle lost. Fight me or flee – and make your failure complete.'

Baron Lucus attempted a battle roar of his own but no one was convinced. Not the commoners, for whom their lord's weakling call was the last thing they heard. Not the knights, who fought for the memory of the wretched boy's grandfather rather than the lord himself. Not Archaon.

Digging his heels into the side of the magnificent beast, the baron urged the hippogryph off the castle wall. Leaping like a forest predator from a tree, the hippogryph pounced on Archaon. The Chaos warlord brought up his shield. For a moment he was lost in the monster, buried in talons, hooves and muscle. With a bellow, Archaon reared and threw the hippogryph and its rider off him. As the thing was tossed back into the battle and bloodshed of the crowded courtyard, Archaon smashed it across the beak with his shield before immediately backslapping the beast further into the surrounding butchery.

Shaking off the impacts, the hippogryph stalked sideways about Archaon. The Chaos warrior and the baron's monster circled one another. Lucus just seemed to be along for the ride. Striking out at surrounding Chaos warriors in spiked plate with his sword, Lucus had his bejewelled blade batted back by the battle-hardened warriors of darkness. The hippogryph reared at one, slicing three ragged talon-tears through the warrior's plate and torso. The second it pecked in the faceplate, shattering the horned helm before snapping the warrior's head up in its hooked beak and tearing it free of his body. Lucus let out a jubilant roar, despite the fact that the victory had little to do with his own personal prowess.

Archaon came in with the *Slayer of Kings*, the daemonsword trailing the glow and shimmer of hellfire. The hippogryph launched itself into the air, beating its wings to keep itself and its rider out of Archaon's reach. Tossing the daemonsword into the courtyard, where it hissed blade first in the dirt, Archaon leapt for the hippogryph's back hoof. Grabbing it with both gauntlets, Archaon used his considerable weight to drag the monster back down to earth. The hippogryph flapped furiously for the sky, feverishly kicking out with both back legs to free itself of the deadweight anchor of Archaon. As the hoof of the other leg struck the Chaos warlord and sent him crashing back to the courtyard floor, the hippogryph flapped over the heads of the knights who were fighting for their lives among the Chaos hordes.

As Archaon got to his feet he saw a squire run across the open space and attempt to tear his daemonsword from the dirt. Archaon didn't know whether the Bretonnian boy intended to use his own sword against him or simply deny Archaon his devastating weapon. The Chaos warlord couldn't help but be a little impressed. It didn't last long, however, and neither did the squire. The *Slayer of Kings* would not move from its position stuck in the ground, dragging the squire back. Seconds holding onto the hilt of the daemonic weapon was enough to scorch the squire's simple soul and envelop the boy in a flesh-melting inferno of hellflame. The daemon U'zuhl had no love for Archaon, but there were few souls dark and powerful enough to wield the possessed weapon, and the Blood God's infernal servant made it a matter of monstrous principle to scorch from existence those unworthy and unwise enough to seize it.

Grabbing a man-at-arms from the throng of battle, Archaon killed him with a gauntlet-clenched punch to the head, snatching up the Bretonnian's spear. Leaning back, Archaon launched the weapon at the flapping hippogryph, burying it in the creature's flank. As the monster shrieked like an eagle about the castle, Archaon ducked and weaved the arcs of poor quality blades and notched axes. Smashing his armoured elbow into the spine of another baseborn warrior, Archaon pulled the warped spear in his grasp over his shoulder and allowed the broken-backed Bretonnian to collapse. Hurling the spear with furious force, Archaon sent the weapon through the baron's plate, skewering his leg to his mount's muscular side. Ducking beneath a Bretonnian knight's battle axe, Archaon slammed the armoured warrior aside with his shield.

Suddenly there was a monstrous explosion from the east wall. Dust rocketed across the courtyard as an avalanche of demolished masonry cascaded inwards, burying trebuchets, mounted knights and Chaos marauders alike. Archaon deflected the slow swing of the battle axe off the surface of his shield before spinning about the grey-bearded knight and slamming the shield-spike straight through his armoured back.

Prising his shield from the blood-spitting knight, Archaon walked back across the courtyard, snatching up the *Slayer of Kings* from where it still quivered in the dirt. In the narrow opening he had used to enter the castle he saw Jharkill, the malformed ogre, holding his shaman's staff. Manfiends and marauders pushed past him, eager to join the butchery inside the castle. The Curseling was with him, the warrior-twin opportunistically slicing at Bretonnian knights who were desperately trying to stem the flow of invaders. As the ensorcelled blade of the twin cut through plate and the flesh behind it, the Curseling's opponents were swallowed up by a violaceaous whirlwind of raw energy that tore the blade-marked victim apart before twisting furiously to nothing. The worm-sorcerer that sprouted from the warrior-twin's shoulder held its staff up high, trailing the haze of the glowing mist and striking castle defenders down with spawn-rupturing bolts of lightning from the headpiece.

The Bretonnian knights needn't have bothered trying to secure the breach. The abominate form of Archaon's slaughterbrute had decimated an entire section of wall and was now crawling across the rubble. The monstrosity of chitinous plate, horn, claw and dagger-filled maw bore the red flesh and fury of its Blood God. It was living decimation and visited some of that potential on Brilloinne Castle. With three tongues flopping out of its mouth, cascading the drool of violent anticipation, the monstrosity smashed its clawed fists through walls, through the foundations of tottering towers and down through the stable structures and courtyard buildings. It snatched up fleeing men-at-arms and bit them in half, discarding what was left before stamping down on a foolhardy knight with its huge hooves, reducing the armoured warrior to splattering scrap.

Winged serpents circled the castle walls, lighting up the ramparts with streams of flame, prompting the flaming, flailing longbowmen stationed there to jump to their deaths. Chimeric predators tore past Archaon, savaging yeomen, squires and knights as they ran from the destructive horror of the slaughterbrute and the monstrosities attacking the castle.

As the abominate creature moved towards the chapel, Archaon found himself running against the terrified Bretonnians, his daemon sword slashing this way and that to clear a bloody path. Waving his shield and the infernal radiance of his sword before the huge monster, he saw the thing stop – its clenched claw just moments from smashing the chapel to brick-dust. Under the control of Jharkill's primitive charms, the thing turned away, suddenly attracted to the flapping form of the hippogryph and the gleaming plate of the baron on its back. Lucus swung his beautiful blade at the inevitability of the beast's closing claws but the miserable nobleman could not land a strike. It was horror to behold as the slaughterbrute snatched the hippogryph and its rider out of the air. Tearing the shiny form of the screaming baron from the saddle, the abomination grasped the winged steed in its fist. Smashing the knuckles of its clenched claw into the courtyard floor to crunch the creature's bones and snap its wings, the Chaos monstrosity flung the hippogryph's broken carcass with merciless force into the north wall. Archaon could hear the screams of Baron Lucus inside the prison of the slaughterbrute's claw. The monster looked down at its shrieking fist before crushing the insignificance of the nobleman, the royal blood of the baron spurting out from between the abomination's knuckles.

Such a sight was too much for even those knights who had pledged to defend the castle when the baseborns turned and fled. With the castle in ruins and the lord to which they owed their oath dead, there was little left at Brilloinne for the knights to die for. As the knights fled, running for the drawbridge that had been cranked open, Archaon left them to his besieging horde. Turning towards the chapel about which the castle had been built, Archaon levelled the thick oak door with a kick. Worm-eaten oak splintered, and chains slipped through rings and dropped before the entrance. Holding the *Slayer of Kings* out before him, the blade blazed brightly in the presence of such a holy place. The chapel interior was resplendent with the gold and silver iconography of the blessed Lady of the Lake and the Grail, from which the legendary Baron Lucus had sipped. As the furious glow of his daemonblade lit up the darkness of shuttered stained-glass windows, Archaon found the chapel to be empty. A hole shattered in the aged brick that made up the back wall had allowed recent entrance into the chapel, and the dust was disturbed evidence of the recovery of the dread treasures of darkness that had remained locked inside.

Archaon nodded to himself. There was no fury. No dark oaths or threats. This was the double cross of which Sheerian had warned him. This was the betrayal and deception he had expected from a sorcerer pledged to Tzeentch. This was the treacherous truth he needed to know, that the Curseling was pledged to Archaon's father-in-shadow, the Dark Master. Vilitch had already consigned the knights and men-at-arms of Brilloinne Castle to spawndom and had taken the dark treasures of the chapel for himself. The castle was now a monstrous trap and tomb – for Archaon.

The Chaos warlord turned around. The Twisted Twin stood there. Both warrior and sorcerous worm watching him. The warrior-twin thrust his blade suddenly through Jharkill's back. The monstrous ogre looked down at the tip of the blade protruding from his chest. He clutched at it with the tiny, claw-like hand of his atrophied arm. The huntsman looked up at Archaon across the bloody courtyard before disappearing in a maelstrom of purple light. As the flesh-shredding whirlwind dissipated – ogre, shaman staff and all – the Curseling stepped forth.

There were fresh horrors all around. The Bretonnian knights and the men-at-arms of the castle had stopped running. The glowing mist that accompanied the sorcerer Curseling and seemed to slip through everything, now disappeared into the ground. With the illusory haze no longer required, Archaon and his Chaos warriors saw the Bretonnians for what they really were: the growing number of the Curseling's spawn army. Misshapen monstrosities of raw flesh, tentacular horror and scything appendages leapt on Archaon's bestial champions, marauders and fiends. The corpses of castle defenders erupted like mounds of mutable horror. Stabbing limbs, snapping jaws and streams of caustic liquid blasted forth from things that, as men-at-arms, had been felled but had waited for their sorcerer-master's signal to reveal the truth of their resilient forms.

Archaon broke into a run. He hacked apart spawn creatures that leapt at him in transformation, dashed extra heads with his shield and stomped, skipped and jumped through a courtyard of snaking tendrils. He decapitated heads that crawled their snapping jaws at his ankles and quivering corpses from which chitinous claws erupted. He did not get far. The worm-sorcerer Vilitch had its staff directed at the charging warlord. As Archaon brought his shield up, the Curseling unleashed a stream of dark lightning that blasted Archaon back across the courtyard and into the chapel.

Shaking the impact from his head, Archaon found himself in a dangerous place. The holiness of the chapel – devoted as it was to the Lady of the Lake through the many pure deeds of Baron Lucus – drained Archaon of his potency. It was like burning in the fires of absolution. His eye burned to open. His flesh burned within his plate. His mind burned with the hallowed nature of the place. Outside Archaon could hear the horror of the battle and the monstrous fury of the slaughterbrute. Archaon felt the ground tremble beneath him at its approach. Like the rest of the monstrosities that were part of Archaon's horde, the abomination was no longer under Jharkill's control. They were slaves to their own dark and savage natures, with some breaking for a cursed freedom while others turned immediately on those about them, savaging the warriors of Archaon's army and the Curseling's spawn with equal ferocity.

Archaon suddenly felt the seething shadow of long fingers around his arm. He felt himself dragged out through the hole shattered in the brickwork of the chapel and when he could open his eye again, he saw that Drei had pulled him free. The chapel suddenly disappeared before them. Grit and shards of stone pranged off Archaon's plate as the chapel was demolished by the slaughterbrute's monstrous fist. With the darkness of the wraith-warrior's arm still alight from the purity of the place, Drei stepped through the dust and rubble of the flattened chapel to engage the abomination.

As Archaon got to his feet and shook off the draining fury of the chapel's consecration, he was set upon by abominations of his own. The tentacles of a rapidly evolving spawn shot out and whipped about his arm. Cleaving through the slime-dribbling tendrils with the *Slayer of Kings*, Archaon felt the huge talons of a winged serpent attempt to snatch him from his feet. Slipping free and dropping back to the courtyard, Archaon rolled. The scaled serpent beat its wings and landed before him, opening the narrow jaws of its mouth to bury its former master in flame. Running at the winged monstrosity with his shield before him, Archaon turned aside the roaring stream, forcing the inferno back at the twisted serpent. Smashing the length of its snaggle-toothed jaws aside with the shield, Archaon turned and brutally hacked down through its long, snaking neck with his daemonsword.

The winged body of the headless monster had barely flapped back into a courtyard stable before another damned creature was on his back. Archaon felt the grapnel-like claws of a chimera on his back and the teeth of one of its several heads crushing the plate of one arm. With a snarl, Archaon barged the nightmare straight into the stone of the smouldering west wall. He smashed it into the unforgiving surface of the wall again and again until the thing's monstrous neck broke and Archaon could shrug the beast off his back.

Archaon found that although Drei had bought him a few moments to recover, his own delay had cost the wraith-warrior dearly. Jumping, evading, weaving and slicing, the Sword of Chaos had slashed at the abominate slaughterbrute with its pair of bone blades. As Archaon charged towards the rampaging monster himself, the wraith-warrior leapt into the furious wing beats of an evasion. Drei was too late, however, and the monster's claw cut through the air, back-smashing the wraith-warrior into a shower of shattered bone and the smeared haze of shadow.

Archaon's own progress towards the unstoppable fury of the beast was suddenly checked by the appearance of the Curseling. Vilitch was hunting the Chaos warlord through the destruction of the flaming castle. As the warrior-twin marched indomitably towards Archaon, the grotesque sorcerer blasted the stables apart with a reality-scorching stream of dark lightning.

Knocked from his feet by the explosion, Archaon scrabbled to his feet with a roar. Trap or not. Expected or not. He would bring this havoc to an end. Archaon broke into a heavy run. With his plate rhythmically clattering about him, he ran along the west wall of the castle. While the warrior-twin impassively marched on towards what he had been told was his foe, the sorcerer was beside itself with feverish, worm-like excitement. The flames. The transformation of spawn. The death and destruction. The smoke-belching castle was a nexus of ruin and change. Directing its sorcerous staff, Vilitch blasted a stream of energy after the Chaos warlord once more.

Archaon ran, barely a hair's breadth before the dark stream. Skidding down to a stop before the bulging foundations of a tower, Archaon allowed the stone to absorb the remainder of the staff's wrath. Looking up, Archaon saw that the slaughterbrute had followed him, its monstrous collection of eyes following the warlord's swift movements.

As Archaon got up out of the dust, the abomination cornered him, its three tongues lolling in monstrous expectation, the throaty thunder of a growl building in the slaughterbrute's chest. The sound was suddenly eclipsed by the ear-splitting cacophony of splintering brick and shearing stone. Archaon had led the destructive power of the Curseling's staff along the west wall, cutting through the thickness of its base. As Archaon stepped back, the wall toppled inwards, smashing the slaughterbrute into the courtyard floor. As the dust rose and the abomination was buried in buckling masonry, Archaon heard the thing's rumbling growl trail off into a bloody rasp.

Scrambling up the mound of red flesh and masonry, Archaon rose and fell with the exertion of the monster's breathing. Pausing amongst the shattered stone, back spikes and chitinous armour of the beast, Archaon turned the *Slayer of Kings* about in his hand. Settling the tip of the blade between the pulverised rock and the armour of the abomination, Archaon took the weapon by the crossguard and leant down on the blade. The daemonsword slid down through the monster's flesh. With Archaon on his knees and the raging blade of the *Slayer of Kings* skewered through it, the slaughterbrute knew pain. It roared its agonies, blood flooding out of its trap-jaw maw, its three tongues slapping around like fish in a dried up lake.

Grabbing the hilt, Archaon twisted the daemonblade in the back of the beast, enjoying the torment that howled out of the monster's brute form. Twisting it around again, Archaon felt the monstrosity's heart burst within its cavernous chest. As the abomination breathed its last, Archon could feel the daemon U'zuhl feeding voraciously on the slaughterbrute's gore-stained soul. He pulled the blood-slick blade of the *Slayer of Kings* from the creature's carcass and allowed it to steam in his hand.

Peering through the thinning dust, Archaon could see his horde still fighting for their lives within the courtyard, Chaos warriors, manfiends and marauders being entwined in the slithering appendages and dragged towards monstrous mouths that were opening in the undulating flesh of the Curseling's spawn. The Curseling itself was being kept busy by Zwei. The wraith-warrior had returned from Archaon's errand, to find the castle in chaos. Slashing both the warrior-twin's ensorcelled blade and the sorcerer's staff aside with expert bladework, Zwei was backing the Twisted Twin up the steps leading to the castle battlements. Skidding down the scree in which the slaughterbrute was buried, Archaon ran for a similar set of stone steps nearby. The Chaos warlord knew that Zwei wouldn't last long against the Curseling.

Running along the blackened battlements and through towers that were still aflame, Archaon gutted and shield-smashed the fire-swathed forms of burning spawn aside, grabbing one by what passed for its legs and tipping it through the crenellations and down the outside of the castle wall.

Running up behind the Curseling, with the slashing fury of Zwei's bone blades forcing the sorcerer back, Archaon suddenly found the staff's headpiece turned about to face him. Knowing that the cursed thing would blast him to spawndom, Archaon turned both the staff and the furious stream aside with his daemonsword, while bringing the edge of his shield down through the shaft of the Ruinous staff. Trapped between the stone of the battlements and the cleaving force of the shield, the sorcerer's staff snapped in two, bleeding a glowing mist about them. Smashing the warrior-twin across the helm with the back of the shield and then back into his face, Archaon saw the stone behind the warrior's skull shatter with the force. The ensorcelled blade came at Archaon but Zwei turned it aside, pinning it against the battlements. Archaon chopped down with the *Slayer of Kings*, the blade chopping the hand holding the ensorcelled blade clean off at the wrist.

Archaon heard the warrior-twin grunt in pain, spitting blood through the grille of his battered helm. Both blade and hand tumbled away down the castle wall, while Archaon held the Twisted Twin against the wall. The worm-like sorcerer writhed and twisted with an agonising frustration, its needle-toothed mouth contorting around a collection of exotic oaths and curses.

'Shut the hell up,' Archaon warned, laying the furnace glow of his daemonblade across the throats of both warrior-twin and his sorcerous brother. Vilitch grew silent, instead revoltingly caressing and calming his injured twin. Archaon watched as, horribly, the skeletal fingers of a new hand eased their way out of the ruined wrist Archaon's sword had left behind. Threading with veins and then blossoming with tendons and muscle, the hand bled new skin through the rawness of fresh flesh. 'I'd like to see you do that without your heads,' Archaon told the Curseling, edging the blood-hungry blade of the *Slayer of Kings* towards their throats. The sorcerer smiled hideously.

'I'll trade you truth for truth,' Archaon told the Curseling. 'I fulfilled my part of our agreement, including the part where I walk into your feeble trap.' Archaon grunted and turned his helm, allowing the destruction of the castle in through his eye slits. Even he had to admit that the trap had been anything but feeble but he wasn't going to tell Vilitch that. 'Now – the Crown of Domination. You promised me the one who knows where it is. You promised me the whereabouts of such a Ruinous individual.' Archaon leant in close, pressing his burning blade ever closer. 'If I hear anything else pass your lips – either set – that isn't what I just asked for, I swear to the dread Powers, I will slash your throats open.'

'...the Dreadpeak,' the Curseling managed, 'where the Worlds Edge Mountains meet the Northern Wastes.'

'Very good,' Archaon said, his blade seething against the sorcerer's flesh. 'See what a good team we make. Now, I don't like surprises. Who waits for me at the Dreadpeak with the knowledge I seek?'

The worm-thing began to laugh.

'Don't test me, sorcerer…'

'Be'lakor…'

'Be'lakor?'

'Be'lakor is the Harbinger, He Who Heralds Conquerors… The Bearer of the Crown,' the Curseling told him, enjoying the warlord's confusion. 'The Crown of Domination is Be'lakor's burden. Only he knows where it can be found.'

Archaon's lip wrinkled into a snarl.

'You know something, Curseling,' he said to the sorcerer. 'I think I'm going to kill you anyway, you monstrous son of a…'

In the radiance of the daemonsword, Archaon didn't notice the sorcerer's own glow. The mist pouring from the shattered staff and gathering at their feet had slithered up about the Curseling. As the Twisted Twin let out a horrid laugh that echoed away to nothing, Archaon lurched forward. The *Slayer of Kings* slipped through the glowing mist that the Curseling had become. With the sorcerer's mocking laughter still bouncing around the inside of his skull and dark magic on the air, Archaon sheathed his mighty blade. Zwei began a search of the battlements.

'Forget it,' he told the wraith-warrior. 'He's gone.'

As the Chaos warlord walked along the battlements, the towers of Brilloinne swirling with flame and staining the heavens black, he looked down on the courtyard. As the Curseling disappeared, his spawn seemed to become disorientated wretches of cursed flesh and monstrous gifts – speared, hacked apart and bludgeoned to death by the dark warriors, bestial champions and savages of Archaon's army. Those monsters that had not fallen in the fighting fled the castle to plague the Marches of Couronne. Gazing out across the battlefield beyond Baron Lucus's castle, Archaon saw that the reinforcements and summoned knights were no more. They had been no match for Archaon's monstrous horde.

Looking beyond the battlefield carnage, the Eye of Sheerian granted Archaon a vision of the standing stones beyond.

Great glyph-inscribed tors that he had recovered on his travels and transported on board his hulks. Standing stones that the sorcerer Sheerian had assured him – if placed in dark configurations – could draw soulfire from lands cursed with the spilling of blood. Archaon had ordered Sheerian and a horde of strongback slaves to have the tors erected before the battle and was sure that he had charged the ensorcelled stones with enough dread power, violence and bloodshed to blow open a gateway to hell – which is exactly what Archaon intended to do with them.

Then, beyond the soot and smoke of the battle, the Ruinous stones that stood and the storm that battered the Bretonnian coast, the Eye of Sheerian showed him sails. Hundreds and hundreds of sails in the distance. Greatships and galleons flying flags of different nations. Bretonnia. The Empire. At the head of the armada surging north out of Marienburg, he could see a great, ornate galleon flying the holy banners of the Church of Sigmar – the cultship of the Grand Theogonist himself.

There was little time. So little time. Archaon turned to Zwei.

'Tell Sheerian to get the stones back to the fleet,' Archaon ordered. 'Tell Captain Darghouth that as soon as the stones and the horde are back on board we haul off immediately and make way. Inform him that a battlefleet seeks to engage him from the south but that we sail north.'

Zwei nodded before spreading his gargoyle's wings and leaping from the battlements. Archaon watched him swoop across the battlefield, carrying his orders. He thought on the Curseling, who had hoped to do his Dark Master proud and strip Archaon's corpse of its treasures. He thought on the Bretonnian king and the Emperor, who sat in distant Altdorf, briefed on the terrible danger Archaon presented. He thought on the Grand Theogonist – whoever he now was – still trying to finish what Archaon had started in the Cathedral of Sigmar so many years before. They would fail. All of them. For Archaon sailed north into destiny.

CHAPTER XVI

'It was Great Grungni told us of his coming. A calamity come of calamities. Daemons born of the land-shaking storm. A prince among daemons risen of their dread number. A doom of horn, wing and terror, walking tall among the darklings, causing mountains to quake and hearts to thump at his passing. He claims the tainted land as his own but Grungni taught us that it was the land itself that would save us. That the depths would be our salvation. That to dig was to dig for one's life. Some say we did not dig deep enough. Some that we dug too far. That the stone of Karak Zhul was cursed long before any dwarf set foot here or desecrated the darkness with pick and shovel. He has found us. The Dark One comes with his legions to reclaim what

> *is his. I write this in my blood, before*
> *it is spilt. So that the sons of Grungni,*
> *the underkin of Karak Zhul, might be*
> *avenged. For our doom has come and*
> *visits his darkness upon our own…'*
> – Dammaz Kron, The Great Book of Grudges

The Dreadpeak
The Worlds Edge Mountains
Grimnir's Day / Passing of Oaths IC 2519

The Dreadpeak shook. The Dark Master was here. At last.

Archaon stood atop the mountain, with the peaks of the Worlds Edge Mountains extending south through the darkness, like the jagged, monstrous spine of all the world. It was here that the dwarfs looked north and turned back, with dread in their hearts, naming the Dreadpeak for such cowardly fears. Below the levelled peak of the mountain, they built what some claim to be the long-lost hold of Karak Zhul – of which no son of the mountains speaks, for the horrors committed there at the beginning of time.

Archaon walked, pulling his cloak about his plate. It was cold up in the heights. Not the cold of the Wastes or the southern continent. It was a rawness, stiffening the lungs and chilling to the bone. It had taken months to get here, but as Archaon walked around the great black circle of standing stones – arranged on the flat, levelled summit of the Dreadpeak – he knew the time had come. After nearly a century searching for the Crown of Domination, he would know where to find the last of the treasures, the treasures with which the Dark Gods had tortured him for so long.

The dark armada had fled the civilised lands of the south. A great fleet had been despatched to destroy them. Perhaps beacons had been lit along the Bretonnian coast. Perhaps Baron Lucus had sent word before the Curseling had taken Brilloinne or perhaps it had been the Curseling himself who had sent word of Archaon's coming. For all the Chaos warlord knew, the Grand Theogonist might have his own ways of knowing such things and had despatched his magnificent cultship at the head of a hastily arranged armada of warships – both Imperial and Bretonnian – to destroy, in Archaon, a common threat. Archaon would not be drawn into such an engagement, however. He was a warlord of Chaos – he did not assume formations and fight battles on land or sea according to long-held traditions or the rules of titled men. He had not assembled an apocalyptic army to see them sent to the bottom of the ocean in cowardly cannonfire.

Hauling off with Archaon's monstrous horde barely aboard and the great black tors loaded, the Cloven Captain took the *Perdición* with the storms that seemed to accompany Archaon wherever he went. Breaking out of the gulf and out into the Sea of Claws – where the longships of northmen and raiders gave them a wide berth – Archaon ordered the dark armada north, up and around the treacherous coast of Norsca. The fleet had followed them. Whoever had been charged with his destruction would not return to the Empire with news that the doom of man had slipped out of their grasp once more. Some flesh-purifying high priest or buffoon admiral, with more titles than sense, would not be able to accept the simplicity of their quarry refusing their offer of an engagement and so had foolishly followed him into open waters, where his numbers counted for something. Despite entreaties from Captain Darghouth, Archaon still refused to engage the armada that was chasing him into the north.

For weeks he watched their bobbing lanterns, enjoying the misery endured by the fearful crew and officers of high-walled galleons, fat greatships of the Imperial fleet and the storm-smashed wolfships and cultships that accompanied them. As frost crept through the creaking timbers and dusted rigging, and the Sea of Claws became the Sea of Chaos, Archaon felt the uncertainty of their pursuers. Unlike his own armada, the ships striking out from Marienburg were not outfitted for such a voyage. Food and water would be running low and the clothing miserably unsuitable for such sharp climes. Still the armada crashed on through the high seas and perverse gales that followed in the wake of Archaon's storm-blessed fleet.

Then it happened. A maelstrom not of Archaon's making tore out of the north – no doubt some horror begotten by the Wastes. The Cloven Captain had an instinct for such dark storms and had requested that the *Perdición* lead the armada into the more sheltered waters of the Serrated Shore, a curved peninsula that saved the dark armada from the worst the storm had to offer. The following fleet were not so fortunate. While Archaon watched in silent satisfaction and the monstrous hordes roared their jubilation from the decks of their ships, the vessels of their pursuers were battered by the unrelenting storm, smashed and wrecked upon the broken lands of the Vestligkyst and the daggered fjords of the Serrated Coast. Despite requests from his own champions to hunt down the wrecked survivors, Archaon ordered the armada onwards, leaving the Sigmarite priests, sailors and officer-noblemen to the bloodthirsty tribes of the Graelings that haunted the coast.

The Sea of Chaos became the Kraken Sea. The Kraken Sea became the Frozen Sea, where Archaon had his sorcerers cut a path through the cracking, creaking pack ice. Finally, when the ice would allow no further passage south-east and the vessels of Archaon's mighty armada became a fleet of frozen remnants, stuck in the warped, white desolation of waters bordering the Chaos Wastes, he called for anchors to be dropped. Disembarking his monstrous army and their mounts, he had the horde craft beast-hauled sleds for his siege engines and dark stone tors. Chopping up the vessels of the fleet to provide firewood, Archaon struck out across the ice on Dorghar, leading the monstrous expanse of his horde on across the pack ice and back onto dry land, heading for the Dreadpeak – the level-topped mountain that marked the dire point where the Worlds Edge Mountains met the Ruinous Wastes.

It had taken days to get the black, sigil-etched stones up

the mountainside. Despite being levelled for the minerals blessing its peak, the Dreadpeak still cast its colossal shadow across the lesser peaks that extended south with the range. It had taken even longer to erect the stones and make dark preparations for their use. A great fire was built on the flattened summit, at the centre of the standing stones. Between what Archaon had learned from the daemon Z'guhl about the drawing and binding of his daemonic kindred to the *Slayer of Kings* and Khezula Sheerian's ancient knowledge of otherworldly summonings – the sorcerer having been summoned himself in such a fashion – Archaon felt ready. Despite his monstrous flesh being a living lie, the Curseling's tongues had spoken true. There was an undeniable darkness to the Dreadpeak. Though no one could know and the dwarfs of the Worlds Edge Mountains spoke not of it, it did feel as if something terrible had unfolded deep beneath the mountain. Perhaps the legendary long-lost hold of Karak Zhul had been here and perhaps it had been here that the daemon legions and their dark prince stalked the dawn of the world and massacred the mountain kin. There was definitely a weakening here. A flaw in the darkness. A chink in the mountainous armour of the world.

'It's time, master,' Sheerian rasped in the thin air. The sorcerer was but a silhouette against the raging fire that lit up the abyssal blackness of the night sky. About the perimeter of the stones, Archaon saw his host of dark sorcerers, all acting under the guidance of Sheerian in the preparations to be made.

Looking out over the edge of the mountain peak, Archaon could see his colossal army camped out in the valleys below. Their camp fires were a rash that spread far between the crooked mountains like a disease or affliction of all the world. Archaon had even sent the strongbacks, spawn and champions that had seen the dark tors to the Dreadpeak back down the mountain. He had left the misshapen Vier to watch over the deathly Giselle, in the monstrous ribcage of her fur-lined wagon-sled. A dark delegation of trusted warlords, chieftains and armoured champions had requested to be present on the mountain – for Archaon's protection, if nothing else – but he denied them, selecting only Eins and Zwei, Sheerian and his sorcerers for company. The daemon steed Dorghar stamped at the rock of the mountain nearby, snorting plumes of its furnace-hot breath into the reedy freeze of the heights.

'Do you think it will be enough?' Archaon asked the sorcerer.

'We are going fishing in the abyss, my lord,' Sheerian answered. 'We have the tools. We have the words. We have princely incantations and the fire of soul-thousands to lure the Dark Master in. Quite the contrary, do not be surprised if we land and bind something worse than Be'lakor.'

'There is nothing worse than Be'lakor,' Archaon told the sorcerer. 'You have the blade?'

The daemon sorcerer handed him the short blade of the sword the wraith-warriors had recovered from the caves below the mountain. The Swords of Chaos indicated that there was no evidence that the Dreadpeak lay upon the mines and holds of Karak Zhul but Archaon knew it in his bones. The dread darkness of the place did not lie. The recovered weapon had been smashed from the grip of a skeleton. It was a dwarf blade, black and serrated with age but made of meteoric iron. Still impossibly strong, Archaon hoped that it had belonged to some lowly sentry rather than a warrior king. Some dwarf who had lost his life in the infernal massacre. An ignominious prison, suitable for the prince that led such slaughter.

Archaon walked out into the space between the towering black tors. The heat from the colossal fire raged and turned the metal of his cursed plate to a flesh-scorching affliction. About him the sigils of the standing stones glowed and smoked with a searing balelight – the soulfire of those slain by Archaon and his horde within their configuration. Standing between them, Archaon felt the world-splitting power crackling at the heart of the nexus. The instability of the rock beneath his boots, the heat from the fire and the air in his lungs. The Ruinous realm drawn up out of the beyond, like the black silt coating the bottom of a disturbed tarn, spuming up through the crystal waters and bleaching the surface with its darkness.

He stabbed the ancient dwarf blade into the rocky earth before the fire. Lifting his helm he spat on the blade, watching the spittle sizzle on metal that had already become uncomfortably hot before the raging fire. Lowering his horned helm, Archaon walked back towards Sheerian.

'Begin the incantations,' he ordered.

The sorcerer's milky eyes fluttered shut. Dark words in a dark tongue proceeded from his cracked lips, echoed by the dread sorcerers standing at the perimeter, between each of the black tor stones.

Archaon waited. And waited. The ritual proceeded long into the night, with sorcerous incantations called like a chorus into the terrifying emptiness of the night sky. The fire raged eternal and the stones glowed with an eerie darkness. Archaon stood with his arms folded and his cloak gathered about him, the fingers of his gauntlet tapping the hilt of the *Slayer of Kings*. Dorghar walked up and down, snorting its infernal impatience.

The incantations grew suddenly louder. Archaon heard the black tors creak and groan. Grit began to bounce about the rocky mountain floor. The flames boomed, blasting out with raging balls of blinding fury, before reaching higher and higher into the black sky. The glowing sigils of the standing stones seemed to melt down the sides of the tors before searing into the rock of the mountaintop. Suddenly the flames went out. Thunder rolled across the sky. Silent flashes of lightning criss-crossed the heavens. When the flames returned, with explosive force, they were lustrous black, like an inferno of raging oil. The midnight flames writhed, twisted and contorted into a shape Archaon recognised. Wings. Horns. A muscular torso and arms. The slash of a tail and the abyssal ugliness of a daemonic face. Be'lakor. The Dark Master.

Straining. Thrashing. Clawing up through his own flaming form. The sorcerer Sheerian had him.

Archaon stepped forward. There were several Be'lakors now. All fighting to be free of the summoning's all but irresistible force. Fearful of the iron prison that awaited the daemon in the form of the ancient dwarf sword. Fifty Be'lakors. A hundred.

'Daemon!' Archaon called through the boom of the oily black inferno. As the fiery phantasms raged, one nightmare shape flickered to stillness. It looked at Archaon, seeming to see him for the first time. 'Dark Prince. My father-in-shadow. Hear me…'

I can hear you, the daemon said, its slick composure at odds with the thousands of other frenzied Be'lakors that fought to be free of the daemon-trap. The Dark Master was both storm and infernal serenity, living the existential agonies of semi-realisation.

I can see you. I feel your dark presence in this miserable world. I smell your fear and taste of your bitter despair. Archaon, who would be Everchosen. Archaon, who will herald nothing more than his own disastrous doom.

'Enough of that, I think,' Archaon told the daemon prince. 'If this flesh is destined to fail, then you fail with it. You tell me what I need to hear, like all fathers to their sons. Spare me, wretched shadow. There is but one thing I want – and will ever want – from you. You are the Herald. You are the Bearer. You, and only you, know where the unholy Crown of Domination can be found: Ruinous right of the chosen, distinction of infernal sovereignty in this world and those never to follow. Tell me, daemon, where can the final treasure of Chaos be found?'

Archaon…

'Yes?'

Archaon, Archaon, Archaon. How can a man who has travelled so far, who has lived the lives you have, who has tasted eternity, not understand the nature of his fate?

'Explain it to me,' Archaon ordered. 'While you still can.'

Your existence is a history of nevers. A madness repeated, falling from the lips of a lunatic. An echo ebbing away to cavernous silence. You are the ghost that has forgotten itself. The shadow passed. Your flesh only lives to know the true darkness that awaits it – once your soul plagues it no more.

'Could the abomination be more cryptic?' Archaon asked.

Like the wayward son, you have pulled away, Be'lakor told him. *You have defied your father's wishes, his hopes for your future. You have forged what you have told yourself to be your own path – yet here you are begging for your father-in-shadow once more.*

'Begging?' Archaon snarled. 'You mistake asking for telling, daemon. Entreaty for interrogation. Invitation for imprisonment. Words don't seem to work on the daemon. Show the wretched thing.'

At Archaon's order, Sheerian and the dark sorcerers gathered about the circle of stones tightened their hold on Be'lakor. The daemon roared, joining the thousands of Be'lakors already raging against their spiritual bonds. The daemon's shadow-form became stretched and contorted. The blade before it rattled in the ground, drawing the daemon in – like the black, iron doors of an eternal prison thrown open wide. Be'lakor's torments sent quakes through both the mountain and sky. The agonies of instability. Infernal fears of imprisonment. Bolts of indescribable energy snapped between the meteoric iron of the ancient blade and the daemon prince Archaon wished to consign to it. The blade glowed to unruly darkness while the great black fire began to die with Be'lakor's hold on the beyond, on the material world, on himself.

'Had enough, daemon prince?' Archaon put to his hated father-in-shadow. 'I am Archaon. My fate is my own. My decisions my own. My existence my own – and I have chosen the doom of all for that existence. I shall trap you in ancient iron, to spend forever in an unworthy blade, wielded by those you consigned to everlasting darkness in this dreadful place. I shall then take this blade – this prison – out to the ocean and drop you into the deepest waters I can find:

lost for eternity in the sands of a dark, watery desert with only carcass-picking crabs for company.

YOU WILL NEVER…

'…find the last treasure of Chaos?' Archaon said as the Dark Master fluxed and raged, the pull of the ancient iron irresistible. 'I'll take my chances. At least I will spend my eternity free to pursue such a destiny. You will not, my father-in-shadow. Besides, the Dark Gods are fickle. Perhaps the next Everchosen of Chaos will be crowned without lowly Be'lakor. After thousands of years, perhaps the Ruinous Powers desire a change. At least one of them does. Oh how he would like to see your failure complete. A world's end without Be'lakor to usher it in…'

ARCHAON!

'Tell me…' Archaon hissed at the dissipating daemon. 'Tell me now.'

THE CROWN WAITS…

'Yes…'

IN THE FIRST SHRINE OF CHAOS–

'Where, daemon?' Archaon roared.

WHERE THE FIRST HUMAN SOUL WAS BARTERED TO THE DARK GODS…

'Your soul, daemon prince,' Archaon said. 'Where?'

YOU ARE UNWORTHY.

'Where?' Archaon bellowed back at the raging daemon.

YOU… WILL… NEVER…

'Wear the crown?' Archaon completed for the daemon. 'Then neither will you! Do it,' Archaon commanded.

'But, master–' Sheerian said.

'Show this abomination the eternity of iron,' Archaon roared. Be'lakor roared. The skies split asunder. Thunder rolled backwards through the heavens. The dwarf blade quivered to a sonorous shriek, glowing with Be'lakor's darkness. The flames boomed and twisted. Dark energies sank a dread chorus, streaming between the Ruinous tors and through the monstrous fire. Thousands of screaming Be'lakors became hundreds. Hundreds became one – a mighty phantasm in flame, clawing, slashing his tail, flapping his wings and tossing the grotesque form of his horned head from side to side, his shrieks, oaths and daemon curses melting the sky.

'Yes!' Archaon roared. 'Yes! Know, monster, what it is to be bound by destiny and a prisoner to your fate.'

Suddenly – with Archaon's monstrous jubilation still echoing about the Dreadpeak – the daemon prince was gone. The oily emptiness of the inferno died. The black, age-eaten blade quivered and glowed with Be'lakor's darkness. Dread energies arced from stone to steaming sword. No one spoke. Thunder faded. The skies flashed with silent lightning and black rain fell on the mountain.

'Master, I...' Khezula Sheerian began but Archaon brought up a single, armoured finger.

The sword's quiverings had built to an imperceptible vibration. Beneath Archaon's boots the Dreadpeak trembled. Cracks felt their way from the daemon-bound blade, through the flat stone of the flattened peak. They creaked and sheared their way through the rock, reaching out to a number of standing stones and creating an eight-point star of ruin. Sheerian and his sorcerers suddenly grabbed for their ears. Archaon felt the excruciating vibration of the ancient blade grow to a mind-splitting shriek. As he screwed his eye shut and grabbed his helm in pain, he heard his father-in-shadow's voice.

Words of monstrous dread and abyssal determination. Both *No...* And *Yesssss...* The ancient iron of Karak Zhul failed. The sword shattered. Shards of wicked iron blasted out in all directions. Sudden. Shocking. Guided by some unholy force. The sorcerers crumbled, slivers of infernal iron protruding from hoods, faces and chests.

Archaon turned to Khezula Sheerian. The sorcerer who had seen so much – with his own misted eyes and the sorcerous Eye that now resided in Archaon's helm – now had two barbed slivers of black metal embedded in his sockets. He tried to say something. Perhaps to Archaon. Perhaps to entreat his warped god. Falling forward on his bony knees, the sorcerer drizzled away to otherworldly flame that snaked across the stone floor and down the mountain. There was nothing left of the sorcerer who had served Archaon so long with his twisted counsel. The two slivers of iron plinked to the floor.

As the metal began to dance on the flat stone of the mountaintop and the freedom of Be'lakor's wrath bled through the rock, Archaon looked down at his own body. A serrated shard of the blade had stabbed straight through his cursed plate, through his stomach, above the hip, and out the back of his armour. His insides burned where the wicked sliver sat, still glowing with the failed containment of the daemon prince. The mountain was shaking with Be'lakor's wrath. The standing stones were rocking back and forth, then fell forward in unison, smashing through the cracked rock of the fire-scorched summit, creating a cavernous sink hole in the top of the trembling mountain. As the summit collapsed in on itself, Eins and Zwei surged for the sky, their wings beating with feverish urgency. Dorghar also leapt from the mountain, the black stallion sprouting black, leathery wings of its own to escape the thunderous calamity.

The rock tumbled away beneath Archaon's feet. He twisted around but the movement was agony with the shard skewered through the side of his gut. His right leg felt wet with blood pouring down from the wound. Archaon clawed at the stone behind him but it simply crumbled away, dragged down with the Chaos warlord by a dark force greater than gravity. A lightless chasm opened up like a monstrous mouth to swallow him whole. As the world became a receding vision, like an eye clouding to unconsciousness, Archaon fell. Rubble tumbled with him. The mountain seemed to roar with Be'lakor's voice. Archaon flailed. He plummeted through the darkness, losing his sense of direction. Seeming to accelerate through the abyssal pit that had opened up through the mountain and its foundations. His vision, his darksight and the sorcerous power of the Eye combined to form a kaleidoscope of shadow overlaying shadow. An obliviate blackness that deepened to an impossible intensity. Up and down, speed and space; these concepts became meaningless as Archaon plunged through the darkling abyss. All he knew was his father's voice echoing through oblivion. His earlier words thundering about him.

THE CROWN WAITS...

...IN THE FIRST SHRINE OF CHAOS–

WHERE THE FIRST HUMAN SOUL WAS BARTERED TO THE DARK GODS...

Then Archaon knew.

...HERE.

CHAPTER XVII

'What good are souls if they are not to be sold?'

– Anonymous

The Dreadpeak
The Worlds Edge Mountains
Grimnir's Day / Passing of Oaths IC 2519

Archaon hit stone. The warlord screamed, although he had not meant to. The impact was bone-shattering enough and would have broken him up into tiny pieces inside were it not for the protection of his hell-forged plate and the wyrdstone that threaded its way through his skeleton. The shard of iron hit the ground at an agonising angle, however, tearing through his insides. Moaning, Archaon scrabbled slowly around, holding his plate-punctured side. Opening his eye he saw nothing but darkness. Absolute. Like pitch poured into his mind. The Eye of Sheerian showed only more of the same. His darksight sizzled with the dank evil of the abyssal shrine. Turning his head, Archaon could see the faint shadows created by blasphemous runes inscribed in the stone of some kind of ancient gate.

Archaon felt the cracks created by his impact spread beneath him. The ancient stone gate to the First Shrine of Chaos disintegrated beneath him. Archaon gritted his teeth against the pain and the torment to come. With the cacophonous crash of the gate giving way, Archaon was falling once more amongst fragments of cursed stone.

Archaon tumbled through the darkest night of his soul. He had walked the polluted Wastes of the world. He had even navigated the empty depths of hell – an otherworldy Realm of Chaos, haunted by daemons and dread entities. Here, however, in a darkness to end all darkness, Archaon felt as if he were falling through the benighted pit-pupil in the eye of a dark god. All Dark Gods. As he saw them, they saw him. He was saturated in the bleak ruination of the collective gaze. He was tempered like a blade, moving between the furnace fires of their abominate love and ice waters of their need, stained black with the cruelty of iron. Phantasmic faces raged about Archaon in the blackness. The faces of men and beasts he had killed. Dark champions he had defeated. Monsters he had destroyed. Daemons he had obliterated from existence. All of them. Roaring for his soul.

Before long, his abyssal drop – accelerating faster and faster through the dark below the world – passed through the depths of an ocean of innocents. The men, women and children who would have to die in the End Times to come. A black, constellation-brimming sky of screaming faces, begging for Archaon's mercy. As he fell, Archaon could read the weakness of the world in them all. Given the eternity they craved, such simple souls would fall prey to the wrath, the despair, the hopes and desires that governed their polluted lives. It burst Archaon's heart and scarred his soul to know it, but Archaon came to understand – in the dreadful darkness – that these mortals had to die in order for the Dark Gods and the monstrous, predatory intelligences of the beyond to soul-starve to inexistence. That was what he was he–

Archaon struck the pit floor. The Chaos warlord roared as his plate warped about his smashed body. The shard of iron was hammered back through his gut, the metal twisting through him like a bent and serrated stake. A horn on his helm shattered and one entire side of his suit was battered flat out of shape. Moaning and rolling over onto his back, he felt for the sword splinter. Grasping for it in the darkness behind his eyelid, he gripped it with both gauntlets. Counting silently to himself, Archaon tore the daemon-shattered metal out of him. Again he bellowed. He coughed. He breathed his ragged breaths into oblivion. He opened his agony-clenched eye. His vision acclimatised to the foetid gloom. There was a miserable light but he couldn't tell where it was coming from. He didn't care. Other senses were being overwhelmed.

As he lay there he was struck by the smell. His laboured breaths took the indescribable feculence of the stench deep into his lungs. He tore off his helm by its remaining horn, gagging for something he could breathe. He retched and gushed blood over the body next to him. He was not alone. There were bodies. So many bodies. Gods, the smell. Rot and pestilence hung over the mound of suffering like a miasma. The gloom was thick with groans, pleading and madness. Insects ran rampant through the plaguescape of diseased forms. Flesh-eating beetles. Fat centipedes. A droning blanket of flies. Archaon tried to stand. Bones broke beneath his boots, leading to more wails of torment. Gangrenous limbs reached out for him. Leprous hands missing fingers scraped at his plate. He pulled his legs away from such pitiless suffering and clambered with difficulty across the diseased mound. Victims had little control over their illness-ravaged bodies – vomiting and making a mess of themselves and those about them. Pox-erupting fevers sent sufferers into a delirium of madness and the twilight was haunted by the laughter of the doomed. People picked rancid flesh from their own bones while the bodies of others bloomed with moulds and fungi that cared not if the nutrient-rich mound beneath was alive or dead.

As Archaon trudged across the never-ending mire of diseased bodies he felt forever pass in the darkness about him. These were the dead and dying he had left in his bloody wake. The millions he would maim and slaughter in the apocalyptic days to come. The famine and disease that would follow in his footsteps. As he strode, climbed and tumbled through the suffering, the armour of Morkar began to creak about Archaon's bones. Some kind of otherwordly corrosion reached through the browning metal. Plates sheared off him, falling into the bodies below. The pus-riddled. The infested. Those ripe with myriad corruptions. Those screaming for help that would never come, grabbing one another for rank comfort. The dead and quietly rotting.

With the rusted armour falling away in a red dust, all else about him disintegrated with the inflicted years. Cloak. Furs. Scabbard. Weapons. The treasures of Chaos. Like a madman – naked and splattered with the filth of the dead and the dying – Archaon clambered and crawled through the grasping limbs and the softening bodies. It was like a gloomy moor. Wet. Stinking. Undulating. Cloaked in a fog of flies and contagion. Before long the laughter became Archaon's own. A dark chuckle. The rasp of laughter. The boom of jubilant doom. The horror of death became a disgusting celebration of life – rich, ripe and overpowering. It started with the ragged wound in his side. It was no longer bleeding. Now it burned with infections and stank of the rot worming its way through his insides. Archaon's skin began to blister. Rashes spread, competing for flesh to ravage. Sores popped and wept down his body. Black blood and pus dribbled from his eyes, ears, nose and mouth in a constant and sickening stream. Maggots and worse squirmed through his flesh. Bits of Archaon fell away. Abandoned. Forgotten. Growths blossomed about his failing innards. He bloated and burst before his skin became a leathery cape thrown over the sharpness of his bones. Even as this withered away to mouldy dust from his stone-threaded skeleton, Archaon stalked on across the benighted landscape of suffering, rot and doom.

There was sick laughter still, but it was not Archaon's own. He was but bone and the indomitable force of will that held him together. The boom of dark mirth quaked through him. With every laugh from cavernous, froth-corrupted lungs, the moaning, fearful grasping and begging became frenzied and intense. The glee of a dark god passed like wet thunder through the realm of suffering – at once the call of a million crows, the chitter of feasting insects, the wailing of widows, the frustration and fury of approaching death and the drone of bells over gravestones. As the laughter shook the very darkness about Archaon, bones began to fall from his frame. His skeleton – that had trudged so far through the endless suffering – began to crumble. His browning bones slipped down through the sea of bodies. He went under, reaching, clawing with skeletal hands as he was dragged down through the writhings of the diseased, the ripeness of the dying and the ancient dust of the long dead.

Archaon felt the clean darkness whoosh about him as he tumbled through the hell of the abyssal shrine. He barely remembered what it was to have flesh. To feel anything but doom. He was falling for so long through the soothing gloom that Archaon fell asleep. When he awoke, he was surrounded by bodies once more. Bodies falling with him. They reached out for him but not in fear, dread or pain. The blackness ached with need and temptation. As he rolled, thrashed and tumbled through the swarm of bodies he saw that they were all the same. A desire from the darkness of his memory. The bodies all belonged to Giselle. A thousand Giselles, sharing the terror and excitement of the fall. Soon there were so many bodies about him – a swarm of flesh – that he could not tell in which direction he was falling or if he still was at all. Giselle, the fledgling Sigmarite sister, bright eyed and unknowing. Giselle the prisoner, thin-lipped and hate-filled of eye. Giselle the lover, her mind and body lost in the madness of the Wastes and the insanity that was Archaon. Giselle, the living corpse, the mouthless horror of emaciation and silence, staring reproach.

Archaon roasted in the fires of the pure flame. An inferno of writhing flesh that burned Archaon with his own damnation. Like a fireball of flesh and dark desires, Archaon fell through a hell of his own making. Archaon could not tell his flesh from Giselle's. One body's from another. They were fused in a spidery arrangement of entwining limbs and twisting torsos. Their hearts thudded as one – in horrible unity through the blackness – like that beating beneath the single breast of a godly Prince of Impossible Pleasures.

Suddenly there was an impact. Hard. Shocking. The clarity was soul-scouring. Bodies broke. Giselle's died. The aching fusion of flesh was torn from Archaon with a glass-slicing precision. Archaon was himself once more. He had endured… once more. Flailing down through the chasmic pit of the First Shrine, accelerating, falling deeper into darkness, Archaon had stuck something. Fragments of it fell about him. Like a crystal wall that his descent had shattered into myriad pieces, Archaon saw himself reflected in the innumerable facets of innumerable shards. Splinters showered about him like rain, creating a flux of impossible colours. In the reflection of each razored surface Archaon beheld Archaon. Archaon who was. Who had been. Who never would be. A mewling infant. An eager young boy. A young man in the making. A warrior, proud and true. A million darknid interpretations of Archaon. The savage. The Ruinous warrior lost on his path. The exalted champion fighting for each and every dark god. Archaon the defeated. Archaon the dead. Archaon the forgotten. Archaons instead. The warlord. The Everchosen. Lord of the Apocalypse. Archaon – end… of… All. Lives all lived in his endless, tumbling descent. A labyrinth of lifetimes. A mind fit to break, tortured by raw possibility and knowing, the endlessness of existence. Archaon screamed for his one life. His single determination. An end to everything known and unknown. A silent, empty darkness for the world and the realms beyond it. He closed his eye for the length of a boundless moment and it was gone.

Archaon hit water. It was like plummeting into rock. If it hadn't been for the wyrdstone that riddled his bones and skull, the impact alone would have smashed him into oblivion. He thundered down into the depths. He could see nothing, but the waters about him were thick, rich and warm. Eventually the force of his descent slowed and Archaon kicked for the surface. As the viscous darkness of the deep met the infernal gloom, Archaon tasted copper. Spitting his last breath, which exploded from his lungs at the surface, Archaon found that he was treading blood in a sea of gore. Like flowing magma the blood burned in patches, lighting the abyssal blackness with a hellish glow. Looking about, Archaon saw that predators of sweeping horned head, serrated dorsal sails and whipping tails cut through the bloody waters. Swimming, Archaon made his way to an archipelago of bone. Colossal ribcages of monstrous beasts and daemons. Small islands of shattered bone and piled skulls, up which the tides of gore washed. Storms of flame danced, seethed and churned across the surface of the red sea, sizzling in the never-ending drizzle of blood spilled from the darkness above.

Archaon hauled himself up through the bones of a monstrous ribcage, perching on a breastbone as the horrors on the blood below sloshed and thrashed to a frenzy. He sat there like a savage, his body dipped in drying blood. Then. Bubbles in the blood. A few at first. Building to a spuming maelstrom of gore. Archaon stood up on the ribcage, attempting to get a better look at the abomination rising from the bloody depths.

It was huge. Monstrous horns. Wings that showered gore from torn membranes of their leathery, outstretched surface. A mountain of red muscle, fused with black-bronze chains and great spiked plate. The bottomless bloodthirsting fury of some great daemon, hunched in its bestial rage. It bellowed its abyssal ire, the grotesqueness of its face stretched back over its colossal, fang-crowded jaws. The force of its territorial roar knocked Archaon from his perch and into the bloody waters. Predatory fiends surged for him with their daggered jaws. Grabbing one around the neck, Archaon dragged it up the shoreline of skulls, pummelling the creature to death. Another surged up the bank, snapping ferociously at Archaon, but the Chaos warlord stamped down on its head with a heel, killing the creature outright.

As he stood there, Archaon found that the monstrous Bloodthirster bellowed still. The slickness of blood dribbled away from Archaon's muscular frame. Firestorms died and skulls rolled back up the shore of the island. The abyssal beast was power incarnate. Violence. Murderous rage as an elemental force. Something about being in the monster's presence brought Archaon back to who he was. A butcher of innumerable deserving foes. A survivor of countless monstrous encounters. A nightmare born of blood. Tested across eternity. He had the dark intelligence of a great warrior, the Ruinous blessings of abominate gods and the death-dealing experience of lifetimes lived and lost.

The great daemon brought its gargantuan arms out of the sea of blood. In one he clutched a bronze battle axe that glowed with the darkness of its infernal craft. In the other was the length of a titanic whip that dribbled flame into the gore.

'Come on!' Archaon roared at the daemonic embodiment of his doom. The monster didn't need any further encouragement. Its arm came up, the searing whip snapped up and around, sizzling arcs of blood from its surface. Archaon turned and ran.

The whip slashed the island to a storm of shattered skull. The daemon stomped its cloven path through the shallow sea of blood. As Archaon leapt for the spine of a long-butchered beast and ran along its length, the Bloodthirster smashed through the titanic, skeletal remains with its great axe. Archaon was once more on the skull-crunching shores of a beach. The archipelago seemed to stretch forever through the darkness and the crashing blood of the sanguine sea.

Archaon could only hope it did. He ran. He ran as fast as he could. When he couldn't run he swam through the rich gore. From island to bone island. Skull mound to mound. Through the ribcages of abyssal behemoths and along the bones of great slain daemons. The Bloodthirster followed like a storm of brass and blood. It smashed through skeletons, decimated isles of bone and colossal skulls that sat in the shallows like standing stones.

Archaon ran on. He could not afford to stop. The blade edge of the huge axe had been sharpened on the Blood God's flinty heart. It hungered for Archaon's blood. In the dull reflection of the bronze blade the Chaos warrior had died a thousand times – cleaved clean in half, smashed to oblivion in a fountain of skull and splintered bone, his head whooshed from his body in a glorious splatter of trailing gore. Each flesh-mulching, spine-shearing, blood-storming ordeal of a death Archaon had avoided by the skin of his imperilled soul. The daemon was an indefatigable force of fury with an abyssal appetite for destruction. And impossibly, Archaon was tiring it. Even such an abominate entity had limitations. The inferno that burned with twice the ferocity could only afford to burn half as long and through an endless series of frustrations, in which the great daemon had smashed the skull archipelago to splinters, Archaon had slowed the monstrosity with its own hate-fuelled exertions.

Crunching to a halt in the skulls, Archaon came to a stop. He was no less exhausted. His mind hurt with split-second evasions and strategies. His legs burned from running. His arms from swimming. His chest from breathing, rising up and down as he stood still on the island. He turned and ran straight back at the storming daemon blasting its way through bone and blood. The abomination was far from spent. It was surprised by Archaon's changing tactic, however, and its arms swung with the infernal burn of an eternity of last efforts.

Archaon skidded down across the skulls. The axe descended with fury and savage precision. For the ghost of a moment,

Archaon saw his blade-cleaved body – split-splattered from temple to toe – in the bronze reflection of the blade. The axe missed, sending skulls rocketing away in all directions. As the great daemon brought up the weapon it found that Archaon was gone. The abominate entity tore its horned head around this way and that. It kicked at the skull shore with is colossal hoof. It peered at the bloody shallows with its tiny, rage-crackling eyes. It looked about at the gore-misted darkness above. Archaon was nowhere. The great daemon unleashed an abyss-trembling roar. The thing had never known such affliction.

Archaon slid down from the pitted bronze of the axe haft. As the blade had buried itself in the skull mound, the Chaos warrior had clutched the thick haft and travelled back with it above the island of bone. As the colossal daemon searched and bellowed, Archaon leapt for the chains and spikes rearing from the embedded plate of the monster's back, riding out the abomination's hellish fury. There Archaon waited. And waited. He held tight to the armoured spikes as the beast went mad, cleaving the dark realm of its nightmare existence to ruin.

Then, as the thing seemed to have no more monstrous rage to give, Archaon hauled himself up the beast's hunched red back and boxed it in a ragged ear. The response was blood-curdling and instantaneous. The great daemon was insane with its own ire. It swung its colossal axe about it, trying to butcher its tiny foe – who seemed insultingly close yet impossible to hit. As Archaon clambered back and forth through the back spikes, the bronze axe smashed and sparked off the embedded armour. Archaon felt the fury of the blade pass by and hung one-handed from a spike as the axe blade bit deep into the daemon's own back. The monstrosity didn't seem to even notice. Pulling himself back up, Archaon held on tight as the abomination stamped through the bloody shallows to shake him free. Archaon would not be unseated, however, riding the great daemon like one of the lost monstrosities of his horde. Again the axe blade came. Again and again. Smashing spikes from the daemon's back and visiting monstrous wounds on itself in the dwindling fires of its fury.

Finally. With the huge bronze axe still buried in its hunched and mutilated back, the Blood God's greater daemon crashed forward into the skulls of a partially demolished island. Archaon rode up and down on the daemon's exertions. The beast was done. It had visited a monstrous fury upon itself and inflicted grievous wounds no being was meant to survive. It crawled up the shore before falling on its muscle-bound arms and the length of its extinguished whip.

Leaping down from the monster's back, Archaon grabbed the tapering end of the whip and heaved it up and around the daemon's monstrously thick neck. All the while the devastated abomination watched him through the scorched orb of a single eye – the other having burst from its frenzied efforts to acquire the Chaos warlord. Sliding the tip of the whip beneath the great daemon's neck, Archaon created an improvised noose. Grabbing the weapon with both hands, Archaon heaved. He heaved for all he was and was going to be. The great Bloodthirster could barely heave its decimated red carcass from the beach of bone but managed to claw at the whip cutting across its throat.

Now it was Archaon's turn to bellow and roar. He hauled at the whip, the muscles of his arms and chest bulging, his bones braced to break. He strained for his survival. For victory. For destiny. As the great daemon breathed its last, its own skull crashing to the shore and its claws falling limply away, Archaon released the whip. He fell backwards into skulls and the blood that lapped up the shore. As he breathed, ached, found his way back from the insanity of his trials, the hellfire about the archipelago died. All was darkness. The clink of skulls and the slosh of blood faded away.

Torches suddenly whooshed to fiery life. Archaon squinted. He was in the depths of the shrine. The First Shrine of Chaos. A place of terrible evil that had scorched the stone black with its malevolent significance. That had damned the dwarfs of Karak Zhul to destruction. That had been the site of man's first fall to darkness. It was here that the Ruinous Powers had first bestowed their blessings on the first mortal pledged to Chaos. A dread, primordial savage of strength and cunning, who had earned immortality and a place at the Dark Gods' side as the first daemon prince.

Archaon got to his feet. He had completed the Ruinous trials as he had begun them. Decked in the hell-forged plate of Morkar, with the *Slayer of Kings* hanging from his belt in its scabbard and the Eye of Sheerian bleeding its balelight from his horned helm. Before him, in the tiny chamber, was a black, stone throne – cracked and ancient – the carved symbols and sigils of the Chaos Pantheon all but worn away by time. The torches crackled either side of the throne. In it sat a skeleton. A former mighty champion of Chaos. The bones of the warlord were warped and spiked with the fell gifts of the gods. On his head sat a simple band of black gold, with its eight points stabbing inwards through the champion's skull. The Crown of Domination. Treasure of the Ruinous Powers, bequeathed to the Everchosen of Chaos and Lord of the End Times to come. Archaon paused for a moment before its reverence and the dread memory of his predecessor.

Archaon clenched a gauntlet and smashed the skull, with all the unceremonious force he could muster. Shaking embedded fragments of bone from the Crown of Domination, Archaon admired its dark simplicity. The crowns of kings might be towering, elaborate things encrusted with gems and devoid of significance. The crown of the Everchosen was elegant in its understatement. It was meant for the darkest of warlords – the most apocalyptic of the dread Powers' warrior champions. Its points were directed inwards, ensuring it could be worn within a helm on the field of battle. It had but one setting at its fore, meant for a single jewel: the Eye of Sheerian with which the crown's terrible power would be combined.

Turning, the grit scraping under his boot, Archaon strode from the shrine chamber. A stone door rumbled aside, the dark sigils that adorned it speaking of the End Times to come. Sunlight, bleak but blinding, was admitted to the chamber, smouldering on the malevolence of the black stone. Archaon peered through the searing light to find he was at the foot of the Dreadpeak. He had no idea how long he had been in the mountain. How long he had suffered the trials of the shrine. What had been an eternity to him might only have been minutes, hours or days in the waiting ruin of the world. All he knew was that he had earned the admiration of the Dark Gods and had been rewarded with their treasures. That now he would be crowned their champion of darkness – their Everchosen – worthy to lead the legions of hell and visit their myriad calamities upon the waiting world. With the Crown of Domination clutched in one gauntlet he ventured outside.

CHAPTER XVIII

'It is said that the day was marked in the heavens by a dread omen. The appearance of a great comet that split the sky in two with its passing. A falling star of tails twin that filled the world over which it shone with fear and foreboding.'

– Urshel, *Signs and Wonders*

The Dreadpeak
The Worlds Edge Mountains
Sigmarsfest IC 2519

Archaon stood on the rocky ledge. The tents of his Ruinous army dotted the valleys and mountainsides, about smouldering camp fires. Everywhere there was evidence of a battle fought and won. Dwarf helms and weapons littered the disturbed earth. Mounds of bodies burned, the flames of the fallen – both dwarf and those of the horde – licked at the sky. Archaon's army had been kept occupied while waiting for him. A dwarf army marching on Karak Zhul, no doubt following some ancient prophecy – as Archaon did – to avenge their mountain kin.

'It seems they arrived too early,' Archaon said.

Or thousands of years too late.

Be'lakor was with him. The shadow of the mountain darkened. The surrounding vegetation withered. Rock creaked and splintered in the dark lord's presence. Small boulders shattered. Archaon's fingers drifted to the hilt of his daemonsword.

Even now, with the world yours to burn, you fear me...

'Take care now, daemon,' Archaon warned. 'I fear we have the eyes of the gods on us this day. You are the Harbinger, the Bearer of the Crown, He Who Heralds Conquerors. You have a role to perform in these dark events. The Ruinous Powers are watching. They will not be denied their amusement.'

Archaon heard calls from the valley floor. Champions and dark knights could see him on the mountainside. Pantheon-pledged warriors dropped bodies they were carrying. Others poured from tents and small camps. Word of his return spread quickly with marauders, bestial champions and dread warriors flooding the area before the Dreadpeak from adjoining valleys. Before long the mountainsides and valleys were swarming with the marauder savages, half-breeds, armoured warriors and dark champions of Archaon's colossal army – doom, as far as the eye could see. Spiked plate. Horned helms. Murderous weaponry. Banners and standards of flayed flesh and bone, bearing the eight-point star of the Ruinous Pantheon. The symbol of a Chaos undivided. Archaon's star.

High above the Ruinous horde, the distant thunder of Archaon's dread presence rolled through the mountains. Above that, a comet blazed across the firmament, slicing the sky in two: a dark omen of the hell the world had to pay and the calamity to come. Archaon slipped his horned helm from his head. He looked up at the sky and nodded slowly to himself. The comet had a twin tail. Like the comet that appeared the night of Sigmar's birth. Like the comet that had adorned the blade of the greatsword *Terminus* – the sigil of his templar order. Another sick joke of the Dark Gods, Archaon decided.

Archaon saw Eins, Zwei and Vier push through the front ranks of armoured warriors and make their way up the mountainside. The wraith-warriors approached, Zwei leading the daemon steed Dorghar by the reins. The misshapen Vier was helping a figure in furs up the incline. As he moved his warped wing, Archaon could see it was Giselle. She walked with difficulty but aided by Vier just managed the slope. She was a vision of skeletal reproach. The skin of her full and once comely face was stretched over her skull. Without a mouth she could not speak, but her eyes said it all. This was the moment that she – and Father Dagobert – had tried to keep Archaon from. It had taken a century but he had done it, much to Giselle's soul-hollow misery. The world would burn and it would be Archaon – the once good man, Diederick Kastner – who would strike the spark.

The Swords of Chaos slowed. The gathered horde fell silent. A monstrous shadow rose up from behind Archaon. The swirling black form of a daemon, bleeding forth from the rock of the cursed mountain. Horned head. A gargoyle's wings. Cloven claws and slithering tail. A great infernal prince of midnight muscle and daemonic visage. A Ruinous Star sat on his chest – an ancient scar – that like a living altar declared that the Dark Gods were unified behind a single, mortal champion of Chaos. Despite his malevolent majesty, the daemon Be'lakor hung his head like a dog. From the sky above, from the dirt beneath their feet and through the eyes of every pantheon-pledged maniac, warrior and warlord gathered before Archaon, the dread Powers were watching.

Archaon turned. He looked up at the monstrous form of his puppet master, his father-in-shadow, his daemonic foe. Thrusting both his horned helm and the Crown of Domination at the abomination's chest, Archaon gave Be'lakor the burning hatred of one eye.

'This is as close as you're going to get to this, Bearer of the Crown. Savour it,' Archaon said. 'Now do your infernal duty, dark prince.'

A bottomless loathing crackled between the two. Archaon turned and presented himself to his vast horde of darkness. The daemon Be'lakor hesitated – the rage of having to crown another, again – tearing at the muscles of his infernal face. He lifted the Crown of Domination and offered it to the sky. Moving around in a circle, the daemon presented it in eight different directions, each time announcing Archaon's coronation in a different dark tongue. Archaon only understood the last of the Dark Master's sullen proclamations.

I present to you Archaon – Everchosen of Chaos, commander of the legions of hell and undoubted Lord of the End Times.

He felt the monstrous darkness of the daemon's touch as he gently lowered the crown onto Archaon's shaven head. The Chaos warlord felt the eternally burning Mark of Chaos rage through his flesh, about where the crown was intended to sit. Like a mantrap of the soul, the black gold of the crown's points snapped shut, piercing both ruin-blessed flesh and skull. Archaon roared up at the heavens. The pain was unimaginable. Like barbs through his very being, the points created a horrific nexus at their centre: an oblivion in his mind through which the Ruinous hearts and dark thoughts of all dread things under his banner were his to know. Archaon cast his gaze across the monstrous horde he had amassed. Warriors, butchers and abominates from the world over. As his gaze passed across them he felt the individual darkness of the souls, their fear of him and the gods he represented, the savage expectation of the slaughter and ruin to come. He heard the whisper of betrayal in champions that he knew he must kill. He knew the dark secrets and strategies that would keep such a colossal army – all fighting for a different world ending dread – unified.

Be'lakor brought the horned helmet of Morkar's cursed plate down over the Everchosen's head. The helm sat snugly – as it always had – with the crown slipping slickly into the space crafted to accommodate it. With a sizzle of sorcerous power, the Eye of Sheerian – already ensconced in a setting at the front of the helm – became as one with the Crown of Domination. Although he had not realised it, Archaon was still roaring his soul-shearing agony and jubilation to the sky. The world had become more than just an experience of the moment. Pain. Emptiness. Expectation. Through the Eye of Sheerian, combined with the properties of the fell crown, the world seared into spectral focus. Beyond the blunt appreciation of what was happening to him – the chill air of the mountains, the agony of the metal punctured through his skull, the thousands of eyes on him, their gaze the burden of dark expectation – Archaon now saw more. A ghostly existence of what had been and what would be. He saw the dwarf army butchered by his warriors of Chaos in the valleys mere hours before and he saw the mountains shake and shed grit, scree and bouncing boulders in some calamity shortly to come. Whereas the Eye of Sheerian had shown him secrets great distances away – across ice, ocean and mountain range – combined with the Crown of Domination it could now cast its gaze both forward and back into events that had been and were yet to be. The sensation was a dread knowing, both intoxicating and fearful. Like a man leaning off a cliff, intending to fall, Archaon obeyed an instinct to pull himself back. It would take some time to acclimatise to the power and overwhelming intensity of the terrible gift and longer to command such abilities. Archaon could think of no better tool, however, to help him usher in the apocalypse than the gift to see the end before it came to pass. With such a dread gaze directed into the days, dread months and dark years to come, Archaon truly had become the Lord of the End Times.

Archaon's roar had been joined by thousands of others. As his voice trailed away, the mind-shattering effect of the crown numbing to secrets unthought and a future waiting to be known, Archaon drew the *Slayer of Kings* and held the blade up. Beside him Archaon sensed that the mighty Be'lakor had taken to a daemonic knee. Archaon's horde did the same, bowing their horned helms and slamming armoured knees into the dirt. Prostrate before the Everchosen of Chaos.

'Daemon, begone,' Archaon hissed at Be'lakor, without even turning his helm. 'I see you, monster. For the first time I truly see you. Stay out of my past. Make way for my future. Now get out of my sight and never sully my presence with your rank darkness again.'

Archaon expected some kind of protest. A threat. A warning. A rejoinder of Ruinous wit. The Everchosen of Chaos turned. Be'lakor was gone. The shadows of rocks, boulders and the Dreadpeak itself seemed to recede and lighten. Archaon grunted.

His Swords of Chaos approached, accompanied by Dorghar and the frail Giselle. Now Be'lakor was gone, he sheathed his daemonsword. Archaon knew what was expected of him. To climb into the saddle. To ride through the roaring jubilation of his colossal host. To lead them out of the desolation of the mountains and into civilised lands of wanton slaughter, flame and darkness. He didn't need the Crown of Domination to show him that.

Vier helped Giselle up to Archaon before backing away. The girl was a skeletal horror – like a wight that haunted the tomb of Archaon's old life. She sank into her furs, the slightness of her emaciated body susceptible to the cold. Long, bony fingers pulled the furs about her. Her jaw moved under the skin stretched across her skull, as though she wanted to say something. Archaon took her skeletal hand in his gauntlet and said it for her.

'Still think I can be saved?' he said, his words a whisper and his humour dark.

Giselle leaned in, holding her fragile form close to the Everchosen's armoured form. He was like a monstrous statue hewn of apocalyptic promise, while she was a deathly echo of the past, so slight and wasted that the rising wind itself would have felled her. The storms that accompanied Archaon everywhere crashed thunder through the skies. Giselle brought her head up next to his, as if to whisper something into the side of his helm.

'Save you?' the girl eternal hissed. 'Who do you think damned you in the first place?'

After everything that Archaon had seen, all the horror he had experienced, he didn't think it was possible to be shocked. The girl's voice – a rasping, suggestive shadow of what it had been – sent a bolt of lightning through the emptiness of the Everchosen's dark heart. Grabbing her by the furs that sat on her sharp shoulders, Archaon pushed Giselle away. The girl's eyes had bleached to an oblivion of blackness and a wretched mouth had stretched itself through the stringy flesh beneath her nose.

'No,' was all the Everchosen could manage.

Excruciating pain once more cut through his side. Looking down, Archaon could see that Giselle had stabbed him. Blinking the shock from his mind, he recognised the dagger. It was a savage thing, both blade and hilt crafted beautifully from the claw of a daemon. Be'lakor's claw. The claw Archaon had chopped from the Dark Master's hand and claimed for his own. Giselle had taken it from him and been busy in her starvation and infirmity. She had slipped it straight through the hole where the shard of sword had punctured the plate. Straight into the agonising sheath created by the old wound.

Giselle was laughing. Girl. Withered hag. Daemon. She was all these things at once. Horrifying and alluring in equal measure, like an abominate daemon of Slaanesh. The girl's scorn cut through him. Clutching his side, Archaon tried to focus through the black torment tearing through his flesh where the daemonic dagger sat. Through the Eye of Sheerian he saw the real Giselle. With heart-stopping horror, Archaon felt his way through a century of haunting suspicions and spectral realisations.

It had been Giselle who had brought the *Liber Caelestior – The Celestine Book of Divination* – to him in the first place. Who with the cruellest weapons of all – pity, trust and even love – had helped to damn him. Had kept him on the dark path, even when she seemed to want to drag him from it. The burn of her touch, her purity, was a torment Archaon had visited upon himself, some part of him wanting to believe. Some part of him desiring a saviour. Desiring a way back. For him, Giselle had been a thread he had unravelled as he wandered the benighted labyrinth of his doom. Through his feelings for her, Archaon fooled himself into feeling as though he always had some kind of way back. At least the strength to end himself before he became an end to all else. Such honesty scorched his Ruinous flesh and lit a fire in the darkness of his mind.

Archaon looked from Giselle to the dagger hilt and back to the girl. The girl who while the world turned, while the champions of Chaos lived and died and Archaon spent a century seeking his doom, had remained ever young. Ever Giselle the girl he had saved from the beastmen in the forest. Ever Giselle, the Sigmarite sister. Even after their time in the Realm of Chaos had changed them, Giselle's affliction should have been her end decades before. Only some living lie, some daemon-thing existing within the dark consecration of Archaon's presence could exist as such. As a skeletal horror bereft of lips. Of words. The daemon had words for him now and they proceeded in the voice of the girl he had known.

'Save me, Archaon, save me,' she cackled in mockery. Then her voice changed, searing with the bottomless hate of the abyss: 'Archaon… save yourself!'

The Everchosen grabbed Giselle's furs and tore them away. As they ripped and parted, the daemon's foul carcass was revealed. A wasted cage of stretched skin and sharp ribs. On her chest, protruding proudly through the emaciation, Archaon could see a mark, a sigil in protruding bone. The Ruinous Star. The star of the Dark Master. The Mark of Be'lakor. The same one that Archaon had found on Gangryss, on Ograx the Great, on the Curseling and the living shadows of the Forsaken Fortress. On Be'lakor himself.

'Kiss me, Archaon,' Giselle taunted, her infernal laughter

everywhere as the abomination leaned in with her ragged mouth.

Archaon grabbed the daemon dagger and heaved at the Ruinous blade. The Everchosen roared his agony and fury to the gods. Moving his gauntlet to the *Slayer of Kings*, Archaon drew the daemonsword. It blazed from its scabbard, already glowing with hate for the Slaaneshi daemon. Giselle's cackling died on the wind as the *Slayer of Kings* passed through her – scorching her furs to ash and smashing her bones to furious oblivion.

As what remained of Giselle bounced and clattered down the mountainside, Archaon doubled over. The Swords of Chaos had already drawn their bone blades but seemed as shocked and confused by the rapid turn of events as Archaon himself. The colossal horde looked on with bloodthirst and wonder, assuming that the Everchosen of Chaos was putting on some kind of brutal, sacrificial display of merciless power.

The searing torment of the wound and the daemonic claw embedded in his flesh became something else. Darkness flooded from the blade, filling him with helplessness and woe. His black heart pumped to a pause while some dread presence deep inside him strangled his soul. It was Be'lakor. The Dark Master had made his play. Archaon had tried to bind the daemon prince to a blade of iron. Be'lakor had used one made from his own flesh, however, to invade Archaon's own. To breach the walls of Archaon's plate and storm the spiritual fortress of his soul. The Dark Master was winning. By the gods, he was winning.

Archaon suddenly reared and roared, the *Slayer of Kings* rattling in his gauntlet. He tried to talk to the daemon possessing his body, mind and being but only found his threats and entreaties bounced back at him through the black oblivion creeping up through him. He was drowning in Be'lakor. The Dark Master – who was bound by dark decree to be the Bearer and not the wearer of the Crown of Domination – had achieved both. Now Archaon was the Everchosen of Chaos, Be'lakor would assume his son-in-shadow's flesh, be the darkness that wore the crown and lead the legions of hell across the face of the world as he had done before.

Archaon started to say something but it was Be'lakor's savage words that passed his lips.

'Die!' he roared. Archaon swung the *Slayer of Kings* – aware of his devastating movements but not in control of them. He demolished Zwei with the daemonblade. The misshapen Vier went to turn the *Slayer of Kings* aside with his crooked bone blade but Be'lakor swung back with Archaon's clenched gauntlet and knocked the wraith-warrior's head from his hunched shoulders. Eins slashed the daemonblade away once, twice… even a third time. Be'lakor was just playing with the Sword of Chaos, however. Lunging forward with unstoppable ease, Be'lakor rammed the daemonsword straight through the chest of the wraith-warrior, steaming its darkness away to nothing.

The Everchosen stood there for a moment. Still. Not thrashing. Not bellowing.

'Flesh of my flesh,' Be'lakor said with Archaon's lips. 'I am yours and you are mine. Soon your soul will be but a forgotten blemish on my own–'

Archaon roared. The mountains rang with his fury. The warriors of Chaos pledged to Archaon's doom lifted their heads. Morkar's ancient plate trembled. The darkness fighting within slowed to a soul-pulverising stop.

Be'lakor was not the first daemon Archaon had fought for his soul. Thunder tore through the heavens above. Archaon reached up and lightning jagged down through the skies to his fingertips.

As Archaon's roar echoed away and a grim silence descended, the Everchosen's plate smoked. With slow, agonising movements, Archaon lowered his hand. With some effort he pulled his boots, one then the other, from the glass about him. Sand, grit and rock had fused to obsidian as the lightning strike passed down through Archaon and into the cursed mountain. Turning, the Chaos warlord saw that his shadow had similarly been melted into the mountainside – except it wasn't his shadow. It was the monstrous outline of Be'lakor. Stepping back, Archaon turned the *Slayer of Kings* in one hand. The obsidian outline began to steam and bubble. The black glass melted. One claw, then another, reached out of the liquid. Be'lakor's horned head broke the surface and Archaon watched as the daemon prince climbed up out of the rock of the Dreadpeak.

Do you know what yo–

'I've spent a century listening to your monstrous self-pity, Be'lakor,' Archaon spat, his words almost cracking under the intensity of the hatred with which he spoke them. 'And eternities trying to escape it. This world has seen your time, abominate. Now it will see mine. You will never be the Everchosen of Chaos – for my reign will be dark, bloody and short, and this world ends with me. And when it does, daemon – with no damned followers, lost warriors or innocent girls to worship you or do your bidding – so will you…'

Be'lakor seethed with dark rage and abyssal frustration. The air crackled and spat about him like a midnight forge. The daemon prince reached out. His shadow sword rose up from the pool of obsidian from which he'd ascended. Taking the monstrous length of the weapon in his claws, the Dark Master levelled the blistering shadow of the blade at Archaon.

'Die…' The daemon proclaimed once more.

'You first,' the Everchosen of Chaos told his father-in-shadow.

The sword of shadow and the *Slayer of Kings* clashed. Each impact echoed through the mountains. Sparks of unnatural energy blasted from the blades as mortal and daemon prince tested each other once again. The shadow blade that seethed darkness one moment and nothing the next. The *Slayer of Kings*, which raged to blistering brightness as the prison blade sang with the daemon's desire to maim, cleave and kill. Archaon held himself to one side, covering his wound and the dagger still skewered through him. Every movement was a muscle-shredding agony that the daemon prince attempted to exploit.

Towering above Archaon, the Dark Master was still the

monstrous, elemental force, swinging his blade with ancient skill and the power of oblivion. Archaon no longer moved through the split-second evasions and desperate attacks that had been his only defence in the Forsaken Fortress. Archaon fought not like a father's son or a master's puppet. He was the Everchosen of Chaos. The world quaked beneath his boots. Archaon fought like he had never fought before. Everything he had ever learned. Every success. Every failure. It all fell into place as the Everchosen expertly turned Be'lakor's blade aside – swinging, stabbing, cleaving, back-slashing and smashing his way across the side of the mountain.

As the titanic battle raged up the Dreadpeak, dislodging tumbling boulders and cleaving away entire shelves of cursed rock, thunder shook the heavens. Lightning slashed at the rock about the pair and Archaon's horde moved up through the valleys to watch them – champions ordering those warriors willing to assist their warlord back to the Ruinous ranks. For Archaon there were no more monstrous lunges, only to cut through the sizzling shadow of Be'lakor's insubstantial form. The Eye revealed strategies to the Everchosen moments ahead of time, prompting Archaon to abandon such futile attacks in favour of those with a greater chance of success. The Dark Master felt the change in his shadow-son immediately. Tested by the Dark Gods and awarded the boon of their powerful gifts, Archaon as mortal champion was a match for the daemon prince – much to Be'lakor's fury.

The huge daemon wheeled about, his tail and wings angling furiously to aid balance while at the same time tearing through the air as weapons of their own. Archaon leapt the monster's slashing tail while jumping between rocks and smashing down through the defensive presentation of the solidified sword of shadow. Archaon passed the streaming glow of the daemon weapon about him and from hand to hand, slashing aside the daemon prince's furious attacks and cutting nicks in the membrane of his great wings.

Archaon rolled as Be'lakor's cloven claw stamped an impact crater into the rock where Archaon had been standing moments before. The Everchosen buried the daemonblade in the cursed stone of the mountain, cutting away stony ledges and sending the daemon prince slip-sliding down the slope in a small rockslide of scree and boulders. Archaon ran, skidded and jumped down the mountainside at his infernal father. A leaping chop of the *Slayer of Kings*, with enough force to split an oak, was met by the shadow blade and turned aside by Be'lakor. Pushing Archaon back at the mountainside, the Dark Master smashed his broad blade at Archaon, dislodging the stone above and sections of rockface that almost buried the Everchosen.

The Dreadpeak shook with the monstrous battle, the mountain smashed by otherworldy blades and the supernatural power of the exalted warlord and the daemon prince. While most of the time both Archaon and Be'lakor were seconds away from being skewered or sliced in half, some raging assaults were more furious than others. When Archaon lost his footing, Be'lakor stabbed the shadow sword under the Everchosen's arm and into rock. Archaon brought the *Slayer of Kings* up immediately, the daemonblade passing through the insubstantiality of Be'lakor's blade and up past the daemon's face. Sparking off the dark glory of his horns, the daemon prince was surprised for a moment before landing a brutal kick in Archaon's armoured midriff and driving the embedded claw-dagger in further.

Landing nearby, Archaon allowed himself to skid away down a sheer slope, landing at the bottom and rolling over in agony. Be'lakor swooped down on his great wings; the Everchosen reared and launched into a blistering attack, which backed the Dark Master out onto a treacherous cliff.

As the battle raged and the mountains shook, the heavens began to darken. Night fell with the twin-tailed comet streaking high overhead and the dread moons rising over the Worlds Edge. The torches of Archaon's monstrous horde moved like a rash through the valleys, circling the Dreadpeak and following the battle around.

As the night wore on and both mortal champion and

daemon prince began to tire, the world felt the abominate gaze of the Ruinous Powers. The mountains glowed with a Ruinous hue while vegetation withered on the mountainsides. The dwarfs, greenskins and ratmen of the range hid in the tunnels and holds while those unlucky enough to be travelling the passes and high trails turned rabid with the murderous appetites of the Dark Gods.

Be'lakor's outlandish bladework – accompanied by his slashing tail and slicing wings – became slower but more determined. Archaon, slowed by his grievous wound and his mortal limitations, had to abandon the more adventurous ripostes and athletic evasions, in favour of savage lunges and decapitating backswings with the daemon-fuelled *Slayer*. Like pugilists at the end of a bout, the pair's attempts to land a murderous blow became laboured, but the monstrous sword swings more powerful. With their blades showering black sparks off each other, glancing plate and the mountain, huge sections of rockface rumbled, cracked and tumbled down the Dreadpeak. On several occasions, curious throngs of Chaos warriors, getting too close to the action, were buried in such rockfalls and gorge-burying slides.

Be'lakor swung his sword of sizzling shadow with monstrous force, sending Archaon skidding across the scree of the mountainside before the Everchosen ran back at him, launching from a boulder and smashing his blade down on the daemon. Archaon swung the *Slayer of Kings* down on Be'lakor again and again, each time the daemon prince taking shelter behind the defensive offering of his blade. The furious onslaught cracked the cliff beneath the Dark Master's cloven claws and sent him tumbling down into the valley amongst the thunder of falling rock.

Archaon allowed himself a moment to catch his breath, his plate rattling with the rise and fall of his chest. He knew his best chance of beating Be'lakor was to reach the valley floor fast. In the ghoulish moonlight, Archaon felt the eye of the Dark Gods – the monstrous pantheon – eager to know if their dread choice in Archaon had been deserved. Half skidding, half running down the mountainside, Archaon made his way for the scree-filled valley. His heart leapt as he saw colossal pieces of rock at the bottom of the collapsed cliff, with Be'lakor's black tail twitching below a titanic piece. Archaon ran about the huge boulder, the *Slayer of Kings* held high. If the daemon prince was trapped, Archaon intended to butcher the monster where he lay. He knew in his dark heart that Be'lakor would do the same. As the Everchosen sidled around, the furnace glow of his daemonblade revealed that Be'lakor had torn himself from the twitching remnant of his tail. The Eye of Sheerian showed the frenzied daemon prince come out from behind another colossal piece of rock just in time for Archaon to get the *Slayer of Kings* between him and the daemon prince's monstrous swing.

Archaon left the ground. He hit the rockface of a mountain across the valley with supernatural force, shattering the rock. Archaon shook his horned helm and tried to extricate himself from the crater in the sheer mountainside. Be'lakor was an abominate shadow, pounding across the valley in great strides. Shaking himself free and with U'zuhl blazing with reproach in the steel prison of his blade, Archaon ran at his daemonic foe. Archaon bellowed and war-cried. The Dark Master roared with inhuman might. It looked as though the two might quake the Worlds Edge Mountain range with the monstrous impact of their blades.

Guided by the Eye of Sheerian and what Be'lakor intended to do, Archaon skidded down through the moss and scree of the valley floor. As Be'lakor turned Archaon threw himself immediately at the daemon. The pair rolled with the momentum, with the Dark Master's stump of a tail thrashing and his wings tearing across the sharp rocks. Archaon sat astride the daemon, smashing him again and again in the face with his sword-clenched fist. Be'lakor grabbed Archaon in a bear hug and pulled the Everchosen to him with all of his infernal might, worming the black dagger in Archaon's side agonisingly through his insides.

As they rolled and separated, Be'lakor could see that the

Slayer of Kings lay abandoned in the scuffle nearby. The daemon scrabbled to his feet and surged at Archaon but Archaon was ready for him. Picking up a small boulder, Archaon launched it at his father-in-shadow, the impact turning the rock to dust against Be'lakor's face. The daemon prince grunted, dazed, but by the time he had recovered himself Archaon had already recovered the *Slayer of Kings*. This time it was the Dark Master's turn to fly – a wing-tangled mess – into the wall of the rockface. Archaon roared up at the night sky as the monstrous daemon tried to pull himself free. Lightning cut down through the darkness, striking the mountain above and dislodging boulders, scree and a section of rockface with an excruciating crack that rumbled its way down to the valley floor and buried Be'lakor.

Archaon would not be fooled again. He ran through the dark clouds of dust billowing away from the collapse. Sinking the searing blade of the *Slayer of Kings* into mounds of shattered rock and scree, Archaon furiously searched for the daemon prince.

'Where are you, abominate?' Archaon roared. 'Face me!'

The small mountain of scree beside the Everchosen exploded, sending shards of splintered rock everywhere. Archaon was knocked half off his feet. Be'lakor stood there, his wings demolished, his tail trailing ichor and half of one of his horns shattered. The Dark Master came at Archaon like a wild beast, swinging the searing shadow of his blade madly at the Everchosen. It was Archaon's chance and the dark warlord knew it. The daemon prince was unbalanced by his exhaustion, his frustration and rage. Calling on his skill, the murderous passion of his daemonblade and the spectral glimpse of future decimation provided by the Eye, Archaon threw himself into the monstrous clash of swords. Feet scrabbled around. Arms swung relentlessly about and the two blades showered dark sparks of abyssal energy about the Everchosen and his father-in-shadow.

Archaon knew he had the daemon prince, moments before Be'lakor did. Holding his ground through several shadow-streaming swipes of the shadow sword, Archaon felt the monstrous blade shimmer back to the world once more. Smashing Be'lakor's blade away, Archaon watched it leave the claw of the monster. Turning into a devastating spin, Archaon clutched the *Slayer of Kings* like a knife and in completing the manoeuvre, slammed the daemonsword straight through the black flesh of the daemon's stomach. Be'lakor was lifted off his cloven claws by the thudding impact before falling to his knees before the Everchosen. The Dark Master roared his agonies to the crowded heavens.

'Just die, you monstrous thing,' Archaon spat as Be'lakor endured his agonies. Archaon took a step back as the abomination looked up at him with murderous loathing and reared to torturous full height. With the raging blade still stuck through his belly, Be'lakor stomped towards the unarmed Archaon.

You are nothing, the daemon howled.

He smashed Archaon into the ground with his claw. The Everchosen bounced off the rock floor of the valley and clattered away. Be'lakor stamped agonisingly after him. As Archaon brought up his helm he saw the colossal shard of rock moments before it was to hit him. Rolling beneath its unstoppable progress, the boulder would have pulverised him to blood and scrap against the rock wall of the mountain. Another came and another, smashing into the valley floor about him like crashing meteorites. One bounced to the ground below his feet, knocking him over with the impact. Be'lakor was on him immediately and although Archaon saw it coming he could not evade the cloven-clawed kick coming for his helm. The impact knocked him off his feet. He landed some distance away in a cacophony of tumbling plate.

Archaon had barely found his way back to his senses when he realised that the skewered daemon prince was standing over him. Pinning the Everchosen to the ground with his clawed foot, Be'lakor smashed Archaon's helm into the rock again and again with his fist.

I am Be'lakor – first of the Daemon Princes. Dark Master of the world with the legions of hell mine to command.

The Dark Master took his foot from Archaon and the Chaos warlord saw in the Eye of Sheerian the horror of what was to come. Hefting a huge boulder above his head, the sword-skewered Be'lakor trembled above Archaon.

'No...' the Everchosen managed.

When it hit, smashing to rock dust on Archaon and his buckled plate, the dark warlord felt himself break up inside. It was like being pulverised between Mannslieb and Morrslieb, clashing about him.

You are nothing, Be'lakor roared at the Everchosen of Chaos. *A twin-bladed sword, who wounds he who wields it. A filth instrument of torture, used by the Ruinous Powers to torment me.*

Be'lakor bellowed through his pain and the frustration of his infernal plans, hefting another huge boulder above his head. Archaon didn't think he could survive another impact. As Be'lakor wavered under the weight of the thing, Archaon tried to clear his pain-addled mind. Coughing up blood that leaked from the side of his thin lips, Archaon spoke the dark words of binding – the incantations the daemon Z'guhl had taught him in the Realm of Chaos. Be'lakor staggered with the monstrous piece of rock while the midnight flesh of his belly burned bright.

'U'zuhl, Skulltaker and *Slayer of Kings*,' Archaon called. 'I release you!'

Be'lakor went to scream something but couldn't. The boulder broke across his back, falling either side of the daemon and almost burying him. He clutched at the *Slayer of Kings* and the daemon U'zuhl, the Skulltaker and Right Claw of Khorne, trapped in the prison blade for as long as anyone could remember, flooded Be'lakor with its boundless fury.

Archaon staggered to his feet and stumbled away, moving from boulder to boulder for support. His leg was broken and his arm – the same arm – shattered, despite the petrified rock that threaded its way through his bones. Blood leaked continually from his mouth and nose, filling his helm with a coppery smell. All Archaon could hear was his own ragged breathing and the horrific wailing of the Dark Master. U'zuhl was tearing the ancient darkness of Be'lakor's soul apart – desperate to feast on the daemon's malevolent essence and assume his dread flesh.

As Archaon staggered away, half watching, half escaping, he saw Be'lakor fall silent. His shoulders rose and fell with the titanic battle that had raged within his being. The battle was over, however, and Be'lakor had won. As Archaon had resisted Be'lakor so the Dark Master had resisted U'zhul. Slipping the *Slayer of Kings* torturously from his belly, Be'lakor held it up. The dull blade started to glow in his claw, burning to a rage-filled intensity that Archaon had never known. The Skulltaker had been free but within moments had been returned to his steel prison once more.

Tossing the furious pollution of the daemonblade aside – not knowing if he could repel another attempt by the Skulltaker to possess him – Be'lakor lifted a trembling claw. He levelled it at Archaon.

Now… you…

The Everchosen of Chaos limped away, staggering from one boulder to another. All the Eye of Sheerian could show Archaon was what Be'lakor might do. The Dark Master was so insane with infernal fury and mindless vengeance that even he didn't know what he was going to do. The ground trembled beneath Be'lakor's step. He seized Archaon around his armoured neck and slammed the dark warlord into the rockface. He smashed him again and leaned in. Archaon could feel the claws of the daemon prince buckle the cursed plate about his bruised neck. Be'lakor was going to crush his throat. Archaon smelled the rank sulphur of the abomination's breath.

I shall wear the crown. I shall be Everchosen of the Chaos gods and stand once more in the warmth of their destructive radiance and favour. None shall stop me. No god. No daemon. Not you.

Archaon felt the vice of the daemon prince's claws close about his throat and the hell-forged plate give. He knew he had but seconds left. Scratching at the punctured plate at his side, Archaon got a trembling gauntlet around the hilt of the claw-crafted dagger. His eye rolled over, white with the agonising pain of its withdrawal. He felt the blade's darkness cut through not only his butchered flesh but also his pantheon-pledged soul. His eye rolled back as the crooks and curves of the wicked blade were freed.

For you are nothing. Nothing begotten of nothing and to nothing you return. You are a footnote in the history of a world destined to burn. Yours was my story to tell and I choose to end it now.

'I'm your son...' Archaon hissed through his father-in-shadow's murderous embrace.

You think that will stop me?

Archaon looked for the Ruinous Star burned across the Dark Master's broad chest. He looked for the chink in the daemon's armoured hide. The cleft Archaon had found in the Forsaken Fortress. The mark of a piercing blade – thrust by one of the Dark Master's many foes – that had yet to complete its journey.

'You... don't... have... the... heart...'

Archaon brought up the dagger and with a single, merciless stab, hammered the claw blade into Be'lakor's chest. A monstrous gasp escaped the daemon. The Everchosen fell down the rockface and crumpled as the Dark Master released him. Stumbling away through the boulders and debris, Be'lakor clawed at his punctured heart and the pumping ichor that gushed from his ruined chest. The abominate's cloven claws suddenly seemed no longer to support him and the beast crashed to the ground in a growing pool of his own steaming darkness. Archaon watched as his father-in-darkness – the twisted daemon prince who had for so long been the source of dread, woe and affliction in his life – died before him. In his final moments of panic, the Dark Master reached out for Archaon, the claw of one hand a pleading emissary of doom. He shimmered with crackling shadow, unnatural energies arcing and sizzling about the daemon. In a last ditch attempt to survive the horror of the wound Archaon had inflicted upon him, Be'lakor was phasing between forms. Between the insubstance of shadow and the last moments of a fell, ichor-coughing existence. Archaon grunted with dark satisfaction. Being crafted from a part of the daemon prince itself, the dagger-claw was doing the same, making it impossible for Be'lakor to escape his doom, as he might a sword swung through the sizzling shadow of his form.

As the pool of liquid darkness grew and Be'lakor sank into his own daemonic gore, the Dark Master steamed away. His clutching claw scraped along the rock with final defiance before slipping back into the obsidian pool. Archaon watched the darkness drain down through the valley floor. Looking up he saw the distant blaze of torches as his monstrous army poured into the valley. The immense moons of Mannslieb and Morrslieb were setting over the Worlds Edge Mountains. Above them the twin-tailed comet that was herald of the doom Archaon was yet to bring blazed across the sky.

Archaon limped through the draining darkness of his father's grave and with difficulty picked up the *Slayer of Kings*. Slipping the daemonsword into his scabbard, Archaon stared back at the spot where Be'lakor had died. The word seemed to ill fit the daemon prince's fate, for the Everchosen knew that he had simply banished the enormous being – the bane of his existence – back to the Realm of Chaos from which he had sprung. Every smashed and aching bone in Archaon's body told him that Be'lakor would be back. He would return as he had many times before to plague the world and the enemies that walked it.

'I'll ensure that there will be no world to return to…' Archaon told the steaming grave. He looked up into the dark depths of the heavens. Thunder rolled in the distance. He knew that the Dark Gods were watching. They would not have missed Be'lakor's failure – the daemon's delicious demise – for the world. 'You hear me?' Archaon roared up at the sky, his threat intended for the fell gods whose soul-devouring existence depended upon the world and its mortal plague as much as the daemon prince they had made an eternity of tormenting. 'Only ash and darkness. An oblivion in which to starve. Choke on it, you monsters…'

EPILOGUE

*'And so the end it came to pass,
Archaon the Everchosen –
at the head of an army vast –
his storm of Chaos yet to come.'*

– Necrodomo the Insane, *The Liber Caelestior*
(The Celestine Book of Divination)

The Borderlands
The Worlds Edge Mountains
Die Zeit der Stürme IC 2519

The Everchosen brought his daemon steed to a stop on the mountain pass. Dorghar's furnace breath clouded on the chill air. He had arrived. As the Worlds Edge Mountains dropped away before him in frost-shattered supplication – peaks becoming foothills and foothills disappearing into thick, dark forest – Archaon knew he was home. To the north he could see the hard lands of the Tsarina: Kislev, ever ready for the dark hordes of Chaos to descend on their desolate land. To the south, however, Archaon cast his far reaching gaze across an Empire ripe for ruin. The Empire – nestling safely in the bosom of civilised lands. Pathetic. Weak. Like a new-born baby: soft, unknowing, defenceless. The victim lands upon which Archaon himself had been forced. As infant. As dark warrior. As doom. The Empire was a festering wound on the surface of the world. Hot to the touch with its weakling gods, its emperors and principalities – lost in the self-importance of its past and delusions of its endurance. Below the spoiling surface, in the empty hearts of its cruel men, the forlorn hopes of its women and fears of its sickly children, it was a land already broken – begging for the blade and the flames of its future destruction. Archaon would be the answer to the Empire's dark and secret prayers. He would be the dark dream of its undoing come true. If the world was to end – and it was – then the Empire, the unhallowed site of Archaon's dread birth and many miserable deaths, was the perfect place to start.

The Worlds Edge Mountains shook. Not with thunder, titanic battles or the wrath of a daemon prince vanquished. Archaon's dark horde – his army of ruin and ending – had grown. The twin-tailed comet, which still scarred the skies with its fierce progress, hung over the Empire like a fearful portent of the horror to come. It led the way to ash, darkness and destruction as it had led so many to the dread coronation at the Dreadpeak. Colossal hordes of Hung maruaders and tribes of Kurgan horsemen, savages pledged to the ruin of the world, their countless number shaking the ground with their passage as shamans and chieftains followed the comet up into the mountains.

At the glorious sight of the comet, warring northmen set aside their tribal enmities, their petty raids and berserker invasions of the hinterland Wastes. Behind bloodthirsty champions in spike and fur, they trudged south through the mountains, along the spine of the world, to find the Everchosen of Chaos: a warlord worthy of their butchery and talents. Half-breeds and beastmen arrived in droves, emerging like a shaggy plague from the depths of dark forests. Then there were the warriors of Chaos. Exalted champions of the Ruinous Gods. Dread sorcerers. Siege engines and wagons. Dark knights in cursed plate, astride monstrous black steeds. New Swords of Chaos to ride beside Archaon into battle and bloodshed. A torrent of pollution, flowing down through the Worlds Edge Mountains like a black river – a cacophony of Ruinous plate, hooves and flesh-flayed banners dedicated to the coming darkness.

Monsters thundered through the peaks, attracted by the unmistakable stench of doom and horror approaching. Horror to which they instinctively wanted to belong. Giants. Abominations of the Wastes. Packs of rabid scavengers, predacious chimeric fusions and hordes of gibbering spawn.

Like the effluence of the world, the degenerates of the Wastes flooded south to join Archaon under an apocalyptic banner of death and destruction. Some followed their dark instincts. Others followed the dread omen of the twin-tailed comet. Champions who saw significance in such a dark sign. All had been pushed before the storm. The endless army that had marched, shrieked and slaughtered its way south, vomited forth from the ruined gate at the top of the world and pantheon-pledged to join the Everchosen of Chaos. They were the world's nightmare. A monstrous host of daemons and infernal princes the likes of which history, even in its darkest hour, had never witnessed. Horrors of the beyond. Things of blood. Of plague. Of dread desire and sorcerous madness. Things of darkness that barely had form, with Ruinous behemoths of greater malevolence and monstrous infernal royalty to lead them. The legions of a thousand hells unleashed. A vast army of calamitous destruction and darkness, like an unnatural disaster that was Archaon's to visit upon the world.

Flooding every pass, crowding the slopes of every mountain, looking down on the victim lands of the distant Empire, Archaon's monstrous host – his dark storm to lead – were amassed along the edge of the world. Their harnessed madness waiting for the Everchosen's signal.

A figure jangled up behind Archaon. The warlord turned to see Gorst, the flagellant trudging forth, pushing through Archaon's abominate ranks. He was skin and bone dressed in scraps. The ancient dragged rusted chains and his head, still caged, stared up at Archaon through the age-eaten bars. As ever, Gorst said nothing. He had followed Archaon across the known world, through unknown realms and followed him still – into destiny. Gorst. The last of a ghostly collection of fading memories. Dagobert. Oberon. Giselle. Archaon was no longer that man. He was more than just a man now. He was doom. He was dread. He was darkness incarnate. He no longer had need of such memories. He was beyond the love of a loyal friend or the placed puppets of infernal betrayal. He was Archaon.

In a slick and devastating move, the Everchosen of Chaos slipped his daemonsword out of its scabbard. Executing a merciless swing of the sword, he cut Gorst's head from his miserable shoulders. The head, still in its cage, bounced before Archaon and his army before it rolled down the slope towards the Empire. Gorst had almost made it home.

Sheathing his sword, Archaon sat in the saddle, his dread plate a hell-forged glory. Dorghar, Steed of the Apocalypse, kicked at the stone floor of the pass, eager to lead on. The *Slayer of Kings* burned furiously in its scabbard. The warlord waited. He soaked in the world as it was in that moment, while the Eye of Sheerian and his monstrous crown showed him the world as he was to make it. Instead of forests, fields, towns, villages, principalities and bloated cities there would be black deserts of ash. Mountainous pyres of bodies burning, scorching the thunder-filled skies. A god-empty darkness in which even those monstrosities that had heralded the apocalypse had fallen to the blade. Monstrosities like Archaon, Everchosen of Chaos and Lord of the End Times.

'This world and all those beyond it will end,' he called through the valleys and vaulting mountains. Archaon dug his armoured heels into the sides of the daemon steed, prompting Dorghar on into the Empire, the Ruinous hordes of darkness at the Everchosen's back. 'That end begins… now.'

'Mortals are free to do as they will. The gods give them no choice.'

– Imperial proverb

ARCHAON:
THE FALL AND THE RISE

The Wastes. The name was well-earned; a blasted, howling wilderness of twilight, blizzard and mind-numbing temperatures. Helmut Horrwitz considered the waste through which he hacked. The squandered humanity. The cost in blood. He tore a rag from a misshapen torso that, moments before, had served as a scabbard for his crusader blade. The material was filthy and rigid with the scalding cold of the place, but it was all he had to wipe the gelatinous ichor from his blessed sword.

They just kept coming. Marauders in spikes and furs. Brute beastmen. Chaos warriors in the dark plate of an even darker calling. Horrors of the flesh. Fiends of the beyond. Wanton monstrosity. The servants of Sigmar might have been in a god-forsaken wilderness, but there was no shortage of wretched foes for consecrated steel. If more of these miserable, misguided things had indeed been forsaken by their gods then there would be precious little work for Horrwitz and his knights of the Twin-Tailed Orb to do there. The favours of corruption were everywhere to behold. Things that had long since shed their humanity begged the Ruinous Powers of this dark place to be twisted in their own inconstant image.

Horrwitz fought on and his templars fought beside him, hacking, thrusting and smashing their way through the hordes. Horrwitz had never seen such a place. The very earth beneath his boots, the sky above his helm, the howling insanity in between: it was all an affront to nature. To the God-King's servants. To the God-King himself.

Horrwitz had fought the threat of corruption beyond his Empire, at its borders and within its rich and dark forests. He had been Sigmar's shield against the witch, the greenskin barbarian, the altered and the warriors of the Dark Gods. Here, in this benighted place, he found all the horrors of his imaginings: the twisted of mind and body; the half-breed; the wielders of gifts abominable and powers unnatural; dark templars, clad in battle-scarred plate and bearing the nauseating sigils of the Ruinous Powers. They swung their blades with a belief as strong as Horrwitz's own, their souls offered to their monstrous sponsors. Their lice-infested cloaks of fur and ragged mantles flowed about them like the sails of damned galleons as they expertly put their shields between the knight's blessed blade and their foetid existence. It was a life of perpetual battle and savagery, however, and the warriors of darkness did not make it easy for him.

They pressed him and they died. Between the filth of horned half-breeds, who came at him with their rude flails, and marauder madmen, mounted on deranged steeds, Horrwitz put down a knight, a champion, a misshapen monster of cursed blessings, somehow still strapped into its plate. The templar's heavy blade turned aside the savage swordcraft of men who had forgotten themselves in the Wastes. It penetrated steel eaten through with rust and an eternity's service at the top of the world, and squealed through armoured torsos and cleaved helms to bring an end to the feverish nightmare of half-lived lives.

And then there was *him*. Horrwitz steadied himself with panting breaths of exertion echoing about the darkness of his knightly helm, the Wastes whirling before his eye-slits and his templar blade flashing forth in frantic service, the creatures came at him, all fang, claw and madness. Amongst blood-stained spear-points, spiked balls on rusted chains, serrated swords and rune-glowing blades, all vying for his death, a death that was only ever moments away, Horrwitz saw *him*.

It was the strangest thing. Amongst the ferocity and the smash of steel on steel, Horrwitz saw a warrior of ruin take to his knees. The sight almost cost the templar his head. His blade only just turned aside the wicked point of a spear, aimed squarely at the faceguard of his helm. He split the weapon down its shaft and then, with a twist of the hilt, the heavy sword snapped the spear in two. Heaving the knightly weapon down and back, Horrwitz did the same to its owner, before pommel-smashing a half-breed thing of horn and snout into the ground and stabbing a Chaos knight straight through the eight-pointed star of his rusted breastplate. As the warrior crashed to one side with a cacophonous clatter, the nameless warrior was revealed once more.

Several of Horrwitz's brother templars lay before the figure, disarmed and disembowelled. Some of their heavy blades had found the warrior wanting. His plate was buckled and split where cleaving chops and thrusts had found their mark. His mauled shield had been smashed from him and his helm was a shattered mess, barely held together with aged rivets and rust. The force of a blow had knocked him all but senseless, demolishing one half of the helm, and a blade tip had nicked his brow. The deep gash leaked blood down his face and through a ragged beard. Blood dripped from his hair and down onto the collection of medallions, charms and Ruinous symbols that hung about his neck on loose chains, twine and sinew.

Horrwitz had seen such dread iconography on the armour and banners of many he had killed in the Wastes. It was quite a collection. Horrwitz thought it impossible to honour so many gods and powers, even if they were Ruinous ones. The kneeling knight blinked blood from his eye and leant on his tarnished weapon, blade in his gauntlets, sword point nestled in the gore-stained earth, with hilt and guard forming a cross before his smashed helm. Horrwitz took several savage steps towards him, hefting the weight of his own blade above his head.

'Defend yourself, slave to darkness!' the templar roared, but the knight didn't move. Blinking blood that went on to steam from his cheek, the Chaos warrior watched Horrwitz advance, but remained still. Within his helm, the templar snarled. Not in fury. Not in rage. His arm wouldn't move. He wasn't afflicted by injury or witchcraft. It was conscience. 'Up, I say, and fight me!'

Another knight of the Dark Gods swept in with an axe, which he ponderously swung at Horrwitz. No less ponderously, Horrwitz moved to one side of the weapon. Moving his eye-slits between the kneeling knight and his attacker, Horrwitz brought his blade down hard on the axe-wielder. The expert and cleaving force of the sword, which he had initially intended for the defenceless warrior, cut down through his attacker.

Hissing through clenched teeth, Horrwitz kicked the demolished knight back off his blade before swinging it about him and cutting down a thrice-cursed altered form. As he completed the turn he found the knight still kneeling before him. He had not moved. He had not taken his chance to escape. He seemed to welcome death.

Horrwitz felt the white heat of his arm. His templar blade was weighty and in his armoured plate it helped to keep the blade moving. His conscience doused the instinct like ice water. He would not become that which he had sworn to destroy. He was a templar of Sigmar. A knight of the Twin-Tailed Orb. He would not become a mindless killer in the Wastes. He would not join the ranks of the lost and the damned.

'Fight me!' Horrwitz roared, but the warrior would not. The templar stomped forward and landed a kick on the kneeling knight, who crumbled with a clatter. Horrwitz smashed the tarnished blade aside with his own before stepping over the prone and armoured figure. Horrwitz turned his blade around and held it over the smashed helm of the warrior. The sword point dangled above his blood-washed face. 'You will oblige me, damn you...'

The Chaos warrior looked up at Horrwitz along the length of his Templar blade.

'I was once a man,' the warrior said, his lips red with blood. 'An honourable man, like yourself. Do me the honour of ending this. I beg of you. Grant me peace.'

Horrwitz went to lean into the thrust, to put his whole weight behind the blade, but he felt suddenly weak. Exhausted. Battle-drunk. He swayed for a moment. The warrior blurred before him but then came back into searing focus. He looked up and about him. His Sigmarite knights had broken the warband. Their unstoppable advance had crushed the corrupted. Their champion had fled and all about them templars were finishing the enemy: bludgeoning with blades, stabbing the last of the life out of felled warriors, bringing peace to the altered and half-breeds where they lay. He turned back to the dark warrior at his feet. He was begging for death. A snarl crossed Horrwitz's features behind his helm.

'I wouldn't waste my honour on you, filth,' Horrwitz told him. 'I won't serve at the pleasure of a man who himself has been a heretic servant of the Dark Gods. You will get no swift and merciful death from me, friend.'

Horrwitz brought up his blade and stepped back. The two warriors stared at each other. 'If you won't fight me then you can take your chances with the Witch Hunter General.' Helmut Horrwitz grunted. 'See if you find any mercy with him.'

Horrwitz was dragging blade-mulched corpses and twitching sacks of warped flesh to the fiery mounds they had built on the edge of the Sigmarite camp. Even with blessed oils, the crackling tongues of flame that felt their way through the twisted limbs were finding it difficult in the plummeting temperature. Above the torment of the fire, Horrwitz could hear the sound of warherds in the distance, the furious braying of beastmen on the wind. The dreadful sound seemed to follow the Sigmarites everywhere, as if the creatures knew the God-King's servants didn't belong in the hellish environs of the Wastes and could smell the purity of their purpose.

Horrwitz dropped the butchered carcass before Sieurs Stenzel and Oberndorff. It was work for menials, but the camp had precious few to service such needs, leaving men of noble birth to stack corpses and stoke burning flesh. The servants had been first to lose their battle with the Shadowlands, either succumbing to the madness the place had to offer or being dragged off into the frozen maelstrom by things that defied description. Anyone not living by the blade or the vigilance of their hate-honed faith became prey. As a result, the camp of gale-savaged tents and wagons was largely made up of hammer-wielding priests of Sigmar, whose ceaseless consecrations made the frozen earth beneath their boots split, Eisenkramer's dour witch hunters and the knights of the Twin-Tailed Orb.

Stenzel and Oberndorff took the corpse Horrwitz had been hauling and, between them, threw it onto the smouldering mound, which was no easy feat in full plated armour. The templars were exhausted and miserable.

'Sigmar's blood!' Sieur Oberndorff spat with the effort. 'I can't stand the god-forsaken noise of those mongrels.'

'It's always there,' Sieur Stenzel said. 'Like it's part of the place itself.'

'Whatever possessed the gods to make such a place?' Oberndorff groaned.

'The Wastes were not made,' Horrwitz told them grimly. 'They were unmade.'

For a moment, the templars said nothing.

'You'll speak to Eisenkramer?' Stenzel asked. Horrwitz nodded slowly, his eyes downcast.

'I'll talk to him.'

* * *

After checking in with the knight-sentries and Father Gerschel, who had taken over the quartermaster's duties, Horrwitz made his weary way across to the tabernacle. The canvas of the large tent was filthy with ash, dust and blood, which sometimes fell as rain from the angry heavens. It was supposed to be a holy place. A mobile temple to house the God-King's war altar that Eisenkramer had insisted they transport through Kislev, the Troll Country and into the Northern Wastes. The tabernacle didn't smell very holy, Horrwitz decided as he pushed through the canvas and entered the stale darkness beyond.

Within the altar chamber, braziers bathed witch hunters and priests in an infernal glow as they conferred in conspiratorial whispers. Father Sternthal, the Witch Hunter General's most senior and surviving priest, swung an incense burner about him on a pair of chains in honour of the twin-tailed comet that heralded the birth of Sigmar. Horrwitz walked through the smoke and knelt before the war altar, the care and attention having been paid to its immaculate workmanship at odds with the mulch-splattered wheels of its wagon flat-bed. The Master of Blades bowed his head and traced a hammer across his heart, asking the God-King for his blessing in this most benighted of places.

The templar's devotions were interrupted by sounds from beyond the canvas partition at the rear of the altar chamber. Behind it he could hear one of Eisenkramer's prisoners being tortured and interrogated. He could hear the harsh, honeyed insistence of the witch hunters, guiding heretic hearts through the trials of forced attrition. He could hear the thunder of the Witch Hunter General himself, compelling his victims to live on through their tortures, so that they might endure more and welcome the light of God-King back into the miserable excuse for their lives. Getting back to his feet, Horrwitz approached one of Witch Hunter General's men. Eisenkramer's torturer put up a filthy hand and gave the templar a surly look before ducking in to inform his master of Horrwitz's arrival. The templar had little taste for the necessities of torture and secretly welcomed the insult.

A few moments later, Wolfram Eisenkramer came forth from the shadows and stood between the flapping curtains. Despite the filth of corruption that he was usually up to his elbows in, the black velvets and white silks that made up Eisenkramer's plain finery were taintless. He ran the finger and thumb of a gloved hand down his starched length of lustrous grey moustache and into a beard that he kept neat. He gave Horrwitz the flint of his eyes from beneath the brim of his conical hat and lit a long-stemmed smoking pipe with an equally long taper.

'A word with you, general?'

Eisenkramer said nothing. He received the questioning glances of exiting witch hunters and a scribe who had been charged with taking down prisoner testimonials in a black, leather tome. The Witch Hunter General dismissed them all with a slow nod, but took the tome from the departing scribe.

As Eisenkramer's staff pushed through the canvas curtains, Horrwitz caught a glimpse of the torturer's equipment that cluttered the chamber beyond. As the witch hunters walked by, he caught the scent of sweat and the fug of blood and violence.

'Master Horrwitz,' Eisenkramer said, drawing on his foul tobacco. He picked up the leather tome and opened it before tapping on the page with his pipe. 'The prisoner you brought me for interrogation…'

The templar ignored him.

'General, there are matters of grave import that demand your attention,' Horrwitz told him.

'Oh, there are,' Eisenkramer said, flicking through the pages and replacing the tome, 'are there?'

'Yes, sir.'

'See, I thought the only matter of import here was the hunting down and destruction of the thrice-cursed abominate known as Archaon.'

'Yes, sir,' Horrwitz agreed. The templar bridled. Eisenkramer puffed on his pipe.

'You have news?'

Horrwitz hesitated. It was nothing the Witch Hunter General didn't already know.

'The half-breeds close on us, general.'

'That is not news,' Eisenkramer told him. 'The beastmen are the very children of Chaos. This ruinous land is the cradle of their degenerate civilisation. What else?'

'Bar the altar steeds,' the templar told him, 'we have eaten all of the other horses.'

'The men are strong,' Eisenkramer said. 'They shall endure. Sigmar wishes it so.'

'The quartermaster doesn't think we can trust the local food sources.'

'I agree.'

'He suspects the water is contaminated.'

'Then it would be a mistake to drink it,' Eisenkramer insisted, relighting his pipe. 'Go on.'

'Eschenback and Strauss are dead,' Horrwitz said. 'As well as your priest, Lowinger.'

'Lowinger... was found wanting,' the Witch Hunter General informed him.

Horrwitz hesitated. Then he told Eisenkramer, 'General, I think that we have pushed north into the Wastes in pursuit of Archaon as far as our resources will allow us. I recommend that we turn back and return to more civilised lands.'

Eisenkramer's eyes narrowed. Smoke coiled like an angry serpent from his pipe. Horrwitz added cautiously, 'At least until we can re-supply, take on horses and replace our losses.'

'You think *he* will stop?' Eisenkramer asked him. 'For water? For horses? You think he'll run for the safety of more civilised lands, Master Horrwitz?'

'No, general, I do not,' the templar admitted. 'But the men–'

'Send you as the emissary of their cowardice?' Eisenkramer hissed.

'No, general,' Horrwitz cut back.

'There is dissention in your ranks, master…'

'There is fear,' Horrwitz admitted. 'Not fear of the traitor Archaon, for whom their hatred burns bright and in whose end lies the hard-won honour of their order. Nor is it for foes faced across the blade in the feverish madness of this place. It is fear that those who lead them in this endeavour have caught such a fever that they lead them about in circles to their doom. But perhaps, God-King willing, we can acquire fresh steeds to speed our progress, and provisions and water to sustain us. We can pick up the trail–'

'The monster is here now,' Eisenkramer seethed. 'Don't you see? We've never been closer. We'll have him. Today. Tomorrow. The next day. We've come too far to abandon the rank scent of his dark deeds, to turn back. This beast is the harbinger of the apocalypse. We take him now, for if we don't, if we let slip the days and fail in this most sacred and required of duties, we shall run out of todays and tomorrows. I will have this heretic under a Sigmarite sword. This star that has fallen so far. I *will*. I'll give him the cold comfort of Sigmar's vengeance.'

'Your threats are no comfort to my men, general,' Horrwitz said, interrupting Eisenkramer's venom.

'Your men,' the witch hunter spat, 'will only find *comfort* on their estates, safe within the borders of their motherland.'

'I'm going to require more than that,' the templar told him with steel in his voice.

'Or what?' Eisenkramer dared. 'You and your men will turn your back on your duty and your God-King? Succumb to the madness of this place? There would be a terrible price to be paid for such heresy…'

The Witch Hunter General's gloved hand snatched at the brace of pistols that sat cross-holstered on his thick leather belt, but the palm of the Master of Blades's gauntlet was already resting like a casual threat on the pommel of his sword.

'As there would be for indulging madness in the one that leads us,' Horrwitz told him. The two men burned into each other. Somehow, Horrwitz had known it would come to this.

It would take time to clear the crusader blade of his scabbard. Perhaps too much time. Eisenkramer's pistol would be ungainly out of its holster and sluggish in its priming. Then there was the question of whether it would deliver its charge at all, the damned things being so unreliable. In truth, Horrwitz didn't want to know who would be swifter in the awkward draw. He didn't want to find out whether his cleaving blade out of its sheath would cut the witch hunter down faster than he could punch his lead shot through Horrwitz's breastplate and chest.

Across the twilight fug of the chamber, the pair heard a dark chuckle. Someone was laughing, the sound slow and shot through with pain. They turned to find that the brawny warrior that Horrwitz had spared out on the Wastes was standing between the curtains, in the entrance to the altar chamber. He looked a mess. Eisenkramer's men had not bothered to clean the prisoner up. He still wore the remains of his plate, including his smashed helm. His face was caked with blood and his ragged beard was sticky and matted. By the look of him, and the slow fashion in which he limped into the chamber, Horrwitz suspected that Eisenkramer's witch hunters had long gone to work on him with their barbarous instruments of interrogation and torture. He jangled as he moved. Thick chains of blessed iron weighed him down, winding about his arms, shoulders and buckled plate like a great metal serpent. A robust lock dangled from the back of the prisoner's neck. Horrwitz had seen heretics in Altdorf imprisoned for months in such crushing restraints before being hung by them from the cathedral walls. Beneath the chains, Horrwitz could see the charms, medallions and dread symbols of the prisoner's many Dark Gods.

'The degenerate mocks us,' Eisenkramer said dangerously. His hand came off his ugly pistol. Horrwitz allowed his palm to slip from the pommel of his sword. The Witch Hunter General narrowed his eyes at the templar again.

'The degenerate is free,' Horrwitz indicated.

'Well, I wouldn't call him *free*.' Eisenkramer took a fat key from a chain about his neck. He tossed the key to Horrwitz. 'Here, he was your prisoner.'

The templar looked down at the key. 'You are finished with him?'

The question was genuine. He had seen very few prisoners walk away from Eisenkramer and his witch hunters, whether they were guilty or innocent.

'Far from it,' the Witch Hunter General said. 'Master Horrwitz, may I introduce Rhaanoc.'

'I don't need to know the heretic's name,' Horrwitz said shuddering. 'And he certainly doesn't need to know mine.'

Eisenkramer ignored him. 'Rhaanoc here is a turncoat,' he told Horrwitz. The witch hunter pointed at the tangled collection of talismans, charms and medallions hanging about the marauder's neck with the bit of his pipe. 'He moves from warband to warband, champion to dark champion, offering his talents to any and all of the Ruinous Powers.'

Eisenkramer tapped the bowl of his pipe out on a scrap of plate still dangling from the marauder's shoulder, before re-filling it with foul-smelling tobacco from a pouch on his belt. 'This is not double-dealing or cowardice. Ruinous champions rise and then they inevitably fall – and when they do it does not go well for their followers. No, what we have here is not cowardice. It's stubborn pragmatism. A most Imperial virtue,' Eisenkramer said, directing the insult at the Chaos warrior.

'He has given you information?' Horrwitz asked.

'Of all my miserable specimens,' Eisenkramer said, speaking of his prisoners and torturer's devices, 'this wasteland wretch tested us, and himself. He screamed, but did not speak. He thrashed, but did not yield. He bled, but did not break. No, Rhaanoc is no coward.'

'Then why waste time torturing him?' the templar asked. 'Why not simply grant him the God-King's peace?'

'That was your duty, sir,' Eisenkramer warned. The witch hunter pointed with the length of his pipe at a talisman in the shape of an eight-point star. It was a variation on a symbol Horrwitz had seen on a number of savages from the Shadowlands.

'This mark, in this crude design, has been observed by my priests and witch hunters on the dead and dying left behind in the wake of Archaon's progress. It is found about the necks, on the armour and in the flesh of his fell followers.'

'This wretch has travelled with Archaon?'

'Aye,' Eisenkramer confirmed. 'For a time.'

'And he confessed to this truth?' Horrwitz asked. Eisenkramer moved around the chained Rhaanoc. He nodded his acknowledgement as he re-lit his pipe.

'A witch or heretic is a receptacle of lying flesh, containing the treasure of secrets within, like a chest. And like a chest, an interrogator need only find the right key to unlock the secrets inside. But there are oh so many keys.'

Eisenkramer was suddenly animated as he spoke about his work. His passion. His calling. Horrwitz's knew his face was a mask of disgust. Eisenkramer nodded to the templar, and a little to himself.

'I know you're upset about Eschenback and Strauss. Strauss particularly,' Eisenkramer said. He moved over to the black leather tome his scribe had been writing in and flicked through the pages. 'But you can blame prisoner… two hundred and thirty-two for that. He claimed that his master…' Eisenkramer consulted the confessional entries. '…Diomedyss the Faceless, believed himself to be the Everchosen of the Dark Gods. That he attempted to bring Archaon's warband to battle in the frosted highlands from which we have descended. At the standing stones of Akhorax. According to the Faceless One's acolyte, Archaon and his brutes ambushed them en route, leaving naught but this miserable wretch alive.'

'The highlands,' Horrwitz repeated absently. 'The standing stones…' Where Eshenback and Strauss had lost their lives and what was left of their humanity in the desperation of slaughter. Their own and that of the warrior wretches about them.

'As you know,' Eisenkramer went on, taking slow steps back towards Rhaanoc, 'we did not find the abominate Archaon there either.'

'We found death,' Horrwitz said. It sounded like an accusation. Again, Eisenkramer consulted his record of forced attrition.

'Arashaq Var,' the Witch Hunter General said. 'Another degenerate warlord with false hope in his Kurgan heart. Like Archaon, a servant of the eight-point star and a champion of evil in all its dread forms.'

'But not Archaon,' Master Horrwitz shot back. The two men locked gazes.

'No,' Eisenkramer admitted. 'To my lasting regret. The traitor must have bypassed the highlands.'

'You sent my men to their slaughter.'

'I sent them *to* slaughter,' the Witch Hunter General shot back. 'It is their hallowed duty to bring the God-King's vengeance to the half-breeds, altereds and marauding savages of this benighted realm.'

'Yet you allow entire hosts to pass us unmolested,' the templar accused, 'on their way south to bring flame and the blade to Sigmar's lands. You trust the word of prisoners without names and pieces of filth like this thing here.'

Horrwitz burned into Rhaanoc with his gaze. Through the discomfort of his agonies and the unbearable weight of the chains, Rhaanoc attempted to hold the gaze, but Horrwitz turned it back on Eisenkramer.

'Only Archaon matters…' the Witch Hunter General said.

'To you!' Horrwitz barked. 'To you he is all that matters. How can you spend time here, in your torturer's tent, trusting the fanciful tales of the damned over the recommendations of your own men?'

'Do you know where I may find the abominate Archaon?' Eisenkramer roared at the templar knight. 'Do you know where the doom of all the world resides, so that I may inflict upon him the wrath of a God-King betrayed, or the necessity of an empire spared its end?'

'No,' Horrwitz admitted.

'This wretch, this coward – who dare face us not – has run for the north. He hides in the land of shadow, where no scout can track his step nor hound follow his rancid scent. All the witch hunter has are the secrets unlocked and intelligence confessed on the frame, on the rack, on the precipice of pain unbearable and agonies traded for truth.'

'The souls of Sigmar's servants cannot be wagered on the word of the damned,' Horrwitz insisted. 'Men will say anything on the rack. Anything to end their sufferings.'

'And they do,' Eisenkramer told him. 'But do you think our questions stop there? Do you think the liar plain, the heretic that lies to himself or the living lies that are the warriors of ruin, are granted their wish? No. The false are granted false respite. For their afflictions must endure as long as they do. Until we find our way together… to the truth.'

Horrwitz watched the dull glow of the brazier glint off the witch hunter's eyes like madness. 'It is a journey shared. Take the turncoat here,' Eisenkramer said, moving towards the chained Rhaanoc standing nearby. 'Apart from the spoiled meat about his heart – where his fell bargain with the Ruinous pantheon resides – he is all muscle. Flesh scarred, inked and tempered by time and brutal necessity. If you are a wanton savage, wandering through the Wastes – fighting for your life and taking the lives of others – you need to be. Without the spiritual safeguards of civilised men and the patronage of gods to be feared rather than appeased, they are but animals, seeking the protection of packs of similar beasts. Like a wild stallion, such creatures must be broken. And when they are, they will take you further. Eh, Rhaanoc?'

'He knows where Archaon is?'

'So he claims…'

'How can you trust the word of the corrupted?' Horrwitz challenged.

Eisenkramer walked over to the altar. Using a silver ladle he poured holy water into a bowl.

'Rhaanoc and I have been through so much together,'

Eisenkramer told the templar, but with his eyes firmly on the brawny warrior. 'Isn't that right, Rhaanoc?'

Rhaanoc gave the Witch Hunter General a stabbing glare. Eisenkramer ladled in another slurp of priest-blessed water.

'Yes... my lord,' Rhaanoc managed.

'Are you thirsty, Rhaanoc?' Eisenkramer asked. 'Can I get you some more water? To drink? To bathe your wounds? To clean the blood of battle and the grime of the Wastes from your body?'

'You would waste our meagre supplies of water on this sack of corruption?' a furious Horrwitz spat.

'And do you, Master Horrwitz,' Eisenkramer snarled, holding the bowl between them, 'have any idea what such holy water does to the flesh of the corrupted?'

Horrwitz did not. But he could imagine. Eisenkramer leant in.

'He does,' the Witch Hunter General seethed. Then he turned back to his prisoner. 'Rhaanoc?'

'No, my lord,' the warrior said, nibbling at his parched lips. A shudder jangled the chains of blessed steel about his bruised and beaten form. The metal of the thick links was already starting to tarnish and brown.

'See, Master Horrwitz,' Eisenkramer said, 'Even small mercies have their place in the arsenal of the interrogator. We can behave like civilised men, even out here in the Northern Wastes.'

Horrwitz watched Rhaanoc's face. He saw the recent memory of unspeakable pain there, the ghost of a warrior's defiance fading before them. He was a fortification overrun. A ship that had been swamped. Rhaanoc the turncoat – who had turned so many times before – had turned again.

'God's bones,' Horrwitz murmured.

'You see?' Eisenkramer said, putting the bowl of blessed water aside and re-lighting his pipe. 'The stallion... broken. We have burned away the lies. Now witness the God-King's power, acting within this unfortunate and forcing the truth from where it was hiding. He has pledged allegiance to just about everyone else in this benighted place and now he pledges it to us.'

Eisenkramer moved about the chained warrior, puffing on his pipe, filling the tent with a silky fug of foul-smelling smoke. He came in close. 'Now, sell-soul, if you don't mind, let us continue our conference. For Master Horrwitz here – to prove your worth to our venture.'

'Yes, my lord,' Rhaanoc told him in a hoarse, strangled whisper. 'Diomedyss the Faceless…' Eisenkramer was back at his book. 'The Faceless One,' Rhaanoc croaked, his broad chest rising and falling with the effort beneath the sapping weight of the chains.

'Yes?'

'Thought himself Everchosen of the Dark Gods,' Rhaanoc wheezed. 'His fell master had deceived him as such.'

'Go on.'

'Arashaq Var traced his bloodline to the warlord Asavar Kul,' the Chaos warrior told the Witch Hunter General. 'He thought to unite the tribes of the Anointed.'

'Hordes Magnus the Pious has long since sent packing back into the Shadowlands,' Eisenkramer said with sickly satisfaction. 'But what of Archaon? Speak of him, turncoat.'

'Archaon is a rising star in the Wastes,' Rhaanoc admitted.

'Yet you left his warband,' Horrwitz added. Eisenkramer stung the templar with a severe gaze. He did not appreciate the knight's interference.

'The bleak skies of the north are afflicted with many such stars,' the Chaos warrior coughed. 'Archaon has many enemies more fearful than Sigmarite servants far from home. Champions, sorcerers and warlords who would wrestle his destiny from him.'

'So, Diomedyss? Arashaq Var?' Eisenkramer asked, tapping his pipe imperiously on the side of the warrior's shattered helm.

'He set one against the other,' the prisoner said. 'Taking the Faceless One himself and sending the Kurgan into harm's way.'

'Into our way,' Horrwitz snapped, the loss of Sieur Eschenback and Sieur Strauss still burning in his chest. Eisenkramer gave the templar a wolfish smile.

'Cold, eh?' the Witch Hunter General said. 'This is why we need intelligence. The Fell Powers twist not only the abominate Archaon's body into a living weapon. They do so with his mind. They cultivate within their servant a savage cunning.'

'He...' Horrwitz said, hesitating. 'He was always a gifted tactician. Not to be underestimated.'

'And we aren't,' Eisenkramer said, before re-directing his questions to the wretch. 'He is close, then?' Rhaanoc nodded slowly. 'Beyond ourselves, who hunts Archaon through the Wastes?'

'There are many.'

'Names.'

'Warriors, sorcerers, daemons–'

'Your mouth seems full of things I don't wish to hear, minion,' the witch hunter said. 'Perhaps a drink to clear your throat?'

'You hear that?' Rhaanoc asked.

Horrwitz listened to the bellows of half-breeds that seemed perpetually on the breeze.

'Beastmen?' the templar asked.

'The Beastlord Khazgar of the Brazen Tusk,' the marauder told them.

'That's better,' Eisenkramer soothed. 'He hunts Archaon?'

'He and his numberless hordes,' Rhaanoc said, 'for the bloody glory of his fell god.'

'The abominate runs before this threat?' Eisenkramer asked.

'He cannot face Khazgar's number without great loss to his own,' Rhaanoc said, lowering his smashed helm and the gaze of his eye through the mangled rent. 'Or else cannot afford to face them at all.'

The Witch Hunter General moved in close.

'Tell me, turncoat,' Eisenkramer seethed. 'You have fought under Archaon's banner?'

'Yes.'

'You know him.'

'Yes.'

'Hunted by the bestial host,' Eisenkramer said, 'without the numbers to engage the Blood God's mongrel… where would he run?'

Rhaanoc said nothing at first. Then, 'Archaon's not much for running.'

'Then what would he do?' Eisenkramer put to him.

'He would hole up somewhere,' Horrwitz said, half to himself. Eisenkramer turned to him before returning the intensity of his gaze to the turncoat. Slowly, the Chaos warrior nodded.

'Where?'

When Rhaanoc said nothing, Eisenkramer brought his lips to one of the marauder's battered ears. 'Like a waterskin, I'll fill you to the brim with the God-King's love. Do you hear me, minion? Don't burn for a master you no longer serve.' Eisenkramer brought them face to face again. 'Where?'

Horrwitz had no wish to see further suffering. He willed the prisoner to speak.

'Rathskorn.'

The word fell from the warrior's lips like defeat. Acceptance. 'Rathskorn Keep.'

A vicious smile spread across the Witch Hunter General's face.

'You know this keep?'

'Yes.'

'And you will take us there, as Master Horrwitz's prisoner?'

Rhaanoc nodded slowly. Eisenkramer looked at the templar. A nasty chuckle escaped the witch hunter.

'I know you will,' he told the chained Rhaanoc.

The Sigmarites left the highlands behind and descended into the mist-smothered valleys below. Helmut Horrwitz listened to the rhythmic *clunk* of his armour as he trudged through the ice and grit. Without his horse he was back to walking in full plate. The cold went through him with its frozen claws and the wind howled through his visor. Rocky rises enclosed the miserable track. Everything felt like a trap. Above was the dark claustrophobia of cloud cover. Meanwhile, every rattling step took the templar deeper within the sea of misty murk into which the Sigmarite cavalcade was descending.

Things moved in the obscurity, prompting Horrwitz to trudge with the length of his gleaming blade out before him. Nothing moved the cloying miasma, however – not the shadows slipping through it, nor the wind or the movement of Imperials through its gloom. Not the remaining horses dragging the deadweight of the altar wagon, packed tents and supplies. Not the warrior priests in mail and robe or the Knights of the Twin-Tailed Orb in their noisy plate and bascinet helms. Not even the witch hunters, wrapped up in their cloaks, their eyes just visible beneath the wide brims of their conical hats.

Horrwitz turned to see that Eisenkramer wasn't too far behind him. Flanked by one of his grim witch hunters and Father Sternthal, the length of the general's pipe protruded from between his hat and the scarf about his neck. Buckled boots crunched through the rime while the leather of one gloved hand rested on a belted pistol. He saw Eisenkramer give him a slow nod.

Turning back, Horrwitz saw the marauder Rhaanoc stumble through the mist. He was still buried in his winding load of heavy chain, the weight of which tumbled him from one side to the other of the path. It was truly a feat of endurance and a wonder that the prisoner hadn't collapsed.

As the templar contemplated the burden of dragging such heavy chains across the Wastes, he felt a pleasant sensation across his own shoulders. A warmth, like sinking into a tavern bathtub, flowed through him. He felt fingers, delicate but strong, knead his aching shoulders and neck. Lighter fingertips traced patterns down his back and across the flat of his stomach. Horrwitz groaned. He was there, in the mist, in the privacy of his helm, in the silky down of his mind – a place he kept safe from the hunger, the biting cold, the torments of battle and the mind-numbing soreness of expanses traversed.

He had only known such a touch once. His cousin Trudi. A forbidden afternoon in the Reikwald, long ago, before the call of squiredom, the chapter house and the God-King.

'Helmut…'

Trudi…

It was as though she were there with him, inside his plate. His true love returned. She kissed him and he responded. His affections were hers and her lips were his.

'Trudi…'

'Knight!'

'My love…'

'*Master Horrwitz!*'

The ruinous warrior Rhaanoc was suddenly and inexplicably between them. His shattered helm. His blood-encrusted face. His ragged beard. His teeth were bared and his voice loud. 'Master Horrwitz!' He was shaking his head and his chains. Horrwitz felt Trudi's light touch on his grizzled chin. She turned it away from the wretch Rhaanoc and back to her own heavenly features. Once again she leant in and kissed him. They were there, in the Reikwald, under the dappled light coming through the trees, with birdsong in their ears.

The templar felt a tug from around his neck. He pulled away. There was the warrior Rhaanoc again. He had forced his fingers between his chains and had pulled the key to his restraints from Horrwitz. Like a contortionist he was attempting to get the key to its chunky lock. The ghost of a warning echoed through the templar's mind. A fire of outrage rose within him.

'Kiss me, my love…'

They were swiftly doused by the intoxicating touch of Trudi's lips on his own. A scream suddenly escaped her. She roared her anguish, almost into his mouth. Horrwitz's eyes fluttered open. The cold was suddenly back. The mist parted and Rhaanoc was there. The heavy chains were coiled at his feet. He was bleeding through his shattered plate. Horrwitz's templar blade was in his hand, stained red with Trudi's blood. With horror, he realised that he had been disarmed, that his prisoner were free and that he held in his arms the murdered Trudi.

'Knight!' Rhaanoc roared again. 'Look down.'

Horrwitz allowed his dreamy gaze to travel to his armoured boots. They were splashed with blood and grit. The floor was littered with shattered bone and skulls. He was half standing in a ribcage.

Horrwitz looked up at the marauder and then back at the cavalcade. Priests, knights and witch hunters were all but lost in the mist, but the templar could hear groaning. Raven-haired beauties of sickly white flesh writhed about them, seemingly inside their robes, cloaks and plate, mesmerising the Sigmarites. The things were a living temptation, all sick beauty and obscene claws. Horrwitz returned to his senses. Trudi suddenly felt cold, clammy and alien on his skin.

'Daemonbreeds!' Horrwitz roared, alerting the cavalcade to the doom of their desires. Trudi's pleasant features drew back like a snarling dog to reveal the daemonette wrapped about him. The knight threw the murderous thing off. It screeched the horror of its unnatural life away before squirming into the blood-soaked soil at Horrwitz's feet. His warning had unleashed simultaneous realisation and disgust in the entranced priests and witch hunters.

There were screams. The screams of templars and priests being feasted upon by their dark fantasies. The screams of expectation and ecstasy all about. Ahead, Horrwitz could see svelte shadows in the mist. Things of unimaginable horror and attraction. Creatures of pale beauty, moving lightly on unguligrade legs and bi-clawed feet. Their sensual forms moved with grace and speed, their lustrous lengths of hair trailing behind them through the mist and wicked pincer-appendages carried like lethal weapons at their slender sides. They were spellbinding and it took everything Horrwitz had left to drag his eyes from the depraved doom of the oncoming daemonettes.

Stumbling at Sieur Stenzel, he helped drag away the monstrous thing that had turned from kissing to tearing out the templar's throat. He drew Stenzel's sword as the knight fought to stem the bleeding, and went to work slaying the infernal creatures that had the Sigmarites in their claws.

As he despatched the lewd monstrosities he saw Rhaanoc swinging the heavy length of his chain about his head. Daemonettes swept in on the warrior, but he smashed them aside with savage arcs of the chain, the unforgiving weight of the chunky padlock like a flail or morning star, bludgeoning the daemons back into obscurity.

With his lip wrinkling in disgust, Horrwitz tore a temptress monstrosity from Wolfram Eisenkramer. As the Witch Hunter General blinked his incomprehension, the horror turned her venomous charms on the templar, snapping at him with her slender pincers. Horrwitz smacked the shears aside with Stenzel's sword. Turning, he swung wildly at another daemonette and another as they came at him. They were fast and moved with a dreamlike grace. Moans and screams scorched Horrwitz's ears as he clipped a serrated claw from one creature's arm before braining another.

Eisenkramer kicked away from an entrancing horror that crawled through the grit and bones towards him. The lustrous river of black hair that flowed from a horned head and trailed behind it gave the monster the appearance of a sensual serpent. As she slithered up on Eisenkramer, her jaw dislocated and a forked tongue escaped her rows of perfect needle teeth. The Witch Hunter General drew his pistol and aimed it squarely at the daemon's grinning face. With a snarl, Eisenkramer pulled on the trigger. The mechanism clunked. The primer hissed. The pistol, however, remained silent. This seemed to amuse the thing as it writhed towards him.

With daemon ichor flying through the mist in a stringy drizzle, Horrwitz ended a warped seductress. The creatures were everywhere, tearing at knights in their plate, screeching after confounded priests, feasting on witch hunters. Like the twilight of some damned womb, the miasma brought them forth. The air stung with their cackling, their passionate shrieks and the snicker-snack of their pincers. The Sigmarites were overrun.

With cat-like agility, a daemonette leapt from boulder to altar, altar to Father Sternthal, and Father Sternthal to Sieur Oberndorff. It was in the air before Horrwitz could work his blade free of the last infernal carcass in which he had buried it. Suddenly his own sword flashed past. The weapon had been tossed through the air, passing blade over pommel. Trailing a black drizzle of daemon blood, the blade took the pouncing creature in mid-air. Abandoning Stenzel's sword, Horrwitz drew back to allow the monster to land in an ugly, dead heap. He turned to find Rhaanoc working up behind him. He had returned the blade to the templar and in doing so had saved his life.

'This doesn't change anything,' Horrwitz roared as he rested his boot on the daemonette and slid his sword from her body.

'My lord,' the Chaos warrior simply acknowledged as he bludgeoned svelte daemons aside. With the monstrosities coming in with their claws under the reach of his improvised flail, Rhaanoc had coiled the lengths of heavy chain about one fist and whipped it left and right with devastating force. Horrwitz found himself biting back an admiration that made him nauseous. The warrior was fearless in the face of the daemon horde. He shattered razor claws to uselessness. He smashed the groaning beasts into the frosted grit of their feeding grounds. He tore predatory daemons from the backs of Sigmarites and chain-mashed them back to their unforgiving god.

As daemonettes died and their ear-bleeding shrieks died away with them, Horrwitz grunted. Such fearlessness and savage confidence no doubt came of making a life in the barbaric insanity of the Wastes. Horrwitz had misjudged the warrior's refusal to fight. He had done more with a simple chain than the warrior priests of Sigmar and the knights of the Twin-Tailed Orb had achieved with their consecrated steel. Eisenkramer had been right. Rhaanoc was no coward.

Eisenkramer...

Horrwitz finished a claw-snapping horror with his sword and turned. His boots took him through the mist, through the disorder and chaos, towards the Witch Hunter General. Eisenkramer was almost lost in the flowing black hair of a serpentine daemon. His arms trembling with exertion, Eisenkramer held the temptress's elongated jaws a fang-scrape from his neck. Horrwitz stamped on through the blood and bones but Rhaanoc got there before him.

Straddling the daemonette, Rhaanoc threw several coils of his tarnished chain about her neck. Hauling her to him, the Chaos warrior wrangled with the monstrosity like some dangerous reptile. He held her there for a moment. Eisenkramer's arms shook before him. The Witch Hunter General found his way to a savage nod, prompting Rhaanoc to drag the horrific creature back into the mist.

Horrwitz offered Eisenkramer his gauntlet, which he took. As the two men stood amongst the bodies of Sigmarites and seductresses, they heard the *crunch* of Rhaanoc finishing the daemon in the murk. About them, surviving pistols put blessed shot through surviving monsters, while consecrated blades and the unrelenting force of hammers pummelled the creatures into the earth of their daemon graves.

Both Horrwitz and Eisenkramer were surprised to see the turncoat Rhaanoc reappear, his chains dripping with ichor. It didn't take the Witch Hunter General long to collect himself and find his way back to the imperious fury of his station.

'You led us into this,' Eisenkramer accused Rhaanoc, but Horrwitz stepped between them.

'It was the prisoner who alerted us to the danger,' Horrwitz told him. The Witch Hunter General looked from the templar to the Chaos warrior.

'They are called the Rapture,' Rhaanoc told them. 'The daemons of Phasma Klatsch, sorceress of the Prince of Pleasure.' The Chaos warrior looked back to where he had despatched the daemonette monstrosity. 'They haunt the trails thereabouts, waylaying travellers.'

Eisenkramer looked about them, up and down the valley. The humiliation of the attack was still fresh on his face and his anger was swiftly spent. He looked to Horrwitz, who gave an all but imperceptible nod.

'How far to the keep?' Eisenkramer put to the Chaos warrior.

'Rathskorn's not far,' Rhaanoc told him.

And it wasn't.

Horrwitz was relieved to see the claustrophobic murk of the mist clear. Behind he could hear the squeak of one of the altar's wheels as priests and the remaining horses dragged it through the frozen mud. He didn't want to think about what such a noise might attract in the highlands around them. The templar cast a glance about their depleted number. The party had paid for their righteous hubris and still the Witch Hunter General was leading them north. North, after Archaon.

Warrior priests and witch hunters seemed to be staying near to the God-King's altar. Some limped close to its blessed form to ensure its protection, while others remained close to ensure their own. Only the knights of the Twin-Tailed Orb advanced beyond the altar's sanctified influence, their blades drawn and their plate bloody with punctures and oozing injuries.

Ahead, Rhaanoc the turncoat led them. The Chaos warrior had tossed his chains at the templar's feet. Horrwitz saw little point in putting him back in restraints. With their grievous losses, they would need every able-bodied man to repel an attack or ambush. He fell short of providing the damned warrior with a weapon, however, and instead walked closely behind the warrior as he tracked them across the Wastes. Rhaanoc said little to draw the displeasure of Eisenkramer or Horrwitz, so it was a surprise when he spoke.

'Tell me, my lord,' Rhaanoc said, his blood-soaked boots crunching through the grit. 'Why do you travel to the top of the world in search of Archaon? Forgive me, but it is plain to see that you do not wish to be here.'

Horrwitz went to answer the prisoner with a brutal rebuke, something to remind him of his place and his lowly station. But exhaustion sapped the templar's remaining strength and the cold chilled his bones. He could barely muster the indignation. He found the question went some way to distract him from the agonies of hiking in full battleplate.

'We're all here to save our souls, turncoat,' Horrwitz grizzled, his breath escaping as a fine mist. 'You. Me. The Witch Hunter General.'

'But Archaon is just one man–'

'He is not *just* a man,' Horrwitz continued miserably. 'Don't you realise? There are texts. There are prophecies. Your former master is not just some wandering madman, seeking the favour of heretic gods, a chosen of some fell power. The Grand Theogonist himself believes that Archaon is the end to all the world. He is a living doom that must be destroyed.'

'And you believe you are the one to do so?' Rhaanoc asked.

'If I get the opportunity, then I will not flinch,' Horrwitz told the prisoner. 'I will not fail. You live only to provide that opportunity, turncoat.' The templar considered. 'But if you think me a glory hunter then you would be wrong. Even if I were, I wouldn't seek it out in this benighted realm. No. I long for my bed. I long for the ancient forests of the Empire. After a lifetime of battle, more than anything else, I long for peace.'

'I would have you get what you want, my lord.'

'Don't blow smoke up my mail skirts, prisoner,' Horrwitz said, his voice trailing off. It was too weak for a warning. It was a forlorn announcement.

'Still,' Rhannoc pressed as he walked on, 'you speak like a man who did not choose his fate.'

Horrwitz grunted. 'I am the Master of Blades,' he said with feeble pride. 'A servant of Sigmar. A knight of the Twin-Tailed Orb. I did not choose this fate. The one we seek chose it for me.'

'How so?'

'My templars and I were selected for this as part of a penitent crusade.'

'Penitence for what, my lord?'

'For the sins of another,' Horrwitz said hopelessly. 'For the sins of Archaon. The man you followed was no northern marauder, No warlord of the steppes or twisted tribesman. He was a son of the Empire. A devout Sigmarite.' Horrwitz shook his head within his helm.

'Is that why you fear him so?' the turncoat asked. 'He knows the Empire. He knows you. He's one of you.'

'One of us,' Horrwitz almost laughed. 'Aye, he's one of us, alright. He was a templar of the God-King…'

Rhaanoc nodded. 'A knight of the Twin-Tailed Orb.'

'Aye,' Horrwitz confirmed, his words laced with shame. 'That.'

'You are here to atone for his fall?' Rhaanoc asked.

'All are to atone for his ruin,' Horrwitz said. 'See, turncoat, it matters not if I fail here. Daily, witch hunters, warrior priests of Sigmar and knights of the Twin-Tailed Orb are despatched to the Wastes to hunt down the traitor. To destroy him. The Grand Theogonist will not stop.' Horrwitz sighed. 'There is the world to save.'

'Master Horrwitz,' the Witch Hunter General called ahead to them, 'about what do you speak to the prisoner?'

The templar pulled back but made the witch hunter wait for an answer.

'Nothing of consequence,' he called back finally.

Following Rhaanoc step by weary step, the Sigmarites were led north. As the valley trail started to descend and the temperature began to climb above a mind-numbing freeze, the brawny warrior came to a stop in his ruined armour.

'Get up here,' Rhaanoc called, but Eisenkramer was loath to take orders from a heretic prisoner. Leaving the witch hunter behind, Horrwitz crunched up through the frosted grit at a rattling jog. There were two armoured figures wandering about their path. They seemed to smell Horrwitz and the turncoat before they saw them and made for the pair with predatory speed and intent that bellied their corpulent forms.

Rhaanoc began to back from their stinking forms. As the Chaos warriors closed, Horrwitz could see they were victims of some dreadful affliction or plague. They had once been knights. Their plate was rusted to ruin, while their hairless skulls sat on swollen throats and multiple chins, and the teeth of their decaying maws were stained red. Their flesh was a stretched canvas of scab, weeping infection and burrowing parasites, while their disease had seemingly caused their bellies to bloat with explosive gases that had eventually burst.

The plague knights groaned ravenously as they stumbled at Horrwitz and Rhaanoc. With ragged, gut-trailing cavities for stomachs, the templar knew the knights could never satisfy their diseased hunger. He could see the insatiability of the unfortunates in their yellowing eyes.

'Don't get too close,' Rhaanoc warned as Horrwitz moved forward with his blade. The plague knights reached out for him with rusted gauntlets, stained black from rooting around in cadavers. They had no knightly weapons. They didn't need them. As wandering plague bearers of infectious flesh, they *were* a weapon.

'Don't tell me my business,' Horrwitz told Rhaanoc, before sweeping forward with his sword. The templar's movements were confident and executed with knightly grace. He cleaved through the limbs of the first before taking its teeth-chattering head. The second lunged for him and he knocked it back, allowing the thing to come at him and impale itself on his broad blade. With the Sigmarite sword buried in the diseased warrior of Chaos, Horrwitz could only watch as it worked its jaw feverishly and hauled itself up the length of the blade towards him. The templar thought he was going to have to abandon his weapon to the thing but something burst or gave within the bloated torso and the monstrosity died right before him. Horrwitz looked at Rhaanoc, who gave an approving nod of respect.

With the threat despatched, Eisenkramer came forward, prompting Rhaanoc on with him. Dumping the diseased cadaver to one side, Horrwitz joined them. Rhaanoc peered over boulders that marked the promontory of a steep headland. Eisenkramer and Horrwitz crouched with the prisoner at the bluff. Below them the valley dropped and widened, once again succumbing to the damp haze of an unnatural mist. Using a brass eyeglass, Eisenkramer peered down before passing the device to the templar. Even without the glass, the knight could see the crumbling black stone of a fat, round keep at the head of the valley.

'That's Rathskorn?' Horrwitz asked.

'What's left of it,' Rhaanoc told him. 'It may not look like much but its walls are thick and have stood not only the ravage of time but also everything the Wastes have thrown at it.'

'Even the abominate Archaon?' Eisenkramer put to him.

'The Wastes are ever changing,' the warrior replied. 'You trust what you know. Archaon favours the keep.'

'He'll be there?'

'He'll be there,' Rhaanoc confirmed.

Horrwitz couldn't see much activity on the walls of the derelict keep. He turned the eyeglass on the open ground before it. He could see shapes and silhouettes moving in the miasma and sickly mist. A host moving on the keep, intending to assault the thick stone of its walls. There were savage marauders, responding to threats and orders. Mounted warriors of Chaos riding up the flanks. Champions of the host in conference with sorcerers beneath shredded banners.

'Who are they?' Horrwitz asked.

'Their banners betray them,' the turncoat said, peering down at the ominous symbol on the warband's standard. Three filthy circles had been stained into the mildewed cloth, forming the wings and body of a fat, black fly. 'It is the host of Lebrus Wormshroud, favoured of the great Lord of Decay.' Rhaanoc nodded at the plague knights Horrwitz had expertly despatched. 'The diseased belong to him.'

'He lays siege to the abominate Archaon?' Eisenkramer asked.

'There can only be one chosen of the Ruinous Powers,' the marauder told them. 'One Everchosen of Chaos. There are few champions in these parts who do not lay claim to such a title.'

'The competition must be eliminated,' Horrwitz said, prompting Rhaanoc to nod in agreement.

'Indeed.'

Horrwitz turned to the Witch Hunter General. 'This could work for us.'

'I'm listening,' Eisenkramer hissed absently. Horrwitz nodded. The pair of them had come so far in search of Archaon, and now that he was close, now that they had him cornered, the Sigmarites could almost taste the prospect of victory. Horrwitz looked back down the eyeglass at the valley floor swarming with the Chaos host and the ancient fortitude of the keep's great, rusted portcullis.

'Tell me there's another way in,' the templar put to Rhaanoc. When the warrior said nothing, Horrwitz pulled his eye from the lens and gave him a stony gaze.

'Perhaps his mouth is dry,' Eisenkramer threatened. 'I have water. Sweet and pure.'

'Tell me,' Horrwitz implored. He would spare them all the time wasted and sheer wretchedness of unnecessary torture.

'For my sins,' the miserable turncoat told him, 'I'll do more than tell you. I'll show you.'

'Where is he?' Eisenkramer roared.

Horrwitz swung his lantern about this way and that, his templar blade glinting with the meagre light it offered. Dust stung his eyes and his nose was fixed in a perpetual wrinkle at the stench. The dark bowels of the keep were thick with the stench of the grave. 'Where's my prisoner?' the witch hunter seethed.

Horrwitz didn't know. The warrior had made his way underground, leading the Sigmarites into a crooked subterranean cave system. As warrior priests and witch hunters lit torches and lanterns to light the way, Rhaanoc had plunged on through the darkness along a route Horrwitz assumed he must know well, a secret way into the keep. An entrance

Archaon used to enter the ruins and routinely usurp whatever beastmen or warbands were settled there. With every twist and turn the prisoner's shattered plate had caught on outcrops, crannies and narrowings, prompting from him grunts of pain.

Finally the rough, jagged tunnel worming its way through the valleyside gave way to collapsed passageways. The stone was ancient and crumbling but essentially angular, betraying the architectural flourishes of dark siegecraft. It was there and then, under the crushing weight of the tumbledown keep, that the turncoat disappeared. He became one with the darkness. It could have been an accident. It could have been by design. Horrwitz couldn't tell. He had almost lost his way several times himself, taking a turn left through some demolished opening when the passage led right. He had almost vanished like Rhaanoc, except down one of the rubble-strewn shafts that seemed to gape open at his feet. Eisenkramer would not be placated, however.

'You have lost my prisoner,' the Witch Hunter General accused, as they made their way blindly through the derelict foundations of Rathskorn Keep, their lanterns guttering in the foetid stench. 'No doubt he sends for his master, to bury us alive in this godless place.'

Horrwitz wasn't so sure. Rhaanoc had been gone some time and there seemed little evidence of the presence of Archaon and his warriors of Chaos. True, the demolished catacombs rang with the screams of priests falling to their deaths and Eisenkramer's witch hunters being crushed beneath collapsing walls.

Enemies announced themselves with their stink. As Horrwitz pushed on – half searching for his lost prisoner, half trying to crawl out of the labyrinthine death-trap – a terrible stench greeted him. It was the mouldy fug of grave earth punctuated with the sweeter zest of corruption. Like fruit that had gone off, the sickly sting of disease reached Horrwitz's nostrils.

Each time his senses were assaulted by the repugnance, he

would find an unfortunate, quietly dying in the darkness. Like the things they had encountered above, the afflicted shambled towards them, their bottomless hunger driving them to crave the freshness of flesh. Some of the diseased seemed genuinely lost, while others fed on each other, their ravenous sickness driving them to feast on their own. How a god, even a Ruinous one, could take pleasure in such degradation, Horrwitz could not fathom. He ended each shuffling victim as he encountered them, granting them the God-King's peace with his blade. Unfortunately, the confines did not allow Horrwitz to maintain as much distance from the infected foes as he might like, and before long he was covered with their gore.

Finally, his exhausting advance slowed to a halt. Casting the light of the lantern behind him he saw the ghoulish faces of Sigmarite priests, templars and witch hunters in half-shadow. Eisenkramer said nothing. He just gave Horrwitz the stabbing glare of his eyes, puffing aggressively on his pipe. The foul-smelling tobacco went some way to masking the scent of corruption.

'What?' Eisenkramer said finally, unable to hide his disappointment and disgust from Horrwitz.

'We're going around in circles,' the templar said. He was watching the silky smoke trail from the witch hunter's pipe. The smoke was drifting away from him. There was a breeze. Horrwitz turned around to find a crack running through the stone wall. It didn't appear to be an exit and Horrwitz had discounted it before. Evidence of a breeze sealed it for the templar, however. Leading with his sword and angling his plate, Horrwitz scraped his way through the narrow opening.

'What are you doing, you damned fool?' Eisenkramer hissed. But Horrwitz pushed on, grunting and heaving, his pauldrons all but becoming trapped between the shattered stone. He could feel the breeze getting stronger on his filthy face. Finally, with one plate-crumpling heave, Horrwitz extricated himself from the gap and stepped out onto what his lantern revealed to be a demolished stone stairwell.

'Steps,' the templar managed, prompting Eisenkramer and his priests to follow. 'Leading up.'

Stumbling up the smashed stone of the collapsed stairwell with the Sigmarites at his back, Horrwitz found that both the breeze and the stench got stronger. The air was rank in a different way: ripe, heavy. The knight of the Twin-Tailed Orb froze as a crack in the wall revealed what passed for daylight in the Wastes. They were above ground, but that was the only good news.

Eisenkramer pushed past the templar. The Witch Hunter General was almost quaking with furious disbelief. Through the gap they could see the keep courtyard. It both smelled and appeared like a temple-hospice during an outbreak of pox or plague. The diseased dominated the scene. The infected were everywhere. Stout warriors stood on the derelict battlements, still and quiet in their rusting armour. The festering bodies of the afflicted were laid across almost every surface. Starving. Listless. Devoid of energy. They were all bloated and displayed the same rotting cavity where their guts and stomach had been. Several were feeding on unfortunates who were so torpid they could not even bring themselves to escape the cannibalistic frenzy.

At the centre of the insanity was a corpulent sorcerer, his mangy robes barely covering his distended form. He sat upon a throne of sloth, his bloated form settled on a mound of similarly suffering followers. His colossal stomach had ruptured and burst in several places but continued to fill with a terrible green gas that leaked from the ragged tears. The symbol of the fat, black fly on his robes identified him as Lebrus Wormshroud, whose banners Rhaanoc had pointed out to them before.

'No...' Eisenkramer hissed as he stepped out through the gap.

'General!' Horrwitz called, trying to grab for the witch hunter. Flies that had previously been content to feed and lay their eggs in the flesh of the afflicted rose in a droning cloud of blackness.

'No,' Eisenkramer rumbled again. He strode across the courtyard with the noses of Wormshroud's diseased unfortunates rising in the presence of fresh meat. Eisenkramer slid a huge silver broadsword from his back. The crossguard was almost the width of his shoulders and the pommel was a decorative Sigmarite hammerhead. As the diseased shambled at him, reaching out with ravenous hands and claws, the Witch Hunter General went to work with the immaculate blade. It seemed like suicide or at least the insanity of blind devotion to his God-King.

It was neither.

Horrwitz understood. Rhaanoc had led them into a trap and, worse, had escaped. The traitor Archaon, who seemed to evade them at every step, was nowhere to be found in the keep. To seal the Sigmarites' fate, they were surrounded by the Lord of Decay's ruinous servants.

'For the God-King!' Horrwitz bellowed as he stepped through the crack in the stairwell wall, just in time to see Eisenkramer draw the long barrel of his pistol and put a single blessed shot straight through Lebrus Wormshroud's bulbous, frog-like throat. As it hit the favoured of Nurgle, the gases within the bloated sorcerer ignited, blasting foul pieces of Lebrus Wormshroud all over the courtyard.

Suddenly the afflicted were everywhere, stumbling at Eisenkramer, reaching out for Horrwitz or scrabbling to feast on the remains of their leader. Warrior priests of Sigmar descended upon them with skull-smashing hammer blows while templars cleaved the diseased in two and witch hunters drew pistols and blasted through the plague carriers. The diseased were up. The all-but-dead were upon them. The infected buried Sigmarites in the corpulence of their rancid flesh and bit into Eisenkramer's men with rotten maws.

It was a massacre. A stinking bloodbath that painted the courtyard of Rathskorn Keep a bilious red.

Moving about the ruined architecture, Horrwitz buried his blade in the dying and half-eaten. He granted the God-King's peace to both the Lord of Decay's diseased unfortunates and his own men. Helmut Horrwitz would not see the knights of Sigmar suffer as the Dark Gods intended. He would not see Eisenkramer's screaming witch hunters become that against which they had fought. He would not see the God-King's priests rewarded with agonies for a lifetime's service. As Sieur Oberndorff, Father Sternthal and the last of the Sigmarites became the instruments of brute mercy about him, Horrwitz found Wolfram Eisenkramer standing before the keep's rusted portcullis. Outside, the mist was clearing. The host that had laid siege to Rathskorn Keep did so no more. The ghostly silhouettes of marauders and beastmen were turning and leaving. Knights on horseback turned their mounts from the keep and the champions of Chaos took their leave.

The Witch Hunter General took the bars of the portcullis in his hands and stared at the departing warhost. They had left a small fire, built on the churned-up track leading to the keep entrance. Standard bearers came forward and dumped the banners of Lebrus Wormshroud in the flames. A cluster of Chaos warriors parted and lowered their helms in almost mongrel-like deference.

A brawny figure came forward. He squinted at Eisenkramer and Horrwitz through the dancing flames of the fire. The pair watched as he tensed his powerful body. His form was battered black and blue. Biceps and pectorals bulged. Fresh scars split. With a grunt, Rhaanoc broke the shattered remains of his plate across his brawny back. Eisenkramer and Horrwitz watched in stunned silence. Rhaanoc pulled rancid steel plate and threadbare mail from his brute form and threw them into the fire. He turned his muscular back to them and removed the rent helm from his head, allowing it to clatter at his feet. The warriors of Chaos came forward with fresh standards. With armour. With horned helm. Furs. Cloak. Shield and sword. They began to dress the prisoner.

'Rhaanoc...' Eisenkramer hissed to himself.

Horrwitz joined him at the portcullis. 'Rhaanoc...'

The men pictured the letters of the prisoner's name falling from the pages of black leather tome in which the Witch

Hunter General recorded his confessions. As the letters tumbled they spelled out a different word. The cursed word that fell from their lips together.

'Archaon.'

'Impossible,' Horrwitz said, a sickening feeling spreading up through his torso. 'It can't be.' Archaon turned in his fell plate and horned helm. The armour of Ruinous royalty. He stared at Horrwitz. Horrwitz stared back.

'Get this portcullis raised,' Eisenkramer snarled. Horrwitz felt the witch hunter haul at the rusted gate and swore that his seething efforts moved it ever so slightly. As Eisenkramer's priests and witch hunters went to work on the portcullis windlass, the two men watched Archaon's own men bring forth an armoured steed. 'Come on!' Eisenkramer roared.

'General,' Horrwitz said as the prospect of what Eisenkramer was doing dawned on him. They had a handful of men but the Witch Hunter General intended to lead them into battle against Archaon's battle-hardened warhost. 'Wolfram, listen to me.'

Eisenkramer wouldn't, though. His gaze burned into the doom of all the world. The chosen of the Dark Gods. The warrior who had fooled them so completely, because he could. Archaon slowly mounted the magnificent black stallion.

'Wolfram, this is suicide,' said Horrwitz. The Witch Hunter General did not seem to hear him. His whole world was the warrior before him. Obendorff and the warrior priests looked to Horrwitz. With grim acceptance, the templar nodded and the Sigmarites lent their weight to the wheel-crank.

Settling into the saddle, Archaon stared straight back at Eisenkramer. Horrwitz watched as the warrior of Chaos gave him a slow nod before turning his steed around. Eisenkramer went wild, tearing at the portcullis as it shuddered upwards, raining rust down on him. Archaon, chosen of the Dark Gods, followed his men into oblivion. As Eisenkramer roared after him, the living apocalypse became one with the mist. Like a rabid animal wanting to be free, Eisenkramer scrambled under the rising spikes of the portcullis.

'General!' Horrwitz called, but he was away, his silver sword glinting in the half-light of day. Struggling to get through the gap in his plate, the templar broke into a heavy run. Within moments the mist had claimed him. He found Eisenkramer staring wildly about, searching for any sign of Archaon.

Then they heard it. The bellowing. The braying. The roars of warrior gors, beastmen and Khazgar of the Brazen Tusk. Horrwitz heard the thunder of hooves down the side of the valley. The beastlord had come to claim Archaon's skull for his Blood God. Archaon, however, was gone, the whisper of a dark and forgotten rumour, lost to the breeze. But he had not left his foe wanting. He had left them Sigmarites who would fight hard for their lives.

Horrwitz brought up his blade, the blade with which Archaon had saved his life, the blade the traitor had returned to him. The bestial bellows were deafening. Silhouettes closed on them: a wall of ferocious horn, muscle and man-hate.

'We've got to get back,' Horrwitz called. The templar knew that the keep was their only chance of survival and the tunnels below it their only chance of escape. Back to the valley. To the God-King's altar. Wolfram Eisenkramer fell to his knees.

'General,' Horrwitz roared, 'we've got to go, right now!' The knight of the Twin-Tailed Orb could feel the quake bestial charge through the ground. 'Wolfram, come on!' The Witch Hunter General was down in the dirt. His blade was buried in frozen grit of the Wastes and the Sigmarite held onto the weapon's great cross guard, his head resting against the sword hilt and the decorative hammer-head that formed the pommel. Eisenkramer was done.

Horrwitz wanted to run, but knew he couldn't. With the rumble of charging monsters closing, the templar tried to steel himself. They were a handful against an army. Death was certain. Horrwitz cast a glance after the ghostly shape of Archaon and his warriors of Chaos. He was about to pay his penance for his comrade's fall in full. The Everchosen of the Dark Gods had set his enemies one against the other.

Eisenkramer and Horrwitz had thought of him as their prisoner when they, in fact, had been his. Shackled to the doom he had planned for them all along.

Horrwitz thought on the words he had exchanged with Archaon on the rise. The lies that had passed between them.

'More than anything else, I long for peace,' Horrwitz had said.

'I would have you get what you want,' Archaon had told him.

Horrwitz's sufferings were all but done. Kissing the flat of his templar blade, the Sigmarite prepared himself for the horror to come, and the peace that would inevitably follow. In that, at least, Archaon – Everchosen of Chaos – had spoken true.

ABOUT THE AUTHOR

Rob Sanders is the author of 'The Serpent Beneath', a novella that appeared in the *New York Times* bestselling Horus Heresy anthology *The Primarchs*. His other Black Library credits include the Warhammer 40,000 titles *Adeptus Mechanicus: Skitarius* and *Tech-Priest, Legion of the Damned, Atlas Infernal* and *Redemption Corps* and the audio drama *The Path Forsaken*. He has also written the Warhammer Archaon duology, *Everchosen* and *Lord of Chaos* along with many Quick Reads for the Horus Heresy and Warhammer 40,000. He lives in the city of Lincoln, UK.